CRYSTAL MOON
World of Grayham

PHILLIP E. JONES

Crystal Moon, World of Grayham
View a high-def, printable – MAP - of Grayham
www.WorldsoftheCrystalMoon.com

Phillip E Jones's Blog and his answers to 'Fan's Questions'
www.PhillipJones.com

Cover Illustrations by: Ian Ferrebee.
Other Illustrations throughout *'Book One'* were created by:
Ian Ferrebee, Angela Woods and Kathleen Stone

Special thanks to Hope Clark, Georgia Carpenter and Janet Bernice for their patience and invaluable input.

I am dedicating this first book to my two sons: Christopher and Chase

This printing was done by:
The Print Media Companies of Southern California, Inc.
3355 East Mira Loma, Buildings 163-165, Anaheim, CA. 92806.
Phone: 714.729.0789   www.printmediabooks.com

This novel is a work of fiction. Names, characters, events, incidents and places are the product of the author's imagination. Any resemblance to actual persons, people or events is purely coincidental.

Library of Congress Cataloging-in-Publication Data
First published in 2008 under ISBN — 978-0-9816423-0-7

Crystal Moon, World of Grayham

ISBN: 978-0-9816423-0-7

Printed in the United States of America
10 9 8 7 6 5 4 3 2

The second print was the release of the:
--Second Edition--
Appropriate for readers ages 13 and up…

PHILLIP E. JONES

CRYSTALMOON

World of Grayham

Crystal Moon

World of Grayham
Book 1 of the series

I would like to thank the illustrators for their hard work!

Ian Ferrebee
www.tigereyegraphics.com

Angela Woods
www.angelawoodsfineart.com

Kathleen Stone
www.vangosmedia.com

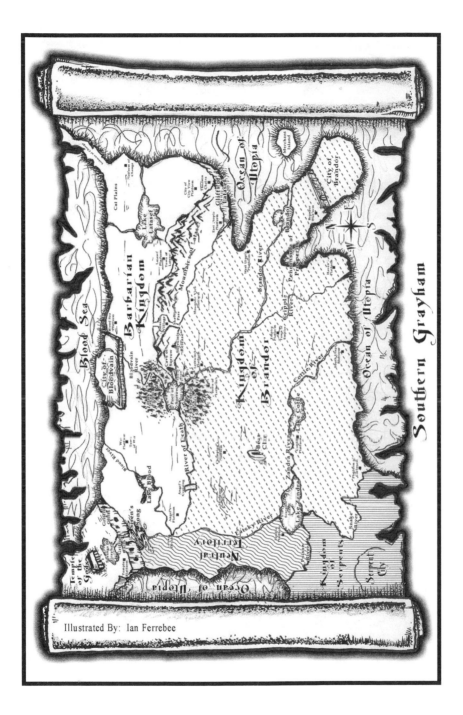

Southern Grayham

Illustrated By: Ian Ferrebee

Stop

Soul to Soul

Hello Reader…   *Jason*

… or should I say, LOST SOUL. I really hate to be the one to deliver the bad news but there's no real way to soften the blow so I'm just going to come right out and say it. You see . . . you and I, well... we're dead or, if it makes it easier to hear . . . we have perished. We can no longer call Earth our home. Our souls exist inside the Book of Immortality and we're waiting for our chance to be reborn on five new worlds.

Yes, I know, none of this makes any sense and you're probably asking yourself, Phillip what on Earth are you talking about? And I would have to answer by saying that Earth just doesn't exist any longer. And also, you've just got to hang in there while I try to explain further.

Just know this . . . I'm really glad your soul was able to be retrieved from the darkness of space and placed in here with me, inside the Book! I know that you're confused and there are many questions, not to mention a fair amount of stress which I'm sure has suddenly surfaced because of my revelation, but it will get better, I promise. Allow me to explain one thing at a time.

First, *The Book of Immortality* has a name—Gabriel. He didn't always have this name, but he has asked me to explain some extremely important things which are for your benefit. So secondly, there were a series of *God Wars* that lasted nearly 3,000 seasons. It was during this period of constant battling by these "so-called" *Deities* that the entire Cosmos ceased to exist. (I say "so-called" because I'm still not convinced that they should be called gods at all.)

Third, but not finally, the places you knew as Heaven, Hell, our beloved Earth, and everything that you ever loved, everything you understood, everything you cherished as your own, exploded into countless pieces of mass which now wander aimlessly through space. Yeah, this news really sucks, not to mention it's thoroughly depressing to know that your soul is stuck inside a book, but again, hang in there with me! Many answers will be revealed as I move forward with the telling of *The Crystal Moon.*

You see, since I was an author back on Earth prior to its destruction, Gabriel asked me to take an accounting of all the many, many facts. I get to share with you the knowledge I've gained from speaking with the other souls that reside inside Gabriel's pages who were involved in these stories. I'll share all the information acquired from questioning those who are still alive, those who were involved in the God Wars, and those who still live on the new worlds. I've taken great care to understand their emotions, their desires, their reasons for doing the things they did and will now share everything with you.

Thus, I welcome you to: *The Worlds of the Crystal Moon.* Let us begin with the first of six stories—***Crystal Moon, World of Grayham.*** I do hope you enjoy my recollections.

**Your friend and fellow soul inside the *Book of Immortality,*
Phillip E. Jones**

Table of Contents

Introduction 1

Chapter 1 – Coma 3

Chapter 2 – Against Our Will 21

Chapter 3 – A Lost Power 51

Chapter 4 – Mental Breakdown 65

Chapter 5 – Broken Back 77

Chapter 6 – First Flight 89

Chapter 7 – Breaking and Entering 97

Chapter 8 – The Truth Be Told 111

Chapter 9 – The Unicorn Prince's Horn 123

Chapter 10 – The Training Blues -or- Should I say, Bruises . . . 139

Chapter 11 – Tough Lessons Learned 155

Chapter 12 – Here Kitty, Kitty 167

Chapter 13 – Kroger the Ogre 187

Chapter 14 – A God Falls 197

Chapter 15 – A Gods Gifts - and - A Revelation 207

Chapter 16 – The Fight 219

Chapter 17 – A Fairly Good Sized Rat 231

Chapter 18 – A Big Stone Statue 243

Chapter 19 – What Irony 255

Chapter 20 – Warning to the Barbarian King of Bloodvain 267

Chapter 21 – A Soul Rescued 283

Chapter 22 – Minotaur 301

Chapter 23 – Duke Barthom Brandor 315

Chapter 24 – Father of Seven 335

Chapter 25 – An Unheard Prayer 341

Chapter 26 – Sick of this Royal Crap 357

Chapter 27 – How a Heart Tastes 377

Chapter 28 – The Vision Begins 393

Chapter 29 – Two Weddidngs and a Funeral 407

Chapter 30 – Justice 433

Chapter 31 – Gods That Like to Bet 455

Chapter 32 – A Babysitting Jaguar 477

Chapter 33 – An Example Made 489

Chapter 34 – No Loose Ends 499

Chapter 35 – Water Mist Mares 509

Chapter 36 – May the Best Man 'Win' 527

Chapter 37 – What a Tangled Web George Weaves 545

Chapter 38 – A Ticket Out of Here 565

Chapter 39 – Surrounded 585

Glossary

Dawn
Time of day when the sun rises just above the horizon.

Morning
Period of time between Dawn and Early Bailem.

Early Bailem
When the sun has reached the halfway point between the horizon and its highest point in the sky, the Peak of Bailem.

Peak of Bailem
Time of day when the sun has reached its highest point.

Late Bailem
Time of day when the sun has passed the Peak of Bailem and taken a position halfway between the Peak of Bailem and the time when the sun disappears behind the horizon.

Evening
Time of day between, Late Bailem and when the sun is about to disappear behind the horizon.

Night
Time after the sun has disappeared behind the horizon until it once again rises and becomes Dawn.

Midnight
An estimated time that is said to be in the middle of the night.

SEASON or SEASONS
There are different uses for the words season and seasons.

Season
The common meaning referring to winter, spring, summer, and fall.

Seasons
People can refer to their ages by using the term season or seasons. For Example: If someone were to be born during a winter season, he or she would become another season or year older once they have reached the following winter season. They are said to be so many winter seasons old.

THE GODS
In order of Power and Strength

Bassorine—God of War

Bassorine instigates wars within the worlds and in this way helps control the population growth on each world. He is rugged-looking, an outdoorsman with human features. He is the oldest of all the gods who have survived the God Wars. He is six feet tall and wears heavy leathers beneath a long hooded robe which he usually keeps open in the front. He is dark-haired with brown eyes and has a scar that runs across his right eye and ends near the corner of his mouth. He wears chainmail beneath his leather shirt, but only a hint of it can be seen. Despite his scar, Bassorine isn't considered ugly. He's a touch boring because he's a little too serious. Bassorine is, by far, the most powerful of all the gods.

Lasidious—God of Mischief and Deception

When Lasidious's eyes are not glowing red and his teeth aren't sharpened to fine points, he's actually quite debonair-looking. He has short sandy brown hair, blue eyes and a chiseled chin. He has tremendous sex appeal and was human before he ascended to god stature. Lasidious is charismatic, charming, witty, and a liar who loves mischief. He's also nearly six feet in height with an athletic build beneath his robes. He normally keeps his hood on no matter what color of robe he wears, only occasionally putting it down.

Alistar—God of the Harvest

Alistar is thin with human features. His hair, sandy brown beneath a hooded green robe, compliments his thin face. Pleasant-looking with soft brown eyes, Alistar is in charge of the world's harvests and determines if there will be feast or famine. He is known to the other gods in the *Farendrite Collective* as having a good nature.

Hosseff—Shade God of Death

Hosseff wears an assortment of different-colored robes and can transform from a human to his normal appearance as a shade. When he is in shade form, the form of his birthright, no facial features can be seen. Instead, a mist or haze fills the hood, giving the appearance of emptiness. His hands also look like smoke and have no definition. Hosseff loves Death and helps to return the souls of the dead back to the Book of Immortality's many pages.

Mieonus—Goddess of Hate

Mieonus, a beautiful goddess with human features, long brunette hair and soft brown eyes. She isn't as elegant-looking as the goddess, Celestria, but she tries awfully hard. She wears an assortment of different gowns and loves the look of lifted heels beneath her feet. With a heart full of hate, nothing gives her more pleasure than to watch the pain of the world's populations as they struggle through life.

Yaloom—God of Greed

Yaloom is a pompous god who thinks of nothing but himself. He loves the finer things the gods have created and surrounds himself with them. His home lies beneath a giant waterfall on the Hidden God World of Ancients Sovereign. His appearance is plain, despite his rich robes and his ring-covered fingers. Although he thinks he is a leader, Yaloom is easily manipulated by others within the collective of gods and they consider him nothing more than a sheep.

Celestria—Goddess of Evil-Natured Beasts

Celestria, the most stunning of all the gods, has elven beauty without a flaw. The blue of her eyes could have been stolen from the ocean's perfect color and her hair cascades over her shoulders and ripples gently as she walks. With no visible imperfection, her every curve and gesture are without fault. Her voice, an angel's voice, is soft and sweet to the ear. Celestria is worthy to be called goddess, even if only judged by her physical features, but beware... her heart is evil and she loves only Lasidious.

Bailem—God of the Sun

Bailem is the only angel to survive the God Wars. Short, chubby, and balding, his remaining brown, short hair is on the sides of his head. This angel god wears white robes with golden trim. His pure-white wings are stunningly beautiful and lay elegantly down his back outside his robes. His tail sticks out through his robe and moves wildly around when he gets excited. Bailem can be a little too serious at times, but does have the ability to lighten up when the mood strikes him. All in all, he is a peaceful being.

Jervaise—Goddess of Fire

Jervaise is a spirit with no true form. Her normal appearance is that of a floating ball of energy. When necessary, she can materialize into a beautiful ghostly being when dealing with the others in the collective. However, she doesn't make it a habit to appear to her followers on the worlds.

Lictina—Goddess of Earth

Prior to Lictina's ascension to godhood, she was the queen of a race of creatures known as the Lizardians. A peaceful being, her job is to make adjustments that will ensure the land masses on each world continue to shift the way they need to. This constant shifting ensures that each world remains stable and serves to release the tension that builds at the center of each world's core. Many of Lictina's followers live on the World of Trollcom. Lictina, as you can imagine by the name of her race, looks like a lizard. She does, however stand erect on two legs and wears elegant looking robes lined with gems. She keeps her hood up at all times. The goddess is self-conscious of her appearance while around the others of the collective.

Owain—God of Water

Owain is responsible to govern the worlds' water supplies. He is very short with long dark hair. His eyes are black and he wears soft blue-colored suits, not being a fan of robes. Owain's parents were also dwarfs and gods, but held little power compared too many of the other gods prior to the God Wars. His mother and father were destroyed in the wars but had enough foresight to place Owain in the protective custody of the collective prior to their destruction.

Keylom—God of Peace also God of Good-Natured Beasts
Keylom was a mild-mannered centaur prior to ascending to godhood. Part horse and part elf, his long dark hair covers his pointed ears and runs down the back of his vest-covered torso. His elfin face is handsome with a small goatee. The bottom portion of his body is a beautiful black stallion with a golden blanket draped across his back. Keylom keeps every square inch of his anatomy well groomed as he is both the God of Peace and the God of Good-Natured Beasts with the responsibility of establishing peace in times of distress.

Calla—Goddess of Truth
Calla has always been a god and is almost as old as Bassorine. But despite her age, she is not nearly as powerful as some of the others. Without accepting the collective's offer to join, she would have perished during the God Wars. She is human in appearance and wears dresses of lace. Calla is not stunningly gorgeous, but she is far from ugly. Calla's title is also her function among the gods.

Helmep—God of Healing
Helmep was a human healer before his ascension. He lived and died nearly 900,000 years ago on a world called Gosslain in the Helgias Galaxy billions of light years from our Earth. He ascended just after his death because of Bassorine's desire to keep him around. Helmep was one of Bassorine's faithful while living on his world and it was this faith that gave him the blessing of godhood. Helmep is the weakest of all the gods within the *Farendrite Collective* and serves as the deity which many of the healers on the World of Harvestom serve. He is handsome, well-built, has short blonde hair, and hazel eyes. In white robes with dark trimmed accents, Helmep is known for his kind heart.

Illustrated By: Angela Woods

Introduction

Sam Goodrich, a strong, friendly, dark-haired man with brown eyes, lowered himself to the edge of the bed. He couldn't grasp everything he had just heard. It all weighed on his heart, suffocating his every thought. Even though he was brilliant— studying with some of the best scholars on Earth and surpassing even their knowledge—he now felt lost, struggling to stay focused.

"How could Earth possibly be destroyed?" he thought. Everything he loved, everything he had worked to build was gone. His family, his friends, and anything he identified with no longer existed.

Insanity rushed in to take control of him. But the firm, gentle and ever-so-powerful hands of a god reached out to touch his head and slowly... Sam drifted off to sleep.

"Rest My Child, Rest!"

Illustrated By: Ian Ferrebee

Chapter 1

𝕮𝖔𝖒𝖆

SAM GOODRICH, once a kind-hearted family doctor, rolled off his opponent's mangled body. His mind was clouded, enraged, and unable to realize his enemy lay lifeless before him in the sand of the arena floor. Using a wooden stave, he delivered another series of thunderous strikes, smashing ferociously away at the arms, back, and head of his victim.

Sam's own gentle soul had turned away in rebuke. It was not until after a voice cried out from the crowd—a voice strong enough to penetrate his insanity that he stopped.

It was Shalee, calling him back from the darkness that had swallowed him whole. Hearing her tender call, Sam suddenly became aware of his victim's motionless, bloodied body as his senses awoke to what he had done. An overwhelming feeling of sorrow once again allowed his soul to embrace him.

Slowly lowering the weapon to the ground... he reached down to feel for a pulse... nothing, not a single beat could be found as he frantically began to move his hand from one side of the neck to the other. He backed away from the corpse, staggered and fell to his knees. Grabbing his head, Sam let out a penetrating cry of remorse,

"Aahhhhhhhhhh!"

His wrenching cry could be heard from the farthest point of the arena.

Sam wept... he was now a murderer...

*Allow me to take you back to a period
just over 14,000 seasons ago...
to a time just before the destruction of Earth.*

DR. SAM GOODRICH put the cold stethoscope on the boy's chest and asked him to take two deep breaths. The child jumped and Sam realized the boy was in good, general health. His flu-like symptoms could be treated with a simple over-the-counter medication, so the doctor wrote out a recommendation and handed it to the boy's mother.

"Mrs. Taylor, thank you for bringing Bobby in to see me. This should do the trick. He'll be just fine in a few days." Sam smiled and gave a few other words of encouragement, then shook the woman's hand before leaving the room.

At five-foot ten, 185 pounds, Sam was a muscular man with washboard abs. He was in amazing shape—and his cardio, not to mention his diet, were impeccable, thanks to the five hours a day he spent training in the world of mixed-martial arts combat for the last six years.

And today was Sam's lucky day... the day of his first professional fight. He had fought as an amateur for the last four years and, prior to that, he spent two years learning the basics, training with his good friend John and as John's life-size punching bag. When he started in the sport—now his passion—he grew accustomed to being turned into a human pretzel, quickly learning that his body could bend in ways he never imagined; all thanks to John who took great pleasure in teaching him.

It was this friend, also a professional fighter, who had been instrumental in Sam's transformation into the machine he was inside the cage. John was nine years older than Sam and one of the few people who took him seriously when he made the decision to learn the sport. Sam benefited from John's experience and knowledge, absorbing it all like a sponge.

Today would be the start of his rise to stardom, paving the way to temporarily leave the medical profession for a career in professional mixed-martial arts combat.

Sam was not your normal fighter. He was known across the

globe for his superior intelligence, testing higher than most well-known scholars of his time. He graduated high school at the age of 10, finished his Bachelors in medicine at age 13, and earned a medical degree before turning 16. In short, he was a walking book of knowledge. His unparalleled ability to rapidly retain data amazed his professors and the world.

But despite his brilliance, he was barred from practicing medicine at such a young age. The medical community felt his age made him too immature to handle real world responsibilities. Even the courts agreed, ruling Sam had to be 18 before becoming a surgeon. Perhaps they were right. Although a genius, Sam was over-confident, hot-tempered and lacking common sense at times.

Yet, he continued to appeal their decisions. And with every appeal came another rejection that thrust a deep jab into his pride and fueled his anger even more—eventually driving him to see a counselor for help with his growing hostility. Tammy, his counselor, suggested a physical outlet, where he could use his body to release every bottled-up emotion. It worked. In fact, it more than worked. Sam entered mixed-martial arts combat training when he was 16, looking for an emotional release and instead, found a new passion.

Later, as his medical career developed, Sam continued training with John every day, deciding to work as a family practitioner, rather than becoming a surgeon, so he had more time for the sport he loved. Using some of the money from his family's trust to open a family medicine practice, Sam's life became a balancing act between his business, patients, training, and fighting.

Thanks to his worldwide reputation, Sam's practice was an immediate success and other eager, high-achieving doctors came to work for him because of the publicity they would receive. Even with all this, Sam kept his personal patient load to a minimum, always keeping time for his passion—fighting.

His practice employed 133 people and included doctors, nurses, and therapists of different medical backgrounds. His mother and father were business-minded people as well, with administrative backgrounds. They handled the day-to-day operations which also gave him more time to pursue his fighting career.

And tonight, Sam's first professional fight would be in Las Vegas. He had to leave work early to catch a plane, since he had to be in the ring within an hour and a half after the jet landed.

Emotions flooded him as he arrived at the MGM Grand, the press and fans of the barbaric sport swarming around the stretch limo. He hadn't even fought in his first professional fight yet, but was already on the cover of ESPN The Magazine. He had to laugh at the headline: *The Smartest Athlete in the World Dumb Enough to Enter the Cage of Mixed-Martial Arts Combat.*

Tossing the magazine on the seat, Sam hoped to give a good show and live up to all the hype. He would hate to be the first athlete to be on the cover with a losing professional record. He grinned at that thought as he stepped out of the limo.

The surging crowd pressed against him as he walked up to the MGM's arena entrance. He laughed inside.

People are nuts, I can't believe this frenzy. I bet if I lose, they won't be so hot for me then!

Women were even shouting out marriage proposals which startled him. One woman lifted her shirt.

"Sam Goodrich, marry me and I'll take care of you, baby," she screamed.

Like any red-blooded male, Sam was not immune to a beautiful woman. He admired her brown flowing hair, long shapely legs, and curvy hips—all perfect. The coolness of the night only added to her beauty... all that is, except her teeth. Her wretched smile exposed twisted gaps you could drive a bus through. Sam quickly moved on, flashing a forced smile as he went by.

A barrage of flashing lights greeted him as he stepped through the door. Almost blinded by their intensity, he managed to work his way through the mob. Not stopping to talk; Sam made his way to the locker room to prepare for the fight. The press would just have to wait until the show was over.

The locker room was a welcomed quiet as he changed.

"Hey Jerome, give me a few minutes, will ya? I need to think before getting myself all worked up. I wish John was here . . . I need him!" Sam said.

Jerome, his conditioning trainer, gave an understanding nod.

"Sure thing man, we need to start warming up, though, so think fast, awwight? You don't need John, bro. You know, John boy sends love. Got to take care of the fam first. Besides, I got your back. We got this under control!" Jerome said, showing a mouth full of golden teeth.

Sam smiled. "Okay okay... give me a minute."

He watched Jerome leave the room. He knew John's daughter needed her father after the accident. Sam would not have even come to the fight, but John insisted. Little Gabby was in stable, but serious, condition from a hit-and-run as she crossed the school crosswalk with her bike. He had said many prayers for her since the accident.

His opponent was tough, a man from Brazil who held a mixed-martial arts combat record of 18 wins and three losses, with 17 of the wins by T.K.O. This guy was a nightmare to face for his first professional fight, and everyone was betting on the Brazilian to hand Sam his first trip to the cage's mat knocked out cold. The press joked that the doctor would be able to stitch himself up and save on medical bills.

After getting ready and warming up properly, the time came to enter the cage. Sam's stomach was uneasy; he bent over in the hallway and grabbed the nearest trash can, vomiting uncontrollably. He wondered if he'd even make it to the ring. He felt weak and chilled; but he stood up, wiped his mouth, and leaned against Jerome's shoulder.

The trainer pushed him back and snapped. "Man up, man. You got this, dog. Use that head of yours and get it out of the clouds, man . . . focus!"

Sam knew Jerome was right. It was time to start thinking through this—he had to take charge of his body and control his emotions. It was time to own the situation.

As they began making their way to the ring, Sam realized the pay-per-view cameras had caught him throwing up on tape. He was sure it would become the cover story for all the sports writers—no matter if he won or lost. Gaining composure, he continued to walk down the corridor and into the arena, enjoying the idea of the press twisting his barrel of vomit into a good laugh.

Most fighters would have been excited by now, trying to psych themselves up, but Sam's mind would no longer allow him to do anything but concentrate. He refused to let the fast-paced environment rule him any longer. As he walked he collected himself, focusing on the task at hand, taking note of everything.

As the cage door closed behind him, Sam stared at his Brazilian opponent and nodded. He felt nothing, not fear nor excitement. He simply stood, evaluating all the weak points of the man's body and systematically calculating how he was going to take advantage of each area to attain victory. It was as if a switch had turned on inside him and he knew his body was prepared from his perfect 12-0 amateur fight experience. Sam had confidence in that fact; the rest of the sport was entirely mental, the easiest part of the sport for him. The doctor was ready to go to war!

The fight started and the two men met at the center of the octagon cage. They touched gloves and circled one another, sizing each other up. The Brazilian threw a couple jabs, which Sam brushed off with no effect. Now he countered with a powerful slapping kick to the inner thigh. The loud smack energized the crowd.

Again the Brazilian attacked, this time lunging forward with his knee, only to pull the knee back and strike with an accurately placed right hand. Sam arched his back, softening the impact, and pushed away with his left hand.

The two men moved in, locking up and grabbing hold of one another's neck. The Brazilian tightened his clinch, pulled Sam closer and scoffed in a heavy accent, "You're not ready for this—go home and leave the fighting to real men."

His insult hit deep, opening up old wounds from the past and awakening the dormant rage within the doctor. Everything in the arena seemed to melt away as his foe seemed to fight in slow motion. Sam's brain processed his opponent's actions by slowing them down and zeroing in on each one.

Once again, the Brazilian in his thick accent taunted him, "I said go home, amateur—you don't have what it takes, boy!"

At that, Sam pulled back and surrendered to the rage rising from the center of his being. He struck the Brazilian with a clean, solid left hook, causing his opponent's ribs to burn with pain.

They separated and again began to circle. Sam landed a methodical jab, followed by another powerful left hook. The Brazilian countered with a jab of his own and followed it by diving in for a takedown. But Sam's rage was in full swing. He brought up a strong right knee, pulverizing the Brazilian's face. Blood spewed from his forehead as the Brazilian fell limp to the mat.

Sam smelled victory . . . a gloriously pungent aroma, emanating from the rage that continued to surge within his body. "I'm ready for this. Don't ever doubt me," he hissed.

Sam threw all his weight on his opponent, surrounding his body with both legs. He buried the heels of his feet deep into the man's groin and threw his arm under his chin. His right arm sunk deep into the throat; his left elbow cupped his right hand to lock it in. To finish the hold, the upper part of his left arm continued upward and he place his hand behind the Brazilian's head and squeezed with all his might as he continued to appease his inner rage. "Never doubt me, punk," he hissed, tightening his grasp. "Die, you putz . . . die!"

It took only seconds for the man to tap and the fight was stopped. Sam had just won his first fight with a rear naked choke submission—but his arms had to be pried from the Brazilian's throat.

As Sam rose in victory from the mat, he appeared calm even though his mind scrambled to quiet the rage pounding inside. Jerome ran to his side. "You did it bro! John boy would be proud. C'mon, get up man, show the fans you appreciate them and enjoy this moment . . . dog!"

Sam knew his fame was about to take yet another giant leap forward and wondered what this new roller coaster would be like. Most men would be thinking about the moment and living it up, but Sam was not like most men. Despite the rage he had just unleashed, his mind was already months ahead of today, planning his next move.

True, he was pleased with his victory since no man had ever taken a path like his. He was in full control of his own destiny, and the world was his for the taking.

Sam turned to face the announcer to answer his questions, but something was not quite right. He fought the awkwardness and shook the man's hand. When he did, the announcer's eyes glowed red as he gave an evil grin, exposing a mouth filled with razor-sharp, pointed teeth. Sam's heart pounded recklessly; he tried to lift his hand to strike at the man, but to no avail.

He was motionless, unable to respond to the orders coming from his mind. His eyelids weighed heavy as if he had gone days without sleep. The overwhelming weight of his body made his knees nearly buckle. He did not know or understand what was happening. Then, as fast as the sensation came over him, it went away.

The next thing Sam knew, he was being congratulated on a nice fight and asked how it felt to accomplish such a great victory. Realizing he was not on his knees, he took a second to get his bearings. He looked again into the man's eyes; this time they were crystal blue, accompanied by a large bright smile. Sam shook the cobwebs out.

"I am happy," he replied. "I have a huge amount of respect for my opponent tonight, and it's too bad that one of us had to lose. I'm just glad it wasn't me," he said with a smile.

The crowd cheered him on; and for that split second, he felt larger than life. Leaving the cage, he turned and looked again at the announcer. The man looked back at him from across the mat. Sam watched as the red glow returned to the announcer's eyes, and a mouthful of razor-sharp teeth began to once again scream their silent threats.

Sam's face showed his fear as he hurried with his trainer back to the locker room. His thoughts raced wildly, but no rational explanation could justify what he had seen. His mind was stumped— and a brilliant mind without answers is a mind sure to go insane.

Entering the locker room, Sam lay down on the bench. As he tried to quiet his mind, a hissing sound filled the room, seemingly coming from nowhere. It pierced Sam's body and reverberated within him. A chill slithered up his spine as he heard the words, "Your wish is granted," then he fell into a coma.

Filled with terror, Jerome ran for help. As Jerome raced down the hall... Sam's body vanished.

The home of Shalee Adamson
Austin, Texas

SHALEE ADAMSON, a shapely, blue-eyed, blonde, pulled into the driveway of an old, rundown house, rushed up to the front door, and walked in without knocking. "Hurry up, Chanice! I'm running late from work and our dinner reservations are in 30 minutes . . . it'll take most of that to get there."

A large woman, sitting on the living room couch, began to cough.

"Hello Mrs. K, how are you?" Shalee said. "Are the pain meds still making you nauseous?"

Kelly lifted her head, and managed to respond between coughs. "I'm sick as a dog. Serves me right, I guess. I should stop sucking on these stupid cigarettes. Thank you for taking my baby with you. She loves you to death, you know. I can see that you're good for her."

"It's easy to love that little girl. She has such a good spirit."

Kelly groaned as she shifted to find a better position, one that did not hurt as much. "That's good to hear. I can't tell you how much my baby has grown since meeting you. The Big Brothers, Big Sisters program is a godsend. Chanice has said more than once that she wishes you were her real sister. She admires everything about you. She especially loves your fashion sense."

Shalee smiled, and then turned her attention toward the hallway. "Chanice, we need to go. I hope you have on the new dress I bought you!"

"I'm coming, I got it on," the ten-year-old yelled from the bedroom. "Mother threw up again, I'm almost done cleaning it up." Shalee looked around—the house was a dump, along with the rest of the neighborhood, overrun by gangs. It was the kind of place she herself had worked hard to get out of. Her family, a bunch of rednecks, had become a statistic, a real-life tragedy.

Only two of her seven brothers broke free from the dive they grew up in and actually made something of their lives. The rest followed in their drunken father's footsteps . . . drinking, shooting up and multiplying like rabbits. They made a bigger mess of things by adding more children to the world who would also grow up without a proper role model.

Despite the obstacles put in front of her, Shalee had grown into a confident woman. She still lived in Austin, like the rest of her family, but put her education to work. After graduating from the University of Texas with a perfect four point GPA, she was now working on her master's in structural engineering and had held a position at a prestigious architectural firm for three years. She had grown accustomed to her new life, right down to her exotic, leather, Jimmy Choo clutch handbag.

Shalee opened the passenger door to her new Lexus. Chanice sat down inside and immediately began to cry. "My mother is killing herself. I don't understand why she's still smoking. It's horrible! Can I come live with you, please? I don't want to go live with my uncle . . . he's so mean."

"Let's take this one step at a time, okay? You know I'll do whatever I can to help you through this. Now, let's focus on some happier thoughts, shall we?"

Shalee wiped a tear from Chanice's face and the young girl gave a brave smile and nodded.

"All right then . . . well, since today's my birthday, what do you say us girls go and celebrate?"

"Yeah, I'm starving . . . happy birthday, big sis!"

Shalee grabbed a CD and popped it into the player.

> *Lately when I look into your eyes*
> *I realize, you're the only one I need in my life . . .*

Swaying to the music, Shalee grabbed her hairbrush from the console and used it as a microphone while she lip-synced. Chanice burst into laughter and started dancing in the car. Then Shalee started singing, making up her own lyrics to the music.

> *My little sister and me . . . oh, oh, we . . . don't know how*
> *to describe*
> *How happy we feel inside.*

Chanice gave her a high five, took the brush and made up her own lyrics.

> *We've got butterflies*
> *We're going to fly higher in the sky*
> *We can become anything wonderful we want . . . we're*
> *like butterflies*

"You got it, my little sister—that rocks!"

Around ten pm, Shalee walked into her home, threw the keys on the buffet table, kicked off her Marc Jacob shoes and made a cup of tea to unwind before heading up to bed.

If I could only get a good night's sleep... I just need one good night before facing another hectic day of presentations, clients and umpteen phone calls. Thank god mother has my Pebbles. I'm just too tired to play with her tonight.

She looked at the picture of her little dog sitting on the coffee table. *What a cute poodle you are . . . yes you are,* she thought in her best doggy voice.

It was later that night when Shalee woke in a panic, sweat pouring from every pore. She wiped her forehead with her pillowcase and swung her legs over the side of the bed. Putting her feet inside the soft pink slippers beside the nightstand, without bending over, she lifted her arms behind her head to help catch her breath. It took a minute before her pulse slowed and her breathing returned to normal. It had been 187 days since the nightmares had begun and her doctor was stumped as to why her mind was taking her on these horrific trips.

Somehow, tonight's nightmare did not seem like the rest. Everything felt a bit off, but she couldn't quite pinpoint why. She slowly stood up from the bed, stretched her arms and arched her back. No relief, at least not like it normally gave. She lowered her arms and looked into the dresser mirror. A frosty breath filled the air as it escaped her mouth. She touched herself, somehow feeling confused as she tried to determine if any of her parts were missing. To her surprise, everything was there; she sighed as she once again watched the chilled air billow in front of her face. She embraced her body with both arms.

What's wrong with me and why is it so cold?

After a moment, she started to laugh and began talking to her reflection. "What's wrong with you, Shalee? Why are you letting yourself act this way? Pull yourself together, go turn up the thermostat and get back to bed." She continued to laugh as she turned to go.

Shalee walked across the room and down the hallway, passing two other bedrooms and a guest bathroom. She needed a drink of water before going back to sleep. As she passed the thermostat, she turned it up.

The blue-eyed beauty was, despite her age, already enjoying the respect of her superiors at work. When she designed her home, Shalee had created a great room, where both the kitchen and living room flowed into each other without separation. Her sense of taste was impeccable. Granite countertops from Africa, top-of-the-line carpet from Europe, imported tile from Spain and trims to match.

Tonight, as she turned on the lights, the colors on her walls seemed dull, growing colder for no apparent reason. The temperature dropped so rapidly that she became frightened. Quickly she headed for the closet near the front door to grab a coat as suddenly, a rush of pain entered her body. Shalee collapsed before she could make it to the closet. Falling to the floor, she caught a glimpse of something out of the corner of her eye as her head slammed into the edge of the coffee table. The glass surface shattered almost knocking her out. As she struggling to pick herself up with weakened arms, blood escaped from a wound torn open by the splintered glass. Shalee's fear magnified, filling her mind with a sense of helplessness as it pooled in front of her. She slipped into unconsciousness as the image sitting in the window, an image she never clearly saw, faded into darkness.

Near the fireplace a tiny little man sat on the sill of the window. No more than two feet tall, his eyes glowed red and his teeth ended in sharp points. He laughed as he scampered across the room, waddling from side to side. He jumped up and landed in a sitting position on Shalee's stomach.

"Your wish is granted, my lady," the dwarf said, leaning forward to touch her chin. As they both disappeared in a cloud of fiery smoke, an echo of laughter exploded waking the entire neighborhood. Shalee was now in a coma—in storage for later use.

The home of George Nailer
Orlando, Florida

GEORGE NAILER was a fit, dark-haired, blue-eyed man, who was always well-dressed. Sitting on the bed next to his sleeping daughter, he ran his fingers lovingly through her hair. She was the apple of his eye. They had spent the day going from store to store looking for the cupcake maker she had been asking for over the last month.

He tried hard to be a good father, loving his daughter with everything he had. She was the only person he had never lied to—or manipulated. He may have been scum, but his little girl was his shining light to goodness. He had named her Abbie—my father's joy—since that's how he felt the day she was born. Her ten-year-old heart was angelic, and that cute little smile... she really knew how to pull him in every time she wanted something. Yes, he was wrapped around Abbie's little finger and, even though he would never admit it, all she had to do was ask and she'd get anything she wanted.

Growing up as an only child of a cruel father, George's life was constant beatings... and sexual abuse as well. George knew he was emotionally scarred, forced to fight his way through his childhood just to get the things he needed. Even getting food was a challenge since his father constantly snorted all his paychecks up his nose. So, at an early age, George turned to hustling and stealing. His perfected skills of manipulation helped his mother pay the rent. But even still his mother often wasted the money on drugs herself.

The past played with his head, an endless loop of loathing, degradation, and shame running through his veins like poisonous venom. Finally, on the eve of his 15th birthday, the poison spilled over and took control. George approached his father from behind as he sat in a stupor watching TV. Then he lunged and beat his father ruthlessly over the head with his fists. His father wailed in pain and shouted for help as George's fists rained down again and again. George slipped further away from reality with each swing. "You're a piece of crap!" he screamed uncontrollably, "You're nothing but an abusive looser, I hate you! I'll make sure you never touch me again or anybody else! I'm not your toy! Who do you think you are? I hate you!"

The police charged in and struggled to pull George off. A moment later would have been too late because George was going to kill his father. He thrashed wildly, fighting against the cops to break free. He screamed at the top of his lungs, "Let me kill him—that scum deserves it . . . let me put him six feet under! Let me kill him! Let me kill him!"

Five months later George's time in a mental hospital had given him time to think. With his father serving 25 years in prison, he finally had some peace. But during those days of recouped sanity, he swore an oath—he cherished and whispered it a thousand times, writing it down to carry with him always: "If I ever have children, I'll protect them—they'll never want for anything. And I'll never touch them in anger or make them suffer. I'll never touch them in an inappropriate manner. My children will NOT suffer like I have!"

And now in his adult life, in spite of his promise, he had struggled in his marriage to Abbie's mother, which caused him to break his oath. Instead of creating a sanctuary of safety for his daughter he gave her a broken home. He hated himself for that but even more, hated taking his daughter home after their visits together. The guilt of failure constantly tore at his heart.

His apartment was small, only two-bedroom but expensively decorated. He rarely spent any time in it though because his hunger for the finer things in life was insatiable. He used others to get what he wanted, including countless women. He spent most of his time living in their homes, emotionally tearing away at them until his needs were met. Once he had everything he wanted, he moved on without a goodbye or backward glance.

George took one final look at his beautiful Abbie, smiled and pulled her door shut. He made his way to his own room and fell across the bed. Tomorrow morning he would press his Gucci clothes and drop his little girl off at her mother's home before heading to work. A big-time client was coming in from out of town and George smiled at the thought of the large commission he'd make. As a salesman for Turkman's RV & Marine, he could sell ice to Eskimos if he needed to, and he'd lie at the drop of a hat to do it, too.

Finally, after a long day of anticipation George's client arrived at the dealership to make her purchase. The RV was fully loaded, right down to the 40-inch flat screen TV with satellite. Brenda Olsen had just come into a lot of money and George's mouth watered as he sized her up. A Southern beauty with a soft accent, her pinned-up blonde hair revealed an elegant neck with an expensive pendant accenting it. She smelled of Victoria Secret's Pure Seduction and her body matched her smile's personality. She was class with a capital "C".

Before she arrived, George took the price sticker off the RV and quoted Brenda a price almost $30,000 dollars over list. His new price was $970,000 and he held to every penny of it. Brenda was an out-of-state referral who had driven all the way from Georgia. He knew from his prequalification over the phone that this would be an easy sale. He knew exactly what model to show and how to go about reeling her in before she set foot on the lot.

During the sale, Brenda did ask to see other models but George looked her dead in the eye and replied without hesitation, "You don't deserve anything less than the best. This is a once-in-a-lifetime purchase. Settling for something beneath your class just wouldn't be right," he insisted as he smiled through his perfect white teeth.

George spent years developing his silver tongue, the tongue of a liar and cheat, and he knew how to use it. He was the *self-proclaimed King of Deception*. Even his own family bought into his tangled web—hook, line and sinker. And even worse, he was the kind of liar who remembered everything he said, which made him dangerous.

He took the initial paperwork to his boss and placed it on his desk. Once the manager signed off on the deal, the two shared a laugh over the buyer's ignorance. Then George took his client into the finance manager's office to get final contracts drawn up.

As George and Brenda waited for the documents to be ready, he buttered her up some more. "Why don't you let me make it easy on you... I can deliver the vehicle to your home in a couple of days, and then fly back here."

"Oh George, would you? You're so generous and accommodating! Why, thank you ever so, you're a peach," Brenda said as she threw her arms around him in a big hug.

"Well, of course, anything to keep the customer happy," George replied, as he thought about a woman from a bar he had been in a few nights ago. He decided he'd ask her along for the trip and they could have a swinging time. The RV was perfect for just such an occasion and would do just fine.

Even as Brenda stopped hugging him George continued making plans. He would drop the woman off at one of the local restaurants before arriving at Brenda's house. Then he could go in alone and make a play for Brenda's affections. He knew she was now a multimillionaire and he could imagine spending her fortune. He wanted that money badly, and would even marry her to get it. He smiled inside as he rejoined the conversation and nodded to something Brenda was saying.

They finished the deal and Brenda prepared to leave—but not without giving George another big hug before she got into her car. "Drive safely, Georgie and bring my "baby" home in good condition."

George smiled, "I'll do just that, Brenda. You take care now. I look forward to seeing you again. Don't miss me before I get there, okay?" Brenda giggled and pulled away.

The next day, George rounded up the lady from the bar and, after a few minutes of smooth talk she agreed that a road trip would be fun. It was noon when they hit the road and the drive was smooth for the first few hours. But George suddenly felt tired and wanted to rest. He had told Brenda he needed a couple of days to get the RV to her home, so he could relax a little now, no worries. He had plenty of time to spend with his new friend before arriving in Albany.

He looked at her and asked, "Mind driving for a bit so I can rest?" Smiling back at him, she said, "No problem." He pulled over and let her have the wheel.

Now what did she say her name was? Oh yeah, Tiffany. George had not made much of a mental note of that fact since his attraction to her was purely physical. He figured he'd probably never see her again once they returned to Orlando. He admired her body and longed for her from his passenger's seat. She was soft in all the right spots. And, although she was older than he was, she was still young enough that gravity had not taken its effect. He knew it would be a great night and he was looking forward to every minute.

Tiffany had only been driving for a few minutes when George heard her mumble something beneath her breath.

"What was that?" George asked. "I didn't hear you . . . say that again?"

The woman pushed her soft, brown hair behind her ear and smiled. Without moving her mouth, George heard her voice echo inside his head.

"Your wish is granted," the voice hissed with a wickedness that frightened him.

The air in the RV cabin suddenly turned cold to the point of being painful. The woman's eyes began to glow red and George could see the razor-sharp points of her teeth. She was pure evil and George caught his breath as he realized he was in big trouble. His eyes became heavy as he slipped into a coma, hearing the echoes of Tiffany's laughter in his mind.

Suddenly, the RV twisted into a pile of metal as it collided with the oncoming semi. The large tanker filled with fuel poured out its liquid everywhere from the gaping hole in its side. As the semi exploded it took the RV with it throwing the following vehicles everywhere. The explosion was a horrific force and tore a six-foot crater out of the concrete. In some areas, the hole was 30 feet across. Cars were crashing in all directions, some as far as 120 feet away.

Police investigating the scene accounted for the body of the man driving the semi, along with the other nine drivers the blast consumed. Victims were scattered in every direction landing in small, charred, bloody pieces. It seemed there was no one driving the RV, the chief of police told reporters, it was as if the driver had vanished. The short, chubby man of the law estimated that, in total, there were over 14 dead, but there was no accounting for the missing souls of the destroyed RV.

Chapter 2

𝕬𝕘𝕒𝕚𝕟𝕤𝕥 𝕺𝕦𝕣 𝖂𝕚𝕝𝕝

IT WAS DARK, almost pitch black, and George Nailer could not see a thing as he woke from his coma. Disoriented, he had no idea where he was; his back ached and his muscles were sore. He reached down and touched the surface he was sitting on—solid, hard, and cold. Now he understood why his body felt so stiff. How long had he been unconscious? There was no way to tell, but it was obviously this floor and his bulging wallet that made him hurt.

George sat there for quite some time, fighting with his eyes to get them to adjust and, after a while, he could make out what he thought were the edges of a room. The nearest wall in front of him was probably 30 feet away and extended so high he could not tell where it ended. In the wall was an outline of what appeared to be two large doors, but he could not tell what they were made of. Turning his head to the left and right, he saw large pillars that also extended up and out of sight. Beyond these pillars, another 30 feet or so were the edges of yet another wall, which stretched up and into the darkness without end. The material the pillars were made of seemed like that of the floor, some sort of marble or other expensive material.

Slowly, he continued to turn and look around. To his surprise, he soon realized he was not alone and a chill went down his spine. Two shadowy figures lay motionless on the floor not far away. There was no wall beyond them, but instead the room stretched into the distance, along with the pillars, far enough that his eyes could not make out the end.

This must be some kind of great hallway or something. I wonder who these two are. I wonder what they're story is? What if they're killers! Man, this place is really creeping me out! I've got to get out of here!

After a moment, he began to whisper under his breath. "What the hell is going on? Where am I? How in the hell did I get here?" As he spoke, his voice grew louder as his emotions took over.

He shouted nervously, "Hello?"

He listened—nothing.

"Hello?" "Where am I? Would someone answer me for hell's sake?"

Still nothing—George and the two motionless figures were alone.

His eyes turned to look at the others lying on the floor as one of them started to move. It was a woman, or at least what he thought was a woman by the sound of the moans. He could only guess because the figure was not in focus yet even though the two figures lay only 15 feet or so from him, within arm's reach of each other.

Her eyes would also need time to adjust and George watched as she sat up. He said nothing, but his mind ran wild with thought.

I wonder if it's safe to say anything.

It took everything in him to stay silent as the woman stirred. He wanted to speak badly, but he knew he had to keep the upper hand in every situation, especially this one. It was clear she was suffering and having a hard time adjusting to the darkness as she started to feel around. Her hand came in contact with the other individual next to her and she jerked back in shock.

"Who's there?" she said in a panic, but there was no answer.

George watched silently.

She's scared out of her mind. At least I'm not the only one. Good... at least she won't be a threat.

Again she asked, "Who's there?"

And George watched, smirking to himself.

Glad I'm definitely not the only one who's confused as hell right now. Okay, this makes me feel a little better. I best stay quiet for as long as I can. Maybe there's an advantage to be had here!

The third figure on the floor suddenly made a noise and started to move. George smiled as he watched the woman jump.

Wow, she's really scared to death. She's terrified! I wish I could see the expression on her face. I bet it's a riot. I can hear her breathing from here. This is classic.

She moved away from the noise and toward George. He had to hold back his desire to laugh.

She would've never moved in this direction if she had any clue that I was here. I should scream, BOO. Oh my hell that would be funny! Okay think, that would be funny, but it would also be a disadvantage. I have to keep an advantage here!

This time, the woman used a much louder voice, **"Who's there?"**

The figure next to her moved again, this time groaning while grabbing at his head with one hand and pushing himself upright with the other.

Okay, this one's a guy. His groan sounds like a man's, George thought as he tried to focus a little harder on the figure. *Just keep quiet and let's let this situation play itself out.*

"I said who's there?" The woman yelled with an even more forceful tone than before. "I have a gun!"

George smiled as he reached down under his pant leg and patted the small firearm that he also carried with him.

Well at least I've got one too.

"Relax . . . relax . . . relax!" the man said, trying to gain his bearings. "My name is Sam, ughhhh." He rubbed his eyes and continued. "Sam, Sam Goodrich, that's who's here."

The woman said nothing. She waited for more information as, unbeknownst to her, George reveled in her anxiety.

She's so scared out of her damn mind that I can feel it!

After a moment of silence, Sam spoke in an authoritative voice of his own. "Who are you? Why are all the lights out? Where the heck am I? Do you have any aspirin? My head feels like a dang truck hit it," he said rubbing his temples.

George watched the woman react and grab for what he assumed would be a purse, which, it turned out, was not with her. Not only was her purse missing, but as she moved closer to him, he noticed that she was wearing her pajamas and slippers.

Wow, nice body, I can appreciate her taste in pajamas. I may not know where I am, but I know a beautiful woman when I see one. Hell . . . I've got to give props where they're due. A guy has got to sit back at a time like this and just enjoy it.

The woman replied quietly, still speaking to Sam. "I don't have any aspirin, I'm sorry." She tried to keep her voice low, not wanting to aggravate his pain any further. She also didn't want to risk frustrating the situation. "If I had some, I would give them to you."

"Dang!" Sam said, looking up, trying to see his surroundings as his eyes also tried to squint into clarity. Questioning the woman in waves, he said, "What is this place? Where am I? Who are you? How long have we been here?"

"I don't know where we are. I just woke up myself and my eyes are still adjusting to the dark. I don't know how long we've been here, and I'm afraid I'm not much help." After a minute, she continued. "My name is Shalee."

"Got a last name, Shalee?" Sam responded quickly.

"Adamson," she answered. "Shalee Adamson is my full name."

"Nice to meet you, Shalee Adamson, I think we've found ourselves in a bit of a pickle here, don't you think?" Sam said with a strong voice as he continued to scan the room. His brilliant mind was already looking for solutions and, as always, he was thinking ahead. His pain began to ease as he moved his neck around and turned to look at Shalee. "You've got to love a good puzzle. Hopefully, I'll be able to see all the pieces here real soon!" he said, with a slight smile that Shalee still could not see.

George deciding the two were not a threat to him, figured it was time to pipe in. "We're in some kind of great hallway," he said quietly.

Shalee, with her back to this new voice, screamed and rushed to Sam's side. Sam seemed to be less of a threat at the moment—which was ironic, since out of the two men in the room, Sam was the only one present who understood the mechanics of how to break someone's neck.

"Who's there?" Sam shouted sternly. "Show yourself!"

"Hell man, no one's hiding. I *am* showing myself. It's not my fault your eyes can't see me yet!" George stood and walked toward them both. "I've been sitting here in the same room, I've just been awake longer than both of you, so my eyes have had time to adjust."

As he walked toward them, he noticed Sam had some sort of fighting gloves on and not much else, except a pair of trunks. There was tape around his ankles, which George figured was from boxing.

The con artist continued, "When you two started moving, I didn't want to say anything until I knew it was safe. It appears we're all at a bit of a loss as to where we are or how we got here. The last thing I remember is driving in an RV with this lady from the bar. Her eyes turned red. It became really cold and I saw her teeth turn into these crazy sharp points. Then I passed out, I think."

"Good on you for keeping quiet," Sam replied. "I admire your tactics. As for me, I was in a fight and the announcer started to question me on my win. It was my first professional fight, and when I looked into his eyes, they were also red. His teeth, just like your woman's, were also very sharp. I felt helpless and couldn't move. The next thing I knew, the announcer's eyes were normal again and so was his smile. I finished answering his questions and remember the crowd cheering me on. When it was time to leave the cage, I looked again and saw the announcer's eyes change back to red. I got scared, man. It was a fear like I've never felt before, and I hurried away as fast as I could to get to my locker room. I remember lying down once I got there cuz I was overwhelmed and really cold. There was a crazy laugh and that's the last thing I remember."

Sam jumped to his feet and looked at Shalee. "What's your story?" he said, extending a hand to help her up.

"Yeah," George added as he watched Shalee take Sam's hand. "What's your story?" The jerk continued to enjoy her fear as he listened to her response.

"Well… ummm… I think I caught a glimpse of someone out of the corner of my eye when I fell in my living room. Not too sure about that, though. All I can really remember is that everything seemed so strange to me. I hit my head on the coffee table." She reached up to touch her forehead and, to her surprise, it was not sore. "That's strange . . . I don't have a mark on me. I wonder …" Shalee's anxiety would have continued to build but something happened to divert her attention.

The great hall filled with an amazing light. The entire group's attention turned to observe this miraculous happening. It was pointless to guess about the purpose of the demon with red eyes and sharp teeth—questions they would not have been able to answer anyway, questions that would have caused great panic and fear. At least for this moment, the light in the great hall was their saving grace.

No matter where they looked to find the light's origin, a source could not be found. The three of them moved close together, standing side by side.

"How is this possible?" Sam said as his brilliant mind changed course. "I don't see any reason for this place to light up like this." He scanned the room intently looking for an answer.

They stood huddled together with Shalee in the middle. She grabbed each of their hands to pull them closer to her. Sam took his hand away and moved clear so he was ready for anything that might happen. George, on the other hand, enjoyed the touch of a woman, and even a frightened woman's touch was acceptable. The manipulator that he was, he took the time to look over her figure once again and admire it.

I like the pink slippers, he thought. *Awe . . . and they have cute, white little bunnies on the top of them. Okay, she's wearing designer pajamas. She clearly has great taste and a stunning . . . well, her everything is stunning.* After a moment, he pulled his mind back to the situation at hand.

They stood there for what seemed to be forever. Nothing was happening so they all had a good look at their surroundings. They saw that the pillars were solid white with no noticeable imperfections. The large double doors nearest them were at least 30 feet tall and about eight feet wide and looked like a precious metal, maybe gold. The floor was polished to a perfect sheen. George looked down, saw himself and winked.

How ya doing, stud? Wow... I'm a looker!

As a group the three turned and looked in all directions. The hallway stretched for what Sam figured to be at least a few 100 yards. Above them, they could see paintings, glorious paintings that appeared to tell stories, but of what exactly they did not know.

There were many angelic beings fighting one another in some kind of intense battle. They all agreed that the ceiling's highest point had to be at least 100 feet up.

After a while of marveling, the three slowly moved to one side of the hallway beyond the pillars. All the way down this side of the hall, about every 100 feet or so, there was another door resembling the one closest to them. Sam counted 12 sets of doors along this side alone and quickly did the math in his head.

"This place must be at least 1,400 feet long. Man, can you imagine the money it took to build this?" Sam said excitedly. His mind raced ahead as he processed everything at once—the fear of the situation, two strangers in odd clothes, the cost to build such an expansive hall and managed to survey it all without missing a beat. He ordered, "George, go check out the other side."

George looked at Sam for a minute and sized him up as if he was going to object, then thought, *Okay, be a team player for now. Do what this guy says. There's a time for everything. No sense getting into an argument now. This chump seems pretty smart. Maybe I can learn something. Maybe I can find a way to take charge of the situation. Play it cool, George, play it cool!*

George moved to the other side of the great hallway and noticed there were more doors there as well. In the middle of the long stretch of doors was a statue tucked behind two of the pillars, previously not visible to them. The statue was in front of another set of even larger doors, which appeared to be different somehow. He could not see their full detail from his current position, but George could see they were different.

"I see a statue in front of a set of bigger doors, but they look different than the others. I can't be sure from here, but it might be worth a look."

Sam agreed, taking the lead and heading in that direction with George in tow.

"What are you two doing?" Shalee shouted. "I'm not moving from this spot. We have no idea what's behind any of these doors. We should stay here." There was fear in her voice. "We should wait right here!"

Both men, almost as if they shared the same brain, replied.

"Suit yourself," as they continued towards the large doors.

Shalee was flabbergasted at their response and, after a minute of standing there alone, ran to catch up with them, yelling as she ran, "Well, just leave a lady standing in the middle of nowhere in her pajamas, why don't you? I look cute in this. What if some crazy person saw me and got some naughty ideas? You don't just find bunny slippers this fabulous. Wait up, guys! Hey . . . I said, wait up!"

Both men turned and smiled as she caught up with them. Sam chided her, "I was wondering how long it would take for you to follow us. I would hate to have gone without you. I need protection, you know."

Shalee gave him a look to kill, realizing he was joking since it was obvious he could take care of himself. She was impressed with his amazing body and, if she had time to think about it, she would have found herself desiring to touch him. His dark brown hair, along with his soft brown eyes, made him exactly her type.

"Maybe we can move together now?" George said in a harsh tone. "This isn't my idea of fun, so the less we have to think about, the better. Please, no more thinking for you, woman!"

Sam ignored George's comment and brushed past him as he continued on. Shalee, on the other hand, gave him the bird as she passed by, and stayed on Sam's heels.

"Women, drama, emotion..." George said as he followed.

They now stood in front of the bronze-like statue. It stood quite tall and had incredible detail. The statue was a man, no more than six feet tall but standing on a base that put him five feet off the floor. He held a wooden-looking staff in his right hand as if he was using it as a walking stick. On his left hip hung a long sword, which clearly was meant for one hand and belted around the outside of his robe. There was a hood that extended up and over the top of his head, hanging just above his eyes. Beneath the shadow cast from his hood was a scar that ran across his right eye and ended near the corner of his mouth. The cut creating the scar had apparently not penetrated deep enough to injure the eye.

His boots extended high to the calf and looked as if they would offer solid protection. The robe beneath his chin, about half way down the man's sternum, was parted and a hint of chain-type armor could be seen, but it was not clear to any of them as to how much of his upper body it covered.

To the right side of the man, but tucked behind the staff, was a four-legged beast that looked like a wolf of some sort. The animal looked peaceful, though, as if it was with its master. They all agreed it was much larger than any wolf they had ever seen.

Across the man's body was a cord that stretched from his upper-right shoulder to his lower-left hip. It extended around to his back and was attached to a sturdy-looking bow. The weapon looked worn, but battle worthy.

As the group moved behind the statue, they noticed a quiver of arrows, in easy reach over the man's right shoulder. The quiver was tucked in close to his neck on the right side and angled down toward his left butt cheek.

On the base of the statue near the man's feet, was a round object that rested on a dragon's back, the dragon acting as a cradle. The sphere had a rough surface and appeared to be made of a gem or some type of crystal. As they looked closer, the group saw that the object looked more like a small planet of some sort and even seemed to resemble a moon more than it resembled an Earth. Even though it was clearly made of a different material than the rest of the statue, it somehow seemed to blend. The sphere was no larger than an NBA basketball and sat nestled in its cradle perfectly.

The platform was at least ten feet in diameter and had smooth edges. There was an inscription that started at the top and circled its way around until it ended near the floor. Both Shalee and George looked at the writings, then at each other and shrugged their shoulders. Sam, on the other hand, had found a starting point and circled the statue as if he were reading.

"What the hell are you doing?" George said as he watched.

"I'm reading."

"Reading?" He shook his head in amazement. "What do you mean, you're reading? Are you telling me that you can understand what's on this stupid thing?"

"There's nothing stupid about it. It's actually quite simple," Sam said, laying his hands across the markings. "Most every language has some sort of pattern to it. If I can figure out this pattern, I should be able to read it. Besides, this can't be any harder than the 16 other languages I've taught myself."

"Holy crap, man, you know 16 different languages?" George said, standing in astonishment. "Where the hell did you find time to learn them all?"

"During my summer vacation when I was nine." Sam acted as if it was nothing out of the ordinary, anyone could do it. He continued on as George asked questions.

"Oh, my goodness, I know who you are!" Shalee said, pointing at Sam. "You're the kid who was all over the TV and the news. I remember you because you and I have the same birthday. I also remember because I was very impressed when I heard about how all your languages were self-taught. I was nine and remember thinking how lucky you were to be going into your last year of high school. I didn't even get through the fourth grade before you graduated. The fuss everyone made about you learning all those languages, wow! My teachers in school talked about you all the time. They told us that if we applied ourselves, we could be as smart as you."

Shalee would have continued except for George's rude interruption. "Oh, shut up," he snapped, "I get it all ready. He's smart. Don't let yourself get too excited or you'll have to swim your way out of this place."

At that, Sam turned, walked up to George and stood in his face. "I don't know who you are, nor do I care, but if you talk to this woman, or any other woman like that ever again while I'm around, I'll have a few things to say about it . . . and I don't mean verbally."

George threw his hands in the air and backed up a few steps. "I feel you, man . . . I feel you. I'll do a check-up from the neck up. Hell, I've got the same birthday as you do too. Maybe I should jump on the whole Sam bandwagon too."

George turned and walked towards the heavy doors and thought. *I know who you are. I remember the news. You've had everything handed to you on a silver platter, Mr. Smartass! Life has been a breeze for you. Try living a day in my shoes, you holier than thou freak!*

Shalee was annoyed with George's antics and turned to face Sam. "So what's it say? Is there anything I can do to help?" she asked, watching the genius at work. "I'm pretty smart myself, so lay it on me. I'm sure I can help."

Sam turned to face her, and with a low, soft, calm voice said, "Unless you have a pen and a piece of paper, I think I'm going to have to settle for using my photographic memory to figure this one out. I need to find the patterns. Some of this seems familiar to me. I feel as if I've seen some of this in my dreams . . . as if it's something I've already learned."

After about an hour, Sam started to point and began to speak. "I think this is a tale of this man's great victories and how he brought home the power to control the worlds that the gods had lost. I'm not sure that I follow it all, but it appears this power is what keeps the planets from colliding into each other. It says here that the planets are all rotating at the same distance around their sun, but on different planetary orbits. It names five planets in this story and continues to say that this power is used to provide the proper separation that the worlds need to keep from smashing into each other."

George Interrupted. "Ya, ya, ya . . . you said that already. Move ahead, will ya, my hell!"

Sam took a long deep breath, calming himself.

"Apparently this power allows each world to support life. In short, the power acts as a governor for the worlds, and every function necessary to support life is what it monitors. This crystal sphere sitting on the statue's base is the source of this power. Apparently the crystal was lost in a large god war of some kind. I guess that it was this man who was able to find a way to retrieve the crystal and return it to the gods.

"It seems he was rewarded with god-like powers for this. The gods who gave him these powers appear to be called, if I'm reading this right, the Farendrite Collective. I can't recall ever learning anything about them before in all that I've studied. I also don't know how many gods form this Collective of the Farendrites, but this is what it says and it does allude to more than one of them. Apparently this man's name, written here on the statue, is Bassorine, but I don't see a last name.

"It seems to me that this part of the inscription here is talking about a prophecy of some sort. It's about how a small group of people, two men and a woman, will be called upon to recover the pieces of the *Crystal Moon*. I assume that this is the sphere's name. Two of the three will fight to recover the crystal, and one will fall to the wayside early, but it doesn't say anything more about what happens to this third person.

"The two remaining will be asked to retrieve these pieces of crystal before all life is destroyed, and the worlds collide into one another. If these pieces of crystal are separated from each other, the planetary orbits will start to shift and chaos will follow until the worlds are destroyed. But if the pieces of crystal are retrieved soon enough and all of them brought together, there will be a reward . . . and permission granted for the races to join together. Apparently, allowing the races to be rejoined is a big deal from the way this reads. I guess it will prove to the gods that the races can get along and live with each other on any planet they choose. I'm not sure how two people going after some pieces of crystal would prove this to the gods, but that's what it says."

Sam shook his head, perplexed, and continued. "So only certain races are allowed to be on certain planets the way it is now. It doesn't explain, however, what it means by races. I can only assume it's similar to races like black, white, Indian and so forth. It does have a date on here, but without a way to reference it to something I won't be able to determine how old this statue actually is. On the bottom, it says to awaken the statue and receive our instructions on how to start the path of our destinies."

"What do you mean our instructions?" George said in a sarcastic, yet frightened tone. "Do you actually buy into any of this horse crap? This could be referring to anyone, not just us. I think it's rather vain to think we're the group it's referring to. I, for one, don't want to be the one who falls by the wayside. Doesn't that usually mean death or something tragic like that? I sell RVs and boats for a living for hell's sake. I'm not a part of any stinking prophecy. Tell him, Shalee. You've got to feel me on this one, right?"

Shalee looked first at George, then at Sam. They waited intently for her answer. "I agree that this all seems really weird. I also agree that I'm just an architect and can't imagine being a part of any kind of prophecy either. But . . ." She paused and continued. "But how fun would it be, even if only for a while, to be able to do something different for a change? I mean, don't you ever just . . ." She shuffled her feet and paused. "Don't you ever just want to be a part of something cool? What if, what if it's . . . ?"

George exploded, "You've got to be kidding me! You're nuts! I must still be sleeping. I have officially met my first genius, who I'll bet is a little off in the head. Don't get me wrong, but how could you be normal with all the crap stuck so tightly in that brain of yours?" He turned to Shalee. "And you take the cake. You're buying into this crock of crap. I knew blondes were—"

Sam interrupted, "You finish that sentence and I'll break you in half! I've never said that I bought into any of this and neither has Shalee. She simply said it would be fun to be a part of something different. I think she means that she wants to be a part of something important."

Sam turned and started to pace while he thought. "Okay, okay, let's think through this for a minute. We don't know where we are . . . no one has come to greet us . . . and we all share the same birthday. We all woke up in the same great hallway and the three of us are standing here in front of this statue letting the unknown get the best of us. Not to mention, we're bickering. I think a better plan is in order, don't you, George?"

George took a long pause. "Okay okay, you're right man, let's just chill for a bit and think! We won't get anywhere if we don't think. I was wrong to get upset. I apologize to the both of you. So what do we do now?"

Shalee smiled, accepted the apology and acknowledged that they needed to keep clear heads. Then, turning to Sam she said, "Well, looks to me like you're the brains of this operation . . . and I, for one, am all ears. Who better to have on our side than puzzle boy?" Shalee grinned flirtatiously, putting her hand on Sam's shoulder.

George rolled his eyes. "Can we just get on with the brainstorming, please? You two can get a room later."

Shalee blushed and quickly changed pace. "Yes, let's brainstorm," she said, flipping George the bird again.

"Okay, let's look at this logically," Sam said. "We have in front of us a puzzle it seems. I believe this is a long shot. Awakening the statue must be a metaphor. Man, I hope that it's a metaphor. I don't think it means that it will literally come alive, but maybe it will produce some sort of message and give us a way out of here, or at least some answers."

Sam started to circle the object once again. The others stayed right behind him as they looked back and forth from Sam, to the bronze-looking man.

"It seems to me that there's only one thing that's not like the others. I'm sure you all have watched *Sesame Street* when we were growing up. Do you remember the jingle? You know the one I'm talking about? *'One of these things is not like the others, can you tell which one?'"*

George looked at him, floored. "Sesame Street, what the hell are you talking about man? Would you like me to go call Big Bird? How about I tell the Cookie Monster to come and help us? Do you see Mr. Rogers around here? My hell, what's your point before I go insane?"

"Yeah, your point," Shalee agreed quietly.

Sam rolled his eyes. It took all he had not to punch George. After a second, he changed his mind and drilled him in the upper part of his right arm. "Shut up and quit being an ass," he yelled as he watched George fall to the floor.

"Damn, that hurts, man," George screamed, grabbing his arm after landing on the hard surface. "Sorry, sorry, sorry, crap, just stop already."

Sam turned toward the statue again without saying another word, calmed himself down by breathing deeply and after a moment, continued to speak. "Okay, the statue of this man, his wolf and the base they're standing on, all look to be made of bronze, but the one thing that's different is this round crystal ball that looks like the moon."

Sam pointed to the object. "Look at it. If you get closer, you can see that it has creases in it. Almost as if it has been put together like a puzzle." Sam quickly counted the pieces and continued. "By my count, I see five pieces in total and this leads me to believe that, with the rest of the statue being basically the same, maybe we should concentrate our efforts on this sphere."

Hearing this, George stood up and walked past both of them. He pushed himself off the floor, wincing from the pain in his arm, then went and stood on the base of the statue.

"Damn man, my arm almost gave out from your stupid punch. You're a bully, this better not bruise or I'll—"

"You'll what?" Sam snapped.

George stared for a moment at the fighter and eventually thought better of the confrontation that he fantasized about winning. He turned and looked down at the crystal. "Let's find out if you're right, ya big bully. Let's take this with us, I bet it's worth something." He bent over and reached for one of the crystal's pieces.

"George, wait!"

But it was too late. George grabbed the piece closest to him, separating it from the rest. Before any of them could say anything, the other four pieces of the sphere vanished, leaving George holding the remaining, single piece.

"Holy crap man, did you see that? The damn thing just disappeared. What do we do now?" George said, looking at Sam. "That just freaks me the hell out!"

Shalee had grabbed onto Sam's arm and moved behind his back. She felt the need to do something, but had absolutely no clue what that something was. She could not explain it, but she knew they were in for a ride.

Sam removed Shalee's hands from his arm, but allowed her to stay behind him. He turned back to George.

"Get down off that thing!"

But before George could take a step the entire thing started to shake. The base of the statue fell through the floor, creating a large hole, sucking George down into it. All that was left was the man and the wolf, floating in mid-air.

"George!" Sam yelled, as he watched George fall into the darkness below. He paused a second and then moved into action. First, he turned and cleared Shalee away from him, motioning her to the other side of the hallway. She went without hesitation, her pink slippers making a scuffing noise as she hurried across the floor.

Sam turned to face the floating remains of the statue, but now the floor had reappeared and both the man and wolf creature were somehow made of flesh.

"So much for it being a stinking metaphor!" he said under his breath.

Not panicking, and having been caught in many stressful situations due to his fighting career in M.M.A... Sam kept his focus, even while Shalee screamed in the background. His brilliant mind thought quickly... *Okay, the man and the wolf are asleep... but I imagine that they could wake at any time and become a real threat. I should dispose of the wolf first just in case. This will leave me with only one opponent to fight if the man wakes up suddenly. I can't hurt this guy too bad because he might have the answers I need to get us out of here. If only I could just disable him and make him vulnerable, then I could get my questions answered without a fight.*

Sam moved swiftly for the wolf, grabbed it by the legs, ripped it from midair and slammed the beast into the floor. The beast awoke instantly, biting at Sam's arm, but missed. Sam had to let go of the creature to avoid its sharp teeth. The animal hurried to its feet and readied itself for attack.

Sam's mind again took over, running the scene in slow motion so he could prepare for the wolf's next move. Now the wolf ran at him, leaping at Sam's throat. Sam quickly moved to his right and, as the animal passed him, struck a crushing right hand to the left side of the wolf's neck. The four-legged beast landed and howled in agony as it turned for another attack.

Sam rapidly studied his opponent, his mind searching for the weak points. Even with all his knowledge, he did not know the creature's anatomy like he did a man's. He figured the best way to defeat the creature was to get it by the throat and squeeze the life out of it. Sam grinned.

Easier said than done, he thought.

The wolf made several more aggressive passes, but each time Sam managed to avoid the attack and hit the animal on some area of its body.

Suddenly things changed... the wolf seemed to have a change of heart. Instead of readying itself to attack Sam, it turned and looked at Shalee. Shalee started to scream. Sam tried to get the creature's attention, but to no avail. The wolf started to move in her direction, slow at first, and then it broke into a run. But the wolf had to pass Sam in order to get to Shalee. The fighter decided it was all or nothing. He took three running steps in the wolf's direction as it passed, calculating the angle of where the wolf would be when he landed.

Sam launched himself into the air. With perfect timing he landed with all his weight on the creature's back, pinning it to the floor. He quickly sat up, raised his elbow high and was about to bring it down on the back of the animal's neck when a booming voice filled the great hallway with a thunderous echo:

"Enough!"

The wolf, Sam and Shalee were all frightened. Sam froze, and the animal lying beneath him stopped struggling. Shalee fainted and fell to the floor.

Sam looked over his shoulder in the direction of the voice. To his surprise, the statued man was now awake and walking toward him. Sam figured quickly that he better finish the wolf off and get ready for the next fight, forgetting something very important: the words on the statue's base. This approaching man was a god, and both Sam and Shalee were the two who would fall by the wayside if he chose.

Sam raised his elbow to strike, but just before he made contact across the back of the animal's neck, he was flying through the air. He slammed hard against one of the pillars closest to where the now walking statue used to sit. He was pinned, suspended high in the air, unable to move his arms, legs and head—even his fingers were frozen solid. He could not even speak.

The man walked slowly over to Sam and looked up at him. "Maybe you misunderstood me. I said that was enough!" His voice was hard, and strong. The power behind it filled the air as he spoke. Sam was helpless.

"My name is Bassorine… **I am the God of War**. I have chosen to use this statue in order to welcome you to Grayham. It is I who will answer your questions and it is I you will listen to when I speak. Do we have an understanding… **my mortal friend?**"

Bassorine waved his arm, and Sam slowly fell back to the floor. His bodily functions returned as he landed on his feet, realizing he was helpless against such great power.

"I understand," he replied.

Sam remembered as Bassorine used the word 'mortal' that he had overlooked the 'god' part of the prophecy when he decided to pick the first fight in his life that would have gotten his butt thoroughly kicked. He said nothing more as he watched the god walk toward Shalee. He stood above her and moved his hand over her body. She lifted from the floor as if floating and slowly regained consciousness.

Seeing the frightened look on her face, Bassorine explained, "Everything will be all right. No harm will come to you, child."

Even the wolf remained calm. The heavy-coated beast now stood peacefully beside the God of War and waited patiently for his orders. It took some time, but eventually Shalee calmed down and moved toward Sam after Bassorine motioned for her to do so.

The wolf limped over to Sam. What happened next surprised both humans. The creature spoke. "You fight well. I can't remember the last time I've been hit that hard. A couple of lucky blows you got in on me, I think. I hope you're okay."

Sam marveled at the wolf's flawed recollection of the fight. He had already moved past the fact that the animal could speak—a fact that Shalee still was dwelling on—and was now working on a way to approach the situation at hand.

"Of course, I'm okay! You didn't even touch me! Why wouldn't I be okay?"

Sam turned his attention away from the wolf, and toward Bassorine, "You said you chose to greet us and answer our questions. You said that I better listen to you when you speak . . . so I'm all ears."

The god smiled as he walked toward the two of them. He motioned for the wolf to come stand by his side. The beast did so without question.

Bassorine spoke as he pointed to his pet. "This is Mosley. He's the finest companion a man, or god, could ever have. He's a Night Terror Wolf. On many occasions, before I became a god, this beast has saved my life. He's loyal to the end, and I've given him an extended life because of his actions. He should live a few hundred more years or seasons if you will, before he joins me in the heavens permanently."

Sam took a few seconds to admire the animal's beauty and then raised his hand as if in school.

Bassorine smiled and motioned for Sam to speak. "Let me get this straight. You're saying that you're a god, and this talking, Night Terror Wolf is named, Mosley. You reside in the heavens, and Mosley here hasn't joined you there yet, but somehow he has managed to appear by your side when you both came to life or whatever is was that you did to make the change."

Sam paused a moment.

"My goodness, I can't believe I'm even saying this. It sounds so ridiculously absurd, crazy, and made up. But anyway . . . you said you used the statue as a means to come and greet us, and we're all here now, in a place called Grayham? Is that about it? Have I got it all straight so far? I'd love to hear you explain all this even further!"

Bassorine sighed heavily. "The statue was to be used as a way to summon me, a conduit if you will, for the purpose of our greeting. The statue has been here for over 10,000 seasons and serves two purposes. The first is to celebrate the mighty victories that I accomplished when I fought to return the Crystal Moon to the gods. The second reason is to hold the Crystal Moon for safe-keeping. When placed in its resting spot, the crystal's pieces work together and send its power throughout the worlds. The Crystal Moon governs the worlds and keeps them all separated with the ability to support life. Keeping the planets separated is just one of its many purposes.

"The Crystal Moon is kept at this place of honor for all to come and marvel at not only its beauty... but to recognize my glory as well. We felt that the statue would be a good test to see how both of you would handle the adversity of this situation."

Shalee had a question of her own. "How do you protect this Crystal Moon from someone taking it? Where I'm from, people steal things all the time. Don't you worry about that?"

"The Crystal Moon is protected by my power and no one can take the crystal unless I release my hold on it."

Sam raised his hand again before he was motioned to speak. "Well, it looks as if someone has found a way to jack your crystal, because it's gone. It vanished just before you showed up. It disappeared into thin air."

The god quickly looked at Sam, took a moment to observe the area and then started pacing while talking to himself. This annoyed Sam as he began to think.

This is some god. Ha... what a joke, he's showing weakness! Gods aren't supposed to do this. They're supposed to be all-powerful and all-knowing beings. He doesn't even speak with any kind of a godly sound for Heaven's sake. He actually sounds just like a regular guy. How irritating is this. Maybe an accent or something... gees!

Sam decided to take control of the situation.

"Okay, it's clear to me that there's something wrong here," Sam said. "Maybe we could dissect this whole situation. Could we start by you answering a few more really pertinent questions? Then you might get some clues about the crystal."

Sam knew his mind was clearly superior to even that of this

particular, so-called god, so he would have to control this conversation in his own way.

Bassorine agreed, motioning for Sam to continue.

"Okay . . . so how did we get here?"

"Your wishes brought you here. This is your chance to have everything you wanted. You succeeded at figuring out the statue's meaning and how to awaken me, otherwise, you would have been sent home. Now you'll be able to stay and enjoy this world. The god Lasidious was the one who retrieved you from your world after you made your wishes."

Shalee listened as Bassorine motioned for Sam to continue. "Okay, we have some issues here. I have a few questions of my own . . . first off, what wishes are you talking about?"

"You both made a wish. I'm sure you remember the wishes that you made on the last celebration you had honoring the day of your birth. You Sam wished to be given the chance to be the best warrior you could be, and to make an impact on the lives of others. Shalee also made a wish. It was for her to be able to, for once, escape her reality and have enough power to actually make a difference in the lives of others. She also asked for an adventure. Both wishes were very noble indeed."

Sam was floored. He thought back to his last birthday party and remembered as he blew out the candles the wish he had made. But—he had no idea the memory had been implanted into his mind by the god.

"I remember the wish, he said, "but I meant I wanted to be the best warrior I could be in the mixed-martial arts combat world. I wanted to be able to touch the lives of others with the fame I gained. I wanted to help people who needed it—not be dragged into something I'm not familiar with or someone else's idea of what I wanted."

Bassorine smiled. "What's done is done. It was agreed upon by the gods to bring you here. Your Gods of Earth agreed as well. Ask your next question."

Sam grit his teeth. How could he argue with a god? Or was this guy even a god at all, with his obvious lack of knowledge of the day's events? He would have argued, but he realized it would be pointless. He couldn't beat Bassorine in a fight and he didn't even know where he was. All he could do was continue asking questions... for now.

"You said the test to figuring out how to summon you was for the two of us to solve, and if we hadn't solved it, we would've been sent home? So you must've released your hold on the crystal. We needed to touch it in order to complete the test, right? Maybe that's how it was taken."

Bassorine nodded in agreement and motioned for Sam to continue.

"I'm sure you knew that I understood many other languages and that I also liked puzzles. I'm also sure you know more about me than I care to guess. So my next question is... what about George? Why was he here, and where did he go when he fell through the floor, along with the base of your statue? What happened to him?"

Bassorine looked puzzled. He stood silent for a minute and turned to Sam. "George . . . who is this, George . . . there should've been only two of you?"

It made Sam happy inside to know that he had a one up on Bassorine. He loved the fact he knew something that this so-called god did not know.

"I'm surprised you don't know this. The writing on the statue talked about a prophecy of a group of three who'll be called upon to recover the missing pieces of crystal. You know, the one about two men and a woman—the prophecy where one of the group's members falls by the wayside, leaving it up to the remaining two to save the worlds and find a way to gather the pieces of the crystal before the worlds collided. The whole 'watch out for the spread of chaos' part was on there as well," Sam said mockingly.

Ignoring his tone, Bassorine took a moment before he spoke.

"This experiment was for the amusement of the gods. Even the gods get bored and need a good diversion every now and then. When I created a prophecy for your greeting, it didn't read the way you've described. The prophecy I wrote was about one man and one woman, not a group of three. It was about the two of you coming into this world and creating an empire of good. You were to make a difference on all the worlds. All the gods had agreed to this and thought it to be a worthy cause—a good diversion to sit back and watch."

Bassorine paced back and forth as he continued.

"Sam, we hoped that your knowledge, along with Shalee's goodness, not to mention her power, would be strong enough to create an empire. We hoped to see this new empire become an example on this world. We also hoped that one day the other worlds would follow in your footsteps, and the races would be rejoined. They would be allowed to live together on any world they chose, instead of how it is now. As things stand now only certain races are allowed to live on specific worlds, and each world is forced to rely on each other for specific needs."

Sam started to speak and then stopped. He started again, and then stopped. Bassorine looked annoyed. "Just speak, Sam," he snapped.

"All right," Sam replied. "I read about the worlds and the power of the Crystal Moon, or what I assume to be the Crystal Moon. I understand the power works to keep the worlds separated and allows for life to survive on them. But if you all agreed that you wanted us to create an empire and set an example, then why did you need this test for us in the first place? Why would you make it so that the crystal ever left the hold you had on it?"

Bassorine replied, "Not all the gods were in favor of this—only the majority and the majority is how we govern the worlds. It was Lasidious, Owain, Mieonus, Alistar, and Celestria who felt that a test should be implemented to see if you were clever enough to undertake such a task. It was Lasidious who said I should allow you to be able to touch the crystal as a way to summon me. The idea didn't seem risky to me . . . therefore, we all figured that no harm would come of it.

"From the sounds of it, it appears that what I've written, or part of what I've written, has been changed. I believe that a trick has been played, a game begun among the gods. The prophecy must have been changed without our knowledge. This could be the only explanation. I fear now that you've been brought into a play for power, and a new plan is in order to stop the spread of chaos that will grow because of this.

"You'll be more instrumental now than ever in saving these worlds . . . and bringing the balance of good and evil back into its proper place will rest on your shoulders. If the pieces aren't returned to me, I fear the planets will eventually start to migrate toward each other. This could be the end of all things that we've created."

"What do you mean we will need to do this?" Shalee finally spoke up. "We didn't ask for this. You said that I have powers. I don't have any powers! You brought us here against our will— against our will!" she shouted.

The god held his hand up... his power silencing her.

"Let me think a moment," he said in a solid voice. He turned and looked at Sam. "I believe this to be the handiwork of Lasidious. He's the God of Deception and Mischief. He must know where the Crystal Moon is. I will check with the others within the heavens and see if they've heard anything."

Sam interrupted before Bassorine could go on any further. "You allowed a God of Mischief to talk you into allowing us to touch your crystal? Why would you do such a thing? That doesn't seem to…"

Annoyed, Bassorine gave Sam a look that stopped him in his tracks.

Sam cleared his throat.

"What about George? He fell through the floor along with the base of your statue."

Bassorine thought some more as he paced. Finally he spoke.

"It seems to me that if Lasidious is behind all this, he must have a reason for George being here. None of the gods knew about George, and I wasn't expecting Lasidious to place you on Grayham just yet. If we had known what he was up to, none of this would've happened. Lasidious can be very sneaky . . . and no one said that he couldn't place you on this world earlier than expected. I wasn't expecting to be summoned by the crystal until Late Bailem."

Sam rolled his eyes as he responded. "If you didn't expect for us to be here until later—assuming that's Late Bailem does mean later—then why did you release your power over the crystal before it was time?"

Bassorine knew he had made a mistake, but was not about to admit it to Sam. The god looked him dead in the eyes, "Who are you to question me? I have listened to you make your judgments and have had enough. I suggest you concentrate on fixing this problem instead of badgering me. Do I make myself clear? I won't have a mortal speaking to me in this manner!"

Sam wanted so badly to tell the god that he was an idiot, but he held his tongue and said instead, "I'm sorry."

Shalee piped in. "Why not just go kick Lasidious's butt and get the crystal back yourself? You could fix this whole mess on your own. While you're at it, you can bring back the base of your statue, place the crystal back on it and put it back under your power. Fix your own mess and send us home. You said it yourself; you're the God of War. Why don't you have this kind of power?"

Bassorine smiled, "Child, it is not that simple. Not all of the gods choose a side in things. Some of us stay neutral in events of good and evil. We believe in free will. I am the God of War, but I don't determine if the war is a good one or an evil one. I love to battle, both hard and fierce, but I don't care who holds the balance of power. When the gods came to me with this idea, I only agreed because of the entertainment it would provide some day. We are gods, and if these worlds are destroyed, we have the power to create new ones. The gods will view this as a big game of chess and you'll be the pawns. The struggle for power will not necessarily be in the form of a war between us, but more the fact that the gods will be trying to keep as many of our chess pieces on the board as possible."

"I'm not someone's chess piece," Sam shouted.

"Me either," Shalee said, moving to the fighter's side.

Bassorine stopped and thought a moment. "You are what we say you are."

Both of them wanted to object but Bassorine silenced them with a motion of his hand.

"The only reason that I care about any of this is because a trick has been played on me. What I had power over has been taken from me. I would like the Crystal Moon back, but it's not essential that I have it to continue existing. I'll help you with updated information as I learn of it while you are on your quest, but I don't have a need to seek revenge within the heavens. I'll just need to play the game better than Lasidious does. He's the God of Mischief for a reason. If you think about it, this really is quite entertaining. Now more than ever, I don't want the worlds to be destroyed. I also don't want to stop these events from unfolding. I smell war on the horizon. This new struggle for power between the races will create glorious wars."

Sam and Shalee were stunned. How could these so-called gods toy with worlds and with each other? It took a moment for Sam to regain his bearings.

"So what about the gods that hate evil, where are they?" Sam said. "Won't they want to put a stop to all of this?"

"There are both good and evil gods among us. There are good gods among us who want peace, love, harmony... but not at the risk of a war between the gods. Also, there are evil gods among us who want chaos, hate and fear, but not enough to fight the others for it. The gods want a simple existence and to be entertained, that's all. We allow each other to influence things on the worlds, but we no longer allow one another to fight each other. If Lasidious is responsible for all of this, which I bet he is, he did nothing more than use the greed or evil within the heart of someone to start these events in motion. The gods wouldn't allow Lasidious to do anything more to a member of any one race other than influence the heart of one that wants to be influenced. This is the extent of how our power is to be used. It looks as if Lasidious has used my statue to deliver his message. He will not do anything to your friend George to harm him unless his greed for the crystal has killed him when he fell. Yes, he will tempt him and manipulate him, but he will not be forced to do anything that he doesn't want to do."

"Holy cow, we're screwed if he's alive!" Sam said, yelling as he threw his hands in the air. "George isn't our friend—he's a jerk! The kind of guy no one likes on our world. You should hear how he was talking earlier. This guy is going to be like putty in this Lasidious guy's hands."

Bassorine walked over to Sam and put his hand on his shoulder.

"Listen to me, son," he said quietly. "It looks as if you're going to be in for a great adventure. I have with me some gifts that the gods have agreed to give the two of you before we started this chain of events in motion."

Shalee, like a kid in a candy store, forgot about everything and grinned at the thought of what kind of gift a god might give. It had to be better than the best day of shopping. She shifted from one foot to the other in anticipation.

Bassorine removed the staff from his hand and gave it to Shalee, but before he let go, he explained. "This is a Staff of Sorcery! It is the only one of its kind throughout all the worlds, make no mistake. Do not judge it by its appearance. This object can wield as much power as its master can command of it. Other staffs exist, but none with this one's potential. Once I let go of it, the staff will bond to you and work for no one else. There's only one problem about having this kind of power . . . if you use too much before you're ready, you can speed up your aging process and provoke an early death. On the other hand, if handled correctly, you can grow with the staff. If you do this at a good pace, you'll be able to extend your life for hundreds of seasons."

Shalee was shaking all over with excitement. She was happy about the gift, excited about the idea she could live a long time—but also scared to death. What if she used the power in the wrong way and made herself grow older, faster?

"How will I know if I have used too much power? Oh, my goodness, I can't believe I'm actually going to be able to do something this cool!"

Mosley laughed when he heard her reaction and spoke with an enthusiasm of his own. "You'll know when you have used too much power. You'll know when you get knocked on your butt and are unable to control the outcome of what it is that you wish to accomplish. The first time you try something and the effects aren't what you expect, you'll understand. You'll learn to feel for the consequence of the power before you command it into your service. You should be able to avoid bad outcomes by stopping prior to finishing your command once you recognize how to trust your feelings. But this will take time and your backside will find a new meaning to the word sore. The great thing about this staff is that even if you spend the first little while messing up and you do manage to use too much power, the effects can be reversed by learning to manage your growth more efficiently.

"Remember, the staff's power is only as good as your own inner strength, so practice as often as you can and start simple. Eventually, as you grow to master your skills and some of the power becomes a natural part of you, you won't need to carry the staff with you at all times. Very, very impressive tool, if you ask me. I've seen similar staffs work before, but, like Bassorine said, this one is special and it's the only one of its kind."

Shalee smiled and turned to Bassorine. "Lay it on me, big guy. I'm ready for this, so let's get started."

"It will be up to you to name your staff," Bassorine said as he let go of the petrified object. Instantly, Shalee began to lift high into the air as the light within the great hallway faded. Her arms flew back and out of control as her chest pushed forward. Wind filled the room as lightning struck both the pillars and the floor around them.

Mosley and Sam followed Bassorine as he stepped back from this spectacular sight. "The staff is bonding with her," the god said. "Soon she'll be tired and need to sleep."

Finally, after a few moments, the lightning stopped. The light returned to the hall, and Shalee slowly fell to the floor, barely able to move. Her breathing was faint, causing Sam to think she might be dying. He lifted her into his arms, cradled her and checked her pulse. It was faint. "What did you do to her?" he yelled.

Bassorine walked over and stood above them both. "She'll be fine. I told you she would be tired, and this would be hard on her. Try not to worry." He turned and motioned to Mosley. "Take Sam's place and give Shalee a pillow to lie on."

Mosley did as he was told and moved under her. Sam let her weight transfer to the animal's furry body and then moved back.

"That should do the trick," Mosley said, taking Shalee upon him.

Sam stood. "So what am I to receive?"

Bassorine removed the bow from his back and the sword from

his waist. He gave the bow first and smiled as he said, "You'll need to name it also. This is the *Bow of Accuracy*. There's no other bow with its abilities on any other world. With this bow you can strike down your enemies from great distances. The enemy must be able to be seen by your own eyes. The bow will not miss if it is used for a just cause. The bow only responds to a master with a good nature and won't allow an evil heart to pull its string. The quiver of arrows will never empty. You can pull from it forever if you like."

The god handed him the sword. "This, on the other hand, is the Sword of Truth and Might. It is also one of a kind. The sword can strike down your enemies with great power and it possesses the ability to search for truth when used upon them. All you have to do is place the blade on your enemies' shoulders and ask it for the answer you seek. The result is self-explanatory."

"So the sword helps me weed through their lies and kicks butt, while the bow lets me hit any enemy I want as long as it's used for good? I think I can handle this. When do we start?"

Bassorine laughed, "Just because you like the sword, doesn't mean you know how to use it. The sword will only work once it feels you have earned its respect. The sword lives and has a mind of its own. You have much to learn . . . and a short time to learn it in. I don't think you want it failing you in battle. Mosley will take you to the city of Brandor. It's up to you to figure out how to wield your new blade and to name it. Your bow, on the other hand, is not so fickle."

Bassorine moved to look at the sleeping Shalee. "I'll come to you once I know more of the Crystal Moon's location. I'm sure the gods will want Lasidious to leave us clues as to where to find its pieces. However, as I've said before, we cannot make him do anything he doesn't want to do. I hope he sees this as only fair so that we all can play a good game. I will see you again soon."

With that, Bassorine disappeared and a new bronze statue appeared in place of the old one, minus the missing Crystal Moon. Mosley looked at it as he allowed Shalee to sleep and said, "I have to admit, I do look good up there!"

Sam smiled and bent down to rub Shalee's back. "I have so

many questions. It looks like I'll have to wait until Bassorine comes back. *Something is bothering me. Bassorine contradicted himself about something he said now that I think back on it.* I need clarification on this matter. Once Shalee wakes up, do you think we should get going?"

"Yes," Mosley replied, "but you can talk to me along the way to the city of Brandor. I may know the answers to some of your questions."

Chapter 3

A Lost Power

GEORGE had heard Sam yelling for him to get down from the base of the statue, but before he could move, the shaking started and his footing slipped. He had tried to reach out and put his hand on the statue's chest, but it didn't help to regain his balance. He wasn't able to grab onto anything to secure himself. The piece of crystal had been in the hand that he had tried to use, and he wasn't about to let something with this much value go.

The floor, to his surprise, had opened beneath the statue, and he had been falling down the rabbit hole ever since. Everything happened so fast he didn't have time to react. The last thing he heard as he fell into the blackness was Sam screaming his name.

The light of the great hallway above him had grown dim as he tumbled over and over. When the hole closed in on itself, he had watched as the last bit of light faded away. His heart raced and his pathetic life flashed before his eyes. Only his little girl would be his last unselfish thought before he died. He closed his eyes tight, pictured his sweet Abbie, and waited for the impact.

The Hidden God World of Ancients Sovereign

"Do you think Bassorine has figured anything out yet?" the Goddess, Celestria, questioned her evil lover.

Lasidious began circling the heavy stone table at the center of the room. Their home was invitingly warm, created by these gods deep within the mountain range known as, The Peaks of Angels. Located on the hidden god's world of Ancients Sovereign, the goddess had softened up the hardness of the rocky walls with many elegant touches. And, just like the Temple of the Gods, the light within their home had no apparent source.

"I'm sure that by now he probably knows that I've pulled a fast one on everybody, Lasidious grinned. "If I know Bassorine, he's thinking this is nothing more than a minor inconvenience to him. I bet he's probably happy. This will definitely start wars and you know how he loves a good battle. I'm sure he'll snap at me a little bit to ease his mind, but I should be able to crawl under his skin and make him really angry if I strike at his ego. He'll think I'm challenging him in front of the others just like we planned. He won't know what hit that thick, scarred-up face of his when I'm done with him."

The goddess moved toward Lasidious. Absolutely beautiful, her eyes could have stolen the blue from the clearest ocean and made it their own. Her hair fell elegantly over her shoulders and down her back as she walked. If an imperfection was to be found anywhere on this woman, it was not on the outside. Every curve and gesture was flawless. Even her voice, an angel's voice, was sweet and soft to the ear. She was worthy of being called, goddess.

Lasidious continued to speak as he watched her pace, seeking to sooth her nervousness.

"Celestria, you worry too much. We have everything under control. We have only used an opportunity the others opened up for us to find someone who wanted power and bring him to Grayham. Besides, the Book of Immortality wasn't even created yet when we stole this human from Earth. How can we be expected to obey a rule that didn't exist? We won't break the new rules within its pages. We'll handle the mortals as we're now required. I won't do anything other than give George a reason to seek out the power he wants. Clever of us, don't you think?"

Lasidious gave them both a verbal pat on the back as his eyes turned red and his teeth sharpened.

"Stop that," Celestria said, "I hate it when you make that face. You know I don't think you're handsome when you do that and I like my cute little devil god when he looks normal," she oozed. "You're much more kissable when you're not making yourself look so mean."

Lasidious shifted from one foot to the other, grinning at his love. When his eyes were not glowing red and his teeth were not pointed, he actually was quite debonair. He had short sandy brown hair, blue eyes and a chiseled chin. He was a tad less than six feet and had an athletic build . . . and Celestria loved every inch of him.

He moved closer to her, a frown creasing his brow.

"I'm sorry, my love, but you know I love you. I won't do it anymore around you." Replacing the frown with another smile, he added, "I hate the stupid story that we've all told the people of these worlds. How we ever agreed to make Bassorine so glorified is beyond me. The people's belief that he was the one who saved the Crystal Moon and these worlds from destruction is ridiculous."

Celestria embraced her god, cupped his face with her hands, and gave him a long, soft kiss. Looking him in the eyes, she placed his hand on her pregnant belly. "We did it because he had enough power to destroy the rest of us. I know neither of us had a death wish and that was one of his conditions before he would agree to create the Book of Immortality   it's the Book that balances the power that Bassorine has over us. It's lucky for us that Bassorine didn't figure this out until after the Book was created. You masterfully manipulated its creation, Lasidious, you clever god."

"I know, but he still has the sword, and we both know that if he figures things out right, he could take it all back."

"Yes, but he's afraid to take the chance. That's why you're going to make him angry enough to try. Have I told you today that I find you amazingly handsome, especially as a master of deception? I don't know what it is, but you and I make a good team."

The goddess touched him seductively as she slowly leaned in. She pressed her body tightly against his and whispered in his ear. "Well, I do know some of what makes us get along." She smacked her lips and licked his ear ever so gently.

As she felt her evil lover tremble with excitement, she continued. "I'm so glad you're unable to lie to me . . . and that we trust each other, my sweet. I don't think that if I were in Bassorine's shoes I would find as much forgiveness as he may for the trick he thinks you've played on him. I have no doubt you'll be able to fuel his fire."

Lasidious looked at her belly and smiled, then frowned again.

"I hate that you made me drink the truth potion to keep me from lying to you. You know I would lie to you if I could—it's just not natural for me to be so sweet and honest, even to you. I never would have drank the stuff if your beauty wasn't so intoxicating."

Once again smiling, he said, "Who am I kidding? Being with you is the best thing for me! Drinking that potion has given me not only you, but our baby as well. This baby will allow us to tip the scales of power and rule the others without all the voting we do now."

The goddess smiled sweetly, an evil intent just behind it.

"Sometimes we have to give in order to get, my pet. You're just lucky that I find you so irresistible, or I would never have wanted you to drink the potion in the first place. With our baby's power and the evil beasts of the worlds that serve me, we should be unstoppable. The dragons can be a powerful force against the others when our child is ready to lead them into battle by our side. It will be enough to take control of everything all of us have created and allow us to rule without opposition."

Lasidious agreed.

"The last vote we had, I was worried the others would be able to tell you were pregnant." Starting to pace, he added, "I sat through that entire meeting, nervous to the point of being sick. If they ever find out about our baby they'll make us mortal before we have the power to rule. It is, after all, against the Book of Immortality for two gods to have a child—since the baby would carry powers far greater than any god has ever had before. The baby won't know how to defend us from the womb but, when he is older, he'll be amazing! The consequences of being mortal are more than I care to deal with. We could be banished from Ancient Sovereign and stripped of our powers. We'd die before our son ever saw the end of his first season . . . this whole plan of ours would come to nothing."

Celestria put her hand over Lasidious's.

"Yes, yes, yes, I know. But, my sweet, you're forgetting about our reward. Neither the Book nor the others will be able to do anything to stop us once our baby is able to command his powers. With both of our powers passing into our child, he'll be able to defend us from the Book. We must hide the baby from the other gods until then and have him live among the mortals until he has become old enough."

"That's the only part of our plan I don't like. He'll be able to defend us from the Book, but the Book and all the gods combined would be a tough fight until he's older."

Lasidious turned and started to pace again.

"That is why we need to create many diversions," Celestria said, "and that's why we brought this other human into the worlds. George has hate in his heart and his desire for power will be easy to channel. All we have to do is influence him to seek out the power he needs to take control of this world, then wars will follow. This diversion will keep the others busy... and their attention off my pregnancy and me. I'm sure they'll be so busy watching you and the mess they think you've created that I should be able to keep them from discovering our baby's birth."

Stopping him now, Celestria pulled him close. "I found a family as you requested, my sweet, and their evil hearts believe that a world with our rule would allow them to seek out the powers they're after. I'll take our baby and put him with a family of elven witches, who are known by the surname Rolfe, from the Clan of Ashdown. They're located in the mountain passes of Vesper, in the Village of Floren on Luvelles. I promised them a sizeable reward. They're easily influenced and they asked for only one thing: to name the baby and have him carry their name until we returned to bring him to Ancients Sovereign. I agreed since it would help our son adjust. Besides, if I know you, they won't be watching our baby for long."

Celestria smiled at Lasidious, brushing her hand through his hair.

"Yes, my love, that will be fine," he said, kissing her softly. "As always, your beautiful mind, that precious evil mind, makes me happy. I couldn't have done better myself. Luvelles . . . I really love that world!"

After Lasidious and Celestria created their home within the Peaks of Angels, they combined their powers to create a shield to keep other gods from entering; making a private sanctuary the others could not break through. This barrier of privacy had become a source of contention among the gods. But when the Book of Immortality had been approached about the matter, it simply responded by saying they had a right to their privacy as long as the laws of the gods had not been broken. The Book determined that the laws had been obeyed and nowhere did it say that two gods could not separate themselves from the others to enjoy each other's company.

The other gods told the Book they feared the couple would be up to no good together and that their spending time alone without proper governing was a bad idea. The Book became angry and told all of them that being a god had its responsibilities and that the consequences of breaking the laws should be enough to govern their actions. The Book did, however, give caution, strongly warning both Lasidious and Celestria that the situation would not be allowed to continue if it felt anything was wrong. If they broke the laws the Book would send them to join the mortals and die of old age

But Lasidious and Celestria knew how to cover their tracks well enough to avoid getting caught—or at least they hoped so. They brushed the threat off; the warning did not stop them. Knowing their plan would take time to implement and develop, they figured by the time everything was in place it would be too late for the Book to do or say anything. It would be forced to serve them.

After the Book made the ruling, Lasidious and Celestria watched as some of the others paired off and implemented the same practices within their own homes. They knew enough of these other couples to know that they would be the only couple willing to tempt fate by having a baby, which turned out to be perfect. The Book's ruling had taken the other's eyes off of them and back in the direction of what all the gods felt were more important matters.

It was in this newly created home of Lasidious and Celestria where they conceived their son . . . and began their long-term plotting. Their plan, implemented over 11,000 seasons ago, would bring them to a higher level of glory than any god had ever achieved before them. Even now, some of the creatures Lasidious created were well over 10,000 seasons old.

"The World of Luvelles is a wonderful world to study magic," Lasidious said, looking at Celestria. "After all, this is where the others agreed to place the Source of all magic, a decision that will end up being their demise."

He turned toward a large, cubed shape cut in the wall that served as a fireplace. Green flames burned within. He stared a moment at their wild movements and then turned his attention back to his goddess.

"The decision you've made to put our son in Floren is perfect. The village is full of magic... the very air smells of it. The most powerful sorcerers, mages, Wizards and Warlocks all gather in one spot to practice the arts. Great things happen there all the time. It will be difficult for the others or even the Book of Immortality to notice our son's growth and development. This will be the perfect spot for our baby to grow."

Lasidious thought a moment longer about the Book of Immortality, then said, "The elven witches should be the perfect, naughty little parents, but we should keep our options open."

Facing the goddess, he added, "Celestria, my dear, it's a good thing you were elven as a mortal before you became a god or our son would not have the proper features to be allowed to live on this world."

He thought about how Luvelles was a world where only Elves, Halflings, and Spirits were allowed to live according to the agreement of the gods. Any soul, if it was not one of these two races, had to have special permission by the Head Master of Luvelles, Brayson Id, to come and study the arts on this world. Yes, there were beasts, giants, demons and other beings, but these did not apply. The gods had only separated and applied rules where each of the following races could exist: Elves, Humans, Barbarians, Dwarfs, Gnomes, Halflings, Trolls, Spirits, and Dragons. Only a few of the five planets created were allowed to contain more than one of these specific races. Every other type of creature could quite possibly be found on all of them.

"Your Elven parents and my human parents have blessed us with the ability to make the perfect little Halfling."

Celestria and Lasidious laughed together.

"So . . . where is our little friend, George? He should've been here by now, don't you think?"

Lasidious grinned and waved his hand near one of the walls beside the table. The rock became transparent, revealing George on the other side. It looked as if he was still falling, tumbling without an end to his suffering. His hair moved, as if a great wind was moving through it. His expressions were delightfully miserable!

"He cannot see us," Lasidious said with a laugh. "I should've told you he was here, but I figured I would let him experience the sense of falling a bit longer. I wanted to give him an awful fright. As soon as you leave, I will go to him and act as if I've broken his fall before he hits the ground. He will be confused—hopefully believing I saved him. I will say that I'm a traveler named Jason who has become wounded. I'll tell him about a map I was looking for, lost by a Serpent King named Sotter near the Pool of Sorrow. I'll tell him that a great treasure is marked on the map . . . and this treasure has a great gift that a man could use to control a kingdom. That should fuel his desire for power."

"Oh my," Celestria said excitedly. "Sotter, I loved Sotter, he was a favorite of mine. I knew him well. I helped him realize his ability to go after the throne of the Serpent King before him. His heart was pure evil. And when he took the throne, I knew he would make me proud. When he finally died, his death bothered me . . . the poor snake lost all his memories before he passed on. That wonderful evil mind went to waste."

Lasidious replied. "It's always hard to lose the children which make us proud the most. I'm sorry for your pain, my love."

Celestria turned to look at her lover. Her sorrow for Sotter vanished as quickly as it came.

"I also know of this map you're referring to—it and the rewards it promises were created for the dwarves of the World of Trolcom.

The goddess Lictina created those items over 4,000 seasons ago. The map was to lead the dwarves into the Cave of Sorrow on the World of Grayham. Then they were supposed to retrieve the Staff of Petrifaction. Lictina had given them safe passage from Trolcom, to Grayham. She expected to be entertained by their venture into the caves. Apparently, she was bored watching their meaningless journey.

"The staff can turn anything to stone and the dwarves were to retrieve it before returning home. The Head Engineer of the mines on Trolcom was to use the staff to turn the mud far below the planet's surface back into stone, creating a safer work environment for all dwarves. I heard that all the gods had agreed with a majority vote to allow the map and the staff to be created, but I was not at this meeting.

"It was Sotter who killed the dwarves and took the map, but he lost it again. I can only assume he wanted the staff's power. Who knows why he felt the need to go after the map anyway? It's not like he could hold the staff in a hand and speak the proper commands necessary to control its power. He's a Serpent King. I can imagine how funny it would've been to see him try, trying to mumble the commands with the staff tucked behind his poisonous fangs.

"I was told Sotter had lost the map and no one knew where it was. Even Lictina had not seen where the Serpent King had left the map and had stopped watching the events after Sotter killed the dwarves. Naturally she was upset when the murders occurred. But then I guess she decided to find other things to occupy her time."

"He did! Sotter **did** lose the map," Lasidious said loudly, rolling with laughter. "Don't you see? Who do you think gave Sotter the idea that the map's treasure could grant him power? I just got his evil little mind thinking he needed the power of the treasure to help him rule. I never told him it was a staff he couldn't use. If I would've told him that, he would've never gone for it. It was his greed and his desire to have everyone fear him that made him go. All I did was suggest it might be a good idea to go alone since his advisors might want to have the power for themselves. I suggested he deserved to have the power that the map would lead him to without any confrontation from the others.

"Celestria, my love, you, of all the gods should know everything about King Sotter, the Lord of Serpents. What was his one main weakness? You're the Goddess of Evil Beasts . . . I know you remember. What's the one thing his bloodline kept the rest of the Serpent Kingdom from knowing to prevent a struggle for power? You mentioned it just a moment ago."

Celestria thought a moment and said, "Ahhhh! His memory failed him and he forgot all things short-term when he slept. I understand what you did now."

She grinned.

"You counted on that fact, didn't you? You knew his short-term memory would cause him to hide the map and forget what he did with it. That was extremely clever, my sweet. So what happened to the map?"

Lasidious realized his goddess was pleased with this revelation.

"Well, it looks like I'm the only one who knows the map's location and just because you are my adoring lover and you're beautiful, I will tell you. Sotter had to stop after he killed the dwarves of Trolcom because he was exhausted. I kept him awake for over three Peaks of Bailem before he attacked them. I made sure he was good and tired afterward. He stopped by the Pool of Sorrow, removed a large boulder from the base of one of the trees, put the map into the hole, and pushed the boulder back on top of it.

"From a distance, I watched him slither up into the highest tree and fall asleep. When our Serpent King awoke in the morning, he couldn't remember why he was there and left the map under the boulder at the base of that tree. It's still there today and, after all this time, the other gods have forgotten about the map being lost as well—all, that is, except me."

Celestria grabbed him and kissed him passionately. "How great you are!" she said with a sensual smile.

Lasidious turned and looked at George again, who still appeared to be falling, "I'll simply tell our scared little friend here that I wish I had the power of the staff, but cannot find the courage to go after it. Once he understands how the staff can help him gain power, he'll want it. Which reminds me, are you still going to suggest to Kepler that traveling with George will bring him great power?

"Oh yes, yes, yes! I think our friend Kepler will make a good travel companion and bodyguard for George—if he doesn't kill him first. I worry that he'll test George. I will work on this suggestion and see if Kepler can be influenced to meet with him at the Pool of Sorrow. Let's say we try to get them both to meet at the pool . . . three days from now?"

Lasidious nodded. "That sounds good. Let's do that. Make sure you stay out of sight from the others. You're starting to show."

"I knew I chose you for a reason. You're the smartest of all the gods. I love you so much," she said as she kissed him one final time. "I will leave now. You need to get our little friend going. I'm sure he's a bit out of it from such a fall. George is going to have a heart attack when he meets his first Undead Jaguar Demon. I would hate for the poor guy to mess his pants before getting started on his journey to power. Goodbye, my love!"

With that, she vanished, leaving behind the sound of her laughter echoing in the room.

Lasidious turned his attention to George and said, "Let the games begin, my friend. You are about to start the adventure of your life."

He held a picture in front of him and looked hard at it. "Well, Abbie, I hope your daddy is ready for all this!"

Welcome to the first edition of

The Grayham Inquirer

When inquiring minds need to know where their favorite characters are.

CELESTRIA is about to meet with the Undead Jaguar Demon, Kepler, to set up a meeting with George at the Pool of Sorrow.

LASIDIOUS is preparing for his introduction with George. The god is looking at his map of Grayham to find the best place to open up the sky and let George fall to the ground. The god has a disguise in mind and plans to teleport them both to this spot. Lasidious will play out his deception as Jason, a traveling adventurer.

SHALEE has woken from the effects that her new staff had on her while bonding with it. She is now on her feet. Sam and Mosley are walking with her, making their way through the Temple of the Gods.

BASSORINE is on the Ancients Sovereign, looking for Lasidious to find out the god's intentions.

Thank you for reading the Grayham Inquirer

Chapter 4

𝔐𝔢𝔫𝔱𝔞𝔩 𝔅𝔯𝔢𝔞𝔨𝔡𝔬𝔴𝔫

NOW that Shalee had slept off the intense effects from bonding with her new staff, Mosley led both her and Sam toward the exit of the great hallway. She had slept for a couple of hours and woke up as if nothing had ever happened. As they walked through the temple, the wolf spoke.

"This temple was built by the gods as a reminder of the importance of the Crystal Moon, not only to this world but to all other worlds as well. This is a place for all to come and worship the gods and thank them for their generous gifts. It doesn't matter which god a person or beast serves; everyone may worship here.

"This particular Temple of the Gods is for the people of Grayham and is the true resting place of the Crystal Moon. There are similar temples that have been built on all of the other worlds, but they hold only replicas of the Crystal Moon within them. All of the temples are protected by the power of the gods from every direction for a half-day's ride on horseback. This protection gives the inhabitants of each world a safe place to worship."

As the Night Terror Wolf finished speaking, a giant, 40-foot-long, sinister-looking serpent with large fangs slithered past them. Shalee grabbed Sam's arm tight as it passed and whispered, "Mosley that was a really big snake. Maybe someone should spray to get rid of those things. Why are they allowed in here? Isn't that some sort of a health risk?"

Mosley chuckled.

"Yes they are allowed inside the temple, Shalee. There aren't any health risks to be concerned about. I just told you that every beast is allowed to worship here."

Sam cut in, "What other kind of beasts come here?"

Mosley shook his head. "Well, all kinds of course."

"That really narrows it down a bit... thanks for nothing!"

The wolf ignored the sarcasm.

"As I was saying before Grayham's temple of worship is where the true Crystal Moon was kept prior to its disappearance, as you have seen. The gods agreed that placing both of you here was a good starting point for your journeys. The temple is located far to the northwest of the city of Brandor."

Mosley pointed to a map to show how far the city of Brandor was.

"It will take us many days to get there."

Changing the subject, Shalee said, "Sam, can you believe the beauty of this place? I still think that snake thing is a bit too creepy for me, but just look at the architecture. It's incredible! No place on Earth can come close to this beauty. I've never seen such exquisite detail. Everything is so grand."

Mosley continued, "There are many areas on Grayham that Bassorine had the gods create specifically to remind you of your old home world. I can only assume that the gods wished for your transition to be a pleasant one. If you're ever able to see the other worlds, their look and feel is nothing like Grayham's."

The gigantic temple doors to the outside world now opened ever so slowly in front of them. Numerous, massive hinges—almost as long as Sam's Mustang convertible—supported the weight of the nearly, 75-foot-tall doors that arched towards each other.

I can only imagine the weight of these things, Sam thought. They've got to be almost two feet thick. No wonder they have to be opened slowly.

"Can you imagine the sound that one of these doors would make if it slammed into the wall behind it out of control?" Sam said. "Can you imagine how much this place cost to build?"

"Mosley," Shalee said with eyes wide, "I look forward to seeing more of Grayham if it's anything like this place."

"I'm sure you'll enjoy yourself, Shalee," Mosley replied, "but the temple is unlike any other place. Grayham does have, however, many wondrous areas to visit."

Once outside, the two humans were at a loss for words. The view was breathtaking . . . it was a moment for a soul to stop and take it all in. Speaking with Mosley, Sam learned that the temple had been built on a large plateau. The structure sat back quite a ways from the edge of a steep drop. The drop, Griffon Cliffs, was about 3,500 feet to the bottom. All around the plateau were natural springs that surfaced and pooled together before flowing over the edge. Many types of beautiful flowers, as well as other forms of vegetation they had never seen before, bloomed around these pools. The sight was glorious, actually beyond glorious. Shalee could have stayed there forever.

Sam studied the area and figured there had to be at least a couple hundred or more of these natural springs that peacefully fed into one other. The sound the waters made as they worked their way into a large pooling area was soothing to the ears.

Moving closer to the edge of the cliffs, the group looked over. Sam could see and feel the energy of the falls and wondered how much water was released into the lands below. Even he could not fathom how many gallons of water it would take to create this kind of natural wonder. The three watched speechless as a large cloud of mist formed. The water from the falls was hitting the rocks below with such a tremendous force that the mist managed to cover a massive area of land.

Mosley spoke.

"Sam, the springs generate enough water to supply three very large kingdoms below, and the entire terrain of what would be left of Southern Grayham slopes away from this area."

"I've never seen anything like this," Sam said, taking a deep breath.

They worked their way clear of the edge and toward a large platform made of wood. Once there, Sam turned to Mosley and started his list of questions.

"Ok, I can see this is clearly not Earth," Sam said excitedly. "So where are we?"

Mosley looked at him confused and responded. "I already told you—you're on the World of Grayham. More specifically, Southern Grayham, on top of Griffon Cliffs is your exact location."

"No, no, no, I mean where in the galaxy are we?" Sam asked.

Mosley looked at him quizzically for a moment before answering.

"I'm not quite sure what you mean. All that is or ever was, since the end of the God Wars over 10,000 seasons ago is where you are. You're on one of the five planets that revolve around the sun. This planet, as I told you before, is Grayham. Nothing else exists, other than the hidden god world called, Ancients Sovereign, but no one knows of its existence or how to get there except the gods and those of us who live in service to a specific god. Most of what I know only consists of these worlds . . . anything more, I cannot say much. I'm not sure what a galaxy is, but it is indeed an amazing name. Does this help you?"

Both Sam and Shalee looked at each other for a moment before the genius finally continued.

"Ok, so you don't know where Earth is, and we're on one of five planets that revolve around the sun. The Crystal Moon's job was to keep us on different planetary orbits, so the worlds don't collide into one another. The Crystal Moon also governs the planets and ensures that they'll support life. I'll just have to accept that for now, I suppose, since you clearly don't know what I'm talking about. At least answer this for me," Sam said, looking to the sun, "How many hours are in one of your days?"

Mosley gave him a blank stare. It was clear the wolf knew nothing about hours. He hesitated a moment, then spoke, "I don't know what an hour is, but I can tell you that we consider a day to be from when the sun reaches its highest point in the sky until the next time it does it again. Does this help?"

"Hell, no, it doesn't help!" Sam snapped. "Of course, a day is easy to figure out. Don't you have any clocks or watches?" he asked, pointing at Shalee's wrist.

Mosley looked at the object on her wrist and asked Sam to explain its function. Once he told the beast how it worked, Mosley looked at Sam and responded.

"We generally plan things around different positions of our sun while it crosses the sky. For example, if you look up, you can see the sun has just risen, and is only a quarter of the way to its highest point in the sky—we call this Early Bailem. When the sun is at its highest point, we call this the Peak of Bailem. When the sun has passed the Peak of Bailem and is again midway to the horizon, we call this Late Bailem . . . all in honor of the God of the Sun, Bailem.

"Just before the sun disappears behind the horizon, we call this dusk or evening. When the sun is gone and can no longer be seen, we call this period of time night. In the middle of the night, we call this midnight and, on the following day when the sun is about to rise just above the horizon, we call this dawn, or morning. It was the other gods who named these times of the day called dusk, evening, dawn, morning, night, and midnight."

Sam grabbed the hair on his head, looked at Shalee, back at Mosley and then spun around with his hands in the air. He laughed, speaking sarcastically.

"Oh, man, these people are so primitive. I wonder where these so-called gods got some of those names . . . Earth, maybe. These people don't even have clocks. How in the hell can you live without clocks?" he said motioning to Mosley while he spoke. "Has no one ever thought to, well, umm, I don't know, maybe create a sundial or something useful for goodness sakes?"

Mosley looked at him, confused. Once Sam realized the wolf had no idea what he was talking about, he turned and adjusted his attitude. He realized that his tone would get him nowhere, and even Shalee was giving him a look.

"Okay, okay," he sighed heavily. "I'll explain what a sundial is later, but for now, Shalee, if you'll allow me to have your watch I'll take the time to get an accurate account of how long the days are here." Sam turned to Mosley and continued. "Can you at least tell me how many days there are in a year?"

Again, Mosley looked puzzled and waited for Sam to explain. The fighter rolled his eyes. "Okay, I'm 23 years old and where I'm from it takes 365 days to make one year of my life." He pointed to Mosley and said, "Do you understand?"

The wolf smiled as he finally thought he understood. "I am very, very old. Many seasons have come and gone in my life."

"What do you mean by *seasons*?" Sam replied. "I've heard that expression a few times now."

Mosley smiled. "The season we now are in is called summer— we determine our age by seasons. I was born in the winter and became one season old the next time winter came. The next winter after that, I became two seasons old . . . and this continued each winter until the age that I am now, which is none of your business. Sam, you said that you are 23, right?"

"I did."

"In what season were you born?" Mosley asked.

"I was born in the spring," he said smiling, knowing full well what the wolf was going to say next.

"Well, we also have spring as a season and a fall as well. The seasons go in the order of winter, spring, summer, and fall, then back to winter again. This would make you 23 spring seasons old. Do you understand?"

Sam laughed. "I understand, but that doesn't tell me how long a year is here. It does tell me how you figure out your ages on this world though, so I thank you for that. I'll just have to figure out how many days are in a year on my own. At least the names of the seasons are the same. Sounds like your gods were too lazy to think of their own names for things when they created these worlds. I swear. I feel like I'm in some sort of dream. How can any of this be real? Maybe I should pinch myself so I'll wake up."

Shalee agreed as she watched Mosley shrug his shoulders. "Well I did tell you that the gods wanted to make your transition from your world to this one as easy as possible. This is a good thing considering that both of you feel that it was against your will to be brought here.

"Maybe the seasons are named the same way that the gods of your Earth named their seasons for this reason! I don't know why you would want to pinch yourself, Sam, but I can assure you that this is all very real, and you are on Grayham. You aren't inside of a dream as you put it. I'm sorry that I'm not more helpful. If I knew anything more I would say it and answer your questions properly. However, I'm sure Bassorine will know the answer to these things."

"Okay, you said the City of Brandor is many days from here," Sam said, "and I'm assuming that if you don't have clocks, then you probably don't have cars either. Are we riding horses? Walking? What's up? Lay it on me, Mosley. You said Brandor is many days from here. What does *many days* from here mean?"

Sam turned and looked at the countryside far below them. Everything he could see was absolutely breathtaking. It was all green and the countryside stretched far beyond his view. Sam took a deep breath as he waited for his answer. He marveled at how clean the air was. It had not been poisoned like the air had been on Earth. It was crisp, clean and pleasant.

Shalee jumped in now before Mosley could answer.

"Yeah, exactly what does many days mean—and by the way, I'm starving. I'm not about to go anywhere else in my pajamas, nor am I going to go anywhere on an empty stomach. After all, a woman needs to look her best when leaving home, and I would really say that this qualifies as 'leaving home.'

"Do you have anything for us to wear? Mine better be cute. You know, you could've at least grabbed my wardrobe if you were going to steal me away from Earth. Hey, how do I make this staff whip up something really fabulous? Will I be able to turn things into frogs and crazy stuff like that?"

Mosley politely waited for her to stop ranting and directed his attention to Sam. The fact that he could answer all three of their questions, despite Shalee's inability to focus at the moment, was refreshing after he had failed to answer the last few Sam had quizzed him on.

"I have the answers to all of your questions. First answer, the gods have left suitable attire for both of you to wear inside the temple. Shalee, I have no idea what you consider cute or fabulous, but if you don't like them, you'll have to talk with Bassorine."

Shalee smiled and tapped the butt of her new staff on the ground. "Don't you worry, once I figure out how to zap him good with this thing, we'll get his fashion sense up to speed."

The wolf laughed.

"The gods will seal the temple to visitors once you've changed. They don't want the beings of Grayham to know the Crystal Moon is missing."

Mosley sat on his haunches before continuing. "Your second question was how many days it will take to get to Brandor. If we travel by foot, it is a 56 Peak of Bailem journey from here to there.

And your final answer is—"

Shalee rudely interrupted Mosley. "Didn't he just say that it was from one Peak of Bailem to the next is how they determine a day here?" she snapped at Sam.

Seeing her expression, the wolf's enthusiasm to answer questions dwindled.

Sam looked at her and responded, "He did, why?"

The woman looked back at the wolf. "If you think for one stinking minute that I'm going to walk 56 days to get to this Brandor place, you're crazy. I'm no Joan of Arc—and I'm definitely not a Mormon pioneer." She looked at Sam then pointed at Mosley. "Who does he think I am anyway: the Crocodile Hunter's wife? For hell's sake, there has to be another way! Where will we sleep at night? I don't even have any money on me for food. This is nuts. I just got a pedicure and my nails done," she said, looking back at the beast. The next statement she screamed at the wolf.

"I don't have any tampons!"

Sam looked at Mosley. He could tell the wolf was confused. He ignored Shalee and spoke instead, to their furry guide. "So you're telling us that we're going to be walking every day for 56 days to get to this place? I can deal with that, but where do we sleep and also, I don't have any money on me for food either!"

Mosley acted upset then winked at Sam in his own wolfish way.

"Shalee, I said it was a 56-day walk, but I said nothing about sleeping. It'll take twice as long if we take the time to sleep. A Night Terror Wolf doesn't need sleep. Did you expect us to stop? I can make the journey straight through."

"Oh, for all the angels in heaven," she shouted! "You've got to be kidding me." She sat on the wood platform and started to cry.

"I said I wanted an adventure, not blisters. I don't even have any suntan lotion for a trip like this and I burn easily. I don't have my makeup. I don't have my hairbrush. I don't have my deodorant. I don't have my perfume. I don't have any clean underwear and I hate this place. I swear that I'll never wish again. Yep, oh yeah, I'll never, ever wish again. Thanks Mom for feeding me a wonderful line of crap about how wishes come true. This isn't even close to my idea of fun. I think I'm going to have a mental breakdown. I don't even have my new purse and it was so cute. Oh my goodness… I can feel the hot flash starting to come over me right now. This had got to be my worst nightmare!"

Tears filled her eyes as she put her head between her knees and continued to fall apart. Sam had to smile at Shalee's reaction. He looked at Mosley before speaking.

"Women, where I'm from, don't find this sort of adventure entertaining unless they are dyk—"

Mosley looked confused, "What is a dyk…?"

"Nothing, nothing, forget I started to say that," Sam said. "It was meant to be a joke, but it would have been in poor taste and not worth finishing. I do hope you have a solution to get us there faster than 56 days." Sam returned the wink and continued to help Mosley get Shalee's goat before continuing. "I'm sure you can appreciate that I'm not a Night Terror Wolf and need sleep."

Shalee lifted her head. "We are humans, Mosley, and I need a soft pillow at night to lay my head on. I'm not cut out for this kind of thing! I cannot look fabulous if I can't get any rest and have blisters all over my body." She lowered her head and kicked out her feet like an angry child before continuing to sob.

Both Sam and the wolf smiled.

Sam continued, "Okay, so how do we get down from these cliffs anyway? They don't look scalable."

The wolf responded, "I do have a solution to get us to Brandor faster. The gods have made the rocks too hard to dig a pick into. Those who have tried to climb them have all died. There are stairs inside the cliffs, but this isn't how we will be getting down."

Mosley turned to Shalee who was still crying and not listening to anything he said. He raised his voice so she would hear him. "I said that I have a way to get us to Brandor without you having to walk for 56 days. So pick yourself up, stop crying, and let's go get the two of you dressed and fed for the journey."

Sam and Mosley watched Shalee wipe her tears on the bottom of her pajama top. The wolf turned and asked Sam to ring the large bell at the far side of the wooden platform. He explained that the only way to get to the top of the cliffs from the land below, without using the steps, is to ride the giant griffons that live inside Griffon Cliffs.

With that Shalee started in again.

"If you think that I'm going to ride some giant whatever it is, you've got another thing coming. I'm not about to get on some creepy, winged thingy. I don't know how to ride stuff like that. Do they bite? I just bet they bite! Oh . . . my gosh, do they smell? What if I can't handle the stench? Will I have to clean up its poop like I had to do with my poodle's back home when walking her? Oh no . . . who's going to take care of my, Pebbles. Mosley, she's gonna starve." Shalee started to yell. "She's gonna starve to death! No one knows she's..."

Mosley had heard enough. He leaned in and breathed onto her face. Shalee immediately fell asleep. Her body slumped over onto the platform.

"She will sleep for a while," the wolf said. "I'm sure that she'll be far more pleasant when she has had a chance to adjust. Are all the women from Earth like this one?"

Sam smiled and responded, "Only the ones worth keeping around. I have to admit, I find her very attractive. I like her sassiness. You'll grow to like her, Mosley . . . besides she's just a tad bit stressed right now, that's all."

"I hope you're right, Sam," the wolf said as he waited for the griffon to arrive. After a while, the massive flying beast appeared from below the edge of the steep drop and landed on the platform.

Sam quickly moved back to the far edge as the giant beast settled down. The force of the wind the griffon's wings generated made standing tough. Sam had to grab hold of the railing to keep from falling. He had read about these creatures but never imagined they were real.

The griffon—part eagle, part lion—was massive and clearly able to carry three or more people. The creature lifted its head into the air and shrieked loudly.

Sam watched in amazement as Mosley walked up to the creature without fear, instructing it in a foreign language.

"I asked the beast to wait until we return from the temple," the wolf said. "We should hurry, they're not known for their patience!"

The wolf told Sam to carry Shalee inside the temple. After Sam finished dressing, he changed Shalee's sleeping body and cautioned Mosley that, if asked, he was to tell Shalee that a temple maid had dressed her. Sam did not want Shalee to know that he had seen her without her clothes. He wanted to ensure that her dignity was left intact. The wolf understood. Sam did admit, however, that he liked the job and was glad the wolf had knocked her out.

Wow... the outfit Bassorine left behind for you makes you look like a princess, Sam thought. How nice it would be if I were your prince... Ha, in my dreams, right?

Mosley showed Sam where to get some food and after putting it into a large pouch, the wolf continued to explain that the journey to Brandor would take six days by air, and fortunately for the mortals, there would be time to stop and sleep.

They made sure they had everything before they left the temple and watched it seal behind them. This would be the last time anyone would enter until the Crystal Moon was returned.

Sam lifted Shalee onto the griffon's back, and then climbed up, securing their new weapons with straps from the saddle that rested on the creature's back. He tied both himself and the sleeping Shalee in, preparing for takeoff. Slowly, the beast walked to the edge of the platform.

Sam swallowed hard as he looked down.

"Hold on! Hold on! This is going to be fun!" Mosley shouted, just before they fell off the edge and swooped into the air. The wolf bit down hard on the leather reigns.

Chapter 5

Broken Back

LASIDIOUS was still sitting at his table, watching George tumble through the transparent wall of the god's cave-like home. He was deciding exactly how he wanted to make his introduction as the fictitious traveler Jason. After reviewing his map of Grayham, the god chose the southern edge of the Enchanted Forest to stage his rescue.

Just to the south of the forest, beyond a large open field, was a place called Lethwitch. He would drop George just outside of town. This would give him enough time to get the needed supplies before heading north to the Pool of Sorrow.

Lasidious had told Celestria that George would be at the pool in three days, which left no time for the Earthling to mess around sightseeing. The God of Mischief hoped George would bump into Kepler as planned and become his traveling companion—if the large Undead Jaguar Demon did not eat him first, that is.

He waived his hand and George disappeared. He stood up from the table, put the picture of Abbie in his front pocket, grabbed the map of Grayham off the table, and a leather pack from his bedroom. The God then vanished.

The Mountains of Latasef
Skeleton Pass

CELESTRIA approached the Jaguar Demon, Kepler. The giant cat, over 23 feet long from the tip of his nose to the end of his tail, had a shiny black coat that was smooth enough to reveal his powerful muscular structure. His claws were sharp as knives, terrifying to most—but not to Celestria, the Goddess of all Evil Beasts.

The cat yawned as the woman approached. His large mouth had seen the death of many men. Kepler's teeth were white except for the yellowish stains at their base that had accumulated from the blood of numerous men's flesh. As he closed his mouth, he stood, stretching his legs, neck and back.

"Who do you think you are to walk within this pass and come into my home like you belong here? Kepler said. "Can you not see the dead which lie with their bones scattered along my pass? Are you not afraid of my skeleton army that I could summon to gut the likes of you where you stand?"

Celestria's face was stern, her voice forceful.

"How dare you to talk to your god this way! I should take you and everything you have and throw it to the Dragons on Dragonia," she said, allowing her voice to echo among the walls of Skeleton Pass. "You will show me your respect, demon."

Realizing who he had insulted, Kepler, bowed down and lowered his head in front of the goddess.

"I'm sorry, goddess. If I had known you were coming, I would have made things more presentable for you."

The giant cat casually pushed a half-eaten barbarian torso behind him with his back paw as if embarrassed about its presence.

"Never mind that, Kepler," Celestria replied as she watched him squirm. "I'm here to inform you of great things that are about to happen. It's time for those who want power to stand up and take it. This will change the powers that be within Grayham's kingdoms forever."

"Sounds intriguing," Kepler responded, "but why tell me this? I have all the power I need. I have ruled my two passes for hundreds of years now."

The goddess walked by him and sat in the place he had been laying.

"Kepler, you know that you've been bored for many seasons now. I know the secret of how you rule this pass. I watch you from the heavens and see how you just lie about wishing for something to happen. I only tell you this because I know there's a man who will be strong enough—and smart enough—to rule this world some day. I have foreseen that this man will be the ruler of all of Grayham, and he'll send this world into a darkness that will make you a very happy little demon, my friend."

He hated how the goddess called him a little demon, but he said nothing to correct her. "Sounds interesting," he said with a hint of sarcasm, "then all I'll need to do is sit here and wait for this to happen. Then I will have my own private world of misery. I can't complain about that, now can I?"

The goddess knew he was more interested than he let on.

"I happen to know this man will be at the Pool of Sorrow three days from now. He should be camped near the outlet where the Pool of Sorrow releases its waters into the Cripple River. For all I know, he may not find you worthy of his company, but I know that a beast of your abilities could be quite useful to this man on his journeys."

"Not worthy of his company?" the demon shouted, letting out a ferocious roar. "I'm **more** than worthy to be in his company. He would be lucky to have me by his side. I would be the best choice as an advisor to the one who rules all of Grayham. I alone can handle this kind of power."

Celestria was pleased with his response, but did not show it. She knew of Kepler's immense pride and hoped it was large enough to take the bait.

"If you're worthy of this man's company, then maybe you should go and sell your abilities to him. See if he accepts your companionship. I warn you, though, Kepler, this is a strong-willed, hot-tempered human. I wouldn't want to make him mad if I were you. I would hate to see you end up on a skewer and cooked for supper."

The beast let out another angry roar.

"I'm no one's supper. I'll go to meet this man and he'll see that I'm a good travel companion. I'll allow him to rule with me at his side. If he doesn't accept this offer, I'll have him for dinner myself before I return home."

"Careful, Kepler," the goddess cautioned. "I know you're strong, but I warn you, don't toy with this human. You'll need to get to the Pool of Sorrow in three days if you're to find this man."

Celestria turned and pointed at what appeared to be the right leg of the barbarian that he had killed earlier in the day. "I will put a blessing on your dinner. This will give you the speed and the stamina that you need to make it in time. It's your decision to make. After you eat this, you'll need to hurry in order to meet him before he leaves the pool."

"That journey would take me at least 30 days since I cannot cross the top of the mountains, but you're telling me that this meal will allow me to make the trip in time? Why are you doing this?"

"Let's just say that it's up to you. I'm doing nothing other than blessing your food and giving you some information. Of all the great cats that serve me, you're my favorite. It has to be your decision to go and fulfill your destiny. I cannot do it for you. However, I need to warn you that I'll be gone for quite awhile after this, and will not come to you again. This is your only chance to grab the power you've always wanted. It will be up to you to make friends with this human and keep him from killing you."

That said, the goddess gave an evil smile and vanished.

The Undead Jaguar Demon thought a moment, turned to the barbarian leg and started ripping the blessed flesh from the bone.

North of Lethwitch

GEORGE was sick to his stomach. The blackness opened beneath him and spit him out like rotten food. He seemed high above the ground and now could only focus on his death. He had been falling for so long he welcomed an end to his suffering. Finally, just before the impact, he closed his eyes and waited. But to his surprise, the next thing George knew he had landed on something soft. A loud scream could be heard beneath him as his descent came to an end.

George waited before opening his eyes. He was not sure if he was dreaming, but he felt alive. He could hear the cries from beneath him. Whatever he landed on was badly hurt. He opened his eyes and slowly lifted himself off a heavyset man. He checked to see if he had broken anything before attending to the fool beneath him. Everything seemed intact, except his clothes which had taken a beating. The man cried out once again, in pain.

"Are you all right? You saved my life, thank you!" George said.

"I think I've broken my back," the man responded harshly.

"Is there anything I can do to help you?" He grabbed the man's bag that he had been carrying and rifled through it to see if there was anything there that could assist him.

"There is a powder in my bag," he groaned. "It's in a copper-tin dish. Add it to the water in my leather hide. It will act as a pain-killer and you can help me get up against a tree or something. I have friends who should be coming by this way soon. They should be able to lay me on their wagon and take me to a healer."

George did as the man said, thinking about what had just happened. He gave the powdered water to the man, which seemed to have an instantaneous effect. The man seemed to become intoxicated and was suddenly quite happy.

"Ahhhhhhhh . . . that's better," he said with a slurred voice.

George took this opportunity to move him against the nearest tree. "Why did you catch me?"

"I didn't catch you. I had no choice. You fell on top of me." The man was clearly feeling no pain as he spoke. "I was walking and the next thing I knew, you landed on me. It's not like men fall from the sky every day. Did you fall from one of the hippogriffs or something?"

"Wow, I am sorry . . . and grateful all at the same time. I don't know anything about these hippogriffs you're referring to. I hope you can forgive me," George said, contradicting the comment within his own mind. "I'm not really sure what just happened to me. One minute I'm on a statue looking at a rock, and the next minute I'm falling uncontrollably to my death. If you hadn't come along, I think I'd be dead right now."

"Lucky me . . . my name is Jason, I'm from Lethwitch. I'm an adventurer and a traveler. Who are you?"

George stood, looking around before answering. He saw a town in the distance as he looked down the gently sloping hillside of the field. "My name is George, from Orlando, Florida, and right now,

I'm at a loss for words. Is that the town you're talking about?"

"Well, George, from Orlando, Florida, well met. I cannot say that the place you're from is familiar to me, but I can say welcome and extend my hand in friendship to you. That town you see is indeed my hometown," the man said with a goofy smile. It was obvious that the drink George mixed controlled any pain he may have had.

"Where are we, and what're you doing out here in the first place?" George asked, turning his attention back to Jason.

"You're between the Town of Lethwitch and the southern end of the Enchanted Forest. I like to travel and recently I found out a secret and I—"

Jason stopped mid-sentence.

George picked up on what the man was about to say and immediately focused intently on listening.

"I have secrets also, Jason," George said, approaching the situation delicately. "It looks like whatever your secret is will have to wait until this back of yours heals. Maybe you could tell me what it is. I'll help you accomplish whatever it was, as a thank you for saving my life."

The RV salesman knew he had no intention of helping Jason, but he wanted to know his secret just the same. He hoped the information would help him figure out the mess he was in, or at least the mess he *thought* he was in.

"I owe you one," George continued. "It's not every day that I break a guy's back while he's saving my life. Let me help you finish your task."

He gave the man another drink and waited for its effects to cloud the man's judgment.

"What could it hurt?" Jason responded after thinking a bit. "You look like a trustworthy fellow. I would appreciate the help. What do you say we split the rewards once you have completed the task? There's enough value and power to go around so I see no reason why we can't share it."

George liked what he heard. The words "power" and "value" suggested this was a task he might want to undertake after all.

Jason continued.

"Don't you ever get tired of being pushed around? I do. I heard of a map that has been lost just northeast of the Enchanted Forest near the Pool of Sorrow. It's actually a lake, but they call it a pool anyhow. The map is supposed to be under a large boulder beneath the tree closest to where the pool's outlet flows into the Cripple River. The map shows where a treasure is hidden inside the Cave of Sorrow. I was going to retrieve this map and come back to sell it for a huge profit. The map is worth an amount of money that I've never had or imagined in my life. This would give me the ability to make changes in my life. The only thing worth more than the map is the treasure the map leads to. I would go after the treasure myself, except for the fact that I cannot find a way to get past the beast inside the Cave of Sorrow. In order to get to the treasure, you must get by him. I am quite scared, to say the least!"

"Wait a second," George interrupted. "This map is worth a large amount of money, so this treasure has to be worth far more than that. Exactly what is this treasure?"

Lasidious, or the man known to George as Jason, knew he had George's full attention. He also knew, from watching George back on Earth, that George was greedy. He would want the treasure and the power that it would bring him. He smiled within as he continued to play the role of the wounded adventurer.

"Well, the map is supposed to lead to a *Staff of Petrifaction*. This staff is able to turn anything into solid stone, but for one problem."

"What's that?"

"The staff can only be used by the dwarves of Trolcom. I'm sure you know of Trolcom. The good thing is: it's worth a lot of money or it could be…"

"It could be what?" George asked impatiently. "It could be what?"

Jason acted as if he was thinking before continuing. He motioned for George to come closer, then whispered. "The staff isn't solid all the way through. Its center holds a liquid. If a man were to drink it, he would receive the ability to turn things into stone."

"Really," George said as he backed away. "That kicks ass. Now that is some really serious power if you ask me. Can you imagine the money we could make with this kind of ability? How could this be real?"

"I assure you that it's all very real."

Jason looked at him and motioned for him to keep quiet and come even closer. He winced, pretending to feel some pain. "I don't understand what you mean when you say that something kicks ass, but I do understand you see the value of this artifact. I, for one, think that it is not the money that we should be thinking about here. If one of us had this power, we could go into the world and take control over all of Grayham. Imagine the wealth that would come from controlling kingdoms. It would be far greater than using the power to make money." Jason smiled wickedly at George. He knew this kind of power would appeal to the earthling's desires.

"Oh, hell yes—if I can get my hands on that staff and drink its liquid, I could gain some serious power." He looked at Jason then added, "Of course, I'll have to take my new best friend with me on this journey once he's back on his feet."

"But, of course," Jason said smiling. "I can tell that you're a man of your word. I just have one question. Do you have the courage to face the beast inside the Cave of Sorrow?"

"Well," George said as he thought for a second. "Courage isn't the problem. The problem would be I'm not the best fighter in the world. What should I expect from this beast?"

"I'll tell you everything I know. The Cave of Sorrow is home to Maldwin, a hideous creature that uses visions of sadness to drive those who enter his cave insane. These visions encourage his victims to commit suicide by walking down the Pass of Tears and throwing themselves into the Pool of Sorrow. They cry all the way down the Pass. Once they are in the lake, they fall deep below the lake's surface; by the time they realize what has happened, they do not have time to resurface before drowning."

Jason pretended to need another drink before continuing. "Any man or creature entering the cave's opening takes the risk of losing himself to the beast's visions. Few have lived to make their way through this cave, but there are those who have done it. The only way out of the cave once you have entered, if you manage not to lose your mind, is to exit through Sorrow's Release. Apparently this exit cannot be seen from the outside, but it can be seen from the inside. It is said to take almost eight days to find a way through the cave."

"Wow," George stood and put both hands on top of his head. "That's nuts. How in the hell am I supposed to do all of this? How am I going to stop him from screwing with me if I go in? How am I going to live long enough to make it eight days? How do I even find my way to this Pool of Sorrow? And once I'm there, how will I lift this boulder to get to the map?" George started to pace with mild anxiety.

"I have said the same things to myself," Jason/Lasidious replied. "I can understand your concerns. In the town is an old mage who has mastered some beneficial uses of magic that may come in handy. This man may be able to help you on your journey. I'm sure he would have some kind of spell that could help you get through the cave. The beast is not aggressive . . . it only uses visions to drive men insane. Maybe if you could find a spell that would allow you to block his visions, you can get close enough to kill him."

"Kill? I've never killed anyone before. I'm not sure I can do it." George stopped pacing and looked at Jason.

"I understand what you're saying, but don't you think this beast deserves to die? His visions have killed many who've harbored him no ill will and simply made the mistake of entering the cave."

George shook his head. He gave the man another drink to keep him comfortable before continuing. "I suppose that he's bad, and killing him would be the best thing to do in order to save others from dying. I like the idea of the reward if I do kill him. Maybe I can handle this after all."

"Good!" Jason replied. "So go into town and buy the supplies you need. I'll give you my map. It'll help you get to the Pool of Sorrow. You can also have my pack. This should give you a little help."

George thought a moment. "Exactly how am I to do that? I have no money to buy anything with. Hell, I don't have a pot to piss in right now. All I've got is what's on me."

Jason eyed George, looking for things of value. He stopped as his eyes rested on his wrist. "Looks to me that what you have on your wrist might be worth something."

The object Jason was referring to was a Rolex that an old widow lady in Orlando had given George. She had come into the dealership to buy a new 45-foot Meridian Yacht, which gave him an excellent opportunity to work his way into her life. He spent six months giving her the attention she had been missing while he collected from her numerous expensive gifts along the way. The widow had paid almost $25,000 for the gift. It was practically a piece of George's anatomy.

"Hell, no," George snapped. "This watch is worth a ton of money. I won't part with it. I can't replace it."

"I understand," Jason said. "It has sentimental value. Too bad, though, I would hate to miss an opportunity to gain this kind of power. The way I see it, you could always buy it back once you have the power to do so."

George thought for a moment, giving the man yet another drink. "I suppose I could always sell the watch for enough to get what I need. I imagine I should be able to have a little cash left over as well. I'll need a larger pack to carry enough food for quite awhile. I'll also need to get this guy to sell me this spell you mentioned. What did you call him again?"

"A Mage," Jason responded.

"I might also want to get a couple of those leather water pouches you have."

"What about a weapon to kill the beast with, some torches for light, a hunting knife and medical supplies?"

George thought a moment, then reached under his pant leg and pulled out his small pistol. "I almost forgot I had this. It's one of the smallest .22 caliber pistols made. It's only able to fire one round at a time. Some of the gangs back home use these guns because they can be hidden in the palm of their hand. It only holds one in the chamber and I usually carry one more round in my pocket." He reached inside his pocket as he spoke, fumbled around a bit and produced the bullet. "The two of these should do the trick on the beast, don't you think?"

"I'm not sure what a pistol does, but, if you're saying it can only work twice, then I would consider purchasing another weapon. Maybe a sword or a dagger of some sort would be good to have as a backup. I would also do a couple of other things. First, I would change the way I talked if I were you. If you respond to the people of this town the way you've spoken with me, they may not understand. I think if you run around saying that stuff 'kicks ass' all the time, people around here will be wary of your approach.

"The second thing I would do is hurry. I heard there was someone else on their way to retrieve the map. It seems that I'm not the only one who knows about it. I would hate to see you lose this opportunity to another adventurer. It was for this reason that I was trying to work up the courage to go myself. You might want to procure more spells to help you catch this individual too, and keep him from getting what you deserve."

"I better get moving then," George said anxiously. "When will your friends arrive so I can leave? I want to make sure you get put on the wagon."

"Don't worry about me. They'll be here shortly and I'll have them take me to Lethwitch to wait for your return. The pool is almost a day and a half from here if you walk, so you better hurry to town. I would want to be waiting for this other adventurer if I were you, and figure out a way to stop him. Maybe you can get some useful information out of him before entering the cave. Now hurry and go!"

With that, George started to run through the field toward the town.

Lasidious removed the picture of George's daughter from his pocket. He changed his appearance back to his normal self. Looking at the photo, he smiled. "Well, well, Abbie, your daddy is working hard. Do you think he can handle all this?"

Laughing, Lasidious vanished.

Chapter 6

First Flight

IT HAD BEEN SIX HOURS, according to the digital watch Sam took from Shalee, since the griffon had dropped from the platform at the Temple of the Gods; Sam was nauseated from the movement of the giant beast. The entire time they had been flying, Shalee had not awoken. So Sam watched the countryside rapidly pass beneath them, awed by the beauty he saw everywhere.

Taking a closer look at the griffon as they flew, Sam noticed that the front talons and the back paws of the creature were now tucked up close to its body to reduce drag from the air passing beneath it. The beast had a beautiful eagle's head, which was pushed far out in front of the rest of its body to guide the way as they flew. The rest of its massive form, other than the gigantic wings, which extended far out on either side, was stretched out smoothly and resembled a lion's body.

Sam took note of the long flat saddle they were sitting on. The large leather surface had sufficient cushion to pad their backsides, and many large lengthy leather straps that allowed for them to tie in. The ride had been relatively safe and, unless the creature decided to roll or make drastic movements, he felt they would finish the flight without any problems.

He looked closer at Shalee as she leaned against him. She had a peaceful look on her face as she slept and he admired her beauty. Just before take-off, he had tied her in with him to keep her safe, and every now and then had pushed her blonde hair clear of her face just to get a good look at how exceptionally gorgeous she was.

He was impressed by Mosley's balance too, and had watched as the wolf bit down on two of the leather straps, one from each side of the saddle, and hung on. After a while, the wolf placed the straps under his front right paw. The beast turned to speak.

"How are you doing back there?" the wolf asked. "The first flight is usually the hardest."

Sam hesitated a second before answering. "I'm doing fine, I guess. How long are we going to be on this thing before it lands?"

A voice shouted from the direction of the eagle's head. "I'm not a thing." The griffon's head snapped around as it shrieked loudly. "My name is Soresym, and don't forget it. You will address me as such if you need to speak of me in the future. I have a mind to roll over and drop you to your death for your ignorance. You should be more respectful with your tongue, human."

Sam quickly realized his mistake and apologized to the griffon, asking forgiveness. The beast accepted his apology and, after a moment of silence, turned his head back in the direction of flight.

"We should be landing on Angel's Platform by dusk, Soresym said. "Beyond that, you won't be traveling with me any longer. My kind only travels between Angel's Platform and the Temple of the Gods. After this, you'll be traveling with my cousins, the hippogriffs.

"We don't like to fly your kind around. I can't stand to be around you humans, or any of the other wretched beasts of this world. The gods require us to do this in order to live within the cliffs beneath the temple. I would not be doing this otherwise. In fact, Bassorine asked me to give you this ride, or I would not have done so. You should've walked down the steps of the cliffs since you're not of noble blood. We'd rather eat you than be servants to the people of these lands, but I suppose it is a sacrifice worth making to keep such a glorious home."

Sam looked at Mosley after apologizing again and chose his words carefully before his next comment. "Is it my imagination or does every glorious creature within this world understand how to speak English?"

Mosley laughed and replied, "No, not all of us "glorious creatures" have the ability to speak your language; most speak a language of their own. Only those in service to the gods can speak all the languages of the worlds."

Sam thought a moment. "I didn't see the steps leading down and out of the cliffs that Soresym mentioned. Where are they?"

"The steps are located inside the cliffs. The gods built them. The common people of the land must use them to get to the temple. The griffons and the hippogriffs are for those who have wealth and noble blood. Mostly kings and nobles have the kind of coin to travel aboard them. If it wasn't for Bassorine, your journey to Brandor would have been a very long one."

Sam nodded and looked at Shalee's watch. He figured by the position of the sun, combined with what the griffon had said about when they would land, the days seemed to be similar to the ones on Earth. He would reset the stopwatch as the sun disappeared behind the horizon and then stop it the next day at the same general time. He hoped to get a good spot on the horizon so his calculation would be fairly accurate. Sam knew that a large change in terrain would throw him off, and wanted as little error as possible. He hoped they would be on the ground when this all took place.

Mosley told Sam that Shalee would continue to sleep throughout the night and most of the next day. He also explained there were many landing platforms scattered all across the land, all of them with a small village, town, or city where they could spend the night. The hippogriffs only flew during the day unless ordered by the kings of Grayham for some specific purpose. And, it was only possible to fly to one landing platform each day due to the distances between them. When they arrived at each village, Mosley would make all the arrangements necessary for the night.

Sam looked at Shalee and wondered how he was going to explain all of this to her. He still had a hard time believing the things that he had learned, let alone trying to make sense of it all to someone else. Animals talked, Griffons, along with their cousins, the hippogriffs, acted as airborne transportation and that was just the start of it. Magic, gods, swords, kingdoms, and everything he thought to be myth were now true. He had no idea about money and how it worked here. He knew nothing of the culture, or even how to speak with the people of this world to make a smooth transition.

He wondered too if his home on Earth was going to get repossessed since he was not there to pay the bills. His mind had so many questions for Bassorine, and yet he was not here to ask him. He could only look forward to the next meeting with the god to get his answers.

Sam moved his hand through Shalee's hair as they flew. He realized his heart was growing warm towards her. She was beautiful and she had been leaning against him the whole time. He imagined that he felt this way because she was the only thing left that resembled anything normal to him. He held her tight as he tried to stop staring at her lovely face.

After flying over the Blood River, a name Sam remembered from his mental snapshot of the map back at the temple, he knew it would not be much longer before they landed. When he saw the platform that stood high in the air, he knew they were getting ready to set down. He looked forward to a belly full of hot food and hoped he would be able to settle his mind in order to get a good night's rest.

Sam smiled as they made their approach. The little village below looked like something from one of those King Arthur movies. It seemed that it was always the people who made their homes within the world outside of the king's cities who lived this way. Their homes looked to be made of stones stacked on top of each other. The roofs were made of large bundles of straw tied tightly together and angled steeply to allow the rain to run off quickly. The entire village was bunched together and looked more like a small town than a village. He could not wait to see how big the towns and cities were if the people of this world called this a village.

Not far from the landing platform Sam saw a stadium or rather, an arena of some sort. It was not large but big enough for hundreds of people to gather. He wondered what kind of sport or theatre was performed there; he'd have to check it out if he had the time. If Shalee were awake she'd probably criticize the fact that the arena's architecture was nothing like the architecture of the rest of the village. In fact, it reminded Sam of Rome, while the rest of the town reminded him of a quaint little place somewhere in Old

Scotland. Mosley was right; Grayham did remind him of Earth in some ways.

As they landed, Sam took note of the watch and stopped its timer: eight hours and ten minutes was the flight time. He grabbed all their gear, along with bags holding their old clothes, and jumped from the griffon. Sam tied the bags together and hung them evenly across Mosley's back, pulled Shalee down from the top of the squatting griffon, and put her across his left shoulder. He was careful not to strike her head against the bow that crossed his back as he adjusted the sword on his hip. Preparing to walk down to the village, Sam saw that the sun was about to fall below the horizon.

"Thanks for the ride, Soresym, it was an honor," he said.

Sam walked to the front of the griffon and looked into his eyes. "Again, I'm sorry for my ignorance. It's easy to see how your kind is far superior to us humans . . . I can see why you wouldn't want to fly us around. I'll make sure that I speak your name with pride every time I say it from now on."

The flying beast turned and looked down at him. "Maybe you're not so bad after all, human. I just may decide to honor you back by calling you, Sam. It's clear to me that your remorse is genuine, and I accept your apology. On occasion I run into one of you two-legged beasts that I take a liking to. I sense that you might be one of those men. I wish you well on your journey. Maybe someday our paths will cross again. Good luck, and may the god you serve be with you as you travel."

Sam laid his free hand on the beast's feather-covered neck. "It was an honor to have met you as well and I do hope we meet again. Fly safe, and may the god you serve be with you too."

Sam turned and looked once again at the horizon. He reset the timer as the sun disappeared. Using Shalee's staff for balance, Sam motioned for Mosley to lead the way. They headed down the long flight of stairs of the giant, wooden platform that rested high above the ground. The quaint village below was now beginning to fill with the flickering, flaming torch lights of twilight.

The Grayham Inquirer

When inquiring minds need to know where their favorite characters are.

BASSORINE is looking everywhere for Lasidious and becoming increasingly angry that he can't find him. He has spoken with all of the others on Ancients Sovereign. No one has any idea where he is. The God of War's voice can be heard throughout the entire hidden god world as he keeps calling for the God of Mischief to show himself.

SAM followed Mosley to an inn, where he laid the sleeping Shalee on a bed. He left with the wolf to go find dinner, and have a mug of ale to calm his nerves.

GEORGE made his way into Lethwitch.

LASIDIOUS was inside his home far beneath the Peaks of Angels. Although he could hear the screams of Bassorine echoing throughout the world, he ignored them. The protection that he and Celestria put on their home has kept the God of War from popping in on him. He is laughing with disdain.

Thank you for reading the Grayham Inquirer

Chapter 7

𝔅reaking and 𝔈ntering

GEORGE hurried through the field towards the town of Lethwitch and then stopped. Looking back at the place where he met Jason, he wondered if his friends had picked him up yet.

Turning back and entering the village, it was only a short period of time before he realized he stood out like a sore thumb. Anyone he tried to speak to would have nothing to do with him because of his clothes. He realized he was still dressed for the road trip to deliver the RV; people just stared at him when he approached, and quickly walked away.

The men of the town were rugged and wore leather clothing for the most part. Some wore softer-looking clothes, made of a material George had never seen. The women had a better fashion sense and wore long dresses—yet still with a rugged look. He smiled to himself.

At least the women feel like it's important to accent their curves. This place is like some kind of Renaissance Beverly Hillbilly's town. How funny is that? I can just imagine how great this place would be for a TV pilot.

I probably smell. Look at me. I'm a train wreck. I must look like some kind of bum to these people. Holy hell . . . I really stick out. These clothes could use some attention. Damn, my new slacks, they're torn across my leg. Crap . . . and my shirt too, this must've happened when I landed on Jason. Poor chump, I can't believe he told me all that.

The pocket of his shirt was hanging limply by a stitch or two. His shirt, pants, shoes, belt, wallet and cufflinks (all by Gucci) were definitely out of step with the town's fashion. His shoes, clearly not meant for sprinting through fields, looked like hell and were scuffed from his rugged run.

George pulled the rip on his pant leg apart to see that his thigh had suffered a good-sized bruise. He figured that his adrenalin had been the reason he had not noticed the pain until now. He knew if he did not figure out a way to blend in soon, no one would talk to him and he would not get to the Pool of Sorrow on time.

Slowly, George walked around the town. According to his watch, it had been a few hours before he found a solution. He was watching as one of the town merchants as he locked the front doors of his store for the night. The older man shook the lock to double-check it, and then disappeared into the next alleyway. He looked at the sign above the door.

Hmmm, I can read the writing. Maybe I'm not so far from home after all. The Old Mercantile, aye . . . Let's let things get a little darker around here and I'll pay this joint a little visit.

George knew that dusk was not the best time for a robbery. Waiting until it was good and dark before circling to the back of the store to break in was the smart thing to do.

He had noticed, earlier, as he walked around town that there were some stables down the road. While passing them, he had seen a piece of iron lying on the ground with a sharp point on one end. He moved quickly to retrieve it. He wanted to make it back to this spot and keep scouting for the right time to make his move.

This had not been the first time in George's life that he had broken into a building. His high school had been his mark four times, his foster dad's home twice. The City Recreational Center near his mother's home had been a target of his over a dozen times when he was 17. He loved to go swimming at midnight. He had a record from all this breaking and entering. He was 16 when he was caught for breaking into the local bar after closing to steal beer for him and his friends.

This place is too easy. It's ripe for the picking. There's no damn security in any of these buildings and with my past experience, I can rip this joint off easily. Maybe I won't need to sell my watch after all!

The buildings of the town were built with a combination of shaped stones and wood. The windows were not made of glass so, if the store had been open, he could have jumped right through them. Large, heavy, wooden doors had been lowered over the top of the openings to cover the holes and large iron hasps held them closed. The roofs were covered with a unique style of wooden shingles that appeared to lock together somehow, but, without climbing up onto one of them, he would not be able to tell exactly how. There were no streetlights or electricity, and many of the town's children were lighting torches that were placed in various locations. The roads were made of perfectly placed cobblestones, and were well maintained to keep any vegetation from growing between them.

This standard of living was far beneath George's own personal requirements. *How could these people live their lives this way? I would never want to live like this. It doesn't look like there's any electricity and I doubt that there's any hot water without fetching it from a well or something and warming it up. Smoke stacks too, I bet there's not a heater inside any of these places either...*

George chuckled.

This place is barbaric . . . maybe I'll even run into a few genuine barbarians one of these days.

When the right time arrived, George circled around to the back quietly within the shadows and prepared to enter. As it turned out, he did not have to use the iron bar in his hand. The door was not fully secured. When he tugged at the lock, it popped open. He slipped inside with a smirk.

You've got to be kidding me. These people are idiots!

He crept through the darkness and was now standing in front of what he thought to be the man's cash drawer. The thief opened it, looked inside, but saw nothing. Nothing, that is except for a small piece of twine that most anyone would have just ignored. George took a closer look, then reached in and tugged at the twine, lifting the base of the drawer up into the air, grabbing hold of it. He removed the thin slab of wood and beneath it were three types of coins.

Bingo . . . it must be my lucky day.

It was dark, but from what he could see, the coins looked as if they were made out of the same metal. But on further inspection, he noticed a distinct difference. There were different names engraved on each type of coin. These names were Jervaise, Owain and Helmep—with a distinct size difference among the three. The largest was Jervaise; the second, Owain; and the smallest, Helmep.

The size must have something to do with their value. Oh well . . . looks like I'm just gonna have to take them all. What a bunch of suckers, who would just leave something like this unsecured. They're too trusting around here. Good for me, I think. You're the man, George . . . you're the man.

He decided to clean the storeowner out. He took one Jervaise, seven Owain, over 50 Helmep coins and put them into a little leather pouch he took from one of the shelves. Then he grabbed some tan leathers, quickly removed his old clothes and put them on. He silently crept around and finally found a pair of wool socks. Boots, he figured were next. He found a pair that looked to be his size and tried them on... a perfect fit.

How can people wear this stuff? I hate this leather crap. I've got to find something better when I can.

Seeing the large leather backpacks near the rear door, he headed for them and dumped the contents of Jason's old pack inside. Next, he balled up his old clothes and shoved them in. Before lifting it, he stuffed one of his old socks inside the smaller pouch full of coins and placed it within the wadded-up clothes inside the new pack.

That should keep these coins from rattling as I move through town.

George reached for a belt hanging from a series of nails on the back wall and was about to put it on, when he heard a noise. Two voices... his heart raced. He was only a few feet from the door and quickly moved to the side of it while putting his back against the wall. He could smell smoke. The men were close enough that the smell of their tobacco had made its way through the crack in the door to his nose. His thoughts ran wild.

Okay, get your pistol. Just shoot them if they come in. Come on George, think. That would cause too much noise and give my position away. Think man; think . . . what about this belt.

He took the belt and stretched it between his hands. George's thought continued to scramble as he looked at it.

Damn . . . this thing is useless. I can only use it on one of them, but what can I do with the other guy? I knew I should've taken Karate. Why didn't I take it when I had the chance? Because I was too lazy, that's why. Damn this really sucks. I don't have the training for stuff like this. There gonna kick the crap out of me if they find me in here. What if they find the money? Holy crap, there gonna be really pissed. Oh, my hell... my heart's going a hundred miles an hour. Just be quiet, man. Just keep quiet, maybe they'll...

"Jonathan Walker Smith!" a lady's voice yelled.

"What?" the man shouted back. "Man, that woman will never leave me alone!"

"I understand," the other voice responded. "My wife is always yelling for me to do something as well."

"Jonathan Smith, you get in here and beat these kids. They won't listen to me," the lady yelled again.

"Be right there, honey." Under his breath, he added so his friend could hear, "You old bat! Can you blame them for not listening to her?"

Both men laughed and then headed their separate ways. George stood still against the wall and waited for his heartbeat to slow down before putting on the belt and heading out into the night. When leaving the store, he locked the door properly after making sure everything inside looked in order. He smiled as he secured the lock.

A good thief always covers his tracks. I'm still gonna have to take karate, though!

George made his way through the town to an inn he had seen earlier that day. He took the backpack and rubbed it in the dirt so it didn't look so new and also added a little character to his leather shirt and pants before heading in. He stood inside awhile, watching the people move about. This time, no one turned a head to take notice of him. He sighed with relief. He noticed the ale people were ordering cost one Helmep coin. He listened as a man ordered a room and handed the lady behind the desk one Owain coin. It was not long before he figured out that one of these Owain coins was worth four of the Helmep. After some time spent observing, he walked to the desk and stood in front of a pretty lady.

"What do you want?" the lady snapped rudely, not looking up from her logbook. "I'm not going to take any more lip from you Cottle boys. I've had enough of your little comments about how wonderful my new dress fits my bosom. That whole city is full of undesirable men or, should I say, children. Don't any of you know how to treat a lady?"

George took a step back from the verbal assault and thought a second before re-approaching her. "Miss, I'm not from Cottle, and, although you're very beautiful, I would never presume to have the nerve to say something that wasn't welcome. I'm sorry you've been treated badly. Some men don't realize that if it wasn't for good women, there wouldn't be any good men... but I do."

The lady stopped dead in her tracks and turned to look at him. She took note right away, George's deep-blue eyes, dark-brown hair, and olive skin captured her fancy. Her blue eyes beamed with satisfaction as she pushed her long blonde hair behind her ears and looked him over from head to toe. She noticed his thin athletic build and was pleased with everything she saw.

"Well now, we have a man who understands how to talk to a lady. How can I help you, honey?" she said, adjusting her bosom to a more ample position.

"Well, miss, I've just come in from out of town and was jumped by two thieves on my way here."

George said this without hesitation as he made up a believable lie.

"I started to shout and all they took was my sword and water before running off. I would've thought that they would've wanted more when they knocked me to the ground, but I think my screams scared them off. They must have gotten nervous. I'm a little shaken, my back hurts, and I would like a room for the night. If you have any water and some food that I might be able to take with me to my room, I would much appreciate it."

George gave a wince for effect, reaching for his lower back as if in pain.

"Oh honey, that's terrible, we can't have that now, can we? Let me see what we have available," the woman said with an eagerness to please. "I do have a room, but I'm afraid it isn't the best one we offer. The bed isn't worth sleeping on, if you ask me . . . but the owner of this inn is too cheap to do anything about it. That would be my mother!"

"That'll work fine. I really need the rest and some food pretty badly so it'll have to do." George grabbed his back and pretended to wince in pain yet again. "This back of mine is telling me just to call it a day." Reaching for his backpack, he gave his best smile. "How much do I owe you?"

"Oh honey, don't you worry about a thing. That room isn't even worth the money. Like I said, the bed is absolutely terrible. How about this? I'll have some food brought up to you and hot water so you can soak that back of yours. You just pay me for the food, and we'll call it even."

"Oh that's very kind of you. You don't have to do this." George was smiling inside as he put the final touches on his deception. "I can pay."

"Nonsense, honey, I'll bring the water up to you myself when my replacement gets here in a while. We have on the menu today boar, hunted locally, and, if you have more expensive taste, sea turtles from the Ocean of Utopia. What would you like?"

The liar's stomach did not necessarily like the idea of either one, but figured he would try the boar since it sounded like the lesser of two culinary evils. "I'll take the boar, I guess. Do you have some bread that you could add to it?"

"Of course, dear," she smiled. "You go and head on up. I'll bring it all to you as soon as it's prepared."

"Thank you, you're a lifesaver." With that, George took the key to his new room, paid her the three Helmep coins for the food and turned to head for the stairs.

"Oh, and one more thing, honey," the lady said with a big smile. "My name is Athena."

"Thank you again, Athena. I owe you big for this."

George returned the smile and started up the stairs, congratulating himself on the deception while evaluating both the woman's personality and her shapely figure in his mind. He liked her soft blonde hair and natural beauty. He did not see any benefit Athena could give him beyond what she had already done, so he decided to be nice when she brought him his meal and not take advantage. He would thank her with a kiss and send her away smiling. He did not quite know why he would stop there, but he did know that this was unusual for him. Something about this woman was intriguing. He wished he had the time to figure it out.

It was only a short while before Athena knocked at the door. She brought the plate of food in and instructed some of the hired help to dump the hot water into the bathing tub. Once done, she motioned for them to leave and turned to face George.

"Is there anything else I can do for you then?" she asked with a big smile. "Perhaps keep you company while you eat?"

"As a matter of fact, there is," George responded. "Come on in and make yourself at home."

While asking some questions about the town, he found out where the mage lived and learned where he could buy a new sword. He took some time and, through some subtle questioning, figured out how the money worked. By the sound of the answers he received from Athena, he hoped that he would have enough money to get the things he needed from the mage because the last thing he wanted to do was sell his Rolex.

George and Athena explored some of their attraction for one other as the evening continued. He asked her to turn around while he undressed and kept himself covered with a towel until he was in the tub. It was obvious that she liked him and he allowed her to rub his neck while he bathed. Once she finished, he gave her a kiss.

"Thank you for the wonderful evening, Athena. I hope you won't be too upset if I excuse myself to get some sleep. I'm exhausted!"

Athena assured him with a soft voice, "Everything is okay. All I wanted to do was make sure that someone took care of you after your run-in with bad luck."

George leaned forward and whispered in her ear as he kissed it softly. "I wish that the women where I'm from were as sweet and as beautiful as you are."

He was surprised at how this sounded; he actually believed the compliment. "I'm sorry, but I'm so tired that if I don't get some sleep, I'll fall apart. Will you eat with me before I leave in the morning? I would like to spend some more time with you before I go."

"I would like that. See you in the morning then?"

"In the morning, I look forward to it!"

George had to admit to himself that he really liked this woman. The way she treated him and the soothing sound of her voice piqued his interest. He was not the type of guy to get involved, but this woman was so much better than anyone he had ever dated back home. She had a class about her that he could not explain. If he had known more of what the future would bring, he would stay a while to explore this possibility further.

George went to sleep that night wondering what had happened to Sam and Shalee. Not that he cared one way or the other about their safety, but more because he was just curious. He looked up at the night sky through the window. For the first time, he realized that the sky was completely dark. There was not a star to be seen except for what he thought to be one of the planets Sam had referred to back at the great hall. He could not be certain which one it was, but the last thing he remembered thinking as he went to sleep was how his daughter Abbie would enjoy this adventure.

In the morning, Athena was there to eat with George. She had kept her word and the liar had kept his. Her sweet smile intoxicated him, and he enjoyed watching her over breakfast, longing to be near her. Her hair, body, soft-blue eyes, and the way she blushed when he complimented her, softened him inside. He wished this moment could last forever.

Once they both finished eating, he held her hand and walked her outside. George gave her a long kiss goodbye and, for the first time, he actually enjoyed a woman's kiss without it being attached to a game or a con. This kiss, to his surprise, was real and full of passion—yet it was also sweet and tender. When he pulled away to leave, he saw the longing in her eyes for him. He wanted her just as much. He smiled and took her back up to the room without saying a single word. Spending valuable time that he did not have, he finally experienced his first act of true unselfishness as he lost sight of himself while pleasing Athena.

Before he left, George assured Athena he would be back. The funny thing was he actually meant what he said. He had no desire to lie to this woman. He would be back to see her and found that he was truly smitten. The same woman he had manipulated the night before to get a room had found a crack in his cold-hearted armor. She had stolen a tiny piece of his manipulative heart and for the moment, turned him into a decent human being. He smiled both on the inside and out as he held her hand for as long as he could before letting go. He was saddened when she went back inside to start her work for the day.

After a minute, he decided that standing in the doorway would get him nowhere and turned back to the business at hand. He had shopping to do and took the time to buy a new sword, dagger, knife, rope, water pouches, torches, and food for his journey.

Finally reaching the home of the mage, George realized that he was nervous. He had absolutely no clue what to expect. He knew nothing of magic or how he would attempt to manipulate the topic.

Just play this one safe, Georgie boy, that's the best bet for this situation I think.

Prior to knocking on the mage's door, he did a quick calculation of what was left. He now had one Jervaise piece, which was worth four Owain. The three Owain pieces he had left were worth 12 Helmep. He still had 33 Helmep, which was this world's smallest currency. By his calculation, the total worth of his coins was 45 Helmep if he broke it down to its simplest form. All he could do was hope he had enough.

George knocked on the door. A tall, thin man answered, wearing a long, bluish-gray robe. He was clearly an older man, sporting a matted beard and a mustache stained from many seasons of pipe smoking. He was not the most pleasant looking man and his hygiene, was absolutely atrocious.

"What can I do for you?" the man asked, his breath stinging the inside of George's nose even from where he stood.

George chocked down his desire to say something rude and explained.

"I was told to seek your help. I'm going into the Cave of Sorrow. I could use a spell that will block the visions of the beast Maldwin and keep them from driving me insane. Oh, and if you have one, I could use a spell to help me trap some food."

"Cave of Sorrow, aye," the mage replied. "Come in, son. You can call me 'Morre'—my brother just left or you could have met him as well."

As George walked past the mage, the desire to vomit rushed threw him as the stench from the mage's body odor clubbed him right upside the head.

Oh my heck... what a disgusting old man, he thought. Take a damn bath for hell's sake.

George struggled to think beyond the stench, swallowing hard before putting a smile on his face and responding.

"My name's George. It's nice to meet you, Morre, I'm sorry to barge in on you like this. Maybe I can meet your brother some other time." *I bet he's just as disgusting as you are,* he continued to think as he waited for a response.

"Maybe, but if you're going into the Cave of Sorrow then you may never get the chance to meet him. I'm probably the only one in these parts, besides my brother, who can help you . . . but only to a point."

"What do you mean 'to a point?'"

"Well, it's like this. From stories I've read, it takes almost eight days to find your way through the cave. The spell I can give you will only last about two days—and I only have two of them prepared . . . and not enough supplies to make more."

"Actually, that should be fine. I only need two because I'm not going to be using the spell until I sense the first sign of the beast. While the spell takes effect, I'll trap the beast and bind him so I can get a large head start through the rest of the cave. And if he catches up to me, I'll use the other one to finish the journey to the cave's end."

"I never thought of that approach," the man said. "It sounds like you may be clever enough to pull this off. What will you use to bind the beast?"

"A rope," George said without hesitation.

George thought to himself. *The real trap will be a gunshot to the beast's head.* But, as usual, he had lied. He knew that he had no intentions of trying to spare the beast's life. He continued.

"All I've got to do is figure out how to trap him once I'm inside the cave."

"That's simple," the mage replied. He turned and led George to the far side of his library. "I think I have three Snare Scrolls. All you'll need to do is read from the scroll after planning where you will lead the beast. The spell sets an invisible trap that'll hold the beast in place for a long while. It won't limit your ability to walk across the affected area. I guess that what I'm trying to say is that you'll be able to walk through the affected area without being trapped yourself. This should allow you to make all your actions look natural while moving within the cave. You wouldn't want the beast to be following you and see you jump over the affected area and give away its location, now would you?"

"Definitely not; I want to make sure that he's captured for sure."

Even though he had not originally planned this approach, George decided that the three scrolls would come in handy. He told the mage he would buy them all.

Morre did some calculations and after a moment, he came to a number that was intentionally overpriced. "That will be 13 Owain."

George did the math and realized he didn't have enough to buy all the scrolls. "Damn," he said. "I'm 7 Helmep short. Is there any negotiating room here, Morre? What can I do to make up the difference? Perhaps I could possibly do some sort of a favor to work it off."

The mage thought a moment and, after a bit of pacing, he turned to George with an idea. "I'll sell you the scrolls for the coin you have on you, if you'll deliver a message to a friend of mine who lives in the Sirens Song. I use the word 'friend' loosely because he's actually a large ball of energy called a wisp—a Wisp of Song. If you can find him, and I assure you he's difficult to find, please give him this magically-sealed envelope. I have found the artifact's location that he asked me to seek out. I'm sure that he'll reward you with an answer to any specific question you may have. Just make sure your question is a good one. The wisp is all-knowing when it comes to treasure or matters of power."

"Wow," George said, stunned. "I'll deliver this envelope once I have completed my task if that is okay with you. I swear that I'll get it done. But first, I would like to know more about this Wisp of Song."

The mage took a few minutes to give him some more details.

"The wisp makes its home within the mist of Griffon Falls. The massive pool hidden within the mist is called Sirens Song. The mist spreads across a large area due to the sheer power of the water hitting the bottom of the falls. This ball of energy hides within the fog. Since the gods have protected the area around the temple, the wisp isn't an aggressive creature. This makes him unlikely to attack. The sphere uses a song to communicate with those who find it. For those who are willing to perform a deed of service, a deed that usually involves much danger, the wisp will give a gift for the information returned. This gift is in the form of a song that the creature creates within a person's mind and discloses the location of an artifact of great power or answers any question asked of it. The task the wisp gives to earn this gift is almost always a risk to the seeker's life. In almost every case, the explorer doesn't return from the attempt. I would just ask it for the answer to a simple question if I were you. I'm sure the sphere will give you the information you ask for after delivering this envelope. You'll be one of the lucky ones, my friend, who doesn't have to perform a deed of service."

George stood there a minute, already thinking of a question for the wisp. He turned and paced a second before speaking with the mage once more.

"I'll get the envelope to this Wisp of Song, you can count on it. I must be going now because I need to arrive at my destination before someone else does. I need to be at the Pool of Sorrow where the pool releases into Cripple River in a day and a half. I have a journey ahead of me so I better hurry. Will you please show me on my map where Sirens Song is?"

The mage pointed to Sirens Song and showed George the quickest path to the Pool of Sorrow. He waved goodbye to George and shut the door. He watched out the window as George hurried down the streets of Lethwitch, then he turned and walked into the library where the goddess Celestria appeared.

"Hello," Morre said, as he changed his appearance. Morre, now Lasidious, quickly kissed his evil lover. "My end is all handled, how about yours?"

"Oh, my love," she cupped his head in her hands and kissed him again, "Oh, you wickedly sweet god, I've truly missed you. Everything is as planned. Did I tell you I loved you today?"

"I love you, too . . . you're everything to me," he replied. They both moved again to the entryway where Lasidious set something on the floor. They smiled at each other, and with that vanished, returning to their home on Ancients Sovereign.

Soon after they took their leave, the door of the home opened and the real Morre walked inside, his natural, nasty smelling odor followed him. The mage looked at the floor of the entryway. As he bent down to retrieve the note lying beneath a small leather pouch full of coins, he let out a huge, juicy sounding fart that creeped through the home like a poisonous cloud. He had to wave his hand to clear the air… grunting at his own disapproval of its foul stench. The smell reminded him of the large, helping of sea turtle he had eaten the night before. After a moment he redirected his attention back to the note. It read…

Dear Morre,

Thank you for the scrolls. I've given you far more than their value since I have inconvenienced you and took them without your knowledge. Please forgive the intrusion on your home, but I assure you it was necessary. I wish I didn't have to leave before meeting you. I have heard so many good things about you. Again, I'm sorry and I hope to one day apologize to both you and your brother in person.

Sincerely,
George Nailer

Chapter 8

The Truth be Told

SAM woke from a great night's sleep after having a delicious supper found for them by Mosley. They had stayed at the village's best inn and Sam was grateful for the wolf's company, admiring the beast as he looked across the room watching him sleep in front of the cold fireplace. The hippogriff was not scheduled to take them to their next destination until the Peak of Bailem.

After a moment, he directed his attention to Shalee, who had slept on the bed with him. He had been careful not to touch her during the night, putting her staff between them. The bed, when he had sized it up the night before, looked to be almost as large, if not larger, than his king-sized bed back home. They both had plenty of room.

Her rest seemed so peaceful. Every now and then, she moved from one side to the other. He was glad for her movement because, as a doctor, he knew it was not good to stay in one position for too long.

She is just so beautiful, he thought. What is it about her that I like so much? I just can't put my finger on it. Do I really like this kind of drama? She is a bit of a diva. But wow... what a diva she makes. I bet those pretty little hands have never seen a day of real manual labor. This woman is gonna be my Achilles Heel! I wish I could lie beside her and hold her.

Eventually, he moved from the bed and walked toward the window. The room felt like he was in some sort of cottage instead of an inn. As his bare feet made contact with the cold, flat stones of the floor he stopped, closed his eyes, and imagined for an instant that he was in a castle. He took a deep breath and stretched. It was a breath that managed to add to his fantasy. He admired how clean the country air smelled.

Sam had always been the type of guy who had to fight with his mind to fantasize. This struggle was something that had always bothered him throughout his life... being a genius had its disadvantages. He could never escape his own need to stay in reality. And, once again, just like most other times in his life, his mind brought him back from his little fantasy of walking on castle floors and dropped him off in the cold reality of a simple village, full of everyday common, simple people.

He moved to the window, looked out, then laughed inside.

At least this reality is something I used to believe was fantasy. At least my mind can't remove me from this reality. It's a refreshing break to get away from things.

The people below were slowly starting to move about. From the smells penetrating the air, food was being prepared somewhere. Taking another deep breath, Sam thought of George.

I wonder where he he's at? Is he dead? If not, what's he up to?

If Sam had known that at this very moment, the same guy he watched fall through the hole back at the temple was now sitting down and having breakfast with Athena, he would have felt a sense of relief. But dwelling on these questions was getting him nowhere. He turned from the window and moved across the room to wash his face. The water he poured from the pitcher had turned room temperature and he knew the slight chill would help get his day going.

Mosley shifted near the fireplace but did not awake. As Sam looked over at Shalee, the God of War, Bassorine, appeared next to the bed. Sam, stunned by this appearance, watched as the god stood over the bed looking down at the sleeping woman.

After a moment, Sam spoke quietly. "I was wondering when you'd be back."

Bassorine turned from Shalee and walked toward him. "There's no need to whisper," he said in a normal tone. "The others cannot hear us. This conversation is only between us two. I'm here to understand your mind, and inform you of our current situation regarding the Crystal Moon. This would also be a good time to answer any of the questions you may have."

"Finally," Sam sighed heavily. "My thoughts have gone in

many different directions, and I've got plenty of questions. But first, what's the situation that you're referring to?"

The god nodded, pulled a chair across the room, and placed it by the window. Looking through the opening, he spoke.

"The Village of Angels, where you are now, has the potential to be a good starting point for your rise to glory, but we'll talk of this later. Many things on Grayham will remind you of Earth as I'm sure you have already discovered. The situation I was referring to is regarding the Crystal Moon. None of the gods have been able to find Lasidious. It's as if he's completely vanished. I had intended to speak with him by now to find out the Crystal Moon's location, but still haven't done so. I was hoping with this information the gods could come together as a collective and vote on how these new events were to be handled. Unfortunately, without Lasidious, we're no further along than when we last spoke. I'm disturbed by this, to say the least."

"Crap! I'm not sure what to say. This creates some concerns for me too," Sam said. "May I ask my questions now?"

"Sam, please don't ask for my permission to speak any longer. I'm here to speak with you without formalities."

"Sounds good to me," he replied. "My biggest concern is that the Crystal Moon is what keeps all the planets from colliding with one another. The crystal provides for the balance of life, right? You said that if it wasn't retrieved and put back in the temple, everything will be destroyed. Exactly how long do we have before this happens?"

Bassorine looked away from the window and then at Sam.

"We have time. The Crystal Moon has been governing the planets for over 10,000 seasons now, placing each planet in its optimal path of travel. The crystal has set the planets on perfectly calculated speeds within these orbits, and has given each the right amount of spin to maintain consistent days and nights. The only thing that will change is that the crystal will no longer be able to change the position of the planets in order to create new seasons. It's good that Grayham is in the middle of a season that is warm and rainy. This should allow for life as normal to keep going within this extended season. People will talk, but no one will understand why the season continues. The best part of the situation is that the crystal has governed all the planets in a similar fashion. The seasons on each world should be similar to the one here."

Sam jumped in, "That's great, but how long will it be before the planets start to drift off course?"

"Maybe what you would consider to be one of your Earth years," Bassorine replied. "Once the planets start to shift, things will change slowly at first, but they'll gradually get worse. The planets, for all we know, could take more than a season to shift since the crystal has been governing them for so long . . . it's how you would say on Earth, a crap shoot."

Sam was anxious—but even more than anxious—he was annoyed that a god would not know the exact answers to his questions. Maybe these so-called gods were simple enough to only have enough power to screw with things on a cosmic level and nothing more. To Sam's way of thinking, a god should be all-knowing as well as all-powerful.

"Is there anything I can do while I wait for you to tell me where the crystal is, so I can prepare to retrieve it?"

"I don't know if you are the best man for the job in light of these new events. You don't have any noble blood running through your veins and, you also don't have the fame to gain an audience with someone on this world who is powerful enough to do something about the situation. This is most unfortunate because I was looking forward to your rise to glory."

"It was the gods' bright idea to bring me here in the first place," Sam said angrily. "And now that I'm here, you're telling me that I'm not good enough for the job? I understand what's involved. I also understand that you might want to keep it confidential that the crystal has been lost from the temple. You could have one big mess on your hands once the people of your worlds find out that the Crystal Moon is gone. Their belief in you will fade once they know you can't stop the planets from colliding into one another. You said we could speak freely, so how about you tell me why you're not powerful enough to keep the worlds from colliding without the crystal?"

Bassorine laughed. "You're very bold when given permission

to speak freely. Maybe I should've chosen my words more carefully with you, Sam. But to answer your question, it took 14 of us
to create these worlds, and the power it would take to keep them
from moving is far too much for us to do on a continual basis. This
is why we all created the Crystal Moon. Each of us poured some
of our power into it. The crystal's pieces were made in such a way
that they could not become drained of their power. I would like to
tell you that gods are all-powerful, but this isn't the case. We have
weaknesses and limitations. If I were to convince the gods to use
their powers to keep the worlds apart, we would soon use all our
power and the worlds would be destroyed anyway."

"So create another Crystal Moon, and replace the one Lasidious
took."

"Like I said, it took all 14 of us to create the Crystal Moon in
the first place and Lasidious definitely would not help us make
another."

Sam thought a minute before responding. He had never thought
of a god as having a weakness before, but the concept strangely did
make sense. It explained how Bassorine didn't know everything.
If there were truly limitations to his powers and his knowledge,
then the term 'god' now meant something completely different to
him than what it did before.

Sam organized his thoughts. "Well then, what you've told me
confirms what I wanted to say. I would think you would want the
people, not to mention the beasts of these worlds, to continue to
worship and maintain a normal life while the Crystal Moon is
missing. What happens when they know you can't do anything
to save them? What happens when they find out that they're ex-
pendable simply because you can create another world with more
people on it to worship you?

"I would laugh at the god I served if he could do nothing because the others allowed one of their own to destroy everything.
You've all taken this free will crap to a whole new level. If you
had me handling this, at least the politics of the situation on Grayham would be handled properly, and you wouldn't lose too many
of your worshipers. If anyone is smart enough and strong enough
to figure this mess out, it's me. So go tell your god friends that I

won't just sit here and do nothing, or you might as well send me back to Earth."

Bassorine stayed cool. He had hoped Sam would summon up the desire to undertake such a task, but he also realized it had to be Sam's decision. Bassorine knew quite well that he had made a mistake by allowing the Book of Immortality to be created. If he had not done so, he would have destroyed Lasidious already and taken the crystal back from him. The god figured that if Sam went after the crystal, Shalee would follow in his footsteps. Shalee was the key to fixing everything. She would follow Sam and her powers would grow as she did. He knew that Sam, of all the men within the worlds, was the best man for the job, but it would not be a small or easy task.

"You have made a few good points, Sam, but there is a lot you still don't know." Bassorine turned to look out the window, his face becoming serious. "I am the God of War and I love a good battle with everything that's in me, but what you are about to do by volunteering yourself is going to be far beyond war. Yes, there will be fighting, but this is about the survival of everything that is left . . . and I do mean everything. Yes, the gods can create another group of worlds, but there's nothing wrong with what is in existence now."

Sam interrupted Bassorine. "You're not telling me something. Level with me, man. I'm not interested in being left in the dark. Something bigger is going on here and I want to know what it is. I'm a big boy and can take the truth far easier than I can lies or deception. What is it that you're holding back?"

Bassorine sighed heavily. He stared at the heart of the fighter. He knew what he had to say was going to sting. "What I'm about to tell you will upset you, but I swear to you it's the truth. There have been many stories created for the people to believe in—most are not true. I would send you home but for one problem. Your world, the one you call Earth, is gone. It no longer exists."

"What do you mean it no longer exists?"

Bassorine looked at him and replied. "I know that a man with your intelligence understands what 'no longer exists' means. I'm saying it has been destroyed. Let me finish what I have to tell you, and then ask me your questions."

The god waited for Sam to nod and then continued.

"When the God Wars started over 14,000 seasons ago, the battle for power eventually extended itself to every galaxy and solar system. The story we created to tell the people of these worlds—the story that I was the one who brought home the crystal to the others—isn't true. I've always been a god, since the beginning of time. This story that I was given god-like powers was made up to give the beings of these new worlds something to believe in. It allows them to have something to be thankful for and gives them faith. This is similar to the way your gods of Earth gave the people something to have faith in . . . something to worship during their lives, rewarding the faithful to a heaven, the unfaithful to hell. The fact is all of the gods used heaven and hell as places to send the souls of our dead to rest. Even the gods who ruled worlds that didn't believe in free will sent their followers' souls straight to hell. They were to be kept there until it was time for them to be reborn. This is where the idea of reincarnation came from on your Earth."

Sam opened his mouth to speak, but Bassorine held up his hand for silence.

"Make no mistake when I tell you that the gods are indeed strong. We are the beginning and the end, but we can be destroyed and have weaknesses. During this War of the Gods, thousands perished, and those of us who survived elected to be governed by rules that we didn't have before. We've done this voluntarily. The laws we implemented have a few things that have been overlooked. We can vote to fix this, but not until the events that have been set in motion have been stopped. The Book of Immortality was created to govern these laws . . . I now regret its creation. I have the power to stop Lasidious, but our laws bind my resolve. I cannot stop him without risking the Book's power and my own destruction."

Bassorine stood up to continue. "Allow me to explain the Book further. Those of us who survived the God Wars decided, as a collective, to create the Book of Immortality. Each of us would pour some of our power into the Book and make it strong enough to govern our actions. Its purpose would be to keep us from warring again for all of eternity and hold our new laws within its pages. If a problem arises, it is for the Book of Immortality to govern the punishment and determine the solution for the problem, not for the gods to get involved. We're no longer allowed to fight each other in order to make things go our way.

"We also agreed, as a collective, that we would no longer control the wills of gods, men, or beasts and give them the freedom to make choices of their own. The Book allows the gods to have free will as long as we don't break the laws within its pages. After all, it was free will that started the God Wars in the first place. Your gods of Earth, along with myself, and others, were among those who supported this concept of free will and ran our worlds this way. We all created heaven and hell. They were created to hold the souls of those that had died. Where their spirits ended up was determined by how they chose to live their lives and how well they followed the rules that their god or gods in some cases, had established for them on their planet. Heaven was a glorious place of happiness, while hell was not so desirable. No matter what, it had to be the free will of men that got them to either place.

"The gods who fought against this concept of free will started the wars—gods that you're familiar with. Ra, Sekhmet and Harrah, they all chose to fight against this concept. The likes of even the fallen angel Lucifer, who you know as Satan, rose up with them and struck down countless numbers, both god and angel alike within the heavens as they drew more to their cause. Once the wars started, it soon exploded out of control and almost everything was completely destroyed. Even the most ancient of gods fell in this battle. In the end, it was those of us who came together to create the Collective of the Farendrites and fought side-by-side as a single unit, survived to see the conclusion of the wars. The war lasted just over 3,000 seasons or what you would call Earth years before they ended. It took those of us that were left another 800 seasons to create this new, smaller solar system. We had to search long and hard for materials to do so since almost nothing remained. These five worlds are all that we have been able to create so far. We continue to bring materials from the far reaches of what used to be other galaxies and store them to try and expand this new galaxy beyond this small solar system.

"The gods wanted you to create an empire here on Grayham to see if the other races would follow in your footsteps. If the worlds followed your lead, we intended to allow all races to be joined. We expected there would be problems with the races joining together, problems similar to the ones you had on Earth with the races that had existed there. But we had hoped with your intelligence, the job could be accomplished. You and Shalee both have good hearts full of kindness. Your intelligence and experiences from Earth could help you to avoid many mistakes in bringing the races together.

"We also hoped that one day we could separate four of these five remaining planets and move them each to a solar system of their own within an expanded galaxy. The fifth planet, known as Dragonia, would be given a new name and become the new hell. This place will punish the souls of all evil beings until they are reborn to try again to live a better life. The dragons of that planet would be given a new home and separated to live peacefully from all others.

"We also plan to create a new heaven and once again bring the good souls there to wait for an opportunity to be reborn. We wanted a place to reward them for their actions and deeds for being good.

"For now, we hold all the souls, whether good or evil, within the pages of the Book of Immortality. The Book keeps them safe until it's time for them to be reborn. Right now, all evil beings are not punished, other than what the Book may see fit to do with them.

"As for me, I'm millions of seasons old and fear this could be the first time since the new worlds were created that an end of all things could come again now that the Crystal Moon is gone. We may have to rebuild life once again after the dust settles. I can only hope the people of this world are strong enough to make it through this.

"Now what I'm about to tell you is most important. Before your Gods of Earth perished in the God Wars, they told me and three other gods about you, Sam. They spoke of the blessings given to you before sending your spirit to Earth. The gods with me that day were Lasidious, Keylom, and Alistar. Your Gods of Earth told us about your superior intellect and how you were the best one to preserve and bring forward through time. I chose Shalee because she would be a good mate for you—having been given the perfect anatomy for bearing children. There were other reasons that I chose her, but all I'll say is that she could be very powerful someday.

"Lasidious must've brought George forward secretly for reasons I don't know. He must've done this without any of us knowing about it. And, if he tried to bring a magical being forward, the gods would have felt this. I cannot think of any reason why he would do this—it simply doesn't make any sense, but I suspect we'll find out.

"After all, it was the Collective of the Farendrites who voted to have Lasidious retrieve both you and Shalee from Earth. We would keep you preserved until we saw a good time for you to be placed on Grayham. We wanted someone with past knowledge of things before all was destroyed to be spared from the destruction and be kept safe until now. As I've said already, the gods felt this knowledge would be essential to building an empire here on Grayham. Your success would be the model for the other worlds.

"I fear Lasidious has taken this opportunity meant for the good of all beings within these worlds and manipulated them for his own agenda. I'm still bound by the Book of Immortality's rules and cannot do anything about this, except hope this can all be fixed. I cannot start another God War over this—the Book will not allow it and the gods also have free will. It appears that Lasidious is exercising his right to make a mess. It's the only logical explanation. He's always wanted a stronger following of both man and beast to serve him. Maybe that's what this is about. Even Lasidious falls under the Book of Immortality's governing, so really all he can do is influence those willing to do his bidding. Unfortunately, the hearts of both man and beast can be easily persuaded to do evil. If you look at your own planet before this happened, your different governments on Earth were about to destroy life with their own weapons of mass destruction.

"The days here on Grayham are identical to Earth's. The number of hours it takes for the planet to spin around one time is the same. You should be able to use this to your advantage when planning your next move. A season is also the same number of days as on Earth; much here will remind you of earth. Your watch will work fine for you until your battery dies. I'm surprised that it has kept its charge while you were in stasis."

The god finally stopped talking. He watched Sam, who was still sitting on the edge of the bed near Shalee's sleeping figure. Sam couldn't think of one single question, his mind and heart were overcome by everything Bassorine had said.

He couldn't fathom the fact that his own personal god of Earth was destroyed, along with both heaven and hell. How could any of this be true? Earth was gone: his family, his house, his car and everything that was familiar to him were now destroyed. The fact that he was one of only three survivors left in all of creation who was spared to live past the God War was overwhelming. The fact that the only beings to survive the God Wars, other than himself, Shalee and George, were the Collective of the Farendrites simply required a complete reboot of his mind. How could he possibly deal with all this?

Bassorine saw the effect all this new information had on Sam. Knowing Sam needed relief from his thoughts, the God of War walked over, touched him on the head and said, "Rest, my child, rest!" With this, Sam fell into a deep sleep.

The god smiled and said, "When you awake, my friend, you'll find a peace within you. You'll be able to understand all of this and, if you still desire to do so, figure out a way to create the glory you need to gain audiences with kings. You're going to need all the help you can get to save these worlds."

Bassorine walked over to Mosley and woke him. He told the Night Terror wolf to extend their stay at the inn and keep watch over them. Before vanishing, the god gave Mosley some ideas on how Sam could gain the notoriety necessary to earn an audience with Southern Grayham's largest royal family, the house of Brandor; then he quietly vanished.

Chapter 9

The Unicorn Prince's Horn

GEORGE finally left Lethwitch. On his way out of town, he passed a group of men who were talking about the robbery that occurred at the Old Mercantile the night before. He smirked, returning to his old self.

Now that was a nice piece of my handiwork. Those poor chumps never saw me coming! What a bunch of idiots...

For the rest of that day and throughout the night, George moved at a slow jog or a fast walk. He knew he must hurry and only stopped to eat or pee on a tree. He thought about the lovely Athena many times, wondering if his little Abbie would like her. He had never brought a woman around his daughter before, but his heart told him she could be the first. He also wondered how long it would be before he could figure out how to get back to his beautiful Abbie. Unlike Sam, George had no idea that Earth was destroyed or that his daughter was dead.

Along the route, there was no shortage of trees. He was told to leave town and make his way north along the Cripple River until he reached the outlet where the Pool of Sorrow flowed into it. The Enchanted Forest bordered all along the west side of the riverbank and was so dense that light struggled to find its way in. George had no desire to go near it; the whole scene was just plain creepy.

He was beginning to feel exhausted from his jog. The weight of his pack had not made his task to get to the Pool of Sorrow any easier. If it had not been for the training he had done while competing in triathlons he would have stopped long ago. He'd heard many strange noises coming from the forest during the night, some of which sounded like screams of frightened animals being killed for food. Each time he heard the screams, a response from something far more aggressive in nature filled his night air. He was horrified; the adrenaline produced by his fear was what kept him moving so aggressively in spite of his body's weariness.

Now that it was morning the noises seemed to stop and he figured it was the only chance he had to get some rest. He looked at his watch; he'd been moving at this pace for almost 16 hours now. His body was about to shut down. He stopped, rubbed his cramping muscles, grabbed something to eat, and laid his head on the stolen backpack for a nap.

He set the alarm on his watch for eight hours and looked over the map that Jason had given him. Some of the town folk said the journey was a solid two-day walk if he stopped to rest at night. He smiled. He had been jogging almost the entire time. He was now within a few hours of the pool—and might arrive at his destination before dark. He could only hope it would be easier to sleep when he arrived, and that the noises around the Pool of Sorrow would not be so frightening.

George adjusted the backpack under his head and used his old Gucci shirt to cover himself. As he fell asleep, he listened to the sounds of the river's movements and plotted his adventures. Once asleep, his dreams were of him, Athena, and his baby girl spending time together. It was a lovely dream of his Abbie flying back and forth between the two of them as they pushed her on her favorite swing.

Back at Angel's Village, Sam and Shalee's room

WHEN SAM AWOKE, Shalee was sitting next to him on the bed rubbing his back. He rolled over stretching his entire body, then sat up with a big smile. Shalee's beauty was absolutely stunning and, for the moment, all he thought about was her. The fighter, teacher, doctor, genius reached up and brushed his hand across her face.

Mosley had been sitting at the base of the bed, waiting for him to awake as well. When the wolf saw that Sam was moving he jumped on the bed and plopped down across his legs.

Both humans smiled and, for the moment, the mood in the room was lighthearted and peaceful.

"Thanks for watching over me you guys. You look beautiful, Shalee. Do you like the outfit Bassorine left for you?"

Shalee grinned, then pulled the cloth away from her waist.

"It is kinda cute. I need to take it in a touch and add a dash of me to it, but I should be able to salvage Bassorine's attempt at acceptable fashion. I do like the… what did you call this head piece again, Mosley?"

"It's called a Gashal."

"Yes, the Gashal, I like the way it lays on my head. The little gems area fabulous."

Sam chuckled.

"You get a beautiful dress and all I got was a rugged leather outfit. Now how fair was that?"

"But you pull it off," Shalee responded.

"I suppose."

Mosley broke into the conversation. "I was wondering when you would wake," the beast said. "I was starting to think Bassorine had knocked you out for good. We haven't left this room except to get something to eat. You slept through all of yesterday and last night."

At that, Sam rose from the bed. The sound of Bassorine's name brought back everything the god had told him. He stood at the window and looked out quietly while the other two sat there confused, watching him.

"You okay, Sam?" Shalee asked.

Sam motioned for them to leave him be for a moment. He mentally reviewed everything he had heard the morning before. He accessed his photographic memory, listing everything he had learned.

1. Shalee was brought forward for the purpose of having my children and to be my mate. **Note to self:** *Be careful how this news is broken to Shalee; she may get angry. I don't know what the other reason is except that Bassorine said Shalee could be very powerful some day.*

2. The Gods of Earth were destroyed in the God Wars, along with thousands of other gods. Only 14 gods, making up the Farendrites Collective, have survived.

3. Bassorine has always been a god. The story that he was given his powers for bringing home the Crystal Moon to the gods is untrue. Bassorine is millions of years old.

4. Earth was destroyed. My family, Shalee's family, George's family—all are dead. My home, car, boat, and my brand new Mustang convertible are all destroyed, along with my medical center.

5. The Crystal Moon is really used for the purpose of separating the planets and monitoring their movements. It controls their distance from the sun, speeds, orbit alignments, rotations and axis tilts; it controls the seasons.

*6. The gods created the Crystal Moon. They don't have the power to govern the worlds themselves. They would run out of power if they tried. Each of them poured some of their power into the creation of the Crystal Moon. **Note to self:** Make sure to ask Bassorine how the gods pour part of themselves into something.*

7. The gods cannot make another Crystal Moon without Lasidious's help. He caused this whole mess so making another one is unlikely.

8. The people of the worlds were told the story of Bassorine's retrieval of the Crystal Moon to have something to believe in; the story is not true, but it does give them something, a sense of faith and peace.

9. It was true that the faithful on Earth would go to heaven.

10. Hell was a real place before it was destroyed.

11. The Book of Immortality is more than just a book—it has its own soul. It is a being the gods created to govern them and holds all the rules the gods live by within its pages. The Book currently keeps all the dead, souls—both good and evil—within its pages until it is time for them to be reborn.

*12. The idea of reincarnation is true. **Note to self:** Who would've ever thought that such a foolish notion was an actuality!*

13. The gods allow all beings, no matter what race, to have their own free will to do anything they want. Even the gods function under the concept of free will and are not allowed to impose their will on the beings of the worlds. The Book of Immortality ensures that this doesn't happen.

*14. The gods originally meant for just Shalee and I to come forward in time. They kept us someplace safe until it was time to place us on Grayham. They wanted us to create an empire and set an example for the races of every world to emulate. **Note to self:** I don't like the idea that I was put into stasis!*

15. The gods didn't intend for George to be brought forward, but Lasidious manipulated this for whatever reason—reasons the gods do not know. The gods cannot do anything about this since, like them, Lasidious has free will. Bassorine has the power to destroy Lasidious, but if he did, he would be punished by the Book of Immortality and made mortal.

16. It is the intention of the gods to separate four of the five planets they've created and give each of them its own solar system.

*17. The fifth planet—Dragonia—is to become the new hell. The dragons will be given their own new world to live peacefully on away from all others. **Note to self:** I can't fathom that dragons are real. Not too sure I really wish to see one and find out for myself though.*

*18. The gods plan to make a new heaven for the souls of those who are good. **Note to self:** I better receive a guaranteed ticket to get in once all of this crap is over!*

*19. The years, days, and hours of this world are the same as those of the now destroyed Earth. Shalee's watch will work fine here. **Note to self:** I'm not about to wear that girly looking thing. I'll figure something else out later. Besides, the battery will die soon anyway.*

21. I don't have any noble blood in me, nor do I have enough fame to do anything. How do I gain it? I need to be able to meet with people in power to get something done around here. **Note to self:** *This really pisses me off.*

Sam had been standing there for a while before Shalee walked up behind him and touched his shoulder. Startled and realizing he was being rude, he said, "I am sorry." Then he faced Shalee, pulled her close and, for the first time, made an advance. If she was to be his mate, why not get started?

"I think you're absolutely beautiful!"

Shalee was shocked by the compliment, but could not keep herself from smiling. The only thing she could think to do was give him a hug in return and a gentle pat on the back. "Thank you, Sam."

"You don't pat," Sam joked. "My friends pat when they hug. I pat when I hug my buddies. I pat my grandma. Let me show you how to hug someone you're interested in." With that, he gently touched her and then wrapped his arms around her, pulling her even closer than before. He held her there for a time and she did not fight it. "Now that's how you hug someone you find attractive," Sam said, releasing her.

"Who said I find you attractive?"

She turned, grabbed her staff and left the room, smiling to herself as she exited the door.

"Ouch, that stings," Mosley said as he looked at Sam. "Nice try, though. I've got to admit that if I were a human, I would've done that myself."

"Well that really backfired," the rejected doctor of love said. "I could've sworn that would've worked. I guess I'm not her type."

"Don't be so quick to judge her, Sam. My wife rejected me nine times before she finally caved in and kept this old Night Terror Wolf."

"Wife, you have a wife? Since when do wolves get married? Do all animals get hitched on this world?"

"Not normally, but I should clarify. My wife died some time ago, 100 seasons ago to be exact. And when she did, I was lost. It took me a long time to stop feeling the pain that it caused my soul. I met her at the bridge of Angel's Crossing. She was traveling with a group, guiding them to the City of Champions. I also happened to be heading in that similar direction with a cure for the disease that had been spreading through the caves of the Bear Clan.

"Her name was Luvera and she was, by my kind's standards, a perfect creature. Her coat, eyes, teeth, body and tail—oh, that tail was exceptional in any wolf's eyes. I would give anything to have her back.

"She was also in the service of the gods and blessed because of it. Many things we had in common back then. We both spoke every language of both men and beast. We talked for four days before we had to go our separate ways. It was destined that I be with her. I think Bassorine was the one who made it possible for me to meet her."

Mosley held his head high as he spoke of her. "Both of us found ways to be with each other and for a while we traveled together doing the work of the gods. Finally, we asked the gods that we served if we could adopt the tradition of marriage—common to humans of this planet—and make it our own. I had to ask her nine times before she finally said yes. Finally, our request was approved and we were united. I was with my wife for over 300 years before she died . . . and cherished her with everything I am."

Sam was impressed as he responded. "Wow, 300 years, that's a long time. The men from the planet I'm from would consider that their own little hell, being attached to someone that long. I imagine it would be nice to find someone you loved so completely that you could enjoy her for so many years. I'm touched. I hope I can find that kind of love myself someday. So which god did your wife serve and how did she die?"

Mosley hung his head as he spoke. "I have never spoken of this to anyone other than Bassorine. I will tell you now, but I don't want to dwell on this once it has been spoken. She served Keylom, the God of Peace, with undying loyalty. Keylom is also the God of Good Natured Beasts. He is a good god, worthy of her service— but it was her service that ended her life."

"How?"

Tears filled Mosley's wolf eyes as he continued. "A Jaguar Demon named Kepler killed her. He's the lord of all the giant cats on Grayham. It doesn't matter if they are alive or undead, good or evil. Kepler uses fear to rule all his feline subjects no matter what god they serve. He's pure evil and has the ability to control the spirits of anyone evil he kills—making them serve his will. He also has the ability to move invisibly within the shadows, even the smallest of shadows. It is for these reasons, along with his massive size, that he dominates this world of cats and commands their service to him."

"He sounds like a personal nightmare. Even sitting in safety here, I worry about crossing his path."

"Kepler is an undead creature. He lives in a place called Skeleton Pass which he has ruled for as long as I can remember. He has a small army of undead skeleton warriors that patrol this area, killing every man who tries to pass through it."

"For real—I mean, you're actually telling me that he's undead and there are things undead under his control that are walking around this world? So how did this Kepler kill your wife and why?"

"I fear that my wife was in the wrong place at the wrong time when she died. I don't believe Kepler had any reason or need to kill her, but she was in his path and suffered because of it. My wife, Luvera, was delivering a message for her god to the Unicorn Prince, Ultonen, who at that time, lived within the Dark Forest. The message was sealed for his eyes only. I cannot speak about the purpose it served. I normally would've gone with my wife, but on this trip, I was detained. Bassorine had a job that required my attention.

"Before I tell you how she died, let me tell you this first. A horn of a unicorn has a few marvelous abilities, even if separated from the rest of the creature. The horn can be used to aid anyone who possesses it. Aside from the healing powers to cure most ailments, all poisonous plants or animals will burst and die in the presence of the horn. When held near, or in the presence of anything poisonous, the horn will start to sweat, giving a warning of danger to the holder."

"Really," Sam interrupted again. "Why would Kepler want something like this? Can poison harm an undead creature like him?"

"No, but it was the horn's special traits that gave the Barbarian king in the city of Bloodvain the idea to hire Kepler to kill the Unicorn Prince for his horn. Kepler was told that if he retrieved the horn, the Barbarian king would stop sending his armies through Kepler's Skeleton Pass when they invaded the Kingdom of Brandor."

The wolf began pacing, becoming more agitated as he continued his story. "My wife was standing in front of the unicorn prince delivering her message when the attack occurred. The prince had his head bowed to her, in appreciation of Keylom's message, when Kepler made his move from the shadows. Kepler rushed from the darkness of the forest and knocked my wife onto the Unicorn Prince's horn, impaling her through the heart. I was told she died instantly and was gone before she fell to the ground."

"Oh, my heaven," Sam said, shocked. "I'm so sorry. Is there anything I can do?"

Mosley looked at Sam and smiled. "It has been 100 seasons as I have said. I think there's indeed nothing that can be done. I know her soul has to be in a good place. I'm sure Keylom saw to that."

Sam knew exactly where her soul was—it was within the pages of the Book of Immortality, waiting for her chance to be reborn but he said nothing to Mosley of this. It was clear that the wolf did not know what happened to the souls of the dead and where they were kept after death.

Sam's mind began churning. "Something had to give that Barbarian king more of a reason to go after the Prince's horn, something more than merely detecting poison. Any of his subjects could have tested his food."

"The murder of the prince served three purposes," Mosley replied. "Two of these purposes were far more important than just the testing of the king's food for poisons. The first, yes, was to protect the Barbarian king from food poisoning. He would hold the horn over the food to see if it started to sweat and give warning. But the second reason was for the horn's healing properties.

And finally, the third purpose was to show the unicorns they were vulnerable to the attacks of the Barbarian king. They would learn that all their numbers could not stop one simple beast employed by the Barbarian king from killing their prince. The king intended to have all the unicorns serve him. The murder of the Unicorn Prince sent a clear message that he was to be feared. To this day, they remain loyal to the king's house out of fear for their lives, despite their powerful magic. The Barbarian king was pure evil and dominated everything in his kingdom through fear."

"Now that makes more sense to me. I understand the desire to use the healing properties and also the message of fear to gain power," Sam said.

Mosley continued. "I haven't told you about the effect the horn had on the king—an unexpected effect even to the king. The Barbarian would use the horn to heal himself. One day he realized that by doing this, he was receiving the benefit of an extended life."

"No way," Sam said, amazed. "Heck, I bet if the Barbarian king had known about that, he would've gone after the horn for that reason alone. If I were in that position, something like that just might come in handy. How long will he live?"

Mosley paused, and then said, "The extension of his life was a side effect of using the horn. The Barbarians are an aggressive race. They fight among themselves for fun. Each time the king would enter a fight, he used the horn to heal himself and his life was prolonged. No one had ever used the horn enough to find out the effects of such constant use. Once the Barbarian king realized the healings were making him stronger and younger-looking, he did things to hurt himself intentionally. He retired to his chambers and cut himself in order to use the horn's healing powers. It isn't known how often he used his horn, but only the gods and a few others knew about these side effects."

"How in the hell could a secret this big be kept from the world?" Sam exploded. "The man is outliving his subjects. Doesn't anyone question this?"

"Of course they questioned, but the Barbarian king didn't want anyone to know his secret. A secret of this magnitude would cause a massive power struggle and start a war amongst the people of

Bloodvain. The king told his subjects that he had found a spring and its waters granted him a longer life. He told them that the spring had dried up when he visited it again to gather water for his sons and grandsons. I wouldn't know any of this if it weren't for Bassorine telling me. Bassorine watched from the heavens as the king used the horn over and over again. The gods were not pleased with the use of the horn, but they do not take away the free will of men or beasts."

Sam rolled his eyes. "Wow, this free will crap can really give everyone a lot of room to cause problems. So what's this Barbarian king's name? I assume that he's still alive?"

"His name was Bloodvain, Bude Bloodvain," Mosley answered. "He recently passed away. His great grandson, Senchae Bloodvain, has taken the throne. Bassorine told me that King Bude told his grandson Senchae about the horn's benefits before he died. The only thing worse than this new king using the horn is that Senchae has been the Barbarian champion for the last 15 seasons. He's the strongest and best warrior the Barbarian kingdom has ever seen. The Barbarians fight to the death when entering their city's arena. The fact that Senchae Bloodvain is still alive should give you an idea of what kind of warrior he is to survive 15 seasons in the arena."

"Wow, now that's impressive!" Sam said, rubbing his hands together. "This guy is someone I can relate to—I love to fight. I just won my first professional fight before I came here, you know."

Mosley quickly interrupted him. "I wouldn't get too excited about this man's abilities to fight. I also wouldn't get any bright ideas about challenging him and living. Allow me to explain to you how the Barbarians fight in their arena. They are an extremely vain race, vain to the point of stupidity. All Barbarian kings throughout history have kept an open invitation with the humans of Grayham to fight in hand-to-hand combat—without any armor or clothes—for the crown. Any human who can beat the Barbarian's best warrior, without weapons and only wearing a cloth to cover his loins, will be rewarded with the King of the Barbarians crown. This means all Barbarians will bow to that human and serve him. Many humans have tried for this power and have failed.

The current champion of the Barbarians, since Senchae Bloodvain no longer fights in the arena, is called Churnach Furgus. In order to fight the kingdom's best, you would first have to beat their second best.

"Bloodvain is a nightmare in hand-to-hand combat, his sheer size alone intimidates any man. He stands over eight-foot four inches tall, weighs nearly 550 pounds, and is easily as well-defined as you are, Sam. He is well known within the kingdom for his ability to fight for long periods without getting tired. The king trains with angered bulls to keep in shape. He strikes the bull, causing the beast to charge at him repeatedly—then meets the creature as it slams into him head on, wrestling the bull to the ground. He does this over and over again while striking the bull with heavy blows. The beast finally hits the ground exhausted and can no longer continue.

"Before Senchae became king, the bull would die and Senchae would serve it to the leaders of his grandfather's army as a gesture of respect. Now that he's the new king, Senchae is loved by his army and doesn't need to rule by fear. He rules through respect and respect alone. He's loved within his army, even though his heart is just as evil as his grandfather's ever was."

Sam was impressed but still looked for a solution. "My experience is that a big man is also a slow man . . . and I'd bet that's his weakness. Admittedly, he may be quite powerful, but if a man were fast enough, he could cause Senchae some damage."

Mosley laughed, "I didn't finish telling you about his training sessions. After he fights this single bull and clears its body, Senchae brings in three fresh bulls and, as before, he makes each of those bulls angry. He uses this as his training for speed, constantly working to avoid the attacks of the other two bulls as he is entangled with the third. Not only does the king have to move quickly to avoid collision with the other bulls, he also has to move the weight of the third bull he is holding. The exercise is intense and far beyond that of any champion before him. The new champion, Furgus, has tried to emulate the king's training. But, even though he's extremely powerful, he cannot fight three bulls at once. Furgus fights one at a time for both power and speed."

Sam sat down on the bed before speaking. "Okay, I'm sold. This guy is bad. How in the heck am I going to gain the fame I need to gain an audience with people of power? How can I fight men like the one you just described and live to tell about it? I'm pretty tough, but also 100 percent sure that both these guys—Furgus and King Senchae—would kick my butt."

Mosley walked to the foot of the bed and sat beside Sam. "I have some ideas, but it will take everything in you to gain the glory you need."

Sam's eyes widened. "So you're saying you can help me figure this out? Then where do we start and what needs to be done?"

Mosley led Sam downstairs for a large breakfast, explaining he would need his strength. They were going to slow down their journey to Brandor and work on gaining the glory Sam needed.

"First you need to learn how to use your sword and bow while increasing your strength and stamina. I've already sent Shalee to begin her education with her new staff. Her training should be entertaining to watch, don't you think? Angel's Village is a great place to start for both of you. And when you're ready, we'll introduce you to the world of arena fighting. We'll be able to make coin there and keep ourselves fed and warm at night."

Sam's voice, filled with anxiety. "Arena fighting, I thought you said that was to the death."

The Grayham Inquirer

When inquiring minds need to know where their favorite characters are.

GEORGE is still sleeping just east of the Enchanted Forest near the Cripple River. Not much to report here.

LASIDIOUS and CELESTRIA are together in their home on Ancients Sovereign. They are working on other plans before Celestria needs to go to the World of Luvelles to spend the rest of her pregnancy.

BASSORINE is still trying to find Lasidious—the other gods are becoming tired of listening to him yell.

SHALEE is on her way to the local School of Magical Studies, where she is scheduled to start training with her staff.

SAM and MOSLEY are having a hearty breakfast, waiting for the man who teaches the local School of Weaponry to show up. This is the man who will train Sam.

Thank you for reading the Grayham Inquirer

Chapter 10

The Training Blues
-or-
Should I say, Bruises

SHALEE left the inn smiling about Sam's advances and sought out the local School of Magical Studies. Angel's Village, according to Mosley, was a good place to train with her new staff. She admired the simple touches of the village. The architecture was not anything to write home about, but it provided a peaceful atmosphere. Simple things were her passion anyway, and, although the buildings could use some attention to their structural integrity, she saw many areas of intricate detail.

Everywhere she turned she saw the pride of the village folk: a sign perfectly painted, carefully placed stones at a well's mouth, cobblestone walkways that ran from the street to each store front and steep, tightly bound, straw-bundled roofs that allowed the rain to run off quickly so they did not leak.

Eventually she came across a young boy who quite possibly was no more than 11 seasons old. He had in his hand a sharpened pencil of some sort, but it wasn't anything like she had ever seen before. Also, on top of an old, smoothed over piece of wood, a good size piece of parchment rested, perfectly placed. He was sitting, facing a group of trees which grew a fruit that seemed to resemble peaches. Her curiosity got the better of her and as she leaned over the young man's shoulder she quickly found herself standing in front of the trees, posing.

"Just stay still for a moment, my lady," the boy said after grabbing her by the arm and placing her in the perfect position. "You'll be my focus. This'll be far better than just drawing some stupid old trees."

"But I don't have the time. What's your name, boy?"

"Trace... my name is Trace Chaslend. Please don't go! Please... I promise to capture your beauty!"

Shalee had to smile. He was an adorable child. His cute, little, chubby freckled face, and his red hair just made her melt. How could she possibly say no to such an innocent request?

"Well as long as you'll promise to get my good side, I'll stay."

"Well that's going to be easy. You don't have a bad side," the boy said with a gapped smile.

"Now, now, now... you already know how to make a lady blush. You're too young to know how to schmooze a woman Trace."

"What does schmooze mean?"

"Oh nothing... you just go ahead and draw your little picture, but try to hurry because I need to get going."

"Yes, my lady."

A while later the boy turned the picture around.

"So what do you think?"

Shalee gasped and instantly thought: *Maybe Bassorine's fashion sense isn't so bad after all.*

"Trace, it's so beautiful. I don't think that I've ever met a young man with so much talent. I will remember your name until the day I die. You have filled my heart with happiness today, Mr. Chaslend.

"I'm glad you like it, but I better go before my mother gets mad at me. I'm causing her to be late. Bye…"

"Bye Trace."

When finally she found the School of Magical Studies, she stood outside a while before walking in. She was nervous, almost to the point of making herself sick to her stomach. It took everything she had to keep from turning around.

The front part of the school was a store. The walls to either side of her had shelves carefully lined many things, both creature- and plant-oriented. The jars were labeled and full of things like baby bat wings, spider legs, mandrake root, dragon scales, snake skins and many other items she had never heard of before. She guessed she had an idea what they were used for though since her favorite show back on Earth was her only frame of reference. The show was about three witches who constantly fought demons in an effort to rid their city of evil. One of these witches had an incredible sense for fashion, but all of them used ingredients such as the ones here on the shelves to make their magical potions.

She was not in the store long before an elderly woman with beautiful, flowing, gray hair and soft features walked into the room holding a staff. The woman was dressed in a white robe, which draped down and covered her shoes. A dark-black, woven fabric was tied around her waist. The outfit did not accentuate her body's curves at all. Shalee instantly thought, *Oh, my gosh . . . I need to call the fashion police and report the crime that had been committed here. If I'm going to train with this woman for any length of time at all, she'll need to be fixed. It would be a shame to allow her beauty to continue to be squandered with such horrid fabrics. Now how do I tell her this?*

The woman's smile grew larger than life as she saw Shalee. She hurried over to her. "You're my new student. Oh, thank the gods that the day has come. I've been expecting you for many, many seasons and have been looking forward to this. My name is Helga Kolinsky."

"Hello, I think, ummm, my name is Shalee," she said, hesitantly. "You said you've been expecting me? How's that possible? I don't recall anyone telling me you knew I was coming."

"No, no, no, child, it's not like that. I have dreamt that you would be coming to study with me for most of my life. I've prepared for this day and longed for it to arrive ever since I was a child. I have much to teach you."

Shalee, needless to say, was a bit unnerved by the woman's confession and started to hurry out of the store. She walked quickly, but, the door was not getting any closer. Looking down, she was shocked to see that her feet were not touching the floor. She struggled to move her legs, but she was going nowhere fast.

Helga Kolinsky laughed as she circled around her. "Oh child, I've known that you were going to try and run out of my store since I was a young girl. Don't you think I've prepared myself for this special day?"

Shalee went from surprised to angry. "Put me down or I'll—"

"You'll what, child?" the woman responded softly. "You're suspended there and cannot move. You'll do nothing until I let you down—and I'm not going to do that, until you calm down and open up your mind. If you'll just think a moment, you'll realize that I'm familiar to you as well. I've had conversations with you in your dreams. You know who I am. Concentrate, child, and think your way through this."

Shalee struggled some more before finally giving up and relaxing. She breathed deeply for a minute and thought back to her dreams. To her surprise, she actually did remember the woman's face. In fact, the lady was one of the few things she had dreamt about that had a peaceful feeling to it. The rest of her dreams had been of terrible creatures and wars, but in these dreams, Helga had dressed much more fashionably, nowhere close to this tragic mess that she had on now.

Shalee sighed as she spoke. "I do remember you. I don't understand how, but I do know you. Please let me down . . . I'm ready to listen."

Helga waved her hand, and Shalee slowly touched the floor. "Well, now that we have that bit of awkwardness out of the way; you and I can work on something constructive."

"I brought coin for the lessons, Helga," Shalee said, watching as the woman moved beyond a large bear rug that hung in front of an opening. It led to a large room in the back.

"Your coin is no good here, child," Helga said loud enough to make sure her voice would be heard by Shalee without question. "We have much to learn and you'll need to pay close attention. Bring that staff of yours and let's get started."

Shalee moved past the rug and into the next room. The room was large and wide open. Large pillows made of leather and stuffed with straw were everywhere. Even the beams, both in the middle of the room and on the ceiling, were covered with this padding. The floors had some sort of mattresses placed tightly side-by-side that covered the entire surface. The only thing missing were a few pieces of gymnastic equipment.

"This is where we'll start your training, child," Helga said with a large smile. "Never mind all the padding, it tends to come in handy every now and then with a new sorceress."

Shalee looked at her puzzled. "Handy? Am I to become a new sorceress?"

"You will see what I mean about the pads and—yes—you're to become a sorceress, if you choose to be one. You, like any other person in this world, have the right to do anything you want, but I would guess you're a little curious, yes?"

Shalee nodded then presented the staff to Helga. "So what do I do with this? I have absolutely no clue where to start."

"First you must name your staff, then quiet your mind and speak with the staff through your soul. I don't mean actually talk with it, but rather learn how to feel its power flowing through you. This is usually the hardest part to accomplish. I'm going to leave now and give you some quiet time to work on feeling its power. Some women find this experience to be quite a pleasure once they understand what to do. There's only one piece of advice I must give you. Make sure to name your staff using a short word, one with no more than two syllables. Trust me on this, it's very important. One or two syllables only, child . . . and nothing more. Don't forget!"

Shalee watched Helga leave the room. She then turned her attention toward the staff. "So are you going to talk to me?" Shalee asked, holding the staff in front of her, laughing. "I can't believe I'm talking to a petrified piece of wood. Anyway . . . okay, first things first . . . I need to name you. What's a fabulous one or two-syllable name?"

Shalee thought a bit then smiled as she remembered a name that made her feel good inside. She would use the name of a magical item from a movie she had seen on Earth. The name just rolled off her tongue every time she said it. It was the name she had given her favorite coffee cup. The cup held the one drink capable of getting her day going in the morning. It was the perfect name fit for her new, petrified, wooden friend. No one was here from Earth to object, so why not steal this perfect name for her own use.

"I think I will call you Precious. Yeah, I like that. How does Precious sound to you?"

Shalee suddenly found a new admiration for the staff. "So how do I feel your power, Precious?" she said, giggling at the thought of talking to the big stick.

Shalee spent the next hour or so in the back room of Helga's store staring at the staff, waiting for something to happen. She looked hard at it, concentrating with everything in her to feel its power. When that did not work, she lay down and held it in hopes that her touch would help her feel something. She wanted to feel its power, even the smallest sign or hint. At one point, she even became frustrated enough to play peek-a-boo with it. To have seen this sight, a grown woman in a room all alone, covering her face and yelling 'peek-a-boo' at a large, petrified, wooden stick was quite amusing. Shalee was sure that anyone seeing this display of idiocy would have put her in a padded room and thrown away the key. She laughed when she realized she already was in a padded room—a more ironic situation could not have been planned if she tried.

Finally, Shalee lay down beside the staff, completely frustrated. Deciding to give up trying to make the thing talk to her, she quieted her mind. It was enough; the staff communed with her, gently at first and then powerfully, sending waves of energy through Shalee's body. The feeling caused her body to tingle all over with a sensation she had never had before. Quickly sitting up, Shalee stared at the staff. She felt amazing, her whole body warm inside. This was good stuff! She wanted more.

She concentrated again, but nothing happened. Now she felt even more frustrated than before.

What am I doing wrong? Am I missing something here? Let me think this through a bit . . . what was I doing when I felt that incredible surge?

Shalee thought for a long time... then finally, it came to her.

I was doing absolutely nothing! I was lying down. That was it: just feeling relaxed—my mind clear of all thought.

Hurriedly, she lay back down and, after a bit, cleared her mind. Once again the staff sent another wave of its power into her, but this time a much stronger one. Her whole body filled with warmth, causing her to tingle in places she did not know she had. There was nothing she could remember that had ever made her feel this good. Shalee sat up and looked at the staff once more and after a bit, she spoke to it.

"Wow . . . that was better than . . . oh my," She giggled. "You can do that to me anytime! Let's try that again, okay, Precious? And I do mean *Precious*. My goodness, I couldn't have named you better if I had thought forever. You keep making me feel like that and I'll never want to leave this room. Would you like to be the first petrified piece of wood in history to have a wife?"

Shalee rolled back onto the mattress beneath her and laughed out loud. She realized how ridiculous the marriage proposal had been—yet, she could not stop smiling and talking to her wooden friend as she lay down once again. This time she wanted the staff to make her feel as good as it possibly could, for as long as she could keep her mind quiet. She told herself to go with it this time and not worry about anything. When she finally managed to quiet herself, the staff again sent more of its power through her.

She absorbed the warmth as her body again tingled. Every hair on her body stood on end and the intensity grew. She started to cry large tears of joy. Her hands grabbed hold of the mattress as the sensation built, this time allowing the feeling to consume her. Shalee was about to have the most incredible experience of her life. And before she had time to think, an intense rush, far beyond anything she had ever felt before, devoured her. Every muscle in her body tightened from the intensity of the moment as she began to laugh with a deep sense of satisfaction. The pleasure of it all seemed to last forever. Finally, her muscles relaxed; exhausted now, Shalee drifted off to sleep.

Sam's Training Begins

SAM had finished eating breakfast with the wolf and they were now on their way to a field just outside the village. Mosley had recruited a local instructor named Barthom Jonas from the School of Weaponry, BJ for short.

As they headed to the field, Sam looked over his sword. He remembered Bassorine's exact words as he handed the sword to him back at the temple. *"This is the Sword of Truth and Might. This is the only one of its kind. The sword can strike down your enemies with great power and it also possesses the power to search for truth when used upon them. All you have to do is place the blade on your enemy's shoulder and ask it for the answer you seek. The result is self-explanatory."*

Illustration by Kathleen Stone

Sam also remembered Bassorine telling him, after he became excited about the sword, "Just because you like the sword, it doesn't mean you know how to use it. The sword will only work once it feels you have earned its respect. The sword lives and has a mind of its own. You have much to learn and a short time to learn it in. I don't think you want it failing you in battle."

Sam didn't know what the god meant about earning the blade's respect, nor did he believe the sword lived. Maybe it was a figure of expression of some sort. As he moved the blade around in front of him, he was surprised at how light the sword felt. He had never spent much time around swords, but the blade was appealing and the markings on the hilt were quite mysterious.

"Hey Mosley, do you know what these markings mean?"

"I don't, but sometimes a magical sword will reveal the nature of its markings to its owner once the proper relationship has been established."

"That's hard to believe."

BJ replied, "Maybe you're not worthy of knowing such things, son."

"Yeah . . . sure," Sam scoffed. "All King Arthur had to do was pull his blade from the stone and his sword worked from day one. Why's this blade so fickle?"

The wolf looked at the fighter. "Who's King Arthur?"

Sam smiled, realizing his point had fallen on uninformed ears. "Oh, never mind."

Finally, they reached the field. BJ faced Sam, motioning for Mosley to step aside, then said, "So how about you show me your blade and tell me its name? A man cannot fight with a sword he hasn't named. That would be a dishonor to not only to the sword, but its maker as well. So let's hear it."

Sam looked at BJ, then back down at his sword. "I haven't named it yet. I forgot about it . . . what should I name it?"

"Only you can answer that question, son," BJ said. He was an elderly man, strong from many years of instructing in the school. His dark hair was graying and his brown eyes were full of wisdom. He wore light leather armor pants and similar boots. His shirt was made of a white fabric that buttoned up the front. BJ continued.

"The naming of a sword must come from within you, son. It would not be very noble to have any other man name your sword."

Sam looked at the blade and thought a moment. "Well, when Bassorine gave it to me, he said it was the *Sword of Truth and Might* so I guess that…"

BJ instantly knelt to one knee and bowed to the sword. Sam lowered the blade and turned his attention to him. "What are you doing?"

"Son, you don't realize what you have in your possession," he said, carefully keeping his head lowered in the sword's presence. "This is a sword given by the gods. I didn't realize it was a godly sword. You just said the God of War Bassorine gave you this sword. This is indeed a great honor. This sword will command great power. One does not simply use a sword like this. A man must ask for permission from the sword itself to command it. I, as your teacher, must ask for permission from the sword to even instruct you with it in your hand. Please son, I beg you to bow before it and ask its forgiveness and let us get permission to continue."

"What?" Sam said, exploding with laughter. "You've got to be kidding me. It's a piece of metal. How in the heck can I ask it for permission to do anything? It's unable to speak. This thing isn't alive—because if it is, it sure as heck hasn't said one thing to me since I got it. Whatever power it's said to have I'm sure it'll come from within me . . . right?" Sam looked at BJ and Mosley, unsure of his comments.

The instructor and wolf looked at each other and took a few steps back. Sam watched them, instantly becoming worried. "What are you guys doing?"

He had no sooner finished his question, when the sword grew red hot in his hand, forcing him to release it. The sword rose from his palm and into the air, then turned and brought its point beneath Sam's chin as if some unseen person were controlling it. The sword made three thumping taps to Sam's jaw with the flat of its blade and started to speak loudly. BJ dropped back to his knees along with Mosley and they both rebowed their heads.

"Sam!" the sword said sternly. "I had such high hopes for you, but it appears you are still an ignorant little boy who has learned nothing since his arrival on Grayham. I have waited for nearly 10,000 seasons to be given to you. I was created, along with your bow, when the gods created these worlds. I must say, I'm deeply disappointed that someone with your intelligence hasn't been able to come into this world and figured out that what you used to think of as normal is long gone. Isn't it obvious that if the Book of Immortality can be given not only a soul by the gods, but also the power to govern them, then maybe, just maybe, a sword of my caliber might be able to communicate with you? It appears the gods have made a mistake... Return me to Bassorine. I have waited for nothing."

Sam was shocked. A sword had just floated in midair and scolded him—then called him an ignorant little boy. This world was throwing his mind some serious curve balls and he wasn't handling it well.

He watched as the sword slowly started to move away as if leaving. He regrouped and chased after it. "Look, I'm sorry. I had no idea I was doing something wrong . . . and I also had no idea that you could speak. I would still like to train with you if you're willing. I'm sorry for my ignorance."

The sword laughed. "It seems to me that for such a brilliant man, you spend a lot of your time apologizing for your ignorance, Sam. If I remember correctly, you also had to apologize to the Griffon, Soresym, for calling him a 'thing.' I hate to admit it, but I find this rather pathetic."

The sword turned and placed its blade beneath his chin once again.

"I might consider allowing you to train with me in your hand . . . if you ask properly."

Sam instantly dropped to one knee. As he started to speak, he realized he still did not know the sword's name so he improvised the best he could. "I'm sorry for my ignorance, and, if you would allow me to, I would appreciate the chance to train with you."

The sword held its position in the air for a long while and observed Sam's mannerisms. Noticing that Sam kept his head bowed and that he was sweating a bit, the sword simply said, "Apology accepted. BJ, you may also train with Sam."

The sword moved toward Mosley and stopped in front of him.

"If it's your responsibility to watch over this human, then I suggest you teach him how to be respectful of the things he doesn't understand." The wolf nodded in agreement and with that, the sword returned to Sam and lowered itself back into his hands.

"Thanks a lot," Mosley said angrily. "Maybe you could stop and think a bit next time. You're making me look bad—and please, don't apologize to me for your ignorance. I'm not in the mood. I'm going to go check on Shalee. BJ, will you please train this fool?"

Mosley then turned and hurried back to the village. BJ stood and motioned for Sam to put his sword back on his hip.

"Until you name your sword, you can't train with it."

He tossed the virgin swordsman a wooden stave and laughingly said, "We'll start with this... it's going to hurt you far more than it will hurt me!"

Helga's School of Magical Studies

HELGA walked into the training room at the back of her store. She smiled as she saw Shalee lying there asleep.

Illustration by Kathleen Stone

"Ah, I remember what that feeling was like!" she thought. The sorceress leaned over and shook Shalee to wake her up.

Shalee slowly opened her eyes. When she realized what was going on and that Helga was in the room, she started to explain what had happened.

Helga listened to her a moment, smiling the entire time as she saw the excitement on Shalee's face. Finally, Helga, motioned for Shalee to be still.

"There's a reason you've been given these feelings. It's the staff's way of keeping you motivated to learn how to master it. When you begin learning how to command your new power you'll make mistakes. We all have. You'll try to use more power than you are strong enough to handle. The effects of this can be harmful to a new sorceress. I should know, I've broken more than one bone in my life while learning. But the good thing about the staff is that, while you're learning, it'll reward you for your success. It is the one thing that keeps a young sorceress from quitting when she fails."

"So you're telling me that every time I succeed and do something good, the staff will reward me with another incredible moment?" Shalee responded hopefully.

Helga smiled again. "I'm saying that for the first little while you will have a wonderful time learning when you succeed. Eventually the sensation from your successes will fade away, and you'll be left with the result of what you are trying to accomplish. Most young sorceresses keep trying to learn beyond this initial period of training because, as they learn to control stronger powers, they also gain the benefit of a longer life from the success of this control. But be careful of the failures, they can shorten your life. If done properly, with careful training, the benefit of your staff could extend your life more than a thousand seasons.

"I'm 247 seasons old and don't look a day over 60. I would have aged better, but I took a road that wasn't so smart when I was younger, commanding power I wasn't ready for. It took me quite a while to reverse those effects in order to live this long. I wanted to be the best teacher I could be for you when you finally arrived. I tried to grow faster than I should've done."

Shalee listened intently. When Helga was finished, she said, "Wow, if you ask me, 247 seasons is a long time. I'm sure you'll be a great teacher. I'm pretty tough. I think I should be able to handle this, so let's get started." She grinned with a playful wickedness as she made her next statement and winked. "So what do you say, let's work on getting my first success?"

Just then, Mosley entered the room from his run back to town. "Yes, let's see her try and get her first success."

Helga left the room. When she came back, she carried a softball-sized steel ball and bent down to whisper in Mosley's ear, "Let's see how she handles a little failure first."

The experienced sorceress moved to the center of the room and placed the steel ball. Then she moved away and told Shalee to take hold her staff.

"Okay child, let's start out with a little something to challenge you." She pointed to a target painted on one of the pads on the far side of the room. "I want you to point your staff at the target, then command the ball to fly through the room and hit that target hard."

"How do I do that?" The new sorceress questioned.

"You'll need to learn the elvish language to command your staff," Helga replied. "All you have to do is say the name of your staff and follow it with the elvish name of the object you are trying to command. You must say this with authority for anything to happen. Eventually, if you become strong enough, you won't need to say anything, but, for now, you must speak with words strong enough to get the desired result from the object you're commanding. The staff will retrieve what you want it to accomplish from your mind and cause it to happen. And it will happen, providing you possess the strength and power to obtain the result. Your thoughts need to be clear and focused. If you don't have the strength or the power, the result will be failure . . . and how this failure manifests itself will vary in many ways, but let's talk of this later."

"Okay, so I named my staff. What is the elvish name for the ball?"

"The name for ball is *koron,*" Mosley said.

Both Shalee and Helga looked at Mosley quizzically.

"What? I speak every language. I work in the service of Bassorine, remember?"

Shalee raised her staff toward the target.

"Anyway, let's give this a shot."

Helga motioned for Mosley to move back.

Commanding the staff, Shalee called out, "Precious, koron!"

The ball launched from the floor and flew quickly across the room. It hit the target with a tremendous force. The padding was destroyed, but that was not all. The ball also knocked a hole clean through the wall and blew up a large wooden barrel full of water across the alleyway.

Shalee bent over, putting her hands on her knees. Trembling, she began to receive the powerful sensation, the benefit of the successful command. Her entire body tingled as she started to laugh and cry at the same time. Eventually she turned to face her astounded audience with a large smile on her face.

"So, I can only assume that's what should've happened," she said, totally satisfied as she continued to giggle. "Oh my goodness, I love this staff!" Looking at the petrified piece of wood, Shalee said, "How precious are you, Precious?"

Helga was stunned. Finally, after a few moments, she said, "Shalee, you're going to be very powerful. I've never in all my years of training seen anyone complete this exercise successfully. I've picked up many new sorceresses from the floor after they slammed into the wall behind you. They all failed to complete this exercise. Quickly, let's try something else! I'm so excited!"

Chapter 11

Tough Lessons Learned

SHALEE was excited by the revelation that no other young sorceress before her had ever commanded the steel ball to hit the target was personally satisfying. Now with Helga in a hurry to start the next lesson, Shalee watched her eagerly. She moved one of the mattresses from the floor and lifted the hidden door beneath it. A dark staircase was revealed that disappeared under the school. Helga turned to Shalee and said, "Use your staff so I can see what I'm doing. The elven word for light is *'me'a'*."

Once Shalee understood how to pronounce the word, she lowered the tip of her staff in the direction of the darkness and spoke loudly, "Precious, *me'a!*"

The stairway and room beneath them lit up. With eyes closed, Shalee stood motionless for a moment, once again receiving the benefit of the successful command. "I think I'm getting the hang of this," she giggled. "Was that the next thing you wanted me to learn?"

The elderly sorceress smiled and started to walk down the stairs. "That's not your lesson. That was far too easy of a command. I just thought I'd allow you one more good experience with your staff before we make things harder. I'll be back up in a moment with your next lesson."

Both Shalee and Mosley waited; soon Helga returned with five pieces of dried wood. She motioned for Shalee to close the door behind her and put the mattress back. Helga headed to the wall opposite of the hole and began to prepare the area. She removed the padding from the floor, walls, and ceiling to reveal an area covered with large sheets of iron. The iron covered as much of the area as the padding had. At the center was the resting spot for the wood.

Mosley motioned for Helga to speak with him privately in the next room after getting an idea of what the sorceress was thinking.

"Are you sure this is a good idea?" Mosley asked with concern.

"What you are about to ask her to do, if it's what I'm thinking, it's something that should wait. It should only be done by someone who has trained for while!"

"Who's the teacher here . . . you, or me? I want to see what her limits are." Helga said, then returned to continue setting everything in place. She left the room, and, after a minute, came back with two pails of water. She placed the buckets close, but at a safe enough distance not to be knocked over in case something went awry.

"Okay, child, there are many forms of fire we can command. There are simple forms like striking a piece of flint to start a campfire. Then there are much stronger forms that burn hot enough to turn things to ash before you can snap your fingers. What I would like you to do is start with something simple, and then we'll work our way up. The good thing about these exercises is that you'll be able to use the same command for each one. The only thing different will be what your mind tells the staff to do. As I've said before, your staff will look into your thoughts for the desired effect that you're after. It will draw from this thought and use your inner strength to produce the outcome. The elven word for fire is *naur.*"

"So you want me to set the wood on fire?" Shalee asked.

"No, child, I want you to think of how you can use fire to create different outcomes. Fire can be molded and shaped to serve you in many different ways. It can be used for more than just destruction and warmth. This exercise will test your mind and also test your limits. Let me give you an example of a way fire can be used that's not destructive."

The older sorceress pointed her staff and spoke her words of power. A thick wall of flame formed. Feeling the heat, Mosley backed to the far side of the room. Shalee watched in amazement as Helga walked into the flame and turned around once inside to wave at her. After some time passed, the sorceress exited the fiery wall and it dissipated.

"Now that's what I mean by non-destructive," Helga smiled. "In my mind, I told the staff to allow only Mosley to feel the heat. The two of us, along with the room, did not feel a thing. As you can see, I'm unharmed. Fire can be used as a tool to create perceptions of power like you just witnessed. Do you see what I mean?"

"That was awesome," Shalee said. "Okay, let me try. Can I do that?"

Helga laughed. "No, child that was very advanced magic. You're not ready to try something like that. You'll need to start simple. It's going to be up to you to figure out what your limits are since you're a much stronger student than I've ever had before. I want you to think of as many different ways to manipulate the wood with simple uses of fire. Be careful not to hurt yourself. You can always combine elven words to make two objects work together as well, but exploring this will be for much later lessons. This concept is far beyond your abilities."

"What do you mean? How can I combine words to make two objects work together?" Shalee asked.

"I'll not answer that question now. I shouldn't have said anything. Focus on what we're doing."

Shalee looked at the pile of wood for a moment and eventually raised her staff. She pointed her new petrified friend, and said, "Precious, naur!" A ring of fire appeared around the wood. The heat could be felt, but was not uncomfortable. Slowly the flame faded.

Again Shalee enjoyed the benefit of her successful command but the strength of her command caused her body to shake so that she had to lean against the teacher until the intensity subsided.

"Well done," Mosley said. "I'm impressed, to say the least. Once you've collected yourself, let's see what else you have in that bag of tricks of yours."

"Oh my goodness," Shalee finally said. "Whew! Oh . . . Well I'm loving this magic stuff! I can't express to you how much I'm enjoying this magic stuff! But give me a minute to catch my breath."

"Take your time, child. This is indeed a wonderful day for you. I must say that I'm a little jealous," Helga said. "I haven't felt this way for more than 200 seasons."

Shalee took her hands from Helga's shoulders. "Well that just sucks for you. Shall we try again?"

Without hesitation, Shalee raised the staff. She prepared her next thought before speaking her words of power, "Precious, naur!" The top piece of wood on the pile instantly started burning—but the ones below it remained unaffected by the flame. The command took a considerable amount of power from Shalee, which caused the benefit of her success to move gloriously within her. This time, the intensity brought Shalee to her knees. She reached down with one hand to balance herself as the sensation grew and tears of joy once again ran down her face. Lasting a much longer time, Shalee finally collapsed to her back and inhaled deeply to try and catch her breath.

Helga looked at Shalee. "I have never seen anyone command fire on their first day. Not only did you command it, you also segregated it to a specific piece of wood and didn't allow it to touch the others. This is the most exciting day of my life. But it's probably best that you stop, child. It's getting late . . . and I think after a day like this, I would personally be exhausted. I've never met a woman lucky enough to shed so many wonderful tears and experience the enjoyment of life quite as much as you have today."

Shalee agreed that she was getting tired, but she wanted to try just one more thing before she left. "What are the elven words for wood and life?"

Helga became instantly worried.

"Oh, child, I don't think it wise to be messing around with combining words on your first day. That isn't something I would teach you for a while. I should never have said anything about it, I'm sorry."

"I understand, but I would still like to know the words. I feel as if I'm on to something here and I really think I can handle it. Just trust me, Helga."

Shalee lifted herself from the floor. Helga and Mosley looked at each other, shrugged their shoulders and took a few steps back for safety.

Mosley whispered to Helga, "This is either going to be really good, or really bad. I'm not sure how you're supposed to be able to judge her at this point. She's clearly not like any of your other students. I say we watch and allow her to keep going until she fails!"

"Agreed," Helga whispered back. "I'll protect us just in case." She waved her hand and an invisible wall of force encircled them both.

Shalee asked again, wondering what the two of them had whispered. "So what are the words?"

Helga answered, *"Taurina* is for wood and *coia* is for life. I ask you again to think about this before doing it—it's not the best idea, child."

"I know how you feel. But how am I to determine what my limitations are if you as my teacher don't know how to judge my progression? You said you've never met anyone who has done what I've done before. Let's see where the line is drawn in the sand."

"Okay, child, but I think we can check another day for what your limits are and where that line is. Maybe you should rest before you try this."

"I'll be okay, don't worry. I'm tough... I can handle a little failure," Shalee said, confidently.

Helga again looked at Mosley. "It's clear she's not going to listen until she finds her own rock wall to run into," she whispered.

Shalee thought for a moment, then a smile spread across her face. "This should be pretty cool and I know that no one on this world has ever seen this."

Remembering something Sam said when they were in the Temple of the Gods; she lifted the staff and spoke in a forceful tone, "Precious, taurina naur coia!"

The remaining pieces of wood jumped from the floor forming a small being shaped like her favorite childhood character: Elmo, from *Sesame Street.* The wooden creature had a coat made of intense fiery fur and moved as if it was alive. As it started to move, Shalee waited, anticipating the reward for her success, but it never came. Something was wrong. The fiery Elmo stopped, turned toward Shalee and suddenly exploded, sending a shock wave through the room. The wave hit Shalee so hard that her body lifted from the floor and moved through the air like a rag doll thrown by an angry child. She hit one of the columns holding up the roof in the center of the room and knocked her shoulder out of joint. Landing on the floor, Shalee's arm twisted under her, snapping with a loud cracking sound that could be heard in the alley outside. She screamed as the pain shot through her body. Having landed in a nasty position, it wasn't even possible to move her without sending another shock wave of pain through her.

Helga darted out of the store and went for a healer, while Mosley walked over to the injured student and breathed his soothing breath over her sending Shalee into a peaceful sleep.

Sam's Training Continues

BJ continued to teach Sam after Mosley left. The wolf called Sam a fool and he was tremendously bothered by that. Now the teacher was delivering hard lessons to many different areas of Sam's body. He'd been hit in the head three times, lower back four times, upper back two times, chest eight times, both arms a combined 17 times and his feet swept from under him another seven times.

BJ extended his hand to pick Sam up off the ground. The novice swordsman had just had his feet swept out from under him yet again and fallen hard. Not only that, but his wooden stave had also been taken from him before landing, adding further insult to injury.

The teacher said sternly, "I've told you many times already to watch your weight when you're moving in to strike. You're leaving yourself wide open. It'll get you killed. A weapon won't be the only thing that your opponents will use against you to win the battle. Not only will their swords be dangerous, but their hands, feet, legs, elbows, and heads are also weapons. You're leaving yourself open for any of these to be used against you. Now get up and watch your balance. Be ready for anything, not just my weapon. I swear . . . I feel like I'm teaching a child of only five seasons."

Sam was frustrated but he was not a quitter. The two men kept at it for a while longer and after a few more trips to the ground, Sam finally held up his hand and motioned for BJ to stop. He limped over to where he had placed his sword and picked it up. Sam bent to one knee and whispered to the blade.

"I've thought of a name for you now. I was thinking of using the name Kael. Would this be all right with you? I think it would be perfect. It means mighty warrior."

The sword answered, "I think Kael is a fine name, but a man should be confident in his decisions. I have already given you permission to train with me. Act like a leader; don't seek my approval. Show me something impressive. I won't allow you to fight with me in any actual combat until I feel you've gained enough skill to keep from embarrassing me."

Sam stood and faced BJ. "I've given my sword a name. I'm going to call him Kael; it means *mighty warrior.*" He lifted the sword and took a stance. "Let's see how you handle this," he said, as he directed the point of the blade toward the teacher.

BJ smiled as he walked to his bag. He set down his wooden stave and picked up his weapon. "This blade has seen many years of battle, boy. I think you need to be taught some humility!"

BJ wiped the sword hilt off with a towel and threw it on the ground. He secured his grip and turned to face Sam. Without a word he lunged, knocking Kael from Sam's hand. A quick swipe with the tip of BJ's blade was all it took to cut just deep enough across the student's thigh to draw blood.

"Damn," Sam yelled as he looked down at the fresh cut. "What the heck did you do that for?

BJ yelled at Sam, "Just because you hold a sword of the gods doesn't mean you understand how to wield the power the sword possesses. You'll come to know these powers if I can get it through that thick head of yours that this isn't some sort of a game. You'll be killed if you enter the arena without the necessary skills. Your stance is terrible, your balance is off, your movements are slow, and your ears aren't listening to me at all.

"I cannot believe that where you're from, they call you a fighter. I don't think in all my seasons of teaching that I've had a worse student on his first day than you. Now stop your whining and let's get moving before it gets too dark. I'm hungry and need some ale."

"Now pick up your sword and quickly put this bandage on your leg. I'll help you stitch it up when we get back to the inn. Dusk is approaching, and we have a nice walk back to the village. With your obvious lack of skills, I can only assume that you'll need to learn how to stitch yourself up as well. You might want to keep a supply of bandages in your backpack when we train. I have a special mud that the Merchant Angels delivered from the healer's on the World of Harvestom. You can put it on your stitches. You'll heal enough by morning so you can continue to train. It won't, however, get rid of the scar. I do hope you learn fast or you're going to be an ugly man before I'm done teaching the likes of you."

It took a while to reach the village and the walk was a quiet one. When the two of them reached the village, they headed for the inn and went up to the room. Opening the door, they saw Mosley and Helga standing over Shalee, who was lying on the bed. Sam immediately forgot about the pain in his leg and rushed to Shalee's side. He looked at the woman and quickly scanned the splints the healers had placed on her arm. Satisfied that all was as it should be, he looked at Mosley.

"What the heck happened to her?"

"Maybe I should be asking you the same thing. You're bleeding with a blood-soaked wrap on your leg. From where I sit, it appears that both you and Shalee have learned a few things today. I can't remember the last time I've seen a man with as many bruises as you have."

Sam quickly looked at his upper body, which he had not bothered covering with a shirt. Smiling, he walked toward BJ and patted him on the back. "I suppose that's the sign of a good teacher. I wouldn't say my teacher is too political with his verbal criticisms, but he'll break through this hard head of mine eventually. This is all new to me but I swear I'll learn if he doesn't give up on me."

BJ grunted and motioned for Sam to sit on the bed. "Shut up and sit down. I don't have all day to teach you how to stitch yourself up, so let's get to it." The teacher pulled a needle made of bone and some thread from his bag.

Sam smiled, took BJ's hands and removed the items from them. "This is something I *do* know how to do. I don't need your help but I could use that mud you told me about. I'll be ready in the morning to train again, I assure you."

BJ tossed the mud to him, threw his bag over his shoulder and walked from the room. "See you bright and early. I'm going to beat you up badly tomorrow! Sleep on that!"

Sam frowned, cleaned his wound, stitched himself up, applied the mud, and wrapped it all with bandages before turning his attention back to Shalee.

"So Mosley, what happened to her and how long will it be before she's back on her feet?"

"I imagine it will only take her a few Peaks of Bailem." Mosley stood up. "I will return soon," he said as he left the room, seemingly uninterested in anything else Sam had to say.

After staring at the door, Sam moved across the room and slowly sat down in the chair near the window, the same chair, in the same spot that Bassorine had sat in. He lowered his head into his hands and began to cry, the emotions of all that had transpired finally overwhelming him. He missed Earth. He missed his family. It crossed his mind to pray, but his god was supposedly dead. A tear fell to the floor. How would he ever manage to keep up such a strong face for Shalee?

The Grayham Inquirer

When inquiring minds need to know where their favorite characters are.

BASSORINE is still upset. He has been unable to find Lasidious. His anger is building, and the God of Mischief is watching part of his overall plan fall into place. Celestria and Lasidious have finished some additional, last minute plotting together in their home. Both gods plan to head out and put them in motion.

HELGA, after leaving the inn, stopped at the healers' vestry. She instructed them to check on Shalee in the morning. She needed to return to her school and clean up the mess the young sorceress had made while training. The explosion had left many of the mattresses charred.

THE OTHER GODS are in the Hall of Judgment, home of the Book of Immortality, located on the hidden god world of Ancients Sovereign. They are speaking with the Book about any options they might have to force Lasidious to come to a meeting, which would hopefully put an end to Bassorine's annoying ranting. Bassorine's anger has become taxing and their patience with Lasidious is running thin. However, the Book cannot do anything but remind them all that Lasidious has done nothing wrong and that it is his free will to show up whenever he decides to.

Thank you for reading the Grayham Inquirer

Chapter 12

Here Kitty, Kitty

HOURS EARLIER, George awoke from his sleep on the bank of the Cripple River. He jumped right up when the alarm went off and hurried once again toward his destination. His muscles were tight and every joint ached, but in spite of the pain he hurried, wanting to arrive before nightfall, or at least shortly thereafter.

To the northeast of his current position, a mountain range extended eastward for as far as he could see. George looked at his map; the mountains started east of the Pool of Sorrow, so he knew he was getting close. His excitement was building. One more look at the map showed the Pass of Tears to be east of the pool and the pass would lead him to the Cave of Sorrow.

Working his way north George began to sense something was wrong. He felt as if he were being watched or, even worse, followed. Every time he looked toward the edge of the forest line, he saw nothing . . . yet something within him knew there was a presence in the darkness. He increased his pace, trying to focus on getting to where the Pool of Sorrow released its waters into the Cripple River. Jason told him, when they met in the field north of Lethwitch, that this would be the area where he would find the tree; the large boulder he was seeking rested beneath it. He knew that under this boulder was supposed to be the map which held the location of the staff within the Cave of Sorrow.

Try as he might to focus on the journey and prize that awaited him, he could still feel the presence of something lingering in the shadows of the forest. He quickened his pace and thought he better not look in the direction of the dense trees any longer. He wanted to give whatever was watching him the impression that he was not aware of its constant stalking.

Finally George reached his destination only to discover to his surprise that the area everyone called a pool was actually a huge lake—one so wide that he could not see its other side. He recalled hearing Jason say the Pool of Sorrow was actually a lake, but the size of it had been reduced to something far smaller in his mind because of its name.

Under normal circumstances, George would have taken the time to enjoy the view, but he had to figure out how to deal with his Peeping Tom. He could sense whoever—or whatever it was—watching him still and it was unnerving. He knew it was just a matter of time before something happened. He didn't know why or what, but the alarm in his head was screaming that he was in danger.

He quickly studied the area where the lake and the river joined and noticed a line of massive rocks that created a path. The path crossed the waterway's outlet and looked to be man-made with the stones perfectly placed across the entire distance of the outlet, calculating the distance to be over 150 feet from start to finish. As he made his way to the crossing, George reached around and pulled his leather pack from his back. He climbed on top of the first boulder and looked at the large flattened surface of the stone. Observing the area around it, he immediately knelt down.

From the shadows of the forest, two yellowish-brown eyes watched as George knelt on the rock. The sun was about to disappear behind the horizon, and the time for the beast to make its move was approaching. Beneath its fur, powerful muscles rippled anticipating the time when he would close the distance between the human and its place of hiding.

Water rushed powerfully through the gap between the first and second boulder. Rising from the rock, George balanced himself and, for a split-second, became distracted by the view. Beyond the

outlet, the terrain made a drastic change in elevation. The movements of the water created a powerful sound below, causing a
temporary lapse in his concentration. He turned his attention back
to the rocks beyond. Jumping was possible, yet intimidating; the
gushing water would easily kill him if he fell.

He counted to three and leapt to the next boulder. As he landed,
he grabbed his ankle and screamed in pain, rolling around on top
of the massive rock before sitting up. Carefully he removed his
boot, keeping the corner of his eye looking toward the forest and
his head low. His face could not hide his anguish and he was sure
that whatever stalked him could see his concern. He rubbed his
ankle, put his boot back on, wincing as he did, and tied it tight for
support. He stood, careful not to put too much weight on the foot,
and tried to take a step. Again he fell to the stone's surface and
grabbed his ankle feeling like a wounded, cornered animal.

As the sun moved behind the horizon, shadows lengthened.
Then, as if a switch had been turned on once darkness presented
itself, a loud horrifying roar filled the air. George turned to look.
Out of the forest, a large, dark figure made its way toward him.
Slow at first, then faster as the beast began to run. He could only
sit and watch in terror as the beast covered ground swiftly, running
towards him. He stood, put his weight on his only good leg, and
swallowed hard. His heart pounded out of control as the thumping footsteps grew louder. Once the beast was close enough, it
launched into the air. But before the beast could land George cor-
rected his posture and balanced his weight on both of his perfectly
good ankles, his injury only a ruse to flush out the attacker. Raising his right hand in front of him George screamed, "Stop!"

Now he watched cautiously as the beast landed on the first
stone and prepared for the final spring with its powerful haunches
that would throw the giant cat crashing into him. The legs again
started to uncoil, but all four paws of the beast were trapped on the
stone. The weight of the cat's upper body continued forward but
the unbreakable snaring of its feet caused the beast to sling shot
back to the solid surface. The creature's face hit the stone before
the rest of its body; then one of its legs, the neck, and lower jaw
crunched and snapped with the impact. George watched in horror

as the beast let out a mighty cry of pain with a sound so deafening he had to cover his ears.

Staring at the beast, George saw that it was a large cat of some sort, but the lack of light made it hard for him to tell. The beast moaned. George jumped from the rock he was on to get a closer look.

Amazing! The Snare Scroll worked, he thought.

He had read the words of power from the magical paper as he knelt down earlier before jumping to the rock he had been on, planning to use the spot as his trap. The only thing left to chance was that whatever had been following him would actually cross the path where the trap was set. As luck would have it, faking an injury drew the beast exactly to where George wanted it.

The sight of the creature was impressive and George was happily surprised that any part of his plan had worked. The power of the magic scroll must have been tremendous to stop such a powerful creature.

I can't believe this magic crap actually works. This place is freaking nuts! Abbie would be scared to death of this thing. I have got to tell her this story! This is so nuts. This is nuts… it's nuts… it's nuts… it's nuts!

As he looked closer, the beast had different shades of brown fur and its broken leg was now bent underneath in a horrific position. The body of the cat was large and George estimated it would have been nearly impossible to fit the animal in the bed of his full size truck back home. The cat continued to moan as George circled the helpless creature. Its lower jaw lay to one side and both of its fang-like teeth had broken off, now resting not far from its head.

George's mind was having a hard time accepting what had just happened. He thought he was ready for anything this world had to offer, but this was the first time anyone or anything had made an attack on his life. His sanity wasn't too solid and was becoming less so by the minute. He remembered seeing this sort of beast in a children's movie he had watched with Abbie not too long ago. He remembered the cat in that movie had similar-looking teeth even though this cat's teeth were now knocked out.

George grew angrier as he realized he could've been killed. "I thought sabertooth tigers were extinct!" he shouted as he stopped to stand next to the cat. "Well, what else does this world have in it?

"I don't think anything in this damn place is normal. Mages, magic staffs, treasure maps and now extinct beasts . . . it doesn't matter... it doesn't matter. Bring it all on; let's see how far from normal we can get."

George had never felt more out of touch with reality in his life than he did right now. But, as he was losing control of his emotions, his loud exploits were being observed from yet another set of eyes hidden nearby.

George moved closer to the cat and taunted it. The cat tried to attack, but the pain its sudden movements caused was tremendous. George watched as the beast went from angry roars to excruciating cries, but he felt no remorse, his heart growing colder with each passing moment. He resented the attack on his life and reaching towards his hip, he now withdrew the sword he had bought back in Lethwitch. Three times he slapped at the cat's broken leg, torturing the beast to make it cry, laughing as he did so. He reached down and twisted the lower portion of the tiger's broken jaw to cause it further pain. Not only did he twist it, but he tugged at it. He was enjoying the beast's suffering and the continuous humiliation of the saber gave him a sick pleasure. George had never experienced these types of emotions, but now he was thoroughly enjoying them.

"Here, kitty, kitty," he taunted loudly, poking the point of the blade into different areas of the giant cat's body and savoring the cries. He was careful to make sure the point entered deep enough to draw blood, but not so deep that it would stand a chance to hit an organ that might kill the tiger too early. The torture he was going to administer was far too enjoyable for him to stop so soon.

He leaned over to pick up the bloody, knocked-out teeth from the rock, then straddled the saber and lowered himself into a sitting position. Dangling the teeth in front of the cat's pain-filled eyes, he jeered, "I'm going to make a necklace with these real soon and tell my children about how good you tasted tonight."

He stood up from his furry chair, circled the beast again, poking it some more with the point of the blade. The whole time he continued to scream and kick at its jaw, laughing wickedly, "Here, kitty, kitty . . . oh, here, kitty, kitty." Eventually he became bored and raised his sword high, pointed it downward toward its neck and plunged it clean threw, taking the sabertooth's life.

George sat down on the cat's lifeless body, opened his pack and removed his Gucci shirt to wipe the sweat from his forehead. He took a minute, allowing his heartbeat to slow down and the rush of adrenaline to stop before he stood up again. Methodically, he severed all four legs of the beast to release the creature from the unseen trap created by the Snare Scroll. Amazed at the beast's weight, despite the missing legs, George cut the tiger into smaller pieces before dragging them from the rock to the ground.

Gathering some wood from the nearby forest, he built a fire near an old, dead tree trunk that lay on the ground. The piece of deadwood, close to the Pool of Sorrow, provided the perfect place to sit near the shoreline. It was clear to George the trunk had been pulled from the forest some time ago. The place he was about to build his fire also had a pit close to the log. The ash in the pit was old, most of it missing as a result of the wind, but at some point others had used this spot to build a fire of their own.

His senses continued to whisper insightful information, making him aware that he was still not alone. Feeling the need for a plan, George cut the dead cat into many tiny pieces of bloody flesh. Once he was done, he put them into a pile and saved a few choice cuts to cook for his dinner and sat on the log. The now experienced slayer of large cats figured that the bloody flesh would serve as a good distraction to any aggressive beast that might come along.

The night had a slight chill to it and the fire provided much-needed warmth while also keeping the area around him lit up. He had collected enough wood to keep it burning hot, tall, and strong until morning. His brief period of Boy Scout experience told him the flames would act as a deterrent for most animals and he smiled to himself in satisfaction.

It took a bit of tugging, but George was able to remove the meat from the end of the skewer. He had chosen a cut from the beast's rear haunch and was eager to enjoy the experience. He marveled at the tenderness, despite the fact it had been held so close to the flame. All-in-all, his first-ever helping of sabertooth was actually a real pleasure. He knew a real chef would have done a much better job but George didn't care; his stomach was getting full and he was satisfied with his success.

∞ ∞

From the darkness, Kepler watched as George pulled the meat from the stick and started to eat. He was nervous, not wanting to startle the man when he approached. The human could release his powers on him just like he'd done with the Sabertooth Lord, which would not make for good conversation. Being cut up like his subject was not his idea of a good time. He decided to approach with caution. Kepler wanted to be seen in the open and avoid giving an impression that he might be a threat. Cautiously he moved forward, making just enough noise as he approached.

The Jaguar Demon had watched everything transpire earlier that evening. The ruler of all the giant cats on Grayham watched from the forest shadows as the brutal slaying of one of his best subjects was sadistically enjoyed. The torture this man had administered to the sabertooth, even to his evil mind, was pointless. Kepler was appalled as he watched the human strike his blade against the beast's broken leg just to cause it to scream in pain. He saw the enjoyable look of pleasure on the man's face as he twisted the tiger's broken jaw. The countless number of times the man poked the point of his blade into his subject to cause further distress was humiliating even to his undead pride. In Kepler's entire existence he had never made one of his victims cry with pain repeatedly the way this human had. The Jaguar Demon had always killed his victims quickly—which made the sight of today's events troubling to even his dark heart.

He had a newfound fear for this man. He thought back to his conversations with the goddess as he approached. "I warn you, Kepler," she said, "this human is strong-willed and has a temper. I wouldn't want to make him mad if I were you. I would hate to see you end up on a skewer, cooked for supper." The demon cat had now seen firsthand what Celestria had hinted at: George had no problem cooking anything he killed and Kepler was not going to end up as a flavor of the day.

He had feared no man prior to tonight. In fact, he was the one responsible for ordering the attack, sending the strongest beast under his rule to go after this man. If the human did not survive, then he was not worthy of his service. The goddess had told him she foresaw this man as the ruler of all worlds and that he would send this world and others into darkness. He liked the sound of that but also knew that a dead man could not do any of this, so why not test his strength right up front? He hated admitting it to himself, but he was afraid to approach the man after seeing how easily he killed his best subject.

The jaguar moved slowly toward the fire but, to Kepler's surprise, George did not stop eating. Did the human not notice him? Or worse, maybe he simply didn't care about his presence. Whatever the truth of the matter, the demon was cautious, assuming the man was not worried about his company, but moving carefully just the same. He believed this human could, at any moment, raise his hand to summon his power and stop any kind of confrontation—even a 1,800-pound Sabertooth Lord had been easy for him to stop.

Kepler turned his nose up as he walked by the pile of bloody pieces and continued to watch the man closely. His mind was calculating as he moved closer to the flames. *"How could this human just ignore me? Why doesn't this man acknowledge me? The human just keeps eating. Should I say something?"*

George knew the jaguar was approaching as the fire cast enough light to see the beast out of the corner of his eye. He thought...

Holy crap... he's huge. The top of his back has got to be as tall as I am. He's gonna kill me. What to do? What to do? Think George, think dang it.

He decided not to lift his head for fear of making any movement other than what he was already doing and continued to eat slowly instead, terrified as every hair on his body stood at attention. The black cat was easily larger than the saber he had just killed which made his heart beat violently against his ribs, creating a wicked surge of blood through his neck. The pulsing created sounds in his ears, strong enough to drown out the creature's footsteps as it drew closer.

George watched as the powerful movements of the cat carried him past the pile of bloody parts and closer to the fire. He was about to jump up from his log and run when the jaguar suddenly stopped. It was all George could do to keep the fear from his face as the solid black cat, with red glowing eyes, amplified his desire to run, but he held firm. He knew running would get him nowhere, other than maybe dead faster. He did, however, continue to eat slowly, not wanting to change anything he was doing in hopes the cat would move on. The bloody pile behind the beast had to smell appetizing to it, so he figured he might still have a small chance of escaping an uncertain death.

George thought to himself... *If I live, I'll never camp in this world again. I'm helpless. I knew that I should've used another Snare Scroll. I don't have the skill to fight this big of a cat. This damn sword won't kill the thing, I'm sure... I'm so dead. I'm so definitely dead. Damn, how could I have been so stupid? I should've used another scroll. Damn those Boy Scout books. This thing isn't even scared of fire. He's just ignoring the bloody pile of food. I'm so dead. Okay, okay, think George. George! You've got to think through this. Okay, just sit here and play it cool. Keep eating slowly. Keep calm and show no fear. Ignore it. Maybe it'll just go away! Oh, my hell, please go away!*

⌒⌒ ⌒⌒

Kepler stood near the fire, motionless. Now not more than 15 feet separated the two of them... and his mind was racing.

"This man doesn't care about my presence. He must be very powerful. He doesn't even look nervous. I've never been ignored this way. I can't let him live to tell about this, it's humiliating. But, if I try to kill him, he'll just use his power on me. I would be no

better off than the Sabertooth Lord. What should I do? I'll just lie down and see how he reacts. I'll move slowly so he doesn't kill me."

George was relieved to see the jaguar lower itself to the ground. The stare of the red eyes continued to burrow a hole into his soul. He kept reminding himself that he did not want to do anything that the massive animal would see as an aggressive movement. From everything he'd read about wild animals, he knew no movement was the best movement. He did not change a thing and nervously continued eating.

Kepler and George continued their mental stand off for a long while... each believing one of them, at any moment, could take the other's life. Finally Kepler became so anxious he had to break the silence.

"Are you not scared, human?" The demon-cat said, careful not to sound too intimidating.

George, after hearing the beast speak, started laughing insanely, not because he wanted the beast to think he wasn't scared, but because he had now run into yet another insane thing this world had to offer. He just couldn't fathom that a giant cat could talk. It temporarily sent him over the edge, laughing so hard it hurt. Tears flowed from his eyes as he laughed uncontrollably, forgetting his life could be in danger. This experience would not have been nearly as shocking had he heard Mosley speak at the temple, but George fell through the floor before the wolf appeared.

Kepler was now more convinced than ever of the human's powers. The man's laughter just added the exclamation mark to his feeling that the human was not worried about him being there at all. He watched the man ignore him as he rolled around acting like a fool with little regard to his presence.

He continued to speak after a moment, "Well, you don't have to be so rude about it. It was only a question. I don't see what's so funny about what I said."

George, through all his laughter, finally heard the beast, taking a few moments to gain his composure. Kepler was worried the man might be toying with him. He figured it was a good idea to say as much as he could before the man calmed down in case he would not have the chance later.

"I had no idea that you humans could be so rude and show so little respect." The cat's feelings were hurt for the first time. "I only wanted to come here and talk. You looked like you could use the company."

He glanced at the pile of food and swallowed hard at the idea of eating one of his own.

"I thought maybe you weren't going to be able to eat all this, and I wanted to ask you for some."

The jaguar waited for the human's response.

George relaxed, took a few deep breaths and reached over to grab one of the pieces of meat next to him. He threw it at the giant cat's front paws and started to laugh hysterically once more. "Here, eat all you want," he said as the insanity swept over him once again.

Kepler's ego had never felt smaller than it did right now. How to react? This human was not afraid of him so his powers had to be great— great enough to allow him to act this way without concern. Now, more than ever, his existence might be in danger; Kepler decided to say something to make the man take him seriously.

"I'm here to assist you in your rise to power. I was told that you were the man to create an alliance with, and together we could bring this world under our control."

This caught George off guard, but his laughter covered his surprise. He took a second to quiet himself, finally sitting up to look at the beast, even though his temporary state of insanity was still not allowing him to think straight.

"Oh, you were, aye? I find this absolutely unbelievable. Why would I want to have a large pussycat travel with me? What are you going to do to help me? Are you going to lick people to death?"

He started once again to laugh uncontrollably. His mind was so far gone now that he made fun of the beast that only a few minutes earlier had him terrified.

The demon, taken aback by George's ridicule, had never been made fun of before, or allowed anyone to speak down to him. The undead beast was convinced that this human would destroy him if he attempted to stop his verbal assault.

"I have skills," Kepler said, now unsure of his own conviction in the statement. "I can do far more than lick someone to death."

George slowly stopped laughing and sat up once more, continuing to hold his belly. "I cannot recall the last time I've laughed this hard. Oh my gosh, my stomach hurts!" He grabbed his belly with one hand and reached up to wipe the tears away with the other. He felt as if he were in a dream.

"I'm sure that your big furry butt has many skills. Quick, show me how flexible you are and lick yourself! I'm sure that will be the ability to get us into power. Why don't we run around and introduce ourselves throughout the land? How do you want to say it to everyone? How about this? My name is George and this is my sidekick, Captain Butt Licker." Again he started to laugh uncontrollably.

Kepler's self-esteem was sinking to an all time low and he was quickly becoming angry. He didn't know what to say to the man that would make any difference, so he decided to walk away. As he stood up to leave, the jaguar said, "I'm sorry to have bothered you, George. And my name is Kepler, not Captain Butt Licker." He lowered his head and started walking away.

George seeing the animal was about to leave, stopped laughing and fought to bring himself back into reality. There might be something here he was missing. Why was this beast under the impression that he, of all the people on this world, was the one the cat should form an alliance with? None of this made any sense, but he never passed up an opportunity to manipulate a situation.

"Hey, Kepler," George called in a relaxed tone. "Come on back and I'll stop being such a jerk."

Kepler stopped and turned to look. After a moment, he turned and continued to walk away.

George had one shot at this. He needed to get the upper hand before there was no hand to play. He knew exactly what he would say.

"Suit yourself, Kepler. I must say I'm disappointed that you're not witty enough to pass my test."

Kepler stopped again without turning around.

What test is this human talking about? Has this whole situation been a test for me to pass? Did the human know I was coming? Could he really have known, and simply killed the sabertooth as a message? If it was a message, it was a good one. I got it, loud and clear. Garesh, I have to know.

Now the jaguar turned and headed back for the campfire.

"I don't like tests!" the demon stated, lying back down near the fire.

George did not miss a beat.

"Let me ask you something, Kepler. I would like you to tell me why I would want your company. What do you bring to the table that can help me?"

Confused, Kepler didn't know what to say, so he just stayed quiet.

"Come on, Kep, talk to me," the manipulator continued. "You clearly want to travel with me. What makes you think that I need a travel buddy? Give me a good reason, and I'll promise never to call you Captain Butt Licker again. Why would I want someone like you assisting me on my quest to dominate this world?"

Until now, George's only concern had been to get the staff. He would figure something out from there, but he did like the sound of dominating a world. He wanted to know more.

"As I said before, I have skills. I'm the Lord of all Cats on this world, and they obey my commands. I also have a few other special skills that may come in handy as we travel. I'm an Undead Jaguar Demon—and the skills I possess can be demonstrated for you," Kepler boasted as began to restore his self-esteem. What the Lord of all Cats did not realize, was that his statements had given George a big clue about why the sabertooth attacked him. It also gave him the idea that Kepler may have seen the events of the night take place, and watched the giant saber die. The demon had all but said, at least to George's way of thinking, that he could possibly be behind the attack on his life. Maybe this big black beast may actually be scared of him!

After hearing the title, Lord of all Cats, not to mention his curiosity about the beast claiming to be undead, George decided to ask a few questions. He hoped that his thinking was accurate and, if it was, he could use Kepler's fear to his advantage. He led the beast down an unsuspecting road of admission as he questioned him.

"So you're the Lord of all the Giant Cats on this world? Very impressive! You're also undead?"

"Yes, I am," the demon responded with pride.

"So you're their ruler. They are under your command, doing whatever you tell them, right? I wish I had that kind of a following. Very impressive indeed," George said, making sure he sounded positive.

"Yes," the demon said again, his pride growing as he sat up tall. "I do have quite the following, as you put it, and they do whatever I order them to do. I can see you're impressed."

"So your orders are the ones they always listen to... and they would never do anything against your wishes, is that right?" George said with an admirable tone.

Again, the jaguar confirmed the statement and pushed his chest out even farther. He was now feeling completely strong once again.

"I told you I had some skills of my own, and I can do far more than lick myself. Are you impressed yet?"

George smiled inside as he now figured it was time to bring the jaguar down a notch.

"Well, I'm impressed, but it would seem to me that I'm missing something here." He changed his expression as he continued, making his statements sound cold to let the beast know he was on to him.

"I'm sure you would agree with me then, Kepler, that it isn't a coincidence that you are here after I had a little run-in with one of your subjects," George said matter-of-factly.

The jaguar's reaction confirmed he was right; the demon had ordered the attack. He also was sure that the demon had seen him kill his subject.

"I'm sure you can see I'm a little angered by this, Kepler."

The demon's face showed the guilty verdict, but he tried to cover it up with a lie. "I swear to you, George, I didn't send the saber after you."

But in reality Kepler knew, despite his denial, what was coming next. His pride had lead to his downfall, moving him down the road to take the wrong fork when it mattered most. He dreaded what his ears were going to hear next.

"You'll never be able to lie to me, Kepler, so why don't you just level with me? You had me attacked and your friend over there died while you watched. Why the deception? You're not really here to travel with me, are you? You really hoped that I would be an easy meal! You best be honest with me because I'm in no mood for anymore of your lies!" Switching to a harsher tone, he added, "I won't travel with you if I can't believe in you, Kepler." He watched for the cat's reaction.

Kepler hesitated before speaking. He was unsure what George would do to him if he lied again and figured that no matter what, he was between a rock and a hard place. Best own up to the attack then try to explain his reasoning.

"I did order the attack and I did watch him die. I wanted to see if you were strong enough to handle the saber. I didn't feel it was worth giving my allegiance to someone who couldn't defend himself against one simple beast. The deception, when I first approached you, was intended to start a conversation, but the things I said about coming here to travel with you were true."

After he listened to the demon's response, George thought a moment. He knew he had a huge advantage over the jaguar as the beast thought he had killed his friend. He was unsure to what extent the beast felt his skills were, so he asked Kepler to explain about what he saw.

The demon felt this to be an odd request, wondering why the human would want to re-live the slaughter, but he did not argue.

"I ordered the attack and watched him run at you. When he leaped into the air, I saw you put your hand up and command him to stop. The next thing I knew, he was lying on top of the stone. I watched you torture him and make him cry out in pain. You held up his teeth and said something I couldn't quite make out. You poked him many times with your blade and finally killed him before cutting his legs off. I saw you drag him from the stone. After cutting him up, you continued to make many smaller pieces of him. I'm not sure what else to say, other than I decided to offer my services to you after that. It was, after all, what the goddess thought I would enjoy doing."

The deceiver had no clue what Kepler was referring to about the goddess, but he did not want to lose his upper hand now.

"Why don't you tell me what other skills you offer as an alliance between the two of us, a skill other than being the Lord of all Cats?"

"I'm able to capture the souls of evil men. I kill them and steal their souls before their hearts stop. I do this before the gods take the souls. I trap them inside the bones of their lifeless skeletons. Once this has been done, they must do my bidding until I decide to release them. I can also hide in the smallest of shadows. This ability gives me the upper hand in many situations where stealth is required. Simple things, the things that affect normal creatures, don't harm me. I walk the world as undead. Things like poison and extreme cold are harmless to me." The demon thought a moment and then continued. "I'm also great at gathering information and pretty good in a fight if it comes right down to it. If I think of anything else, I'll let you know, okay?"

George liked a lot of what the jaguar said. He figured it couldn't hurt to have the beast travel with him as long as he could maintain the illusion that he had powers. He would travel with the beast for protection and use his illusion of power to command Kepler. He wanted to keep this fantasy strong until he was able to retrieve the power of the Staff of Petrifaction. Then, once he was able to turn things to stone, he would re-evaluate his need for the demon.

Turning to Kepler, he thought of two questions. He hoped the answers would make the next couple of steps in his journey much easier.

"Okay, so how do you feel about lifting heavy boulders? Are you immune to the effects of the beast inside the Cave of Sorrow?"

Kepler responded with a "yes;" it was everything George wanted to hear. They decided to call it a partnership (for now) and as the night was late, they turned to sleep. It was only a few hours until sunrise and there was a big boulder to find. As George went to sleep, he contemplated how he was going to maintain this illusion of power. He would sleep well and dream of his daughter Abbie, along with Athena. And this time they would take his little daughter to an amusement park and eat cotton candy. It would be a pleasant dream.

Kepler, on the other hand, was relieved that he was able to accomplish the task that Celestria had recommended. The demon was happy to be in George's service and still in one piece. He sighed and decided to go and sit on a nearby boulder to ponder the day's events as the fog began to move in across the lake.

Illustrated By: Angela Woods

From a branch, high above in a nearby tree, Lasidious watched the uniting of the two travel companions. He lowered his eyes to the rock at the base of the tree. It was this large stone that the map rested beneath and it would soon be discovered. He realized he had been right about George's ability to seize power and hoped the earthling could distract the gods long enough for his child to be born unnoticed. He needed this diversion to hide Celestria as well so she could give birth to their baby without fear of discovery.

He enjoyed the luck involved this evening with George, but he knew that this kind of luck simply followed those who were clever enough to find it. Smiling, the god vanished.

The Grayham Inquirer

When inquiring minds need to know where their favorite characters are.

IT IS A NEW DAY and everyone is up and moving in their little part of Grayham. Celestria and Lasidious are inside their home, once again, on Ancients Sovereign.

GEORGE is with Kepler at the Pool of Sorrow. After waking up, Kepler sent for help to move the boulder that supposedly set atop the map.

SAM is training with BJ in the field just outside of Angel's Village. The fighter in training is being humbled by yet another series of beatings, despite showing significant improvement. Kael, Sam's sword, commented on Sam's learning ability, saying he was a quick study, and doing much better than the day before.

THE HEALERS have attended to Shalee, replacing her bandages and applying more healing mud to her arm. She is tired from the experience but not in too much pain. Despite her failure with the staff, she smiles as she looks across the room toward the fireplace. She is holding 'Precious', commanding the fire to do many different little things—making sure to only use simple commands so she could enjoy the benefits from her successes.

HELGA is working on a few new lessons for her protégé. The older sorceress has every intention of making Sha-lee practice with her broken arm. She plans to retrieve her student from her room at the inn not long from now.

MOSLEY is talking to the manager of the Angel's Arena, setting up Sam's first fight to give the earthling a taste of the intense competition in Grayham's arenas. This particular battle will not be to the death, but neither will it be without injury if Sam does not fight well. The competition—wooden staves as the weapon of choice—will continue until a cry for submission is uttered. In this fight, Sam will also be required to inflict enough pain on his opponent to make him yield. Compensation for a victory would be ten Owain coins . . . or only two, if he lost.

BASSORINE is in a meeting with the Book of Immortality trying to convince the Book that Lasidious is up to something. He tells the Book that both Lasidious and Celestria cannot be found. But the Book does not give him the answers he wants to hear and is reminding Bassorine that its pages contained no law requiring either of these gods to check in with the others. The Book also reminds Bassorine that if a meeting of the gods is called for, attendance is not mandatory, and Lasidious does not have to show. According to the Book, Lasidious has not broken any rules and everything he has done up to now is acceptable.

Bassorine tries to object, but the Book of Immortality reminds him again that if free will is ever taken away from any soul by Lasidious, then the Book will feel an emotional wave of sorrow flowing through its pages. Since no rules were broken, the Book has felt nothing; therefore, no steps needed to be taken. The God of War storms out of the Hall of Judgment, screaming for Lasidious once again. He regrets the creation of the Book.

Thank you for reading the Grayham Inquirer

Chapter 13

Kroger the Ogre

The Home of Lasidious and Celestria
Ancients Sovereign

BOTH GODS, now in their home on the World of Ancients Sovereign, laughed as they listened to Bassorine scream. They also were thrilled with their successful pairing of George and Kepler, created at the Pool of Sorrow.

"You should've seen Kepler's face when George was torturing the Sabertooth Lord," Lasidious sniggered. "It was all I could do to keep quiet. And when Kepler decided to introduce himself, he was so careful about it. You should've seen George keep his cool when he saw the giant cat. How that man ever knew to use the Snare Scroll to trap the saber in the first place is beyond me. I thought for sure he was going to get his head taken off when Kepler sent the Saber Lord after him. It looks like our little George is smarter than we figured and has pretty good instincts.

"Truly, my love?" Celestria purred, rubbing Lasidious's forehead with her thumbs. "Do tell..."

"It was perfect. He set his trap and played at being injured—a beautiful deception. I was so proud of him. He even had the nerve to laugh at Kepler and make fun of him. He told Kepler that his only skill was licking his balls. And, as if that was not enough, he called him Captain Butt Licker. I nearly died when I heard the insult! Kepler was too scared to do anything about it. I think he believes George has powers. I still can't figure out where George got the nerve to do all that. I would have thought for sure he was going to mess in his pants when Kepler showed up."

Celestria cupped her lover's face in her hands. "You're so cute when your vicious mind overflows with pride." She kissed him and touched her belly. "Your baby grows, my sweet, and I'll be leaving for the Village of Floren soon. I'll need to stay there until the baby is born and no longer use any of my powers. As we discussed, we can't allow the others to track me down—and using my powers will only increase the risk of that. I want you to be patient. I won't be able to be with you, but I'll always be thinking of you."

Lasidious and Celestria kissed passionately, then agreed it was Lasidious's responsibility to carry out their plans until the baby was born. Celestria kissed her evil lover once more, and then left to spend the remainder of her pregnancy with the elven witch family, Rolfe.

The Pool of Sorrow

GEORGE and Kepler were waiting. It would take the rest of this day and most of the next before Kepler's summons for help to remove the boulder from beneath the tree was answered. He sent one of the dead Saber Lord's relatives north to fetch help from a giant ogre named Kroger.

Angel's Village

HELGA walked through the door of Shalee's room unannounced to get her student moving for the day. The elderly woman caught the young sorceress in training, using her staff to command smaller successes and then enjoying the small satisfactions from them. Shalee was in the middle of one of her pleasurable tear-filled moments when Helga barged in. The older Sorceress had to laugh. As a young sorceress in training herself, she had done something similar—only she had been smart enough to lock her door.

Shalee was embarrassed by the intrusion and jumped out of bed, her face damp from her tears of joy. She tried to hide her embarrassment behind a pillow.

"Don't you knock?" Shalee snapped.

Helga fell to the empty bed. Holding her stomach with laughter, she tried to answer but could not.

"Yeah, very funny," the younger woman said, turning away to hide a smile. "I bet you did the same thing and know what I was up to. You can't blame me, ya know. 'Precious' has given me a lot of happy thoughts."

"Oh child, you don't have to tell me. I didn't leave my room for days when I first began my training. My teacher was very displeased with me to say the least."

Both women laughed, and the moment of embarrassment vanished, replaced with a perfect time of bonding as Shalee taught Helga how to give a "high five."

"My friends and I gave each other high fives back on Earth when we felt something was special or funny. Would you like to be my new best friend—I think you and I could be good together? Besides, I could really use a friend right now. I have cried so much since learning that all my loved ones are dead. I really wish the pain would go away!"

Helga was ecstatic, "Oh, child, I love that idea. I would like nothing more than to be your new best friend, anything I can do to help ease your pain. I know what it's like to lose a loved one!" Helga gave her new best friend another high five to celebrate.

"So, now that I've had my first failure, the rest of it should be smooth sailing, right?" Shalee asked, changing the subject.

"Let us hope that's the case, child. We best get going though. I have a few things planned we need to get right to. I hope you don't fail again. I would hate for you to break the other arm and not be able to practice for a while."

"You know it, girl," Shalee said with sass as she threw up her good hand for another high five. Both women enjoyed the moment, then Shalee changed her clothes before heading out.

Now returned to Helga's school, Shalee was anxious to get started. She was amazed at the healing properties of the mud that had been used under her bandages. Even though she had broken her arm the night before, she could tell that the time it would take to move past the injury would be minimal. Her arm was significantly improved already.

Once again in the padded room, Helga removed a few of the mattresses from the center and replaced them with four large buckets of water. Turning to Shalee, she said, "This exercise is similar to last night's but this time I want you to manipulate the water in different ways and don't even bother asking combine words."

Shalee smiled and did not argue. She looked at the four buckets, and, after a minute, she asked Helga for the elven word for water. The sorceress gave it to her, figuring it was a simple request, but Shalee really had other ideas. She raised her staff into the air and shouted, "Precious, nen coia!"

Helga looked at her student and threw up her wall of force to protect them both just in case. Shalee fooled her teacher by combining the elven word for 'life,' coia, with the word for 'water,' *nen*. All the teacher could do now was wait for the outcome and hope for the best.

They both watched apprehensively as the water began to lift into the air and form into a shimmering image of a falcon. The detail the command had retrieved from her mind when creating the flying beast was spectacular. Shalee's memories had come from the nature channel back on Earth and the falcon had been her favorite ever since. The bird looked like a piece of crystal, except for its graceful movements in flight. After a while, it began to make sweeping passes above their heads as the staff responded to her changing thoughts. Eventually, she could feel her power beginning to fade and decided to end the command by flying the bird over the top of Helga's head and allowing the water to fall on top of her. She would have laughed at the sight of her wet teacher, but the success of her command was beginning to build. She lay down quickly and allowed the rush to consume her. She fell asleep and could not be awakened for the rest of that day due to the intensity of the experience. Sam had to come and carry Shalee back to their room. Helga followed and tucked the covers around her, in awe of her student's power. It had taken the older sorceress almost ten seasons of her life to accomplish what Shalee had done in two days. She smiled inwardly, and wished that she could give her new friend a high five.

The next day, near the Pool of Sorrow

THE GIANT beast man hurried to respond to Kepler's summons. From his home in the Dark Forest, Kroger, an oversized ogre, emerged and crossed the boulders at the outlet's crossing. The Dark Forest started on the north side of the outlet's crossing and circled that side of the Pool of Sorrow to the River of Death far to the west. The only thing separating the Dark Forest, from the Enchanted Forest was the pool, the outlet into the Cripple River, and the River of Death. The Enchanted Forest circled the southern side of the pool and terminated at the River of Death to the west, as well.

George heard the thunderous footsteps as the giant approached, watching in amazement as the massive beast of a man made the stones shake as he crossed them and dwarfing the rock where the 1,800-pound Saber Lord was killed.

As the ogre got closer, Kepler explained that Kroger was cursed at birth with gigantism with his own father leaving him in the Dark Forest for dead. Kroger's mother died giving birth to him as his size in the womb was too much. Even though it was not Kroger's fault, his father resented him from then on. Kepler explained that Kroger had been raised by the most unlikely of families that had taken him in as their own—a group of Dread Gorillas; no one could explain why they had done this. The Dread Gorillas were so fierce that they ate their own if a weakness was found; but perhaps they saw the ogre as unique, and respected this difference enough to let him live.

The ogre was easily 30 feet tall and wore furs to cover his midsection. His feet were bare, toughened from many years of exposure. He carried a massive club with spikes and two straps ran up his chest and over his shoulders to support a massive pack that George figured could hold a small car. The pack had something inside, but George could only see the bump the object made. Kroger was not a handsome creature; scars covered his body from years of wrestling with his gorilla family in play.

Luckily for George and Kepler the giant could cover great distances in a short amount of time or they would still be waiting for him to arrive. Kroger had run the same distance the saber had traveled in a quarter of the time when coming to deliver the message from Kepler.

In spite of his difficulties, the giant was a happy person, singing as he walked over the crossing. George could tell from the sound of his voice that this big guy was not one you would expect to score high on an IQ test. The ogre reminded George of a large child with Down syndrome.

Dusk was approaching and George now took charge of the situation. He introduced himself to Kroger, treating him with respect. After a few minutes of befriending him, he excused himself for two purposes: to empty his bladder and to let Kepler instill the proper amount of fear in the giant's mind about George's perceived powers.

Once George rejoined the group, he asked Kroger to remove the stone and the giant did as he was instructed, lifting the rock with ease. As he watched Kroger playfully toss it up and down, he figured it probably weighed close to two tons. The only reason he had any close estimation of the rock's weight was due to the ones that were delivered to his home for his landscaping. George smiled when he watched the ogre throw the rock into the torrent waters beyond the outlet's crossing. The deceiver marveled at such immense power, thinking that this guy would make a good bodyguard some day.

George jumped into the hole and moved the dirt around. It took a few minutes, but he finally uncovered the map. He did not understand how this piece of paper could look so new, but he said nothing. The weight of the stone that had been sitting on it should have destroyed it, yet the paper had not absorbed any moisture from under the rock. It was as if the map had been drawn that morning. George did not dwell on this fact because just like everything else in this world, it was just one more peculiar thing.

Kepler and Kroger were curious about the map, but George

pulled it back to keep them from seeing it. "Easy, my powerful friends," he said. "There's going to be something in this for all of us, but, for now, I will ask you to let me figure out a plan. This map is going to help us gain a tremendous amount of power if we do things right. Just be patient, and we'll have everything we could ever want."

Kepler really wanted to look at the map, but figured George was not stupid. If he said the map was going to help them gain power, then he could only assume the human knew what he was talking about.

Night was coming soon, and George wanted to study the map. He ordered the duo to gather wood for a fire and soon they were all sitting by the flame. Both Kroger and Kepler stared at George while he memorized the map. He was shocked at how easy it was to read; the location of the staff was clearly marked, resting behind a hidden door which guarded it. The great part about the staff's location was that it rested just inside the cave's entrance. The bad part was that, once inside, there were only two ways out. The map listed both ways, the first was to make it through the cave's eight-day walk and find the exit called Sorrow's Release. The second was to find the beast within the cave and kill him to release his control over the entrance, risking a confrontation with the beast.

George remembered what Jason told him back in the field near Lethwitch about this beast. He said it was a hideous creature that uses visions of sadness to drive anyone insane who entered the cave. The visions made his victims commit suicide—they walk back through the Pass of Tears, weeping and throw themselves into the Pool of Sorrow. They swim deep enough that by the time they realize what has happened, they do not have time to surface before drowning.

The idea of dealing with the beast was of little concern to George. He remembered that Kepler had told him he was immune to the visions of the beast. The beast was unable to use his visions on the cat because sadness was an emotion his demon's heart could not feel.

With his mind working overtime as he studied the map, it was only a couple of hours before he had his plan.

"Okay, I have a job for all of us to do, but first I'm hungry," George said as he rubbed his belly. "What do you guys say we get something to eat?"

"Food!" Kroger shouted. He reached into his gigantic pack and pulled out a dead bull. He ripped it apart and offered it up to the group.

George laughed, realizing what the bump in the giant's pack had been. He thanked him for the meal, watching as Kepler and Kroger now ate their supper raw. George, on the other hand, found a stick to hold his meat above the flame.

After everyone was done eating, they sat by the fire while George explained his plan. Once done, he put the scroll in his bag and lay down, suggesting they all get some rest before heading out in the morning. He placed the bag under his head to keep curious minds out of it and went off to sleep.

The Grayham Inquirer

When inquiring minds need to know where their favorite characters are.

THE NEXT MORNING, George, Kepler and Kroger are up and on their way through the Pass of Tears traveling towards the Cave of Sorrow. They plan to camp a safe distance from the cave once they arrive. George wants to avoid any unexpected encounters with the beast, Maldwin. They will review George's plans before entering.

SAM, Mosley and BJ are on their way to Angel's Arena. BJ wants to give Sam an idea of what to expect before his first fight. The fight is scheduled as the last one of the evening. Sam, however, is not sure the idea to put him in the arena so early after starting his training is a good one. The trainer wants to get Sam some practice to familiarize him with the sandy surface of the arena floor.

SHALEE is once again with Helga after sleeping through the night. She still feels very weak and they have decided to stick with simple commands as they continued her training. The past few days have been wonderful, despite her broken arm, but using the staff has taken a lot out of Shalee. The rewards 'Precious' has given her have been exhausting; she has never shed so many tears of joy in her life...

As training continues, the rewards she expected from these simple commands were no longer happening. Helga explained that Shalee has moved to an advanced skill level and from now on, the benefit of easier commands would add small extensions to her life.

CELESTRIA is now with the elven witch family on the World of Luvelles. She is posing as a distant relative of the family. The story, if asked, is that she has traveled to be with them until her baby was born.

LASIDIOUS finally plans to make his appearance to the other gods. He has sent word for the *Book of Immortality* to call a meeting inside the Hall of Judgment. The Book invites all the gods to attend this meeting and, as expected, with the exception of Celestria, every god informs the *Book* they will be present.

Thank you for reading the Grayham Inquirer

Chapter 14

𝔄 𝔊𝔬𝔡 𝔉𝔞𝔩𝔩𝔰

𝔍𝔫𝔰𝔦𝔡𝔢 𝔱𝔥𝔢 𝔥𝔞𝔩𝔩 𝔬𝔣 𝔍𝔲𝔡𝔤𝔪𝔢𝔫𝔱
Ancients Sovereign

THE MEETING was held in the Hall of Judgment—the home of the Book of Immortality. The vanity of the gods had ensured everything on Ancients Sovereign was breathtakingly beautiful and the room they was no exception. But it was difficult on this day to enjoy the beauty of this place as many harsh words were being thrown around by those in attendance.

"I'm outraged at the deception . . . and theft of the Crystal Moon," Bassorine said as he yelled at Lasidious.

Most of the gods were now sitting around the table within the Hall of Judgment, but some of them, due to their individual body compositions were unable to sit. They stood and listened to Bassorine scream across the table's surface.

"I would never have released my hold on the crystal if I would've known it was your intention to steal it."

Lasidious laughed in a taunting manner. "Who cares if you're outraged? I have broken no laws within the Book's pages. I'm the God of Mischief for a reason. Did you really expect nothing to happen when I suggested you release the power you had over it? Deception is what I do, idiot. Did you really think I felt it would be wondrous for you to appear to the earthlings in a glorious fashion when they touched it? I couldn't care less how you appear in their eyes. I was pleasantly surprised when you agreed to do such a stupid thing. It was your own vanity that drew you into my plan. You're pathetic, Bassorine."

"What?" the God of War screamed. "It was my vanity. How was I vain?"

"You have the biggest ego in this room. It didn't take much to convince you that appearing to them after they touched the crystal was a creative way for you to look... *ALL MIGHTY!* It was your vanity that liked that idea, or you would've never agreed to it."

Bassorine tried to speak above Lasidious, but he began to stumble over his words. He was not good at verbal confrontations, especially when angry. It sounded as if he was babbling as he spoke. It was easy for the God of Mischief to take control of the conversation.

"Your babbling only helps to make my next point. Face it, Bassorine; you're not the brightest of the gods. When it comes to thinking long term, you should leave it up to us. You can plan a war, I give you that, but when it comes to anything important, you should leave it to the rest of us to handle. There would be nothing created if you were the only one left alive after the God have no imagination. If it weren't for your power to help create the things that the rest of us thought of, power that we all have as well I might add, you would be useless. Everyone around this table knows I'm right! Now that I think about it, you definitely are useless. We all know that everything would have been created without you anyway."

Lasidious could see Bassorine moving toward the edge of his seat as he continued. "Let's face it: if you had any brains at all, you would've never allowed the Book of Immortality to be created in the first place. The funny thing is, not only did you allow it to be created, but you allowed me, of all people, to manipulate its creation. Thank you, Bassorine, some of the loopholes within its laws are simply wonderful. I've just got to say it... you're the definition of stupidity!"

The other gods jumped back from their positions around the table as Bassorine responded angrily with a few well-thought-out statements. Keylom, who had been unable to sit because his body would not fit in a chair, cringed as his hoofs clacked against the hardened floor. The sounds the beautiful centaur's weight made only added to the tension in the room.

Bassorine stood, drew his sword, jumped up on the table and began to walk across it. He was headed for Lasidious as he threatened, "I'll show you who's stupid! Let's see how stupid looks when I'm standing above your lifeless corpse."

Before anything more was said Bassorine flew across the room and slammed hard into a nearby wall, falling to the floor with a thunderous thud. The room shook from the collision and the thick marble wall was severely damaged.

The Book of Immortality rose from its golden stand. The Book realized the meeting had gotten out of control and it was time to take action. The stand was the Book's resting place since its creation and it stood above the table by only a few inches, closest to Bassorine.

It was the Book who had knocked Bassorine into the wall with its power. In all the years since the gods had created it, they had never seen it use any of the powers within its many pages. Until now, the Book had always settled things with logical communication. Everyone in the room was stunned, even Lasidious, although he had counted on it to happen. It was the God of Mischief's goal to put the Book in a defensive position, forcing it to protect him.

All watched as Bassorine picked himself up from the floor and dusted off his long leather coat. The Book spoke.

"Bassorine, this meeting will not become a battlefield. You *will* not harm Lasidious. He has the free will to say anything he wants, just as you do. I suggest you calm yourself before you do something that will require further action."

All the gods now stood, watching for Bassorine's reaction as the God of War finished shaking off the debris from the marble wall; he lifted his head high. Everyone knew he was the strongest—able to destroy each of them. But it was the Book's job to keep the gods from fighting and its power was not to be taken lightly, no matter how powerful Bassorine was.

Bassorine was the only one of them with a weapon that could destroy the Book. Angry, he debated in his mind what his next move would be. When the gods created the Book of Immortality, they had left two weaknesses: one was Bassorine's sword. The gods had agreed that they needed a way to take back control from the Book if it ever became necessary, but they did not leave much room for error when doing so.

Bassorine now calculated these facts, knowing he'd have only one shot to destroy the Book—realizing another one could be created, if needed. With the Book out of the way, he could destroy Lasidious. If he did this, it would set an example to the others that they should never deceive him again and, even better, he would once again be all-powerful. Lasidious's actions could be his excuse to take back this power.

Lasidious, sensing Bassorine's hesitation, took a few more calculated shots at his ego. "See what I mean, you big ox? You're an idiot. Only you would attack me in front of the Book. You're not strong enough for that. I think you've lost your edge. You should accept the fact that I have taken the crystal. Go bury your head in the sand. You're nothing more than a sheep—you need someone to follow." Lasidious now laughed at Bassorine's expense while the others were on edge because of what he had just said.

The God of War's pride swelled deep inside him and his hatred for Lasidious grew stronger with every breath he took. His desire to destroy the Book and take his vengeance on Lasidious was cosmic. The deception of the god, along with his verbal bashing and the attack from the Book, clouded his judgment. He could not think of a time when he had wanted to fight more in his entire existence. Bassorine watched Lasidious smile and laugh hysterically at him, daring him, taunting him, luring him to attack. With every breath he took, Bassorine sized up the Book, calculating the best way to destroy it.

Then finally, he quieted his mind and took a few deep breaths. After a moment, his decision was made. He would fight. He was ready to go to war. Methodically, he began walking toward the group, acting as if he was going to put his blade away. Reaching the heavy table and seeing that the gods were beginning to sit back down, he quickly lifted his sword into the air. The blade began its deadly descent toward the Book of Immortality. None of the gods had expected this move, except for Lasidious.

The God of Mischief had hoped this day would come—this moment had been a part of his plan all along. He knew that one of the

laws within the Book's pages was for the gods to protect its existence and it could be defended with any use of power necessary,
without punishment. Lasidious knew he didn't have the power to
hurt Bassorine, but he didn't need it. Then again, if this part of his
plan failed, he would be dead. He was also aware that Bassorine's
blade was the only thing in existence that could destroy the Book
of Immortality. Other than that, the only weakness the gods had
given the Book was a slower reaction time. If Bassorine could
catch it off guard, its reaction would not be fast enough to fight
back. All Lasidious needed to do was buy the Book some time; he
was ready to do this.

As Bassorine's blade arched through the air, Lasidious reached
forward with his hands and sent a wave of force strong enough
to push the Book out from under the thunderous slam the blade
made as it hit the golden stand. The force was strong enough that it
continued through the stand and the stone table, cracking the floor
beneath. The Book flew from the table and landed on the floor
across the room unharmed. Lasidious quickly sent another wave
of force into Bassorine and knocked him back. Doing this bought
the Book additional time to respond. He was not strong enough to
knock Bassorine into a wall like the Book had done, but he only
needed to take away the god's balance long enough to allow the
Book to react.

It took Bassorine only a split second to regain his balance. He
leapt across the room toward the Book, trying to make up for the
lost time. Once again, his blade arched through the air and met its
target with a thunderous collision—but—by this time, it was too
late. A powerful field of protection surrounded its pages.

The repercussion of the two powerful forces colliding together
sent everything in the room thrown hard against the opposite wall.
The collision of bodies surrounding the table was strong enough
for them to break through walls and land in the countryside beyond the structure. Except for Bassorine and the Book of Immortality, the gods were now lying in the grass with pieces of the hall
around them with a billowing cloud of dust choking the air. The
rest of the structure fell on the two in battle. It took a while for the
rumbling to stop but not before the sounds of the event could be

heard as thunder throughout all the worlds.

Silence now... the gods lying on the grass eventually stood to look at the spectacle. With the dust settling, all that was left was an enormous pile of marble.

The gods looked at each other and waited. They were about to declare both the Book and Bassorine as destroyed when they heard a noise from under the pile's center. Lasidious swallowed hard at the possibility that it could be Bassorine. If it was... he would be dead. Bassorine would not find forgiveness within him. The God of War's blade would split him in two.

Slowly the pile of marble started to shift and lift into the air. The pieces floated away and settled toward the edges of the rocky debris. From the center of the pile rose the Book of Immortality. Lasidious exhaled with relief as he watched the Book Float over to the group, the Book announced, "Bassorine is gone and will no longer be with us! I have destroyed him!"

Some of the gods fell to their knees while others stood in disbelief. They had all known Bassorine and, despite their differences, admired the god. But they quickly shook off their loss, realizing there was one less being more powerful than them at the top. Lasidious allowed his evil heart relished the fact that this part of his plan had fallen in line.

The Book spoke once again. "I'll need a new Hall of Judgment and I want it built right away. If anyone breaks another law, they will meet the same fate as Bassorine. It is also within the pages that for every fallen god, a new one must take the place left behind. It is also in the laws that this new god is to be chosen per the wishes of the fallen. I will announce the new god's name when we convene to honor the Mighty Bassorine's passing.

The Book floated to Lasidious. "Is it your intention to allow everything created by the gods to be destroyed? If it is, then it's your right to do so, and no one will do anything to stop you. There's no rule that says you cannot take or destroy the Crystal Moon. I cannot fathom why you all could've forgotten such an important rule, but this appears to be the case."

Lasidious responded, "I don't want the crystal or the worlds destroyed. I'm simply bored, and wanted to play a game. I've scattered the crystals and have given them individual hiding spots. There's one piece on each world at this moment, but this could change."

The God of Mischief smiled.

"I intend for us all to play a game, if you so choose, of course. I have each piece of crystal protected. No one can touch them, except for me, now that Bassorine is gone. You'll be given a choice to join a team. Those of you who join me will create a team of evil and try to collect three of the five pieces of the crystal. The other team will be one of good and will need to collect three pieces also. For every piece of crystal collected and placed together, it should allow enough power to be sent to the worlds to keep them in place and buy us some more time to finish the game.

"The planets should not start to shift for about a season. I would imagine that every time we add an additional piece of crystal to the others, it should give us an additional season, even if the crystals are split between the teams. These pieces will still work to govern the planets as long as two of them are bonded together. If my team wins and collects the majority of all the crystal's pieces, the worlds will fall under our control. We'll govern the Crystal Moon as a whole . . . forever. If the other team wins, then the worlds will be dominated by good, and they'll likewise be given control."

"What will keep you from cheating?" Alistar, God of the Harvest, questioned. "You'll have a distinct advantage over our team."

"I give the Book my word that I won't cheat. If I do, I'll volunteer to be destroyed," Lasidious responded. "This should be enough to keep me in line. If I find it difficult to play fair, I'll resign from my team and watch. I've never been much for teams anyway so this may very well happen."

"Sounds fair," Mieonus, Goddess of Hate, responded.

Lasidious clapped his hands, rubbing them together, he continued.

"The influence we have over our followers will be our weapons, or tools you might say, to manipulate. You could even call them our chess pieces. If I remember right, Bassorine loved chess." The God of Mischief smiled at the thought of Bassorine's destruction, then continued. "We will play a game fit for the gods. The only rules are that we cannot force our pawns to do anything they don't want to do. As the laws of the Book of Immortality state: 'Free will is to be cherished above all else.' The second rule is that all the worlds will continue to trade merchandise without interruption, since it is necessary for their survival. None of us will do anything to influence this trading to stop, or the game will end and the crystal's pieces will be destroyed. The goal is to get the beings of the worlds to strategize for the pieces of the Crystal Moon and fight to capture them. The team that captures three of the Crystal Moon's pieces first . . . will win."

Lasidious moved to a piece of stone debris and stood on top of it before making his next statement.

"If the game is not played, then I will destroy the Crystal Moon. The worlds will follow eventually, destroying themselves and our followers. However, without Bassorine, we will be unable to create another Crystal Moon to govern them. We will then have to rebuild and start over. I think we all remember how boring that was. I'll be my team's leader and you can now choose to play or not."

Lasidious smiled and said, "Who would like to be on my team?"

The gods looked at each other. As expected, they all enjoyed the thought of this new diversion. Of the 13 remaining gods, Lasidious now had a team of eight, including himself and Celestria. He watched as Bailem stepped forward and took the other team leader position; with the remaining four falling in behind him.

Before Lasidious left, he shook the hands of his team and called for a meeting in his home. He informed them he would allow for their entrance and gave them a period of the day to be there to start the planning.

Bailem did the same as the Book of Immortality made one final statement before they all left. "It appears that this follows the rules of free will, and I don't see any laws within my pages being broken. The game has now begun!"

The Grayham Inquirer

When inquiring minds need to know where their favorite characters are.

LASIDIOUS—God of Mischief and his team are in his home, deep within the Peak of Angels. The gods present at this meeting are Yaloom—*God of Greed,* Mieonus—*Goddess of Hate,* Hosseff, the Shade—*God of Death,* Jervaise—*the spirit Goddess of Fire,* Lictina, the female Lizardian—Goddess of Earth and Owain—*God of Water.* The one god missing from the meeting was the goddess Celestria—*Goddess of Evil Natured Beasts.*

Planning began and Lasidious informed his team of what had transpired so far. He told them of George, Kepler, and Kroger's alliance. He gave them up-to-date information, telling them the group was on its way to the Cave of Sorrow. He was unable to give his group the exact location of the first piece of crystal that had been placed on Grayham because of his promise to the Book of Immortality, but he did say he might change his mind and put two pieces of the Crystal Moon on Grayham instead of one. They all agreed that the things Lasidious had done up till now were good, and congratulated him on his destruction of Bassorine.

BAILEM—an angel, now, the God of the Sun was also holding his own team meeting. The gods present at his home were Alistar—*God of the Harvest,* Keylom—*the centaur God of Peace,* Calla—*Goddess of Truth*

and Helmep—*God of Healing.* None of them knew where to start. All they knew was that the first piece of crystal was somewhere on Grayham. The meeting seemed somewhat pointless but they did hope to recruit the new god to their team once the Book introduced this individual.

SAM has finished his early morning training, now familiar with the arena. Back with Shalee he still has time before his fight to think about it all and he's worried, using Shalee as a sounding board. Sam's fight is to be the last fight of the evening; and by all estimates, the fight should end before dark. He just wants it to be over with.

HELGA is working hard to figure out stronger lessons for Shalee. The older sorceress had given her pupil a few days off in order to accomplish this. **Bassorine had visited Helga in the middle of the night prior to his destruction.** He told Helga that Shalee could handle an aggressive growth in her skills. He would not say why or how her student could handle this, but he did say that she was not to speak of their conversation with Shalee or anyone else. The God of War had left her wondering about many unanswered questions.

CELESTRIA is helping the witches clean their home and prepare her baby's room. She hasn't been this excited about anything since she became a god. It has been well over 100,000 seasons since she set up anything without using her powers and she found this to be quite a challenge.

MOSLEY had stayed with BJ after Sam's training. When the fights started at the Peak of Bailem, the trainer excused himself and headed for the nobleman's seating box to watch the fights. Mosley then left and was looking for Sam when the Book of Immortality appeared in front of him.

Thank you for reading the Grayham Inquirer

Chapter 15

A God's Gifts
and
A Revelation

"MOSLEY, we must speak," the Book of Immortality said before teleporting them both back to the World of Ancients Sovereign. The Book did not give Mosley the chance to say anything when they arrived but rather continued talking. The Night Terror wolf could only stare at the Book's black binding as the thin slit that functioned as its lips, opened up and the words poured out of it.

"Mosley, I have much to say and little time to say it so listen carefully. Some of what I'm going to tell you will be upsetting, but the time for emotions will need to wait. I realize none of this makes any sense at the moment, but I assure you it will very soon. I ask you to be strong. And when the time is right, you can grieve if you need to.

"Bassorine has been destroyed. You are to become the new God of War. You... were Bassorine's choice."

Mosley knew of the Book, but had never seen it before, nor did he understand its function. He managed to set his surprise aside and focused on what it had just been said.

"Destroyed.... how could've Bassorine been destroyed? That's not possible... is it, and what do you mean that I'm to become a god? Why would I be given a chance to become a god? This doesn't make any sense!"

"There isn't time to explain. I can't afford for the others to know of our conversation. I must hurry. You're to be given godly powers and it will be your job to fulfill Bassorine's role as the new God of War, that's all I can say at this time."

The Book of Immortality did not wait for a response; he immediately began to impart the powers of the gods to Mosley, enlightening him to the ways of the gods. The knowledge of everything the Book knew to be true was forced into the wolf's mind like the destructive nature of an avalanche mowing its way down a tree-covered mountainside. Even the fact that his wife was not waiting for him in the heavens and that her soul only rested within the Book's many pages was now known and this hit Mosley hard. All he could do, for what seemed to be forever, was stare at the Book and wonder which page her soul rested on. Mosley tried to organize his thoughts but found this much information to be overwhelming.

"Mosley, I'm sorry for the abruptness of my actions. It'll take some time for you to adjust. According to the laws within my pages, you're allowed to bestow two gifts on anyone you choose. Then you must say goodbye to those you love and return here, to live on the Hidden God World of Ancients Sovereign.

"The gifts cannot be wealth, knowledge or love. They must be something that will aid a person, or beast, through life. The gifts cannot give any one being or person the power to control the free will of others. For example: the ability to fly to get from place to place . . . or the ability to tell jokes and make those around them laugh, would be considered good gifts. Again, Mosley, I'm sorry for any inconvenience this may cause you, but there are things that must be done, my friend, and done quickly to ensure the safety of **Bassorine's secrets.** They must be done to ensure the future. Search your memories. I've given you everything you were meant to know. The day grows short, now go!"

The Book disappeared, leaving Mosley to teleport himself to wherever he wanted. Mosley thought about it for a moment and spoke out loud, but no one was there to listen.

"What if I don't want to be a god? I mean, don't get me wrong, I like the idea, but you could have at least asked me first. Maybe I would've wanted to spend more time on Grayham. I didn't want to know there wasn't a heaven or that my wife's soul was put into a Book, even if it has a soul. How can I get rid of this deep pain? I don't wish to mourn my wife again. Can someone talk to me, please? What a way to give a god his powers . . . this is very anticlimactic, you know!"

Mosley always wanted to be like Bassorine and figured the Book of Immortality already had this knowledge, but what a remarkable way to make it happen. Thinking it through now, he eventually came to realize the power he held. He commanded the feeling of loss for his wife to hide deep within him; he would deal with his emotions later. Once the pain subsided, he smiled.

"Hmmmm, this god thing could come in handy."

Coming back to reality, the wolf knew he did not have much time. He had to be back on Ancients Sovereign by nightfall, no time for long goodbyes. He had to get going, but wanted to try out his new name on for size.

"Hello, I'm Mosley, God of War." He said aloud as he trotted around. "Hey, look at me . . . I'm Mosley, God of War." He liked the sound of it. "I'm Mosley, the new God of War. Don't make me zap you." The wolf laughed and said it many more times in many different ways. He could only hope that his fighting skills were better as well, but he would have to find that out some other time.

For now, he concentrated on the fighter and, before he knew it, he was standing in front of Sam. Both Sam and Shalee were caught off guard by the sudden appearance of the wolf-god. Shalee jumped back, raised her staff, and almost yelled a command before she realized who it was. Sam reacted by throwing himself into a defensive posture and raised his hands, ready to strike.

Mosley balled up to cover himself, a reaction not necessary for a god, but an old habit developed through the years; that would have to change. He slowly opened his eyes when nothing came of the commotion. He looked into their confused faces and gave a cute, wolfish grin. "Hey guys, what's up?"

Shalee sighed heavily before talking. "Mosley, you scared the bejesus out of me. Since when do you know how to pop in and out like that?"

"Yeah, what the heck was that?" Sam added, trying to calm down.

Mosley responded after a moment. He was not sure where to begin, so he decided he would answer questions later. "I have a lot to say to both of you, but most of it will have to wait. I won't answer questions right now, Sam, because you have to fight in a bit. For now, I'll say that Bassorine has been destroyed."

"Destroyed? What are you talking about?" Sam snapped.

Mosley responded, "That would qualify as a question, Sam. I said no questions until later. I need you to listen for now. I'm here for a reason and need you to let me do what I came to do. Bassorine was destroyed and it was his choice that I take his place."

Mosley, prideful, stuck out his furry chest before continuing.

"I'm the new God of War, but not as powerful as Bassorine... yet. More power will come in time but for now, I must bestow two gifts on someone before I return to the god world. I'm giving them both to you, Sam, if you'll allow me to."

"What do you mean bestow on me two gifts? And what do you mean you took Bassorine's place and you're the new God of War?" Sam said, confused.

Mosley smiled. "Sam, you're unable to refrain from questions no matter what the situation. I would've expected as much. I'll put it this way. All you need to know is I'm now one of the gods—and I'm here to give you two gifts. Do you want them or not?"

Sam looked at the wolf and was dying inside to ask another question, but thought better of it.

"Well, of course I want them, big guy. Anyone would want a gift from a good-looking, furry god like you. Lay it on me, buddy."

Sam spoke with a touch of innocent sarcasm and a big smile on his face. He was not sure if he believed the things the wolf had said, but, the last time he doubted something on this world, a sword had scolded him for his ignorance and tapped him on his chin. He didn't wish to look foolish again.

Mosley smiled and continued.

"We both know your rise to glory is going to be a long, hard road. What I want to do is help you speed your journey up a bit. The gifts I can bestow must be something to assist you in your life. I have thought about what to give you and my decision is this: you will receive a gift to assist you in the arenas of Grayham. I want these gifts to increase your ability to fight and be a natural part of your body."

Sam became excited as he heard the words "increased ability to fight." Maybe he shouldn't be so hasty; he'd give his four-legged friend some credit. He was practically crawling out of his skin as the new god continued.

"I'm going to grant you greater natural strength for the first gift. You'll be able to lift about four times your body weight above your head. For the second, I'll endow you with greater natural reflexes. This will allow you to move quicker and respond as fast as your mind can think. We both know that will be fairly fast. You would like both of these gifts, yes?"

Sam was like a child in a candy store. He could not stand still waiting for Mosley to tell him what to do. His doubt in his furry friend vanished. "Yes, yes, yes, yes, yes, and yes! What do I have to do to get these gifts? Did I tell you, Mosley, that you're now my number one best friend?"

Mosley laughed and looked at Shalee who was as excited about Sam's gifts as he was. "I think our fighting friend here is going to get an aneurism from all the excitement."

"I agree, so what does he have to do?"

"That's the great thing about it," Mosley replied. "He has to do nothing other than allow me to let the gifts flow into him!"

Without hesitation, Sam readied himself. "Heck, let's start flowing then, big guy!"

Mosley walked over to Sam and touched one of his paws to Sam's left foot. The transfer of power was instantaneous. The fighter felt an electrifying surge move through his body... not painful, but rather a soothing current moved through him as his body accepted the gifts. He could feel his strength increasing. His feet felt light as he watched his body change. He looked at Shalee to confirm that what he thought he was seeing was actually happening. He saw her nod. His body was growing bigger and stronger.

Shalee stood aside and could see the affects the gifts were having. Sam's height was increasing as she watched and his muscle mass grew. His legs, arms, chest, back, and neck all became thicker . . . and, to her wondrous delight, that was not all. She loved all of this new Sam, but his overall new look was just as wonderful as before; she had always desired him.

Sam's new six-inch-taller lean frame held the additional weight perfectly. He had just enough body fat to look healthy. His shoes burst open, allowing for the growth; his pants were not only too short but shredded. Shalee grabbed Sam's old pair of fighting trunks and made him put them on. Sam dropped his pants and, for the first time, Shalee saw the fighter in all his glory. His shoulders were broad and his arms were like cannons. The neck was thick. His jaw line had tightened enough to accent the perfection that already existed. His abdomen called to her—and the rest, well, Sam was perfection.

Shalee lost herself in him, admiring what she had longed for since they met. The staff was a grand thing but now Sam would get all her attention. It was time for her become Sam's new girlfriend.

Shalee lost herself in the moment; saying things that were completely out of character and downright unladylike... things left best to the imagination. Both Sam and Mosley looked at her in shock.

Embarrassed, realizing what she had done and blushing bright red, Shalee apologized immediately. "Oh, my goodness, just listen to me, I'm so sorry. I don't normally act this way—I don't know what came over me. Can we forget I said all of that? Please, Sam, don't be angry with me! I'm very sorry!"

Sam listened to everything Shalee said and looked at the new god and winked. "Looks like you've given me more than two gifts after all, Mosley; the ladies now won't be able to resist me."

He turned to Shalee and smiled. "I'm glad you like the new look. I've always liked yours as well." He addressed Mosley once again. "You really know how to hook a brother up, my friend."

Sam looked over his new six feet-four inch, 275 pound frame and marveled at its splendor for a while. Excited, he blurted out without thinking, "Well, I'm sure I can make some strong babies with Shalee now, isn't that right, Mosley?"

Mosley rolled his eyes at both the humans—neither one of them had much self-control.

Shalee looked at Sam. Her mood went from anxious embarrassment to utter surprise and soft-heartedness. She moved to him and looked into his eyes, softly speaking as she held his gaze. "You look at me like that? You see me as the woman you would want to have your children? If I had known this, I would've never walked out of the room the other day and made you believe I didn't feel the same for you. I've always found you attractive, Sam. I promise I'll never play you again. If you still want me, I'm yours!"

Mosley rolled his eyes again, feeling awkward this time as Sam pulled Shalee in close and kissed her lovingly. "I do want you," he said softly. "You're forgiven for the other day and, just so you know, I spoke with Mosley about how to pursue you. You would've been chased. I was willing to enjoy your desire to play hard to get. This new look just made my job a little easier, it seems. I guess if it's all right with you, I can skip the hard part of chasing after you and become your man?"

Shalee smiled big and stroked Sam's face, saying everything without speaking a word. For the first time, they allowed each other to feel the passion they had both avoided for this long.

He kissed her again in farewell and headed outside to the village. He wanted to find a new pair of leather fighting pants before entering the arena. There were only four more fights before they called his name.

Shalee stood in complete silence. Her heart was at peace; no woman in Grayham could be happier than she was. After a few minutes watching her, Mosley finally broke the silence.

"I hate to ruin the mood but I need you to listen to me," he said. "Did Sam tell you everything Bassorine had told him?"

"Well—Sam told me some of it, but I was so tired. I know Earth was destroyed, and I'm not sure how I feel or how to *deal* with that. I miss so many people and it's hard to believe they're gone. I have been trying not to think about it. It hurts way too much. When I've got time to think, all I do is cry." Tears began to run down her face.

"Shalee, Bassorine brought you here for the purpose of being with Sam. He had hoped the two of you would form a union and have children, but I assume Sam didn't tell you that he knew this part."

Shalee wiped away the tears and responded with a sniffling chuckle. "That little devil, he was going to pursue me no matter what I said. Wow, I could have played much harder to get if I'd known that. I think that's so cute!"

"I'm glad you feel that way," Mosley sighed, "But there is a much bigger reason you're here . . . much, much bigger than having Sam's babies."

"As if having his kids isn't enough of a responsibility . . . what else can you throw at me? Motherhood can be a real challenge, you know."

"I'm sure you're right, but what I didn't know until after being enlightened and receiving my powers from the Book, was that Bassorine had told the Book of Immortality many secrets after its creation. Did Sam tell you about the Book of Immortality?"

Shalee thought a moment. "He said it was where all the souls go since heaven and hell are destroyed, but it all sounds entirely made up and fake to me!"

"That is part of what the Book does, but it also holds the laws of the gods. The gods have to live by these laws no matter what." The wolf god thought a moment and continued. "The information I'm about to share with you was given by Bassorine and protected by the Book of Immortality at all costs. Bassorine didn't share this information with anyone else. I would not know any of this now, but it was Bassorine's wish that I be told. Bassorine instructed the Book to divulge this information only to me if something were to happened to him."

The wolf took a deep breath, and then said, "You will grow to have abilities far greater than that of any sorceress before you, has ever had. Your gods of Earth spoke with Bassorine before you were born. It was a secret meeting that only Bassorine and your gods of Earth knew about. The gods that traveled with Bassorine back to Earth, only went back with him 23 years after you were born. Bassorine was the only one to meet with your gods of Earth the first time around. It was during this secret meeting that he asked the Earth gods not to divulge the information they had shared between them to the others—and they didn't, making sure they kept this pact sacred.

"It was at this secret meeting where your gods were asked to give your unborn fetus the ability to absorb the energies that live all around you. Bassorine asked your gods to allow you to channel these energies at a much higher level than those who are normally able to do so. He requested that you be given a gentle heart and strong will. This is why you learn so quickly and are so kind. This is also why you are so stubborn and display a bit of drama. You have the ability within you to become a god without having to ascend! You could be the most powerful woman, even more powerful than the gods without having to leave for the god world."

"Wow, a god? I don't know about that. What do you mean by energies?"

"I don't think it's possible for me to describe these energies in terms you would be able to understand, so I'll call them miniature beings that cannot be seen living all around everyone. It's these beings that only certain souls can absorb into themselves. They flow into you when you command you're magic and become a permanent part of you."

"So you're telling me these life forces enter my body and stay there? What happens once they are inside of me?"

Mosley smiled at her concern. "Let's just say they are the building blocks of your magical foundation within your soul. The bigger you can make your foundation, the stronger you'll become. The powers you'll be able to command will be tremendous."

Shalee interrupted him. "So why did Bassorine ask the gods of Earth to do this? Why did he choose me?"

"It wasn't that Bassorine specifically chose you, but it was more a matter of your birth order; you were the next soul to be sent to Earth after they spoke of Sam's abilities and what skills he would carry with him throughout life."

"So you're saying I was just lucky," she chided with a big smile.

"It would appear so," Mosley responded. "According to the knowledge the Book of Immortality has given me, Bassorine knew that the gods wanted to create a Book to govern them after the God Wars were over. They all liked the idea, but, when they had discussed what the weaknesses of the Book would be, he wanted a back-up plan to ensure that the Book could be destroyed if it ever needed to be. He was the God of War for a reason, and he never failed to create a good tactical plan. He knew his sword could destroy the Book, but he also knew that if for any reason he was to fail, someone else would need to fight to destroy it."

"Why would Bassorine want the Book destroyed?"

"He didn't want it destroyed when he met with the Earth gods. He liked the idea of the Book, but he didn't completely trust the others. He wanted to make sure that if any of the gods found a way to control the Book someone would be strong enough to take back the control that was lost. Bassorine felt that the Book could be used as a weapon if it fell into the specific control of one of the gods. Now that Bassorine is gone, you're the one who would need to take this control back if it is ever lost. Right now, the Book of Immortality governs itself and is a pure being without evil. But if one of the gods finds a way to manipulate this and forces it to do evil, I'm sure you can imagine the problems that could arise. I cannot be sure and have no evidence that any of the gods are trying to get control of the Book, but you're the only one who'll be able to summon the power necessary to take back this control."

Shalee stood in silence a moment. "I'm not powerful enough for this. How do you expect me to fight the gods for control of the Book? I'm not able to command that kind of power. I can't even fathom this concept!"

"You'll be able to someday, Shalee, I assure you. The only reason I'm able to tell you this now is because the others don't know that I have been given my powers yet. This knowledge is sacred. This is my only chance to say anything without the worry of being watched. The Book of Immortality has passed this information to me after Bassorine's destruction for a reason and knows you could be the only thing to protect its existence if any of the gods find a way to take control of it. Make no mistake—there are those living on the hidden god world that are deceitful and hungry for power."

Shalee responded. "I believe you. I can only imagine with that kind of power that, there must be a ton of temptation to go with it. So what do I do?"

You'll become very powerful, but this power will also make you a target. I want you to be careful and, even though you are going to learn how to command powers like no one has done before you, unexpected danger will find you because of it. Don't use your powers unless you must, and try to avoid attention."

Shalee laughed in frustration. "How can I become powerful if I don't use my powers? It doesn't work that way. I have to use them in order to be able to grow stronger. It sounds to me like I'm screwed. This is a damned if I do and damned if I don't situation."

"I understand how your power works, Shalee and I know you must command them to grow stronger. I agree that you find yourself sitting on the blade of a double-edged sword. It is up to you to find a balance and try to grow without attracting attention. You can do what you want, but this is my warning to you. You'll know when you have become strong enough to worry, and then you can make the needed adjustments. I must leave before I run out of time. I have many goodbyes to say before I leave, and I suspect that someday you'll join me there. Speak of this conversation to no one, not even Sam."

"Why can't I tell Sam?"

Mosley sighed deeply. "You will be putting him in danger if he knows. I'll protect your thoughts so that this information cannot be stolen from you. Guard it well."

The wolf touched his paw to her foot to protect her thoughts from theft. Shalee asked him what he meant by protecting her thoughts, but he did not answer. He simply said to trust him.

"Just remember I'm the only one of the gods who has the knowledge of what Bassorine has done. Do not speak of this, and protect those whom you love, Shalee. Will you please tell Sam I forgive him for not saying goodbye, and I understand his excitement? Tell him I wish him the best in his fight. I also wish you well, Shalee. I'm sure this won't be the last time we speak. You can help Sam with your abilities if you put your mind to it, but I cannot tell you how to do so."

With that, the new Wolf-God of War vanished.

Chapter 16

𝕿𝖍𝖊 𝕱𝖎𝖌𝖍𝖙

SAM was angry when he came back from looking for a new pair of pants and Shalee was dying inside because she could not tell him anything Mosley had told her. It was a good thing for her that Sam had returned with an issue to attend to. It gave her a chance to focus on something else. She had never been good at keeping secrets but knew how important it was that she did not expose this one.

Sam had worked himself into a panic and was storming around the room.

"I can't go out there looking like this! I will be the laughing stock of the village. These trunks are too tight. I look like a giant Richard Simmons. I will be hung out to dry before I go out there looking like an enormous queer."

Shalee smiled and threw him his old pair of torn leather pants. "Put these on as best you can . . . I have an idea."

"Why would I do that? They don't even fit," he snapped.

"Just put them on as best as you can," she said, not liking his tone. "Let me try something. I have an idea that could fix both your pants and your boots."

Sam did as he was told and pulled the shredded mess on to his body. He watched as Shalee raised her staff and pointed it at him.

"Wait! What the heck are you doing with that thing? I don't want you blowing me up or something. Save all that hocus pocus for someone else."

"Don't be such a baby. I know what I'm doing. Now stand there and be quiet so I can concentrate."

Once again, she lifted her staff and pointed it at the leather pants. "Precious, lanne," she said with an authority that surprised her new boyfriend.

To his amazement, the leather started to grow and add to itself as if it were alive. It did not take long before he was standing in a perfectly formed piece of clothing.

"Holy cow, that's awesome! I'm going to thank you for this later!" he promised, lifting her in the air and planting a big kiss on her.

Shalee enjoyed the kiss, but in the back of her mind, she realized the staff had not rewarded her for the success. There would be no more tears of joy and she knew the intimate relationship with her petrified, wooden friend would soon be over. However, she grinned because now she had a replacement—her relationship with Sam. The timing could not have been more perfect—and she wanted to make Sam happy.

Sam lowered her to the floor, and Shalee once again commanded her staff to repair his boots. Like the pants, the leather mended itself and formed perfectly to his feet. Sam bent over to kiss her again as BJ walked into the room. All that the trainer could see was the large back of a much bigger man. Not recognizing his student, the trainer quickly turned to excuse himself, thinking he was in the wrong place.

Sam quickly called to him, "BJ, wait, it's me—Sam. Don't go!"

The trainer turned back, reentered the room, and stood there stunned. He could see it was Sam's face but nothing else resembled the man he knew. He rubbed his eyes as if he were in some sort of dream and looked again.

"Sam," BJ said slowly. "Is that you?"

"Yes, it's me. You aren't going to believe me when I tell you, but I have been given some gifts by our new God of War, Mosley."

The trainer pondered a moment before speaking. "Well if you mean your size, I can see that. Are you referring to the wolf? Isn't Mosley the wolf?" BJ was confused. "I thought Bassorine was the God of War?"

Before Sam could respond, the bell of the arena sounded. It was his turn to fight. On the way out of the room, he told BJ that he would explain everything later and made sure the trainer would watch his fight very closely. He wanted to get as much feedback from him after the fight as he could.

Sam was the first to enter the arena. He still did not know who his opponent was. As he entered, the crowd cheered. The atmosphere reminded him of the professional fight he had in Vegas, except for being outside and the mat being made of sand. The arena and style of fighting were far different than anything he had ever known, but the screams of the crowd remained the same. He raised his hands into the air and allowed himself to enjoy the moment.

He walked across the sandy surface to his position and grabbed his wooden stave. He moved it around, surprised that his actions were much quicker than they had been before. He smiled inside, realizing this was more of the benefits from Mosley's gift.

Then, his opponent entered the arena.

As if a light switch had been flipped, Sam's demeanor changed. He was all business as he sized up the man and moved across the arena floor to take his place. The adversary was a few inches shorter and much leaner. He did not look to be much of a threat until he started to move the wooden stave wildly around with great precision. Sam had never seen anything like it. The man's movements were so fast. Sam muttered under his breath, *"This is gonna hurt!"*

As he crossed the arena to engage the opposition, Sam reminded himself that there were no rules. In this world, a fight was a fight. No matter what happened, there was no referee to complain to about it. It did not matter if he took a shot to the groin, head-butt in the face, had sand thrown in his eyes, or any other cheap shot, he still had to fight his way through. It was the truest form of fighting a man could compete in.

The wooden staffs collided hard as they met, echoing across the arena as the people began to cheer. A quick crushing elbow followed—smacking the side of Sam's head and then another stinging strike fell against his upper back. He watched the man spin around effortlessly as he moved from one strike to the next. The force of the blow to his back made his nerves scream and was strong enough to knock him into a stumbling fall, but he managed to control it with a roll to his feet. Though a severe blow, he once again stood ready to defend himself. The pain sent a thunderous message: *"Pay attention!"*

Now the adversary attacked with the tip of his stave. The thrust—part of a combination of moves—was meant for Sam's belly, but he blocked it. The spinning leg following it, however, threw Sam to the ground and on his back.

As he fell, Sam saw the man continue the sweep back to his feet. Another powerful, potentially life-ending, downward strike headed his way, but again he managed to block it just before it made contact. If it had crushed into the side of his head the fight would have been over as well as his life.

Sam brought his leg up, twisting for the right angle as he did, and slammed his foot hard into the backside of the man's knees. This brought him to the ground, but his foe managed to land solid, ready to swing. Sam quickly rolled away to avoid the wicked slice which barely missed hammering into his face as he stood to ready himself for the next advance.

Sam backed up, taking the time needed to regain his composure. He moved far enough away to think, beginning to replay the downward strike meant for his head in his photographic memory. Even though the strike had been blocked, he realized it would have ended his life if it had connected. He knew his opponent was trying to do far worse than make him quit. Even the swing that had missed his face was powerful enough to cause permanent damage. His rival was not trying make him submit—he was trying to mutilate him.

Sam replayed both attempted strikes a couple more times in his mind. He felt like a dog backed into a corner. He knew he was out of his element and that turned his fear into an angry storm. He readied himself, but this time he would deliver the pain. He no longer had an opponent . . . he had an enemy.

The enemy rose from his knees and slowly moved toward Sam. Noting the change in Sam's eyes, he approached with caution. Sam began to circle his foe as his anger grew with each breath.

Some time passed as both men continued to size each other up. The opponent suddenly threw himself into a roll as Sam's raging mind took control and slowed every movement down so he could easily be defended. He watched his enemy come out of his roll and attempt to deliver a strike, but Sam was ready for him and blocked the blow. As his mind continued to slow down the advances, he blocked three other strikes meant for his head, stomach and groin. Uninjured, now Sam forcefully countered with a punch that landed solidly on his enemy's temple. The hilt of his wooden stave assisted the blow's impact, and his knuckles sunk deeper than normal.

Clearly stunned, his rival tried to reach out for him but Sam quickly spun away, escaping the man's grasp and keeping him off balance. As he exited his spin, he sent his stave cutting through the air towards his enemy's reaching forearms, breaking his left arm in the process. A loud crack filled the air sending the crowd into a frenzy.

Sam watched his enemy's wooden stave fall to the ground but, despite his broken arm, the man moved to retrieve the weapon he had dropped. Sam had no compassion; his rage had grown far too great and he was now out of control. The sound of the man's arm breaking, along with the crowd's cheers, fueled the fire inside of his hardened heart. He wanted vengeance for the attempt on his life, and once again he replayed it in his mind.

Sam struck his foe again, stopping him from retrieving his weapon and breaking the man's other arm as he reached for the staff. Another loud cracking sound could be heard, but this time it was not only his opponent's arm that broke. The contact was severe—severe enough that the wood of his weapon splintered into many pieces. Realizing it was now useless to defend himself with, Sam quickly adjusted. He forcefully snatched one of his adversary's limp arms and twisted it—enjoying his cries as the broken bones ground against each other. Sam yanked unmercifully, pulling toward him, feeling the limpness as if it were a wet rag. His enemy fell forward. Unable to catch himself, the man's face broke his fall, slamming him into the sandy surface of the arena as his scream of pain pushed the sand from his mouth.

With no opposition Sam's next strike was wide open. With both arms broken his enemy was unable to lift himself from the ground or defend himself in any manner. Sam's rage-filled insanity took no note of this helplessness and now without hesitation he jumped into the air and landed with a crushing knee to the base of the man's neck. A loud crunching sound covered up the cry of surrender. The screaming fans were fueled by the noise—the force of the strike leaving his opponent out cold. Sam was fighting like a merciless, rabid dog, unable to think of anything but the all-out victory.

He reached for the broken, right arm and twisted it into a triangle position behind his foe's back and woke the man from his unconscious state. He would have called out and surrendered, but he could not find the power to do so. Sam's boiling adrenaline ignored his enemy's defenseless position as again he raised his right leg high into the air and brought his 275 pounds down as hard as he could. It landed on top of the enemy's shoulder blade where his knee dug deep into the area between the scapula and the man's spine. The force was enough to break not only the scapula to the ribs beneath. The ribs tore violently away from the spine and, once again, bone-crushing sounds filled the arena.

This time the spectators did not cheer; they had become quiet, understanding the severity of what had happened to the fallen warrior. They all knew that this fight was not one meant to be to the death. But Sam's mind was cold and still in full survival mode. He couldn't consider the man's future, nor was he able to feel compassion for him as he was sure *this* man had tried to kill him. His angered fury forced him to keep going; Sam was now an insane torturer, not a fighter.

He rolled off the dead body and toward the stave that had been kicked away. His mind was clouded . . . unable to realize that his enemy was already dead. He delivered another series of thunderous blows, striking over and over again to the back, arms and head, ferociously tearing away at them like an enraged beast. Sam was lost to his own gentle soul, which for the moment could not claim him and turned away in rebuke. It was not until a voice cried out from the crowd to stop, that he gave pause.

It was Shalee—the only voice strong enough to bring him back from his insanity. Hearing her voice, Sam became aware of the man's lifeless body and his feelings returned and embraced him; the gentleness of the doctor produced a sorrowful remorse over what he'd done. He stopped and backed away from the body, grabbing his head with his free hand. Rage turned to disbelief, then horror and finally a tragic grief filled his soul.

He moved in and knelt on one knee. Slowly, he lowered the weapon to the ground and reached to feel for a pulse. Nothing, not a single beat could be found. A wave of emotion swept through him as he realized the consequences of what he had done. After letting out a penetrating cry from his knees, he fell back to a sitting position, brought his knees up, buried his head in his forearms, and wept uncontrollably.

The crowd was silent—not a whisper or comment, only shocked looks as they stared down at the arena floor watching Sam cry. The only sound heard was his sobbing. It was the first life he had ever taken. He not only took a life, but lost himself while doing it. He knew he was now a murderer . . . the antithesis of a healing physician. His heart weighed him down so that he could not move.

BJ calmed the nobles and instructed them that it would be a good time to leave. Once everyone had cleared the box, he ran to the arena where Sam continued to sit. The trainer had been in many fights in his life and knew full well the emotions that his distraught pupil was feeling. He once had lost control in the arena himself and paralyzed a young minotaur for life.

BJ arrived to find Shalee had already taken Sam into her arms, doing her best to comfort him. BJ reached down and lifted her up, motioning for her to come a few steps away and speak with him.

"Shalee, I admire your efforts to comfort him, but Sam's pain is something you can't fix. Until you have been in his shoes, you can't understand his inner torture. Please go back to the inn and wait for us there. I'll bring him to you. He's broken no laws and will not face any consequences."

BJ gave Shalee a quick wink and continued. "This is actually a good thing. This kind of gossip will spread quickly and will work in Sam's favor. As he fights in the other arenas of Grayham, his opponents will know of this outcome and this will instill fear in them, giving Sam an advantage."

Shalee had a hard time understanding BJ's candor. The barbarism of this world made her sick to her stomach. She whispered, "How can killing a man be okay, BJ? I should stay with him, he needs me! We're not from here. This isn't okay where we're from."

BJ pulled her close. "You need to trust me Shalee. Please, do as I ask and go. Men are the same . . . no matter where you're from, and this is not up for debate. Now go!"

Frustrated, Shalee did as BJ asked. She motioned to Helga that she was ready to go, grateful to have someone to talk with. However, before she left, Shalee asked BJ to do her a favor.

"Please tell him that I'm here for him when he's ready . . . and always will be." Having said what she needed to, Shalee left.

BJ moved to Sam, watching the arena mortician carry away the dead man on a stretcher. He turned his attention to the weeping fighter. "Are you going to sit there all night and feel sorry for yourself, or are you going to stand up, dust yourself off, and act like a man?"

Sam lifted his head but did not respond. He stood up and brushed himself off and began to walk.

"I know how you feel, Sam," BJ said, walking alongside him. "I once paralyzed a beast when I became enraged. The arenas of this world carry with them a lot of emotion and just as much death. You aren't the first to kill someone in the arena. You will come to terms with this, I promise. In a short while from now, your name will be known through the world. You, my friend, are going to be considered great some day."

BJ put his arm around his fighter, encouraging him all the way to the inn. When they arrived, he stopped Sam outside. The trainer spoke sternly but softly. "Sam, I want you to look in my eyes and let me know that you've heard everything I've said."

"I heard you," he replied. "I just don't know how to move on from here. I feel lost. I've never killed a man before. How do you move on from something like this? This goes against everything I believe in. I'm a doctor. I never wished to be a murderer!"

"You don't get over this. A man must learn from his experiences and use it to grow into a better person. You've done something awful . . . and I understand your pain. I also have beliefs and values, but sometimes we must adapt in order to survive. You'll be okay and you will eventually find peace again. You're a fighter, and we all understand the risk evolved when we enter the arena.

"The opponent you faced tonight has killed 12 men. I didn't know this until one of the nobles mentioned it. I would have stopped the fight, but it's against the laws of Grayham to do so. Only you and the man you faced could stop it. If you wouldn't have killed him, he may have killed you."

Sam thought a moment and realized BJ was right. The blow intended for his head could have killed him. "I see your point, and I agree he would've tried to kill me. This is just a tough pill for me to swallow right now. I need time to think!"

"I can tell you how I got over my anxieties if you really want to know. But you have to promise to take me seriously—and do exactly as I suggest. Are you going to listen to your trainer, Sam?"

"I promise, please tell me what to do," Sam said, expecting to hear some kind of great wisdom from the older man.

The trainer nodded. "I want you to take this seriously. Like me, when I had my experience, you also have something going for you like I did. Upstairs you have a beautiful woman, and there is no better counsel than a woman's touch. I want you to do what I did. Go up there and allow her to fix this. Women have a way of making things better. Shalee can make your pain seem less evasive and you'll heal much faster. If you still don't feel any better in the morning, I want you to come and find me."

BJ pulled Sam close and gave him a hug. "You'll be okay, son . . . I promise. You and I are going to be like father and son. I think that you're growing on me!"

Sam smiled slightly and returned the embrace. "I could use a father right now. Thanks BJ . . . you're not so bad after all."

After a moment, Sam entered the inn. As he did, almost every face in the place stopped and turned to watch him pass on his way up the stairs. The news of his victory had already reached them and no one uttered a word. Sam stopped and took a deep breath as he stood in front of the door to his room. He turned the knob slowly and entered...

To Sam's surprise, Shalee greeted him with open arms. She did not speak nor did she try to make anything better when he started to cry. She pulled him close and after sitting him on the edge of the bed, she held him for a moment. She lifted his chin from her bosom and whipped the tears from his eyes. Leaning forward she now kissed him ever so softly. Her eyes were filled with longing to be with him and she realized Sam's sadness was beginning to fade. Again she brushed her lips gently across the other areas of his face. Her checks met his, their warmth made him tremble. When she closed her mouth across the top of his ear and began to nibble, he was lost.

Sam took control and pulled her aggressively toward him with an enjoyable intensity that Shalee had never experienced before. Their longing for one another fueled their passion and they loved away the night.

The Grayham Inquirer

When inquiring minds need to know where their favorite characters are.

IT'S A NEW DAY in Grayham, time to rise and shine. Sam is lying with Shalee's head on his chest. The night had been explosive, passionate. Shalee feels extremely satisfied and her heart is filled with love. BJ was right; Sam feels much better. The lovers decide to snuggle for a while before getting up.

THE BOOK OF IMMORTALITY is preparing the ceremony to honor Bassorine's passing. The event will be held on top of the Falls of Faith, where Bassorine used to go and sit when he wanted to think. The other gods, once the ceremony ends, will turn their attentions to other things as if the late God of War never existed.

GEORGE, Kepler, and Kroger kept their fire going all night and are now cooking breakfast. Kepler had caught a meal for them just before they settled down for the night. They will go over the plans George made one more time before entering the cave.

BJ and Helga meet for breakfast and to discuss Sam's fight from the day before. They find as they talk, that they have much in common. Although neither speaks of it, there is a romantic interest growing between them.

CELESTRIA makes the best of her stay with the witch family, teaching them new potion recipes. She can't believe the family called themselves witches. They were idiots, but she knew they would not draw attention to her baby after he was born.

MOSLEY woke up inside his new home. Bassorine left behind a perfect place and the wolf was admiring his new view. He stood outside and looked into the valley below, taking a deep breath from high atop Catalyst Mountain.

LASIDIOUS is thinking through his plans for the near future. He misses Celestria and knows the time is approaching for him to step down as his team's leader. But he's okay with the change as it is just one more part of his master plan.

Thank you for reading the Grayham Inquirer

Chapter 17

A Fairly Good-Sized Rat

Illustrated By: Ian Ferrebee

The Cave of Sorrow

GEORGE took a deep breath. "Okay, so let's go over the plan once more before you go inside, Kepler. Kroger and I will stay out here and give you time to find a good spot to hide within the cave's shadows. We'll wait until you're set, then I'll climb to the top of the cave's entrance and hide while Kroger bangs his club hard into the ground to capture the beast's attention. Hopefully, he'll have enough curiosity to come and see what all the commotion is about. If he does, it should lead him past you. I want you to wait until he gets close to the cave's entrance before you try to push him out. Remember that you'll have to stop short of the entrance because of the spell the beast uses to control it. Even if it leaves the cave, we don't know what will happen to you if you try to exit. Once the beast is out, I will kill it with my gun. If I'm unsuccessful, then Kroger can bash it into a flat little pancake.

"Do we all understand that it may take a while for the beast to hear the commotion and come looking? It is, after all, one hell of a big cave. I'm counting on the walls inside to echo the sounds of Kroger's club hitting the ground."

Both Kepler and Kroger nodded. The demon headed inside as George watched the time on his Rolex. After a couple of hours, he climbed to the top of the cave and signaled for Kroger to start pounding at the spot he had circled on the ground.

The God World of Ancients Sovereign

MOSLEY awoke and stepped outside onto the porch of Bassorine's old home. The view was breathtaking. The cabin overlooked two valleys, one to the east, and one to the west and both valleys were filled with grazing animals. The home sat high on top of Catalyst Mountain. Bassorine had given the mountain its name. This had been his way to remember the many wars he had been the influence behind or better yet, the catalyst for.

The home itself was not unique, but none of the other gods lived in anything like it. Bassorine had been a rugged god and the dwelling he left behind was nothing more than a log cabin. When the god had visited Earth, he had seen that style of home; it suited him. And now, it fit Mosley as well. The wolf figured he might stay and worry about building another one later, if at all.

Today was a special day for Mosley. He would have a chance to meet all the gods for the first time. The Book of Immortality had said his introduction would be short and to expect a rush of interest in him after Bassorine's passing ceremony was over.

He spent a good portion of the night howling gleefully at the many different abilities he now possessed. All of them were useful, but he especially liked the fact that he could think of a rare steak and it would appear before him. He had enjoyed three or four of them before he went to sleep, ignoring the fact that he would never need to eat again if he chose not to. Now, he had to look good for the ceremony, knowing the gods were snobs. A bath, no matter how much he hated them, was in order since he didn't want to turn up any noses.

Back at the Cave of Sorrow

HOURS passed while George sat patiently above the cave's entrance, listening as Kroger continued to slam his club hard into the ground. It caused a dreadful noise, which taxed his nerves. A hole formed at the center of the clearing as a result of the devastating slamming—a good five feet across and equally as deep, with trees resting atop the pass shaking with every hit. George told himself it might take a while, but he had not calculated on the boredom he would feel sitting in one spot for so long.

Suddenly to his surprise, something scurried out—which could not have been the beast. The creature was not hideous at all. George opened and closed his eyes in disbelief, straining to get a better look. It was a large rat of some sort, still small enough to fit into his pack. He watched closely as the rat rose up in front of Kroger and looked toward the giant.

The ogre grabbed his head, lowered himself to the ground and once he was sitting on his large butt, he started to cry. George knew for sure by the way Kroger was reacting that it was Maldwin. The visions had an instantaneous effect on the giant. He realized that he needed to protect himself before anything else happened. He read from the scroll that Morre had given him with the giant's booming cry covering his voice as he spoke its words to release the spell that would shield his mind. As before when he used the Snare Scroll, the paper vanished into thin air when he was done.

A new plan was in order. The original plan was not going to work since Kroger was no longer any help. He knew his pistol would work fine since the beast was small, but his intentions had changed and shooting the rodent was now a last resort.

Watching from above, George observed the way the visions affected Kroger, and an idea started to form in his mind. He would make himself known to the rat, acting in a similar manner to the ogre. But instead, he would not sit on his butt and cry, but rather he would pretend to be sad as he walked around and try to get close enough to the creature to trap it. Adding the rat's abilities to his new group would be a nice benefit. If Maldwin's ability were salvageable, killing him would be a waste.

He climbed down from the top of the cave, careful to make as little noise as possible. For the moment, Maldwin had his back to him. In his mind, George ran over the plan once more. He still felt it was worth a shot, especially with the scroll protecting him. What harm could it do to try? He questioned his judgment one more time, but the answer was the same. The rat's talent may come in handy . . . he had to try. The plan could backfire, but he was prepared to shoot the creature if needed.

He reached the ground and noticed that Kepler was close to the entrance, but back far enough not to disturb the magic cast upon it. He turned, pulled his old shirts from his pack and wrapped his hands for protection in case the beast decided to bite.

George was now within 10 feet of Maldwin; the rat still had no idea he was there. Suddenly George lunged into the air and landed on top of the creature, who let out a squeal of terror as George closed his covered hands around the critter's body. Lifting Maldwin into the air, the successful hunter of rats laughed.

"I got you, you little snot!" he shouted. "Your visions don't work on me. I bet you never saw it coming did you?" George carefully set the terrified little creature on the ground, pinning him there, waiting for him to tire.

Maldwin squealed uncontrollably, but struggle as he might he could not break free or bite his captor to release the grip. George laughed as he watched. Eventually, Maldwin became tired and his body relaxed. George adjusted his hold to one hand, then reached under his pant leg and drew his pistol. He pointed it at Maldwin's head and spoke to him.

"Can you talk, rat?" He waited for a response as he tightened his grip. "I asked if you can talk! Every other damn thing in this world can talk, so you'd better be able to." When nothing came from the beast, he continued. "This is the last time I'll ask you . . . and if I hear nothing, I'm going to kill you!"

Again nothing, George lifted his pistol and was about to pull the trigger when suddenly the rat spoke. "As sel a ip te yalema quay!"

The words were clearly a language, but nothing George could understand. "English, you little freak, speak English. Do I look like I speak Ratanese?"

From inside the entrance of the cave, Kepler shouted, "He wants you to spare his life and he'll do anything you want."

"You understand this . . . this . . . this—"

"He's a rat," Kepler snapped. "What's wrong with you? I do understand him. He's scared of you, stop yelling at him. You've made your point, yelling no longer serves a purpose. Besides, your letting the excitement affect your brain."

George thought a moment.

Okay I have to think faster than this. Be smart, George.

"Well, don't you have many talents... it looks like having you around is going to be quite useful. I have a linguist and a politician all wrapped up in one big, furry, undead, jaguar demon. This is going to be the start of a long, beautiful friendship, my friend. Remind me to treat you well as we travel, Kepler. I shouldn't have doubted you or your abilities . . . you make me proud!"

George made sure that Kepler saw his big smile, knowing that this simple reassurance would go a long way. The jaguar seemed nervous around him the last few days, so he figured being complimentary, however untrue it was, would help him relax. Yes, his manipulative mind was truly working better now.

Kepler did feel a sense of relief when George said these things, and shouted from the cave something that only he and the rat could understand. "Uh uyat gote say."

George watched the rat twist its head after hearing Kepler; and responded, "Le fuat yoor tekle."

Kepler walked from the cave and back into the open. He moved close to George and sat down. "I told him to release his magic on the entrance and I would help him talk with you. What would you like me to do? Do you want me to translate?"

The manipulator thought a moment. George had no idea how stupid he was about to sound. "That sounds good, Kepler, thanks a lot. I have so much for you to tell him. Tell him that it's clear that neither you nor I are affected by his visions. Tell him that I don't intend to kill him. Tell him that I would like it if he would join us on our travels. Tell him that we intend to seek control of this world. Tell him I offer him a chance to do something other than live in the cave and that I would like to employ his ability to use his visions so that we can put them to better use. Tell him that killing everyone who enters his cave is pointless and will solve nothing and that if he does travel with us, soon there will be amazing rewards for him. Tell him a life of luxury will follow and that you and I will soon rule this land and he would be wise to stay with us. Tell him I've decided to ask this of him but if he says no, I won't harm him. Tell him I want something from inside his cave, and after I have retrieved it, I'll let him go if he decides not to join us. I think that if you tell him all that, it should be good enough for now."

Kepler smiled as a jaguar would. He looked at George and for the first time since they had met, he decided to make a joke. "Really, that's it, nothing else? Are you sure? Are you absolutely positive that's all? You want me to tell him, tell him, tell him, tell him, tell him, tell him, and finish it off by telling him some more. Are you sure that you don't want me to tell him something else? You might want to tell him you need to know his mother's name. You might want me to tell him you need to know his sister's name or you might want me to tell him you need to know his aunts' and uncles' names while I'm at it. I can tell him you need every family member's name, right? I would hate for you to miss an opportunity for me to tell him something. It's not like you've given me enough to tell him yet. Will that be all I should tell him or would you like me to tell him anything else? After all, telling him is what you want, right? How about I tell him right now? Should I tell him right now, boss man? Tell me what to do. Please tell me. If you don't tell me, I might not know when you want me to tell him!"

George caught the sarcasm and rolled his eyes. "Just tell him!"

The demon cat laughed hard and, after a few moments of speaking with Maldwin, began to translate, "Okay George, he said to tell you . . ."

George broke in quickly. "Okay, I get it all ready. I sounded like a bloody idiot. You've made your point."

Kepler chuckled. "All right, he'll travel with us . . . and he also hates the cave. He's lived in this place only because he and his family were trying to avoid being hurt by the humans of this world. Much of his family was killed by them, so he's hated your kind ever since. He only uses his visions as a way to defend them. He's the sixth generation to live in the cave. He has many relatives inside, but he's the only one who has this ability to use the visions to make the humans go away. The little guy can manipulate the visions for many different kinds of emotions, not just sadness. He said there is only one within his family who can command the gift at any given time. It was the gods who originally gave this gift to them. The skill is passed down to each generation, and his family decides who will be given the gift when the one who possesses it dies. He doesn't know the name of the god who gave them the gift, but he thinks it was a woman.

"Apparently his family was originally given the gift as a way to help out with some sort of test. He doesn't remember the details of the test, but he does know that this is why they received the power. He knows a group of dwarves were to be kept out of the cave. The family was to use this gift on them, but the dwarves never showed up. I guess they had something to do with the test. His family decided it was something they would use to keep the humans away once they had the power; it is a comfort to them."

Kepler's dark heart remembered the reason why the dwarves had died. He had been friends with the Serpent King Sotter long ago, and knew it was the snake who had murdered them, but he never knew why the snake did it. The King had a runner deliver a message asking him to keep his cats from attacking in the Enchanted Forest. The message was that he had some dwarves to kill near the Pool of Sorrow, and that they had a map of his kingdom. He was going to go get it back and did not want any interference from Kepler's subjects. The message never said what the dwarves were doing at the pool, or anything about them going into the cave. He had only pieced it together from what Maldwin had told him.

Kepler suddenly realized George had the map. He could only guess, but he figured that George intended on making the serpents serve him, or use it in some other way to gain power over them. The map must have secrets of how to do that, and the demon now wished he had cared more about what the Serpent King was doing. He didn't know why the map would take George inside the cave if it was about the serpent's kingdom. Back then, he had ignored the ruler of the snakes because he knew of the king's problems with his memory, having hidden successfully countless times within the shadows of the Serpent King's underground city. But why would the dwarfs need to enter the cave as a test? That must be the reason George was going into the cave. Was this why Sotter wanted the map back so badly? He would wait to find out once the human exited the cave with the answer. George did, after all, say he had something to retrieve. He thought it best not to say anything for now since he couldn't do anything about it anyway. George was too powerful and would destroy him if he tried to force the answers out of him. Besides—his friendship with the man was growing, and he could see that George's mind looked for an opportunity in every situation. Maybe this was not a bad alliance after all.

Kepler continued. "Maldwin said that if you give him and his family a place to stay, a place safe from harm, he will travel with you and be loyal. He has asked me to get your word that you'll provide this place once you have gained the power to do so. He has also asked us to seal the cave once you have whatever it is you seek inside. Apparently his family can use other smaller escapes they have created through the years to seek food. He wants to say goodbye to his family before we leave. This is very important to him. He promised his loyalty many other times in the conversation as well."

George thought a moment and looked at Kepler. "Do you believe what he says and feel we can trust him?"

"I do believe him and I think he could come in handy. I must admit, I like the way your mind works. This little guy doesn't have an evil bone in his body, but he'll do whatever it takes to protect his family. I would allow him to come if I were you. I think I can teach him to speak with you as we travel."

George smiled. "Tell him." He stopped and realized what he said. He was about to do it again. He took a deep breath and continued. "Oh, my hell, don't *tell* him anything . . . *inform him* that I'm agreeable to everything he's said and wants. I would like him to stay out here with you while I retrieve what I've come for."

"When I come out, Kroger can seal the cave after the rat has said goodbye to his family. Oh, and please ask him to give Kroger some better visions. I'm sick of listening to the big ox cry. My hell, I'm about to go nuts. All this sobbing is killing my ears. I would hate for the big guy to smash our little friend here into a rat pancake once he releases him from the sad crap he is seeing. Maybe some happier thoughts would be a good idea to stop this from happening."

Kepler communicated everything to the rat and it didn't take long before Kroger's crying turned to smiles. The big guy warmly hugged himself and started to sing in gorilla tongue. George rolled his eyes at the sight. "You've got to be kidding me. The retard is snuggling himself now. How did I ever sign up for this? I don't remember the application for this job asking if I ever had any experience with gentle, giant morons! Give me a break," he said, throwing his hands up, and entering into the cave. "I'll be back soon. Keep an eye on them both, Kepler, will ya please? I think you'll love it, if I can find it."

The demon watched as he disappeared into the darkness. He couldn't wait to finally get the answers to his questions. What did the dwarves want in the cave and was it the same thing George was after? He pondered this a bit, allowing himself to get lost in thought, and could not figure out why he hadn't connected the dots until now.

Finally, he turned to face Kroger. He also understood gorilla. This reason alone allowed him to befriend the giant long ago. The knowledge of the language had saved him from being smashed into jaguar mush by his club. He shook the thought off and watched the simple-minded, big fella sing. The song was a lullaby his gorilla mother had sung to him as a baby when going to sleep. Even Kepler's vicious heart had to smile at the sight of this pathetic-looking sweetness.

George made his way into the cave and opened the map. He waited for his eyes to adjust. Realizing more light was needed, he pulled out a torch from his pack. He fumbled around in the dark and came across an old antique cigarette lighter passed down from his great, great grandfather. This was actually a lie he told everyone. He had really stolen the lighter from a Vietnam veteran while doing some charity work for the VA hospital in Orlando. He refilled the old lighter not too long ago and could use it many more times before it ran out of fluid. It was a one of a kind and he carried it everywhere he went, despite the fact that he didn't smoke.

He lit the torch and studied the map once again. Once he had his bearings, he headed for the secret door. The cave was moist and wet inside, the floor slick and smooth, like massive amounts of water had raged through them through them for years. He'd have to be careful of his footing. He would have grabbed onto the walls for better balance but they were just as slippery as the floor. It was clear why it took eight days to go from one end of the cave to the other. Hurrying would only cause him to fall. There was one good thing about the smooth wet surfaces though: when light was cast on them, it reflected and lit the cave nicely.

It took him an hour to get to where the door was marked on the map. He sat the torch down to free up his hands, careful not to let any of the moisture on the floor extinguish the flame. He moved toward the walls and reached out to feel around. Thinking there was some kind of hidden latch or switch to toggle. He moved his hands all over, feeling his way... but found nothing.

Frustrated, he went for the torch and picked it up. He held the burning stick high above his head and let the light fill the room. He might need to ask his new rat friend for assistance. That is when he noticed a spot, about 20 feet deeper into the cave, where the light was not reflecting. George moved toward the area and stood in front of it, again holding the flame high. It was as if the light went through the wall and outlined an entrance, yet it still looked to be solid.

It was worth a shot. Again his hand reached for the slick surface. He intended to feel around the wall, but instead the solid-looking surface faded away in front of him. His hand had destroyed the magic's illusion as it passed through and revealed the path ahead. Without wasting any more time, he stepped inside and followed the short corridor that opened up into a room. This world continued to surprise him. At every little turn something happened, whether it was magic snare scrolls catching big cats, rats speaking, undead demons walking, giant ogres lifting or magic staffs hiding . . . it was all amazing.

At the end of the corridor, he found a room, not deep, but long. Turning his head to his left, he finally saw what he was here for ... it was just sitting there in all its glory. The staff rested on top of a heavy stone table not more than 30 feet from him.

He became nervous as he approached the table, his mind wild with thought.

I've seen something similar in movies back home. Okay George, just move slowly, watch every step. This room's floor isn't like the others. It's not wet either. Something has protected it and has kept it safe from the elements. Every footstep could be your last. This is taking forever; it's only 30 feet for hell's sake. Now I know how Indiana Jones must've felt. I'm so dead. I'm gonna get my head taken off by some kind of blade. What if it comes out of a wall? What if it hits me between the legs? I don't want to lose my privates. This place has to be trapped. Find the traps George, you can do this. What if I can't do this? What if I've come all this way and now, I'm cut into tiny little pieces? What if I should turn around? Maybe that's what the people who made this place want me to do. They want me to turn around and that's when I'll take a spear to the gut. Something is gonna jump out and get me. I'm so dead. I'm so dead.

His mind continued to race as he looked for possible booby traps. When the staff was within reach, he scanned the table and the area around it, the mental torture he imposed on himself intense.

Why is this room so different than the rest of the cave? If the staff is so powerful, it should have traps to protect it. Why haven't any of the traps cut me up yet? I could still die if I lift the staff and it's rigged to kill. That's the answer. The traps are rigged to go off when I take it. The stinking staff is the trigger! Why didn't I think of this until now? I'm in my own personal hell. I'm so dead!

Sweat built up on his forehead as heavy as when he ran marathons. He scanned the table, walls, ceiling and floor for anything out of the ordinary. He could not see anything but a few small cracks. Overall, nothing was there that seemed alarming. Standing frozen in place, he could not make himself reach for the staff. He knew it was a trap and his life was in danger. He scanned the room again, his heart pounding. George knew if he did not take the staff, he would live for now. But he also knew that he would not be able to defend himself once Kepler figured out he was powerless. Either way, he was sure he would die.

Damned if I do . . . and damned if I don't.

He was in a bad spot and now, more than ever, he wanted to go home.

Finally, after what seemed like hours of standing there staring at the staff, he gathered the courage. Reaching out to take it, he breathed deeply, slowly letting it out and then breathed deep again. Counting in his mind, *ONE... TWO... THREE...* he quickly lifted the staff from the table and ducked down. He expected things to fly out of the walls as he closed his eyes tight and waited for the final blow, but nothing happened.

Nervously, he stood up and looked around. He was still in one piece, but the experience had left him shaken. He began speaking to the empty room. "I guess there are no poison arrows on this trip, aye guys?" Looking around for someone to answer, George realized his insanity and started to laugh, breathing freely once again.

"I certainly hope a big rolling rock doesn't chase me out of here, guys. Thanks for the staff. I promise to put it to good use." Slowly George worked his way out of the room. Despite his cynical joking, he continued to look over his shoulder for a large rolling boulder... but one never came.

Chapter 18

A Big Stone Statue

GEORGE decided, before leaving the cave, he would stop long enough to drill a hole in the butt end of the staff. He wanted to drink the liquid inside its hollow center and ingest the power Jason told him about. The wood was hard; even with the sharp point of his knife; it was taking forever to make a hole. He looked at his watch and realized he had been at it for over five hours. But finally, the staff gave way and revealed the liquid within. He held the hole tight to his mouth and lifted the staff high. He directed the flow to pour into the back of his throat beyond his tongue, avoiding the taste as much as possible, just in case it was vile.

He thought the draining would never stop. It was difficult to take in this much fluid without tasting it no matter how hard he tried. Luckily the drink went down smooth and it did not trigger a gag reflex. He swallowed all of it, careful not to miss a single drop. Lowering the staff to the ground, he waited for something wonderful to happen. He thought of the movies and pictured how the receiving of a power should look. But nothing happened, not a single tingle or quiver did he feel. No white light, lightning or loud noises; George only experienced an upset stomach from drinking so much so fast.

Maybe Jason was wrong. Maybe the liquid in the staff didn't give the power to turn things into stone after all. He thought he should feel differently somehow if it had worked. He looked at the staff lying on the cave floor. After a moment, his thoughts focused and he grabbed it tightly. Try as he might, the staff would not change. He had to be doing something wrong, or Jason was misinformed. He hoped, with everything in him that it was just a matter of time before he figured it out.

When he exited the darkness of the cave, the sun had already gone down. Everyone was sitting by a fire that Kroger had made. It was Kepler who noticed him first.

"I thought you were never going to come out of there. Pretty slick in there, isn't it? I thought maybe you might have fallen and hit your head."

"It's definitely slick. It took me forever to find what I was after." He threw the emptied staff toward Kepler's feet. "Here it is!"

Kroger became excited when he saw the staff. "Oh, George you got pretty stick us play with. Kroger like play stick. Let him have," the giant said as he reached down to pick it up. The staff broke under the weight of his hand, leaving a sharp point on one of the pieces that wedged beneath one of his huge fingernails. The beast man cried out in pain and big tears began to flow from his eyes, falling heavily to the ground. Kepler tried to console the gentle giant, but nothing worked. The demon could not get him to stay still long enough to remove the massive splinter.

"It hurted Kroger," the giant screamed as he sobbed. "Stick mean to Kroger. Make stick stop pain to Kroger. I no like stick no more, George." He threw himself on the ground and held his finger tightly with his other hand.

Kepler stood there, lost as to how to handle the situation. Kroger's foot slammed down from his fit, nearly smashing Maldwin.

"George, make stick no hurt Kroger, George. You give Kroger mean stick. I no like stick no more, George."

This carried on for quite some time. The giant baby rolled around without regard to the safety of the others. At one point, he caught a couple pieces of the wood in the fire and sent them flying. Everyone was running around to avoid being squashed. George had seen enough; his breaking point had been reached.

George exploded with all his energy. "Shut up, you stupid retard! If you don't shut the hell up, I'll leave you here by yourself!"

Everyone became quiet, even Kroger. Babysitting the big giant was going to be a big pain in the butt and George knew it.

"Kroger, listen to me," George screamed. "Sit up right now!" The giant did as he was told. "Don't make another noise. I want you to stop your whining. I'm going to fix your finger and you're going to stay still. If you don't do this, George will be very mad at Kroger. Do you understand me?"

The giant nodded as another tear fell to the ground and splashed next to George's foot. He sighed and stuck his hand out. As George walked toward it, the giant turned his head, took a deep breath and held it as he prepared for the pain.

George snapped out a few more comments before he removed the big splinter. "I've never seen a bigger baby in my life. You would think someone was going to kill you, Kroger. I'm so sick of listening to your whining. I just want you to be still a while."

With all that being said, George reached out and grabbed the sliver. He sized up the situation and leaned in to lay his other free hand on the end of the giant's finger. Suddenly, to his surprise, the skin started to turn gray and began spreading. Quickly the grayness moved past his finger and throughout the giant's hand. George jumped back and moved away, watching in horror. Nothing could be done to stop it; he knew this was going to look bad to the others. He looked at Kepler.

"What's happening?" Kepler said excitedly. "What did you do to him? This wasn't necessary. Stop this now, George."

The giant watched as the change moved up his arm. "What happen me? I no feel my arm. It sleeps, yes?" The beast man was confused and could not understand. He continued to speak. "I make sleep stop, arm wake. I wake now. You see, George."

The Ogre's arm was heavy now as it turned to stone. Kroger struggled to lift it into the air. The collision it made when it slammed into the ground shook the area around them, adjusting the fire which rekindled itself. The entire forearm crumbled into rubble. Kroger now understood it was George's fault that this was happening to him. "My arm rock, George. Why you do me this? You hurt arm more. Why? Are George not friend to Kroger? You no like Kroger no more? Kroger like George. Kroger be good. George to fix Kroger. Please, George, no make Kroger die."

Kepler nervously backed away from his human travel companion. "You're turning him to stone. His whining was not that bad. Stop it before he dies."

George had no idea what to do. He looked at the ogre and spoke softly. "I didn't mean to do this Kroger. George does like you. I'm so sorry, big guy. You're my friend and I'm sorry. Please forgive me."

The grayness was growing faster now, passing through the giant's shoulder. Soon it would reach his heart and there was nothing he could do to stop it. All he could do was stand there and watch. Before the last beat could be finished, his heart became solid and the giant knew it was over. Kroger's eyes, filled with confusion as he looked deep into George's heart. George could feel his heart breaking.

Kroger's speech grew softer as the last of his air left his body. "It okays, George. I like George, me still friend." That was the last thing the 30-foot-tall, gentle giant would ever say.

Kepler slowly walked around the statue. He didn't know what to think. He felt George had done it intentionally, but his demeanor, standing with his head lowered, said something different. He had even apologized to the giant and it seemed sincere. Was it an act, or was he truly sorry and could not stop the change? How did he do it?

The rat asked the jaguar demon what to do, and, for now, he responded by telling him to stay put. He needed time to get to the bottom of this. Why would he want to turn Kroger to stone? The giant would have simply left if he had been told to. It did not make any sense. The ogre could have been a tremendous ally.

"George, I don't want to make you mad, but this doesn't seem to be something a man with your intelligence would do," the demon said. "Even with his whining, the big guy could have been an asset to us. Will you please explain your logic here? I would hate to think you're this irrational, temper or no temper. This seems stupid and not something a man seeking power would do before he gets it."

"I know, I know, I can't explain this," George replied. "I didn't mean for this to happen. I never wanted to harm the big guy. I have no idea how to control this power I received from the staff. I didn't think it worked. I need to figure out how to control this quickly, or I'll be turning everything I touch into stone."

"What are you talking about? Are you saying that you can turn anything to stone and you have no clue how to control it? This is the power you went into the cave for? How could this be? The staff is broken! Don't you have to use the staff to control the power? It broke, so how could this be?"

The demon was having a hard time concentrating with Maldwin shouting in his ear. The furry critter was confused and scared. He wanted to know some answers. The cat turned to the small beast and again asked him to relax while he figured it out.

George looked up, motioned with his hand for Maldwin to calm down and moved to sit down. He reached down to balance himself on a tree that he had Kroger fetch the night before. He asked the big guy to bring him a small stump to sit on, but instead, he returned with an entire tree. He had laughed when he saw it and figured that, to Kroger, it probably was small. George had called him his adorable, retard that night.

Before he could finish lowering himself, he noticed a bug was resting where he intended to sit. He reached down and flipped the centipede-looking creature from the spot. The creature flew through the air and before it hit the ground, it was rock solid. He backed away quickly and so did the others.

"See what I mean? Now what? The staff had a liquid in it that I drank. I was supposed to be able to turn things into stone when I wanted to, not every time I touched something. The power should work in such a way that I can walk up to anything and change whatever part of it I choose. For example let's take you, Kepler. I should be able to walk over and touch you and turn your leg to stone and leave the rest of you unharmed. It looks to me that no matter what I do, it's all going to turn to stone. I'm all ears if you have any ideas on this. I swear to you that I didn't want to hurt Kroger. Sure, he was a retard, but he was also likable. I would never hurt someone I had an alliance with on purpose, no matter how much they annoyed me. I would send them home first. It makes no sense to kill my friends. I might have needed him someday!"

Kepler explained the situation to Maldwin. The rat was freaking out and asking a million questions. He was not going to stop, so it was best to talk with him. As he explained the situation, the rat's mood seemed to settle down quite a bit. When the rodent finally calmed down and was able to reply that he understood, he related a story of a similar situation he had been involved in. The creature had come close to killing his own mother when he received the gift of the visions. He could not control them at first. It took the family watching around the clock to keep his mother from jumping into one of the deep shafts inside the cave. The point Maldwin was trying to make was that he could understand how this whole situation could be a tragic accident. But, despite his understanding, the rat asked the demon to tell George to avoid touching him.

George waited patiently for Kepler to translate. When Kepler finished relaying everything to him, he felt much better. The alliance with the two of them was strained, but still intact.

George looked at Kepler. "So what the hell do you think I should do to get control of this?" he said anxiously. "I don't want to accidentally turn you and our little rat friend here into statues. Do you have any ideas?" He moved back to sit on the tree.

Kepler thought a moment. This was new to him; his abilities had always been under control. After a bit, he came up with a solution.

"Okay, so it seems to me that you'll need to be able to practice in order to figure out how to command the power. Since you've left the cave, I've seen two things turn to stone that you've touched. The first was Kroger, and the second was the bug. I've also seen two things that you have touched that have not turned to stone. The first was the staff that wedged under Kroger's fingernail and the second was the tree when you touched it to lower yourself down onto it. So if I'm right in my observations, you have only turned things to stone that are made of flesh and blood. I think that you need to start practicing. Seems simple enough and—"

George interrupted. "I can't go around touching every living thing I see. I will kill it all and leave a trail of stone that leads right to us."

Kepler laughed and replied, "No, no, no, what if I told you that I have things you could practice on? Things already dead, made of bone. Bone is a part of us, so you should be able to practice on them. You won't have to kill anything, I promise."

George sighed, "I would say that sounds a hell-of-a-lot better. Where will we do this, and what things are you referring to?"

The demon looked at Maldwin, then back to George. "Well, it seems to me that we promised this little guy that you would seal the cave, and without Kroger, this will be impossible for us to do. So, my plan is, I'll summon 300 of my skeletal warriors from my pass. You can practice on them until you learn how to command the power and make it work. I can summon more if need be, but once we get to 541, I'll be fresh out of ideas and you'll have to practice on living creatures. This should also solve our problem with Maldwin here. We both know that for a while you won't be able to control the power, and we'll have a few intimidating look-ing statues on our hands. I suggest we start at the mouth of the cave and, as you go, we'll leave these stone skeletons along the entire length of the pass. This will leave quite the impression for anyone who comes this way. I think our little friend here will agree that his family should be safe. The skeletal warrior statues, com-bined with this big ogre here should frighten most anyone. Even I would hesitate if I saw something like that—and I command these warriors."

George became excited once again. "That's an awesome idea. Are you sure you don't mind me practicing on your warriors? What about your home and the protection they provide?"

Kepler smiled and jumped up into Kroger's stone lap to lie down. "I said you had to stop at 541. I never said that's all the warriors I commanded. I'll still have an even 100 guarding my pass. I can always create more as we travel. I do like man flesh you know, especially the evil ones that I can make serve me. There is something I'll want for this, but I'll call in that favor later. Do we have a deal?"

"It's a deal." George moved to shake his paw but thought better of it. "We'll have to shake on it later, I think. When will the war-riors arrive?"

Kepler let out a low roar. Behind him sat two rocks at the base of the cliffs. Two black jaguars made themselves known to the group and appeared before George's eyes. He had a clear view from where he sat and watched the beasts jump down within the light that the fire cast in their direction. They were equally as large and intimidating as Kepler—seeming to appear out of thin air.

George's heart rate went through the roof, but he maintained his position on the tree. Kepler had his posse with him this whole time and he had not known it. It was not a good feeling, but he'd be damned before he'd show any weakness to the cat. He had been through this once before with Kepler, but this time he had a true advantage and not just his bluff. He calmed himself down and waited for more information.

Maldwin, on the other hand, despite the human's inability to control his new power, jumped up and sat next to George for protection. The little rat was having one hell of a bad day. His world had been turned upside down. He had been jumped on, threatened, pinned down, yelled at, and negotiated with, joined George's group and, if that was not enough, he was sitting here with three very large cats not far from him moving in his direction. He felt like dinner. Cat and mouse was not a game he wanted to play today.

"George, allow me to introduce my brothers, Keller and Koffler. The three of us are identical to one another. I'm the oldest, by only moments at birth. This is how I create the perception that I'm everywhere within Skeleton Pass. We work together to keep everything within the pass under our control. I will send my brothers to collect my undead army. It will take 12 Peaks of Bailem before they arrive."

George took a deep breath and responded. "So you're the oldest and the leader?"

"I am the eldest and the leader. The power to control the skeleton warriors is only mine to command, but I've given my warriors commands to follow. My brothers can use these commands to send word for them to come. My brothers will be good to have around at times, and could help us out when needed."

"Well, I guess I can see why you're not concerned with keeping your home protected. It looks to me like you have plenty of backup," George responded. "Twelve days is a long time. Why don't we leave Maldwin here? We can run to Lethwitch and stock up on some supplies? This will kill a good six or seven of those days. If we take our time and stay a couple nights, it will give me an opportunity to experiment with this new power and maybe I can find something to put over my hands. When I touch my clothes they don't change to stone, so maybe a pair of gloves would act the same way."

Kepler agreed and sent his brothers back to his home. He looked at Maldwin and told him that it would be awhile before they left the area. The rat said he understood and would wait until they returned. With that, George and Kepler headed for Lethwitch.

The Grayham Inquirer

When inquiring minds need to know where their favorite characters are.

IT'S A NEW MORNING on Grayham, and Sam is getting ready to catch one of the hippogriffs to travel to his next fight. Shalee is making the trip with him, along with their trainers. The next arena is located just outside a town called Lethwitch. They intend to stay there a week before moving on to the next town.

Upon further communication with BJ, Sam decides that if he is going to gain the fame needed to meet the King of Brandor, he must fight twice a week over the next 11 weeks—22 fights in all—and hopefully win every one of them. His ambitions are adding up to one city, town or village each week, until it is time to fight in the City of Champions for the Golden Chalice of Brandor.

MOSLEY attended the ceremony honoring Bassorine's passing. He has also decided to join Bailem's team. He is with them now, giving them a rundown of everything he knows, or at least everything Bassorine would have wanted him to share.

MALDWIN called his entire family out of the cave. They have gathered around the stone statue of Kroger as the rat explains that he will leave with his new travel companions and soon they will have a better, safer place to live. He can only hope that George will be okay with the size of his family. There were easily over 150 of them—and all were asking questions.

GEORGE and Kepler are on their way to Lethwitch. They have walked through the night and both agreed to stop for a rest after the Peak of Bailem. George set the alarm on his watch to ring five hours later, and shows his jaguar friend how the Rolex works, since he was asking questions about the device... questions George wishes to avoid answering.

CELESTRIA is going nuts. The elven witch family has been nagging her to answer all the questions their small minds can conjure up. If it were not for her baby's safety, she would have left already.

ATHENA is sitting behind the counter at her work, going through the logbook and singing. She has been happy since her breakfast with George, and looks forward to seeing him once again.

LASIDIOUS is ready to step down as team leader. All the gods have been called to a meeting, scheduled for Late Bailem. He plans to announce where he is going to put one of the pieces of crystal.

Thank you for reading the Grayham Inquirer

Chapter 19

𝔚𝔥𝔞𝔱 𝔍𝔯𝔬𝔫𝔶

®eorge and Kepler's Napping Spot

"OKAY, so you have your Rolex watch," Kepler said after hearing much of what George had explained. "I understand it keeps what you call 'the time' according to your Earth's day, which has 24 hours—and it takes 24 hours for your sun to rise, travel across the sky, then rise again. And I understand what you call a 'minute.' You know, I think it would make things much easier if we had something like your Rolex to plan our days by. You should keep track of this so-called time and see if one of our days is similar to one from your Earth. But what I don't understand is how you got here."

"Well, that's the fuzzy part for me too... one minute, I'm driving with this beautiful woman in an RV—I'll explain what an RV is later. I was delivering it to a customer's house, and the next thing I knew, her eyes changed color, her teeth grew sharp and the cold... oh, the cold was like little needles to the skin. The next thing I know, I'm waking up in a great hall with huge pillars and golden double doors. I was one of three appearing in that hallway. Once I realized the others weren't a threat, I introduced myself. They were both from my world and, like myself, had no idea what was going on. The man said his name was Sam, a pompous chump, if you ask me, but he was quite smart. The woman, wow, she was annoying and not worth talking about. We found a statue, and this guy Sam was able to read what was on it. It had a prophecy about the three of us and also talked about a crystal. I think he called it the Crystal Moon."

The jaguar demon interrupted. "The crystal, you mean the Crystal Moon in the Temple of the Gods?"

"Don't know for sure. I can't remember since everything was so crazy that day. The inscription on the statue talked of man's great victories and how he brought home the power the gods had lost to control worlds. Apparently this power, which Sam said the Crystal Moon generates, is what keeps the five planets from colliding into each other. It said something about the planets all rotating the same distance around a single sun. I know there's more, but I'm not recalling it right now. Wait, I do remember that, according to Sam, it named the five planets in the writings and some guy named Bassorine was given powers and made god-like."

The demon jumped in again. "I know what you're referring to. The place you are talking about is the Temple of the Gods above Griffon Cliffs. The man you speak of is the God of War, Bassorine... he is powerful, but we'll get to that in a minute. You're right—the Crystal Moon, which rests on the statue of Bassorine, does send out the power necessary to keep the five worlds separated. Bassorine's power protects the crystal, keeping it safe so no man or beast can take it and throw the worlds into chaos."

Kepler stopped talking when he saw the expression on George's face change. "What is it, George? You seem to be bothered by something."

The manipulator started to pace, bothered, and anxious. "Maybe we can keep walking while we talk. I have a gut feeling I'm not going to be able to sleep once you hear everything."

"Sure, we can walk, but you're making me nervous. What's the problem?"

"Well," George sighed heavily, throwing his backpack across his shoulder (and making a mental note that it did not change to stone), "You said the crystal was protected and that this so-called god Bassorine—"

"There is nothing *so-called* about the power of the gods. They are to be feared and respected. If you know what's good for you, I would talk respectfully about the gods. They are all powerful."

George turned to Kepler. "If this so-called god was so all powerful, I wouldn't have been able to take a piece of his crystal before I fell through the floor, now would I? Didn't you say his almighty power protected it? I shouldn't have been able to take a piece of it then, right?"

Kepler came unhinged.

"You took a piece of the crystal? Do you know what you've done? You've doomed us all! Now the planets will collide and destroy us all!"

The demon began pacing while George watched nervously. The cat was clearly angry, and George was not sure if it would end in a confrontation. Eventually Kepler took a few deep breaths, realizing his outburst was getting them nowhere.

"So where is the piece of crystal and what do you mean you fell through the floor?"

George hesitated, eying him up and down for a moment. "Now keep calm when I tell you this... I don't know where the piece is."

The demon let out a deafening roar. George prepared himself for the worst, holding his hands up in case Kepler attacked. The demon's explosion stopped and he gave George an evil look that cut through the man's soul. With an unmistakably cold tone, he said, "So you're telling me you have enough power to remove the crystal and you took it—and you have *no* clue where you put it?

What else haven't you told me?"

George was scared, despite the fact he had readied his hands to turn the cat to stone. He knew the Undead Jaguar Demon could sense his fear this time.

"I said I had no idea where it is because I fell through a floor when I touched the crystal. I lifted up one of its pieces... and it wasn't just me who thought we should touch the crystal. Sam thought the crystal was an answer to a riddle written on the statue."

"You lie!" Kepler screamed. "I've read the statue a 100 times, and it says nothing of a riddle."

George snapped back. "Hey, I didn't ask to be brought to this ridiculous world. There was a riddle, and if you call me a liar again, I'm going to get really pissed off."

"Okay, okay... then finish your story."

Angry, George continued. "The statue said something about three people fighting to recover the crystal. One will fall to the wayside early, but it didn't say anything further about what would happen to that third person. The statue said we were to wake it up, and Sam thought it was a metaphor. The only reason we touched the crystal was because it was the only part of the statue that didn't look like the rest. It was all made of bronze, but the crystal looked like... well it looked like a stupid crystal! We figured that was the answer to the puzzle. So when Sam said it looked like it had five different pieces, I jumped on top of the statue's base and grabbed one of the pieces. The next thing I knew, the rest of the crystal pieces disappeared into thin air, except for the piece I had in my hand—"

"You had a *piece* in your hand?"

"Yeah, yeah, yeah... then the floor started to shake, and the base of the statue I was standing on fell from under my feet through a hole... and I fell through the hole with it. I remember the man and his wolf didn't fall with me though. They stayed suspended in air as I fell away from them. I can only assume the one the statue talked about falling by the wayside was me. I don't know what happened to Sam and the woman, Shalee. It felt like I fell forever before the darkness opened up and I landed on a guy named Jason, just outside of Lethwitch in a field south of the Enchanted Forest. I had no clue that, by touching the crystal, I had started a cosmic problem."

Kepler returned to pacing. "George, put your hands down. There's no struggle between us... we're allies. Have you not learned anything from your experience with Kroger? We may get angry, but we don't fight amongst ourselves. I don't believe you could make up such a ridiculous story, so I'll accept it as fact."

He slowly lowered his hands and waited for the demon to continue.

"All right... so you fell through the floor and the crystal disappeared. You have no idea where the people are—the ones with you in the temple—or any idea of where that piece of crystal is? Mmmm... you clearly have enough power to get past Bassorine's hold on it. All this appears to make sense except for a few things."

"What *things* are you talking about? Tell me, and I'll clear them up for you if I can."

"You said you fell on a man named Jason... how long ago was this?"

George thought back. "About 10 days ago."

The demon shook his head in disbelief. "So since you arrived here 10 days ago, you have learned about the map, killed my subject that I sent after you, found out about the cave... and learned the staff was inside and went in to retrieve the power to turn things into stone? I would like to know how you learned of all this in such a short time."

"That's easy to explain," George said. "I also forgot to tell you that I robbed the mercantile in Lethwitch to get money to pay for the scroll I used on your friend." The liar gave a wide grin.

Kepler laughed loudly for a moment and then realized what George had said. "George, what do you mean you used a scroll?"

George knew he had said too much. He sat on a mound and started flicking tiny ants, sending the newly made stone statues flying everywhere. He was going to level with the jaguar and tell him the truth. "Like I said before, I landed on a guy named Jason. He was a big guy and when I landed on him, it broke his back. He was in a lot of pain, so I reached in his pack and gave him a liquid that killed the pain and made him talk way too much. Jason told me about the map and the secret it had on it. The map would lead me to where the staff was located inside the cave. He told me I wouldn't be able to command the power of the staff by using it, but there was a way I could get the power out of it—drinking the liquid that filled the hollow staff. If I drank the liquid, it would give me the same powers the staff would have given to its intended owners. Apparently the staff was meant for some dwarves to use."

"Dwarves—what dwarves?"

"Well Jason told me the dwarves were from a place called Trolcom. I've no clue where that is. When your Saber Lord attacked me, I got lucky. I felt something in the forest watching me so I knelt down on the rock crossing and used something called a Snare Scroll and set a trap. It was dumb luck that he ended up in the trap. I was overcome with anger when I tortured him. It wasn't until I drank the fluid inside of the staff that I gained the power to keep you from killing me. I was bluffing you the whole time to stay alive. I have no power other than the ability to turn you to stone."

As George finished telling his story to Kepler, he flicked another tiny ant statue toward the feet of the demon. "So... how do you like me now?"

Kepler had to laugh. "You played the game well, George. You know, you really surprise me, my friend. To think that after I saw you kill the saber, I feared you. When I approached you that first night, you just sat on the log eating—totally ignoring me. I figured you must've been powerful and simply held up your hand to stop the attack. Using the Snare Scroll was brilliant. And on top of it all, you were lucky enough for it to work. Of course, it made me sick to my stomach watching you torture him. But that whole time, you did it because you lost your temper? Interesting... because, I was just as scared of you, as you must have been of me. It kills me to know that you have only just now found a real power to command. Granted... it's a good power, but you couldn't have kept me from killing you before this. What irony. Well, George, my friend, I'll enjoy this until the day I cease to be on this world."

Kepler rolled on the ground laughing. "When I think back—the look on your face when Kroger was turning to stone, it's funny, knowing what I do now. You didn't have any clue what was going on, and I bet you were frightened. I bet you thought your alliance with me was ruined because of it. It's a good thing I thought you had demonstrated a real ability to think your way through a sticky situation or you would've been traveling solo. But don't you ever worry about me, George. I'll be your ally and swear to you my loyalty. I like your style, I really do!"

"Well, you should've seen your face when I was ignoring you at the fire that first night. You looked puzzled. I was about to crap in my pants and take off running. When you walked up, I was scared out of my mind but figured I better not make any sudden movements. I had no idea you saw me kill your buddy until later. When I fished for the information to see if you saw me kill him, I got lucky. Let's just say that it was a shot in the dark that turned things into my favor... and I used it to gain the upper hand. You know, it's funny now that you mention it, and I'm with you... enjoying the irony of it all. I do believe we make quite the odd couple... you and me."

Kepler laughed a while longer with George and finally he sat up and faced him. "As funny as this all is, we still have a problem. The crystal is missing, and the worlds will end some day. I wonder how long we have until that all happens."

"I don't know, but if Bassorine had his power on the Crystal Moon so that no man or beast could touch it, then why was I able to? I had no power to do that. I'm just a guy with a quick wit who wanted to gain some respect. Something else has to be going on here if he's as powerful as you say."

"Perhaps," the demon responded. "I agree that you shouldn't have been able to move the crystal, so I'm sure everything will be revealed in time. For now, let's rest a bit and continue to Lethwitch when we wake."

Lying down, George reset the alarm for a few hours later. Before he went to sleep, he reached for his wallet. He wanted to look at his baby girl's picture and dwell on her for a minute. When he opened the wallet, the photo was missing. Frantically, he rifled through the compartments of the leather billfold—it was nowhere to be found. His eyes were so heavy, the exhaustion of the last few days overwhelmed him; he cried himself to sleep. His dreams made up for the missing photo. He dreamed of Abbie and Athena.

Back at Angel's Village

SAM and Shalee have walked up the stairs to the top of the landing platform with their trainers. To Sam's surprise, the Griffon Soresym has just brought the last of the servants from the Temple of the Gods. They are grumbling about the temple being sealed and being out of work. The fighter walked over to the giant flying beast.

"Hello, Soresym. How are you?"

The eagle head turns and looks at Sam, surprised to see Sam's head sitting on top of a much larger body.

"You look familiar to me, but the person I know with this face is much smaller. Who might you be?"

"Soresym, my friend, it is me... Sam. It's a long story, and if we were riding with you, I'd tell you all about it. Let's just say that one of the gods gave me a gift. It is a pleasure to see that you're well. I've thought of you many times since our meeting."

"Ahhhh... Sam, it is indeed unexpected to see you here. I see you are also well. I have also thought of you and would love to hear the story some time. Maybe you could tell me this story about how you have grown so much. You look like you have changed quite a bit. I would probably have ignored you, but I do recognize this woman. I see your female companion is now awake. The last time I saw you, young woman, you were unconscious. Who might you be, little lady?"

Shalee looked at Sam. She was a little unsure of how to react. Sam quickly stepped in, seeing her hesitance. "Soresym, I would like you to meet my beautiful girlfriend, Shalee."

"I see," the griffon responded. "Hello, Shalee, I'm sure you don't remember, but I'm the one who gave you a ride from the top of Griffon Cliffs to Angel's Village. I'm glad you're feeling better."

Hesitantly, Shalee responded. "Thank you, Soresym. I really don't remember much of that experience, please forgive me."

"Nonsense, child, don't worry about it. Your boyfriend here made enough ignorant comments when we first met to make you look like an angel, I'm sure." The griffon chuckled a bit and looked at Sam. "So, Sam, where are you off to today? If you would like, I can give you a ride. Ever since the gods shut the temple, the rides I give back and forth are few and far between. I have told the others this was going to be my last trip for a while anyway, so maybe I'll tag along with you and you can fill me in on how the gods added this extra size to your frame."

"Well, since the last time you have seen me, a lot has happened. I think we would love to fly with you... and I would be more than happy to fill you in as we travel. Please forgive Shalee, my friend. She's quite nervous about this whole flying bit."

The griffon laughed and comforted her. "There isn't much tur-bulence, and the weather is perfect for flying today. Go ahead and climb on up. Don't worry, I can easily carry the four of you, but it may be a tight fit so you may have to sit close together."

Everyone climbed aboard and sure enough, they had to tuck together tightly. BJ sat at the rear just behind Helga. He had been watching the older sorceress and thought she was beautiful. He took the opportunity to reach around her waist. Pulling her in close, he quietly whispered in her ear, "I'm doing this for your safety."

Helga managed to twist around to look at him and saw a sly smile and adorable wink. She accepted his obvious advance and nestled in tight against his chest. She put her hands on top of his and enjoyed their ruggedness. Neither Sam nor Shalee were aware of the exchange as they only had eyes for each other.

As they took off, Shalee felt disappointed that she had not ex-perienced this, the first time, and made a mental note to no longer throw fits about things she knew nothing about. Sam and the giant griffon began to converse and talked for the entire trip.

Back on the World of Ancients Sovereign

MOSLEY was still in his meeting with his new team members. He had explained to them that he knew everything the Book of Immortality knew of Lasidious's plan to make everyone play the game. He was about to tell them all he knew of the third person the other gods did not know about.

"His name is George. He was brought forward by Lasidious because he feels the human can be easily manipulated to accom-plish things on his agenda. From what I know of him, Sam said he was a mean-spirited man, and Shalee didn't like him either. As we all know, there were clear plans for Shalee and Sam. When I became enlightened, I decided to give both my gifts to Sam to help his rise to glory. I think this will help our cause, and allow him to gain an audience with the King of Brandor much sooner. I think we all know the game Lasidious is playing is going to be hard fought from his side. If he wins, it will be miserable for many of your followers. We don't want him to collect the majority of the crystal pieces and bring darkness over the worlds. We'll need the Kingdom of Brandor on our side to fight for the crystal... and Sam will need to be a key part of this."

Bailem spoke up. The god was short, heavyset, with blue eyes and balding brown hair. He was pleasant to look at, wearing golden robes with dark trim. Bailem's long tail hung to the floor; his angelic wings hidden beneath his robes. He had been the only angel to survive the God Wars, and had become the god known as the God of the Sun.

"So if I might ask, what were the two gifts you bestowed on Sam to help his journeys in the arena? I think we all know he won't gain an audience with the King of Brandor unless he defeats each arena's best fighter. If he does make it to the City of Champions and wins, all of us know who he'll have to fight in Brandor's arena... the champion of Brandor, Justin Graywind, is the General Absolute and has never been defeated. Every opponent who has entered the arena with him has died before he could be carried out of the arena by the healers."

"I can tell you the healers working in that arena are good," Helmep said as he broke into the conversation. The God of Healing was tall and thin, well built with blonde hair, hazel eyes and wore a white robe with red trim. He was handsome and his smile carried a wonderful charisma. Helmep continued. "They are the best of all the healers who serve me on Grayham. Justin Graywind does not leave any room for them to work. When he's done with his opponents, they are done. Of 54 fights he has had in the arena and won, all of them ended in death."

All the gods at the meeting were getting sidetracked, so Mosley called for order. "Don't forget that we can get Sam invited to Brandor if we make some simple suggestions. The two gifts I gave Sam were increased strength and greater agility. This should help him to gain his audience. His girlfriend Shalee will be able to assist him as well with her sorcery. Now as much as I would like to keep talking about these things, it is time for the meeting that Lasidious has called. I suggest we head over there."

Everyone agreed and vanished. When each of them reappeared, they found Lasidious and his team sitting on the grass outside the newly constructed Hall of Judgment with the Book of Immortality. The new hall was identical to the old one, just as the Book had insisted. It was normal for the gods to snap their fingers and create anything they wanted, so the new hall had been constructed quickly.

"I'm glad everyone is here," Lasidious announced. "I have decided that, rather than putting a piece of crystal on each world, there will need to be at least two pieces of the crystal on this world in order for them to be rejoined quickly. I'll announce where the first piece has been placed soon. Until then, I would work on strengthening your positions within this world and be ready for anything. I thank you all for coming and I will now excuse Celestria and myself from my team. I don't think I can keep from creating an unfair advantage if we play. I'll watch and continue to give you information on the crystal's pieces. Your teams now have equal numbers. I suggest you look for ways to strengthen both good and evil on this world. I'll see you all in 60 Peaks of Bailem."

With that, Lasidious vanished, and left the other gods looking at each other in confusion. The God of Mischief's next destination was the town of Lethwitch.

Chapter 20

Warning to the Barbarian King of Bloodvain

LASIDIOUS appeared in front of the Mage Amar, who was the brother of Morre, whom Lasidious had impersonated the last time he had been in Lethwitch. Amar worked in his brother's store—the same store where George had purchased his magic scrolls—whenever he was on the World of Grayham. He was an older man, hair gray, but, unlike his brother, he did not wear a beard. The magic user had been startled when the god appeared, but throughout all his years, he had come to expect the unexpected and was able to dismiss the shock quickly. Amar realized who was standing in front of him and bowed before his god.

"Hello, Amar," Lasidious said. "It has been awhile, my friend. How's your brother, Morre?"

Amar kept his head down and replied. "Hello, my lord, my brother and I are well. To what do I owe this pleasure?"

"Amar, please stand up and look at me. I'm here to talk as friends, not as your god. I'm glad that you're both doing well, but I'm here on business, and to inform you of some things."

The mage nervously rose. "I don't understand."

"I know, my friend, but the other day I was here in your store and took a few of your scrolls and sold them to a man named George. There was also a note from this man, thanking your brother."

"I know of the note. My brother told me about it. He said he had been paid way too much for the scrolls, but why would this cause your visit? There was more than enough money left behind to cover the expense, far more. I was fine with things and have since heard my brother say that he has made replacements. I would've paid better attention to what kind of scrolls had been taken, but I had no idea I would receive this visit, my lord."

"I'm glad you were all right with the finances of the transaction, but this isn't why I've come. I don't care about the scrolls. The man I spoke of will be seeking power within this world. He'll be arriving in Lethwitch a few days from now. He's the type of man I know you have been waiting for. I know you wish to seek out your own path of glory... and this man could help you. If you choose to, it might be wise for you to align yourself with him until it benefits you to leave. His heart is as dark as your own, and I think you could act as good council to him. He currently travels with the Undead Jaguar Demon, Kepler."

"Kepler? My lord, Kepler is a vicious killer without any honor! Can he be trusted? I have heard many stories about the men who have tried to go through his pass. He kills without mercy, as if for fun."

Lasidious laughed. "Kepler can be trusted, Amar... and you have also killed for fun, without mercy. The jaguar has honor, but this isn't something that you would know about. Like you said, you have only heard stories. The man I speak of is also ruthless, and he's not from this world. He has traveled here from the past. It's in his character to seek as much power as he can obtain. He has already aligned himself with the beast Maldwin from within the Cave of Sorrow, as well as Kepler. He even had an alliance with Kroger before he killed him."

"Kroger, you mean the ogre from the Dark Forest, my lord?"

"Yes."

"Kroger is a gentle giant, my lord. Why would he want to kill him, and why would I wish to travel with a man who does not respect his allies?"

Again Lasidious laughed. "Amar, I know you have also killed an ally or two in the past. I think you forget with whom you speak."

Amar bowed his head. "I'm sorry, my lord. It's not every day I speak with someone who knows my secrets. Please forgive me! How was he able to align himself with the beast Maldwin? The creature's visions are deadly to all men."

"There is no forgiveness necessary, Amar. I find your evil mind quite pleasant, but, to answer your question, George is immune to the visions. He needed the scrolls he bought from your brother to protect Kroger's mind, not his own. The giant was with him when he went to the cave, and it was at the cave that George killed Kroger by turning him to stone."

Amar's eyes widened. "He turned Kroger to stone? That's a treasured power. There's no one on Grayham, other than myself, who can command it. Did he use a staff or spell?"

Lasidious smiled inside as he continued. He knew the mage would be impressed with the information. "He commands the power but is having a hard time controlling it. The great thing about his ability is that it is natural ... he uses neither a staff, nor a spell."

Amar could not believe his ears. "How is this possible, my lord?"

"I told you it would be wise to align yourself with him. Maybe you could be his counselor and teach him how to direct the power. You have been to Luvelles and trained under your good friend, Head Master Brayson. You understand the dark arts better than anyone on Grayham. Both of us know you're the most powerful mage on this world! I would, if I were you, keep this to yourself and not share it with George."

Amar once again bowed. "I'll do whatever you ask of me, my lord!"

"No, Amar, I'm not here to ask anything of you. I'm simply here to inform you of things that are happening. I want to see you become powerful someday. It's an idea that you may want to think about. You must want this for yourself. I don't wish to make you do anything that's not your heart's desire. I'll give you a vision of what George looks like. If you choose to befriend this man, your wisdom would come in handy to him... and your rise to glory would soon follow. I wouldn't take your brother along. We both know that his service to his god is for good, and wouldn't agree with your desire for power. You should make this decision on your own. And if you choose to pass, I'll still look fondly upon you. After all, we're friends, are we not?"

"Yes, my lord, I would like to be your friend. I've never seen myself as a friend to a god. I've always lived to serve you, my lord."

Smiling, Lasidious put his hand on the man's shoulder. "Amar Gregory, you are my friend and I extend my hand to you this way. You're a free man, with free will... and I respect you as the man you've become. I couldn't be prouder of the way you've served me, but it's time for your glory if you choose it. I'll sit and watch from above as your biggest fan."

Amar was happy with the way his lord had spoken to him. "Maybe it would be best if I took my staff and went to find this George, my lord."

Lasidious agreed but reminded the mage that George would not arrive in town for a few more days. The god suggested that it would be wise to gather all the materials he would need to travel with his new allies. He watched Amar run from the store and into the night. The God of Mischief had three simple words to say before he left for his next destination: "What an idiot!"

With that, he vanished.

The Next Morning
City of Bloodvain

LASIDIOUS waited patiently within his pen for the Barbarian King of Bloodvain to arrive. He had taken the form of a thick-horned, black bull and was due to enter combat with Senchae Bloodvain for his daily training. He threw himself around inside the corral, playing the part of a raged animal, and tore some of the fencing apart. When the handlers tried to approach, he sent them flying through the air, landing in awkward positions and breaking bones.

"Looks like we have a very spirited one today, my king," the general of the Barbarian army commented. "I've never seen this bull before, but I dare say he's going to try and put up a fight, sire. He's much bigger than all of the others you've fought."

King Senchae Bloodvain nodded at the general and other high-ranking members of his army. Removing his clothes, he looked across the arena while tying up his long hair. He was an enormous man—slightly over eight feet, four inches tall. It was customary for the Barbarians to fight to the death... and today would be no exception. King or no king, he would fight in nothing but the furs covering his loins. If today was his turn to die, then so be it. He weighed nearly 550 pounds with muscles bulging everywhere. He was well known within the kingdom for his ability to fight for long periods of time without becoming tired. Today, as he did every day, he would train with angered bulls to keep in shape. He would beat the first bull to death and feed it to the leaders of his army later that evening.

Now ready, the king looked at the bull and said, "General Furgus, it does appear to be a fine bull indeed. I hear your son, Churnach, won his fight yesterday. He makes our kingdom proud. Wasn't that his eighth victory since I surrendered my belt as champion to him?"

"Yes, my king, it was indeed. He still talks about one day being able to train as hard as you, my king. He tries hard and is finally able to handle two bulls for his agility training, but I believe it will be some time before any man can match your skill with three, sire."

"Let us hope, General that this isn't true, and your son shall one day be as good a champion as I was. For now, let's kill this bull for dinner and bring in the other three after. How does that sound?"

"My king, as always, I look forward to watching this... and I'm sure we will dine well tonight before we sleep with all our women, sire."

"Indeed general, you keep all your women and I'll just stick with my queen. I would hate for her to bring down her wrath on me. She can be quite forceful, you know, for a woman. Besides, a man who respects his wife lives a good life."

Both men enjoyed the fantasy of the queen's power over the king, but the general knew that his king's loyalty to his queen was given out of respect and not fear. Senchae would never look at another woman. He held true to his vows with the queen, despite the evil in his heart.

The City of Bloodvain was home to the Barbarian King. Senchae was the type of man who governed his army and high council through respect. Unlike his grandfather, Bude Bloodvain, and most other kings before him, he had achieved this respect throughout the Barbarian kingdom's arenas for over 15 seasons prior to taking Bloodvain's throne. Every fight in the kingdom was to the death. The vanity of the race as a whole kept the challengers coming. He was then—and still is today, even though he does not compete in the arena any longer—considered to be the most feared Barbarian champion ever to live.

He was the strongest and quickest Barbarian the kingdom had ever seen. Since he was crowned king, Senchae sat on the throne ruling with a strong hand and yet, still trained harder than any other throughout his entire kingdom. Unlike his grandfather, he maintained a belief that the respect of his army should be earned, not commanded. The king used this respect to command the army, but he still used fear to keep control of the rest of his kingdom. His heart was as evil as his grandfather's, and killing was just a game. The leaders of his army and the high council were allowed strong opinions, unlike his grandfather's monarchy because Bude Bloodvain was a much weaker king, and had to control his armies through fear of his crown. Senchae chose to listen to his men before making a decision, but the men knew it was the king's right to make a decision... and when he did, it was final.

"So General, what do you say we let dinner out of his pen so I can toy with him a bit?"

"Yes, my king. Release the bull!"

Lasidious exited the holding area where he had waited patiently, or at least as patiently as an angered bull would wait.

"This one looks tough, sire," the General shouted from his seat in the king's box, adding, "Best watch your back side with those horns, sire. They look to be a good fit if you ask me."

"I could always trade you places, Furgus. I know that such intercourse would be a pleasure you would like far more than I. I saw the way you were looking at this fine animal earlier. I dare say that you looked to be in love!"

The other members of the king's army laughed hysterically and the General accepted the slam graciously. "Witty indeed, my king, I must remember who I jest with next time."

"Indeed, Furgus, but you know I have nothing but respect for you and the other leaders of my army," Senchae said as he watched the bull charge.

Lasidious lowered his head. Bloodvain, grabbed a horn in each hand, then used Lasidious's momentum to throw the bull to the ground. The god landed hard, followed by the king's crushing punch to the side of his neck. Keeping in character, the bullish deceiver bellowed in pain, digging his hoofs into the sand. Slowly, he rose for another attack. Lasidious snorted, shook his head forcefully for effect and charged again, allowing the king to throw him once more before taking the offense. Much to the bull-god's amusement, the General and his men cheered wildly for their king.

Lasidious knew that what he planned next was going to be accepted by the king's men and interference would not be an issue. In the Barbarian kingdom, if you entered a fight, it was to the death and the king was no exception.

Again Lasidious charged and allowed Bloodvain to grab his horns. This time, he held firm as the big man tried to twist him for the throw. When the king could not complete his maneuver, he was caught off balance from the attack. The bull-god drove him hard into the ground then rose to drive his head into the king's groin area, careful not to do any long-term damage, but effective enough to stun Senchae and pin him down.

The General ordered his men to stay put. He reminded them that it would be an insult to help their king, so they obeyed the order.

The god threw his bull body hard onto Senchae, putting much of his 2,200 pounds on him to keep him pinned. He watched as the giant man struggled to free himself, punching the bull's body several times. But the blows were ineffective. Bloodvain could not find the leverage to injure his opponent.

Lasidious lay there, careful not to put too much weight on Senchae, and waited for him to tire. But the king did not tire but rather realized the bull was not trying to fight any longer. To his surprise, he was able to relax, hoping the bull would get up and leave. Senchae figured he would wait—but then was caught off guard.

The bull spoke to him. "King of Bloodvain," Lasidious said, quietly.

The king shook his head, closed his eyes and reopened them. He was not sure he heard correctly and was further stunned when the bull continued to speak.

"My king, I have news that I bring to you. Right now, in the Kingdom of Brandor, a man is seeking great power."

Senchae responded, "How do you speak, beast?"

Lasidious snapped, "Shut up, great king, or I'll kill you now. Listen to me or this meeting will become quite unpleasant for you. Do you understand?"

Senchae nodded his head, waiting for the bull to continue.

"As I was saying, in the Kingdom of Brandor a man is seeking great power. He will come to your kingdom. This human is to be feared. You will not have to find him, he'll be coming for you. Your kingdom's reputation will be damaged if your champion loses to this human. It is your choice, and I know you have your laws, but if I were you, I would handle this myself. You'll know this man when you see him. He travels with an Undead Jaguar Demon named Kepler. I know you're familiar with this demon cat. He was the one hired into your grandfather's service in the past to retrieve the Unicorn Prince's horn. The cat now serves this human. The man can fight like no other human you have ever seen. My king, the looks of this human are deceiving. He'll destroy your champion. The only one in your kingdom that is strong enough to face this man is you. Now, I'm sure your unicorn horn can dull the pain that I've left in your groin. I have come a long way to give you this message... and now, I'll take my leave."

The king watched as the bull rose, walked back into the holding area and down into the stables below the training grounds. He stood and, after a short time, followed the bull. By the time he arrived at the stables, the bull was nowhere to be found. King Senchae Bloodvain was left standing alone and confused.

Two and a half days later
The Town of Lethwitch

WHEN GEORGE and Kepler arrived in Lethwitch just before the Peak of Bailem, the whole town seemed to be in a big stir. Kepler decided to stay outside the town because of the reaction he would get from the people. It was far too hard for the demon to move around when there were not enough shadows in the middle of the day to hide within.

The excitement in the air was evident. George followed the crowd to the outskirts of the east side of town near the Cripple River. Cheering erupted from the inside of the arena. He wanted to go inside, but lacked the coin. He was forced to live vicariously through the others going in and out.

After speaking with some of the people, he realized the fights were like the gladiatorial combats held in ancient Rome. Unlike that civilization, the gladiators of Grayham were all free men, not criminals or slaves forced to fight. No, these combatants were glory seekers. And, as long as anyone could remember, the games had always been a part of their culture.

George needed to find money fast so he could watch the fights. He gathered from listening that the competition would last for the next two days.

Smiling to himself, he headed back into town for a familiar spot. It did not take long before he once again was standing outside the mercantile. It was the middle of the day, so he walked in to look around but the store was empty. He figured most of the town's people were at the fights. By his count, there were only two people in the store: an elderly gentleman behind the same counter he had robbed before and an older woman, maybe the man's wife or assistant. By the way she stocked the shelves George figured she had worked there a while. Given her attention to detail, he would have put money on it that both of them were the proprietors.

The old man saw him and came out from behind the counter to greet him. "Hello, friend, how may I help you today?" The woman heard the greeting and also stopped what she was doing and came over to stand next to the man. "Hello, son, not a bad day out today... may we assist you with something?"

"Hello, yes, it's a nice day out. I was looking for a pair of gloves and thought that maybe a nice place like this would have some. Do you think you could help me?"

"Oh, sure we can, young man," the gentleman replied. "This is my wife Jane, and my name is Carl. We carry a wide variety of items, so let me help you find what you're looking for."

The woman excused herself and headed back to stocking boots while her husband showed him the gloves. The area was near the boots, but on a shelf closer to the middle of the room. As George followed the man, he scanned the room to see if anyone else was around. It appeared they were alone. Jane was busy adjusting the boots, so George took a deep breath and reached out to touch Carl on the back of his neck. His transformation was instantaneous. George could tell the stone-figured man was going to topple over. He had been in mid-stride when the manipulator touched him. Hurrying, before the woman could hear her husband's stone body hit the floor, George reached over and touched her forearm. Jane's transformation was just as quick as Carl's, but she did not fall.

The killer watched as Carl broke in two as he hit the floor. The commotion caused George concern so he quickly went to the door and looked out to see if anyone had heard. Fortunately the street outside was quiet; no one had noticed a thing. Now he did not hesitate. George headed for the money drawer and sure enough, the older couple was as trusting as before. George found an amount equal to almost 14 Owain coins then bolted the back door shut and created a sign to hang in the front window. The sign read, "Closed for the fights —See you all in four days."

He grabbed a pair of gloves, exited the store, locked the door, and moved to the alleyway. Once there, he took a deep breath and laughed at how easy murder actually was. He put on his new gloves as if nothing happened, and headed out to buy a gift.

He found some flowers and went to the inn where Athena worked to surprise her. But his timing was terrible... she wasn't there. The lady behind the counter recognized him, smiled, and told George that Athena would be back tomorrow night, and she would make sure Athena received the flowers.

George smiled as he thought that at least something in this world was the same as Earth... flowers still meant something to women. He wrote a note and attached it. The note said:

Dear Athena,
I wanted to give you these flowers to let you know you're on my mind. I miss your beautiful face. Your smile is like an angel's. I'm sorry I missed you, but I will be back, soon.
With fondness, George

George left for the arena, feeling bummed that Athena would not be in town until tomorrow night. But then, he figured it was for the best since he could not control his power right now anyway. He was about to buy his way into the arena when a familiar voice shouted his name. "Oh, my goodness, George, is that you? I thought you were dead!"

He turned and watched as Shalee ran towards him. She was wearing a white dress, black lacy sweater—but nothing like you would find on Grayham. The outfit clung to her bosom and waist, with her blonde hair pulled back in a ponytail, exposing a graceful jawline, George could only smile as he watched her approach.

He pretended to care as he started to speak. "Oh, wow, I was wondering what happened to you. Look at you, looks like you figured out a way to add a little kick to the boring clothes they wear around here."

Shalee looked down. "Oh, this was a gift from Sam after he won his first fight. He spoils me. I had to adjust the waist and bodice, plus take the sleeves off... then make a matching sweater from this interesting black material I found at an adorable little fabric store near The Mercantile. I swear the place looked so tiny, but they still had some cute things for sale. I think the women around here like my fashion. You wouldn't believe how many of them come up and ask about it. Maybe I can start a trend!"

George ignored most of what she said but had focused in on the part about Sam winning his first fight.

"Sam, he's fighting? So he's also here with you? Tell me what's going on with you guys."

"Sure, but first, tell me what happened when you fell through the floor. I was horrified! I didn't think we'd ever see you again. I thought you were dead."

George made up a lie. "I fell to a room below and was knocked out. The next thing I knew... I was in this town. Nothing too exciting has happened since. It's been kind of boring, if you ask me. Not much to talk about. So tell me about you and Sam."

"I'm just so glad that you're okay. Well, let me see, where do I start? The place where we woke up was a temple controlled by the gods. Sam and I have been working ever since to gain the fame he needs to win an audience with the King of Brandor... and I've been trying to work on my powers with my staff here." She held up the staff. "Precious, I'd like to introduce you to George."

The liar was intrigued to hear more. "Well, hello, Precious. So Shalee, when did you start naming large, petrified sticks and what do you mean by your powers?"

Shalee took a deep breath. "Wow, where to start? Well, since we last met, I've become a sorceress in training. I'm really excited about it because I'm kind of good at it. I'll have to show you someday... I think you'll be impressed."

"That's crazy! What about Sam? What's his story?"

"Sam is doing well. He's a fighter in the arenas of this world. He fought yesterday and won his second fight. He has another one tomorrow. He kind of loses his mind when he gets in there, but realizes now that it's necessary in order to gain an audience with the King of Brandor. I swear it takes me hours to calm him down afterwards. He has killed both men. He gets so enraged, it's scary to watch. Even though he has killed his last two opponents, he's becoming well-known, and fast. Last night, everywhere we went after the fight, people came up to him and treated him like a celebrity. The people of this world seem to love barbarism. I don't understand it!"

"Are we talking about the same guy I know? I realized he was a tough guy and all, but I didn't think he was that much of a stud."

Shalee smirked. "Oh, he's the same guy, all right. There is one big difference, though. The new God of War, Mosley, gave Sam a couple of gifts—one enhanced his body composition, making him a much bigger guy than the last time you saw him."

"I thought the God of War was Bassorine?"

"He was, but then he was destroyed and Mosley has taken his place. You would like Mosley. We traveled with him before he ascended and became a god."

"What the hell are you talking about, Shalee? Are you telling me that you've actually traveled with a god since we arrived here?"

"That's exactly what I'm saying. I know what you mean, though. Sometimes I sit in my room and think this all has to be some sort of dream. It's so hard to believe that everything I thought to be fantasy is real. I've been on Grayham for about two weeks now and so much has happened to me. I have cried so much!"

"No kidding, I'll second that motion. I wish I could say my life has been as exciting as yours."

Shalee looked at his hands. "Why are you wearing those gloves? It's kind of warm for that, don't you think?"

"It's a long story, don't ask."

"Okay—well, I would take you to see Sam, but he's training with BJ right now, and I'm waiting here for Helga to go inside and watch the fights. I've been training so much lately that I need a break."

George interrupted. "I assume Helga is your trainer from the sounds of it."

"That she is. Even Helga likes my fashion—and I've got her wearing it now. Hey, you're welcome to come and sit with us. I'll buy you an ale or something."

"I'd like that," George replied, thinking he could care less about Shalee's fashion sense. "Maybe we could all have dinner tonight so I can see Sam and catch up."

Later that Evening

SAM was with BJ when Shalee came in and told him about running into George. The fighter was interested in meeting for dinner, so he proceeded to get dressed and tended to his trainer's wounds.

"It looks like the old man is going soft on me," Sam said as he applied the healing mud to BJ's leg.

"Give me a couple gifts from the gods and watch what I do to you, young man," BJ grumbled.

Both Sam and Shalee laughed. After a moment, BJ lightened up and began to laugh as well. They all headed out to meet George for dinner.

The Grayham Inquirer

When inquiring minds need to know where their favorite characters are.

SAM and Shalee are making their way to the tavern across town to have dinner with George. Amar is sitting at the bar observing him. Lasidious is also sitting in the tavern—invisible to all—watching the events unfold.

CELESTRIA has retired to the room that has been provided to her by the elven witch family. She is having a pleasant conversation with two squirrels sitting on her windowsill and watching them eat the nuts she set out for them. Their conversation is a great stress reliever after her interactions with the witches. They are driving her mad. She is counting the days until her son's birth—and her departure.

MOSLEY has just left a meeting with his team of gods. They were all in agreement that he should visit, Keldwin, the King of Brandor.

ATHENA is singing as she cleans the dishes at her mother's home. She is excited about her flowers. They had been brought to her from work. She could not wait to see George again. She read the note over and over again, anxious for her shift to start tomorrow night when George would be back.

SENCHAE BLOODVAIN is holding the Unicorn Prince's horn close to his groin. The healing power the horn possesses is starting to soothe the pain. He cannot believe how black and blue both of his inner thighs are. As he contemplates the talking bull's words he is struggling with his pride. Never before has he been in a near-fatal position. He always was the dominant one. Although his men did not regard him any differently—their respect still intact—something still gnaws at him. He would have preferred an honorable death to the bull's mere departure. But taking his own life now would be cowardly, so his only option is to swallow this bitter pill.

Thank you for reading the Grayham Inquirer

Chapter 21

𝔄 𝔖𝔬𝔲𝔩 ℜ𝔢𝔰𝔠𝔲𝔢𝔡

GEORGE waits for his dinner companions to arrive as he finishes his second mug of ale; quietly a gray-haired man approaches wearing a robe and holding a staff; he sits down at George's table.

Holy crap, he thought. Who's this character? This freak looks just like Merlin.

"Look pal, I have people coming so you might want to take a hike!" George said.

Smiling, the man replied, "I will make this quick, George."

Amar watched the surprise on George's face, and then continued.

"Yes, I know your name; I've been sent by someone to assist you on your journey. I know you need help with your—well, let's just call it your gift—since we are in mixed company. I can teach you how to control it. With my council, you can master it quickly."

The liar leaned forward across the table. "Who the hell are you to tell me that I need your guidance... and who's this someone that supposedly sent you?"

The mage leaned forward. "Lasidious sent me, and my name is Amar. You bought your scrolls from my brother's store."

George feigned a lack of interest. "Who gives a crap what your name is? I didn't ask you to sit at my table, nor did I ask for your guidance. Am I supposed to know who the hell this Lasidious is? You're wasting my time, and I think it's best if you go before I make you wish that you had."

I hate presumptuous people, and this guy is really freaking me out, George thought.

Before Amar stood up from the table, he said, "I'll be outside the arena at the closing of the games. If you want my help, get back to me. Think about this in the meantime. How could I possibly know about your gift? I'm here for a reason." With that, he left.

Now more than ever, George was confused.

How could this old man have known who I am... and about my power? There's never a dull moment around this place. I have so got to write a book about this for my Abbie.

George decided he would find Kepler after dinner and ask about this Lasidious character. Kepler could track Amar down and bring him when it was time to head back to the cave. He lifted his drink from the table, slammed down the rest of his ale and waited anxiously for his guests.

When Sam and Shalee finally arrived, George could not stop staring at the fighter's transformed body.

"Holy cow, man, look at you! You're a horse. Put an axe in your hand, throw a red-checkered shirt on you and call you Paul Bunyan. I thought you had muscles before, but this is sick. Shalee told me where you got the size from."

Sam quickly interrupted him. "That is a conversation that is best left for places a little quieter, don't you agree? I have a lot to tell you about this world and many other things we've learned since we've arrived. I'm hoping to compare notes and see if we each know something the other one doesn't."

George looked around and figured it was a good idea to wait. So they changed the subject and had a nice dinner. After the meal, they left the tavern and headed for the inn.

Lasidious watched the three of them leave. He remained invisible and followed them to the inn where he could hear their entire conversation.

George was glad to learn that the inn was not the same place where Athena worked. He did not want to mix business with pleasure. This meeting, in his mind, was all about gathering information—it had nothing to do with friendship. He could care less if either one of them even existed, he just wanted the information.

Everyone filed into the room, and Sam started to speak.

"So it's nice to see you. I'm glad you didn't die when you fell through the floor. I thought for sure you were a goner. Before Bassorine's destruction, he made me think that you might have survived since Lasidious had plans for you."

Lasidious smirked when he heard this. He had taken a position in a chair across the room and was maintaining his invisible cover.

"What the hell are you talking about? That's the second time I've heard that name today," George said. "I don't even know a Lasidious. I woke up outside of this town and have been here ever since. Who's this Lasidious anyway?"

"He's the god who retrieved us from Earth. He was only supposed to bring the two of us, but he brought you as well. The gods don't seem to understand why, though. Even Mosley, the new God of War, is clueless. Shalee and I were supposed to create a new empire as an example for the worlds, but it looks like this has been put on the backburner now that the Crystal Moon is missing. Shalee was brought forward to be my mate."

Shalee slapped Sam's arm and took this opportunity to act like she did not already know what Mosley had told her. "Hey, you never told me that part!" She wanted to tell him the rest of what she knew about her powers, but she remembered the wolf told her it was dangerous to say anything.

"Maybe we could talk about that later, babe," Sam said.

George jumped in, "Poor girl, you have to sleep with this big guy... Yuck! Well, I don't know anything about this god Lasidious, but maybe I'll meet him someday. If he has plans for me, then he better say something soon because I've got to get back to my daughter."

Sam looked at Shalee, both of them knowing George's daughter was dead. Sam decided to lead into it slowly. "I think both Shalee and I have been so overwhelmed that we lost sight of your disappearance. I'm grateful that you're okay."

"I agree man, it was very stressful when we arrived," George replied. "I didn't handle things very well. I hope you both will forgive me for the way I acted that day. I really would like to catch up with you both. No one on this world has any clue of the things we share in common. It would be nice to keep this bond, if you guys don't mind. Maybe we can figure out a way to get back home."

"We forgive you, George, and I'm sure we also need our own little slice of forgiveness for things said that day. I remember flipping you the bird if recollection serves me right," Shalee said, a bit nervous about what was coming.

Sam glanced out the window and chided jokingly, seeing an opportunity to lighten the mood before he gave George the bad news. "I'm sure we all agree that I'm the only one innocent of any wrongdoing that day. It's not like I punched anyone in the arm or anything."

They all laughed.

Sam's face grew somber as he began to tell George everything he knew. "So you already know about the five worlds and the Crystal Moon, but what you don't know is that these gods created a Book after the God Wars destroyed everything. They call it the Book of Immortality and it holds all the souls of the dead. There's no longer a heaven or hell... and no matter if a person is good or bad, everyone ends up in this Book until it's time to be reborn."

George responded. "That's pretty deep... sounds fake!"

Sam continued telling the story of how Bassorine being given god-like powers was a big lie that the gods told the souls of these worlds to give them something to have faith in. "Bassorine told me that the gods of our Earth sent our souls to heaven or hell, depending on how we lived."

"So all that crap was true," George responded. "You're telling me that what the Bible said is true... and I would've gone to hell for all the things I did on Earth? Wow, I'm glad hell was destroyed then. This all sounds so unreal to me, but, with the way this world is, I'm inclined to believe anything."

Sam was unsure how to respond. "I suppose that if you were worried about your soul, it is good that hell is gone. But there's something else you need to know."

"Okay," George said cautiously.

"Everything was destroyed in the God Wars. The only thing that exists, are these five worlds."

George laughed in disbelief. He repeated back all he knew so far. "You're trying to tell me this guy Lasidious is a god, who was told by the other gods to bring you two to Grayham. He was only supposed to bring you and Shalee, but he somehow tricked the others and brought me here for reasons that no one knows. You two were supposed to be an example on this world and these so-called gods presumed Shalee would want to be your mate and have your babies while you run around ruling an empire. I would say that gives new meaning to the word presumptuous. Is this story for real, because it seems like a gigantic pile of horse crap to me?"

"I swear it's true, George."

George looked down at the floor. "It sounds so farfetched to me, like some sort of fantasy. You're saying everything was destroyed in the God Wars? Nothing remains of our gods of Earth? If the only things that remain are these five worlds then..."

Sam watched as he saw the light come on in George's head. Shalee grabbed Sam's arm and held it tight, remembering how she felt when she learned that everything was gone.

George started to cry uncontrollably as he came to the realization of what Earth's destruction meant to his life. He reached for his wallet. Remembering the picture of his daughter was missing, he crumbled to the floor. Shalee rushed to his side, but he held his hands up and motioned for her to stay away. "Don't come near me," he urged and backed up against the wall. "I'm dangerous and you need to stay back." His grief was hellish; the memories of his daughter filling his mind, the pain of her death tormenting him.

"She was so young," he sobbed loudly. "I loved my daughter

more than anything. She was so perfect. She loved me no matter what anyone said. She didn't judge me or look for my faults. She loved me because I was her dad. Oh god! My baby girl... my baby girl... this really hurts man. Your daddy loves you, baby," he screamed as he looked up to the sky. "I know my baby is in heaven." He wailed as he remembered. "Oh, my goodness, there is no heaven. How can she find a safe place for her tender soul to rest if there's no heaven? I don't know how to stop this pain. My little girl won't know Athena."

The dreams of his baby girl going to the park with them both would never come true. The thought amplified his pain and ripped his soul apart. "My heart, oh it hurts. I have to go! I have to go! I have to go now!"

George picked himself up and ran across the room toward the door. Before he left the room, he turned and looked at them both. "I'm afraid that this is where we part. I need to find a place for me now... I'm lost. Please *don't* follow me."

He slammed the door behind him.

Lasidious stood up from his chair, maintaining his invisible cover. He walked through the solid door to see where George was going. He did not want to lose sight of him now.

Shalee started to follow, but Sam grabbed her. "You can't stop his pain. No matter how bad you wish to be able to. He needs to figure this one out on his own," he said softly.

"What if he kills himself? I can't imagine a child of mine dying." Shalee fell to the bed crying. Her sympathy for George's pain was pulling at the core of her heart. "I wouldn't be able to deal with that kind of guilt."

"He won't kill himself. He's a better man than that, and something tells me he'll fight back and land on his feet. He mentioned a woman's name, so maybe he has a shoulder to cry on."

George's heart was devastated as he walked down the hallway with the invisible god, Lasidious in tow. He became more enraged with every step. His hate was enough to fuel the whole of Grayham twice over. His mind questioned.

How could the one good thing in my life be stolen from me? How could these so called gods destroy everything I consider precious and dear to my heart? Why did my baby have to die?

His mind screamed this agonizing cry over and over again until he was lost in tormenting sorrow.

Why did my Abbie have to die? Why did my Abbie have to die? Why did my Abbie have to die?

He stopped at the top of the stairs and looked out across the dining area of the inn. People were sitting, drinking, unaware of the danger lingering at the top of the stairs. He removed his gloves.

"The gods have taken my baby girl... now it's my turn. I'll kill your followers. I'll have my vengeance. I'll kill'em all," he said under his breath with a reinforced evil. "An eye for an eye... just like the good book said!"

His eyes grew dark, changing color as he scanned the room. The beautiful baby blue filling them slowly faded and was lost to his hate. They now held the blackness of the darkest night. Never again would their color return, as the last piece of goodness in George's heart vanished forever.

Lasidious watched with concern as George's eyes changed color. The god knew this was not good for his plans. He decided to follow George until he could fix the problem.

George clapped his hands together and scanned the room. He decided to kill everyone below, starting with the men and working his way to the women. He flew down the flight of stairs. He touched them all as they ate, repeatedly telling himself that everyone must die. The taste of vengeance was sweet. He would kill every follower of the gods... kill them all.

The town would have had more deaths that night, but it was late when George exited the tavern. He headed toward the southern edge of the Enchanted Forest. Along the way, another 29 people made the transformation into statues. Once he arrived, he lifted his head to the sky and screamed for Kepler.

After a bit, the giant cat appeared from the shadows, sensing the shift in George. Something inside the demon warned him to keep his distance. The blackness of George's changed eyes burned its way right through the demon. The torch and the way it lit his face amplified the intensity of his dark stare. The demon waited for orders.

George screamed out. "I want you to go into town and find a man named Amar. He works for his brother Morre who owns the magic store. I want you to do this before morning and tell him to come find us. I'll be waiting in the forest for your return."

With a steel-cold tone, George warned Kepler.

"I would leave right now if I were you. I'm in no mood for conversation."

Kepler wanted to object, but he did not want to argue with the hate flowing from this human. For the moment, he would do as he was told. He turned and charged for the shadows of town.

George headed into the forest, found a clearing and started a fire. He lifted his head toward the starless sky and shouted. "Lasidious... Lasidious, I know you can hear me if you're a god. I know you're watching me. I'll kill everything that I see if you don't show yourself."

"You called," Lasidious said, appearing as Jason. Slowly, he morphed into his true form. "I'm here. What is it you wish to say to me?"

George darted toward him and grabbed hold of the god's hand. To his surprise, nothing happened. Lasidious only laughed. It echoed in George's brain. Lasidious lifted only a finger and George was forced back, suspended in air.

Once George's body had floated a good distance, the god lowered his finger, forcing George into a sitting position.

The gods were allowed to defend an attack according to the

Book of Immortality to make a point. On the other hand, they were not allowed to kill the soul responsible for the attack. No law had been broken.

The god surrounded the area with an invisible field, allowing both of them to talk freely without fear of being heard by the other gods. "How bold of you, George, but did you really think you were going to turn me into stone? Are you unfamiliar with what the term god means? Didn't you think I would have enough power to stop something so trivial? Do you think I would've told you how to get this power if I couldn't defend myself against it? Think, George. This is very unbecoming of you. I would've expected more, much more. Now, how about we start again? You can speak to me as if I'm someone you respect."

George screamed at Lasidious. "Why would I want to respect you or any of the gods? It was your fault that the God Wars happened and my daughter died because of them. Why don't you kill me now and get it over with? You've taken everything from me... everything that means anything to me... I have *no* desire to listen to anything you have to say."

Lasidious thought a moment and leaned forward. "George, I know your heart and what you have lost does not necessarily have to be gone forever."

George turned his head. The blackness within his eyes held the gaze of the god without waver. "My daughter is dead. I don't care about anything else that you and all your heavenly counterparts have destroyed, but I do care about her. She was everything to me, my light, my soul, my smile, my comfort, my desire to keep going in life... and the only person I ever truly loved. I never would lie to her—and I lie all the time. I never would hurt her, yet I hurt others all the time. I'm lost without my baby, and you took her from me. I have nothing to live for since you destroyed Abbie, along with everything else in your damn war. What could possibly be so important that you had to destroy my little girl? Why don't you go take a hike? I want nothing to do with you!"

Lasidious laughed as he reached in the pocket of his leather pants. "I will pretend that you didn't speak to me this way George. Look at this." He pulled out a picture of George's daughter and gave it to him. He watched the man tremble with tears as he held the picture near his heart. "Sometimes what we think is lost, George, isn't really lost at all. Your daughter's soul is resting in the Book of Immortality. This book holds all the spirits until it is time for them to be reborn. I retrieved your daughter's soul when the Earth was destroyed and placed it in the Book."

"You what?"

"I knew this day would come and we would have this conversation. I can get your daughter for you, but it will take some time. I have a plan, put in place long ago. I thought you would be the right person to help me carry out this plan. I saved you by bringing you here before your Earth was destroyed. Once I learned of your daughter, I went back for her soul. She was lost in the darkness of space that had once surrounded your destroyed Earth... and I pulled her from it. There were billions of souls there that day, but I only retrieved hers from this darkness. I asked the Book of Immortality to give her soul good dreams. The Book agreed to do this, but questioned why I would do something completely against my nature."

"Yeah and why *was* that?"

"I told the Book that, every now and then, a soul as tender as your Abbie's touches my evil heart. That was the end of our discussion, and I poured happy thoughts into this page along with her soul. She is living an existence where she is at peace with you, George. In her reality, you are the best dad and take her to the park every day. You play with her and get ice cream cones."

"You mean she's all right?"

"Completely—I even gave her a little dog called 'Tidbit.' This vision and other pleasant ones play over and over for her... so she's reminded of how great her loving dad is every single day. She laughs as you both get ready to go home and the dog pees on your foot. You retire to the home you had before you came here. She even thinks her mother is happy and that you have a great marriage. See, George, I've given her a pleasurable existence."

George wiped tears from his cheeks.

"I would say that, other than the ex-wife part, it sure seems to be a pretty good thing you've done for my Abbie, Lasidious. So are you telling me that you can bring her back to me? When can this happen... soon?"

The god smiled.

"I'm saying that thanks to me, your life was spared from the destruction of Earth. I'm telling you that I should be able to one day rejoin you with your daughter. Holding the power to bring your daughter to you is the key and I have a plan to gain this power. For now, I'm bound by the laws set within the Book of Immortality, but I have plans to rectify this problem. For that to happen, I need someone here on this world to take over power and create some distractions. That is necessary for me to move freely while the gods stay busy watching everything unfold. In other words, I need a smoke screen, George. I believe, if we work together, you could see your daughter again... soon. We could have this all done in one of your old Earth years if we work hard at it. However, my entire plan is contingent upon one thing... your being strong enough to create those distractions. Now, I cannot make you do this; you have to want this on your own. It has to be your own free will that chooses to undertake such a task. What do you say, George? Are you with me on this?"

"I'm with you on two conditions. When you finally get the power to retrieve her, you do it immediately... and I'll need to be updated on our progress as we go. I also want to have enough coin where I don't have to worry about things. If you agree to this, I'll bring a hell to this world like no one has ever seen until my baby is returned. I would think that this will keep those other chumps off your tail."

"Agreed," Lasidious said smiling. "It's too dangerous for us to have these meetings. We would not want one of the other gods to listen in and diminish our advantage. If you will open your mind to me, I can keep our conversations between us. No one will be able to look into your mind and retrieve anything we say... and it will allow me to update you without us meeting like this. I'll be able to talk with you in your dreams. George, I'll do this as part of our agreement, but as I said before, this all has to be your choice."

"Then this is what I choose. Let's get this show on the road," George said as he rubbed his hands together.

Lasidious touched him on the head and, after a minute, he moved away. "It's done," he said.

"What, that's it? How anticlimactic. I didn't feel a thing. You need to work on the special effects of gift-giving. Hell, when I received the power from that staff, all I ended up with was a tummy ache. You need to step it up a notch next time, okay? You really suck at this!"

The god laughed. "You and those movies locked in that head of yours. They make me laugh, George. I know about your special effects from Earth and we'll work on it for next time, okay?"

"Hell yeah, that does sound good... maybe some lightning, some thunder or how about crap catching on fire or blowing up with a lot of rain following right behind it to put it all out?"

"I get it, George. You want drama, and I'll show you some. I've cleaned up your mess in town. The people you killed once again live. I'm glad I had my eye on you, or you would've stirred the pot beyond well done. You need to be more cautious of the trail you leave. People would've been scared and started talking. Imagine if someone identified you and an angry mob came after you? You're not immortal, my friend. You don't need that excitement just yet. The time for this will come."

Lasidious walked to him and touched his head once again. His eyes turned back to the soft blue they had once been.

"I don't think your new girlfriend would have liked your eyes looking so evil. I'll no longer visit you unless it is in your dreams or unless I'm completely sure that it's okay to appear face to face. Your Abbie is waiting, so make me proud."

The god vanished just as Kepler showed up.

The demon said hesitantly, "Has your mood changed or should I go for a while? Your eyes look much better."

George had not known that his eyes were a problem until Lasidious had said something—and now Kepler had made a comment about them as well.

"Relax, Kepler, I have nothing to be mad about any longer. I'm sorry for yelling at you. So what do you say we get some information out of this mage when he gets here?"

The demon turned and looked into the trees. Amar stepped forward. The mage moved to the fire and sat near him. "It took me some convincing to get him here. I don't think he likes me!"

Kepler smiled as he moved away.

George focused his attention on the mage. "Amar, I'm glad that you've decided to join us. Please, come and sit down. Let's finish our conversation from earlier. How do you think you can help me, and why do I want your help?"

The King's Castle
The City of Brandor

MOSLEY appeared before the sleeping king in his bedroom chambers. When he woke him, the king jumped from his bed and grabbed his sword, readying himself for battle. Mosley hurried to speak. "Easy, Keldwin, I'm not here to hurt you. I hope I've found you well. How's your son, Aaron?" The wolf intended to make a point with the king. The king was not going to take kindly to being woken up.

Hearing his name, the king looked harder through the darkness, waiting for his eyes to adjust. "Mosley, is that you?"

"It is indeed me, and I've come to speak of important things. I request you get dressed and gather the leaders of your army, then meet me in your throne room."

"Since when do you give orders to a king, Mosley? And who gave you permission to call me by my first name? What on Grayham possessed you to think that entering my chambers is permitted?"

Mosley continued to push the man's patience. "Keldwin, I think you'd be wise to join me in the throne room. I'm not just anyone, and I would look at it as more of a request. You can come to the throne room or not, but I'll be there."

"I'll have you flogged, wolf! How dare you talk to me this way! Guards! Remove this pest from my room!"

"The guards cannot hear you, King of Brandor. This "pest" is no longer just any wolf. I've been given a gift from the gods and now, I'm one of them. I would appreciate it if you would gather your men and meet me in the throne room... if you please!"

"Mosley, you bore me with these lies. You... a god—since when would the gods want the likes of you to join them? Now leave me to my rest, and I'll forget you had the arrogance to enter my chambers."

"I'll leave as you request but . . ." Mosley smiled within himself as he made his next statement. "I guess that I'll have to seek out better men than you to listen to what I have to say."

Keldwin, upon hearing this insult, became furious and attacked Mosley. He lifted his blade high and brought it down across the wolf god's back. The blade passed right through as if thin air had been struck and crashed hard against the stone surface beneath him. The king watched in horror as Mosley turned and faced him. The wolf growled and showed his teeth. His dark fur stood up on the back of his neck as he maneuvered the king into a corner. Once his royal butt was pressed tightly against the wall, Mosley spoke again, snarling.

"I asked politely, Keldwin, and you can do as you choose, but I would think twice before you turn your blade on me again, old king. I am indeed the new God of War and demand respect from the likes of you. Gather your men and bring them to the throne room. I and some of the others will speak with you."

"Others, to what others do you refer?" the king said, frantically.

"The other gods of course," he replied and vanished.

When everyone had made their way to the throne room, the group consisted of the king, his son Aaron, the General Absolute, Justin Graywind and the gods: Mosley, Helmep, Alistar, Keylom, Calla, and Bailem.

Bailem stepped forward and prepared to introduce everyone. He kept his beautiful white wings close to his back and adjusted his robe to a better position around his portly belly. His tail moved back and forth as he spoke.

"This conversation is private to those of us in this room. We cannot be heard by anyone on the outside so all of us can speak freely. Mosley, please tell the king why we've come."

"Keldwin, your god, Bassorine, is no longer with us. I have taken his place. We haven't come here to make any demands, only to inform you of events that will soon happen. You'll need to strengthen your army to its full potential and make ready for war if you are to survive. There's an evil building its forces, the likes of which this world has never seen. For now the threat is minimal, but it will soon be powerful. The Crystal Moon has been stolen from the Temple of the Gods and has been divided into five pieces."

"Who took it?" the king demanded, forgetting temporarily the company he was keeping.

"The god Lasidious has decided to play a game with the fate of all the worlds. He told us two pieces of the crystal will be placed somewhere on Grayham. The gods within the heavens have been divided into two groups. The first is the one you see before you. We will be assisting you if you wish. The second group's objective is to put all the worlds into a darkness that'll last forever. If we don't secure at least three of the five pieces of crystal, all will be lost and the World of Grayham, as you know it, will be a dismal place."

"And, if we succeed?"

"If we succeed... the world will be without evil and your bloodline shall rule forever. The other three pieces of crystal are scattered on the other worlds. It will not be your problem to figure out how to secure the third piece. We would like you to prepare yourself to go to war for the two pieces that remain on this world. The two pieces need to be rejoined soon to buy the worlds some time and keep them from colliding into one another, destroying everything."

The General Absolute spoke out. "If it is a matter of war, my king, I would like the chance to ask questions, sire."

"By all means General, go ahead."

The general walked forward and approached the gods as if they were normal men. "I don't follow a few things. You have said that an evil builds, yet I have no report of this from my runners. Our only foes are the Barbarians, but we haven't been at war for many seasons now. I've heard nothing of any plans of an attack."

Bailem stepped forward. "I understand your concern, General, but we assure you that this force does indeed strengthen itself and will make itself known without warning. Like we said before, the gods are divided in the heavens. If you think that they aren't strengthening their positions with the people of this world, you are indeed without clear thought."

The leader of the king's army rubbed his head as he moved around the room. His bicep bulging as his arm moved back and forth through his long hair. "Your point has been made. I'll get every man called into service to prepare for battle. Exactly how long do we have before we see the first signs of this movement?"

Keylom, the God of Peace, stepped forward. "General, you know I hate war, but we don't know this answer."

The king moved forward to speak. "You would ask me to call every man in my kingdom into service and wait for an undetermined amount of time? The finances for such a calling would be tremendous and ruin our kingdom's economy."

Alistar, God of the Harvest, stepped forward. "Keldwin, your crops are due to be harvested in 45 Peaks of Bailem. I'll bless the soils of your land. Your crops will become bountiful. You'll be able to use the finances from such an abundant harvest to fund your army's preparedness."

The king responded. "It would take three different full harvests to make that kind of coin. I would like to know what your intentions are to address this issue. Without your help, Brandor will have to take its chances and wait to call our men into service."

Alistar turned and thought a moment. "Send word to every farm, village, town and city that when they harvest their crops to be careful to leave the roots of anything harvested above the ground. If they do this, I'll bless the soil. When they awake the following morning, their crops will be grown again. For crops growing beneath the ground: When one is pulled from the ground, replace it with a new seed and the soil will produce another by morning. This will continue until three full harvests of all your crops have been gathered. I assure you they will be abundant."

The general walked forward. "This is good, but how will the people of this land gather this much of a harvest and get it to Merchant Island to be sold?"

Once again, Alistar answered this question. "General, I'll bless an area of soil outside of each city, town, and village. You can use this area to plant and harvest Garanto trees, which will grow and become as tall and as strong as if they had grown for an entire lifetime. Use this wood to make many harvesting wagons. Use them to carry the harvest to the coastline cities of West Utopia, Haven, South Utopia, and Carlosam. Once there, you can use the king's fleet of ships to transport the harvest to Merchant Island. Make sure you have the people in your kingdom stock their homes well. This will assure your men that their families are fed. These harvests will give your economy enough coin. You should be able to harvest enough of these trees to rebuild much of the run-down areas of your lands as well. I'll bless large areas for this. You'll need to build massive barns to store what you are unable to get to the coast until your next trip."

Alistar thought a moment and continued. "Your first harvest is not for a while, which gives you time to build your wagons. I'll leave now to bless these areas and will return to tell you where to plant your trees." The god waved his hand near the wall. Bags of every kind of seed appeared, each bag clearly marked. "I've placed similar bags throughout your entire kingdom. You can find them in your royal storehouses." With that, Alistar vanished.

The king walked up to Mosley. "It appears that there's work to do. I apologize for my arrogance earlier. I think the general will agree that we'll need to use our army to get all this accomplished."

"Wise king," Mosley said. "I'm sure the arrogance would have been similar on my part if someone claiming to be a new god was popping in on me as I slept." He smiled to reassure Keldwin that all was well. And with that, all the gods left for Ancients Sovereign.

Chapter 22

Minotaur

Just Outside the Town of Lethwitch

AS THEY SAT around the fire within the Enchanted Forest, George informed Amar of the trouble he was having controlling his new power. As they talked, he tried to discuss Amar's life—not his own. He did not want to lose any advantage that he and Kepler might have. He could tell Kepler had picked up on what he was doing and at one point, the cat even winked at him to confirm that he understood.

George realized the mage could be helpful in learning how to use his new power and controlling it would prove to be simple. Kepler's skeleton warriors were not going to be necessary.

Amar had grabbed ten rats from the cellar of his brother's store before coming to see him and threw them in a small cage. One by one, he pulled them out and instructed George. It took only four deaths before he had his first success. George was able to limit the transformation to a single leg. The rest of the rat had been spared a solid death, hobbling around in front of them.

Kepler was impressed. "Well, it looks like you're getting the hang of it. Maybe you'll be able to keep from killing us all now."

George shook his head and pulled another rat from the cage. This time nothing happened at all. He smiled as he tossed the rat into the air and Kepler snatched it in his mouth. Again, he reached in and pulled one more and lifted it into the air without changing it.

"That's very good, George," Amar said, "but can you change its heart without turning the rest of it?"

"I can try," George responded. "But how will I know if it worked if I can't see it?"

"Because it'll fall over dead, stupid," Kepler said in a condescending tone. "It is, after all, the heart you're turning to stone. I think that's a pretty major thing that keeps the body going, don't you, genius?"

George realized how stupid his question was, smirked, shook his head and directed his attention toward the rat. The critter began to shake. Seconds later, George tossed the dead rodent onto the ground. He watched Amar cut it open so he could witness his handiwork. Sure enough, the heart was the only thing turned to stone. Everyone around the fire—including the invisible god—cheered at George's success.

Reaching in the cage again, George threw another one to Amar for inspection. This time he had changed just the lungs, as he had intended. Again, everyone praised his work. By the time, he arrived at the tenth rat, he had become good enough to change a specific toenail and then he let the creature loose in the woods. George was pleased with himself, to say the least.

After a bit, he sat next to Kepler. Amar was talking to the jaguar when Kepler felt the hand touch him. He sprang to his feet. George laughed.

"That's not funny, George," Kepler growled.

The jokester rolled on the ground with amused satisfaction. "Oh, my hell, you should've seen your face. Amar, did you see his furry black face freak out? He almost crapped himself."

Amar laughed, and soon Kepler calmed down to laugh at his own expense.

Some time went by as they relaxed by the fire, and then George broke the silence.

"Kepler, go back to the cave and fetch Maldwin. Your brothers need to know that the skeleton warriors aren't needed after all. Amar and I will return to Lethwitch and prepare for the journey to the Siren's Song. In 20 Peaks of Bailem, we'll meet at Angel's Village. After we reunite, we'll head west to the Latsky Divide, and then turn to follow the Latsky River north to the Siren's Song."

Kepler asked, "Why are we going to the Siren's Song?"

"For more power... of course, I need to speak with the wisp inside the mist and give it something."

This seemed to satisfy the demon and he headed for the cave. Amar walked with George into town. On the way, the mage informed George that his family had once served in King Brandor's court. The mage said that they could take the hippogriffs to Angel's Village. When he realized that George had no clue about the flying creatures, he explained. George liked the idea. Amar told him the journey to Angel's Village would only take two Peaks of Bailem by air—and that they could take their time.

Lasidious decided it was time to leave. He had learned enough and his presence was no longer necessary.

George liked the idea of flying on the hippogriffs. Leaving much later than initially expected would allow him to watch Sam's last fight. He could also spend time getting to know his beautiful Athena. He decided to get a room at the inn where she worked and make sure he was there when she showed up.

When they arrived at the inn, the two men shook hands and parted ways after agreeing to meet at Early Bailem on the 17th day. George continued inside the inn. The lady behind the counter smiled as he walked up.

"Back already, I see," she said. "I don't believe we've met properly. I'm Susanne, Athena's sister. I had the flowers taken to her at my mother's house. I'm sure she loved them. She's just south of here, visiting our mother's farm. My sister has never gone home to talk about anyone, except you. I hope you're worth it," she said giving a half-serious-half-questioning laugh.

"Oh, I wouldn't count on it," he responded with a smile. "I'm a big pain in the butt... and I don't think I would pay even one Helmep for me."

Susanne smiled and laughed with him. "So what're you going

to do to keep yourself busy until she arrives?"

"I was thinking about going to the fights. Do you know when they start?"

The woman turned and grabbed a local event calendar. "It looks like they start at the Peak of Bailem. Is there a particular fighter you're interested in?"

"I have an old friend fighting and want to watch him. This will be his third fight. He has won his first two."

"Could you tell him that Athena has a single sister? I always have room for a strong man in my life."

"I will, but I'm not sure how his girlfriend would like that. She's a sorceress."

"Well then, I want no part of it. I would hate to be turned into a frog or something awful like that."

"Thank you for your kindness, Susanne. Will you tell Athena what my room number is when she arrives? I look forward to getting to know you better, too. Hopefully, I'll meet the rest of your family someday."

The Next Day: Lethwitch Arena

GEORGE watched the fights and was amazed at the brutality. Many men were carried out on stretchers, followed by a trail of healers. He hoped Sam was good. The champion of the Lethwitch arena was undefeated, with 11 wins—some of which ended in death and Sam was the unlucky one to be his opponent. The schedule said nothing about the champion like the other fighter profiles had. It simply said he was the 'Beast from the West' called Herogon.

The fight was to be with a sword and shield, no body armor—to the death. When George asked around he learned that combatants would enter the arena in nothing but a loincloth, sword and shield in hand.

He wondered what was going through Sam's mind. If he could find a way inside the fighter's preparation room below the arena, he would ask. He had tried earlier, but had been stopped by two guards.

∞ ∞

Shalee was standing over her boyfriend, rubbing his shoulders. After a minute, she moved away and picked up her staff. She looked at the trainers and asked for some time alone.

"Are you ready?"

"I'm as ready as I can be when you do this. You know this scares me when you use 'Precious' on me. Yeah, you made my pants grow, but are you sure you can make this work? I really don't want to end up like some kind of magical hamburger."

Shalee laughed. "Don't be silly, I wouldn't want my baby to be hamburger either. I do like hamburger, though... so maybe..."

"Not funny, babe, can you please get this over with? I trust you know your stuff so I'm shutting up."

The sorceress gave him a quick kiss. "Make me proud," she said and lifted her staff. "Precious, tiuka helma." Her voice was strong and forceful.

Sam could feel a difference in his skin. Even though his appearance had not changed, he knew the command had worked. He grabbed hold of Kael and used the blade to test the effect. He watched as the razor sharp blade of the gods crossed his skin, leaving no mark behind. "Wow, that's pretty cool, not even Kael is cutting into me."

Kael decided he had a few things of his own to say. "This doesn't mean your opponent's blade won't kill you. It only means your skin has toughened and smaller wounds will not open as easily. Strikes with his hands and feet or even the blunt force of his shield should feel less painful. But if he is able to stab you with the point of his blade or make a solid deep slice, you will die. Do not make the mistake of thinking you're invincible."

"Thanks, Kael, leave it up to you to bring a brother down," Sam joked.

The magical sword had come to understand Sam's humor. "I think you need to prepare your mind, Sam." The sword floated over to Shalee. "Will you excuse us, please? I have something to say to Sam before he goes into the arena."

Shalee had never heard the sword speak before. She was caught off guard, even though she knew it could. She shook it off, kissed Sam and did as the sword requested. When she left, the blade settled down beside the fighter. "Sam, I would like you to fight with me today."

Sam could not believe his ears. Until now, Kael had said that he could not wield him in anything other than training. "Are you sure, Kael? You're not worried I'll embarrass you?"

"I have something to tell you before you can take me into the arena, Sam. I need to tell you what the markings on my hilt mean."

The fighter was all ears and waited patiently for the weapon to continue speaking. "The message reads:

Bound by honor and righteousness,
a true warrior that has lost everything
will command this Sword of Truth and Might.
His wisdom and valor
will be his true power to lead the masses.
The power of the 'Elvish' word
will strike his enemies down before him."

Sam replied, "Kael, that's good and I'm grateful you told me the meaning, but I don't know any of the elvish language."

"Val arrna, it means storm of power," Kael responded. "All you need to do for now Sam is remember two words. When you engage your enemy, it would be wise to say these words. They will allow me to fill your body with energy. I can guide your movements and assist you in striking down your enemy. You'll need to be careful though. You don't want the people finding out you wield a sword given to you by the gods. All you need to do is place me near your mouth and speak the words loud enough so I can feel their power. I'll do the rest and assist when you need it. Unfortunately, I cannot help you in the arenas where swords are not permitted. Today you'll kill your enemy quickly."

"Do we have to kill my opponent?" Sam said with a shock. "I don't wish that on anyone."

In a soft voice, the sword said, "Sam, this fight is with two men who wield sharp weapons. Do you really think there's another way? This fight... will be to the death. It says it on the event schedule."

"You know I don't read the event schedule. It gives me anxiety. Wow, I..." Sam hesitated. For the first time, he realized he was going into an arena to kill someone intentionally. He knew his first two fights had ended with the deaths of his opponents, but that was because his foes were trying to do more than subdue him. In this fight, he was going to kill or be killed. He had to find the rage within him to get through it.

The bell of the arena sounded, jarring Sam from his thoughts. He only had a couple of moments to find his position. He headed out with Kael in his hand.

The crowd erupted as Sam entered. George marveled at how well known he was. They chanted his name while stomping their feet. The fighter moved into his position and held his hands high to absorb the energy of the screaming masses.

When Sam saw his enemy walk through the arena doors, he was shocked to see the beast. It had a bull's head, a massive human torso and powerful, cow-like legs that ended with sharp hooves. He knew the type of beast from books he had read as a kid. It was called a Minotaur—the same type of creature BJ had paralyzed when he was a younger fighter. Long horns, at least two feet in length, extended out on either side of the beast's bull head and the creature towered over Sam.

He watched the beast release a bellowing sound like an angered bull and the crowd erupted with cheers. The creature's muscles tightened when it threw its arms to its side, level with the floor of the arena.

From the intense feeling of the crowd and his opponent's evil stare, Sam knew he would die if he did not fight ferociously. He surrendered to the rage that was beginning to build, fueling him and calling upon his inner demon, locked away in his mind. It was screaming to be freed... Sam opened its cage. The hate poured out of him, changing his entire demeanor. His heart turned to ice and Sam walked in to engage his enemy.

Lifting Kael to his face, Sam closed the distance and spoke the words, "Val arrna." Although he did not feel a difference, he trusted the blade had heard his command. The two combatants collided in the center of the arena. Sam thrust his shield hard into his opponent's, and as they pulled apart, both swords crashed hard into one another, sending their malicious sounds throughout the crowd. As quickly as the blades met Sam pulled his away and slashed at the bicep that held the Minotaur's shield. A large gash opened and the tip of Kael cut to the bone beneath. Blood shot everywhere. His enemy dropped his arm and screamed horrifically. The arm was dead to it, and Sam knew he no longer had to fear this part of the creature's anatomy.

Sam circled and prepared for his next advance. He shot in and the blades tore at each other violently. Sam dropped his shield and followed this strike with a left fist to the snout of the bull's face. He stepped to the right, and spun out of his step by bringing his left leg through, planting it and pulling his right leg back as he moved the Sword of Truth and Might through the air in a slicing motion. As his right foot planted, the blade not only finished cutting the bottom of the creature's arm off below the elbow, it also opened a gash on the beast's left side. Once again the beast cried in pain, and Sam watched his enemy fall to its knees.

Sam backed away and stopped attacking. To his surprise, he was in control of the rage within him. He circled and waited to see if any additional confrontation would follow. He listened to the crowd as they called for death. He was angered, but he did not want to kill the beast. Slowly, he started to walk toward the arena doors, taking his eyes off his opponent. He threw his sword up above his head as he felt the Minotaur's movement behind him, and blocked a downward strike that wielded enough force to have split him in half. He fell away from this strike, rolled forward and spun to one knee. He had placed his free hand behind him, filled it with sand and stood up.

He watched his enemy advance and, as it drew close, he threw the sand into its eyes. Sam caught the swinging arm that held his opponent's sword with a clean, cutting strike of his own that chopped through the beast's elbow. He watched as the weapon fell to the arena floor with the lower arm still gripping it. His enemy was blinded, and it could not clear the sand from its eyes. He listened to the cries of pain as he moved around the miserable creature. Blood was pouring from all the fresh cuts, and the arena floor was saturated. The doctor in him waited for the staggering beast of a man to bleed dry and fall to the ground. After a moment, the cries of his enemy made him realize that he was prolonging his suffering, and he became sympathetic. Moving in, he raised his blade to his side, brought it around and cut the head from the beast. The crowd was frenzied as he grabbed one of the horns and lifted the severed piece of anatomy into the air.

Sam exited the arena carrying his enemy's bullhead. When the healers stopped him in one of the hallways to collect it, he tried to send them away. He said he was going to stuff it and put it on his wall some day. The men looked at each other, not sure how to respond. After a minute, Sam grinned. He tossed the head to them and said he would keep the next one. The healers were unable to grasp why he would want to do such a thing, explaining that the Minotaurs were allies of the Kingdom of Brandor. Doing something like that would be considered disrespectful. Sam acknowledged their point and sent them away without arguing.

Once they were back in the preparation room, Sam and Kael talked. "So it looks like you did me right, Kael!" Sam said excitedly. "You really took it to that son-of-a-gun. The way you made me move was so smooth. I've never felt like that. The beast didn't even touch me once."

"I don't follow," Kael replied. "I did nothing to help you."

"What do you mean? I said the words you told me to and we had ourselves a victory. I've got to admit, I felt great with you guiding my hand."

"I did not guide anything, Sam," the blade responded. "I was ready to help you if you needed me, but this victory was all yours. I didn't have to assist you even in the smallest way. It was your instincts that felt the Minotaur's attempt to strike you from behind. It was your speed that cut through the creature's arms, side and head. All I had to do was enjoy the pleasure of the warm blood that covered my blade... and if you don't mind, I would like to be cleaned up now."

Sam smiled as he removed the blood from Kael. It made the fighter feel good inside to know that he had won this battle with his own skills. It was not long before Shalee, BJ, and Helga came into the room, excited about his victory. They wanted to meet for a celebratory dinner. They made their way to the local tavern. Tomorrow was going to be an early day. They would not be able to stay out late. The plan was to catch a pre-scheduled ride with Soresym to the Town of Mountain View for Sam's next two fights.

That evening, over dinner, BJ and Helga found each other's eyes and playfully flirted with one another. Both trainers were careful not to allow their students to see the momentary exchanges of quick smiles and subtle winks. It was clear to BJ that something was there and he wanted to explore this possibility of Helga's companionship further.

After dinner, BJ excused himself and asked Helga if she would join him for an evening walk. When Shalee offered to tag along, he declined and said it would be nice to pick another trainer's brain about their student's progression without the students present. Both Sam and Shalee thought nothing of it and soon retired to their room.

After the two trainers managed to put some distance between them and the inn, BJ reached down and took Helga's hand. They walked east out of the city and made their way to a bridge which had been built to span the distance over a river which flowed south from the Pool of Sorrow.

They found that their attraction for each other was mutual. It was on this beautiful night, with a clear sky and both the Worlds of Harvestom and Luvelles in clear view that BJ kissed Helga for the first time with the gentle rippling of the river's water passing beneath the bridge.

Athena's work

ATHENA started her shift and was still happy about receiving the flowers from George. She knew it was just a matter of time before he showed up, and she would get the kiss she so badly wanted. She moved all about the inn, singing as she did her odd jobs. She was dusting the bar when her man finally arrived. She flew across the room and into his arms.

"Hey handsome," she said full of excitement. "I'm so glad you're here, I just can't stand it."

George pulled her close and gave her a big, warm kiss.

"I missed that smile of yours. I'm going to be in town for a while. I was hoping that you and I could work on getting to know one another better. Maybe we could take some time, pack a little dinner, and find a nice spot to eat somewhere one of these nights."

Athena liked the idea and excused herself for a minute. She ran into the back room where the kitchen was and, after a few minutes, came out with a basket full of food, telling George she was free for the night. As they left the inn, they held hands and walked south out of town. Athena told him she had the perfect place for them to stay the night. He smiled at the thought and pulled her close.

It was a 15-minute walk before they came to a natural spring that boiled to the surface. It filled an area 60 feet across. A gazebo-like covering sat in the center and a quaint bridge led to the covering. The natural romance of the spot was perfect, and they stopped to dine.

The conversation was without pause and they enjoyed each other's company. Between the constant kissing and touching, they managed to leisurely finish their meal. Eventually they continued on in the dark toward a place only Athena knew. The planets above in the night sky reflected enough of the sun's light to give a soft glow and served to guide their way. When they arrived, George saw a cottage that was about twice the size of his old apartment back on Earth. The stonework was meticulous and great care had been put into every detail.

Athena walked to the door and opened it. "Mother," she said loudly. "I brought home that cute man I was telling you about.

Can we stay in the spare room?"

George was taken aback by the forwardness of his new girl-friend, but after a second of thinking it through, he stepped inside. He shouted, "Mom, we're home!"

Retiring for the evening, he lay with Athena. And for the first time in his life, he snuggled with a woman without expecting more. He knew his goose was cooked—this woman had his heart. All he had to do was figure out a way to make sure she ended up in his life, but he knew that would come in time. He rolled over, pulled her close, and gently drifted off to sleep.

The Grayham Inquirer

When inquiring minds need to know where their favorite characters are.

THREE PEAKS of Bailem have passed. Kepler is with Maldwin at the entrance to the Cave of Sorrow. The jaguar realized, on his way to the cave, that he was going to run into a problem, so he commanded one of his giant feline subjects from the Enchanted Forest to travel with him. The rat refused to leave as expected because his family would not be protected while he was gone. Without the stone, skeleton warrior statues that had been promised, Kepler knew it was pointless to argue with him.

To fix the problem Kepler told the rodent that he would have 100 of his warriors monitor both the cave and the Pass of Tears. They would not leave and Kepler would order them to protect his family. Maldwin agreed and Kepler sent word to his brothers by way of his feline subject. Once Maldwin instructed his family to stay hidden until the skeletons arrived, they left for Angel's Village.

SAM, Shalee, BJ, and Helga have arrived in the town of Mountain View a few days ago. They all were impressed with the scenery. It had taken six and a half hours for Soresym to fly the distance. They worked out a new meeting time for the Griffon's return. Soresym enjoyed the reports of Sam's fighting adventures.

YALOOM, God of Greed, took over the leadership of Lasidious's old team and they are plotting. From what Lasidious told them, they have decided the best thing to do is to put the Barbarian Kingdom in a strong position for the war they know is coming. By the time they are done, an assassination on the King of Brandor's son, Aaron Brandor, and the General Absolute, Justin Graywind, is finalized to be put in motion.

MOSLEY spent the previous day mourning his wife's soul. He hated that she was within the Book of Immortality and is now with his team. They watched from the God World as the King of Brandor sent his runners throughout his kingdom to deliver his orders. Alistar has told Keldwin the locations of the blessed soils and Keldwin has ordered the first harvest of the massive trees which will be used to build the wagons.

Building these oversized wagons is going to be quite the task and the wood continues to be harvested quickly. The runners have called for meetings with the nobles in each city, town, and village in order to explain what must happen. They also informed the nobles that two of the king's engineers would arrive at each location to help with the proper design and construction of the wagons. The final approved drawings show that each wagon will have nine axles and 15 horses are needed to pull them.

GEORGE and Athena spent the last three days on her mother's farm. After that first night, they both agreed to stay in the guesthouse and not in her mother's spare room.

CELESTRIA is still months away from delivering her baby boy. The elven witch family is testing her patience. She wants to destroy them all, but she continues to remind herself of the goals she set with her evil lover. She has retired to her room to speak with the squirrels.

LASIDIOUS is with the Wisp of Song, deep inside the mist of Siren's Song, below Griffon Falls. He tells the creature about the envelope he gave to George, and that the human would be traveling to meet with him. In return for the envelope, he asks the wisp to tell George how to win the crown of the Barbarian King.

SENCHAE BLOODVAIN is still on edge from his run-in with the talking bull. He is sitting in his bedroom chamber holding his Unicorn Prince's horn. He has skipped his training for the first time in 16 seasons.

Thank you for reading the Grayham Inquirer

Chapter 23

Duke Barthom Brandor

BJ took Sam to a quiet place outside of Mountain View to train with Kael. The clearing they were in was surrounded by trees at the base of the Mountains of Latasef. BJ had trained here as a younger fighter many years ago but today, Kael, Sam's Sword of the Gods' would be doing the training.

"Okay, Sam," Kael said, "I have already taught you the command— val arrna— that allows me to help you guide your movements. It is the basis for every other word that will be added for other actions. The next word you must learn is naur. What I want you to do is hold me up and speak all the words at once. You will need to speak more forcefully than you did when fighting the Minotaur to release the power of these words."

Sam thought he understood and lifted Kael into the air. "Val arrna, naur," he said forcefully. The blade burst into flames. Sam dropped it to the ground.

"What are you doing?" Kael screamed as the ground caught fire. The blade went cold and BJ stomped out the flames. "Why did you drop me?"

Sam was speechless for a moment and then responded. "I didn't want to get burned . . . I'm sorry."

"You *wouldn't* have been burned. It's your command that releases my power. This means that you're protected from anything you tell me to do."

"I'm protected? So I won't get hurt... that's cool! May I try again?"

"Yes, but don't drop me!"

"I said sorry already. I won't drop you again."

"It's okay Sam, go ahead and do it."

"Okay, but I am sorry. I didn't mean—"

"Just shut up and do it again," BJ snapped.

Sam lifted Kael up high. "Val arrna, naur." The blade ignited and he began to move it around. He touched it to his skin and was shocked, despite the sword's explanation, to see that the blade felt cold to him. He held it out towards BJ. "Can you feel any of the heat from it?"

BJ responded, "Of course I can, stupid. Kael already told you how it worked. Have you become dense?"

Kael continued to speak. "Sam, now that you have commanded the power and it is active, you can build on it, like you would the stones of a home's foundation. Let's say you're in a fight and have commanded my flame, but now the enemy is lining up in front of you. You need to bring them down much quicker. You can extend my area of coverage without changing my weight or balance. You can swing my blade at will and not worry about your allies around you. This power will only cut your enemies down and pass right through your friends without harm. I want you to hold me up and say the word . . . *ngw*."

"Wait a second," Sam said before going any further. "So after I do this, let's say there is an enemy on the far side of BJ. Are you telling me that I can pass the blade right through BJ's body and only kill the enemy beyond him?"

"That's exactly what I'm saying and it doesn't matter if an enemy is beyond him or not. If you consider him to be a friend or ally, then I *will* pass right through him. We are connected spirit to spirit."

"No way, this has to be the coolest thing I've ever heard. Okay, so how do you pronounce that word again?"

It took a couple of times for Sam to learn how to pronounce it as the word had no vowels. Once he understood, he lifted the sword and released its power. Sam was floored to see Kael's blade extend neatly another eight feet. He moved the sword around and it felt as if nothing had changed. Even when he brought the sword to his side, the blade adjusted to pass through without hitting the ground and then re-extended itself again. Sam spun around smoothly and, after a bit, he caught BJ off guard as he passed the blade right through him.

"Watch it, boy," BJ screamed. "Just because you know it won't hurt me doesn't mean I want it tested on me. If I could, I would kick that sorry butt of yours."

Sam smiled and he held Kael to his side and moved to stand by the trainer. "Don't be mad, big guy. You know I love ya."

BJ grumbled and moved away. "So what's next?" Sam said, as he looked at Kael.

Kael's magic subsided. "I can see you like this. Let's try a new one. The word for ice is *khelek*. I want you to do the same thing, but this time instead of commanding fire, I want you to command me with the word for ice."

Sam lifted the blade and said his command: "Val arrna, khelek ngw." Kael once again extended and an ice-cold flame appeared all around his blade. "Oh my gosh, this is so cool! But why would I need to have both fire and ice? Why not just stick with one?"

"For such a smart man, you can ask the dumbest questions. Do you think that you would fight a fire-breathing dragon with a sword of fire when it is immune?"

"Okay, I see your point. Are you telling me there are dragons on this world?"

"No, I did not say that, but some enemies will have an ability to withstand certain powers. The dragons live on the World of Dragonia. I don't imagine you would need to worry about them. But one day you may find yourself in a fight where you'll need to use a different type of power to strike down your enemies. I'll also teach you the words for water, poison, and lightning."

"If I'm fighting these kinds of beasts, then they may have magic of their own. How will I defend myself against them?"

"At any point you feel you need protection, you can use the words *var* and the name of what you need to be protected from. For example, you could say *Var alu*. This will protect you from an enemy that uses water as a weapon. If you need to protect those immediately around you from this same foe, you can use the words *Vara alu*, which will extend the area of protection to 15 feet around you."

Sam thought a moment. "So let me give you an example. Let's say I'm fighting one of these fire-breathing dragons. I would say

Val arrna, ngw khelek to bring forth the icy flame on your blade, and then I would follow this up with Var naur to protect me from its breath of fire. Is this what you're saying?"

Kael confirmed and they continued with the training.

Shalee and Helga are shopping

SHALEE purchased a new belt designed with many pockets sewn into it. Helga explained that many useful substances could be kept in the pouches and Shalee would be able to command her staff to retrieve them when necessary. But before Helga could explain anything else and per Shalee's character, she pointed her staff at the belt and commanded Precious to change the appearance into something more fashionable.

"I think I can wear this now," Shalee said laughing. "I wasn't about to wear that hideous thing."

"Everything is fashion with you," Helga said, shaking her head. "Will you pay attention now, child? We need to put some key in-gredients in those pockets so you can command Precious to com-bine them for the effect you want. It's like cooking; when you bake bread, you need different ingredients. Your staff is able to summon fire, lighting, ice, and wind naturally. You won't have to worry about those since they can't be kept in a pouch anyway. But now we have 25 pouches to fill so we should choose wisely and prepare an arsenal of commands that will use the ingredients available to you."

"I agree we need to choose our ingredients wisely, but we won't need to prepare an arsenal of commands."

Helga looked at Shalee quizzically. "How so, child? I've been doing this for many seasons now, 247 to be exact, and I think I know what I'm doing."

"Well, you taught me that Precious can read my mind," Shalee replied, "so that means all I need to do is command my staff to *create* and let her look into my mind for the desired outcome."

Helga moved to the other side of the room. She sat down and thought a moment. "You may have a point, but it would require a lot of power. I have spent my whole life saying each word for every ingredient I use. What you're describing seems too simple, but it also sounds possible. We'll try it once we fill the pouches. I can't imagine that you have this kind of power yet, but we'll see.

"You will need to make sure you buy more ingredients as they get low. The staff will only need to draw from a very small amount of each ingredient no matter how large the effect, but you'll eventually run out."

Once again, Shalee smiled and looked at the older sorceress. "Why would I do that when all I need to do is tell Precious to multiply what's already there? Once we have the supplies, I'll never need to go to the store to buy them again."

Helga was floored.

"I can't believe I've lived this many seasons and never tried to do that. I have always waited till I ran out and found a place to buy more. Poison can be expensive, you know!"

Shalee laughed. "Watch this. I'm sure it will work."

She went over to the store owner and asked the lady to bring her a vial of poison. The lady did as requested and produced the vial. Shalee asked for a bowl. It took a moment, but the lady returned with one and sat it in front of her. Shalee lifted Precious and spoke her command and it was not long before the entire bowl was full.

Both Helga and the lady behind the counter were amazed. Helga took a little bit of the poison from the bowl and put it inside a cup. She lifted her own staff and did as Shalee had done. The sorceress flew back, landing on her butt as she failed.

"Holy cow," Shalee said with a panic. "You failed. Are you okay?"

"Help me up will ya! Other than my pride being hurt, I'm fine!"

Shalee smiled. "Well, there is a bright side to your failure."

"And what would that be?"

"Well, at least you didn't waste all the coin that you've spent on ingredients all those seasons."

Shalee picked Helga up from the floor as the older sorceress grumbled. Shalee turned and looked at the lady behind the counter. "Care to try?" she said smiling.

The woman declined and said she didn't have the power to command something of that nature; her staff was best left under the counter.

The three women enjoyed choosing the 25 ingredients. Shalee had everything she needed—a vial of water, poison, sand, cloth, steel that had been ground to a fine powder, straw, sulfur, dragon scales—four different types—and various other creatures' parts. She had a vial of explosive powder and three types of oil—one of them simply for nothing more than cooking. With the power Shalee used to multiply the woman's inventory, she did not end up paying for any of it. It was a successful day of shopping, and they left to go out of town and try a few spells.

Later that Night, Just South of The City of City View

MIEONUS, Goddess of Hate, arrived behind a tavern south of City View. The cliffs nearby had been the point of entry for Brandor's Army 75 years ago when they attacked the Barbarian's Kingdom. At that time neither the city nor the tavern existed. The King of Brandor back then, Jahronus Brandor, had sailed his fleet beneath the cliffs to unload 10,000 men. Prior to this, 200 of his finest men had scaled the rocky walls. They had carried with them long thick ropes and, once at the top, they signaled for the fleet to come and secured heavy iron chains to the top of the cliffs for climbing.

The army had used a special catapult that had been attached between two of the king's largest ships to throw a massive iron ball to the top of the cliffs. The ropes were woven together to keep them from snapping. Once this had been done, they wrapped these ropes around the backside of a number of large trees to act as a pulley. The men secured one end of this much larger, woven rope to the big ball, and dropped the other end to the ships below. Large iron link chains were secured to it, and the ball was pushed over the side of the cliff to lift the chains upward.

Due to the ocean's depth, the army had to devise a way to sever the rope before the iron ball pulled the chains up and around the trees, then back into the ocean forever. They created a series of special bladed harpoons to make sure they didn't miss. The men fired over 40 shots in the direction of this reinforced rope. It was the job of the 200 men at the top of the cliffs to make sure that when the rope was severed, the chains did not fall back in the opposite direction.

These 200 men had thrown their weight on the chains and driven special iron bars between the links. The whole operation would have failed except for the cuts the chains made in the trees. The cuts stopped the progression of the chain long enough for the men to secure it properly. The army climbed up the chains, and began their invasion on the Kingdom of Bloodvain. And now there was a tavern that had gained its name due to this activity...The Iron Chains.

Mieonus had been assigned to plan the assassination of the King of Brandor's son, Aaron Brandor, and the General Absolute, Justin Graywind. The goddess knew that inside this tavern was a relentless killer named Dawson Drake. He skillfully killed his victims and was the deadliest assassin in all of Grayham.

Dawson Drake, known only by the name "Double D", had not used his real name since his first assassination at the age of fourteen. His father had been a drunken piece of garesh and beat his mother. She had been the type of woman who loved Double D with all her heart and could not defend herself against the advances of her husband. After a long night of merciless beating, Double D leaned over and picked her up off the floor. She made the mistake of saying in a blood-filled, raspy voice that she would give her last Helmep if someone would kill her husband; her son took her up on the offer. After he attended to her wounds and she lay down to sleep, Double D took her last two Helmep coins as payment from her secret stash and entered the darkness of the night. He left with murder on his mind, stalking his father from the shadows as he returned from yet another night of heavy drinking. The situation was perfect for a killing, with him and his father being the only ones around. He crept up on the much bigger man and buried both his daggers deep into each one of his kidneys. As he stood over the man he stared into his eyes and watched him take his last breathe, knowing it was his own son that had ended his life. It was just the beginning of Double D's merciless career.

The assassin was always a hard person to find, and the only way to get in touch with him was through a man called Assistant Kane. Once contact had been made with Kane, it was difficult to get Double D to accept the job for anything less than 25 Yaloom coins, the highest denomination of currency in the land. The goddess knew that when she entered the tavern Double D would not find her request welcome; it would be a tough sale to get him to accept such the job.

Mieonus decided not to approach him as a goddess, but rather she would show up as Assistant Kane himself. She needed a way to deal with the irritation of the assassin if he became angry. She moved her arms in front of her and, as she did, a new appearance emerged... she was now a tall, thin, handsome man with long black hair in brown leather pants and a black shirt.

Slowly the goddess worked her way into the tavern heading for a spot at the bar next to Double D. As she sat down, she spoke to the assassin with a whisper.

"We need to talk, Double D. I see you're still hanging out with the Barbarians. How do you avoid being killed?"

The assassin was a shorter man with an athletic build. His hair was long and he was dressed in black from head to toe. He was not ugly, but he was also not considered handsome. His eyes were brown and his long brown hair fell across his eyes as he looked down at his ale.

"I thought I told you never to meet me in person, Kane."

"I know, but there are extenuating circumstances," the goddess replied.

"I don't care what kind of circumstances you have come to me under. You know how I work and this isn't the day that I'll make exceptions."

Kane stood up from the bar. "Too bad you feel that way. The job would have paid us 100 Yaloom. We would have been rich. I'll see if Tiara wants the job." The goddess left the bar and started to walk down the trail leading into town. The next thing she knew, she was laying flat on her back with a dagger to her throat.

Double D whispered softly. "Move and I'll cut you through. What possibly could be such an important job that it would pay 100 Yaloom, Kane?"

"Someone wants the son of the King of Brandor and his General Absolute dead. Will you please let me up? This is not how I want to do business tonight. Maybe we could walk and discuss this."

"That kind of job is a suicide mission! Why would anyone want to attempt such a thing?"

"Well, I'll leave and tell them you said it can't be done. I'm sure they'll find someone to go for that kind of coin."

"I never said it couldn't be done. I said it was a suicide mission . . . suicide for everyone but me. I wouldn't do the job for such a low price though. It'll take twice that much."

The goddess laughed and started to walk away. "I'll tell them you said that also, but don't expect me to return with an answer."

"Kane," Double D called after him, "One-hundred-fifty then." The assassin watched as the man kept walking. "One-hundred-twenty-five and that's my final offer. Don't push me, Kane."

"Deal   you know where to find me for your money when the job is done."

"I need supplies for the job. I need an advance."

Kane turned and looked at him. The goddess threw a bag filled with coins and watched the assassin catch it.

"I see you came pretty sure of yourself tonight, aye Kane?"

"I'm a business man. That's what I do." And with that the goddess walked down the path and out of sight.

17 Peaks of Bailem Have Passed Since Parting With Kepler

GEORGE walked up the stairs of the landing tower with Athena, to find Amar waiting for him at the top. The time he spent with Athena was wonderful, and he was 150% sure he wanted this woman to be in his life forever. He told her he had to travel to the Siren's Song to meet with the wisp, which surprised him. When he tried to tell her a lie about where he was going, he found he could not do it because of his deep love for her. He told her the truth and the woman did not question him. She smiled and told him to be careful and simply asked when she would see him again. Again he told her the truth saying he did not know exactly, but that he would try very hard to see her as soon as he could. He wanted her to believe in him so much that, the previous evening at dinner, he gave her his Rolex and asked if she would consider moving to wherever he settled down. She said it would be okay as long as they could visit her family every now and then. He liked that answer and, as they had done every night, they went to her mother's guest house.

George greeted Amar and turned to kiss his beautiful Athena. "Tell mother I said goodbye, okay?"

Athena liked how he had taken her mother in as his own.

"I'm sure that both my mother and sister will be asking me 500 questions when I get to work. I've never taken this much time off in my entire life. My sister is expecting all the naughty details. The great thing is that I don't have to embellish and make it all up this time." She moved in close and put her head to his chest as she giggled happily. "I love you, George," she said.

This was the first time he had heard those words from Athena's mouth. He looked into her eyes and said, "I love you too." For the first time in his life he had told a woman that he loved her without it being some sort of a game.

Amar also said goodbye to Athena and, as they both climbed onto the back of the hippogriff, George displayed a smile that would not go away. The hippogriff launched into the air, and the two love birds gazed at each other until they were nothing more than a tiny speck.

The City of West Utopia

SAM won both fights in the Town of Mountain View and had now arrived in West Utopia. He beat both of his opponents in the arena and, like before, all his fights ended in death. His record was now a perfect seven wins with zero losses, all by way of permanent knock out.

Now, Sam and Shalee planned on taking the day off from training. They wanted to spend some time together without the crowds that have been following them. Sam's rise to glory was starting to show some real promise and the break was necessary for them both to stay sane.

BJ and Helga bid their students a good day and took the opportunity to run off and spend some quality time of their own with one another. Their secret relationship had blossomed since their first kiss just outside of Lethwitch and it was becoming tiresome to create excuses to hide the fact from Sam and Shalee that they wished to be with one another.

Grayham was similar to Earth in yet another way. It had its own version of the paparazzi, but instead of the constant snapping of photos, they wanted the fighter to sit still and allow himself to be drawn. These drawings would be hung on the information boards that could be found at the center of most any populated area. With the time it took to sit for an artist, Sam and Shalee both figured they'd much rather have the photographers from Earth in their face.

But finally, they were able to pack a lunch and just past the Peak of Bailem they headed out. As they were leaving town, a young child dressed in fine clothing ran up to them and bowed. The boy was holding a note in his hand.

"Can I help you, young man?" Sam said.

"Your presence is commanded at Duke Barthom Brandor's home, sir."

Sam looked at Shalee and laughed. "Well, who are we to turn down a request to go meet our first duke?"

Shalee laughed as the little boy interjected. "This is not a request sir. It's an order to come to his home."

"And if I don't wish to come, young man?" Sam said angrily. "Maybe I don't wish to come, boy."

"Sir, I beg you to come. If you don't, I'll be beaten for being incompetent."

Sam looked at Shalee as she slid in close to him. "Well, you did say you wanted glory, sweetie. I suppose that with your glory, we'll have to put up with some pompous jerks every now and then."

Smiling, the fighter turned back to the boy. "Alright boy, lead the way."

The child led them through the city and up a hill to some large estates. They reminded Shalee of the Roman architecture she had studied in her free time back on Earth. The whole scene was fascinating.

Sam, on the other hand, was not so impressed.

"You would think the gods would have at least given the people of this world some other ideas for their architecture. It's like they stole all their ideas from Earth. Yea, I know it was supposed to make our transition easier on us, but give me a break already. It's not very unique if you ask me. Everything since we have arrived on Grayham, though beautiful, is from some period of our history back on Earth before its destruction. Can't they come up with something original at least?"

Shalee rolled her eyes.

"Who says that these were our ideas in the first place? Maybe these same ideas have been used before Earth was ever created in some other culture, in some other world."

Sam nodded his head in agreement. "Point made, you might be right I suppose. It wouldn't surprise me after all that we've learned. But I wonder what the other worlds look like that the collective has created. Bassorine did say that they are different than Grayham. I just wonder how different."

As they continued to walk, massive columns lined the road leading to the duke's home. The detail of the sculptures that had been chiseled into the columns, were remarkably life-like. Beautiful grape vines stretched between each of them and were held by the chiseled stone hands of the sculptures' outstretched arms. The fruit was being harvested by slaves. The cobblestones of the road were perfectly placed on top of tamped rubble beneath to allow for the drainage of water.

The Duke's home was enormous making both visitors feel anxious as they entered. They were taken to a large room and, as the doors to the room opened, a group of people greeted them. Shalee was relieved that she had made both of them dress nice for their special day together.

A fat, jovial man walked up and introduced himself. "Welcome, welcome, my name is Barthom Brandor and I'm the Duke of West Utopia. I have heard much about you prior to your arrival in our fair city, Sam, but I don't believe that I know who you are, young lady!" The duke kissed her hand.

"My name is Shalee. It's nice to meet you, Duke Brandor."

"Sam, I believe that a woman as beautiful as the one on your arm should be given the right to call me by my first name if that's all right by you, sir."

"By all means, I'm sure this would make things far more pleasant for the lady."

"Then it is settled. Shalee, you can call me Barthom and, since I have extended the courtesy to your lovely companion, I will allow you the same privilege, Sam."

"Thank you, Barthom," Sam responded. "To what do we owe the pleasure of being called to your home today, sir?"

"I watched you fight today, Sam, and I must say that your reputation as it spreads through Grayham is an understatement. I don't believe that I've seen such a presence in the arena since my king's General Absolute. I dare say that you could find yourself in the arena with General Graywind himself some day. This would be a fight I would dare not miss. He, like you, has killed every single man who has ever entered the arena with him. I do hope you're able to make it that far and shove his vanity right down his throat."

The entire room erupted with laughter.

"Seems you have earned a room full of fans, Sam, and I'm sure that we'll all be following your career."

Sam and Shalee found that their day with the noble and his friends to be a pleasant one and, as they left, their host sent them off with a few gifts. Sam received a set of finely crafted black leather armor. The seal of the duke's home, a red dragon, was embedded at the center of the chest piece, arm bracers, and greaves.

Shalee was given six bolts of expensive fabrics of assorted colors. She realized though that she did not have any place to put them. She'd been so busy running around with Sam and staying at one inn and then another that she hadn't even thought of getting a place of her own. She spoke with him about the problem as they headed back into town and decided they would go back to the inn and discuss the issue with Helga.

Helga and BJ were sitting at the bar of the inn drinking ale when the two arrived. They saw the older couple flirting with one another but didn't say anything. BJ was about 61 and, even though Helga was over 247, she did not look a day over 60. They stood in the background and watched as Helga reached over and touched BJ's arm. It was clear there was more to this relationship, but neither Sam nor Shalee had noticed it until now. Slowly Sam crept up on them and, right as BJ touched Helga's hand, he cleared his throat loudly.

The trainers jumped.

"Well, look what we have here," Sam said with a fatherly voice. "I guess I'm going to have to start keeping a better eye on you two kids. We leave you for the shortest time and come back to find you flirting. I'm shocked."

"Oh, get lost," BJ said with a smile. "Old people have lives too, you know. I never would have thought I could look at another woman after my wife died, but all this traveling with Helga has given me a new perspective. We have something here that's good for the both of us."

Helga sat on her stool, embarrassed about being caught. "Sam, please know that we still intend to make sure your training is the best we can offer."

Shalee jumped into the conversation. "I don't think that ever crossed our minds, Helga. The idea is rather charming really. Sam and I were talking the other day about the two of you and agreed you both are like, well, parents to us. You're not just our trainers, you're our friends. We've grown to see you as family and love you both."

Helga started to cry at the sentiment. BJ looked at Sam and rolled his eyes as guys do when this kind of thing happens. He stood and placed his arms around her and said, "Well, the cat has been let out of the bag. We can be more open with our love now."

"Love, you guys have been doing this long enough to use that kind of word?" Sam said. "Where was I when all this courting took place?"

BJ turned to Sam. "Well, since you and Shalee consider me as a father, the place you have been when Helga and I were courting is right there with my daughter. This incestuous relationship you two have going must stop." The trainer smiled as he sat back on his stool.

Everyone laughed. Helga was able to stop crying and slapped BJ on the arm for being crude. "He's always talking that way. He can be so naughty. Why last night he said—"

Shalee grabbed her ears and spoke over Helga. "This is T.M.I. This is T.M.I."

Sam agreed, chuckling. "Too much information," he confirmed.

Helga and BJ laughed at the phrase and tuned in to what Sam had to say.

"Shalee and I just received some gifts from Duke Brandor." He pointed to the leather armor. He had set the gifts down across the room prior to sneaking up on them. Shalee's fine fabrics were also on the pile. As soon as BJ saw them, he jumped from his stool and ran over to take a look. Lifting the chest piece from the floor, he held it up in front of him. The excitement could be seen on his face as he threw it up and over his head to try it on. The armor was far too large for his smaller frame, but it didn't curb his enthusiasm. "Sam, do you realize what this means?"

The fighter moved over to stand next to his trainer. "It means we have met our first noble I guess, why?"

"It means far more than that, Sam," BJ responded. "It means that the house of Brandor will be talking about you as your career develops. It means that the king himself knows who you are. The nobles are talking about you now and this is good. When something like this happens, a fighter usually receives an invitation to come and fight before he completes his 11 city, 22 fight requirements. So far we've completed three cities. If we can win our next few fights, I'll bet that if you win convincingly in the City of Haven, you'll get an invitation to come to the City of Champions before you finish your second fight in the Town of Empire. Sam, all you have to do is make your victories have large statement attached to them and we'll be on a fast track to the King of Brandor's personal Tournament of Champions.

"There is far more than fighting at this tournament. It's a city-wide event that lasts for ten Peaks of Bailem. Sixty-four fighters are invited and none of the fights are meant to be to the death until the last two. If a fighter survives his last two fights, he's then given a chance to fight the General Absolute. Many want the glory attached to this, but all have died from this choice. The general is a merciless fighter and, although he's an honorable man, he believes that the arena is a beautiful place to die. The leader of the king's army steps into the arena fully prepared to die, and is equally prepared to kill."

The trainer took the chest plate off and placed it on Sam as he continued.

"The first day of the tournament is to celebrate the 64 fighters and the General Absolute. The next seven days of the tournament is held and the field is narrowed until only one fighter is left. On the ninth day, this fighter is given his chance to face the general. The tenth day is the highest form of glory a fighter can achieve on our world. The winner of this fight is celebrated and invited to the king's personal dining table in his castle. For as long as I can remember it has been the general who has been celebrated. I don't think he cares about dining with the king, since I imagine he probably does this often as the leader of the king's army. If you could beat the general in the arena—you would be one of the most powerful men in the Kingdom of Brandor. Only the king and his son would be above you."

After hearing the trainer's speech, Sam was excited. He agreed that he needed to make an impression in his next few fights. He was about to order an ale when Shalee tapped him on the shoulder. He turned and saw a look of fright in her eyes.

"What's wrong, babe?"

Shalee put her hand on his chest. "Didn't you hear the part where BJ said that everyone of the general's opponents have died when they fought him?"

"I heard it, so what's the big deal?"

"He's killed everyone—that's the big deal. I don't want that to happen to you. I love you!"

"He also said I didn't have to fight him if I didn't want to. So let's not worry about it." He said this to make Shalee relax, but knew he would fight, if given the chance.

Shalee seemed to be okay with the answer. After a moment she turned to Helga and asked if the sorceress would make a quick detour to the City of Brandor and find a place for them all to live.

BJ thought it was a great idea. Being this close to Brandor, it would only take four Peaks of Bailem to fly down and find a home. Helga could make her way back afterward. All she had to do was take a separate hippogriff to Brandor. She could find a suitable home and catch one a few days later to meet up with them in the City of Haven. He suggested she even take the cloth Shalee had been given and leave it there. BJ said he would go himself, but he would not have time to get back before Sam's next fight. Helga agreed to leave for Brandor the next day.

Retiring for the evening, Shalee watched to see Helga slip into BJ's room. She smiled as she went to bed herself, crawling up next to Sam, she said. "You can see the love in their eyes for one another. I think it's cute!"

Sam just rolled his eyes.

The next morning the group headed for the landing tower. While walking through town, they all noticed a higher level of military activity. The king's soldiers were carrying trees to the mill. Sam stopped one of the men and asked what was going on. The man said the king had given orders to build harvest wagons. The king himself had received word from the gods that the harvests were going to be bountiful and the wagons would be needed in order to transport the bounty to the coastal cities.

"Why is the harvest being transported to the coast?" Sam asked BJ.

"The harvests are shipped to Merchant Island to determine their value and then distributed throughout Grayham," BJ said. "Each world has certain benefits they provide to the others. Goods are exchanged between the worlds and delivered back and forth by the Merchant Angels."

Sam was curious about the angels and asked more questions. BJ continued to explain.

"The gods have created a group of beings whose sole purpose is to move the merchandise back and forth from each of the worlds. The merchandise is delivered to each world's Merchant Island and, after a value is established, it is distributed into the population. No one has ever seen a Merchant Angel. There are special areas of the island that the Angels assemble to gather the goods and then take those goods away when everyone is gone.

"Sometimes, when government officials from two worlds agree to allow a member of another race to visit, it is the Merchant Angels who transport them. The ride is said to be dark and miserable. The gods have created special containers to transport live beings, but the entire ride is spent in the dark and takes two Peaks of Bailem or more depending on which world you're going to. For example, when a criminal is caught, they are sent to the World of Dragonia as punishment. If the dragons don't kill you, the other criminals living there will… or maybe the demons."

"Dang, that's crazy," Sam responded as they arrived at the base of the landing tower and began their climb to the top. "So can you at least eat on this journey?"

"I don't know anything more about it, Sam. Maybe you'll have to do some research later on it."

Once at the top of the tower, they stood on the platform and waited for BJ to lift Helga up onto the sitting area of her hippogriff. He blew her a kiss as the giant beast lifted into the sky.

Soresym showed up not too long afterward, right on schedule. It was the first time Shalee had been standing on top of the tower when one of those magnificent creatures landed. The wind created from the beast's wings as it landed made her thankful for the tall railing that lined the entire perimeter.

She walked over to the griffon and smiled as she put her hair back in place. "So much for looking cute for you today, Soresym," she said jokingly.

The griffon chuckled as the remaining three climbed on board. They lifted off to wing their way to the City of Haven.

Chapter 24

A Father of Seven

World of Luvelles

LASIDIOUS is on the World of Luvelles visiting with the Source, an ancient dragon the gods have provided with a home. The Source's job is to test all those that seek magic's greater power and determine if they are capable of looking into the Eye of Magic. If deemed capable, the Source grants them access. It is not enough to be just capable. The seeker must also be truly worthy by the Eye. If they are—the seeker lives. If not—the seeker's soul is swallowed by magic, and their body locked within the Eye forever. Since Lasidious does not want to make another appearance before the gods at the moment, planning the future is in order and the Source is a good place to start.

Just Outside
The City of Haven's Gates

BRANDON SMITH, a strong-willed, handsome family man, comes from a long line of farmers and makes his home near the City of Haven. Not only is his family known throughout the valley for their kindness, but they are also known for their ability to make well-crafted, iron shoes for the area's horses. He is a good father to seven beautiful children while his wife Josephine, is an average-looking woman with a heart of gold. After bringing six boys into the world, she was finally blessed with a beautiful little girl.

Family comes first in Brandon's life and, even though he is busy with them, he also maintains a strict training schedule, which he follows after the children go to bed. His wife puts the children down every night after dusk, then Brandon trains in their barn with three of his good friends. He goes on to participate in the fights each season when they come to Haven.

Brandon named his sons Brandon Jr., Jonathan, Mathew, Jasper, Mark, and Chase. His little girl, Adriana, is now three seasons old and her brothers, starting from oldest to youngest, are twelve, ten, nine, eight (twins) and five seasons respectively. His oldest, Brandon Jr., is a strong boy who has worked with his father in the fields of their farm since he turned eleven. It is the same age Brandon's father and his father before him had put their boys to work... a family tradition.

Jonathan is an athletic child and spends countless hours playing with his father's wooden training swords. He was almost eight before he could carry a stave properly, but once he could, his mother couldn't keep the thing out of his hands.

Mathew is quite the fisherman. If he cannot be found, he is probably on the river going after the "big one." It was only five nights ago that he came home carrying enough fish to feed the entire family. Brandon made sure the boy received the recognition he deserved and helped the boy prepare the meal for a special celebration of his catch.

Twins Jasper and Mark are mama's boys. They are the mischievous ones of the family, but know when their father speaks, they'd better listen. They do, on the other hand, run rough shod all over their mother. It took a while but she finally figured out their weakness. When the two boys would get out of hand, she would send them out to pick a sturdy switch off some nearby trees. When they returned, she would place them on the table and inform the boys that the switches were for their father to beat them with when he came home. The kids knew it would hurt, and it was this style of mental warfare that usually put them right back in line. Most of the time, Josephine would find a reason to let them off the hook before Dad arrived home. It was actually quite rare for her to allow them to get the switch on their rear ends, but she would, when necessary. For the most part, however, the switches just served as a friendly reminder that she meant business.

Chase was the charismatic one of the bunch. He not only had his grandmother and grandfather wrapped around his little finger, but all the neighbors as well. He was the kind of kid who could talk to anyone despite being only five seasons old. His mother's friends loved pinching his chubby cheeks. Brandon had taken his son into the city last spring and stopped at a local place to eat. Melted goat cheese on potatoes—Chase's favorite food. On that particular day, three beautiful women who were leaving the eatery stopped, pinched Chase's cheeks, and called him "cutie." Chase had turned his head and, even at the early age of five seasons, watched their beautiful backsides all the way out of the door before turning back around and saying, "Dad, every girl in this town . . . loves me!" Brandon had laughed and rubbed his hand through the boy's hair before heading home.

Adriana, the baby of the family, had thick blonde hair and facial features like her father. She was also spoiled—a real daddy's little girl. She thought her father walked on water. Josephine had taught Adriana how to butter Brandon up when she wanted something. If Brandon had an Achilles' heel, Adriana was it.

Brandon Sr. met Josephine when he was a boy in school. They were the same age and now, at 30 seasons old, they had been together as a couple since he asked his wife to go steady with him at the age of only ten seasons. When Brandon was 16 seasons and of legal age to leave his father's home, he went to his wife's father and asked for her hand in marriage. Because their fathers were good friends, permission was granted and a beautiful wedding was celebrated not long after.

Josephine did not waste any time starting their family. She became pregnant on her 17th seasonal celebration. Children had been an experience that forced both of them to change quickly, but they managed to hold their vows sacred and grew together.

It was on Brandon's 18th seasonal celebration that he became old enough to fight in the arena and had been fighting each summer season ever since. It was just before his wife had given birth that he won his first fight. The money from the victory helped them start making payments on a piece of land he wanted to purchase from his father. His father was a good man and loved by most everyone. On Brandon's 20th celebration, after he had struggled to make his way for the last four seasons, his father decided Brandon had learned how to be a man and let him have the land without having to pay any more. That day had been a wonderful celebration that the entire Smith and Rosslyn families had attended. Both families were from the area and numbered over 197 strong.

Today was another great day and Brandon's family was getting ready to head into the city and watch their father fight in the arena. Brandon had been an arena fighter for 12 seasons now. When the fights would come to Haven each summer, he used it as an opportunity to make extra income. They would drop Chase and Adriana off at the grandparents' house before heading to their favorite inn. The only thing that changed throughout the seasons was how many kids attended with them.

After checking into the inn, Brandon went down to the arena at dusk and, as he always did, he read the fight schedule for the next day's events. Just like every season, he had absolutely no information about whom he was fighting, but he did notice that his opponent was his same height and about 30 pounds heavier.

Brandon was the only fighter who never entered the lottery because of his connections, and was also the only fighter that did not travel from place to place. His dad's brother was the event planner and, as his uncle had done every season, he saved the one fight without weapons for Brandon. His wife had been firm that no weapons were to be involved, and had insisted that he not fight with anything that could split him open. So his only option had been to fight hand to hand. It was his good fortune and the fact that his uncle was employed by the arena that allowed him to fight in the same event each season.

The next day Josephine woke them all and, as per tradition, they made their way to the inn's dining area. This was the one time the kids could order whatever they wanted. They laughed and told stories over a diverse selection of food and, after breakfast, Brandon left for the arena after kissing them all goodbye.

"I love you all. Maybe after the fight we will go to grandpa's house and swim in the pond." He embraced each one separately before heading out. He did, however, stop when he came to his lovely Josephine. He kissed her softly and looked her into the eye. "I consider myself blessed each day to have you as my wife. You're my reason for living. I love you so much!"

The look of his wife's face said it all. They embraced again and after another soft kiss, he was off.

The bell sounded. It was now time for Brandon to take his place on the sand of arena floor. As he entered, all the locals knew him and cheered. He looked to the area where his family sat and waved at his kids before blowing his wife a big kiss. He crossed his arms over his chest to express his love for all of them. Once this had been done, he turned and prepared his mind for the fight.

The cheers of the crowd melted away as he watched his opponent enter the arena. The reaction of the crowd seemed abnormal. They seemed to express concern, but Brandon didn't know why; he'd never seen the man before. This was new to him since most fighters' careers lasted less than a season; most fighters were usually dead or stopped fighting due to the wounds they suffered from their battles.

Despite the crowd's moan-filled concerns, Brandon readied himself and the signal for the fight to start was given. He moved towards his foe and each of them touched fists in the center of the arena. He threw himself into a roll and grabbed a handful of sand. Coming out of the roll he threw the sand in the man's eyes and followed up with an assault, striking powerfully at his foe's face and ribs. He moved around his opponent, then jumped on his back to put him in a choke hold. He was surprised at the man's power, and suddenly he was picking himself up off the sandy floor.

Brandon watched as the man wiped at his eyes and again darted at him. He planted a crushing fist to the side of his foe's face, then moved back. To his bewilderment, his opponent was still standing which meant he'd have to charge again. This time he landed a crushing kick to the chest sending the man rolling backward on the ground—a roll which didn't stop his opponent as he quickly returned to his feet.

Brandon was shocked. He'd never seen a man take this much abuse and still be standing. Both strikes had been solid—any other man would have fallen unconscious. He realized he'd need to try something stronger, maybe an elbow to the side of the head. He jumped high in the air, intending to come down across the blind side of the man's face, but instead, was hit with a massive fist to his own throat. The shot slammed Brandon to the ground. He thought to pull himself up but found he couldn't move. It was not because his opponent was holding him down; in fact, his foe was still grabbing at his own eyes, fighting to clear the sand. No, this was different... he couldn't breathe. Any more movement would only shorten the air supply he had left. The strike had crushed his windpipe; it'd be the last time he could look at his family before leaving this world.

He stumbled over to the area where they sat and gave his wife a look of anguish and love. He saw the pain on her face as she cried and longed to take it from her. He watched her pull the twins close and bury their faces in her dress to keep them from watching. Brandon Jr., Jonathan, and Mathew all stared at their father with horror. There was nothing they could do. He crossed his heart with both of his arms one final time and pointed to each of them to show them a father's love.

Slowly his air ran out. Gasping for more, he couldn't find the oxygen he needed, and fell to his knees instead, fighting the convulsions of his body with everything in him, not wanting his children to see him suffer. He won that battle, and then felt for his own pulse... but could not find one. His family slowly faded from his sight forever.

Sam stood on the arena floor and watched the crowd after wiping the sand from his eyes. He wasn't getting the normal reaction he was accustomed to since his first fight in Angel's Village. He walked over to the fallen warrior and, feeling a need for compassion, placed his arms under the lifeless body and lifted him from the ground. The crowd's reaction told him this man was well-loved and would be greatly missed. Sam looked up into the seats with

Brandon in his arms and watched as a woman in the first row stood with all her children and wept uncontrollably. Tears filled Sam's eyes as he held her gaze.

Chapter 25

An Unheard Prayer

SAM carried Brandon's body from the arena and into the healer's room, where his body would be prepared and given back to his family for burial. This had been the type of fight Sam felt he could make his opponent submit. His training session the previous day had been dedicated to that style of fighting. He hoped to secure his victory without causing another death, but it was not meant to be. For this man to be lying here lifeless was devastating.

He looked down at the motionless figure and watched as the healers gave way to the mortician. The people adored this man, a local farmer and an ironworker. He overheard from the crowd that the woman in the first row with all the children, was his wife. He thought back to how she wept when he looked up at her. The dead man's sons were strong little boys who held their ground and didn't look away. The oldest boy even nodded at Sam as he held his father in his arms.

"What's this man's name?" Sam asked the mortician. "It's clear to me that he was someone important around here."

A large lady dressed in black responded. "His name is Brandon Smith, or was Brandon Smith. He was a father of seven children—six boys and a girl. Everyone who lives here knew him. His whole family is beloved. He has fought in this arena for 12 seasons."

"Is it okay if I wait here until the family comes? I would like to express my regret for their loss."

"Suit yourself, but I don't know how well you'll be received by them."

After a little while, Brandon's wife walked into the room alone. When she entered, Sam was standing over her husband's body with his back to her. She paused, clearly caught off guard by his presence, swallowed hard and moved to the opposite side of her husband's body. Sam watched as she leaned over to hug Brandon and kiss him on the forehead. She did this for what seemed to be forever and, to Sam's surprise, maintained her strength.

Slowly she rose and stood up straight to face him. She started to speak but then stopped quickly to catch the tears that wanted to escape. After three long, agonizing, deep breaths, she said, "What's your name, fighter?"

Sam wanted to make up a name and run out of the room, but he found the nerve to speak. "My name is Sam."

"Well, Sam, my name is Josephine Smith and this is my husband Brandon. My husband would have been proud to know you. With the way you handled yourself and the respect you showed by carrying him from the arena, he would have found you to be a man of honor. He would've believed his death to be a good one. My husband felt that to die in battle was honorable. And as much as I would like to be angry with you, Sam, I cannot dishonor my husband's death with these emotions. I would like to invite you to his passing ceremony tomorrow. I'm sure my husband would feel honored if you attended."

Quietly a young boy walked into the room. Sam watched as he moved close to his mother and, as she had done, bent over to kiss his father. As the child stood back up, he handled himself with a presence that Sam felt to be far above his seasons. He walked around the table his father lay on and stuck out his hand. Sam took hold of it and they shook. The little man looked into his eyes and nodded before leaving the room.

His mother spoke after the boy left. "That was Brandon Jr. He's sad, but my husband taught all our sons that fighting in the arena was glorious. He told them that if anything were to happen to him that they should hold their heads high and be men about it. They'll cry when we get home, but my three oldest boys understand how their father wanted them to act. My twins, on the other hand, are with their uncle. They're not old enough to understand."

Sam started to cry and fell to his knees, apologizing for her loss. His emotions were so intense that Josephine comforted *him* and encouraged him back up to his feet.

"Don't cry, Sam, my husband would've found this to be a praiseworthy death. His wish would be that you don't mourn him, but rather celebrate him. After his passing ceremony, I'd like you and your family to come to the farm and celebrate him with us. I would appreciate this—if it wouldn't make you feel too uncomfortable."

Sam confirmed that he would be there for both the burial and the celebration, asking where he was to come and apologizing one last time. As he expected, Josephine was gracious and told him everything he needed to know. Saying she would see him later, she then placed her hand on his face to reassure him before leaving.

Sam left the room himself, joining BJ and Shalee who were waiting for him. Without saying a word, they left together for the inn. Once they had settled into their room, BJ explained that the other fights had been canceled in Brandon's honor. The arena's banker told BJ they were going to pay every fighter as if they had won both of their fights. He also said that most of the city would shut down for the burial.

"Can you imagine how many people will be at this burial, Sam?" BJ asked.

"A populated area isn't even considered to be a city until it has reached 16,000 souls. If most of these people knew this man and his family, this will be a very big event."

Sam finally spoke.

"I can only imagine what it would be like to be so well loved by a community of people that everything shuts down upon your death. I don't know how I can get back into the arena again . . . and how I'm going to face all these people? You should have seen his wife. She was so gracious and kind. Even her son was strong. Going to this man's passing ceremony and the celebration afterward will be far worse than stepping into the arena."

This time Shalee pulled BJ aside and said she would handle this one. The trainer left the room and she turned to Sam and said, "Sweetie, this man knew what he was doing when he entered the arena. He knew there was a chance of not leaving alive. Brandon was a good father and taught his children that the arena is a place of honor."

Sam interrupted, "Yes, I know that, for hell's sake. But the man didn't have his wife using magic to help him absorb punches like you do for me. This man should have easily beaten me. The punches he hit me with, not to mention the kick to my chest, should have knocked me out. He died because I cheated him out of his victory. There's no honor in that. How can I face these people knowing what I know?"

Shalee moved to him and placed her hand on his heart. "I want you to listen to me, Sam, and I mean listen well. You trained to make this guy submit, not to kill him. I saw you swing. You couldn't even see when you made contact. It was nothing more than luck that you won. Both of us know there's much more at stake here than one man. If we don't find a way to gain an audience with the King of Brandor and to find the pieces of this stupid Crystal Moon, everything will be destroyed. Now answer me this: with what you know about this man, don't you think he would have wanted to die so that you could go on to save the rest of his family?"

Sam did not know how much he agreed with Shalee's logic, but he agreed that whatever it took to save the rest of this world had to be done. He figured he would be strong when dealing with Brandon's family. He would give them the money won from the fight at the celebration honoring Brandon's passing.

The memorial was like no other funeral Sam had ever been to. It was held at the Peak of Bailem since it was Brandon's favorite time of day. Brandon had always said that a hard-working man's day was about over by this time since they woke up so early.

There were thousands of people who surrounded the family as they stood on top of a hill. They lifted Brandon into the air and lay him on top of a pile of wood. Josephine and all the children surrounded the pile with torches. For the first time since he had been in Grayham, he listened to a prayer being shouted from the hill down to the people below. The prayer was addressed to the god Bassorine.

Sam started to cry. He knew that their words were falling on ears that did not exist any longer. He did not have the heart to tell them that their god was dead. And maybe it didn't matter since every soul ended up in the pages of the Book of Immortality anyway. Why destroy the beliefs of a family in mourning... it just didn't seem right.

To his surprise, Brandon's father called Sam over to stand next to Josephine and gave him a torch. As the man squeezed his arm, he looked at the fighter and said, "My son would have wanted you to light the fire with his family. It's a privilege to have the man who defeated him in battle honor him in this way; it will also help start the healing process for this family."

Sam took the torch and looked at BJ. The trainer nodded that this was correct as he turned to light the fire.

Late Bailem had come and gone and the party was just getting warmed up. Sam was sitting on one of the many chairs the family had set up around the farmhouse watching a scene like nothing he'd ever experienced before. As far as he could see people were eating and laughing across the farmer's land. No one appeared to be sad, not even the family. They all celebrated to honor their fallen hero.

When it came time to give the toast, each of Brandon's nine brothers took a turn talking. Hubert, Brandon's father also spoke, followed by Brandon's wife. Once she had finished, Josephine turned to Sam and unexpectedly asked him to make a toast of his own.

It was agonizing. It was not the idea of speaking in front of thousands of people, but the pressure of speaking about a man he knew so little about. The fact that so many people loved Brandon, a man he killed, was unnerving. He thought for as long as he could, then addressed the crowd.

"In all my seasons as a fighter, I've never met a man who was so beloved by everyone who knew him. I consider myself blessed to have met such a man. I only wish I could've known his qualities outside of the arena. From what I know of Brandon's life, I believe he would have been the kind of man I would've cherished as a friend. I will forever remember this day because of the love that has been displayed here. I know Bassorine will reward Brandon for a life well lived. So let's raise our glasses and celebrate this man . . . shall we?"

The crowd erupted and cheered as Sam finished his speech. Everyone moved around him and placed their hands on his shoulders. After things calmed down, Sam turned to Josephine and whispered in her ear. He handed her a bag full of coin as he did.

"I've decided to give the winnings that I've received from your arena to help ease this family's burden without Brandon. Take it . . . and know that I care about you and your family."

"Sam, you are truly a good man. I . . . I will...." Overcome with emotion, Josephine held the bag close and began to cry. As the women around Josephine sought to console her, they realized what Sam had done. It was not long before the entire gathering knew of Sam's generosity. He would leave Haven with a reputation as not only a fighter known for his barbaric victories, but also as one known for his compassion and kindness. His actions on this day would catapult him to a new level of glory.

Five Peaks of Bailem Have Passed Since Celebrating Brandon;s Passing

GEORGE, Amar, Kepler and Maldwin gathered at Angel's Village before continuing on to the Siren's Song, a journey that took over four Peaks of Bailem. It had started to get dark when they entered the mist, which reminded George of a cool, foggy evening in Florida.

The moisture in the air thickened as they walked and created a climate that gave life to vegetation unlike anything George had seen before. After walking awhile longer, they stopped and lay down to get what they hoped would be a good night's rest.

As they slept, George dreamed of his little Abbie and, in his fantasy, Lasidious had returned his baby girl to him along with

Athena. They went fishing and Abbie caught a good-sized trout on her first cast, which almost pulled her into the water because of its size. The day was good until darkness fell across the pond. The next thing George knew, he was standing alone and both of his favorite women were nowhere to be found. He called to them but there was no answer. He knew the darkness had swallowed them and he started to panic. He screamed for them over and over again, desperately hoping for an answer, when suddenly a speck of light appeared. It was small at first, but it grew larger as it came closer. The light became a large sphere; he was scared but could not run. He looked frantically around him to find an escape, but all he could see, beyond the light, was blackness. The ball was floating through the air and, as it was about to crash into him, an electrifying scream filled his head.

George woke with a start and sat up. Confused, he scanned the area around him. All of his companions were asleep, the campfire was still going, but his clothes were saturated from the moisture of the mist. Something made him feel as if he should leave the group. He could not explain this feeling, but knew it had to be done.

He stood up, careful to not make any noise, grabbed his pack, and walked toward t he river following it north. The elevation was changing quickly and it was not long before he was hiking through the darkness. The hillside grew steeper, elevating his heart rate as the river gushed by in a torrent making its descent over the rough terrain.

He kept moving, pressing ahead with sheer determination. Eventually he reached the top of the hill where the area flattened out in front of him. He stopped now to take a few deep breaths before continuing. He was not sure how long it had taken to get to this point, but it had been quite the hike.

An extremely large pond stretched out in front of him for as far as he could see. He should not have been able to see anything, but some strange glow filled the air above, allowing him to get an idea of where he was. To the far side of the body of water, Griffon Falls could be heard crashing into the rocks below. It was the force of the falls that clearly caused the mist to fill the sky.

From the depths of the water, a light appeared and made its

way to the surface. It continued to rise until George saw that the light was the same sphere from his dream. He knew now it was this creature that had called him to this spot. The water fell from its smooth surface and soon the ball of energy floated in front of him.

There was a long silence as he stood there watching. Then, as he was about to say something, the air filled with a song. The sound was beautiful, glorious in fact, and he could understand the song's lyrics even though they were in a different language. Through its song, the sphere called itself a wisp. The creature told him that it knew why he was here and asked for the envelope he carried. George removed it from his pocket and held it in front of him. This seemed to satisfy the wisp. It asked him if he was prepared to give the envelope up in exchange for information.

George nodded and once again the song spoke to him. The sphere said that he could ask one question and, once the answer was given, George would need to leave its home. The power seeker already knew what his question would be and without hesitation agreed to the terms.

George asked, "How should I use my ability to turn things into stone to gain the power necessary to rule this world?"

Again the song of the wisp filled the air. Soon George knew all about the Barbarian Kingdom and how strong their vanity was. He learned that there was an open invitation to any man within the Kingdom of Brandor to fight the Barbarian's best warrior. If one man could beat him in hand-to-hand combat, the Barbarian King himself would surrender his crown.

The fight would be to the death with both combatants entering the arena in nothing but a loincloth. No weapons would be used, only the fighters' natural abilities as the Barbarians would not allow anyone in the arena that used magic. The Barbarians also would not know of his ability and he could enter the arena without suspicion.

The light of the sphere became blinding, and George had to cover his eyes. When he lowered his hands from his face, the wisp was gone and so was the envelope. He had to wait for his eyes to adjust before heading back to camp but he was excited now that he knew how to put his power to its best use. He would make his way to the City of Bloodvain, and challenge their best to a fight. He wore an evil smile all the way back to camp.

As he made his way down the mountainside, the others were awake and the night was fading. They all had been worried but, with as much ground as there was to cover, they figured that staying put was best. George informed them of his meeting with the wisp and that their plan was now in place... he would fight for the Crown of Bloodvain.

"What, are you nuts?" Kepler said. "The Barbarians are the most ruthless fighters in all the land. They don't allow magic in the king's arena. There's no way you'll even be allowed to challenge their champion."

Amar jumped into the conversation, "I agree with Kepler. How do you expect to be able to do this when you're using magic? Without it, you would be pummeled into a pile of garesh."

"What the hell is garesh?" George responded.

Annoyed, Amar replied, "You know, garesh, when a horse lifts its tail and drops it to the ground."

"A pile of garesh, he says. I think I like that term. I'm gonna start using it."

"I like cheese!" Maldwin chimed in. The group turned to the rat and started to laugh. He wanted to get in on the conversation and this was the one phrase Kepler had taught him that everyone could understand.

After a bit everyone stopped laughing and George continued. "The Barbarian king won't allow anyone to enter his arena that uses words of power or magical items. The king will only allow fighters to wear fur loincloths to cover the family jewels."

"Family jewels?" Amar said quizzically.

"It's another name for your midsection. You know, the part that hurts when I kick it for interrupting me when I'm talking," George snapped.

Amar smiled. "I apologize, by all means, please continue."

"The king won't let me in the arena in anything but a cloth to cover my family jewels. There are no weapons allowed. Think about this for a moment, guys. I don't need to speak words of power or use magical items. My ability works naturally and all I have to do is touch someone. Not only that... but I can turn a specific part of his best fighter to stone and they'll never know it."

"Yes they will," Kepler responded. "They harvest the heart, lungs, kidneys, liver, and the brain before placing them in jars for their burial celebrations. They'll know if you have done something when they open their champion up and see his insides are stone."

George thought a minute before responding, "So what do they do with the rest of the body?"

"Well," the jaguar hesitated a moment and continued. "For those Barbarians who are held in high regard, they send them out onto the Blood Sea and burn their bodies while on board. Eventually the sea swallows them and everyone goes home to celebrate."

"Then there you have it. I'll only turn the parts of him to stone that won't be cut from his body and the sea will cover up the truth. I'll turn the inside of his Adam's apple to stone or maybe the inside of a small part of his spinal cord so he cannot get the signals from his brain. This would give me some time to move in, smack him a few times and run. I'll figure it out before we get there, I'm sure."

Amar looked at Kepler as he paced back and forth. "When Lasidious told me I should travel with you, George, I didn't imagine that you had this kind of nerve. If you pull this off, you'll be king of the entire Barbarian Kingdom. We'll be enemies of the entire Kingdom of Brandor. George, my family lives in Lethwitch. If we become enemies of Brandor, will you promise me that we won't ever attack Lethwitch?"

George agreed that this presented a problem. His Athena and her whole family were also from Lethwitch. He agreed not to attack this area, not because he cared for Amar's family, but because he cared for Athena's.

After a while George started to pace. He had an idea and pulled his map out. He told Kepler it would take him at least 20 Peaks of Bailem to reach the Blood Sea landing platform. Since he could not ride the hippogriffs, a perfect opportunity to work on this plan now existed. He said that Kepler should go to the platform and wait for the rest of them to arrive by way of hippogriff.

Amar broke in and stopped him. "Okay we've got one problem already. We cannot fly all the way to the Blood Sea platform. The hippogriffs fly there, but they won't take someone out of Brandor and fly them into Barbarian territory. The rule of the kingdoms states that no one can fly into a kingdom that you're not from. The only exception to this rule is Angel's Village because it is protected by the gods. The closest landing tower anywhere close to Bloodvain's is in Gessler Village. This is a place where the roughest crowds from both kingdoms have a tendency to migrate. This village is considered neutral territory and not owned by either kingdom."

Now Kepler jumped in. "That's because I dominate the passage to the village through fear. Gessler Village has been a good supply for my brothers and me to build our skeleton army. We stay out of the village for the most part, but the only way to get to it is by hippogriff or through our pass. We catch at least nine or ten victims a year walking through our pass and kill them. I can only use the evil ones for my army, though. Never could quite figure out why the good ones would even bother going to Gessler, but they do. Maybe it is because that's where some of the finest metal for armor is mined."

"Kepler, will you get to the point already?" George snapped.

"Okay, okay, sorry! I think what Amar is trying to say is that you'll need protection in Gessler since the crowd there isn't a pleasant one. I have an idea that should work. Instead of meeting you at the Blood Sea platform, I'll make my way to Gessler, but it will take me 23 Peaks of Bailem. I want you to arrive the next day. My brothers and I will be there hiding in the shadows in case you need us. Just get off the hippogriff and make your way to an inn called The Bloody Trough. You won't see us unless you're attacked. When night makes it easier for us to move around undetected, leave your window open for us to enter through."

George responded, "Kepler, it absolutely scares the crap, wait, I mean it scares the garesh out of me that you can hide like that. I cannot tell you how happy I am that you're on my side. That's a good plan. We should do it. Will you please ask Maldwin if he can project his visions to a group of people all at once?"

The demon, although unsure where George was going with this, asked the rat. "He said yes, but if it is too big of a group, they'll all see the same thing."

"Exactly how big is too big of a group before they start seeing the same thing? How many people can he project his visions to before he has to stop?"

Again Kepler asked and responded to George, "He said more than three and they'll need to see the same thing. He has projected his visions to his entire family before. He said before the collapse in the cave, his family totaled over 500."

The manipulator smiled and started to plot. "Holy cow, 500 and I bet he's got no clue if he can do more than that. So what we know is that three or less, he can project separate visions and more than three, they all need to see the same thing. Is that what he is saying? Oh, and express to him that I'm sorry about his family dying like that."

Again the undead cat asked the rat to confirm and responded, "He said that is exactly right and he imagines he can do much more than 500 at once."

George grabbed his chin and then started to ramble off a plan. "OK, so let's figure out what the three of us will do until Kepler gets to Gessler. I think we should go back to Lethwitch. We can take the hippogriffs from Angel's Village once we get there. That part of the journey should take us four Peaks of Bailem. With the two days of flying back to Lethwitch, it will leave us seventeen Peaks of Bailem before we need to leave for Gessler. We can spend time with our loved ones there and work on the problem regarding rival kingdoms.

"We can introduce Maldwin to everyone who we'll need to move out of the Kingdom of Brandor. Once we take over the throne, we'll need to bring them to Bloodvain with us to live in the castle. I don't know how else we'll be able to guarantee their protection unless this happens. I'll take our little rat friend here and introduce him to Athena's family as my pet. He can use his visions to manipulate them and gain their affections. He can make them think that they need to come to a meeting of great importance.

We can hold the meeting in Athena's mother's barn in the middle of the night. Amar, you can also take Maldwin to get your family to come as well. Once they all show up, he can give them all the same idea of how great it will be to live in the Barbarian kingdom under our protection.

"Maldwin will need to end these visions by making them feel it's important to come each and every night to another meeting. I want him to do this until they believe that it is indeed a good idea to be with us. Amar, we can depart for Gessler and leave Maldwin behind to stay on Athena's farm until we send word for our families to come to us. This should give our little rat friend plenty of time to brainwash them all. Kepler can keep his skeleton army under control, and they can provide safe passage through both his passes and Gessler Village. I suppose he might want to brainwash them to like skeleton warriors also. Do you think you can explain all that to him, Kepler?"

"Well at least you didn't tell me to tell him that you said to tell him this time. I would hate to listen to that again. Should I tell him now?" the demon said, poking a little fun.

"Just shut up and tell him," George said with a laugh. He was starting to feel a strong bond with the giant cat. His feelings for Amar were still up in the air. Beyond learning to control his power, he still didn't see much use for him. He figured he would take a wait-and-see attitude.

Kepler laughed and went over the plan a couple more times with George. He wanted to make sure that he did not mess this up since he would not be there to fix any problems. The jaguar suggested they walk as he informed the rat of the plans. They walked until the Peak of Bailem before Kepler stopped them and said his conversations with Maldwin were complete.

"The rat will do everything you want him to, George. The signal for him to know who to use his visions on will be given by squeezing his tail softly. Maldwin will take care of the rest and he has asked for one favor in return."

"So what's the favor?" George said.

"He wants the two of you to leave him a nice pile of food behind the barn before you go to Gessler."

George turned to look at the rat and before he could even say anything the rat looked at him and said, "I like cheese!" The rat grinned as he showed his two large front teeth and twitched his nose.

The group laughed at the fact that this statement actually fit the conversation this time. Kepler told the rodent that he would have his pile of cheese when the boys left for Gessler. Not long after that they split up, parting ways for their own destinations.

Three Nights Later

DOUBLE D had made his way through the first part of Skeleton Pass and was now sitting on a stool at The Bloody Trough Inn. The inn had gotten its name before it was built. Long ago, when people first began to travel to Gessler, the center of the village was used for watering the horses. The people built a six foot high, 30-foot-long, slightly-sloping rock wall on this spot. Twelve different troughs, six on each side, also formed out of rock, had been laid into its base. A small, natural spring nearby continually produced enough water for the entire area. The people of this village had figured out a way to direct some of this water up to the top of the wall. Once there, gravity directed the fresh water down to each of the troughs below.

One night, while the village slept, a horrible double murder was committed and the bodies were thrown across the top of the wall. The two headless figures plugged the flow of water on one of the sides and, by the time morning rolled around, the trough was full of stale, discolored water. The blood not only had covered the rock edges but it turned the water that was left inside red. Even though over time the stains faded, this one specific trough had been labeled. The family who built the inn decided to name it The Bloody Trough after that incident. The inn had been built over the troughs and to this very day, a man could take his horse into the tunnel and leave it to drink.

Double D was drinking his ale and contemplating his trip through the second part of Skeleton Pass when an unexpected event happened. He had previously been paid by one of the nobles of the Barbarian Kingdom a season ago to kill another barbarian for sleeping with his wife. This type of job was not one that he normally would have accepted, but the pay that was being offered was up front and substantial.

When he took the job, though, someone talked. When his target heard that he had been hired to kill him, he ran before Double D could set things up. As always in life, things have a way of coming full circle. That particular barbarian just walked in to sit at the bar. The assassin knew that the man would have no idea what he looked like so he decided to talk to him a bit.

"How's it going tonight? Is it still raining out there?"

"Hmpff," the man grunted.

The assassin smiled at the shortness of the exchange and decided to ask another question. "So where are you from, friend?"

The man did not respond and kept drinking. He figured he would try again. "Say friend, where are you from?"

The barbarian turned to look at him and replied rudely, "I've no desire to talk to you. Your one of those pathetic excuses of a man from Brandor. I'd sooner spit on you."

The man from the north was a large man, over seven feet tall; like most Barbarians, he was also very strong. His long, dark hair hung to the right side of his rock-jawed face. The coldness of his eyes would have scare most men, but Double D was not most men.

The killer walked to the far side of the room and took a seat. He would now wait for the big man to leave and go out to the waste shed to relieve himself. Watching him pound down one drink after another, the killer figured it would not take long before the need would arise.

When finally the barbarian did go, he drunkenly stumbled out into the night. The assassin followed him, watching from the shadows as the barbarian opened the door to the shed. He gave the man a few seconds and pulled a cloak from his pack and put it on. He took the hood and lifted it over his head and as he did so, he vanished.

Quietly, Double D opened the shed. The big man turned to look in his direction. He stepped inside and let the door shut. He watched as the Barbarian grumbled and turned to continue to pee. The men from the north liked to drop their pants down to their ankles; they didn't seem to care much for privacy or meekness. This didn't bother the assassin at all; in fact it made his job easier.

He moved towards his prey, pulling out his long knife laced with a deadly poison. He moved closer to the man, the tip of his blade now just a matter of inches from his buttocks. The blade—13 inches long, two inches high and 3/8 of an inch thick—had hooks along the top that rolled back towards his hand. A sharper blade could not be found within all of Grayham. As the assassin shoved the blade hard into the man's butt, he lifted up in the direction of the hooks and ripped the knife out. He ducked just in time to avoid the large man's elbow as he spun around.

The assassin darted out, leaving the barbarian alone in the shed full of garesh, screaming to death. That was Double D's cue to keep moving. He walked to the other side of the village and entered the second part of Skeleton Pass.

Chapter 26

Sick of This Royal Crap

Three Peaks of Bailem Have Passed Since George Left Siren's Song

SAM, Shalee, BJ, and Helga arrived at the Town of Empire five nights ago and Sam has already won his first fight. The fight had been to the death and his ribs had taken an awful beating. They were badly bruised and would need a couple of days to heal.

Shalee continued to work with Helga to increase her powers, astonishing the older woman with her successes. Shalee has still only suffered just the one failure since her first day of her training in Angel's Village. For privacy, they had been practicing just outside of Empire in a heavily wooded area. Not one soul has bothered them and the spot proved to be a great place to go back to each night.

Tonight was beautiful and the skies were clear. Shalee still had not gotten used to the fact that there were no stars in the sky as she looked up with the only two objects she could see being other worlds; but she had no idea which ones they were.

Helga watched as Shalee commanded Precious to rip a massive tree from the ground and send it flying high through the air. Both ladies laughed as they had to catch themselves from falling when the massive trunk, almost eight feet in diameter, crashed hard into the ground. The area around them shook and the noise was earth-shattering. Helga had to put up an invisible wall to protect them both. The limbs splintered off in all directions from the collision and one other tree toppled over from the force. They continued to giggle and wondered if they had awakened anyone back in town.

Both women decided to stop training for the night and cautiously start a fire where they could sit for a bit to talk.

"Oh, my goodness that was loud," Shalee said as she rolled with laughter.

"I know, child, I know, I had no idea you were going to send it that high into the air. I hope no one comes out here to yell at us. I actually bounced off the ground when it hit."

"Oh my goodness, you should've seen your face when it was coming down. I knew you were going to put up your protective wall."

They continued to laugh as Helga realized that the younger sorceress was commanding powers that most did not obtain in their entire lives. It didn't make sense to her how such a thing was possible, despite Bassorine's visit. Shalee had long since passed Helga's abilities and really, the only reason the student needed her around was for emotional support. Providing this type of support, along with the fact she felt like a mother to the young lady, was the main reason Helga stayed. She thought back to what Shalee had said to her and BJ back in West Utopia. It was time to let her student know she had surpassed her abilities, hoping her student would continue to need her for more than magical support.

"Shalee, I have something to say to you, dear, and I must admit that I'm nervous about telling you what I've got to say."

The younger woman could see the worry-filled eyes of her friend. "What is it, Helga, why the long face?"

"Well, child, I have been trying to figure out how to tell you that I cannot teach you anymore."

"Why, do you have someplace to go? Did I mess up or something? I can fix it if you're upset with me."

"No, no, no, child, it's not like that. I'm not mad, nor do I want to stop being around you. It's simply that your powers have grown beyond mine. I cannot teach you because you are better than I am, dear."

Helga moved to Shalee, pulled her close, and hugged her.

"I'm sad to say this, child, but I fear that I'm not of much use to you any longer."

Shalee returned the embraced and after a second pulled away, tears filling her eyes as she spoke.

"I already knew that my abilities were beyond yours. Just because you cannot teach me any longer doesn't mean I don't need you. You, BJ, and Sam are all I've got. I need you now more than ever and you'd better not ever leave me. Who will I talk with and who will shop with me when Sam needs me to buy stuff?"

Shalee smiled as she wiped her eyes and moved to sit down.

"Do you want me to stay with you then, child?" Helga asked as she looked for confirmation.

"Yes, of course... I need you. You're like a mother to me. The mother I had back on Earth is dead and she would have been happy to know that you're taking such good care of me."

"Well, then it is settled. Now you're stuck with me for good." Helga sat down next to her. They embraced.

Thinking about continuing to advance her skills, Shalee said, "Well, if you're not able to train me, then who is, and where do we find this person?"

After a moment Helga said, "We've already been to a place that has such a person. His name is Amar and he lives in the Town of Lethwitch. He's much stronger than I am and could teach you much more. He's the only person in Grayham who can help you grow beyond what I've taught you. He's one of the few men who has traveled to the world of Luvelles and studied the magical arts. If you'd like to we can seek him out once we've gotten Sam to the City of Champions."

"I don't want to leave Sam until he has met the King of Brandor. I hope he can keep his winning streak alive. I can't handle watching him get any more stitches. His ribs looked terrible. Let's pass on finding Amar for now. I'm sure I can think of something to challenge myself until the time is right. All we have to do is think of something absolutely absurd to try and, bam, we have another lesson, yes?"

Helga laughed. "I suppose you're right. Maybe you can try to rain down fire or something like that. Who knows what you're capable of?"

Shalee agreed, then changed the subject. "We need to find a way to get the king to listen to Sam. Maybe you and I can figure out something clever to speed this whole thing up." Shalee smiled and again hugged her friend.

∽ ∽

Unbeknownst to the two women, they were being watched from the shadows. The evil stare of the being from within this hiding spot were filled with disturbed thought.

∽ ∽

The sorceresses stayed up through the night and spent most of it talking about girl stuff. When morning arrived, it was time to go back to town and eat breakfast with the boys. The ham and Greggle eggs were delicious and, as always, the conversation quite pleasant. Afterwards everyone prepared to go to the arena for Sam's fight.

Later that day with the Peak of Bailem passed, Sam had already entered the arena and crushed his adversary. There wasn't any part of his opponent's anatomy which had resembled anything human. The lottery landed him the battle of man vs. beast and it was the first fight of the day. He had fought a bear that resembled a Kodiak originating from the caves of the Bear Clan. He was their only champion who represented them for the last 16 seasons.

Sam was allowed to use a dagger in the battle, but he didn't bother. When the bear charged, Sam used its momentum to drive it into one of the sharp stakes that stuck out from the arena gate. The fight lasted only a few moments. Afterwards, Sam requested the pelt from the Arena Master, but, due to the alliance the Bear Clan had with the King of Brandor, his request was denied.

When Sam tried to leave the arena, there were many guards posted at the door. BJ ran up to him. "There's a rumor going around that someone of great importance is here. No one is allowed to leave until this person speaks."

"Who is it? I have a stinking headache, my stomach, and ribs hurt and the pain's been getting worse all day. I don't care what they have to say or who it is. I want to go back to the inn and get some sleep."

"They're not telling anyone who it is, but it's usually a member of the royal family who is given this kind of privilege. I hope it is Duke Jonathan Brandor. He's a great man, and talking to him would be good for your career. If we can get you in front of him, it would help tremendously."

Sam rolled his eyes. He was so tired of hearing about his career. The idea of killing anyone else made him want to puke. His head hurt and he was growing tired of fighting up the food chain to talk to a stupid king.

"Well whoever it is, BJ, I'm sure he puts his pants on just like you and I do. Maybe let's just tone it down a notch or two and relax some. I'm not in the mood for dealing with some pompous jerk throwing his royal weight around today."

A voice from behind Sam spoke.

"Pompous jerk, he says. I heard you were a strong man, Sam, but I wouldn't have imagined that you viewed royalty with such disregard."

The royal personage that addressed Sam was well-dressed and had clearly heard everything Sam said as he walked up behind them.

BJ knew who was speaking and backed up against the wall, bowing on one knee. Sam didn't care in the least and turned to defend his position.

"It's not that I view royalty with any disregard, I'm just not in the mood to kiss someone's butt today. I have a headache, I feel sick and all I want right now is get some sleep. Who in the heck are you anyway?"

The fighter went on ranting as BJ tried to get his attention. As he carried on, the prince listened.

Finally, BJ shouted to get Sam's attention. "Sam, shut up, the man you're talking to is Prince Aaron. He's the King of Brandor's son.

Sam whirled around.

"So what . . . like I said before, he puts his pants on just like I do, unless there's some kind of royal secret I don't know about."

The prince laughed and cut in.

"Sam, Sam, Sam, my good man, I can see you're clearly out of sorts today. I'm glad I came today and not my father. He would've had you beaten for such words. I, on the other hand, would like to think I can understand people's frustrations. Maybe we could walk a bit and have a nice conversation, just the two of us. I have come a long way to see you and I would appreciate the company. I'll have the healers fetch you something for your headache."

Sam turned and looked at the prince. He took a few deep breaths before responding. "Sure, no problem, but I need to relieve myself first. I'll be right back."

While he was gone, BJ attempted some damage control. The prince assured the trainer it was unnecessary, but it didn't make BJ feel any better. The prince continued by telling the trainer that everyone was allowed a bad day every once in a while and he'd already been assured by Duke Barthom Brandor that Sam was a true gentleman. They would talk and he was sure the conversation would be a pleasant one.

When the fighter returned, the prince took Sam and headed toward the cobblestone streets. The king's army cleared the way as they went and barred people from stepping outside their business doors.

"Sam, Duke Barthom Brandor has spoken highly of your character. I've also heard about what you did for the Smith family in Haven after your victory over Brandon. I've never heard of any fighter giving his winnings to the family of his fallen opponent. Once I heard of this generosity, I spoke with my father and he was quite impressed. He told me he would be holding his tournament early this season since we may be going to war. I informed the king that, with your reputation and the way it has spread in such a short time that, we should invite you to participate in his tournament. It seems you have turned the heads of the right people, Sam. The rumors were right about your skills. Since I received my father's permission, you now have two more victories to your name. The king's tournament will start in seven Peaks of Bailem and I would like to see you attend. I don't normally deliver invitations myself, but I wanted to see what all the fuss was about. So, Sam, what do you say?"

Prince Aaron had sandy blond hair and blue eyes. His frame was not a fighter's frame, but he was fit. His robe was black with gold trim and on the back rested the crest of Brandor, a red shield with gold-lined edges. At the center sat a golden scale to symbolize justice.

Sam was grateful for the invitation, but his mind was thinking about the upcoming war.

"You said we may be going to war soon. So is this what all the wagon building is about and the additional army activity everywhere? Are they not really for harvesting? What can I do to help?"

"I can see why people like you, Sam. You have just been extended one of the highest honors a fighter can be given, yet you're more interested in what I've said about the war. It's refreshing to see such an unselfish nature. To answer your question about the wagons, I first need to know that you'll swear to secrecy on this subject. Sam... can I trust a man like you?"

"Of course you can trust me. I swear it. Heck, I can keep my yap shut for some good dirt."

"I don't think that I've ever heard someone talk as you do, Sam. I find it entertaining. The wagons are for the harvest. The gods Mosley and Alistar have promised us that there will be three bountiful harvests within a short period of time. We need the wagons to get it all to the coast. From there, the king's fleet will take these harvests to Merchant Island."

"Okay, so if Mosley is part of this, then it must be serious. How's he doing anyway? Has he been back to see you since he gave you this information? I was hoping to say a few things to him when I bumped into him again."

The prince gave Sam an odd look. "You know Mosley? How can this be that you know the new god?"

Sam smiled. "I was the first one to talk to him after he became the new God of War. I know that Bassorine was destroyed. Mosley gave me a couple of gifts and told me to find a way to gain an audience with your father."

The prince took Sam's arm, led him into a pottery shop and ordered his guards to clear the area. Once this was done, he spoke, "Who have you told Bassorine is dead?"

"I have told no one but myself, Shalee, BJ, and Helga. We are the only ones who know. I would not allow that kind of information out before I knew how to properly use it. I understand the importance of keeping quiet."

"You've done well, Sam. We'll speak of this more in Brandor."

The prince reached into his robe and produced a pouch, tossing it to Sam. As the fighter caught it, a heavy clinking sound was heard.

"In that pouch there are 25 Jervaise coins," The prince said. "If my math is right, it will equal what you would have won in ten victories in the arena. This is your reward for being so gracious to the Smith family. It's also meant to give you the means to come to Brandor and stay comfortable for a while. I think it would be wise for you to leave with me in the morning. You can bring your friends and we'll finish this conversation with my father."

Sam was unsure how to react so he tossed the bag in the air and caught it before responding.

"I guess I'll see you in the morning then."

He watched as the prince stuck out his hand for him to kiss it. Sam took the prince's wrist, turned it over to expose the palm and shook it. He followed it up by saying,

"Where I'm from, Aaron, we show respect in different ways. I have much to tell you, but for now, I'll ask you to be patient with my ignorance of your customs. I'm not from this world but maybe I can explain about all of this on our way to Brandor."

The prince was shocked at the fighter's manner, but then he looked down and secured Sam's hand in the same manner, allowing his arm to be moved up and down.

"We call this a handshake where I'm from and friends do this. I do hope this will be the start of a good friendship," Sam continued.

"I hope so too, Sam. I look forward to tomorrow's conversation and the explanation of the world you're from. I didn't realize the customs of the other four worlds could be so different."

"I'm not from any of your worlds and I have much to tell you. See you in the morning then?"

"Agreed," Aaron replied.

With that, the prince walked out of the store, escorted by his guards.

When Sam arrived back at the inn, BJ, Helga, and Shalee were waiting for him at the bar downstairs. BJ was a wreck, worrying that Sam would say something that would upset the prince. Both women were trying to calm him down since his ranting was getting a little loud. Sam walked in behind the three of them just in time to hear BJ make the following statements.

"Then the bonehead said, with the prince standing right there, that he puts his pants on just like he does! If that wasn't bad enough, he said that maybe there was a royal secret to putting their pants on. I was so embarrassed. I wanted to sink into the ground. So much for getting an early invitation to the City of Champions, I'm sure that has all been blown to garesh."

Sam smiled. He tossed the bag of coins over BJ's shoulder and watched them land heavily on the bar.

"You're right; we didn't get an invitation to the City of Champions."

BJ shouted, "I knew it. He messed it up. What'd I tell ya . . . you're a bonehead!"

Sam rolled his eyes.

"I may be a bonehead, but we did much better than just being invited to the City of Champions. Look in the bag, ya old grouch!"

Once BJ saw what was in the bag he closed it tight and whispered. "This is a substantial amount of coin. Where did you get this?"

"Why, the prince, of course. I sold him a new secret of how to put his pants on! He was so appreciative that he invited us to his father's tournament in Brandor. It is being held early because of the war that may come."

BJ exploded with excited laughter.

"The prince gave you this and invited us to the king's tournament? Why would the prince give you this much coin and pay you to come fight?"

Sam looked at BJ and whispered, "Have you ever heard of keeping quiet so the whole world doesn't know that we've got this kind of coin on us? Let's go up to the room and talk."

Once they were in the room, Sam explained how he had received the invitation to the king's tournament and the purse of money. The prince wanted them to meet with the king because of everything he knew about the gods. Sam informed them that they were leaving for Brandor in the morning with Prince Aaron.

BJ responded, "So we're leaving for Brandor, and we'll be meeting with the king? What should we wear, Sam? I don't have my best clothes with me or my armors."

Sam looked at Shalee, "Looks like someone's star struck."

Shalee laughed. "Maybe they have room on this world to start a celebrity magazine. BJ would love it."

"What're you two talking about?" Helga cut in.

"Oh nothing worth explaining," Shalee said.

"Well I'm not going to see the king looking like a beggar," BJ announced. "I'm going to buy some nice clothes. You all might want to do the same."

Shalee walked over to Sam, and nestled up into him, speaking in her cutest voice, "Baby, don't you want to take your loving, precious, wonderful, sexy, kind, generous, perfect little magic-user shopping? Don't you want to spoil me a little bit? I'll make it worth your while."

Sam rolled his eyes at BJ and sighed. "See what you've started, old man? Let me have the coin and I'll go buy us *all* something."

Sam and the Gang are off to Brandor

THE GROUP was due to meet with the king the following morning; and now, Sam and Shalee were about to go to bed, but instead found themselves in a conversation about how aggravated Sam was feeling.

"I'm sick of all this royal crap," Sam said. "Ever since we met the prince, I've bowed more than I care to. I'm telling you right now that I'm not going to kiss this king's butt tomorrow. If he can't have a normal conversation, then screw him.

"I miss home, babe, and I'm at the end of my rope with this world. I had the world in the palm of my hand back on Earth and I didn't need to kiss anyone's royal behind. I don't have anything on this world. I just know that I'm going to have to suck it up tomorrow and kiss this guy's royal butt to get anywhere. Crap, this really chaps my hide.

"I know I need to be more patient, but I've killed so many people since I've got to this world and for what? It was all just to get *here*, and now that I am here, I'm half crazy and about to lose my mind. We don't know if this guy will even listen to me. How am I going to make a king believe that I'm here to create an empire and set an example for the worlds? How am I going to get him to let me go after the Crystal Moon's pieces? He will see me as a threat if I tell him the gods want us to be the example for the other worlds to follow. I need a break! I need a stinking vacation!"

Shalee could only smile at Sam's outburst.

"Would you just relax? Maybe you don't have to kiss his royal behind after all. Just be bold with the king, and know that I've got your back. I realize the way the king and his son treat people isn't the way you would do it. So maybe if you show them that you're strong, you can get somewhere with them. Just shake the guy's hand like you did Aaron's and see how it goes. I know that you don't like the politics of this place. Maybe you can use the fact that we're not from here to cut through all the red tape. If that doesn't work, just piss him off and I'll do my thing. We'll command his attention and make him listen. After all, we have been sent here by the gods; let's act like it. Let's take charge of the situation."

Sam turned, walked to the window and looked through it. They had been given a room in the castle by the prince. The king's city stretched as far as he could see, with architecture completely different from the Roman style of West Utopia. It reminded him of something King Arthur would live in. Although it was built with great attention to detail, he liked the other city better; West Utopia simply had more class. He was surprised that the king would allow his kingdom's cities to have so many different looks. If he were king, there would be some sort of consistency in the architecture. He thought to himself: *Isn't this hodgepodge of different looks something that should bother Shalee and not me? After all... she is the architect of the group.*

After a moment he turned to face his sorceress lover.

"So exactly how would you have my back? What do you mean we should take charge of the situation? I can only assume you're referring to using your magic. I don't know everything that you can do with that staff of yours. Give me an idea of what you're talking about here. Give me some news that'll make me feel better. I really need it right now."

"I can do far more than that," she said, scanning the room. In one of the corners of their castle suite, she saw a potted plant with loose gravel. She grabbed it, ripped out the plant, and handed the pot to Sam. With that, she moved to the other side of the room.

"I want you to take a handful of that gravel and throw it at me as hard as you can."

"What? I can't do that. I'd hurt you."

"Don't be so sure, stud," she responded with a laugh. "I wouldn't tell you to do something unless I knew I was going to be okay. So just throw it, you big girl."

"Are you absolutely sure?" Sam said with a look of uncertainty.

"Just throw it and I'll make it worth your time." She licked her lips to emphasize her point. "Do I need to say more?"

Sam smiled wickedly as he grabbed a handful. He reached back and threw it as hard as he could.

The sorceress had already lifted Precious and was speaking her command. The pebbles stopped in front of her and stayed suspended in mid-air. She moved around them, methodically circling the floating stones a few times as she plucked them one by one from the air and turned towards her lover. She handed them to Sam as she spoke, allowing her hand to massage him as she moved it away.

"Can you put the rest of them back for me, babe? I'll be in bed waiting for you."

Sam smiled as she walked by and patted him on the behind. She was removing her clothes as she moved across the room. He turned back to face the floating rocks and gathered them into the pot as quickly as he could.

The next morning after Early Bailem, Prince Aaron guided Sam and the rest of the group into the king's throne room. As the prince entered, everyone bowed. Aaron signaled for them to come forward and approach the throne. As Aaron had instructed earlier, they did as they were told and lowered themselves to one knee, waiting for the king to enter. It was a long wait... which angered Sam. He was sick all these royal protocols wasting his time. Bow here, bow there, bow, bow, bow and bow again was the only thing he seemed to do in this stupid city.

Aaron sent one of the slaves to inform the king they were waiting, but somehow this news did not seem to create urgency on his father's part. After being on their knees for what felt like forever, the king finally entered. They all lowered their heads and waited for the signal to lift them.

"Stand, fighter, let's have a look at what all the commotion is about," the king said to Sam and watched as his order was carried out. "I must admit, you appear to have a presence about you." The king motioned for the rest of the group to stand and continued. "Everyone stand. I welcome you all to Brandor."

They did as instructed without saying a word. Sam, however, was not one for all the formal gesturing and stopped the king's party in full stride. He was not about to spend all day on these meaningless formalities.

"Look," he said in a matter-of-fact tone. "I'm sure we can spend all day with this formal greeting of one another. I would even bet that under different circumstances it is fun and has its place, but can we skip to the part where we get something accomplished? I have knowledge of things that you may want to know. The quicker we get going, the sooner we can win this upcoming war."

As Sam was speaking, BJ was squirming inside. He knew that this was not the way things should be done and he expected the king to explode with anger.

Shalee agreed with Sam's feelings. Although she didn't show it, she was more than ready to back him up. As agreed the night before, they wanted to get something accomplished and were not about to be brushed off without being taken seriously. She was holding onto Precious, more than ready to make an impression.

The fighter walked right up the steps to the king's throne and stuck out his hand. This caught Keldwin off guard. He was unsure how to respond so he looked to his son for guidance as the guards took a readied stance around them.

"I told you his mannerisms were strange, Father. He says he's not from this world and he has been brought here to create an empire to serve as an example to the other worlds. Apparently, it was he and his friends who were involved in the Crystal Moon's disappearance. Sam said there were three of them that came to this world from a place called Earth. From what he told me on our journey, there was supposed to have been only two of them, but

Lasidious deceived the gods and brought a third."

The king stood and moved behind his throne. He didn't care much of what he'd heard and he especially didn't like the part about Sam creating his own empire to be an example to the other worlds.

"So you're the ones responsible for taking the Crystal Moon. Don't you know what this has done to the fate of all the worlds?" Sam ruined his momentum and interrupted with a voice loud enough to cover the king's.

"Keep your royal britches on, Keldwin! Put your listening ears on and pay attention. No one said we're responsible. Aaron said we were involved and he also said that Lasidious had deceived the other gods. I knew this was going to be a waste of our time. If this is all you managed to get from your son's words, then I'm disgusted and would never serve a king with such a weakness."

BJ was about to die inside as he listened. He knew what was coming next. Sam would be hung before sunrise. For that matter, they all would be hung.

The king was astounded at how Sam spoke to him.

"Guards, seize them all and take them to the dungeon."

This was Shalee's cue for her to take action. She jumped to her feet and yelled, "Precious, iluve sal." Everything in the room froze. The only ones who could still move were the king, Sam, and herself.

Keldwin looked around before turning his head to Shalee and unsheathed his sword. In turn, Sam brought Kael from his resting spot on his hip and pointed it directly at the king as he yelled,

"Val arrna, naur." The blade burst into flames.

"Not so fast, Keldwin."

Shalee watched Brandor's leader lowered his sword as she moved through the frozen figures.

"My king, you're being far too hasty. It seems to me that you've let your crown go to your head. You're not listening. If you'll pay attention . . . right now... I'm calling you, 'my king.'"

Shalee passed her hands across the blades of Keldwin's soldiers as she continued to speak. "Your men keep their weapons sharp. You must be proud of your army. I would ask that you open your mind and realize that your way isn't the only way. We're not from your world and we won't spend all day kissing your royal back-side."

The sorceress continued up the stairs that lead to the throne and walked behind Keldwin. She rubbed her hand over the top of his shoulders and could feel him tremble as she did. She continued,

"Where we're from, we treat others the way they treat us. You are not giving us the respect we deserve, my king."

Shalee floated back down the stairs and removed the weapons from his guards' hands as she continued to speak.

"We have no intention of bowing to you until you speak with us as equals. You'll treat us with respect and as friends. Once you've done this, you'll have our loyalty and we'll adopt your customs. We'll conform to your silly illusions of respect. People don't respect you because they bow to you, Keldwin. They respect you because you have earned it. I would imagine that your people bow only because they fear your crown."

The sorceress placed the swords at the king's feet and backed up.

"I watched as you hid behind your throne to command your guards to seize us. It is a sign of weakness and I don't respect a weak man. I would only respect a king who has the nerve to get something done with his own two hands. I respect a man like Sam here. You need a man like Sam helping you, Keldwin. I won't stand here and allow you to make a mockery of this great man. You haven't earned our respect to command us to do anything yet, my king. If you want me to bow, I suggest that you stop this nonsense before I become angry."

Shalee moved back up the stairs and removed the king's sword from his hand. She turned it around and tapped it on his chest. "You don't wish to see me angry, do you?"

Keldwin shook his head, unable to speak as the sorceress continued.

"We have been brought here by the gods and we have no intention of leaving here until we find a way to save these worlds. I think we all should work together, don't you? You'll find a spot within your army for Sam and it'd better be an important position. Consider this a non-negotiable request. We have come here to help find the Crystal Moon so I'm sure you can understand my position on this matter."

The sorceress lowered Keldwin's sword to the floor with the others. She stood and brushed her hand across Keldwin's face before moving to stand behind Sam.

"Do we have an understanding, Keldwin? If we don't, speak now. I suppose that if it is necessary, I could always use a much stronger magic than you have just witnessed to make my point."

Keldwin felt defeated as he sat on his throne, but took the time to think for a moment. He was a handsome man with long, dark hair that complemented his brown eyes. He also had the body of a fighter and looked nothing like his son, Aaron. His wife had been a beautiful handmaiden whom he married after taking the Crown of Brandor many years ago. His decision to marry a woman without royal blood was not well accepted, but in time, she became loved and accepted by all. It was her fair complexion that colored their son's appearance. She had died not long after giving birth to Aaron, and the king never remarried because his heart would not heal.

After a few long moments, the king responded quietly. "Is anyone hungry . . . or is it just me?"

Sam laughed and grabbed the man's hand, pulling him up from the throne. He put his arm around his shoulders and spoke.

"Now that's the best thing I've heard all day. Do you have any pancakes?"

Sam and the king were about to leave the room when Shalee commented. "My king, no one will remember this day's events and we'll now adopt your customs. Thank you for listening, sire."

The king forced a slight smile and responded anxiously, "It appears that maybe I was being hasty. We have much to talk about over breakfast."

Sam and the king turned and walked for the doors.

After they were gone, Shalee stood by the doors before releasing her magic, allowing everyone to move again. Some were confused by the absence of Sam and the king and kept looking back and forth from their empty hands to the pile of the swords. She giggled as Helga winked at her. She pretended to give her friend a high five as she left the room to catch up with the men.

Helga turned to BJ.

"I may not be able to teach her how to command her powers anymore, but I can still teach her how to be a vixen with them. I guess it all went as planned."

BJ looked at her. A hundred questions filled his eyes.

"What are you talking about woman, what's a vixen ... did Shalee teach you that word?"

Helga smiled and kissed his lips softly as she responded, "She did but it's nothing for you to worry about. Just wait till I teach you how to use the phrase ... *who's your daddy!*"

Taking him by the hand, she led BJ and Prince Aaron to follow after the king.

The Grayham Inquirer

When inquiring minds need to know where their favorite characters are.

SAM, Shalee, BJ, Helga, and the prince spent the rest of the day with Keldwin. All parties enjoyed getting to know one another. They shared information that needed to be exchanged. And now with Late Bailem approaching, the king is about to give an address, giving the details for his upcoming tournament.

DOUBLE D is still traveling to Brandor. He is now only three Peaks of Bailem from the city gates.

GEORGE, Maldwin, and Amar are due to arrive in Lethwitch on the morrow and have decided to stop for a night's rest. They will sleep at an inn located inside the City of Champion's gates, not far from the landing platform

KEPLER is on his way to Gessler Village. His trip is uneventful. When he reaches the northern part of the Dark Forest, he asks Hestin, a Grave Raven, to deliver a message to his brothers. He wants all the jaguars to be at the Gessler landing platform when he arrives.

THE GENERAL ABSOLUTE, Justin Graywind, is with the army's high-ranking officers. He is being briefed on all the field reports needed to create new orders. As expected, the wagons are being built in an orderly fashion. Each populated area of Grayham will have more than 70 new harvest wagons ready within the next 17 Peaks of Bailem. The carpenters and engineers are working with the king's army through the nights.

The general knows they only have another 20 Peaks of Bailem before the harvest. He orders his men to scatter throughout Grayham and make sure that all men, no matter what their normal occupation, are helping in the process. He also follows up on the progress of the harvest barns in certain key areas and has given his officers enough coin to hire 200 men to build these barns. After a few more orders are given, he closes the meeting and makes haste to join the king at his dining table.

CELESTRIA is still living with the elven witch family. She has now taken up walking to avoid them as much as possible.

LASIDIOUS has been on the World of Luvelles. It was five nights ago, though, when he felt the power of Shalee from afar. He excused himself from another long conversation with the Source, and went to see what was going on.

Lasidious put a warning spell on Shalee the day he brought her to the Temple of the Gods. He also secretly listened in on a conversation between Bassorine and the Book of Immortality in the Hall of Judgment. The late God of War had told the Book that Shalee was special and would command great powers one day. This news prompted Lasidious to put the warning on her. At that point, Bassorine became suspicious and put up a barrier through which Lasidious could not hear any more.

Lasidious would never have dreamed that Shalee could become so powerful so soon. Something more had to be behind her growth, but he did not know what it was. Whatever the reason, he needed to find a solution or George would be in trouble.

That night, Lasidious watched Shalee and Helga from the shadows near the Town of Empire. The tree she launched into the air was massive and the power necessary to do so was substantial. He was glad he had introduced George to Amar sooner than expected. He knew their relationship would be short-lived. George would not want Amar around if he felt threatened by his powers and Shalee's powers would definitely command Amar's attention.

Once George had an idea of how strong Amar actually was he would turn him to stone. Lasidious knew also that he would need to implement another part of his plan sooner than expected. He needed to appear to George in his dreams and offer him some helpful information. He just hoped that the Earthling's hunger for power was strong enough to stomach the next step.

MOSLEY had been watching from the hidden god world, and had enjoyed every moment of what happened in the King's throne room in Brandor. He was impressed with Shalee's speech to the king, and decided it was time for a little appearance during the king's upcoming dinner. He has grave news to deliver to King Keldwin.

Thank you for reading the Grayham Inquirer

Chapter 27

How a Heart Tastes

WHEN GENERAL JUSTIN GRAYWIND finally arrived, he apologized for his tardiness and introduced himself to the group. He took his normal position to the left of the king with BJ and Helga on his left. To the king's right was Prince Aaron, followed by Sam and Shalee. The king ordered the servants to bring their meal as he filled the general in on everything he knew, conveniently managing to avoid saying anything about the events in the throne room.

After a bit, Keldwin explained how the general was the champion of Brandor's arena and like Sam, had killed every man or beast that entered the arena with him.

Upon hearing about Sam's successes, the general commented, "This is most impressive. You have come to our world and adapted well. I'm sure you'll be a worthy opponent in the arena when we fight."

Sam looked at Shalee, who seemed angry. He had told her before that he wouldn't fight the general and now that he knew the full extent of her powers, he wasn't about to break his promise. The fighter was unsure how to respond, but as it turned out, the king ended up saving the day.

"General, I wasn't planning on having the two of you fight each other. I have plans for both you and Sam to work together to strengthen our kingdom. With this man's knowledge and his abilities in battle, I was planning on placing him under your command." The king avoided explaining his fear of Shalee's powers and Sam's sword.

"I understand," the general responded. "It'll be nice to have a sergeant who's as well-trained in battle as you."

The king looked at Shalee and took a deep breath. The sorceress was now looking directly at him, waiting for his response. He knew that the general was going to be displeased with his next statement.

"No, General, Sam will not be just a sergeant. He'll be your second in command."

"What?" the General said explosively as he stood up from the table. "You can't be serious. What does this man know of commanding an army?"

Sam was about to interject and inform the general of his extensive knowledge of the wars he had studied back on Earth, but suddenly, Mosley appeared on top of the massive table startling everybody. Both Sam and the general drew their swords; but once they realized who it was, lowered their weapons.

Justin bowed and was the first to speak.

"I'm sorry, lord Mosley. I didn't know you'd be coming. I meant no offense by my actions. Please forgive me."

"General, it is perfectly acceptable. You're a man of war, I would expect nothing less."

Sam and Shalee took an entirely different approach to the god's appearance. They reached up, pulled him close, and hugged him.

"Mosley, how are you?" Sam said, squeezing the wolf tighter as he continued. "It hasn't been the same without you around. One minute you're traveling around with us and, the next minute, you're off with the other gods ignoring me. I miss ya, buddy!"

Shalee could not contain her excitement. As she spoke in her cutest doggy voice, she rubbed her hands through his fur wildly, "Oh my goodness, I missed my Mosley." She laughed as she kissed his snout.

Mosley couldn't stop himself from laughing. Shalee was a favorite of his and her advances, despite the obvious looks of confusion from the king, were welcome in his heart.

"I missed you also, Shalee, but I'm not so sure about you, Sam," he said grinning wolfishly.

"Dang," Sam responded with a big smile. "Bust a brother in the chops when he's down, why don't you?" Sam gave the wolf another big hug and sat down.

After a moment of continued looks of disbelief between both Justin and the king, the wolf began to speak seriously.

"I'm sorry I've been absent, but I've been attending to important matters. Being a god isn't all it's cracked up to be. The others have become lazy and haven't been of much help either. I'm glad to see that you've finally made your audience with the king. I watched the entire event unfold from the god world when you met in the throne room."

The king felt uncomfortable that Mosley had seen what had happened and hoped the wolf wouldn't say anything in front of his general. Mosley could feel the reluctance of the king and turned to relieve his worries, projecting his thoughts into the king's mind. They were heard by the king only because he wanted to hear them.

"Don't worry, Keldwin" Mosley thought, *"Your secret's safe with me. I will not tell the general of your fear of Sam and Shalee."*

Upon seeing the king's relief, the wolf god addressed all of them. "I agree with the king's choice to place Sam second in command of the army. It's the best thing for this kingdom."

The king sighed with relief as he spoke. "Lord Mosley, is there anything else we should know?"

"I'm here to inform you that Sam was chosen by the gods to help create an empire for the other worlds to view as an example. I tell you this, Keldwin, the knowledge this man has will benefit your son and his armies. It's hard for anyone in a time of war to set an example for others to emulate, but this is the very reason he's here. It's not necessary for Sam to be the leader of this kingdom, but to help your son create this empire; he'll be the most important part of it. I hope you and your general have enough strength within you to let him help make your son's kingdom the example the gods want it to be. If you can do this, the other worlds may adopt your customs and the gods would allow the races from each world to be united. It's your choice, Keldwin. This kingdom will need all the men it can find for this, not to mention what must be done to secure the two pieces of Crystal Moon on this world."

The king heard everything the god said, but, like his general, he was concerned about how Mosley had phrased a few things. The wolf had referred to his kingdom as his son's, actually referring to it as such more than once; it caused him to worry.

"Lord Mosley, you spoke as if I won't be here to see these things happen. You have spoken of my kingdom as if it wasn't mine and made it my son's. Is there something to become of me?"

Mosley jumped down from the table and moved to the king's side. "Keldwin, I hate to deliver this news, but your body is fighting a disease and has been for quite some time now. Your body's ability to fight this is beginning to weaken. By morning, you'll start to feel the effects of this disease and your healers won't be able to stop it from killing you. I'm here to bless you so that you can see the end of your tournament. This will be my gift to you. As per your custom, your son will become the king, and the general will become his advisor. This will leave the position of General Absolute open. The second in charge of your army assumes this position. By default, Sam will be the new General Absolute. I believe that to be a wise move. Your confidence in this man isn't misplaced. The move will be a hard one for the officers in your army to accept, but I'll be present when you tell them. I feel sure the loyalty of your people will remain strong."

Prince Aaron anxiously waited for the god to finish speaking. Once done, he jumped from his seat and argued with Mosley that his father should not be allowed to die. The king held up his hand and silenced him, then let his son know it was okay.

The king stood and started to pace. He moved along Sam's side of the table as he spoke, "My son is strong and will make a fine king. Once I die and the general becomes Aaron's new advisor, Sam will become the new General Absolute. I agree, Lord Mosley, that this is per our custom."

Keldwin hesitated then continued. "Aaron, you don't have an heir. I suggest you get busy and find a wife. You'll need children to survive you once I am gone."

The king turned to look at his son.

"I know this isn't the timing you've envisioned for finding your wife, but you've enjoyed sowing your royal oats long enough. It's now time for you to do your duty by finding a queen. I want you to promise me that you'll do this soon after I'm dead."

The prince looked at his father and hugged him. "I promise, Father. I won't let you down, sire. I'll lead the people with the wisdom that you've taught me."

The king smiled and, for a moment, allowed himself to be proud. After a bit he continued. "It is my wish that from now on, until the moment I'm dead, when we aren't in the company of others, that everyone in this room calls me by my first name. Let us talk as equals. I would like to enjoy this pleasantry before I die. I find myself wanting friends right now, not loyal subjects. This isn't something that I wish to command to be done. I want it to be from your hearts. It's acceptable to say no."

Everyone in the room spoke at the same time, calling him Keldwin as they confirmed their acceptance of the idea.

After a moment of silence, the king kissed his son on the forehead and said, "But you still have to call me Father." He smiled and hugged the boy one more time making a treasured memory for them both. Shalee and Helga started to cry.

After a heartfelt embrace, the king turned to the general.

"You best get Sam ready to be placed as second in command, Justin. You should also inform him about our efforts to collect the upcoming harvests. He'll need to know everything about our army."

The general stood from the table and responded. "My king, I mean Keldwin, it will take at least 10 Peaks of Bailem to instruct this man."

Mosley responded. "Justin, do you remember me saying that Sam was chosen by the gods?"

"I do, Lord Mosley, and I'm okay with that, but it doesn't mean he can learn such a tremendous amount of information in such a short time."

Sam laughed and commented with a big smile, "Justin, prepare to be impressed. I think you'll find that I'm more than capable. You only need to speak the information once for me to have it committed to memory. The faster you talk, the quicker we'll be done."

Justin looked at Sam. "I can speak for days about our policies and our army."

Sam turned to the king. "Keldwin, if what Justin says is true, then I'll be ready to be sworn into command in a couple of days, trust me." He turned and winked at Mosley. "Tell them, big guy, about my mind and how it works."

Mosley laughed. "Sam is able to see anything that someone says as if it is written in his head. Everything that is said he remembers. He can quote you conversations from when he was only two seasons old without missing a word."

The general turned to look at his soon-to-be second in command and responded, "This is very impressive. Second in command might be a waste of your skills, Sam. A messenger might be better position for such a memory. With a mind like yours I could send many unwritten messages throughout all Grayham and not worry about my letters being opened by the enemy. It sounds like you just might be able to handle that!" Justin made sure he smiled big so everyone would know he was being clever.

The king laughed along with the others and spoke to the group,

"I'll announce Sam's position to the officers at Early Bailem. I'll have the cooks prepare a hearty breakfast and instruct the hippogriffs to fly through the night if need be to get them to their destinations. They will also swear to complete silence until we have announced the changes to the kingdom. Justin, you'll spend the next three Peaks of Bailem briefing Sam. We'll have his ceremony before the royal courts and the kingdom on the fourth Peak of Bailem when the tournament begins. This announcement will be made inside the arena and the word will spread. Many of the arena's fans will already know of Sam's victories and with Mosley present..." The king hesitated and turned to the wolf.

"Lord Mosley, we have a problem. No one in our kingdom knows that you're the new God of War. How will your presence create an authoritative impact on my officers, let alone the fans of the arena, or even Grayham for that matter?"

"Keldwin, don't worry... call your meeting in the morning with your officers and I'll make a grand entrance. Have your runners spread word through the city that Bassorine has been destroyed and a new God of War has ascended. Make sure the news spreads like a fire. On the day the tournament begins, I'll make an entrance like no one has ever seen. I'm sure we will turn the heads of the people and give them confirmation that I am indeed the new God of War. After this, the people will recognize Sam's new position. Announce to the fans that I'll be coming so that no one panics when I make my entrance."

The king thought a moment.

"I believe this will work. My Lord, if you were to speak in support of everything that is being done, it would truly help to ease their minds as well. Would you do this?"

"Yes, it is a wise thing to have me address the people. I'll speak at both events and tell your subjects that there are gods in support of your decisions. I agree with you, Keldwin, this will work."

Mosley bowed to the king, said his good-byes, then vanished.

The general clapped his hands and three slaves ran into the room. He told them to find his officers and make sure they did not leave the city without first attending breakfast at Early Bailem. The slaves bowed in agreement, then left to fulfill the commands.

The general looked at the group and said, "Well since we're all on a first name basis here, would you all be in agreement that we should toast to these new events on such a fine night?" He smiled big as he lifted his glass high. "Here's to my new friends and a four-legged wolf-god."

Everyone lifted their glasses in a mutual cheer: "Here, here!"

Later that night in the City of Champions

GEORGE, Maldwin and Amar stopped for the night as George figured they'd arrive in Lethwitch tomorrow before Late Bailem. He was anxious to see Athena, and wanted Maldwin to put their plan in motion right away. The plan was for Maldwin to brainwash Athena's family into believing that living with George in the Barbarian's City of Bloodvain was a good idea. He would introduce the rat to her relatives and let the rodent do the rest of the work.

They had checked into the inn closest to the City of Champion's landing platform; it was also conveniently located just inside the city gates. The flight on the hippogriff from Angel's Village had been uneventful, but George enjoyed the ride. He told Amar that he would see him in the morning as they walked by the mage's room. He was exhausted from the trip and was more than ready to lay down.

He had been carrying the rat in his pack since the beast was too small to keep up taking advantage of the time to teach the beast some new phrases. He actually started to bond with the little guy and now was quite fond of the rodent, making it easy to tell Athena that he was actually his pet... it was no longer a lie. After a quick bath, he ate a couple of biscuits and finally lay down for a night's rest.

It was not long before he was dreaming of his little Abbie and the beautiful Athena. The dream was pleasant, but Lasidious interrupted. The god needed to have a conversation with him and now requested the approval to enter George's dreams. As agreed that night in the Enchanted Forest, George opened his mind.

Lasidious spoke: "George, my friend, how are you doing in your travels?"

"I'm sure you already know. So why don't we skip right to the point of why you're visiting me. What can I do for you?"

The god laughed. "I suppose I do make too much small talk at times, but I've come to tell you something important. I fear there's something that could stop us from achieving the power necessary to get your daughter back."

George responded, "Okay, so let's figure this out and move on. What do I need to do?"

"As always George, you don't disappoint me. The woman you arrived with on Grayham has discovered she has incredible powers. This will present a problem for us, George. I need to know how you feel about Amar."

"Why? What does Amar have to do with Shalee?"

"He has nothing to do with her right now, but once he finds out about her power, he'll seek her out to destroy her."

"What the hell are you talking about?" George replied sharply. "Are we talking about the same Amar that I know? Why would he seek out Shalee? This guy isn't even worth having around. He is a spineless wimp if you ask me. You should've seen the look of concern he had on his face when I said I wanted to fight for the Crown of Bloodvain."

"I agree that Amar doesn't have the backbone for great things," Lasidious said, "but he is the most powerful mage in all of Grayham. I told him he should keep his powers hidden from you until the time was right. If he goes after Shalee, he'll become very powerful and impossible for you to control. This will destroy your chances to get your daughter back. I don't want this, George, do you?"

"Well hell no, I don't want him to mess things up. I think you already know that. So what can I do about it other than turn his ass to stone, or is that what you want me to do? Is that even possible with him being so powerful?"

"I don't want you to do anything that you don't want to do. The choices you make need to be your own, not mine. I'm going to tell you a way that you can become as powerful as Amar, George, but it needs to be your choice."

"I'm all ears. Lay it on me, and he's a dead man."

Lasidious laughed.

"A person's soul doesn't immediately leave their body when they die. This is a lie that that the gods have told the beings of all the worlds. We did this to stop those who would attempt to do exactly what I'm about to tell you. Only the most ancient of elves on Luvelles still have this knowledge. Under the right circumstances, a soul can take hours before it leaves for its new home within the Book of Immortality."

"What do you mean by 'in the right circumstances'?"

"I mean you would have to kill Amar to take his powers, George. The problem is that you have to do it just right in order for his soul to stick around."

"That's all I have to do? I don't even like this guy, so are you saying that if I kill him in a certain way I can get his power? I'm all ears."

"I'm saying that killing him is part of it, but it is more complex than ending his life. It requires you to be an artist." Lasidious waited for a response.

"Okay, so let's get to the details and I'll go drop his ass. I'm cool with Kepler and Maldwin, but Amar is a real chump. I couldn't care less about him or his family. I vote we bust him up."

Lasidious was surprised at how cold George had become since his arrival on Grayham. Now that the human had taken life, he loved the rush it gave him. The god knew that George was loyal to those he cared for and it made him the perfect machine to do his dirty work. Without his loyalties George could not accomplish their overall goals. He was happy at how his choice to bring this earthling forward was turning out.

The god responded, "I will tell you, George, but it could be more than you can handle."

"Look," George said rolling his eyes. "Spare me the drama and tell me what I need to know. If this is what it takes to get my Abbie back, then I'm game. Amar is a dead man as far as I'm concerned."

"Well, this is the only way to ensure you won't be stopped by Amar's power once he goes after Shalee and kills her. He's already very powerful from his trip to the World of Luvelles and the addition of Shalee's power would make him unstoppable on this world. The Head Master of Luvelles doesn't make friends with just anyone. This should tell you about how strong Amar actually is."

"How in the hell did Shalee get so friggin' powerful anyway?"

"I don't know, George, but how she got her power, does it really matter right now? Don't you think we should figure that out later?"

George thought a moment. He was suddenly glad that he'd let Lasidious into his dream. "Okay, I agree; it's a good idea to figure out what the deal is with Shalee later. So tell me what I've got to do right now. I'll make it all happen while he sleeps in his room."

"Your love for your daughter is strong. I hope it is strong enough to do what I'm going to tell you next."

"Come on man, get to it already."

"You will need to eat his bloody heart before his soul leaves for the Book of Immortality, or his powers will be lost to you for good."

"I have to eat his heart? My hell, man, that's disgusting. I don't think I like you very much right now to be honest. I like your sick mind, Lasidious, but that's gross. I mean, so what if his power escapes and goes to the Book? It just means he won't be a threat to me any longer."

Lasidious sighed. "Come on, George, you're smarter than that. I told you Shalee's a dominant force and Amar wants her powers. If you're not able to command his powers, then you'll lose the battle with the Kingdom of Brandor. She's going to be one of the many people that could destroy you *without* Amar's powers.

His powers can make you untouchable to most everyone on Grayham. Once he figures out he can have all this power without you, then you're going to be a waste of his time. He'll get rid of you, George."

"Okay I see your point, but eating his raw heart isn't my idea of a delicacy. Hell, I don't even have a bottle of wine to chase it down with. This isn't *Silence of the Lambs*, you know."

"George, as always, you and your references are intriguing but to get serious, you'll need to keep Amar from moving and from speaking his words of power. If you can do that you can open up his chest while he's still alive, rip his heart out, and take the first bite before it stops beating."

"What do I look like, Lasidious, some kind of Doctor Frankenstein or something? Even if I could do that, how will I keep him from dying from the shock before I can get him opened up? I don't have any kind of anesthesia to knock him out while I cut him open."

The god agreed. "Well, at least you're thinking in the right direction. You won't need any medication, George."

"Okay, I'm all ears. I would love to know how to this is possible."

Lasidious projected a vision of the human spinal cord to George's mind. "If you look at this image, you'll see a spot on the human spinal cord that you earthlings called, the dorsal horn. If you turn this area to stone, he would not be able to get the signals of pain to his brain. It will keep him alive so he doesn't die from shock."

"Damn, Lasidious, you're one morbid S-O-B, you know? I love the way you think. So how can I get his chest open?"

"You'll need to crack his sternum and pry his chest apart to expose the heart. You can do this with the tools you'll find at the Smith's barn outside the city. This will be a noisy job. The Smith lives inside the city's walls so no one should be there during the night. If you decide to do this, you'll need to take Amar with you. It'll be far too loud to crack open his chest inside his room. You must take the first bite of his heart before it stops beating and do not stop eating until it is all gone. You cannot stop his soul from finding its place in the Book of Immortality, but you can strip the power from it before it goes."

"Okay, I can do this," George responded. "But I swear, if it tastes like garesh, I'm going to haunt you forever, Lasidious."

The god laughed. "I'm sure that it won't taste pleasant, but it'll be worth it, I assure you, George."

With that, the dream between the two of them faded and George was left dreaming of his little Abbie once again. Slowly his little girl turned to him and yelled, "Dad, get up and save me!"

George awoke with a start and left the sleeping Maldwin in the room. He went to the mage's door and knocked. When Amar answered, he told him he could not sleep and asked him to take a walk with him. Shaking his head in dismay, the mage decided he'd get dressed and go, if for nothing else, out of curiosity. It was not long before they left the inn.

George made small talk with Amar as they walked out of town. He spoke of how much he missed his little Abbie and wanted her back. He explained that he had made a pact with Lasidious and that the god had promised him he would return her if he took control of the Kingdom of Bloodvain. Every answer the mage gave George about how he would do anything for a daughter of his own if he had one served to strengthen the killer's resolve to eat his heart.

When they arrived at the barn, the lock was secured. George said, "I need a hammer from inside. Amar, why don't you use some of your hocus pocus to unlock this?"

The mage laughed and held up his staff. He spoke the simple command and the lock released. Both men entered and George took a seat on a wooden bench near the forge. He looked at the mage and spoke.

"Sometimes I feel like I'm going crazy. I miss my family, Amar." The liar was now in full manipulation mode. "I want to tell you something. When I first met you, I didn't like you very much, but I've really grown fond of you over the last few days. You remind me of my uncle back home, and I really need someone that I can trust in my life. I was wondering if you needed a friend, and how you felt about being friends with me. If you don't want to . . . hey, I'll understand and I'm really sorry that I've bothered you." He finished off his deception with some tears to add effect.

Amar sat next to George. "I don't have any problems with being your friend. I would actually prefer to travel this way and I have also wanted this as well, but I've had my doubts. I didn't think you cared for me much. I'm surprised at your request. What made you decide this?"

George responded and played the part by hugging the mage. "I've been so alone since my arrival here. I can't tell you how grateful I am that we'll be friends. It makes me happy to know I won't be lonely any longer. I have some news for you that will make you happy as well, my new friend."

"What kind of news?"

"Well, it's like this. I know where you can gain a significant amount of power above what you already command. I know of your power, Amar. I also know that this woman will increase your power if you seek her out and take it away from her."

Amar looked confused. "How do you know of my power? I have said nothing of it."

"I'm a smart man, Amar. Now that we're friends, I'll tell you her name if you want to know it. This is my way of showing you that it's my true desire to be your buddy."

"George! This is valuable information that you're giving me. I definitely would like to know her name." Amar thought to himself, *"If this is true, I'll be unstoppable. I can take the Barbarian Kingdom on my own. I'll dispose of you George and keep the throne for myself."*

"Friends for life, right?" George said with a big smile. "Let's take this foursome all the way until we rule this world!"

"I agree that the four of us will dominate," Amar said with a calm voice as he anxiously waited for the name. He would leave instantly and teleport to her location once he knew where she was. He could come back and kill George later. He would also need to kill the rat and Kepler. He would not want to leave anyone alive that would have a desire for revenge. This would mean Kepler's brothers as well.

George spit in his hand and stuck it out. "Where I'm from this is how we become friends."

The mage looked at him confused.

George laughed and explained, "You spit in your hand and I spit in mine. Once we shake, we become brothers. We'll become true friends. You do still want to be my friend, right?"

Amar smiled. If all it took was one handful of spit to get the information he needed to dominate this world, then it was worth it. He lifted his palm, spit in it and extended it.

George grabbed his hand and smiled as he shook it up and down. "Amar, I'm so glad you fell for this line of garesh."

Amar's eyes widened and he started to speak, but it was too late. His tongue and lips were now stone. He ripped his hand away and tried to move, but his feet were heavy. They were also stone and both of his hands were beginning to change. The pain was severe as he watched the grayness cover them. He tried to move again but became unbalanced from the weight in his shoes. He fell backwards to his butt. George walked up to him and touched his nose to put the stone blockage on his spinal cord. Instantly the pain stopped. Amar wanted to call forth the power to stop his attacker, but he could not.

"I guarantee you, Amar, that you won't feel a thing," George said as he pushed Amar flat on the ground. "Just lie back and relax for a bit. It'll all be over soon."

George laughed as he ripped the mage's robe apart. "Yuck, I hate a hairy chest. Allow me to get rid of this for you." He took his knife and started to cut away the flesh to expose the sternum beneath. "Ya know, I hate to say this, Amar, but I'm not really a doctor. I'm not even qualified to be doing this. This may leave you a little bit out of it when you wake up. Ha . . . who am I kidding . . . you're not ever going to wake up once I'm done with you! I should probably say that I'm sorry, but I think you already know that I would be full of garesh. I think I'm actually starting to enjoy this! Hmmm . . . who would have ever known I had the talent to be a surgeon?"

George leaned over and looked Amar in the eye. "You wouldn't have any idea how I should bust your chest open, would ya? Maybe this hammer and chisel will work. Awe . . . you don't like that idea. I can see that you're a little upset with me. Stop giving me the silent treatment. Gees... you act like you've got a tongue made of stone or something!

George laughed wildly.

Amar wanted to respond to his attacker's wicked chuckles but all he could do was watch as his pumping heart was torn from him and then cringe as George took the first bite. Slowly the light faded from Amar's eyes.

Outside the barn, Lasidious stood and watched as George finally found the special effects he had asked for. The light show was spectacular. He knew Amar's powers were now George's to command. He wondered how the heart had tasted. He would appear to George in another dream later this night and teach him how to use one of his new powers. The great thing about George's new abilities would be that he could command them all naturally. He would never need to speak any words of power or use magical items. This was the god's most fascinating creation yet and it was all done within the laws of the Book of Immortality. He had not taken anyone's free will, but George had. He loved loopholes.

Later that night, George lay down on the bed in his blood-soaked shirt. It was not long before he went to sleep. But his sleep was short-lived because Lasidious appeared quickly to him. The god now took just enough time to teach George how to teleport from place to place, teaching him that he needed to be familiar with the area. If he were not familiar with where he was trying to go, he could kill himself.

When George asked how, Lasidious answered by telling him that mages have been known to teleport themselves 20 feet underground and die, all because they did not know the area well enough. George asked Lasidious if Athena's mother's farm would be safe since he had been there so many times and the god replied it was.

Lasidious told the new mage that he would need to appear to him some other time and teach him more, but he didn't want George anywhere near the city when the rumors about the dead began to spread. He informed George that the lady downstairs was suspicious due to his bloody shirt and had already called the guards who were, at this very moment, on their way up to check it out.

The dream ended and George lifted himself out of bed and moved to the far side of the room. He picked Maldwin up, closed his eyes, and concentrated as Lasidious had instructed.

The door to the room burst open and guards entered screaming for his surrender. They had their swords held high, but the room was empty.

The next thing George knew, he was standing outside his soon to be mother-in-law's farmhouse. He was about to knock on the door, but decided to address the blood on his clothes first. Taking up his knife, he set Maldwin down on the ground, and turned away so the rat couldn't see what he was doing. Then he cut the top of his head, allowing the blood to drip down his face.

He knocked, deciding to feign an assault—saying he had been jumped again by the same guys who tried to rob him the first time he spoke with Athena. He concocted a story of how he had obtained the upper hand this time, allowing the mother to tell Athena the story so he would not have to tell lies to this beautiful woman.

The door opened and to his surprise Athena standing there. She freaked out when she saw the blood and pulled him inside, shutting the door behind them. Maldwin looked up from the ground, unsure about what he should do, so he sat, staring at the door until eventually it opened and George scooped him up to bring him inside.

"Sorry, little guy," he said. "Babe, this is Maldwin. I know he is a rat, but I really like this little guy and he's my pet, so don't freak out, okay?"

Athena responded in a scolding voice, "George, put the rat down and sit. You're a mess. What happened?"

Chapter 28

The Visions Begin

ATHENA cleaned the blood from George's face and stopped the bleeding. She asked many questions but George wouldn't answer them. She wanted to know what happened and all he would say is, "Don't worry about it, babe, I'm okay." Each and every time he said this he gave her a kiss and changed the subject. After a while, his beautiful girlfriend gave up and stopped questioning him. George was glad he had been able to avoid telling her a lie. The manipulator felt bad enough that Maldwin was going to manipulate the minds of her family, but he would not deceive her. He had to draw the line somewhere.

The next morning, George could see that the rat was anxious. He figured it was because he had teleported them both without Amar in the middle of the night. The blood all over his clothes didn't help any either. When he had a moment away from both Athena and her mother, he took the rat outside to console him. He used one of the phrases he had taught him on their journey back from the Siren's Song, making sure his smile was big when he made his statement. Wanting his furry ally to feel settled he said, "Everything is 'A-okay,' man!"

The rat looked into his eyes and then, after a moment, he relaxed and twitched his nose. It was clear Maldwin wanted to say something but did not know how, so George waited patiently. After a minute, the little guy said the only thing he could think of. "I like cheese, George!"

The liar smiled and took him back inside. "Hey mom, do you have any cheese?" Once Mary, Athena's mother, produced it, Maldwin scurried into a corner and started to eat. After a moment, George turned back to his future mother-in-law and smiled. "He's cute, don't you think?"

"If you like giant rats, I guess he would qualify as cute. That's not really my idea of a fine pet though." Mary pulled out a chair and sat down.

"So what have you been up to, George? You seem to find yourself getting beat up a lot lately. Athena told me the night she met you, you had gotten jumped outside of town. Now you show up at our door last night all bloody and refusing to offer an explanation. Do I need to worry about you, mister? I don't really want to think that you find trouble so easily!"

George moved across the room and stood in front of her. Putting his hands on her shoulders, he looked her dead in the eye.

"I assure you that I'm not trouble," he said. "I've had a little bad luck lately for sure, but I think everything is going to be okay. How could things not be good when I've got so many beautiful women in my life?"

His charismatic line of garesh seemed to pacify Mary and he gave her a hug. "Don't worry about me, Mom. I'll take care of your little girl!"

She leaned back far enough to catch his eyes and slapped her hand on his chest softly. "You better, the two of you have much to discuss." As she finished her statement, Athena entered the room. "There are preparations that need to be made, George. You need to talk with your girlfriend."

"Mother," Athena shouted. "I was going to tell him later today, but you just had to stick your nose in it, didn't you?"

The elderly woman walked up to her daughter and kissed her cheek. "That's what I do, child. I'm entitled, young lady, because of what I went through to bring you into this world. Love you, sweetheart."

She smiled and left the two of them standing in the room. George looked at Athena quizzically.

"So you were going to tell me something today? What is it?"

Athena took a deep breath and moved close to him. She hugged him for quite some time. It was obvious to the master manipulator that he was being buttered up for something big so he played along. What she had to say was clearly creating some distress within her but George knew whatever it was, he would be okay. He loved her enough that whatever help she needed, he would figure something out.

"Honey?" she said softly.

"Yes, sweetheart, what is it?"

"You know I love you, right?"

George knew it must be big, or she would not be leading up to the knockout punch so slowly. He was too good at this game not to recognize a set up when he heard one. He played along.

"Yes, baby, I know you love me with all your heart."

"You know I would do anything for you, right?"

"Yes, I know you would do anything for me."

"You know my family likes you, right?"

George put his chin on top of her head. "Yes, babe, I know your family loves me."

"You know I would go anywhere with you, right?"

"Yes, I know you would go anywhere with me."

"I really, really do love you, George!"

"Babe, you're stalling! I love you, too! Why don't you tell me what it is, so we can talk about it? I promise that I'll be there for you, no matter what."

Athena started to cry as she hugged him even tighter. "I won't get mad if you leave me." She had never been in a real relationship before and the men she had dated only treated her badly. She loved George with all her heart but she was afraid that he wouldn't want her after what she had to say.

George sensed what was going on and he smiled, knowing there was really wasn't a problem at all. He pushed her back so he could see her eyes, then held her gaze with a passion that he had saved for only one other in his life before. The memory of his little Abbie filled his heart.

"I will take care of both you and our baby, Athena. I'll never leave you. I have a few things to do before the baby's born, but I promise you that your family will see how strong our love is."

"How did you know?" she responded with a shock. "I have told no one other than my mother and sister. I was waiting for you to come back before I said anything else."

"How about we just say that you're terrible at the way you deliver bad news? Besides, what made you think that I'd feel that this was bad news anyway?"

"I don't know, but you're the only man I've ever been with," Athena said. "I was worried you wouldn't want me when you found out. I've always been treated terribly by the men I've dated. I've given you so much more of me than I have anyone else but I was frightened anyway, I guess!"

George pulled her close, hugged her passionately and told her to get ready. He assured her that he loved her and wanted to take her out to get something to eat. The fact that he was the one to take her innocence only made him feel that much stronger about her.

When Athena left the room, he took Maldwin in his arms and scratched his furry little neck, something he'd learned to do on their way back from Siren's Song. He called to Athena's mother and, as she entered the room, he gently squeezed his tail. The rat looked at him for confirmation and George nodded. He set the rodent down and pulled the woman towards him to ask his question.

"Mary, I have something to ask you. I want to marry your daughter and I would like your permission."

The woman's smile stretched from ear to ear as she grabbed him and hugged him tight. "I knew you would be good for her. So when's the wedding?"

George explained that it would be best to do it within the next few Peaks of Bailem since he had to travel some more. He wanted to make sure Athena was not showing when they tied the knot. He assured Mary that he would be settled down before the baby's birth and that they would all be taken care of.

The woman accepted his answer and they set a wedding date. Once agreed upon, she darted out of her home for Athena's sister's place, and started planning. The wedding would be held the day after tomorrow.

George turned to look as Athena came back into the room. She was now out of her pajamas and in a beautiful, full-length dress. "Is this cute enough for you?"

He put his arm around her and placed his free hand on her tummy.

"I will love you until the day I die... I have something to ask you over breakfast. Are you hungry?"

The King of Brandor's Breakfast With Military Officers

SHALEE, BJ, and Helga were not allowed to attend the king's meeting since it was for military ears only. Shalee already knew what was going to happen, but BJ felt left out and decided to leave for a walk after they woke. His pride was hurt and the girls let him go while they went shopping.

The night before, the group had taken the General to see their new home, walking together as they drank their ale. Afterward the General took the group to a large estate that rested a mile from the arena—the home of the army's second in command. He had previously told Sam that once he was sworn in this palatial home would be his and Helga would be reimbursed by the king's treasurer for the expenses on the other home. Both men, as well as the girls, could not believe their good fortune, but they waited until they were back in their quarters before discussing it.

Shalee spoke with Helga in an excited voice, "Wow, did you see how big that place was? It wasn't what I imagined living in back home on Earth, but I think I can work with it, girl." She threw her hands in the air to give a sassy high five which the older sorceress returned with attitude. "You go, girl!"

BJ looked at the two women and said, "What the heck is all *that* about? You two women do some pretty silly things! Shalee you teach her too much of this Earth talk. I don't even recognize her now."

"Oh, lighten up you, old fart," the 247-season-old woman said laughingly. "Shalee only taught me a few mannerisms from her old home. There are plenty more I need to learn, too. Besides, I think they're fun! You're just gonna have to love them with me!" She leaned over and gave BJ a long and passionate kiss.

"You just wait until I explain the phrase, 'who's your daddy' to you."

Both Shalee and Helga laughed and again did a high five.

Sam said, "Women from Earth sometimes act a little off-in-the-head. Don't even try to figure them out because it's impossible. They come from a planet called Venus anyway."

When Shalee heard Sam's snide remarks, she gave her lover boy an evil grin and lifted Precious into the air.

"Let the games begin," she said as she stalked her man, slowly walking towards him. Sam had played this game before and knew what was coming as he ran away from her and the two began chasing each other around the room. Shalee sent tiny electric shocks from the tip of her staff into Sam's buttocks. Time after time the macho fighter jumped into the air screaming like a little girl. "I love you, baby . . . ouch. I love you, baby . . . ouch." Even BJ had to laugh.

The next day Sam woke up early, kissed his beautiful sorceress and told everyone goodbye. He assured BJ that once he could do something about the situation that he would have a place of importance for him by his side very soon.

Sam went to the king's dining hall to wait for Keldwin with everyone else. Finally, the king entered the dining room and greeted his officers, thanking them for coming, and shaking hands before changing the tone of the meeting.

Sam could see the slight hint of pain on Keldwin's face. The effects of the disease were already beginning to bother him.

The king continued, "I have called everyone here, not only to sit at my table and eat a fine breakfast, but to discuss issues of great importance. We will eat in a moment but first we have matters to address." The king moved around the long table as he spoke. His officers totaled, not including the General, 11 men. Michael, the General's second in command, the same man who was about to be temporarily demoted, was sitting next to Sam near the head of the table. He would be given his position back as soon as the King passed on and Sam moved into the spot of General Absolute. The other ten officers, each a leader of his own legion, occupied seats of importance with the Prince sitting at the far end of the table. The King's army was just over 50,700 strong and the Kingdom of Brandor always had the advantage over the Barbarian Kingdom's numbers. The King continued.

"I have a few things to say, some of which will not make you happy, but I've received word that these decisions are the right ones, directly from the gods themselves."

The room filled with whispered commotion as they looked at each other, the serious tone of the meeting increasing. The General finally stood and called everyone to order so the King could continue.

Slowly the king walked behind each officer, circling the entire table before resting behind his own chair. "Bassorine, God of War, has been destroyed."

Before Keldwin could get another word out, the table once again became agitated and questions filled the air. The general stood and spoke loudly, "Didn't I just say that this meeting will come to order? There will be no more speaking until the King has finished."

The officers knew not to question Justin's authority as his reputation as a mighty warrior was respected. Everyone quieted down and once again the King took the floor.

"As I was saying, Bassorine is gone, but a new God of War has taken his place." The royal man's eyes scanned the room as he watched his officers throw each other glances. Never, in the entire life since he had been king, had a god made his presence known to the leaders of his army. He knew this would shock them since, until now; the gods had kept to themselves. The King had never met Bassorine, but he knew Mosley from the work Bassorine had him doing before he ascended.

He waited a minute for them to digest this information before he continued.

"The god that has replaced Bassorine as the new God of War is Lord Mosley. The wolf will be joining us for breakfast this morning."

He knew this statement would get some reactions since most of his officers had met Mosley in the past. The table once again buzzed with commotion, but the King stopped the General from yelling at them, deciding to allow them to talk among themselves a bit before he continued.

After a moment Keldwin raised his hand the room quieted.

"As I was saying gentlemen, Mosley is the new God of War and—"

The King didn't get in another word before the room suddenly filled with a mighty wind, intense enough that each man had to steady his glass. As the wind settled, a brilliant light appeared a few yards behind the King's chair. The men shielded their eyes... and when the light dissipated, Mosley was standing in its place. Despite the King's warning that the wolf was coming the frightened men backed away from the table. The General covered his mouth with both hands and turned his back to the men to keep them from seeing him laugh. The King did not show any emotion at all. For the next few moments, the room was in chaos.

Sam, knowing what was coming, was not frightened in the least. He moved to a clear area of the room away from the table and knelt on one knee along with the king, the Prince, and the General Absolute, adding to the importance of the god's appearance. The four men stayed in this position with their heads lowered, without saying a word, until the rest of the frightened men gathered their nerve and eventually knelt as well.

Mosley had added some additional size to his appearance for the occasion and actually looked to be twice his normal size. He sat on his haunches and pushed his furry chest out in a majestic posture, looking absolutely stunning, with his white teeth and tail and coat brushed to a regal shine that was better than perfection. Sam thought there was no finer example of a wolf-god than Mosley had now become. With everyone kneeling, the god finally spoke.

"Great King, I request to be a part of this meeting. I'm not here to force my opinions, but I have things to say that will be useful. Please stand, Keldwin, so that we may talk."

The King rose and followed Mosley to the far side of the room where they could speak privately, their backs to the others. Mosley leaned in towards Keldwin to speak.

"So do you think they bought it? They did seem a bit nervous, but I feel that an impression has been made. What do you think?"

"Oh, I very much agree. The men will listen to everything you say now."

"Do you think the entrance was dramatic enough?"

"Oh, more than dramatic, the men have never seen anything quite like it, I assure you."

"How are you feeling?"

Keldwin hesitated before answering. "I feel as good as a man can, considering the fact that I know I'm dying."

"I understand... please kneel in front of me Keldwin so I can give you the blessing that you'll need in order to see the end of your tournament."

The men watched their King take a knee. Mosley touched him on top of the head with his paw and a glow surrounded Keldwin's entire body as he hovered above the stones of the floor. Eventually the King returned to earth and rose to his feet.

"May I give them an order, Keldwin?

"Please . . . by all means, my Lord!"

When they turned to the group, Mosley commanded them all to sit with an assertive voice. Everyone moved quickly. The wolf watched the anxiety on their faces.

"Great King, I will sit a moment and listen as you speak."

Keldwin loved being called a great king in front of his men. It gave him renewed vigor to carry on with the meeting.

"Thank you, Lord Mosley. I was about to tell the men that there are some changes coming to our kingdom."

The King turned to his men and forced a smile as he continued.

"I'm dying, and will be dead not long after my tournament."

The room buzzed with commotion once again and this time the king allowed the General to explode.

"I said to keep quiet. The next man I have to tell this to will be put on the arena's lottery. I feel bad for the soul who has to face me."

All the officers knew this was their last warning and no one would dare speak again unless they were asked to; but Sam, on the other hand, sat across from the General thinking he could defeat Justin if given the chance.

"Michael, I will be temporarily removing you from second in command and placing Sam here in your stead. When I die, Sam will become the new General Absolute and General Graywind will become the advisor to my son. Then Michael, you will return to your responsibilities and assist Sam in our upcoming war."

The King turned to look at Mosley for confirmation that what he said was correct.

"This is correct, Great King," the wolf replied in a strong voice.

The King continued. "Are there any questions?"

The first one to raise his hand was Michael. "My King, with all due respect and I sincerely mean no offense, but who exactly is Sam that, he is able to show up as if out of nowhere and move into a position that I have earned?"

The General was about to jump out of his seat and rip Michael apart for his ignorant nerve, but the King was wise and recognized the situation. He held his hand up to Justin.

"The last time I checked, Michael, I was made king and any position that is given is because I choose to allow it. If I remember correctly, our laws, laws that my family created with the Royal Courts and the senate, allow me to have the final authority in times of war. The gods themselves have told us that war is upon us. I've already ordered the General to activate our armies as you also know. So I would ask you to explain to me, Michael, why it is you feel that you have the right to question your King? Do you question the knowledge that the gods have about Sam? It was by referral of the gods themselves that Sam has come by this position. It's true, he's not from this world, but he is a warrior with a great tactical mind. A referral such as this would be foolish for me to ignore. Who here at this table would agree by raising your glasses?"

Everyone in the room lifted their drinks saying, "Here, here."

With one more issue settled, the King continued.

"I'll announce Sam's new position at the start of my tournament. I expect all of you to leave here after breakfast and carry out your duties as General Graywind has ordered. I've already sent word for the hippogriffs to fly through the night if need be to help in carrying out my orders. Each of you has an important job to complete now for your kingdom."

The king turned from the table and looked at Mosley.

"Do you have anything you wish to say, my Lord?"

The oversized wolf-god moved close to the table, lifted his front paws up onto the edge and looked down at the men. "The gods themselves have brought Sam to this world along with his soon-to-be-wife, Shalee. They are powerful beings and worthy of your respect. I would hope that this relationship does not need to be tested before you accept that they are worth following. I leave you now, but will be watching you from the god world." With that, the wolf began to dissolve into a million little pieces that floated up and through the roof.

Once the room settled down and the King saw that everyone was calm once again, Keldwin turned the meeting over to Sam before making his exit with his son and the General.

Sam stood and moved to the head of the table.

"Does anyone have any questions?" he asked.

The soon-to-be-second in command (Sam) was still thinking about Mosley's comment that Shalee was his soon-to-be wife. Up until now he hadn't even thought about it, but he had to admit that he liked the idea. He would have to address this idea again after he finished with the men in front of him.

Every single officer had a hand in the air. Sam sighed as he pointed at one of them to begin.

Later That Afternoon, Just After the Peak of Bailem

IT WAS OVER BREAKFAST that George asked Athena to marry him. She was delighted of course, and dragged him immediately to a jeweler friend of hers. George smiled as he paid for the ring, ignoring the fact that the money came from the pockets of Amar's dead body. He realized too that this was the first time he had given someone other than his daughter a piece of jewelry. His first wife had bought her own. He enjoyed giving instead of receiving, and he watched as his beautiful Athena's smile grew.

Before they left, the jeweler told them that she would have the ring ready the next day, early enough to retrieve it before the wedding. The next stop was to buy the new bride a gown, and George something to wear that would make him look dashing. Both items of clothing would be ready to pick up at the same time as the ring. After they were done shopping, Athena took him back to her mother's to thank him properly. As always, George treated her with selflessness and passion.

It was now just past the Peak of Bailem and George figured he'd better get up and put his plans in motion. He asked Athena, if she were to ever move, which of her family members she would want to be near her. Athena answered his question and, after she did, he asked if she would take him to meet them all. She agreed and, as they left Mary's home, George grabbed Maldwin. He threw the beast in his pack and headed out holding Athena's hand.

It would take most of the afternoon to find each of these family members. By the time they were done, though, Maldwin had learned the faces of everyone he would send his visions to.

George and Athena stopped by a dairy outside of town and he purchased a block of cheese for the rat, then headed back home. On their way out of town, George noticed military personnel moving around and asked Athena what she knew about it.

"Giant wagons are being built for the harvests, harvests that will be extremely bountiful because they were blessed by the gods. Some of the town's men have been hired by the King to build barns on the other side of mother's farm to hold it all," she replied.

The only reason she knew this was because everyone in town was talking about how the King of Brandor had paid men to carry out his orders, a very unusual way of doing things.

Where was Kepler when he needed him? George knew the demon would be able to get answers as he stalked around unseen. He would have to find out what was going on after his wedding.

As Maldwin shifted in his pack, George remembered what Kepler said before they separated: the rat would need a quiet place to send his visions. George took the little guy to Mary's barn and left him with his block of cheese. Kepler also said it would take the rat some time to reach everyone and get them all to come to one of their midnight meetings. The manipulator hoped the first meeting would be held the next night.

The next morning, George woke up, kissed his beautiful fiancé's soft lips, and excused himself to check on Maldwin. When he arrived, the rat was sleeping soundly on a bale of hay, the block of cheese untouched. Quietly, the new mage walked over to him and whispered so he did not startle the beast.

"Maldwin, Maldwin, wake up little guy."

Slowly the rat stirred. When he looked up at George, the mage could see he was exhausted. The furry rodent pulled his way over and set his head on George's lap. George rubbed his head and spoke to him softly assuring him that everything was okay. The visions the rodent had sent to everyone must have been hard to deliver. He didn't want to push his little ally any harder and now gently supported the rat's head as he moved out from under him and lowered Maldwin to the hay. He was about to make his exit when a faint voice called to him.

"George, everything is 'A-okay' man," Maldwin said as he watched the mage turn and look at him.

George smiled, walked back into the barn, tore off a chunk of cheese and laid it next to the little guy's paws before leaving the barn.

The meeting that Maldwin had set for all of Athena's family was held that night and everyone was beginning to show up. As they came into the barn, Maldwin extended his vision to each of them. With all present and sitting on the hay, the family members closed their eyes and became absorbed in the vision Maldwin was feeding them. They learned of the wondrous idea of living with George in the Barbarian Kingdom and how peaceful it would be there for them.

Meanwhile, George and Athena had left for a wedding getaway. Besides, George did not want his future bride to be manipulated by the rat's vision.

George smiled as he walked down the road holding her hand; his plan was coming together. As they walked, Athena put her head on his shoulder. He was tired and wanted to get back to his future mother-in-law's home as soon as the coast was clear, knowing the wedding would come quickly after getting to bed so late. He hated late starts. By the time he rested for a bit, hurried to town, grabbed the ring, the clothes, and returned to the farm to get dressed, it would be Late Bailem; barely enough time to say, "I do!"

Chapter 29

Two Weddings and a Funeral

WHILE ATHENA was introducing George to her family, about the same time the new mage had secretly squeeze Maldwin's tail to inform the rat of who to send his visions to, excitement was been building in Brandor.

Sam left the breakfast meeting with the officers of the King's army and hurried out into the city to find Shalee. He was shocked at how hard it was to find a woman who stuck out like a sore thumb. When he finally found her with Helga, they were in one of the local jeweler's stores. The heavy-set man behind the counter was placing a gem into an elegant, tiara-like headpiece when Sam walked in. The comment Mosley made kept circling around in his mind. How ironic that he should find his mate in a jewelry store—it only heightened his anxiousness.

"Hey, babe," Sam said, giving Shalee a kiss on the neck.

"Hi, sweetheart, I'm just looking for a good reason to spend your hard-earned coin on me. How was the meeting? Did Mosley make a good showing?"

"He was impressive all right. He showed up with some very solid special effects and made himself look twice his normal size."

Shalee looked over her shoulder and grinned at Helga. "So did everyone freak out?"

"Yeah, did everyone freak?" The older sorceress chimed in.

"Oh, they freaked out all right, but Mosley said something that has been sticking with me all morning."

It was easy to see that Sam was hesitant to talk about whatever it was, but that did not stop Shalee from asking.

"So what did our furry god friend say to get you so worked up? Do I need to take you back to the castle and help you relax? I could always chase you around with Precious!"

This did not bring the normal smile to Sam's face that it usually did and Shalee knew something serious was on Sam's mind.

"I'm sorry hon, what's bothering you?"

Sam looked at her with an intensity she never saw before.

"Mosley said that you and I were going to be married."

Shalee didn't know what to say.

"Did you say anything to Mosley about this?" Sam queried, "maybe when I wasn't around or something?"

"No, I wouldn't do something like that," Shalee said, "but, I've got to say, I do like the idea. He's really a smart wolf!"

When Sam heard this, the concern he had about talking with her suddenly vanished, enabling him to be his usual bold self and approach the conversation with more self-confidence.

"Well then I too agree with Mosley; I like the idea as well. I'm so glad you feel the same. Come, let's find the King and ask him to marry us tonight.

"Oh Sam, I can't think of anything better. To be married by a King, it sounds delightful and romantic!

"Let's go then," Sam said, "we don't have much time since Keldwin will be leaving us soon. I think we should go ask him to do it right this very second."

Helga screamed happily at the top of her lungs and started to run insanely around the shop. "My babies are getting married, my babies are getting married! Hey . . . what is a second? That does mean right now, right?"

Shalee watched the woman's antics and laughed lightly. "I'll explain it later, but yes… it means now!"

Helga shouted again. "So go get married already!"

"I guess we're getting married then... "Mom" has spoken."

The brilliant-minded doctor, fighter, lover, soon-to-be commander and friend was suddenly engaged. He grabbed Shalee, lifted her up, gave her a big kiss, and rushed her off to find the King.

As they hurried to the castle, Sam asked Helga to track down BJ. He wanted the trainer to be his best man, knowing that Shalee would naturally choose Helga to be her maid of honor. Everything else would take care of itself. All they had to do now was find Keldwin. When they all finally came together and entered the throne room, they found one of the servants and sent him to fetch the King, making sure he relayed the message as urgent. Then the four of them kneeled on one knee as they waited for him to come. The wait seemed like forever, but it was only a few moments. Even though the King had been sleeping, he came quickly, thinking it may have something to do with Lord Mosley.

Keldwin entered the room and saw the four of them kneeling with reverence. "Sam, what is it that you so badly needed. Why did you wake me?"

Sam knew exactly how to answer his question. "Keldwin, do you remember telling us that you wanted us to treat you as a friend when others were not around?"

"I do."

"Well, I'm here to do just that. I have decided to marry Shalee and there's no one I would want to perform our ceremony more than you. I can't think of a better friend to give this honor to. We would like this to be our gift to you before you die!"

The King was speechless. Never in all his years as King had he been so touched. For the first time, he felt like he had real friends other than Justin Graywind if Sam believed him to be approachable enough for something as important as this. He knew this would be the one special day that Sam and Shalee would remember for their entire lives and being a part of it was indeed, a gift—and quite the honor. Feeling so blessed, the King began to weep.

Keldwin walked toward the group and motioned for them to stand. He gave each of them a hug and, when he came to Sam, he kissed his forehead and smiled as he spoke. "You've honored me and I would be pleased to perform your ceremony and honor you in return."

The King clapped his hands and three slaves ran into the room. He spoke to them as they entered. "We have much to do. I want my royal seamstress, cook, jeweler and carriage driver brought to my throne room immediately!"

The slaves ran from the room and the king turned back to face the group. "This wedding will be one to remember. I'll marry you after the start of the tournament. We will wait for Mosley to make his entrance and then, after I announce your position as second in command, Mosley will speak to the people and ensure them that the gods approve. You then can be married in front of thousands of my people from all over my kingdom. This type of event has never been done before in the arena. Everyone will know you throughout the land. Once the first day of the tournament is over, we'll retire to my grand ballroom and invite the nobles to celebrate your marriage. We'll have a grand feast. This will be my gift to you."

The four were elated and surrounded their King in a big group hug. After a moment, Keldwin clapped his hands and told the slave who appeared to make sure they did exactly as Sam and Shalee commanded. Once this was done, he excused himself and went back to bed.

Both Sam and BJ left the palace, but just like boneheaded men do on occasion, they figured that they would leave the planning of the wedding to the two women. They headed into the city mindlessly to grab a few ales.

Normally Shalee would have been upset that she had been abandoned, but Precious would make quick work of the tasks at hand. The young sorceress had a special wedding dress in mind—as most women do why they begin to plan their weddings as young girls—so she ordered the seamstress to bring an assortment of fabrics to the throne room. When the woman finally arrived with the different fabrics, Shalee and Helga lined them up against the wall to get a good look. The ladies talked quietly for a bit and agreed on the perfect combination of colors....a predominantly white dress with a dash of pink for accent. Shalee raised Precious into the air and spoke her words of power. The seamstress stood in disbelief as the fabrics lifted from the floor and, for an instant, disappeared into a big ball of light. When the light faded, a beautiful, flowing masterpiece was left floating in air.

The women cheered and hugged each other, giving the seamstress a hug as well, who reacted with utter confusion. Laughing gaily, Shalee retrieved the dress and tried it on. She was stunning of course... a beauty without equal. The lines of the dress accented her every curve perfectly and the pink accent brought out the glow of love in her face. She took off the dress and gave it to the seamstress, asking her to make sure it was put in a safe place.

When they walked through the kitchen doors, the head cook

seemed to be displeased that they were in his domain. Shalee laughed and told Helga that even the chefs on Earth were protective of their kitchens. She moved around the room and saw everything was in order, scanning the entrance to the kitchen to determine exactly how big of a cake she could make, she grinned. Each requested ingredient—with the exception of the cinnamon, since no one had a clue what it was—was present and accounted for. Even the pile of wood she requested was stacked next to the counter as ordered. Once again she lifted Precious and spoke the words of power.

Again the magic created a blinding light. Some time passed, but when the light faded, a cake like no other appeared on a large table with wheels. The creation was nine different levels, all supported by perfectly shaped wooden columns. Many different shades of icing worked together to tell a romantic story of love. Angels, made of hardened sugar, dressed in yellow robes, were sitting around the edges of the cake, their legs draped over the side, wings spread, and hands folded in front as if praying. Nine of these heavenly figures sat on the first level, their numbers reduced by one with each level as the cake ascended upward, until finally—a sole angel rested on top. This angel was dressed in a red robe, also made of hardened sugar. His perfect, white-feathered wings were spread and circled forward to protect two figures with them: the figures of Sam and Shalee.

The king's head cook was astonished by the beauty of the pastry. Over six feet tall, the bottom layer alone had a diameter nearly six feet wide. Shalee had even created a small cupcake for the chef to taste. He was delighted and left her with a standing invitation to come into his kitchen anytime.

The women left and made their way to meet with the jeweler. Shalee used her magic again to create the rings; but this time the lady who brought the gems screamed when she saw the magic work. The poor woman darted out of the room and, despite Helga running after her, would not come back.

All-in-all, the day was productive. When Shalee retired for the night, she laid her head on Sam's chest. As she rested, the sorceress suddenly realized in the middle of the night that everything was not done: she had forgotten to make Sam's tux. Once again she sent a servant for the seamstress with a message to bring materials that would be fit for a groom. When the lady arrived, Shalee made it quickly so they could all go back to bed, thanking the seamstress with a hefty tip.

Wedding Day

SAM and Shalee planned to marry just after the Peak of Bailem. They dressed together, mutually agreeing that the old Earth tradition of the groom not seeing the bride prior to the ceremony was ridiculous.

Helga and BJ had already left for the arena and now it was time for the couple to leave. They headed out of the castle and joined Keldwin, the General Absolute and the Prince who were waiting for them in the king's carriage, all of them dressed in their best military regalia completed with armor. The king was the first to speak.

"Shalee, I must say that I've never seen outfits quite like these before. I'm impressed. I wish that my kingdom had more of your fashion sense."

"Thank you, Keldwin. If you would like, I'll make you something special for the final day of the tournament. It will enhance your good looks and make you quite debonair."

"I'd like that, but it is our tradition to wear our best armors. Maybe you could do something special to make *them* look better."

"I would be honored, Keldwin."

"What a bride you'll be on this wondrous day. Your beauty would make the gods jealous."

"Here, here," the General responded. "Sam, you're a lucky man. If ever you have a day that you need a break from such grace, you can send her my way."

Sam laughed and looked at the Prince. "And how are you today, Aaron?"

"I'm fine, thank you," the Prince replied, "but I would like to know what the name of your outfit is. I think I would also like to have Shalee make me one someday."

Shalee did not give Sam the chance to answer. "Oh Aaron, you would look handsome in a tuxedo."

"Tuxedo," the King said laughing. "That's a funny name, but if you say it enough, it could grow on you, I suppose."

"Agreed," the General responded.

The pleasantries of the conversation continued until the group finally arrived at the arena. As they entered, the people cheered for their King and every woman who lined the hallways marveled at the beauty of Shalee's dress. Even the men admired the couple's outfits.

"Shalee," Keldwin said, pulling her close. "Are most of my people admiring your fashion to the point that they don't notice their King's arrival, or is it just my perception?"

Shalee kissed him on the cheek and whispered in his ear, "What can I say, Keldwin? When you look this fabulous, they just love you."

"I can only assume that fabulous means, very beautiful?"

"You know it!" Shalee responded, grinning as she slid her hand sideways through the air and snapped her fingers with a sassy sexiness.

The King chuckled and continued with her arm resting atop his.

When the Peak of Bailem arrived, trumpets sounded to signal the start of the tournament. The King, along with Aaron, Justin, Sam and Shalee, walked to the center of the arena and waved to the crowd as they waited for Mosley to arrive.

The daylight suddenly turned to darkness as the clouds lowered to a position just over the arena. They looked angry and lightning struck the arena floor. The clouds finished their descent and settled on the sandy surface. Now nothing could be seen and the screams from the frightened crowd filled the air. Sam was unable to see Shalee, even though he was holding her hand. When the clouds finally dissipated, all that was left in their place was a larger than normal-sized wolf god. The crowd's fears vanished with the haze and screams were replaced with cheers as once again Mosley made quite the impression. The King waited a bit and then held up his hand to silence the cheering crowd. Sam was impressed at how quickly this massive gathering could become quiet.

Now the King signaled for the announcement to be made. A large man, standing at the top of the arena, shouted down to let everyone know that Sam would be taking the place of Michael as second in command. As expected, there was a lot of commotion as the crowd puzzled and buzzed about the decision... this was Mosley's cue to speak. Deciding to make his point on an even larger scale, the wolf quickly grew to 40 feet tall before starting to speak. The crowd silenced, watching in horror.

"People of the Kingdom of Brandor, hear me!" Mosley's voice matched his giant size. "The gods are aware of your King's decision and know that Sam will only serve to strengthen the leadership of your King's army."

Keldwin admired the god's ability to make a point. He turned towards Sam and motioned for him to bow which Sam did. The King then used his sword to swear him in; when Sam stood, he was the new commander. Now, only three people in the kingdom held more power than he did. As he rose, the crowd cheered welcoming their newest military member. The royal group gazed over the crowd and seeing that Mosley's message was successful, it was time to move on.

The wedding was next and Keldwin signaled for everyone to take their places. BJ and Helga made their way to the center of the arena where 30 well-dressed men carrying long trumpets formed two long lines facing each other in front of the king. The trumpets were made of silver and were thin, while the men were dressed in black with silver ruffs extending from their chins to the bottoms of their coats. Their shoes gleamed with perfection in the sunlight, contrasting well against the white sand of the arena floor.

Sam and Shalee were given room to stand in front of the King for the deliverance of their vows with the Prince and the General taking their places behind Keldwin. The armor of the three men had been polished for this occasion and they lowered their arms as they stood at attention.

Mosley decided to give Sam and Shalee a gift and he moved to the side of the King, sitting next to him with head held high; then he announced in a thunderous voice:

"This wedding is considered blessed by the gods."

The people cheered as the wolf gave the group a look, extending his powers as a god and enhancing their ability to be heard by everyone.

Once the vows were complete, the King bound them together with a ceremony, motioning for the couple to kneel and join hands. He took his sword, lifted it high into the air and blessed the union by slowly lowering it to touch each of their shoulders. Once this was done, he commanded them to stand and announced to the Kingdom of Brandor they were now bound for life.

The crowd cheered and the trumpeters lifted their instruments high. A tunnel formed as the music filled the air indicating it was time for Sam and Shalee to leave the arena. The King kissed them both on their foreheads and waited for the couple to begin their first handheld walk as husband and wife. Keldwin, followed by Aaron, Justin, BJ and Helga, then walked behind the couple in single file as everyone exited. Once the musicians cleared the sandy surface, Mosley was the only one left. He made a grand exit, once again expanding himself into a giant, then lifting his head high into the air and howled before vanishing.

After a time, the crowd finally settled down and the first fight was announced. The stadium erupted again as the tournament began.

Sam and Shalee went back to the castle to begin their life together. Later that evening, the party began with royalty filling the king's ballroom. Unannounced, Sam stood up on a table in the center of the room to call for a toast, tapping on his mug of ale to command attention.

Once everyone had their eyes on him, he looked at Shalee and said, "To my beautiful, loving wife, you know my most intimate mind and my weaknesses. I cannot hide my gratitude for allowing me to love you. I embrace the sharing of all our secrets. The change in me is all due to your cherished love. I will be forever blessed. So here is to my beautiful wife, my companion, my heart and soul, I will be forever grateful. I love you."

Shalee rushed to stand beside him on the table and a long passionate kiss followed as the room filled with applause. After a moment, Sam held his glass high in the air and spoke again.

"It has come to my attention that the people of Brandor have never seen a wedding cake. My lovely wife has prepared this special gift for you. With your permission, my great King, let us have the cook bring it out for these fine people to partake."

The king agreed and clapped his hands. From out of a large set of double doors, a massive cake appeared on a polished wooden cart.

The delicacy was a hit.

BJ and Helga, after saying a few words of encouragement to the newlyweds, managed to quietly sneak away to be alone. They moved to the center of the royal garden behind the king's castle and lay on the grass, giggling as two lovers do when falling heavily in love with one another and breaking the rules to do it. They both enjoyed the idea of the garden being considered off limits to the commoners and being somewhat naughty only heightened their experience.

In the darkness of night, lying in each other's arms, they looked up and admired the worlds of Harvestom and Luvelles as they shined down from a starless sky. The two worlds managed to light up the garden ever so slightly and give it soft romantic glow.

No words were spoken as the interlude sang a song of its own allowing the lover's lips to discover their special brand of happiness.

After a long while had passed and only after an even longer embrace, BJ looked into Helga's eyes.

"You know that I love you... I love you more than I've ever loved any other. You've taken this old broken heart of mine and given it back to me whole and renewed. You've helped me feel once again. For so long… my heart was hard… but you've managed to soften it. I'll always cherish you for this great gift you've given me!"

Helga's heart melted.

"I love you too, you big grouch!" She smiled as she nestled into him. "I love you too, BJ," she whispered seductively, "with all my heart."

Meanwhile, at Mary's Home

GEORGE and Athena were also due to be married this evening. When Late Bailem arrived, George was finished with all the running around he had to do. Although it was a little later than expected, he now stood in front of an assistant to one of Brandor's senators in the torchlight to receive his vows. Athena's mother had tried to get the senator himself to perform the ceremony, but every senator from each of the kingdom's villages, towns and cities were at the King's tournament.

Mary and the senator had been friends since childhood. Even though he was from a royal bloodline, they found each other irresistible, often running off together despite the laws that forbade it. They continued in secret until his parents found out and put a stop to their relationship. Royalty did not like to mix bloodlines with commoners, despite what the king himself had done many seasons ago. Mary hated the King for this, often wondering what her life would have been like with Ralton Brandor. But as she looked at her beautiful Athena on her wedding day, she realized that this was the life she was meant to have.

The ceremony was going to be simple and Athena's entire family was in attendance. George's heart was filled with happiness and for the first time in his pathetic life, he was committing to something lifelong other than his daughter. He would no longer use women for things he needed or wanted. He would simply have to rely on his charisma to get what he wanted without any added bonuses. He would be loyal to Athena and give her, at least in his mind, the respect she deserved. There was a new child on the way and he was not about to let this one have a broken home.

The assistant kept the vows short, but sweet. The family cheered as the couple went to her mother's barn for the party, creating an atmosphere that reminded George of some kind of hillbilly square dance back on Earth. Everyone was having a good time and there was even a potluck dinner laid out on many tables. The only thing missing was a wedding cake... and a whole lot of class. They settled for fresh fruits dipped in a sweet cream as a dessert and George told himself he would marry Athena again once he had more wealth to do it right. George took Athena for a walk just before midnight. Since the entire family was there, Maldwin sent his visions to them and once again, they all saw how great it would be to live with George in the Barbarian Kingdom.

The newlyweds went to their favorite spot, the same spot where they had their first meal. As they sat in the gazebo in the middle of the pond, George kissed his new wife and held her close. They stayed there for hours; when finally he decided that Maldwin should be done, they prepared to leave. He kissed his Athena one last time.

"I have a surprise for you."

"You do, what's my surprise, honey?"

"I'm able to do things that will allow me to come and see you more often as I travel. I need to show you what it is so you can understand how I can find my way home to you every night. I want you to keep this surprise a secret though... will you do that for me?"

Athena looked at George, her eyes filled with confusion. "I thought you said your travels were going to take you far to the north?"

"I did."

"So how do you expect to be with me if you are there and I'm here?"

George smiled and pulled her close. "I'll show you, but you have to promise to keep it a secret between us. Will you do this?"

She was hesitant to agree, but she embraced him and put her head on his chest, which was her favorite place to be. "If it lets us be together, then I promise."

George smiled. "Close your eyes, babe."

"Why?"

"Trust me... just close them."

Once she had done so, he closed his own. When they reopened them, they were standing in his mother-in-law's guest home. Athena screamed, backed away from George, and started speaking wildly. "What kind of sorcery is this? How can I be in my mother's place?"

George expected her reaction.

"Honey, sit down."

He took her arm and guided her to the table where he pulled out a chair. He watched her face as the seat's legs screeched across the floor.

"George, are we really at my mother's guesthouse? How is this possible?"

The mage pulled another chair close to her and sat down. "I thought you would be happy that I can come and see you each night. Once I get to where I'm going, I'll be able to come back and forth every night until it is time for you to come and be with me. Doesn't this make you happy?"

Athena started to cry. "Why didn't you tell me about your abilities before we said our vows, George?"

He did not know how to respond. "Let me ask you this. If I had told you, or shown you, before we got married, would it change the fact that I've always loved you and have been good to you since the first time we met? Would it have stopped you from wanting to marry me?"

Athena looked into his eyes. "No, George, I love you and I would die if I couldn't be with you."

"Well, if you love me no matter what," he said brushing his hand softly against her cheek, "then why are you so upset about something that will allow us to be together? I have the ability to do so much more than what I've just shown you, but it has nothing to do with how I love you. I love you because my heart wants to be yours. I'm sorry that I've upset you... will you please forgive me?"

Athena melted at his plea and stood with him to embrace. She once again put her head on her favorite place and cried. "I'm happy that I'll be able to see you often, but this scares me. Whatever it is that you can do, whatever these things are, I think it would be best for you to show me sometime. I don't want to be scared all the time."

"Baby, you have nothing to be scared of. I will always protect you and your family. I'm much more powerful than you realize, that's all. Just know that when I leave here, I'll be going to set up a wonderful home for us. I won't let you or our baby down."

Athena whimpered a little as he pulled her close, then whispered to her new husband, "I'm so glad that I have you. I've never been this happy and I want to be with you. I want you to do whatever it takes to make sure that we have a happy home and that our baby has a good life. I'll follow you anywhere."

With that, the newlyweds kissed, George lifted his bride into his arms, and carried her into the bedroom. He would enjoy the night and leave in the morning for Gessler Village. He no longer had Amar with him and the cost to fly on the hippogriffs was steep. He had 13 Peaks of Bailem left before Kepler would be in Gessler Village but with his new powers, it would only take him seven days to get there. He wanted to become familiar with the village so he could teleport back and forth as he pleased. He figured that the more places he became familiar with, as Lasidious had instructed in his dreams, the easier it would be to get around this world.

As the newlyweds went to sleep for the night, George dreamt of his little Abbie. The dream was sad and his little girl kept screaming to him, "Daddy, save me." He tried to run towards her but was unable to do so for reasons he couldn't figure out. The dream was hellish, but thanks to Lasidious, it was cut short as the god asked to be allowed into his mind; George gave him access.

"George, we need to talk."

"You could've shown up a little earlier, you know. The dream I was having of my Abbie was awful. Are you sure she's okay, Lasidious?"

"Yes, she is, George. Like I told you before, her soul is in the Book of Immortality. I've given her many good thoughts of you and her mother. You don't need to worry about your little girl, she's safe."

"So what do you want with me tonight?"

"Well, first I think congratulations are in order. I see you have a fine woman lying next to you."

"How do you know I'm lying next to Athena . . . are you here?" George was starting to feel uncomfortable that the god knew so much. "I'm dreaming, right?"

"Yes, George, you're dreaming. I know many things and I keep track of my favorite subjects."

"Okay, so what do you want?"

"Well, it's not so much what you can do for me, George, but

more what I can do for you. I have come to enlighten you on the rest of your powers."

"Do I need to do anything?"

"No, all you need to do is lie there. I will enlighten you with everything you need to know. When you awake, you'll be hungry and thirsty. I know that your journey to Gessler begins in the morning, but it may take a bit for you to feel strong enough to get going."

George agreed to let him do his thing. Lasidious filled his mind with the details of his powers and after a few lengthy explanations, the God of Mischief left. George woke with an awful thirst. He asked Athena to prepare him a meal and he drank all the water in not only the guesthouse, but the main house as well.

Athena was surprised at how much he ate; it actually took until Late Bailem before he was finally able to get on the road. He said goodbye to his beautiful wife and made sure that Maldwin understood he was leaving. In parting he had one last thing to say to the rat: "Everything is 'A-okay' man."

The Next Day, Late Bailem is Approaching

DOUBLE D made his way into the city of Brandor just after the Peak of Bailem. The closer he came to the city, the larger the presence the army commanded. It had taken him a long time to get close to the arena, and Late Bailem was approaching. He could only assume, since darkness was falling, that the crowd was cheering for the final fight of the evening.

The assassin quickly decided when the perfect time to kill the General Absolute would be. He knew from previous trips to this city's arena that during the King's tournament, the General always fought the winner on the ninth day. He would take the opportunity to dispose of the general then. For now, he would simply use the next six days to scout the castle for the best place to kill the Prince. He wanted to make a statement and he needed to find a place with plenty of room, planning to kill the King's son in front of as many people as possible. He also wanted to guarantee a clean get away since this assassination would not be an ordinary killing. This murder would have a horrific scene, disgusting enough that all the Kingdoms of Grayham would talk about it forever. He wanted everyone to talk about how sadistic the slaying of the Prince had been with the news of it traveling everywhere as a statement of his "artistry."

Double D couldn't find an inn to check into as everything was booked for the tournament. He wanted to speak to as few people as possible anyway, so he scouted the area until he found an old man who had left the tournament by himself. He watched from a distance and followed the man to his home, arriving behind him as darkness fell.

He looked around to see if anyone was looking, pulled his hood over his head, and became invisible. He still hadn't washed the blood of the dead barbarian back in Gessler Village from his cloak and thought to himself that it was good that he couldn't be seen. He walked to the front door, opened it, and slipped inside. He could hear the man in his bedroom singing as he prepared to clean himself up and get into his bathing tub. Ignoring the man, he moved through the rest of the home looking through bedrooms that had not been opened in quite some time. Not a thing was out of place... the beds were perfectly made and a layer of dust was on the nightstands next to them. It was the home of an unmarried man. Even the bathing room that was meant for the woman of the house had nothing in it. This sad old man was a perfect find. From the looks of things no one would be coming to visit anytime soon. Double D smiled.

The assassin waited for the old man to lie down and fall into a deep sleep before making his move. Slowly he put his pack on the floor of the room and shut the heavy door ever so gently. He walked towards the bed, moving as silently as a cat, keeping his breathing normal. He had done this so many times now that it was all second nature. He reached down and pulled the covers back to get a better look. Ready to grab, he now had his target in sight and he reached forward with both hands—but suddenly pulled back just in time to stop himself from sneezing... a close call. Once again he reached forward and concentrated on his target. This time there were no interruptions and he finished the job, reaching with both hands to snatch a pillow from the spare bed in one of the guestrooms. He fluffed it up and quietly crawled beneath the covers. He had much to do tomorrow and wanted to be up and gone before the old man woke.

Over the next six days he scouted the castle and settled on the spot he would assassinate the Prince. He moved freely around the royal house, even in the middle of the day, keeping his hood up and remaining invisible to everyone. The plan was perfect and required just the right set of circumstances to carry it out. Tomorrow the General would die.

Gessler Village

GEORGE arrived in Gessler with Kepler not due to arrive for another six Peaks of Bailem. There was still plenty of daylight and the mage asked around until he found the Bloody Trough Inn. He figured out which room's window would be best for Kepler to enter through as they had planned and he paid the owner of the inn to reserve the room as he left to survey the area. The mage needed to find the perfect spot to teleport each time he came to the village and, after a while, he stumbled across the entrance to one of the village's mines. About thirty feet to the left of the opening was a tree tucked up against the hillside. He walked over to it and looked around its base, quickly realizing there was enough room between the hillside and the branches to make his entrance. Just to be sure, he watched to see how many people came and went from the mine; there was little traffic. This area would work for sure.

Using his sword, George created a pocket in the tree's limbs, clearing away all the branches he felt might interfere. At the base, he smoothed the ground to make sure it was level. By the time he was done, he was familiar enough with the area to avoid a mistake in teleporting here. He stood inside his wooden cocoon and looked around, memorizing every detail until he was confident everything was committed to memory. He walked to the other side of the village and took a practice run. Crossing his fingers and taking a deep breath, the mage closed his eyes. When he opened them, he was standing behind the tree, tucked perfectly in his little alcove. A big smile crossed his face, satisfied with his success. The next stop was his mother-in-law's guesthouse. George closed his eyes and disappeared.

The General Absolute Prepares for Battle

DOUBLE D arrived at the arena early and hid beneath the stadium where the fighters prepared for battle. He knew the General would pass this way to take his position on the sandy floor when the trumpets sounded. He had been invisible in his cloak since leaving the old man's home, and was now tucked in the wooden rafters above the staircase that ascended to the fighting area.

It was about time for the trumpets to sound for the final time, and the assassin reached inside his pouch to produce a tiny dart. He had laced its tip with his finest poison and put it into a skinny tube about 12 inches long. As the General passed, Double D planned to blow through the tube to send the dart into the General's neck.

The poison's effects would not be instantaneous, but were strong enough to kill Justin after some time had passed. The General's body would react to the poison in such a way that the healers would misdiagnose the problem. By the time they figured it out, their patient would be dead. And, with the adrenaline flowing through his body, the man would die much faster than normal. He lifted the weapon to his mouth and waited.

The trumpets sounded and, as expected, the General ascended the dark staircase. There were torches on the walls, but there was only enough light to keep the men from falling. Watching as the General passed beneath him, Double D blew hard into the tube as soon as he saw the base of the man's neck. The dart flew through the air, hitting its target accurately and delivering the wicked poison into the General's blood stream. Justin reached back and slapped at his neck, knocking the dart into the shadows below.

Double D watched as the men around Justin questioned if everything was okay. He held his hand up to see if there was any blood, but the darkness of the passageway prevented him from seeing clearly. The assassin was apprehensive for a moment, but the General shrugged it off as nothing more than a mild irritation. The murderer relaxed and watched as the big man continued to the sandy surface of the arena, smiling as the crowd erupted with pleasure at the sight of their champion.

Justin Graywind absorbed the screams of the adoring fans into his very soul. He had been in this position countless times before, and his nerves were chiseled from the hardest of stones. He walked out into the sunlight and took his spot where no other fighter had been allowed to stand. The big man lifted his sword in the direction of his opponent and, to honor him, pulled it back in front of his face before bowing.

The General watched for the King to give his signal for the battle to commence and then he turned to begin his assault on his new enemy. The man ran swiftly toward him and Justin met the advance with equal measure. The two warriors' blades slammed fiercely into each other, the men spinning in unison as if their actions had been finely choreographed; their blades met yet again with a horrific power.

General Graywind backed away and nodded to his foe as he smiled, acknowledging the skill his enemy had displayed. Then he attacked again; one volley after another, a series of metal clashes followed from many different angles. Then, the General's big foot made solid contact with the man's chest and sent him flying backwards.

Justin motioned for the man to stand, and smiled as the fans screamed with pleasure from the exchange. He circled for a bit, feeling his excitement growing. He lived for this atmosphere. This was what his heart beat for. He circled and held his arms high, absorbing the chanting of his name, and waiting for his enemy to engage.

But something was not right.

As Justin turned to face his foe, his eyes began to dim. He reached up to rub the cloudiness out of them, but it didn't have any effect. What was wrong? He felt fine but for his eyes... it didn't make any sense.

Through the fog he caught a glimpse of his enemy's attack and his instincts took over. He stepped to the side of the advance and sent a crushing blow to the side of the man's face with his fist. The impact was enough to send his enemy to the ground unconscious. The General began to realize he probably didn't have much time before he wouldn't be able to see at all; and now his chest was beginning to hurt. Toying with his opponent was not wise while in this condition, so he followed up his strike with a downward stab of the sword to the back of the man's head. The point of the blade passed through his skull and exited the right eye. The mighty Graywind left his sword there and grabbed his chest in pain.

The crowd, not realizing what was happening, erupted with sadistic joy! And the General, despite his condition, raised his hand to acknowledge them. Stumbling towards the center of the arena, his sight was almost completely gone now and his breathing was all wrong. Justin dropped his arms and stood motionless. He was frightened, the way children are frightened when they're sure something is under their bed at night. The same man who had seen bloody wars was actually now scared. The beast in his own bedroom closet was emerging to take him.

The crowd continued to cheer but he took no comfort in it. Coldness came over him as his heart pounded mercilessly against his chest. He grabbed at it, lifting his voice to scream for the King's healers, then collapsed to his knees.

The crowd silenced as they watched in horror. The King, realizing that something was terribly wrong, commanded his medics to hurry. Justin's breathing was short... before the healers could arrive, he was gasping for air that he could not find. His lungs began to fill with blood, and the weight of his body was becoming too much to handle. Falling backwards, he couldn't see the sun's brightness and the only sound he could hear was the blood in his lungs bubbling with every short breath he managed.

Sam jumped from the King's box and ran towards Justin. The healers were taking too long. Sam laid the leader of the army flat on his back and lowered his ear to the man's mouth. He heard the gurgling of blood in the man's lungs and knew there was no saving him with the medicines of this world. He called for Shalee. She lowered herself to the sand and ran to his side. Pointing to Justin he said, "Use Precious... hurry!"

His wife cried as she explained that her powers could not be used this way. She saw the horror in Sam's eyes. She lowered herself to lift Justin's head into her lap.

All anyone could do was watch helplessly as they surrounded the dying man. The King moved in to take Shalee's place, and leaned over to whisper in Justin's ear, "You will always be my champion, my friend," he said with conviction.

Soon, the last gasp of blood-filled air escaped the warrior's body and his eyes closed forever. The King, full of rage, called for his guards to secure the arena commanding that no one be allowed to leave. He screamed at his healers with misplaced anger.

"What good are you if you can't stop this man from dying?" He screamed with an agonizing pain in his heart. He and the General had been friends since they were boys. Justin's father also served under the late King of Brandor as a high-ranking officer. They had the same teacher when studying the arts of war and countless times, his friend had thrown him to his back when practicing. The boys had done everything together: hunting, fishing, riding, playing and, when they were old enough to appreciate women, hunting of a different kind. The General had always been much more of a skilled fighter than the King and when he ascended the throne, he watched his friend fight his way up to becoming the military's finest leader. When Justin beat the previous General Absolute, Keldwin gave him the job as leader of his army.

Now their friendship had come full circle. The memories of their lives together were surfacing and Keldwin was shattered.

The King made everyone wait until the General's body was cleared from the arena floor. Then one by one, as the spectators left the arena, each was searched for any clues that may pertain to his death. There was no logical reason for this man to die. He had not even been struck by his foe. His pointless death tore at the King's mind and he could not let it rest. He marched around the arena screaming orders. The people who watched were full of nervous anticipation of what he might do having never seen their King act this way before. No one could predict what royal power he would invoke to appease his irrational mind.

The search for a killer lasted through the night while the King found solace with Sam in a small, secluded room off the arena, collapsing in the future General Absolute's arms to weep. Even the Prince had never been this close with his father. Sam motioned to the Prince that everything would be okay and quietly sat with Keldwin until he could pull himself together.

Eventually, he said, "Keldwin, I need you to listen to me. I know your pain is great right now, but remember how Justin would have wanted his King, his friend, to remember him."

The King pulled himself away from his counselor and replied, "I don't know what to do. Sam, I need you to tell me how to act. My heart is destroyed. No one knew how close we were. We've been friends since we were boys. I confided everything to this man. When my queen died, my son Aaron was devastated but it was Justin who helped me be the father I needed to be to ease the boy's pain. What do I do, Sam?"

"I think you already know what your friend Justin would say. He would tell you to be strong and remember him with honor. He would tell you to live and enjoy the last few days of your own life. He would say that he looked forward to being reborn with you someday and that he admired you. He spoke of his admiration for you when he was preparing me for my position."

The King's face softened. "He admired me, Sam?"

"He did. He admired you for your military mind. He admired you for your strength and your honor. He told me of some of the things you did as children. I believe, Keldwin, that your friend believed he couldn't have had a better friend than you. If he were the one in your place right now, sire, he would be just as devastated as you. I would tell him the same thing that I'm telling you. Be strong and honor your friend. Don't be sad. Celebrate him. That's how you would want him to honor you, if the roles were reversed."

"Sam, you're right. I'll honor Justin and keep my head held high. Thank you for your counsel. When I die, my son could have no finer advisor than you."

Sam thanked the King for the compliment and walked with him to the room where Justin lay. Until now, Sam hadn't realized the exact situation he found himself in. When the King died, he would be the second most powerful man in the entire kingdom. He swallowed hard as he walked his King into the other room. If he knew that the Prince might also be dead within days, he might not have been able to function.

They stood above the General's body watching the healers as they tried unsuccessfully to figure out what had been the cause of the man's death. The King would not allow an autopsy, knowing Justin would not have wanted to be torn apart to satisfy their need for answers. After a while, Sam encouraged the King to come with him and reminded him there was still one day of his tournament left. Even though the General had lost his life, he had still won the fight. He could think of no better way to honor Justin than to have the celebration to honor his passing in the same arena that the General had loved so much.

Keldwin loved the idea and called his slaves. He ordered them to spread word within the city that the ceremony to honor the General would be held after Late Bailem tomorrow in the arena. The slaves scattered to tell the news. Sam walked with the King to the royal carriage, comforting and keeping him company during the ride.

Sam was completely exhausted when he arrived in his room where Shalee was waiting patiently for him. They avoided talking and went straight to bed instead.

When Late Bailem arrived the next night, the arena was filled with royalty, nobles, and every member of the senate. The adoring fans of the General filled what was left of the seats. The King's 200 guards lined up in four formations around a tall platform in the center of the arena. The King entered, followed by Aaron and Sam. Shalee, BJ, Michael and a few other officers who had been able to make it back from their assignments were seated in the King's box. Keldwin led Sam and Aaron to the top of the platform to stand next to the General's body and they took turns saying their final goodbyes, touching the blade of the warrior's sword before leaving Keldwin alone with him.

The King knew that Justin would not want any words to be said, and he decided to honor his old friend one last time. He bent over to kiss his forehead and lit the fire before descending the stairs. The arena sat in silence as the flames consumed the structure. No one was allowed to leave until the last bit of life from the fire died. This was the Kingdom of Brandor's way of showing respect. The dying of the fire signified that the General's soul had ascended to the gods.

The next day, Sam was brought into the throne room and sworn into the General Absolute's position. Michael was returned to the position of second in command and Sam sent word for all officers to return home before the King died. Eight slaves delivered the royal message that officers were to be given access to the hippogriffs so they might arrive before the King's demise. Observing the King's demeanor, Sam knew Keldwin did not have many days left to live.

The Grayham Inquirer

When inquiring minds need to know where their favorite characters are.

FIVE MORE PEAKS OF BAILEM have passed since Sam sent the slaves to retrieve his officers throughout the kingdom and they have all finally returned. The senators who remained in the city after learning of their King's failing health, were directed to the King's throne room along with the officers. The King was now very weak and wanted to make an announcement before dying. What he would say to all his men was of the utmost importance. The King had spent much of the last two days working on the details of the passage of his crown with Aaron, Sam, and Michael.

DOUBLE D is hiding in the castle, waiting for the perfect time to kill the Prince. He was sitting in the corner of the room with his hood pulled up to hide his presence, when he learned of the King's failing health. The King told his associates where he wanted his viewing to be. The way Keldwin had described how his casket would be placed was the perfect set-up for Double D's murder plans.

GEORGE kissed his Athena goodbye and teleported back to Gessler to meet with Kepler. He is now in his room at The Bloody Trough, napping and waiting for the jaguar and his brothers to enter through the window.

CELESTRIA is now only 40 Peaks of Bailem from giving birth. She has sat the elven witch family down to have a long conversation about how they were wearing on her nerves. They have promised to change their attitudes a great deal because of this stern little talk.

MOSLEY is going to attend the King of Brandor's meeting and wanted to make sure the transition of power was perceived to be supported by the gods. As it turns out, his team has decided to take an interest in this event and is now in route with him. The gods also know that Double D is in the city and they are curious. Although they can't assist in this matter, they want to show their support of the King's decision to turn his crown over to the Prince before he dies. Mosley, although pleased his team is coming with him, is having a hard time imagining the reaction of those in attendance when the gods make their appearance.

LASIDIOUS is planning to entice the Serpent King Seth to make a trip to see George in the city of Bloodvain. He knows that George is now only seven Peaks of Bailem away from the Barbarian King's city. If everything goes right, and he still has his doubts that they will, the mage will be king by the time the reptile arrives with his military leaders. He hopes George will steal the crown and create an alliance with the Kingdom of Serpents for the upcoming war. So far the ex-earthling has impressed him, but taking the Crown of Bloodvain will be difficult. The Barbarian King has a group of mages counseling him and, even though none of them were as strong as George, they could combine their powers to defeat him.

He only hoped one of two things would happen. The first: George would think of a plan to deal with the King's magic users before entering the arena. The second: the Barbarian mages would be too vain to work together to kill George. Either way, all he could do now was cross his godly fingers and hope for the best. He had given George all the weapons necessary to gain power. He ordinarily would have given him a solution to defeat the Barbarian King and his mages as well, but this was a much different situation.

The Book of Immortality's rules forbid any god from providing information that would change the balance of power on any world. It was okay to tell George that killing the King would bring him power, but he couldn't give him any advice on how to do it. Up until now, he hadn't crossed the line, but he definitely had walked right up to the edge of it. If George succeeded, he would be the king of the entire Barbarian Kingdom. It would be the largest balance of power change that Grayham had ever seen.

Lasidious was not paying attention to the situation developing in the Kingdom of Brandor and he had no idea that the balance of power was about to change there as well.

SENCHAE BLOODVAIN was training harder than ever before. Since his run-in with the talking bull that pinned him to the ground, he had been preparing for the human's arrival. His mind had not been able to find rest.

ONLY FOUR, PEAKS OF BAILEM remain until the harvesting of the crops across the Kingdom of Brandor. All of the new, oversized harvest wagons are nearly finished and the massive harvest barns are complete and ready to store the excess until it can be taken to the coastal cities. Sam has dispatched part of the King's fleet to dock at these cities and wait for the wagons to arrive with their cargo.

Thank you for reading the Grayham Inquirer

Chapter 30

𝔍𝔲𝔰𝔱𝔦𝔠𝔢

SAM arose from Justin Graywind's chair with his new armor in place to symbolize his position as leader of the king's army. It would be his last hour as general because by meeting's end he would be the advisor to the new king, Aaron Brandor, and Michael would move into his spot as General Absolute. The only person in the entire kingdom who would be more powerful than Sam would be Aaron Brandor himself. Over the last couple of days, he had gotten to know Keldwin's son and there were many things he admired about the royal offspring. They were about the same age with many of the same likes and dislikes. All-in-all, he figured that his service to Aaron would be a real pleasure.

Sam started the meeting:

"Gentlemen, I've called you all here to listen to the king's wishes. He's very weak and any questions you may have will need to wait until after the king has left. The prince and I will address them at that time. The king is on his way and—"

Before the general could finish his sentence, Mosley and the rest of the gods on his team appeared around the table. The men reacted a little defensively from the surprise visit and Sam did some quick thinking to calm everyone down.

Mosley spoke first.

"General, we're here to listen and show our support. We have no need to participate in this meeting, but our presence will be good for the kingdom."

Mosley had recently learned of Double D's presence in the city and this was the real reason he wanted to come to Brandor. He wanted to say something to Sam, but he had to abide by the same laws as Lasidious. Although his team had no idea what was about to happen in the Barbarian Kingdom, the law was still clear: no god could provide the mortals with information or instruct them in how to handle an event that changes the balance of power. This rule prevented the gods from gaining more followers through such powerful manipulation. He knew if the assassin killed Aaron, the laws of the land would automatically make Sam the new king. Aaron did not have any sons or a wife to survive him and Keldwin's queen had died some time ago. It was once the law that the crown would go to the eldest relative if the king did not have a direct descendant or queen, but now the senate's new law said the crown would go the highest-ranking member of the military. After today, that would be Sam.

This law had been made when the family of Brandor fought for power many, many seasons ago. The fighting had left the kingdom vulnerable to attack with many losing their lives when the Barbarians invaded. When the enemy was finally driven back to the north, the senate was created and the new law was passed. The surviving family of the king would still be royalty and with an eternal royal bloodline, but the king's advisor would become king.

Sam once again took control of the meeting.

"My lords, we are honored with your presence and blessed to have you stay and watch over these proceedings." Sam sent a messenger to inform Keldwin of the god's attendance so he would be prepared when he entered the meeting.

A moment later the king did enter sitting in a wheelchair pushed by the prince. Everyone except the gods kneeled in reverence. The king motioned for them all to stand and take their seats. Aaron pushed Keldwin to the head of the table. When the king saw that everyone was settled, he spoke in a weakened voice.

"Thank you all for coming."

As he spoke, the coughing began, spewing blood into his hands as he covered his mouth. No one dared to react since they didn't want to dishonor their king.

Keldwin continued.

"I have come to tell you all that I'm giving my crown to my son, Aaron. From the very moment I finish addressing you; Aaron will be your king. I expect you all to serve him like you have served me. Sam will become his advisor, and Michael will become the new General Absolute. There have been many changes because of my poor health and General Graywind's passing, but I have confidence that my son will lead this kingdom with honor. I hate to say farewell, but, when you see me next, it'll be to say your goodbyes and honor my passing."

The king took time to say each man's name and bid them farewell before he motioned for a servant to take him to his chambers.

Once Keldwin was gone, Sam led the group and bowed to their new King, Aaron Brandor. While this was taking place Mosley was staring into the corner of the room, looking right through the magic of the assassin's invisible cloak. He was careful not to allow Double D to notice, but he needed to see the killer's appearance as clearly as possible.

King Aaron now addressed the leaders of his army and the senate.

"Much needs to be done to make this kingdom ready for the upcoming harvests. In addition to my father's ceremony, we need to make sure the crops are harvested efficiently. I would like to hear the status reports from those of you who carried out General Graywind's orders."

The King spoke with the authority of a seasoned veteran and Sam was impressed with the young man's powerful presence. The meeting lasted until the middle of the night with the king giving direct orders to senate members to make the preparations for his father's death. He laid out the orders for a proper viewing of his father's body: first the family of Brandor would be given a chance to say their proper goodbyes, then the common folk would be allowed into the castle to pay their respects.

Aaron was pleased with how Justin Graywind had been honored when the fire to celebrate his passing was lit in the arena. He told the men that his father would be honored in the same way, knowing that not only Justin, but also his father too, would approve of the idea. It would bring their friendship full circle. Once this last ceremony for his father was completed, the arena would never again host a passing celebration.

The new king left the room and Sam called a close to the meeting. He waited for everyone to leave while motioning to Mosley to wait a moment. When they were alone, Sam spoke to the wolf-god. But Mosley's attention was elsewhere as he watched to make sure that Double D had left the room. Sam watched the wolf's eyes and became curious since he could not see anything but the walls.

"What were you looking at, my Lord?"

"Nothing Sam . . . what can I do for you?"

"Everything is changing so fast... I'm feeling a little overwhelmed. I'm wondering if you could give me one of those fancy blessings of yours to help me sleep tonight. I'd be very grateful, my Lord."

"Sam, you and I don't need these formalities between us when others aren't present. How about we continue as we were before I became a god... Let's treat each other as we used to?"

Sam smiled.

"You mean the way you called me a fool when I started my training with BJ? Like the time that Kael yelled at me for not respecting him as a Sword of the Gods? I can think of nothing better than to go back to our old ways and create more fond memories."

Sam moved in and lowered himself to hug the wolf's neck.

"Thanks for being there, old friend!"

Mosley enjoyed this exchange, but could see that Sam had something else on his mind as well.

Sam took a deep breath then said, "I was wondering if you could make sure that both Justin and Keldwin's souls are allowed to communicate with one another. You know . . . when they arrive inside the Book of Immortality. They were such good friends and it irritates that there's no heaven. Can you do anything about this and get the Book of Immortality to allow two old friends to continue their relationship within its pages?"

"I may be able to," the wolf replied. "I can talk with the Book and see if they can speak with each another. It's strictly up to the Book to make the final decision, but it seems like a simple request."

"Thanks, Mosley. That's all a guy can ask for."

Gessler Village

KEPLER and his two brothers jumped through the window into George's room. Standing around the bed, they watched what they thought to be a sleeping George, and joked as they looked down at the mage.

"Aw, how cute," Kepler said with a chuckle. "I didn't know that something so ugly could look so pathetically adorable."

Keller, one of his twin jaguar brothers, laughed and said, "Don't give him too much credit; he's still a human. They don't have the ability to be cute. But the poor, furless freaks try, though."

Again they laughed as Koffler, the third brother, made an attempt to jump in, but he was not known for his wit. "Yeah, yeah human, yeah can't give him credit without being furry, you guys."

Kepler and Keller looked at each other and rolled their eyes. After a minute, Koffler realized his brothers were mocking him.

"What, what... hey mother said you guys need to be nice to me."

"Mother was destroyed a long time ago, stupid," Keller replied. "Do we need to take you out back and bloody you up a bit?" He said turning to look at Kepler.

"I hate to say this, but I think every family has a member that's just not all there."

Both undead jaguars laughed at their brother's expense.

"What?" Koffler said angrily.

George suddenly sat up, catching the three cats off guard.

"If you guys think I'm ugly, I'd hate to tell you what I think of your looks. Every time I see you, I feel I should put out a saucer of milk and say, *'Here kitty, kitty'.*"

"George, that's not funny," Kepler said. "You know I hate those words, especially when *you* say them." He looked at his brothers. "That's the same thing he said as he stood over the Saber Lord and tortured him with the tip of his sword."

The other dark cats muttered among themselves about George's poor taste in jokes.

"Looks like we are even then, doesn't it?" George asked.

"I suppose," Kepler responded. "Where is Amar?"

"I killed him!"

"You did what? Why?" The room became tense.

"Because I found out that he'd hurt our chances to take over the throne of the Barbarian Kingdom."

Kepler started to pace.

"And exactly how did you come by this information?"

"Lasidious told me he'd create problems. Do you remember the woman I told you about... the one I came to this world with? Well she has come into a lot of power. Lasidious revealed that Amar had been to the World of Luvelles to study the dark arts and that he planned to kill Shalee to take her power. If I allowed this to happen, Amar would've become powerful enough to destroy all of us and take the throne for himself. I wasn't about to allow that to happen, so I led him into a smith's shed outside the city of Champions. I turned his mouth, his tongue, his feet, and his hands to stone before I ripped out his heart and ate it."

"What?" Kepler said, astonished. "You ate his heart? Wasn't it enough that you killed him? What could you possibly gain from eating everything you kill? Would you have eaten Kroger also if he wouldn't have been stone?"

Hearing Kepler's ranting, George smiled.

"Of course I wouldn't have eaten Kroger. I only ate Amar's heart because it was the only way to steal his powers before his soul left his body."

"What are you talking about?" Kepler growled.

George figured he'd show the beast instead of argue with him. He lifted his hands into the air; once they were level to the bed, he turned his palms up and lifted them further making all three jaguars rise from the floor. Both Kepler's brothers became angered and started to growl, but George silenced them with a glance. Kepler, on the other hand, reacted calmly.

"Okay, I get the point, George. You have his powers. So you're telling me that you had to eat his heart to get them and that this was the only way to steal them from his soul before it ascended?"

"Ding-ding-ding, we have a winner," George said as he lowered everyone back to the floor. He turned to Keller and Koffler as he did. "Please relax and everything will be alright."

"So what else can you do, George?" Kepler questioned.

The mage smiled.

"I can do many, many things, but let's talk about it on our journey to Bloodvain."

The giant cat agreed. George stated they would leave in the morning. The rest of the mage's night was splendid. He told Kepler and his brothers he would be back at Early Bailem and that he would meet them on the far side of the village. Then George stood and closed his eyes. When he opened them, he was standing over his beautiful wife. He leaned over and ran his fingers through her hair. When she woke, she smiled, and made room for him to crawl in beside her.

The Next Day: the Castle of Brandor

AARON stayed with his father throughout the night. Keldwin had intended to go to the throne room and pass the crown from his head to his son's, but found he was too weak to get out of bed. He tried to apologize to Aaron, but could not get most of the words out. Breathing his last, a father said to his son, "I am proud of you, boy!"

These six simple words tore at the Aaron's heart and he cried uncontrollably, draped across his father's body.

Sam found him kneeling by his father's bed with his head lowered into one of his father's palms. He lifted the young king from the floor and led him out, signaling for the healers to prepare Keldwin's body for viewing while servants were sent to tell the senators of the old king's passing. Now the senators would do the jobs Aaron had assigned to them as Sam comforted his royal friend. Keldwin's viewing was scheduled for the next day at the Peak of Bailem, with the celebration to honor him to follow after dark.

He took the king out to the royal garden and sat him down, speaking gently in an effort to console him.

"Aaron, talk to me. Let's get this off your chest so you can breathe again, my friend."

"Sam, I'm fine. I think that I've had more than enough moments to prepare for his death ever since Mosley informed us that he would die. It hit me hard, but I've shed many tears today already.

I'll continue to grieve, but not without performing my duties to the best of my abilities. My father would have wanted it that way. The last thing he said to me before he died was that he was proud of me. Many men never get to hear their father saying something so special to them."

Sam helped Aaron from his seat before speaking,

"And I thought I was going to have to counsel you. You have it all under control it seems. What do you say we go and get a mug of ale? I don't know about you, but I could really use one right now."

The king agreed that the idea sounded pleasant, and both men headed for the royal kitchen with their arms draped across each other's shoulders.

In the City of Serpents

SETH, the serpent king, was slithering through his underground kingdom toward his royal rock, a serpent's version of a throne. Far beneath this boulder with a flat top was an underground lava flow. The heat from the molten river produced enough energy to warm the rock and, since Seth was cold-blooded, this was the large snake's favorite place to rest. It was also the same rock that his great-great-great-grandfather, King Sotter, had rested on many long seasons ago. His kingdom, for the most part, did not interfere in the matters of the two dominant human kingdoms of Grayham. But now and then his snake army needed to chase their soldiers away so they could continue to live peacefully. His kingdom spread from south of the Poison River where it left Lake Zandra to west of the Snake River, which also exited the same lake.

His kind was known for their deadly poisons and thus, maintained a simple existence. They sold their poisons and various other forms of plant life that grew in the marshy areas of his kingdom to Merchant Island. His reptilian population did not have any need for wealth, all the coin collected from the sales of their goods was kept in an overflowing underground cavern. Selling these items kept the other two kingdoms out of his borders and allowed them to live without worry of invasion. His kingdom had been doing this for so many hundreds of seasons that he couldn't remember why they had started doing it in the first place. When he became the new king, he continued to do what worked and kept it simple.

There were four different ways into Seth's cavern, all of which were guarded by two of his reptilian guards. These soldiers were not there to protect from outside invaders but rather to protect the king from his own kind. Every now and then, an ambitious, up-and-coming snake champion would feel strong enough to try and take the king's rock in an attack. The personal bodyguards always managed to spoil the attack and life, as usual, moved forward. If a serpent was strong enough to fight his way to the king and kill him, then he was given the throne and he would remain king until he was either killed or died of old age. The rock would then be passed to another snake within his bloodline.

When Lasidious showed up in front of Seth's boulder, the snake was warming himself and taking a nap. The Serpent King's soldiers attacked the god but Lasidious, careful not to hurt them, put a wall of force around himself and watched as the giant reptiles slammed wildly into it.

The god made sure that the king was the only one who could hear him. "Seth, I have come to speak with you."

The serpent hissed, "So I see. Who are you to stand in front of my rock?"

Lasidious responded to the snake king's ignorance. "I'm Lasidious."

The reptile knew this name belonged to a god, though he had no knowledge of what the God of Mischief looked like. He knew that his ancestors had served Lasidious for centuries. Even in stories about Sotter, his great-great-great-grandfather, there was mention of this god's name.

He ordered his guards to settle down and humbly asked, "So what is it that you need, Lord Lasidious?"

Lasidious knew that the Serpent King's hissing would drive him mad so he decided to tell the giant snake everything he had to say and let him dwell on it.

"Seth, you've proven to be a good king over your kind. You've continued the ways of the kings before you and this has kept outsiders from crossing your borders. I'm here to tell you that a great threat has emerged that will destroy your way of life. The Kingdom of Brandor has decided that they will go to war with the Barbarians soon."

"War?" Seth hissed.

"Yes. The war will consume your borders as well and will not stop until you're all dead. The only way for you to protect your way of life is to ally your kind with the Barbarians. They have a new king who is very powerful, although he is not a Barbarian himself. He defeated King Bloodvain in a battle for the crown. If you ally yourself with this man, both of your kingdoms can work together to defend yourselves from the advances of Brandor. Once they've been driven back and their bid for power is stopped, you'll be able to continue your life as normal. This is a friendly warning, Seth. What you do with this information is up to you. The man's name you'll need to seek, if you choose to, is George. I wish you luck in whichever decision you make. I must take my leave."

Before Seth could respond, Lasidious disappeared. The Serpent King looked at his soldiers. After a moment of pondering, he called for his council and announced that they would be taking a trip to Bloodvain.

Keldwin's Viewing is Close at Hand

SAM woke up early on that special morning while Shalee continued to sleep. After Sam left the room, Shalee opened her eyes and after a long stretch prepared to take her morning bath. Dropping her towel to step into a tub of warm water, the sorceress suddenly let out a loud shriek, ran to the bed, and pulled the blanket over her. Mosley had materialized unexpectedly in front of her.

"Mosley! What're you doing popping in on me like that? Dang it! Can't a girl have some privacy?"

Mosley smiled wolfishly. "Don't worry, Shalee, you're not my taste. You don't have long enough fur, or a bushy enough tail for me to find any satisfaction from seeing you without clothes. Now if you were to put a bushy tail on you, I just might—"

"If you finish that sentence, so help me, I'll turn you into a godfrog," the sorceress said with a cold look.

The wolfed laughed and turned his back to the woman. She wrapped up again in her towel and the wolf turned to face her.

"Shalee, I've come to tell you something you should know as a sorceress. I want you to think about this and make sure that it's heavy on your mind at all times. This will be the one thing that will keep you alive when other magic users find themselves facing death."

"Holy cow, Mosley, you really know how to ruin a girl's bath. You pop in here unannounced, tell me I don't have a cute enough tail, tell me you have something I need to know and then scare the crap out of me by saying that if I don't think of this all the time that I could die. Nice work! You're now my number one favorite god of all time. I think I'm going to change your name to Mosley, the Wolf-God of Bad News."

Shalee laughed as she ruffled her hands through Mosley's fur.

Despite the fact that he'd come for a serious discussion, Mosley enjoyed the woman's antics and did not mind her affections either. After a minute he pulled away and asked Shalee to sit. When she did, Shalee left a clear view. The towel had ridden up and Mosley quickly turned his head.

"Um, Shalee, could you please?"

Once she realized what he was referring to, she squealed and pulled the covers over her. "All you boys are the same no matter what species you are. Human or wolf, you're all dogs and every stinking one of you put your eyes where they don't belong."

Once Mosley stopped laughing, he continued. "Shalee, I need you to take me seriously. I cannot tell you why I've come to say these things, but I can tell you that it's for a very specific reason."

"You're scaring me, Mosley!"

"You should be scared, Shalee. You always need to be on the lookout for things that don't seem normal. You should always have a plan for when these things happen. If there is one lesson you can learn from me it's that your powers can take control of most any situation if you're ready.

"I have to go now, but remember, be ready no matter what. I'm sorry I cannot say more. Our conversation today has been just between us.

"Always be ready, Shalee... always be ready."

With that, Mosley vanished leaving the woman sitting on her bed shaken and trying to process this new information. After a while, Shalee took a faster than normal bath to make up for lost time, and headed out to be with Sam.

Aaron decided to change the place where his father's body was to be viewed and had Keldwin moved to the royal theatre. Double D heard the changing orders from across the room where he sat invisible just a few feet from the king. The fact that the late king's body would now be on display a short distance from the stage curtains made his job of killing Aaron even easier. It all but guaranteed him a smooth getaway. He departed immediately after the announcement so he could familiarize himself with the layout of the theatre.

The assassin stood on the stage where a few souls were preparing for the viewing. Carefully, he dodged invisibly around them, plotting his escape. It did not take long before he felt he was ready, prepared for anything unexpected that might happen.

Eventually the morticians entered the building carrying Keldwin's body. They entered from the back to avoid the masses of people who had come from all over the city lined up for miles to say goodbye. Double D watched as they placed Keldwin not more than five feet from the curtain. Seeing the placement and knowing his escape route would be perfect, he relaxed further, and then smiled to himself. Even though he was invisible, he always had a plan in case something went wrong; it was the very thing that made him the assassin he was today.

He listened as the people talked about how they would usher everyone up on stage to say their goodbyes—viewers would walk up one side of the stage, pay their respects in front of the casket and exit on the other side of the stage. To keep everyone from standing outside in the streets, they would bring in the family of Brandor, followed by the senate, and then the high-ranking officers of the army. These first VIPs then would sit in assigned seats and everyone else would be ushered in to fill the seats that remained. This way, everyone could be cycled through until the last person was gone.

The part of the plan discussed next caught the assassin's attention. Aaron had decided that he would address the people. Ten guards, five on each side, would stand at either end of the casket. The casket itself would be placed parallel with the front of the stage. The back side of the casket would be wide open for his approach.

To the far side of the stage would be the king's throne. His advisor, the General Absolute and their wives would also be joining them. All Double D had to do was wait for his target to lean over his father to say goodbye. When he did, it would be the last breath the man ever took.

The assassin was not concerned about the guards. He knew they wouldn't be able to find him once he darted behind the curtain. Their reaction times would be slow as the king wanted his guards at attention and facing the crowd below the stage. He couldn't have dreamed up a more perfect scenario if he'd tried.

Double D watched as the Peak of Bailem passed and the doors to the theater opened. Just as planned, the family was ushered to their seats first, followed by key members of the senate and their families. These first two groups were placed one behind the other in front of the stage. The members of the military and their families were next, numbering 900 souls. With the other 3,000 seats filled, it would be the biggest assassination to ever been seen in all of Grayham. If not for his greed, Double D would have killed Aaron for free.

Quite some time passed before the theatre was filled. Double D watched as Sam stood up from his seat next to his lovely wife, gave her a quick kiss on the top of her hand, and walked to the center of the stage.

"Ladies and gentlemen," Sam shouted to make sure everyone heard. He waited a second and continued. "Please, everyone come to order."

The crowd quieted down.

"In a few moments your king will be arriving to make his way through the theatre. Your king has requested that no one speak until he has said goodbye to his father and has addressed you. Once the king has left the building, you may talk amongst yourselves and walk up to the stage after the last member of the senate has exited the building. You'll be told when it's your time to pay your respects. I ask that all of you show respect for the dead as well as for your king."

Only a moment or two went by before a young, well-dressed servant boy approached Sam. He whispered in his ear that the king had arrived and was waiting outside the doors to be introduced to the crowd. Sam rose and signaled the trumpeters to ready themselves.

He then shouted, "Ladies and gentlemen, please rise for your king. I give you… King Aaron Brandor."

The trumpets sounded and filled the massive room with wonderful music as the king entered through the double doors and walked to the stage. Sam waited until Aaron climbed the stairs to his position then lowered himself to one knee and bowed his head, symbolizing the respect of the entire audience who could not kneel from their seats. Sam kissed the king's hand before being signaled to rise, whereupon the king embraced Sam and whispered in his ear, "I find much strength in you, Sam. Thank you for that."

The advisor was touched at the compliment and embraced the man once again before taking his seat. Aaron turned to face the audience and began to speak.

Shalee listened from her seat next to Sam as the king gave his memorial speech. She was still bothered by Mosley's words which had left her with a heightened sense of awareness. She scanned the theatre looking for something out of the ordinary, but couldn't find anything. But the sorceress held tightly to Precious as she directed her attention to Aaron.

"You'll always be remembered, my great king."

These were the last words Aaron spoke as everyone now watched him make his way to say goodbye to his father.

Double D waited on the other side of the casket and looked across as Aaron approached. His knife was ready and laced with poison to ensure he completed the job if he made an imperfect thrust. This was the same knife that killed the big Barbarian back in Gessler Village. He waited for the right moment... then quietly he stepped towards the head of Keldwin's coffin and moved his arm into a coiled position.

As Aaron stood above his father, tears fell from his cheeks but the assassin felt no compassion. The pain that filled the king's eyes could find no soft spot in Dawson Drake's killer heart. In fact, Double D actually smiled as the grieving man leaned over to kiss his father on the forehead.

He would allow for Aaron to have this final kiss. As the young king began to lift himself up, the assassin plunged his knife under his chin, pushing it up and through the top of Aaron's head. Double D smiled as he savored the penetration as the blade pierced through the top of Aaron's head. The pleasure of such a wicked act was intoxicating to him.

Anxiously, Shalee had watched the king move across the stage toward the coffin. Mosley's earlier comments had scared her to the point that she had used Precious to heighten her senses. Something was not sitting right in her gut, though she couldn't explain what it was, she was ready. As the sorceress watched the king bend over to kiss his father, she almost exhaled with relief when the hole in the king's head opened and blood spurted everywhere.

This would be the last time the killer's blade would kill anyone. He would leave it behind, buried in the king's skull to make a statement as he made his escaped.

"Let's go get my money," Double D said to himself as he let go of the knife.

Shalee, seeing the knife appear in the king's head, slammed Precious against the ground as she screamed, "Precious putta iluve." Everything in the entire place stopped moving, both seen and unseen. Now the sorceress stood from her chair and moved in quickly to look at the scene.

Blood was everywhere... with drops of blood falling from the knife suspended in midair. She gathered her emotions and then looked more closely. How could a knife just appear like this? Looking even closer, Shalee saw one of the drops of blood was out of place, falling toward the other side of the coffin. As she studied it, she determined that this would be impossible, unless the drop had fallen from an object that was moving away from the king's head.

Shalee moved back over to Sam and released him from her magical bond. She held her hand to his mouth and quickly explained the situation. It took Sam only a moment to look at the scene and bring himself up to speed. Slowly he moved around the guards and to the backside of the coffin. As he did, his foot tripped upon one of the extended legs of the assassin.

"Something is here," he whispered.

Shalee reached down to touch what felt like soft cloth. Upon further investigation, she realized it was a leg. Slowly she began to rub her hand along the bottom of it, toward what should be the rest of the body. When her hand crossed the midsection of the person, she was appalled to discover he was aroused from his activities. She pulled her hand away.

"Oh my gosh, Sam, it's a man . . . and he's . . . Yuk, just come and see! He must get his rocks off this way. I can't touch this pig any more. You're going to have to do it."

Sam shook his head and moved in to take her spot. He took a deep breath and sure enough, the guy was excited to be there. He moved his hands disgustedly up the rest of the killer's body until he came to his head and realized the killer had a hood on, which Sam now pulled back, revealing the rest of the assassin's torso. Both Sam and Shalee jumped back a few steps and caught their breath.

"So what should we do with him?" Shalee said.

Sam didn't answer right away, but circled the frozen figure instead, rifling through his pockets. "I want to know who we're dealing with here."

"Be careful!" the sorceress said, even though she knew there was no chance that the killer would move.

Sam reached in and pulled out a small wooden case with the initials "Double D" burned into the top in a beautiful script.

"I guess this guy calls himself Double D."

"Who cares what his name is?" Shalee snapped. "What're we going to do with the creep? I can't keep these people still like this forever, you know."

Sam agreed. He lifted the assassin from the floor and carried him back towards the coffin. He straightened Double D's legs to a perfectly balanced position and placed his hand back on the butt end of the knife that protruded from the king's skewered head.

"What are you doing?" Shalee asked in a frantic whisper.

"I'm making our frozen mannequin here look guilty. We don't want him getting away now, do we?"

Shalee liked this plan. She took the cape from the killer's back and held it up in front of her. She figured that one of these days it might come in handy even with the situation she found herself in at the moment.

"You've got to be kidding me; there's blood all over this thing.

Your mother would be appalled if she had any idea that you left your clothes so filthy."

(The assassin still had not cleaned away the blood from the Barbarian he'd killed back in Gessler.) The sorceress draped it over her arm with two fingers as if it was diseased.

"Can you please focus?" Sam snapped at his wife. "Help me with him. You can criticize him on his lack of fashion sense later!"

They put Double D into position and took their seats after adjusting Aaron's weight so he fell towards the coffin. Shalee slammed Precious into the floor and commanded everyone to be released from her magic.

The next thing Double D knew, he was standing with the handle of his knife still in his hand and the weight of the king falling towards him. He released the blade and looked up at the crowd... everyone could see him! He heard Sam shouting for the guards to seize him as he snatched at his hood... but only grabbed at the air. He ran for the curtain, but one of the guards tackled him to the floor before he could take his first step. Nine different blades of the king's guard were pointing down at him.

Double D was captured.

The theatre was frantic and everyone was screaming as they saw their king fall, bloodied, across the top of his father. Sam took center stage and looked at Shalee. Motioning for Shalee to use Precious on his voice, he yelled, "People of Brandor, I command you to sit down and be quiet!"

Everyone stopped at once and looked at their new king. Most of them didn't realize it yet, but Sam was about to make the chain of authority well-known. He shouted again with the thunderous assistance he had been given.

"King Aaron has been murdered. I will not have you frantically making a mockery of this man's death. Sit down!"

Everyone began to take their seats as he turned and motioned for the guards to bring Double D to the front of the stage. The guards knew instantly that Sam was their new king and did not hesitate to obey. He ordered the morticians to take Keldwin and Aaron from the room and return with them in clean attire, inside two new coffins. Sam turned once again to face the people of Brandor.

"People of Brandor, you will stay with me until our two kings have been returned to us. There is justice that needs to be delivered here and I intend to give our fallen kings the respect they deserve. We won't leave until this has been done. Do you all understand?" Michael, as if he had been prepared to say it all along, stood from his chair and shouted. "King Goodrich has spoken. Hail King Goodrich."

The entire theatre was now aware of Sam's new role and responded appropriately, "Hail King Goodrich!"

Eventually the morticians returned with the bodies of the late kings. During their absence, Sam made Double D sit on his knees and face the crowd with his hands tied behind his back. Confessing to his profession and crimes, he was forced to admit he had also slain General Graywind. The new king spoke to the crowd while they waited and told them all who Double D was. After doing so he spoke of honor and valor to lift the spirits of those in attendance.

"These two fallen men were warriors and leaders. They will be missed. Double D has dishonored three different men with his actions and they will receive the justice they deserve."

Sam turned an event that was meant for a viewing of the dead into a pep rally of sorts. He did not want these people to leave without having closure, knowing full well that all three of his fallen friends would approve.

When the bodies were in place Sam commanded that they be tilted to face the direction of the people. Michael ordered six of the ten guards to hold the two fallen men in position. Motioning for the remaining four guards to lift Double D to his feet, he made an announcement.

"People of Brandor, on this day in front of our beloved kings who've fallen tragically, there will be justice. This man will tell us why he killed our great leaders."

Double D spat on the floor. "I will say nothing!"

Sam pulled Kael from his sheath and commanded the blade to bring forth its fire. Quietly, he asked the sword if it was ready for some action. The blade confirmed that it was, and he lifted the sword high after the response.

The people within the theatre were awed by the blade's power as once again, Sam addressed the people.

"People of Brandor, I hold in my hand a sword given to me by Bassorine himself before his destruction. This is Kael, the one and only, Sword of Truth and Might."

The entire theatre and his military all began to watch him with great admiration as their murmurs filled the room. They all knew how treasured such an item was and the fact that their new king possessed it was quite a shock.

"I will use this sword to strike down our enemies. I say that we should start with this man right here. What say you?" He pointed the tip of the sword in the killer's direction as he finished.

Everyone in the theatre erupted with excitement. Seeing their late king's murderer brought to justice gave them great pleasure and they all screamed in unison, "Hail King Goodrich, hail King Goodrich, hail King Goodrich."

Sam brought his hand up to silence the crowd and commanded the blade to change to another type of flame. Kael brought forth the destructive forces of water as Sam looked at Double D. "Why did you kill these men?"

The assassin spit on the floor and cursed him. Once again the crowd erupted with anger, shouting profanities at the killer. And once again their new king held his hand up and commanded their silence.

This time Sam lifted Kael and asked the question as he placed the blade of the sword on Double D's shoulders. The man screamed in pain as the watery-flame tore at his skin. He wanted to spit on the floor but Kael's power overwhelmed him.

"I was hired to kill them. I did it for the coin!"

The people screamed and cursed the assassin.

Sam lifted his hand in the air to silence them.

"Who hired you?"

"I don't know who hired me for the job. I get all my work through a man called Assistant Kane. He pays me when I'm finished."

Sam held his hand high to keep his people quiet as he asked his next question, "When are you to meet this man to get your money?"

"I don't know. I usually seek him out after a job is done."

The new king realized that the assassin was telling the truth as Kael confirmed his story. He only had one more question to ask before bringing down his judgment. "What's your name, murderer?" Sam yelled.

Double D screamed horribly to avoid the question. Kael had a hard time breaking through the man's determination to stay silent. The killer had not said this name since he was a child and it pained him to such a degree that he screamed in agony as the memories of his dead father haunted him.

"Dawson Drake, my name is Dawson Drake," he cried breaking into wracking sobs as he finished his words.

Sam motioned for his guards to steady the man and he spoke for all to hear. "Dawson Drake, I hold you responsible for your actions. The murders that have been committed against both King Aaron and General Graywind will be brought to justice on this day, in front of the people of Brandor."

Sam was not about to make this man's death easy on him. He was enraged at how this piece of garesh caused so much pain to so many people in such a short time. He took Kael and placed the point of the blade against the assassin's right shoulder and commanded the fire to come forth, slowly pushing its way into the assassin's flesh. The killer cried out as the very heat cauterized the wound to keep it from bleeding.

The crowd cheered as they watched their king twist the partially buried weapon. The louder the man screamed, the happier the people became.

Sam withdrew the sword and again used Kael in the same manner, except this time, he dug into the opposite shoulder. The screams of the killer were horrific as the crowd continued to savor his torture.

The new king continued abusing Dawson Drake for a while longer, until he was satisfied that the pain had degraded the man to the point of no return. After having the killer placed into the perfect position, Sam then lifted Kael into the air, commanded the blade to quiet its powers and brought the sword down on top of Double D's head as hard as he could. The force split the man in two as if a warm knife had cut through a stick of soft butter. After a few seconds, his weight shifted and both halves opened up like a fisherman's net dropping its catch on the deck. The life spilled out of him as his guts spewed all over the stage and his two halves fell in opposite directions.

The crowd erupted as they cheered their new king's actions, screaming with sounds of praise and asking the gods to grant Sam long life. After a moment, he held his hand up once last time to silence them and commanded his guard and every member of the military present to leave and build a platform to celebrate the passing of these two great men with the task to be completed before midnight.

Speaking to the crowd once again Sam said, "I command everyone to go to the arena after Late Bailem. We will celebrate these great men and light the fires to set their souls free."

The people of Brandor cheered their new king one final time, then Sam took Shalee by the hand and exited through the back of the theatre.

Chapter 31

Gods That Bet

The Hidden God World of Ancients Sovereign

LASIDIOUS went to the home of Yaloom on Ancients Sovereign to deliver a message but when he arrived he found the goddess, Mieonus present as well. Yaloom and Mieonus were watching the assassination of Aaron take place as they glared into a massive indoor waterfall that fell smoothly into a large pool far below the level where they now stood. This perfectly flowing sheet of water was a lot like watching a giant TV, except for the fact that the images being portrayed where real and currently happening as they watched. Yaloom had added this feature to his home many, many seasons ago when he had created it.

Yaloom, the God of Greed, had exquisite taste. His home represented nothing short of the best. Though he, himself was plain to look at, his fingers were covered with priceless rings. He was extremely self-centered and his home showed his vanity. The pool at the bottom of the water fall had diamonds that shimmered from the bottom of its depths. The water from this pool then continued on and cascaded over many other smaller falls before exiting the structure. The base of this mansion, built into the center of a 1,100 foot fall, had a hole that opened near the cliff and released the water down the remaining 500 foot drop below.

Every ounce of the fall funneled into the home before it exited at the bottom. Despite the massive amount of force that poured into the top of the structure, it was pleasant where they sat. The god had engineered this mansion in such a way that the deafening sound was carried away from the main level in which they sat. He had smoothed the walls inside to quietly direct the water to allow for good conversation.

Lasidious intended to call a meeting about the pieces of the Crystal Moon's whereabouts as Yaloom's team had made a grave tactical error in bidding for the first two pieces of the Crystal Moon. But instead he watched the events unfold within the waters, seeing everything that was happening in the royal theatre of Brandor. Realizing that the images were of current events, it was too late for him to do anything to stop them. He watched as the assassin shoved his knife into Aaron's jaw and through the top of his head and then he saw Shalee stop time and release Sam from the magic to help her figure out how to deal with the situation. Although he was angry, he admired the way the two humans worked together. He could even tell that *Mosley was sitting on the stage, but the people did not know that the God of War was there.* Lasidious knew this because of the orange glow that surrounded the wolf within the water's projections.

"Why would you have wanted this assassination?" Lasidious screamed at both Yaloom and Mieonus after watching the guard tackle Double D. "What on Grayham would you expect to accomplish by doing this?"

Yaloom responded defensively. "The Kingdom of Brandor will be weakened by this assassination and Keldwin's death. Both the army and the government will be disorganized for the upcoming war."

The God of Mischief was very angry.

"Don't you realize what you've done? I'm surrounded by idiots!"

"We aren't idiots," Mieonus snapped. "We have manipulated this whole event and it will benefit the plans of our team."

"Your team . . . most of your team is doing nothing. There's so much more that could be done. You order one little assassination and expect that it will win your team the Crystal Moon? The other four members of your team haven't done anything constructive to help you at all. They sit around bored and just watch everything unfold. It's as if they could care less about the destruction of these worlds. This assassination isn't going to accomplish what you wanted it to at all."

"It will!" Yaloom shouted.

Lasidious snapped back and trumped his voice with his own. "No, I repeat, it will not help you. In fact, the two of you may have very well ruined your chances to secure the first two pieces of the Crystal Moon. You have created an even stronger leadership in Brandor. How could you be this stupid?"

"Stop calling us stupid or we'll—"

"You'll what? You'll do nothing because you're scared of the Book of Immortality and what it'll do to you if you tried. So spare me your threats. You don't even understand why I'm angry, do you?"

Yaloom screamed. "Well then why don't you stop yelling at us and explain?"

Lasidious took a few deep breaths and continued, speaking in a calmer tone.

"The brilliant mind of Sam and the power of his wife will not create a weakness. Have you forgotten how smart Sam is and the fact that Bassorine gave him the Sword of Truth and Might? Have you forgotten that Shalee is able to draw from a source that will make her a powerful sorceress? Granted, this'll take her a while to accomplish, but she's already a phenomenal power on Grayham. For you to make her a queen is ridiculous. Bassorine brought her here for a purpose. Don't you think there was a reason for this? He must've known something we don't. And whatever his secret was, I intend to find out."

"How could we've known how powerful she was?" Mieonus said, "we weren't watching her. How could we have known that Sam would end up as king and Shalee, the queen, when we instigated these assassinations? There wasn't any way of knowing that Mosley gave Sam his gifts and that they would help him get an audience with the king. We couldn't control the changes that the king made in planning his tournament. When we started this plot in motion, we didn't know that Sam would be given an invitation to come and fight. He didn't even fight in the tournament and somehow he—"

"—Yet somehow he found a way to become king without lifting a finger in Brandor's arena, Lasidious interrupted, throwing his hands in the air. "You would've known most of these things by paying attention. Come with me, I'll show you what the situation is really like. Meet me at Brandor's theatre next to Mosley. Make sure that you make yourself invisible before you get there."

With a grunt of frustration, he disappeared.

When Lasidious reappeared, he was standing next to Mosley on the stage, invisible to the people who filled the royal theatre of Brandor. The wolf god had been watching the events undetected and the four gods now stood together to watch. They said nothing to the wolf at first, as they watched Sam twist the flaming hot blade of Kael into Double D's shoulder. This was going to be an event worth watching, so each of them took a seat on the floor.

Sam commanded the blade to bring forth its watery power to question the assassin and the gods listened as Dawson Drake cried out his name. The agony of the assassin's screams, along with the smell of his burnt flesh, filled the air as Sam dug the blade of fire into his body. The people cursed Double D gleefully as he cried out. When Sam was finally done, they watched as Kael sliced through the killer, spewing his guts across the stage.

Lasidious decided it was time to make conversation that could only be heard by the four of them.

"Mosley, I see you've managed to get Sam into the best spot possible to use his full potential in the upcoming war. I've got to admit, I'm impressed, my four-legged friend. Not only have you made him a king, but you've convinced him to make Shalee his queen. I should keep a better eye on you from now on. It looks like you're a born manipulator just like me."

The wolf turned and looked at his fellow gods. "Sam *is* impressive to watch isn't he? It really didn't take much more than a few simple suggestions. I wouldn't say I'm a master of manipulation like you, Lasidious. I wasn't even a god when I first started helping Sam. I could tell him what to do rather than make suggestions like we have to do now. I had an unfair advantage, don't you think? It is easier to make things happen when you don't have to obey the laws of free will within the Book of Immortality."

Yaloom cut in.

"Fair or unfair, I'm impressed." The god began to polish one of the many rings on his fingers as he continued.

"I should have been watching more closely to see what was

going on in Brandor. I had no idea that you had Sam in a position to become king. I decided to watch the assassination and I've ignored everything else. Mieonus and I felt that this would weaken the kingdom but I fear we've made a big mistake by not watching Sam and Shalee to see what they were up to."

"Ya think?" Lasidious snapped. "It's bad enough that Mosley found a way to get Sam into the position he did without the two of you knowing, but you also killed the two people that were left above him. You just handed the crown to Sam within a matter of days. Nice work, guys. Remind me why you're gods again?"

"Okay, we get it already," Mieonus snapped. "So it's clear that this isn't what we intended to happen. But answer me this one question: what have you been up to that's so important?"

Lasidious smiled wickedly. "I just might have to show you if you're really interested."

Mosley took this chance to brag. "Sam has taken complete control of this situation. Look at how the people love him for his leadership. I must say that I'm surprised at how Shalee's powers are advancing. She has only failed to command her staff once. When the assassin attacked Aaron she was the one who noticed something wasn't right. She stopped time and was able to make sure the killer was caught... I've got to admit those two are turning heads everywhere they go."

"Yes I know, I saw both of them do all this while watching the images within Yaloom's waterfall," Lasidious responded. "She's quite impressive."

Mosley changed the subject.

"So I finally found your little buddy, George."

"Really," Lasidious said without showing his surprise, "I was wondering when someone would find him."

"Yes, I sensed him when he teleported yesterday just before Early Bailem to meet up with Kepler and his brothers on the north side of Gessler Village."

Mosley turned and now looked directly into the God of Mischief's eyes.

"And what did you find out? It seems to me that our little game is coming full circle now. It will be harder to trump one another since we all know what to look for."

The god knew he could still speak with George in his dreams if he needed to and whether or not Mosley was watching would not be an issue once he spoke with the mage. This was going to make things easier to keep an eye on the gods involved in the game.

"I found out they were headed north into the Barbarian Kingdom," Mosley answered. "It seems to me that if he's able to teleport, someone must be giving him some good information on how to find powers of his own."

"Really," Mieonus cut in. "I thought you were staying neutral and allowing the teams to do all this."

Lasidious laughed.

"No, I said I wouldn't cheat and tell either one of the teams anything in an unfair way. I said I wouldn't help the team I originally was on unfairly. I pulled myself off your team so I could do what I wanted to do. As it turns out, it was a good idea that I *did* do my own thing because the two of you don't seem to have a good grasp on how to get anything done."

"Will you stop with all the little digs!" Yaloom snapped. "We get it already. You're the 'master of manipulation.' That was made clear when you found a way to kill Bassorine with the Book."

Yaloom paused, then said grudgingly, "It was quite clever if you ask me."

"Thank you, Yaloom. There may be hope for you yet," Lasidious said with a verbal pat on his own back.

Mieonus rolled her eyes. "Could you possibly have a bigger opinion of yourself? For your sake, I hope the air in that big head of yours doesn't leak out."

Mosley cut in. "I will be watching to see what George is up to from now on. I noticed that he teleported without a spell or staff. We all know that without using a staff or any words of power that he's controlling very advanced magic for this world. He's using his magic naturally and we both know the only way he could accomplish this."

"You're very perceptive, Mosley," Lasidious said. "What else is that wolf brain of yours thinking?"

Both Yaloom and Mieonus agreed with Lasidious that his perceptions were accurate, although they did not know why they were agreeing and waited for the wolf to answer. They hoped to be clued in with his response.

"Well," Mosley said softly. "We all know that he had no natural magical abilities when you retrieved him from Earth. The others would've known that you had deceived them if you tried to bring a magical being forward. The only way he could have gained these abilities is by eating the heart of someone before their soul left for the Book of Immortality. So how about we level with each other and you tell me how I'm doing so far?"

"Just because I created two teams doesn't mean I don't have any agendas of my own. All I've done so far is tell the horse where the water was. He chose to go and drink it. I have been very careful not to break the rules of the Book of Immortality as I'm sure you have been. Just like you, I've done nothing more than make a few simple suggestions to motivate him and start him on his road to glory."

"I wouldn't call eating someone's heart a simple suggestion," Mosley responded. "I would like to know whose heart he ate. So who was it that he had to kill for his powers?"

"I think whether it is a simple suggestion or not is a matter of opinion. I'll answer your question as to whose heart he ate, but everything I say to the four of you from here on out is under the rule of Fromalla."

Mosley thought a moment before responding. He knew that Fromalla was the rule, or rather the law, that was created by the gods and written in the pages of the Book of Immortality. It was created due to the overwhelming lack of trust that the gods had for each other after the God Wars were over. Even though they fought on the same side during the wars, once they were over, a battle of a new kind started. Each of them had been bidding for as many followers as they could get to increase their powers when the worlds were created. In the process, they shared each other's secrets to try and undermine each other's campaigns.

It had been Bassorine who called a meeting to suggest that everyone vote to pass this law. The rule was long and covered all angles. It basically meant that if two or more gods were together and shared something that was said to be under the rule of Fromalla, it could not be divulged to any of the others without penalty of being made mortal.

"I agree that our conversations will be under Fromalla," the wolf said. "So who's the person George killed?"

Lasidious looked at Yaloom and Mieonus before speaking and waited for their responses. He watched as both of them nodded their heads and agreed to obey this law as well.

Once satisfied that they were all in agreement, he continued. "The mage Amar, from Lethwitch is whose heart he ate," Lasidious said with a chuckle.

The other three gods gasped. Mosley said, "Are you referring to the same Amar who studied under the Head Master on the World of Luvelles?"

"Yes, I am referring to *that* Amar."

The wolf shook his head as he continued. "How was he able to do this without Amar using his magic on him? This man was easily the most powerful mage on Grayham."

"Yes, he was very powerful, but he also didn't have the drive to go after the kind of power George does. The powers that Amar commanded were wasted on his inhibitions. He was scared to do anything with them. Sure, he had his moments of courage, but when it came right down to it, he was a sheep."

"Okay, so Amar was a follower and not a leader, but that doesn't tell me how George killed him."

"I was getting to that, just relax. It happened like this. He shook the mage's hand and turned the most critical parts of him to stone."

Again Mosley was confused. "Okay, I'll bite, how did he do that?"

Lasidious decided to lie back on the stage before he responded. "I told him where the Staff of Petrifaction was within the Cave of Sorrow. He went in to get it and drank the liquid inside of its hollow center."

"Never mind the fact that he got past Maldwin," Yaloom jumped in. "I'm sure that's another story of its own. So how did he learn to control the ability to change things to stone once he drank the liquid inside?" Yaloom asked.

Lasidious smiled again. "Well the funny thing is, it was Amar himself that taught his own killer how to control the power that killed him. Quite the irony, don't you think?"

Mieonus, Goddess of Hate, shook her head and pushed her long brunette hair clear of her face as she smiled sadistically, her brown eyes showing her pleasure as she continued.

"I'm sure you enjoyed yourself when you watched him die. I know that I would have. Well, it seems you've been positioning George for great things, Lasidious. What is it that you feel he will be able to accomplish with these powers?"

Lasidious laughed at the question.

"Now, now, now, you all don't think I'm going to give you every piece of the puzzle, do you? You'll just have to tag along with me and see."

"Well, you can't blame me for being anxious to know more," the goddess laughed. "But you still haven't told us how he killed Amar with the power that the staff's liquid gave him. Just because he turned his tongue to stone doesn't mean he still couldn't use his hands. Amar did command some of his powers with just a movement of his arms, you know. Those powers had progressed past the use of words."

"Don't be so hasty to misjudge our good friend George," Lasidious said as he lifted a finger into the air to make his point. "He's a crafty man, I tell you, and extremely smart. He turned Amar's tongue to stone like I said, but he also did other things to him. To keep him from running or fighting back, he changed his feet and his hands to stone. Once the mage was immobilized and could not feel any pain from the stone blockage that was put on his spine, he finished the job. It was this stone blockage that kept him from dying of shock. My little buddy, as you call him, Mosley, used the tools from a smith's shed outside the City of Champions to break open his chest. He ripped out his heart and took the first bite before it quit beating. I have to give him credit. He ate the whole thing a lot faster than I could have. I've never had much of a stomach for blood."

"That's wonderful," Mieonus clapped as she responded excitedly. "I must hang out with you more often Lasidious. You seem to play in a much better sandbox of evil than I do."

Lasidious laughed, "What do you say we head over to the arena and watch them light the fires to celebrate these men passing on? We can talk more there."

"That sounds like a good idea, Lasidious. I haven't been to an

event like that in a while," Yaloom commented as they all disappeared.

The gods sat on top of the highest point of the arena as they
watched the fire consume Keldwin's and Aaron's bodies. Sam lit
the wood with Kael's flame and sat in his new throne within the
royal box to watch.

Four Days Later

THE HARVEST for the Kingdom of Brandor was moving forward as planned and the crops were replenishing themselves as
promised by the god Alistar. Today was the last day for collecting these harvests and every bit of it would need to be stored in
the barns. All 770 harvest wagons were making their way to the
coastal cities with bounties so plentiful that virtually every man
with a wagon was helping in the effort. In total there were well
over 18,000 wagons on the roads, each full and overflowing with
crops.

To the north in the Kingdom of Bloodvain, the Barbarians had
also collected their harvests but there was nothing special about
this event. Life moved forward as usual for everyone—everyone,
that is, except Senchae Bloodvain and his mages who would be
meeting George outside the city walls. The Barbarian King's
scouts had located the man along with his jaguars, and returned
to inform Senchae that their little visitor should arrive at the city
gates around Late Bailem.

Senchae wanted to confront the human before he challenged
him in front of his military. The warning of the talking bull had
made him fearful that he would lose his crown to this man and he
was not about to let things go that far. He would meet the man with
his mages and kill him before he had the chance to step foot inside
the city.

But the meeting was not 'til later and presently, there was good
meal to be eaten first. At that very moment, Kepler, Keller, Koffler
and George were sitting down to have a nice breakfast. They were
about a half-day's walk from Bloodvain and figured they'd arrive
by dark. Keller caught a nice baby fawn, and the mage was sitting
by the fire with his stick outstretched to cook his portion of it.

"Yuck," Keller said. "How can you stand to eat it that way? You're cooking the flavor right out of it, George."

"Yeah, the flavor out of it," Koffler added in his normal idiotic response, his mouth full of bloody flesh.

"Shut up, Koffler," Kepler snapped. "I'm in no mood for your stupid antics today." The demon turned to George. "We're not far from the city now, so what's the plan?"

"Well, I was thinking that as soon as the four tigers you sent for arrive we'll continue on to Bloodvain. As I said before I'll make all the giant cats, except you Kepler, invisible to everyone, but the two of us will still be able to see them. Six invisible cats should give us a slight advantage, don't you think?"

"I like the idea of backup," Kepler said. "But if you win the arena fight do you really think the king's mages will let you just take over the kingdom? I don't think they'll want a, and I mean no offense by this, they don't want a pathetic outsider running their kingdom. I think we both know their invitation to come fight for the crown would be revoked if you actually won. I really doubt they'll just fall down and serve you."

"Kepler, my friend, my black, furry friend, you underestimate me still after all this time. Allow me to show you how I'm going to get the people to love us and stop the king's mages at the same time."

George reached into his pack and pulled the sleeping Maldwin from it.

The demon looked at the rat and was instantly up to speed.

"So you teleported to Lethwitch last night and retrieved the rat."

Kepler said hello to Maldwin in his own language.

"So what do you want me to tell the little guy to do? I could tell him, you said to tell him, that I should tell him that you said telling him was a good idea, to tell me something that I could tell you, so you could tell me, to tell him it's a good idea, for him to tell me, to tell you that he understands."

George laughed, "You're never going to let me live that one down, are you?"

"Nope, never gonna, George," Koffler said with a stupid laugh as he started to choke on his food.

Both Kepler and Keller yelled at their brother as if they were using the same mind.

"Shut up, idiot!"

They all laughed for a minute before George continued.

"Anyway, I want you to ask him, not tell him, to please give the Barbarian people a vision of how great we are when I give him the signal to do so. I want to be able to walk around the kingdom with you and not worry about our safety. I also want him to send his visions to the king's mages if we find ourselves in trouble with them. Just tell our little friend here to keep a good eye out for them and cover our backs."

Kepler did as he was asked and told Maldwin what George wanted from him and the rodent said he understood. Before they started the last stretch of their journey to Bloodvain, George waved his hand over the tigers to hide their presence, then asking Koffler and Keller to ask if they could see the beasts. Once the demons said they could not, George asked Kepler... the jaguar demon confirmed he could see them just fine. Once again George waved his hand to hide Kepler's brothers, then the group was on its way to take the crown of Bloodvain.

The four gods—Lasidious, Mosley, Mieonus and Yaloom—now in their invisible state, watched the conversation between George and the cats.

"I guess I understand what George is up to now," Mosley said as he watched George, Maldwin, Kepler and the six invisible large cats head out for Bloodvain. "It will be interesting to see how this turns out. He's very smart and obviously a decent tactician as well."

Lasidious smiled. "I was worried about how he was going to take the crown, but I must give him credit. He actually has a pretty good plan. When I told him about the staff, I never expected he'd turn the rat into an ally too. He intends to use Maldwin's talent as a tool to accomplish his goals. If he does everything right, he just might pull this off. I do wish though, that I could tell him exactly how to do it... I'd like more of a guarantee that this is going to work."

Mosley nodded.

"I know what you mean. I wanted to tell Sam that Double D was about to kill Aaron, but I'm just as bound by the same law that you are."

The deceiver laughed. "Sometimes we gods make the damnedest rules, don't you think?"

"Agreed," Mieonus interjected. "But I suppose the rules have their purpose or they wouldn't have been made."

"Besides, I think it makes the game more fun," Yaloom said as he turned his attention away from George's group. "Shall we follow them to see what happens?"

Lasidious responded. "Yes, let's do follow them. It will be interesting to see how this plays out."

"Being a god and having the ability to summon anything you want kills the idea of betting on whether George will become king," Mosley sighed as they began to walk. "I liked betting much better when I was mortal."

"Well," Lasidious responded, "We could always bet, but instead of getting things for winning, we could force the looser to do stupid embarrassing things as a punishment for their choices."

"I *like* that idea," Yaloom said, "Then we wouldn't nearly as bored and it would surely give us a few laughs. Let's swear on the Book of Immortality that we have to do these things, providing it doesn't embarrass us in front of our followers of course."

Lasidious smiled wickedly. "I'll agree to that, how about you Mosley?"

"I think I can do that," the wolf laughed. "This is easily the most childish thing that I've ever agreed to… but it'll be fun. I've got to admit thought… I never thought that as a god I would be doing something so idiotic."

Later That Evening Outside of Bloodvain

THE GODS walked to a large rock and took their places to watch the meeting. Senchae and his mages were now within eyesight of George and they dismounted their specially-bred horses and tied them to a nearby tree. Everyone now walked towards each other on foot.

Both sides were cautious of the other as they drew closer, but George was very relaxed. Yaloom was the only one who could not sit. He had lost the first bet about when the mage would dispatch his invisible cats to circle behind the Barbarians so he had to stand with his robes draped over his right arm and a red bow placed over his privates until the next bet was lost.

"This isn't what I had in mind," Yaloom said with disgust.

"Shut up and pay attention," the other three said as they watched the two groups converge.

George took a deep breath as his group stopped in front of the Barbarians. The king was massive, a true force of nature, the likes of which George had never seen before. He whispered to Kepler, "Holy garesh, this guy has muscles in places I never knew existed. Maybe you should tell Maldwin to be ready."

"Agreed," the demon whispered back. "Maybe we should be careful." The demon spoke to the rat in his own language to make sure he was prepared to use his visions.

After a moment George smiled and addressed Kepler again. "Don't worry, my friend, I've got it all under control... I have a plan." George quickly took note of the positions of his six invisible cats. As instructed, they had crept up from behind the king's five mages and readied themselves to attack.

The group traveled on a well-used road of packed dirt that lead to the city, and stopped by a rock surrounded by trees and which also held the invisible gods. They were seemingly alone and George loved the idea. Speaking first he addressed the king.

"I'm assuming you are Senchae Bloodvain."

The big man responded angrily. "Who are you to call me by my name? You're a sorry excuse of a man and haven't earned the right. I should kill you where you stand for such disrespect. I'm a king and you'll address me as such."

Kepler watched as George began to laugh. The big Barbarian didn't know how to respond. Kepler had seen George do this before and it made him nervous. He remembered what he felt like when he was unsure of what George was made of and he knew the mage was going to pick a fight.

"Do you meet everyone outside your city's walls?" George asked. "I think someone told you I was coming. You obviously know I'm here to take your crown off that thick head of yours... it'll look much better on me than atop that nightmare you call a face."

Without waiting for a response, he gave the signal for the cats to attack, and squeezed Maldwin's tail to send the king a vision of helplessness. The powerful claws of all the tigers, along with Kepler's brothers, tore into the sides of the unsuspecting group of magic user's heads—the sheer force of their blows knocked all but one of them unconscious. The man, though he tried to speak his words of power, did not have enough time before Keller's jaws closed on his throat and tore it apart as his life poured on to the ground in a pool of red.

Senchae grabbed his head and fought off the visions fed to him by Maldwin. To everyone's surprise he walked toward George, who reacted by lifting his hand and pinching his fingers together as he lifted his arm high into the air. The Barbarian started to float and grabbed at his throat as he began to choke. George grinned as he thought back to yet another one of his favorite movies on Earth.

The gods standing nearby on the rock were making bets. Lasidious was the first to speak. "I bet he takes him prisoner," he said as he looked at the others.

Yaloom responded anxiously as he hoped to be able to put his robe back on. "I say he kills him now!"

Mosley was next. "I also think that taking him as his prisoner is the best move."

Mieonus laughed as she chimed in. "I also agree that George will kill him now. I think his emotions will get the best of him."

The mage spoke with a coldness that Kepler had never heard before. "I told you I was here to take your crown, you moron. Did you really think that I'd come unprepared? Do you think you're so powerful that you could kill me so easily? I should snap you in half."

As George spoke he became louder and louder.

"I should have my friends eat you for dinner!"

George waved his free hand and the cats appeared below the gasping man as he hung suspended. "Do you really want to die, King of the Barbarians?"

Senchae had to search for the breath to respond. "I'll die before I serve you. Kill me now."

George lowered the big man to the ground, but instead of choking him, he bound his arms and legs with unseen bonds. Slowly he moved his face only inches from the large man.

"You'll die, don't worry about that, but not before I use you as my puppet. There are many things I can do to you that'll make you cooperate with me. We can do this the hard way where I choke you to the point of suffocation before bringing you back from a near death... or you can do as I say. When I'm done, I'll spare your family a painful death and allow them to have a peaceful existence and enjoy their lives. The only person that has to die after I get your crown . . . is you. I'm sure you don't want your family to suffer do you?

George paused, waiting for the king's answer.

So what do you say, Senchae?"

"My family would rather die than serve you," he said, spitting in George's face. "Even my son would not serve a swine like you."

George wiped the spittle from his cheek, not allowing his emotions to control the situation. He took a few deep breaths as he thought about how he would react if he were in this big man's shoes. He wouldn't have given any more information about his own son if he were in Senchae's position and now he realized he had an opportunity to use the Barbarian's information against him... but he needed to know more. He'd have to trick the big man to get any additional information.

"So how is your son, anyway?" the mage asked as he slowly led the Barbarian into his set up. "Is he still as proud as his father?"

The reaction was just as George expected.

"Of course he's proud, he's a Barbarian King's son. We're not like you pathetic swine from the south. We are a people of strength."

"Funny you should say that, Senchae; from where I stand, looking down at you, there isn't much strength in front of me. I see a sorry excuse for a king who would rather kill his family than admit to his own weaknesses."

The Barbarian screamed with rage.

"Take your magic away and you would be nothing! You'd be just another weak excuse of a man from the south."

George laughed.

"Does your son have the same weaknesses that his father does?"

"You don't know my son. All Barbarians are strong. You'll die for your insults, you'll see."

The king twisted and turned, struggling to break free of his magical bonds. Once again the mage laughed and this time George spit in the face of his enemy to anger him.

"Even my daughter, who is only eight seasons, could beat your son in battle. Do you think we should see whose kid is stronger and let them decide our disagreement?"

George hoped that the king's son was close to the age he used for his fictitious daughter. If he wasn't, there was a backup plan as always.

"Hah," the big man scoffed. "Your child commands magic like you or you would not be wasting my time with this nonsense."

"She doesn't command magic, Senchae, but she's pretty good with her hands and feet. I'd be willing to bet everything I have that she would kill your son in the arena of Bloodvain."

"Your child without your magic is no match for my son. You're wasting time talking about this. I'll never serve you and my family will not serve you either. They would rather die first, you piece of garesh."

Once again the king spit in the mage's direction. George figured the big man's reaction was a sign that his son wasn't old enough, or he would have accepted the challenge. It was now time for plan B. He turned to his jaguar friend and spoke to the demon as if the Barbarian was not present.

"Kepler, I thought you told me these people from the north were strong. This man won't even let our children fight for the crown. Don't you think this is a pathetic display of weakness? I think we should spread the word of how weak they actually are."

Kepler had an idea of where the mage was going with his questioning as he could already see the Barbarian biting his tongue, his pride baiting him.

The undead cat responded, "I agree, George. I'm disgusted at what I've seen here today. I would've thought that a man from the north would've had enough pride to accept such a challenge. Maybe his son is actually a daughter, and he doesn't want us to know it."

George laughed and out of the corner of his eye, he could see that the king was about to blow up. "How true that is, I think our big friend here has no clue that his son should be wearing a dress."

Both Kepler and the mage laughed wildly to instigate a reaction... and that was all it took. Senchae's pride now gripped his emotions.

"My son is not a girl and I'm not your friend. If he were old enough to fight your daughter, I would allow him to do so. I would get no greater satisfaction than watching your daughter die in my arena."

George turned the heat up a notch, screaming at the man with his next statement, taking a stab at a confession.

"Are you telling me your son is so weak he can't beat a girl of only eight seasons? You're lying to me, Senchae. You're scared to put him in the arena."

Bloodvain screamed in return.

"A boy of three seasons cannot be expected to know how to fight. Let it be! You and I can settle this!"

The king instantly realized he had said too much and given the mage the information he was fishing for.

Now he softened his voice.

"Please, there must be a way to settle this dispute. I can give you anything you want. What is it that I can do for you?"

George once again started to laugh. He had indeed gotten the information he was after. Then he stopped and after a moment of dead silence, looked wickedly into the eyes of the begging king and spoke in a tone that made the gods feel a chill run up their spines.

"I want your son to die, Senchae," he hissed.

The king screamed as he watched George give orders to the demon jaguar. "Kepler, please take one of your brothers with you into the city when it gets dark. Find Senchae's son and bring him to me. I'll need your other brother to stay behind so I can communicate with the tigers." George leaned over and whispered to the jaguar, "I would prefer the smarter of the two if you don't mind."

"Ha . . . I understand. I will take Koffler with me, but what of the noise the child will make when we carry him out? We'll be discovered when he cries."

George took out a piece of cloth from his pack, tore a long thin strip from it, and tied it on Kepler's neck. He waved his hand across it twice and the strip of cloth disappeared.

"This cloth will make everything you carry silent. Even if the boy screams, as long as you have him in your mouth or even hanging from your teeth, he won't be able to be heard. I suggest you take the baby in the middle of the night and use the darkness of the city to make your escape."

The demon responded as he listened to the cries of the Barbarian king. The big man was begging George to stop.

"Hiding and using the darkness is what I do, George. We'll be back." The two demons ran towards the city in the fading light.

Once they were gone, George turned to the crying king and smiled. After a moment, he found the anticipating eyes of the four tigers and asked Keller to give the order for the large cats to drag Senchae's dead mages into the trees.

"Tell them they can dine on their flesh if they wish."

Keller gave the order, then responded.

"I'm sure they'll enjoy the meal, but I still don't think they like you much."

"I don't need them to like me. I just need them to obey you."

"Agreed," Keller said and moved into the trees to join his feline companions in severing the limbs for their meals.

George listened to the deep growls of the feeding cats for a moment, and then turned back to the king. He lifted his hand into the air and the man began to float. He used his magic to carry Senchae's big frame into the brush, taking another piece of cloth from his bag to use as a gag. He wanted to keep the road clear until Kepler returned with his brother and hoped they'd arrive before dawn. In the back of his mind he knew the king's guards would come looking for him if he was gone much longer. He could only assume the Barbarian had left his city without the knowledge of the others, since he had intended to confront George before he made it to the city. He was glad that Lasidious had warned him that this may happen, but he had been frustrated that the god could not tell him how to kill the Barbarian King and successfully take his crown.

The Grayham Inquirer

When inquiring minds need to know where their favorite characters are.

NIGHT has fallen across Grayham. George built a fire that he could put out quickly if need be. Maldwin ate his cheese and fell asleep. The mage commanded two of the tigers to stand guard over the Barbarian king and directed the others to watch for unwanted visitors from the edge of the tree line.

MOSLEY, Yaloom, Mieonus and Lasidious sat by the fire invisible. Yaloom and Mieonus are in the betting penalty box since they were wrong about George taking Senchae as a prisoner. Both gods are wearing each others' clothes.

CELESTRIA is now only 32 Peaks of Bailem from having the baby. The elven witch family is more pleasant to be around since their last conversation. The goddess had cooked everyone dinner and, despite her obvious lack of talent for the culinary arts, the family ate the dried-out platter of meat she set before them.

SAM is elated to hear the news that Shalee is going to make him a father. Both of them just returned from a dinner with the members of senate, where they announced her pregnancy. At that dinner, some of the senators also expressed a concern. They still had no idea when the war would take place, and wondered if the full mobilization of the military was necessary. Sam reminded them of the god's warning to be prepared. He also reminded them that the kingdom would not have had the three separate, bountiful harvests if not for the blessing of Alistar. The gods expected them to use the money to keep the army ready. This seemed to please the members of his government. It was now just a matter of time before Merchant Island would assign a value to the first shipment of the kingdom's harvests. Soon these harvests would be dispersed throughout the land and the kingdom's treasury would be full of coin. The funds to support the war would no longer be an issue.

Thank you for reading the Grayham Inquirer

Chapter 32

A Babysitting Jaguar

"THIS IS SILLY," Yaloom snapped as he walked around in Mieonus's high heels. "I don't like this game we're playing one bit. I never dreamt I'd be doing something this stupid. Lasidious, your cunning mind is absolutely dreadful!"

"Oh shut up. Quit moving that sniveling snout of yours," Mieonus said, with arms crossed and gleaming eyes full of irritation. "I have to sit here in your stinky, body odor-filled clothes and I'm not whining, am I?"

Yaloom stumbled as one of his heels doubled over, sending the god flying face first into the flames.

"It appears we have our own personal jester," Lasidious said slapping his knee. "Yaloom, you look like a fool!"

"Ha, ha, ha, very funny, enjoy your little moment at my expense, go ahead but you'll lose a bet soon enough and it'll be my turn. I'm sure we'll see who's laughing then."

The wood shifted as the God of Greed pushed clear of the fire and they all watched nervously as George looked in their direction. They knew now that the mage felt their presence as he had waved his hand in their direction.

"That's odd," George said as he waved his hand a second time. He was sure something was there, but his attempt to reveal the unseen did not work.

"Why would the fire do that? The logs shouldn't shift like that," he muttered. He waved his hand a third time for good measure and still nothing. He shrugged his shoulders and continued waiting for Kepler to return.

Before dawn, the jaguars returned with the child. As soon as the Barbarian king saw his baby boy he cried hysterically, begging George to listen to him.

"I'll do anything you want. Please don't do this. He isn't even old enough to understand why you're killing him. If you want my crown, then take it."

George ignored the plea and took the baby from Kepler's mouth. The child was screaming. George knew that as soon as he took him, the morning air would be filled with the frightened child's cries and, hearing them, Senchae would want to stop his boy's execution.

George took the child by one leg and lifted him up. The baby's face showed the horror as the mage dangled him upside-down. Senchae cried for the safety of his son.

"Please, please, I beg you to spare his life. Do what you want with me just let him live. He hasn't seen enough seasons to die this early. What is it you want? I'll do it... I'll do exactly as you command."

Finally, the king had said the words that George wanted to hear. His manipulation had come full circle and he now had a marionette whose strings he intended to pull. He lowered the baby back to Kepler's mouth to shut him up.

"Okay, time to bet. I think George is going to leave the child behind with Keller and take the king back into the city," Lasidious said.

Mosley placed his bet next.

"I say he does the same thing except he leaves Kepler behind since he has the cloth to keep the child quiet."

As soon as Lasidious heard his logic he said, "Damn, I forgot about that, Mosley. Good call, my furry friend."

Both Yaloom and Mieonus saw an opportunity to get back into their own clothes, so they agreed with Mosley. Lasidious rolled his eyes.

"You two are nothing more than sheep."

The entire group laughed. Once again George turned his head in their direction and waved his hand to reveal the presence he felt... but nothing happened.

"He knows we're here," Yaloom said. "Do you think he's powerful enough to reveal our location?"

"Come on, Yaloom. You can't be serious. He may feel a presence around him, but he isn't powerful enough to reveal us."

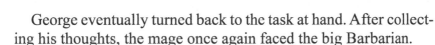

George eventually turned back to the task at hand. After collecting his thoughts, the mage once again faced the big Barbarian.

"Your child cries to live, Senchae. Why would I let him breathe another day with the way you've spoken to me? I know you came out of your city to meet me and I also know that it was without the knowledge of your army's leaders. You wanted to kill me before I had the chance to challenge you. So tell me why I should change my mind. Why wouldn't I kill this boy of yours?"

Senchae, all 550 pounds of him, cried like a baby as he answered.

"I'll give you my crown if you want it. If you let him live I'll do whatever you tell me to do. He's too young to die before his time. I give you my word as a king that I'll do this. I swear it on my father's grave. Just take him back to the city and I'll go with you peacefully."

George stood up and yelled at the king as he grabbed the baby from the demon's jaws and held him high into the air. Again the chilled morning air filled with his cries.

"Do you take me for a fool, Senchae? Do you think that I'm so stupid that I'd go into the city without any insurance?"

The mage lowered the child back to the jaguar's mouth and moved to within inches of the king's tear-filled eyes. He hissed as he spoke.

"You'll go with me, Barbarian, but I'll leave your baby behind with my demon friend here. If you make so much as one wrong move... your son is dead. We will go into the city and release your son once I send word that I have the crown. As to your fate, you'll die in the arena today by my hand as payment for sparing your little boy's life. You'll be given your burial at sea and I'll harvest your organs myself. If you try anything stupid, I'll turn your son into stone."

George reached into his pack and took out a small worm that he had found under a rock earlier. He lifted it up in front of the big man's face and smiled with an evilness that sunk into the heart of the king. The worm's flesh turned a solid gray before George crumbled it up and dropped the dust to the ground.

The Barbarian cried at the hopelessness of the situation.

"I'll do as you ask. Please just give me your word that you won't kill him once this is done."

"What's the boy's name, Senchae?"

The man sobbed, "His name is Sadridz Bloodvain."

"I'll spare the child... I give you my word on this." The mage sat down. "But if you so much as think one wrong thought, I'll gut him like a fish."

"I understand what must I do? My military leaders will be wondering where I am soon, and it is probably a good idea for us to get going."

George agreed and began giving everyone orders.

"Kepler, stay with the boy and keep an eye on him. When he gets hungry, feed him some of the bread from my pack. If I'm not back by tomorrow night or if anyone tries to rescue the child, kill him and get out of here."

He made sure the king was paying close attention to everything he said.

"Tell Maldwin that it's time to implement our plan with the king's people and inform the tigers that I'll be taking them into the city with me. Make sure they know they'll be unseen just like before. Ask them not to attack unless I give the signal."

The beast did as he was asked.

"Keller, once we're in the city, can you give the order for the tigers to attack if need be?"

"I can do that, just say the word," the demon replied.

George looked at the king as he walked over to Kepler. He lifted the baby by his leg and smiled as the child cried. He dangled the boy in front of the frustrated father.

"Are you sure you're ready for this, Senchae? I'm only going to give you one chance to get it right." He pointed to Kepler's teeth as the mighty cat yawned. "I'd hate to see your son torn apart by those jaws."

"You don't need to remind me any further. Please just allow me to say goodbye before we go. I won't ever be able to see him again so please, allow me this last request."

George waved his hand and the Barbarian could feel his magical bonds release. "I'll grant this, but don't overestimate my generosity."

The big man shook his head and crawled over to his son and took him from the mage's hands. He turned the child right side up and cradled him in his arms, quieting his cries.

George allowed the Barbarian to hold his child for quite a while before he ordered him to put him down. The big man shook his head and took his heavy shirt off to make a spot for the boy to sit. In the back of the George's mind, he was thinking.

There just might be a better use for you, Senchae. Killing you and your family may not be necessary after all. I'll investigate this further on our way into the city. Oh, crap . . . I've got to prepare for the Serpent King's arrival. My hell Lasidious, you could have given me more time.

George barked out an order. "Let's go, Senchae, we don't want to worry your men!"

"Agreed," the Barbarian replied. "So how do you want to do this?" It was like the king was a new man since he had the chance to say goodbye to his son. He seemed at peace, resolved to the idea of his death.

"Well . . . I may have thought of an idea that would make us both happy. I'll tell you about it along the way. You may not have to die after all."

∞ ∞

"Dang, Mosley, you won," Lasidious said. He left Kepler and took the rest of them just as you said he would. Looks like I lost the bet . . . what do I have to do?"

"I have a few ideas if you want a couple, Mosley," Yaloom interjected.

"So do I, there are so many things we could do to him," Mieo-nus smiled as she rubbed her hands together.

Mosley laughed and began to follow George. As he passed Senchae's son, he touched the boy's head with his paw to give him peace. Kepler was sitting near the child and the wolf god decided to appear to the cat. He informed the others that he would catch up to them saying he wanted to comfort the frightened youngster. The others agreed and left him behind.

There were other reasons the wolf wanted to stay behind but he did not want the others to know. He needed to look his wife's killer in the face. He knew the laws within the Book of Immortality bound him from taking revenge, but this would give him closure. Although he could not punish Kepler for her death, he needed to let the demon know that he *knew* he had killed her.

Once the other gods were gone, he allowed himself to be seen by the demon as the jaguar immediately took a defensive position.

Mosley said, "Relax, Kepler, I'm here to speak with you. Do you know who I am?"

"I do," the demon responded anxiously. "I know of you and I know you took the place of Bassorine. What do you want with me?"

"I know that I'm not the god you serve, Kepler, but I'm the god who is watching over this baby. I've blessed this child. You won't be able to kill him. I have also made sure that he keeps quiet for you until George gets back. Please make sure you play with him and keep him entertained." Mosley nudged the boy with his snout and the child chuckled. "I think you'll find the child willing to play now."

The demon shook his head. "You want me to do what? I'm not his father. I don't do playing. It's degrading enough that I have to sit with this foul creature in the first place."

"No, no... you aren't his father, but you will be the one I'm angry with if this child doesn't find his stay here in the woods peaceful."

The wolf growled at the cat as he continued. "It's the least you can do for me, Kepler, since you killed my wife when you attacked the unicorn prince. I'm still not completely healed from the events of that day; so do you think you can manage to keep this baby happy for me?"

"I never meant to kill your wife, Lord Mosley, I swear it. She was in the way... I didn't even know who she was. Her death wasn't intentional. The weight of my body knocked her into the prince's horn when I went after him. I meant her no ill will."

Mosley growled again.

"She ended up dead anyway. You don't need to talk of it further, Kepler. I'm not here to seek revenge on you. I'm here to ask you to take care of this child for me. Don't let any harm come to him. Play with him and make him smile... that's all I ask of you. There's no reason for this child to suffer while he's out here. Play peek-a-boo with him or something."

"Peek-a-boo? I'm not a babysitter. I don't know how to play with a child."

"Just play with him and forget your pride. You'll make a fine toy for the child. Kids love furry things. Let him pull your tail, bite your ears, poke you in the eyes and grab your tongue. The baby will get a kick out of it, I assure you. He can use your coat to wipe the snot from his nose and you can lick him clean if he messes himself. I'm sure you're willing to do this for me. We can consider this small task as my way of forgiving you for killing my wife. It's your choice, Kepler. What do you say?"

Mosley looked the cat square in the eyes.

"I give you my word that I'll take care of him, Lord Mosley." Kepler said bowing. "Thank you for your forgiveness!"

With that, the wolf god disappeared and ran to catch up with the others.

Meanwhile, George was talking with the king as they traveled.

"You know, Senchae, we could handle this in a better way. It's obvious now that you're a man who's willing to give your life for your family. I respect that. It's also obvious that the people you have surrounding you aren't all that powerful . . . like yourself. The mages you had giving you counsel were weak. You know this, right?"

"It would appear so now that you mention it. I was fighting off your rat's vision when you killed them so I don't remember much."

George laughed.

"Well, you'll have to take my word for it then."

The mage hesitated a moment and continued.

"I'm wondering... do you find the people of the south to be pathetic because you perceive them as weak?"

The Barbarian hesitated to answer, but George assured him it was all right. "Speak freely . . . let's talk as friends, Senchae."

"What in the name of Grayham is he doing?" Lasidious asked as he listened in on the conversation. "This is certainly a twist I didn't see coming. If he does what I think he's going to do, it will be brilliant. Yaloom, do you see the brilliance in this?"

The God of Greed had a "deer-in-the-headlights" stare when Lasidious looked at him. Mieonus wasn't much different. Lasidious snapped out a retort in frustration.

"Where's Mosley when I need someone to speak with who understands strategy? You have got to be kidding me, you two. How in all the worlds could either of you be gods?"

He didn't wait for a response but instead turned his attention back to the conversation between George and Senchae.

The mage could see Senchae's hesitation and reassured him once again.

"Look, Senchae, I already know how you feel. So give me a straight, honest answer."

"Yes," the big man finally spoke up. "We feel the people of the south are weak, but I've never met anyone like you. I must say you've changed my mind in some ways!"

"George . . . my name is George and I allow only my friends to call me that. You can also call me George if you wish, Senchae."

The big Barbarian was now more confused than ever.

"I don't understand."

"I imagine you wouldn't, so let me explain. The more I think about it, the more I feel you and I can help each other. Your goal is to defeat the people of the south, correct?"

"Yes, but what does this have to do with you and me?"

"Maybe the two of us can work together to kill everyone who won't serve us in Brandor."

"I'm listening," Senchae said without hesitation. "I like what I'm hearing so far."

"Well, you need a consulate to protect you, and I want to have the power to defeat the Kingdom of Brandor. The two of us can join forces and achieve our goals together."

George stopped and looked up at the big man.

"I don't need to be king. The two of us can accomplish great things without sacrificing your life. You can keep your position as king. We'll even go back right now to get your son and bring him with us. You'll announce me as your counsel, and I'll use the rat's visions to subtly give your military leaders the idea that everything is okay. All I want is for my family to be treated as you would treat your own, and we'll need to feed all my animals."

George moved his hand around. All six of the invisible cats appeared next to Maldwin, who had been walking with them. The rodent jumped into George's arms and began twitching his nose wildly. He still felt like dinner being around all the big cats.

Maldwin looked up at the mage and bravely said, "Everything is 'A-okay,' George."

The Barbarian king laughed at the rat.

"So you want to form an alliance and I still get to be king? You want to kill everyone in the south and take over their kingdom. What else do you want me to do for you?"

"As I've already said, my king," George said, bowing to the ruler with his manipulative mind now in full swing, "I want you to provide for my family and my pets. I also want you to use me as your counsel, and allow for my powers to protect you when I'm around. I never wanted to kill you, just get you to listen."

Senchae could not believe his ears.

"I was convinced you were going to kill me."

"My king, did you really believe that? Think about it for a moment. Your city wouldn't listen to an outsider without your support. If I hadn't commanded your respect, you would've never taken me seriously? Besides, you intended to kill me, so I didn't have much choice. I couldn't allow you to rip me apart, now could I?"

Senchae laughed.

"I suppose I did put your back up against a wall." The king pondered these new ideas for a minute. "I like the idea of the two of us becoming allies. We could go after the lands of the south, but that will take a much stronger army than I command. What other tricks do you have to help us with this campaign?"

"Well," George grinned, realizing he was in, "Kepler is lord of all the giant cats. You can see the alliance I have with him. And, between the demon's cats and his Skeleton Warrior army, we'll have a powerful force against Brandor. There is one other thing that I'm working on as well, but you'll need to set aside your pride to make it work."

The Barbarian king was intrigued, if not a little annoyed by George's words... "And what would this be, George?"

The mage smiled when he heard the big man say his name, knowing for sure that the Barbarian was truly his puppet.

"The Serpent King Seth is on his way to meet with me. He thinks you're dead and I'm the King of Bloodvain. So you can see we have a small problem. I thought that you would make me kill you, but, as it turns out, we are going to be able to do great things together. So how do we handle this situation now?"

Senchae thought a moment and then responded, "We could always send my scouts to find him and meet with him in his territory instead of having him here. I don't think he has any idea what I look like."

George thought a moment. "I don't know that we should go to his home without having an alliance first. Is there a place outside the city where your scouts could bring Seth? We could pretend I'm king until he leaves. Then I'll follow him back to his kingdom once we have an alliance. I'll familiarize myself with his home once I'm there so I can teleport back and forth to give him important information. We should be able to coordinate our attacks on Brandor this way."

The king smiled. "I like this, but I don't understand why the Serpent King would want to get involved in the affairs of war when his serpent kingdom has lived peacefully for so long."

The mage laughed.

"That's an easy question to answer. Someone put it into his head that Brandor is going to attack him." George smiled widely as he gave the Barbarian the impression that it was he who had done this.

"You really are an ambitious soul. I would've never thought of that. I hate snakes, George. Maybe you and your rat can do this meeting on your own. Besides, he thinks I'm dead. I'll tell my scouts to tell the Serpent King that you're their king. That seems simple enough. You can hold this meeting south of where we met. I have a home there that I use as a getaway sometimes, so by the time you have your hidden cats, my guards and your rat, you should be fine, right?"

"I agree," George replied. "What do you say we go back and get your son? Maybe we could cook a good dinner tonight when we get to your castle."

"That sounds good, but I wouldn't expect my military leaders to be overly receptive tonight. They are Barbarian men after all. To accept this change will challenge their pride."

"I never saw that one coming," Mosley said to Lasidious. "I think it's smart to form this alliance with the king. If he had killed Senchae, I don't think he would've ever gained the respect of the Barbarian people. This way, over time, he'll become accepted with the king's support."

"I agree with you, Mosley," Lasidious said. "I'm becoming more and more impressed as we go. It's brilliant. He can always dispose of the king later. It will be interesting to see how he handles the king's military leaders and the Serpent King, Seth."

Mieonus responded. "Your buddy George is worthy of being a king some day, Lasidious. I hope he pulls this off." The goddess found herself becoming a fan of the mage as well. She was definitely going to keep an eye on him. "I think that I'm going to take my leave and go home."

All the gods agreed and made their exits with Lasidious smiling big as he vanished... he had avoided the consequences of the lost bet.

Chapter 33

An Example Made

GEORGE, Senchae Bloodvain, the Barbarian king's son, Maldwin and Kepler, along with the rest of their feline companions, arrived at the king's castle. As the group entered the city, they turned many heads—most men didn't travel with seven man-eating cats and an oversized rat.

Bloodvain was a rugged, wooded city. The whole scene reminded George of a national park, only with people living in it. The king explained how the entire city was built within a heavy forest that extended to the north where the tree line ended at the beach of the Blood Sea.

The Bloodvain River flowed from the Pool of Sorrow, through the Dark Forest and through the center of the king's city. Heavy, wooden bridges spanned its depths and the river was full of fish. In the short time it took to cross into the town, the group had seen two different men catching their dinner.

As they walked through the trees, George's frustration grew. Everywhere he looked, the place reminded him of log cabins— a lifestyle he loathed. But he was careful to keep his feelings to himself, not wanting to strain his new relationship with the king. It was bad enough he had been sleeping on the ground, something he would not have done back on Earth. But now he would be spending the rest of his life in a wooden shack. He hoped the king's home was much nicer. If it was, he would find a room there to live in until he could build something better. He was not about to live like an animal. And he really missed his Gucci clothes.

As they approached the castle, George saw that Senchae's home was nothing more than a giant lodge. It was much nicer than the rest of the city, but it looked like the home of the Brawny Paper Towel man. It was not a place for George. He would have to figure out a way to renovate the place, but for now it would have to do.

Everywhere George looked he saw trophies of the king's great hunts. Heads of deer, boar, mountain goats, Minotaur, mounted fish, and various birds hung all over the walls. Life-sized, stuffed animals were scattered throughout the structure as well. He saw bears, gorillas, buffalo-looking beasts and after the third stuffed cat, he stopped the king to point out a big problem: Kepler and his posse were becoming upset. The idea that members of their feline family were being used as trophies was not sitting well with them and George insisted this issued be resolved immediately. The king had his servants remove all the trophies of every cat in the castle lodge, apologizing to the big cats. This seemed to suffice for now as Kepler calmed his subjects.

Once they were in the throne room, the king's general entered with some high-ranking officers of the Barbarian army, completely missing George standing nearby with his feline partners. He expressed his concern over the company that his king was said to have been keeping and told his king that there were rumors spreading throughout the city that the king's visitors were undesirable.

When he heard this, George, being the wisecracker he was, had to comment.

"I wouldn't call us undesirable. I'd call us diversified."

The leader of the army snapped his head around and realized he had spoken in front of the company of his king. He turned and bowed to Senchae as he spoke, "Sire, I'm sorry for the interruption."

Bloodvain laughed.

"General Fergus, allow me to introduce you to George Nailer. I met him just south of the city and I've brought him back to be my advisor."

"What!" Then, realizing his tone, the Barbarian added, "My king, your advisor, how could you possibly let this, this—"

"—This what, General?" George interrupted, "Are you suggesting that I'm not capable of doing the job? Or are you bothered because I'm not a Barbarian?"

Fergus looked at his king, silently asking permission to confront the man from the south.

Senchae smiled. "By all means, General, I give you permission to speak freely. I told you they would react like this, George."
George decided to say something to stir things up. He realized this guy was good, if not better, than anyone else to start a confrontation with.

"I can handle this, my king," he said.

The thought of George calling Senchae his king angered the Barbarian general. "You're one of those pathetic souls from the south. Who are you to come into my homeland and act as if my king is your own?"

The manipulator stared at the general.

"I'm the guy who is going to be protecting your king from now on. It seems to me that you have a shortage of qualified people around these parts. Where were you when the king's mages failed him last night? Where were you when the king's son was taken from his bed in the middle of the night?"

"Bah, I don't answer to you! I should kill you where you stand for your ignorance."

"Ignorance... the last time I checked, there was no ignorance in true statements! Let's face it, General Fergus; you were nowhere to be found during either of those events. You didn't know where your king was and I'll bet no one knew his son was gone until this morning. How am I doing so far, General? Maybe you should use the word insolence, because it's a better description of how I'm speaking to you... I'm pretty sure that I'm being insolent."

The leader of the army pulled his war hammer from his hip and pointed it at George. Each one of the six cats took defensive positions and growled in a frightening display of power that warned the overzealous barbarian that he was making a stupid decision. Even Maldwin was ready to use his visions if the mage squeezed his tail. His nose was twitching wildly from the excitement.

"It seems that you have help and that you don't fight your own battles," Fergus said as he scanned the room. "If you didn't have all your cats, you'd be a dead man right now."

George laughed as he looked at the king. "Maybe a demonstration is in order."

The king stood from his throne and spoke to the General. "Are you sure you know what you're doing, my friend? I'll allow you to fight if you would like but if you get blood on my trophies I'll want them cleaned. I warn you though, it's a mistake to fight this man. He's not as weak as you might think."

"Of course I know what I'm doing. I can protect you, my king. You don't need this swine from the south. Allow me to kill him and I'll show you that I should be the one in charge of your protection, not this piece of garesh." The general rolled his hammer around in his hand.

The king gave George a glance before giving the okay to fight in his throne room. He only had one question. "What of your cats, George?"

The mage turned and motioned for them to move toward the walls. He lowered Maldwin to the floor and asked Kepler to call the rodent to him. "Tell the tigers I don't need their help. Make sure they don't interfere." He turned to Maldwin, held up his thumb and said, "Everything is 'A-okay' man!"

"Everything is 'A-okay' George," the rat responded, twitching his nose.

Again the general rolled his hammer in his hand. "Are you going to play with your mouse or are you going to fight?"

"Well, maybe there are others whom you could invite to your throne room to watch this man kick my butt. I'd hate for the people of your great kingdom to miss such an event."

Senchae understood what the mage was thinking and, despite the General being a friend of his, he still lived by the code that those who instigated fights should follow through with their threats. He knew that George was going to make an example out of his General and. Bloodvain respected the tactics of the mage, so he decided to allow an audience. He had given Fergus a chance to back off of his comments, but the big Barbarian had pursued the issued to this course of action. It was long since passed the time for apologies.

The king clapped his hands summoning his servants, then sent them to retrieve all those who were in the castle-lodge to bring them as witnesses. It wasn't long before the room was packed with onlookers with an area cleared for the men to fight.

Senchae looked at both of them and explained that this would be a battle to the death. He was anxious to see to what extent

George would go to make his point.

Fergus nodded in agreement to the king's statements, then looking right at George, and said. "This is to the death, swine. You leave our kingdom right now and I'll let you live. Go back to your pig-of-a-mother and crawl back into the hole you came from."

The mage smiled in return.

"Are we fighting or are you going to talk me to death?"
Kepler and his three brothers growled as they cheered. "Kill him, George!"

Maldwin was excited and screamed as loud as his tiny body would allow him to, "I like cheese, George!"

Everyone in the room turned, including General Fergus, and looked at the rat. After a moment of awkwardness, the angry Barbarian shrugged his shoulders and turned his attention back to his enemy.

"What can I say?" George said, with a sinister grin. "He likes his cheese!"

Without another word the Barbarian attacked and swung his hammer towards George's head. The mage dodged the advance, rolled out of the way, and stood up.

"General, come on now, is that the best you can do? I heard you were better than that. Please don't disappoint me by missing again."

Fergus screamed as he made his next advance, again missing the quicker, smaller man.

"How could you be the leader of such a powerful army? Your movements are slow! My king, maybe you need a new leader."

Neither Senchae nor Fergus knew that the mage had used his magic to assist his speed. George would toy with Fergus a bit more before taking the offensive. "You could try and hit me this time, General, or is that hammer to heavy for you? If I'm not mistaken, that's what it was made for, right?"

"You talk too much for a dead man," Fergus snapped as he once again charged in for another air-filled blow that smashed into the floor without hitting its target. This time he wouldn't give George the chance for another comment but rather lifted his hammer quickly and took another big swing. Again he hit nothing but air.

"I'm disappointed in you, General. You can't be serious. My

king, is this the best our army commands? I guess they can't all be built for war as you are, sire." George knew he made Senchae sound stronger with his comments and slammed the General's pride at the same time. Point made... it was now time to demonstrate how powerful he *really* was.

The mage waited for the next swing of the General's hammer. As expected, he raised the weapon over his head. George lifted both his hands just as the hammer started moving towards him. A wicked storm of lightning shot out of the tips of his fingers and slammed hard into his enemy's chest sending the Barbarian flying across the room and crashing into the king's throne. The chair crumbled under his momentum. The General and throne slammed into the wall. The General slid unconscious to the floor.

Kepler was shocked by what George did and the air filled with anxious murmurs. The jaguar knew his friend had stolen Amar's powers, but he didn't realize he'd become that powerful. The undead cat had seen many mages throughout his years, but none of them had commanded this type of power. He needed to have a serious conversation with his partner.

"Damn," Senchae said, disappointed. "That was my favorite chair. George... you broke my chair. It has been in my family for many generations. Could you please kill him without breaking anything else?"

The mage grinned. "Allow me to fix it, my king." He waved his hand and the many shattered pieces of wood floated around the room as the crowd cried out with fear. The king gave them a look to quiet them down. The wood pieces came together magically uniting until the chair once again rested in one piece.

"I trust that's better, sire?" George said, watching the king shake his head; then he went to stand over his unconscious opponent. Looking around the room for rope, he found none... but then he noticed the wooden rafters that spanned the room. He stabbed one of Fergus's feet with his dagger, and let the blood flow from it. He turned and lifted his hand in the direction of the unconscious Barbarian who was now floating toward the wooden beams.

Screams filtered from the crowd and the king once again ordered silence. With the Barbarian now resting tight against the beam, the mage took his free hand and with a forced motion of his wrist, draped the General's arms around the beam. The mage made sure that the Barbarian's arms overlapped each other as he walked directly beneath his dangling feet. He touched the general's bloody foot as it drained down his boot, listening to the anguished sounds of the crowd. As he touched the General, his arms turned to stone.

Once again the king demanded silence and motioned for George to continue. The mage walked over to Kepler and whispered in his ear; the giant cat now allowed George to sit on his back as he moved near the repaired throne.

The undead beast stood tall and let out an angry roar to wake the General. George knew the people were taking all this in like a sponge and, once they left the room, would gossip throughout the city about the day's events. And now he wanted to leave an indelible impression. Saying his final words before killing his enemy from the cat's back would be memorable, something they would tell their children's children.

As Fergus became conscious of his situation, he cried in pain. George lifted his voice and said, "General, you aren't worthy to serve our king. You can't command an army when you're every action is filled with a pathetic weakness. It's now time for you to die!"

The mage lifted his hands once again and lighting shot forth from his fingers. He continued to do this until every last cell in the General's body was thoroughly cooked through. The smell of burnt flesh filled the room, a stench George wouldn't stick around for. He called all the giant cats around him, making sure they were all touching one another as he looked at the king.

"My king, I take my leave now and will return to you in the morning." The mage touched Kepler's back, motioned for Maldwin to jump into his arms, and they all disappeared.

The Grayham Inquirer

When inquiring minds need to know where their favorite characters are.

GEORGE and his companions appeared in Athena's mother's barn. The mage took one of the Corgans, a large cow-like looking beast from its stall and turned its lungs and its spinal cord to stone, providing the rest of its flesh to feed his giant feline friends. The large piece of meat simply fell over and become one big rare steak. Before he left to look for Athena, he waved his hand across the bloody scene and made it invisible. Maldwin was still in his arms when he entered the house, so he gave the little guy some cheese to satisfy his hunger.

Now lying in bed with his beautiful wife, he talked to her pregnant belly. Athena was happy with her husband's affections and rubbed his head. He planned to go back out to the barn later and clean up the mess, then leave for the Barbarian king's throne room in the morning. He knew that the impressions he made in Senchae's palace-lodge would be the talk of the barbarian's rugged populous when he got back. Despite his love for his beautiful, pregnant wife, he was anxious to return and see the results of his handiwork.

SAM was sitting with Shalee at breakfast feeding his lovely wife grapes when Mosley appeared. The god informed them that Lasidious was holding a meeting to announce where the two pieces of Crystal Moon had been hidden.

CELESTRIA was bored until she thought of a project; she would learn how to make an Ospliton pie. An Ospliton fruit-tree grew not too far from the elven witch family's home and the two squirrels she had been feeding from her windowsill helped her pick the best fruit. She now had a basketful and was carrying it back to the house.

SENCHAE BLOODVAIN left General Fergus's body hanging from the rafters. He called for the Barbarian's family to come and collect him for his burial on the Blood Sea. From the looks of it, there would not be anything left of his organs to harvest since his guts had been fried to a crisp.

The Barbarian king spent many, many moments after George's departure explaining to his military leaders that he wanted war; it was time to take control of the Kingdom of Brandor for good. He bragged about his new advisor's powers, using the lifeless General as a visual aid to convince them he was right in allying the barbarian people with the mage. All-in-all, the meeting went well.

As Senchae sat to eat his breakfast, he realized his army could actually win a war against the south. With the Serpent King's army, Kepler's giant cats and the Skeletal Warriors all fighting alongside his own Barbarian Army, he would soon be king of all of Grayham. He smiled as Sadridz ran into the dining hall screaming happily for his daddy.

LASIDIOUS was with Yaloom and Mieonus. He informed them that his meeting would be held before Late Bailem in the Hall of Judgment, then left to go meet with George... there were a few matters which needed to be discussed and he couldn't wait for the mage to dream again."

Thank you for reading the Grayham Inquirer

Chapter 34

No Loose Ends

WHEN LASIDIOUS appeared to George, Athena had just left her mother's guesthouse to fix them something to eat. The mage was sitting in a hot bath that he had conjured up and he wasn't fazed in the least when the god appeared.

"Hello, my friend," Lasidious said as he looked down at the deceiver. "I felt speaking to you in person would be a pleasant change, don't you think? How are you?"

George smiled. "I'm sure you already know how I am, Lasidious. You were watching me the other day outside Bloodvain and you know the Barbarian's so-called castle is a joke. It reminds me of an oversize Elk's Lodge from back home. It figures I'd end up trying to take charge of a bunch of rednecks. I'm going to have to renovate that place, maybe even rebuild it. I won't live like Grizzly Adams, Lasidious. I need a little class in my life."

The evil god chuckled.

"I'm sorry you don't like the king's style. The Barbarians are a rough people."

"Really," George mocked with disgust. "I would've never been able to tell that. Those damn redneck idiots, not to mention all their stuffed animal trophies they have all over the place, they drive me nuts. I bet the king's wagon is on some cinder blocks in the royal barn. Once we take over Brandor, I intend to take full control and send that big blockhead Senchae back to the north. I'll stay down here and run the south."

Lasidious laughed at his ranting.

"I'm sorry you dislike it up there, George. Not to change the subject, but it's true I was watching you the other day. It's also true that I wasn't the only one."

"Really," he replied, "And who else was watching? Did you all get the show that you were after?"

"And more, much more . . . the four of us were impressed. You did some things that even I wasn't thinking of. I was worried about how you'd work your way into the hearts of the people of Bloodvain and I must admit I agree with you that killing the king wasn't a smart idea after all. I applaud you for your decision to use him as a tool though—and how you dangled his son in front of him to find the Barbarian's breaking point was an exceptional work of evil. So, how did it go when you got to the city? I wasn't there for that or watching from my home on the god world."

"Well, you would've shared in my delight!" the mage said, lifting a cloth to wash with. "Do you mind if I finish while we talk?"

"By all means…"

George began to wash and explained the events from the night before.

"It's safe to say the General didn't like me much and when he threatened me, I made an example of him. With the king's approval, I toyed with him in front of the entire castle staff until he was thoroughly degraded, telling him he was weak in front of everyone. He tried to hit me with his hammer many times, but I kept avoiding his swings and tore at his pride. Then I killed him."

George paused a moment to retrieve the soap.

"I hit him with lightning and followed that up by draping his arms over one of the wooden beams in the king's throne room. I made sure they were crossed over top of one another before turning them to stone. As I let him dangle there, I sat on Kepler's back and asked him to give a mighty roar to wake the unconscious idiot up. You should've seen the looks of the people when the demon filled the air with his ferocious cry. Even I felt the chill from it. Once the General awoke, I sent my lighting into him again and kept at it until he was Kentucky-fried."

Lasidious interrupted, "Kentucky-fried, George?"

George laughed loudly, "It means I cooked him until he was a crispy-looking Barbarian. I didn't hang around to do a taste test, though."

"Well done, well done, my friend. This will give you quite the reputation in Bloodvain. With the king backing you up I bet the people will be more apt to listen to you even though you're an outsider."

"We shall see," George responded. "When I left Senchae's throne room last night, I teleported the seven cats, Maldwin and myself and left the General hanging from the ceiling."

Lasidious smiled.

"I wish I had a hundred of you, George. You continue to impress me. I look forward to the day I can retrieve your daughter."

The mage smiled at the thought of his baby girl and continued. "So how do you think I should handle the Serpent King when I meet with him?"

The god walked to one of the bathing room windows.

"I'm not able to give you that information, George. It is against the gods' laws. You'll have to finish the events you started in motion without me assisting you. Besides, with the way you have done things so far, you don't need me telling you how to win friends and influence people."

"Winning friends and influencing people... an excellent resource book for me back on Earth. I used that book as my Bible to learn manipulation. I wish I had it here so you could take a gander at it, Lasidious."

"As do I, it sounds like a fine read. But I actually have a reason for my visit today... I want to warn you to be careful when you talk to the others. The gods are watching you and we can't afford you to say something you shouldn't when they are present. I don't wish to have our plans found out!"

Lasidious disappeared before Athena walked into the room.

"Who were you talking to, honey? I thought I heard voices in here."

"You know me, babe, and all the babbling I do," he said as he stood from his bath and grabbed a towel.

Shalee Trains to Increase Her Powers

AFTER BREAKFAST Shalee left Sam for the royal gardens. The queen wanted to work on her magic and she had all the workers leave the area. Over the last week she had made significant advances in her powers and could now command most of what she had learned without using Precious. Today she was walking around the garden passing her hands over flowers, making them magically grow. And now she was about to make her first attempt at teleportation.

When Helga arrived, the ladies embraced as they always did.

"You know, child, I've never been able to command this magic. All I know is that for you to make it work without killing yourself, you'll need to be familiar with your destination. There is only one other on Grayham that can use this power and that's Amar."

"Exactly how would I kill myself? If I fail you mean? What could happen?"

Helga cupped Shalee's face with both of her hands before answering the question. "You could appear too high above the ground and fall to your death if you don't teleport again fast enough. You might appear under a large rock, inside a wall, under the ground, deep below the surface of a lake, in a lava flow or, if you're really, really lucky, you could appear with your head stuck in a horse's backside. But hey, no pressure, sweetheart, I'm rooting for you." She winked.

"Ha, ha, ha, very funny, smart-aleck, thanks for the confidence builder. I'm so glad I called you for support. Right now I can't remember why I love you so much. Will you please remind me?"

"Because, child, you know that you need your adopted mother."

"Bah," Shalee laughed as she threw her hands in the air. Before they spoke again, they moved to a spot she had picked out.

"I've been studying this spot for a while now," Shalee said. "I figured that this would be the spot to start. I'm not sure what to do to make this happen, though. For some reason, I already knew that I needed to be familiar with the place that I intended to teleport to . . . don't ask me how!"

"That's very insightful child, but where is Precious?" Helga questioned.

"I want to do this without the staff. I want to work on commanding my powers without that kind of crutch."

Helga looked worried.

"I understand your desire to master your powers, but do you think it's wise to try and teleport without the staff? Maybe you can use the staff to get a feel for it and then try again without it later."

"No, that won't work. The staff uses words and the way I have been using my magic lately is without being verbal."

The older lady looked astonished.

"Since when have you started doing that? I have to whisper to command powers without my staff, but even then I can only do simple acts. Do you remember when I lifted you off the floor in Angel's Village? I still had to whisper under my breath to hold you there. You're telling me that you're controlling your powers without words at all?"

"I am," Shalee replied.

"Oh child, that's unheard of. I don't know of anyone that has the ability to do it. Amar can command many of his lesser skills without words but he does it with just the use of his arms. And I don't believe he can command this type of magic without his staff."

The queen smiled.

"Well, I'm able to control most everything without my staff now or without using words. I don't know how, but it seems natural."

"The gods have blessed you, child," Helga responded. "I think we both know that this is your decision since I can't teach you further."

"So shall we give it a trial run then? I'll stand over near that statue." Shalee looked at the stone figure. "You know what, Helga?" the sorceress said, sidetracked.

"No, what is it?"

"Some things don't change from my world to this one. Even back on Earth, we had these statues of men that didn't have their privates covered. On Earth this was considered art, but I think it's silly. What do you think?"

Helga thought a moment, and then grinned with a suggestive twist. "I like the look very much. Don't we all like them rock solid, child?"

Both ladies laughed heartily and gave each other a high five. They each kissed their hand and touched the statue for good luck.

"Now BJ and I just—"

"—Stop!" Shalee cried as she covered her ears. "I don't want to know about my adopted dad's personal life... T.M.I... too much information."

Again the ladies laughed, but then got serious.

Helga spoke first, "If you aren't going to be using words of power, then you should try concentrating. Try closing your eyes and focusing on what you want to happen. That's what I'd do if I were in your shoes."

Without answering, Shalee closed her eyes and took a deep breath, then thought of the nice grassy area next to the rose bushes. She pictured herself standing there... then after a second, she heard Helga scream.

"Oh, child, child, child!"

Shalee did not want to open her eyes. She could not tell if her friend's tone was good or bad.

"You did it! Oh, my child, you did it! I'm so proud of you."

Shalee opened her eyes and gave a big grin, then she and Helga had a long, strong embrace.

Sam walked up on them. "Is there something you two need to tell me, babe? What's going on here?"

His queen grabbed him, winked at Helga, and told him to close his eyes. The next thing Sam knew, he was standing in their bedroom. He would have said something, but Shalee held her hands over his lips to stop him from talking.

"We have something to celebrate. Just relax."

She licked her lips seductively. Sam smiled.

The King of Bloodvain's Throne Room

GEORGE teleported to an area near the wooden bridge outside the king's castle lodge, arriving with all his cats cloaked for invisibility. He wanted to know how he'd be received if the people thought he had arrived alone and, to his surprise, the people in the city bowed to him as he passed.

Leaving Maldwin visible, the rat sat inside his pack with his head sticking out. As the mage entered the throne room, three Barbarian men and four large women were collecting the General's body. One of them climbed onto the beam where Fergus hung with the goal to break his stone arms apart so he could be lowered. George didn't know it, but the man who took the hammer to the general's arms was his own son. As he stood there, no one spoke to him. It was not until the king showed up that George learned the man with the hammer was the new champion of Senchae's arena.

"His name is Churnach Fergus; he's the General's son. I wouldn't expect a warm reception from him if I were you. I had a long conversation with the family to calm them all down and they understand that the General challenged you first, but still..."

George turned to the Barbarian king and made sure that he was the only one to see his smile. "Well, this is a bit awkward then, don't you agree?"

The big man, despite the complete lack of sensitivity in George's reaction, had to smile. "Walk with me for a minute, my friend. I think it's best if we take our leave for now and allow them to have this time to grieve."

The king walked with George into one of the hallways before saying, "It should only take the Serpent King about 20 Peaks of Bailem to arrive. Do you know how long he has been traveling so far?"

"I do," the mage responded.

George had no sooner said this than screams echoed from the king's throne room. Both men glanced at one another and ran back to the doorway. As they entered, bodies were flying everywhere and falling lifeless to the floor. The king looked at the horrifying sight as he heard the angry roars of the invisible beasts. After a few moments, the only one that was left alive was the Barbarian champion. He was swinging wildly through the air, but it was not long before he was lying dead as well.

George waited for the commotion to stop. He waved his hand through the air. Seven blood-soaked cats appeared standing over lifeless bodies. Some of them had large mouthfuls of fresh Barbarian.

The mage looked confused as he glanced at the king. He shrugged his shoulders. He took a second to gather his thoughts and said, "Kepler, what's going on here?"

The demon responded, "The son of the General said that they were going to kill you, George. The other two men with him said they should do it now while you were close and not heavily guarded. The women agreed with them and said you were ripe for the picking. I figured it wasn't wise to wait for them to attack so me and my friends, well, let's just say we took care of it."

"I can see that," the king responded before the mage could reply. "Your friends are already creating quite the body count, George. Maybe we could save the rest of it for the people of the south from now on, if that's okay with you."

Kepler walked over to the king, looked him straight in the eye, and growled coldly. "The big guy, Churnach Fergus, the one you said was your champion, stated his king wanted them to attack. He said they all would be rewarded for killing you, George." The jaguar watched closely for Senchae's reaction.

Bloodvain turned and looked George dead in the eyes. "I swear to you, my friend, I said nothing to him about a reward for killing you. I have sworn my alliance to you and I won't break that promise... on my son's honor."

The demon stared at the king's eyes and made his judgment. He knew George would be angry and think that the king was untrustworthy because of his statements. The demon spoke up before George could use his magic to kill him.

"George, please, may I speak with you a moment?" Kepler said in a tone that redirected the mage's attention. "This is important. You can kill him in a minute as easily as you can right now. Please speak with me in private."

The king found he was unable to move as George followed the demon through the bloody mess to the other side of the room. Senchae had been bound like this before, and he knew it was pointless to fight the magic.

"What is it, Kepler?" he said angrily. "I should've killed him already."

"No, George, I lied to the king. This family said nothing of attacking you."

"What? Why the deception? I must not be following your logic."

Kepler sighed, "I figured that the General's family was angry. I don't believe in leaving loose ends. Without them around, there's no one to seek revenge. It also gave me a chance to see if the king was loyal. When I told Senchae his champion said what he did, I watched his eyes to see if there were any signs of deception. If he had any ill will towards you at all, I'd have known it. The king truly considers himself to be aligned with you. I don't think he'll be a problem.

"Besides," the demon continued sarcastically, "It has given me and my followers someone to kill. If you look behind you, I now have some fresh Skeleton Warriors to command. Granted, it will take a while before their flesh rots off, but in time, they will be a fine addition to my undead army. Don't you think?"

George turned and looked at the bodies as they rose from the floor. They stood in front of the demon. The mage had to move out of the way to allow them to fall into formation for Kepler to command with his thoughts. Without a word being said, the dead left to sit among the trees for the animals to feed on.

The demon said with a smile, "I find it easier and faster to leave them in an open area of the forest. The animals and the bugs can clean their bones faster this way. Give it about 10 Peaks of Bailem or so and we'll have some fresh fighting skeletons that can't die. The only way to kill them is by using fire or . . ." Kepler stopped his sentence. "Well that part doesn't matter."

"I already know, Kepler" the mage replied. "You die, they stop working. You know you're one sick cat, right?" George said as he patted Kepler on the head. "I love you buddy, your my furry ally… your secret is safe with me."

George walked back across the room and waved his hand at the king. He did not offer an explanation of the events, but spoke with Senchae as he released his power over him.

"Nine Peaks of Bailem," the mage said as he walked by. "The Serpent King has been traveling for approximately nine days now. So where does this leave us?"

The king stared into his bloody throne room and did not move. After a moment, George yelled from down the hallway, "Senchae, are you coming or not?"

Chapter 35

𝔚𝔞𝔱𝔢𝔯 𝔐𝔦𝔰𝔱 𝔐𝔞𝔯𝔢𝔰

IT WAS ALMOST LATE BAILEM before Lasidious showed up at the Hall of Judgment to announce where the crystals were. The god knew that the others, including the Book of Immortality, had been waiting for him... all of them sitting patiently around the big table that the Book's golden stand rested on.

"Thank you all for coming," Lasidious said. "I feel it's time to give you all the location of the first piece of the Crystal Moon that has been placed on Grayham."

Mosley interrupted.

"I was under the impression that you were going to divulge the location of *both* pieces of Crystal."

"And I'll do just that, my furry friend, but not today," the God of Mischief said with a smile. "Shall I continue or does anyone else have questions?" Lasidious looked around the table before continuing. "As I was about to say, the first piece has been placed on Scorpion Island at the center of Lake Zandra. I'll—"

Alistar, one of Mosley's team members, interrupted. Adjusting his green robe and running his hands through his short sandy brown hair, he looked directly at Lasidious with a pair of soft brown eyes which only managed to compliment his thin face.

"Lake Zandra is haunted by the Water Mist Mares that you created when we made these worlds. They're deadly. The people of Grayham make it a point to stay away from its shores because they know the mares can destroy the armies of all the kingdoms on Grayham if they weren't bound to the waters of the lake. How do you expect anyone to cross the lake in order to get to the island? The mares patrol the surface of the waters and even if they aren't there when the people try to cross it, they'll definitely be there before they get to the other side. We all know what will happen then.

It will be a quick death, not to mention what the Scorpion King would do if they managed somehow to set foot on his island. I don't see any way for either side to get this piece of the Crystal."

Lasidious laughed.

"Do you think I'd put the Crystal where it stood no chance of recovery? There's no fun in that; and I've told you already that I don't want the worlds destroyed. This is just a game... the Mist Mares have a weakness, don't you remember?"

Everyone in the room nodded their heads in acknowledgment regarding the weakness of the mist mares, but none of them remembered what it was.

Calla, also a member of Mosley's team, spoke up. She brushed her long blonde hair aside as she sat properly with her lacey dress tucked tightly between her legs.

"Okay, so what's the weakness?"

"Hah, you can't be serious. Do you really think I'm going to tell you that? That would ruin the game," Lasidious said, laughing again at his own cleverness.

Mosley shook his head at the ignorance of his team. They had known the God of Mischief for too many seasons to know better but still insisted on asking questions that would never be answered. The wolf decided he better take over the conversation.

"Lasidious," the wolf said, walking around the table. "Please correct me if I'm wrong, but you wouldn't have fun if there wasn't a twist. I believe you may have a clue, or some kind of riddle we could reveal to the people. At least that way, they might stand a chance to fight the Mist Mares."

Lasidious smiled at the wolf.

"You know, Mosley, I'm proud to have you as one of us. Sometimes I get sick of how witless these others are."

The room exploded with anger. Mosley and Lasidious held each other's gaze, a mutual respect passing between them. The fact that they were pursuing different goals did not seem to matter. Lasidious ignored the fuss a bit longer then turned his attention back to the table.

"Pipe down already, I don't care if any of you dislike how I feel about you. If it were up to me, the only one in this room I'd keep around would be Mosley. If I had the power to do so, I'd destroy you all."

The god glanced around the table at the angry faces. When he came to Mieonus and Calla, he decided to calm them down a bit. "Now that I think about it, I would also keep you two lovely goddesses around. You too, Jervaise, you're a beauty when you decide to materialize and join us. You're all far too beautiful to destroy. But you, Lictina... now you're about the most unsightly thing I've ever seen. Put your sick-looking tongue back in your mouth and sit down!"

Those complimented commented on Lasidious's good taste while Lictina lowered her Lizardian-shaped figure into her chair and continued to express her hostility along with the males.

Now the Book of Immortality spoke up, the voice commanding everyone's attention. "I don't know why you're getting worked up! It doesn't matter how Lasidious feels. As long as he doesn't act on his impulses, he's allowed to hate every last one of you. You all came here for a reason. Maybe you should just get the information you came here for and leave until Lasidious is ready to give you the location of the next piece."

Once the room calmed down, Mosley spoke. "So, like I was saying, maybe you have a clue of some sort on how the humans should handle the mares?"

Lasidious smiled and reached into his pocket. He produced two scripted scrolls and laid them on the table.

"I have written a riddle on each of these. Both of them read the same. I'll give one to each team. If any of you try to give the answer of this riddle to the people of Grayham or assist them in any way, the scroll will disappear and return to me. If this happens, I'll destroy the Crystal Moon... and we all know what that means."

The god handed Mosley and Yaloom the parchments and waited for the wolf to walk to the table and lower the parchment from his mouth to the surface.

⊰

Water Mist Mares of Zandra.
Beautiful, but yet so deadly.
A sole reflection.
Their nature is in war.
To govern the lake from shore to shore

⊱

Mosley finished reading. "Sam will figure this out before he's done reading it. He'll have the answer without me telling him a thing... it's pretty clear what you're trying to say here."

Yaloom looked at Mosley. He played with the rings on his fingers as he spoke. "Are you saying that you understand what he has written? What's so clear about it? Explain to us what you know."

The wolf shook his head in disgust. "Yaloom, I'd rather leave you in confusion so I can be sure you won't give the answer to George."

"Who says I'm going to give this to George?" Yaloom snapped. "Maybe I intend to take the information elsewhere."

Mosley shook his head again and turned his attention to Lasidious.

"I think you're right about the intelligence in this room. I've never seen this much ignorance. You know I'm right about your riddle... you know Sam will figure out how to defeat them."

"I agree. It's hard to get one over on him with his superior intellect, but I don't think it will be as simple as you think. There is a twist I assure you."

Lasidious smiled as he patted the wolf's back.

"When can we meet again to discuss the second piece of Crystal?"

"In ten Peaks of Bailem," Lasidious said. "Remember, you aren't to assist the people of Grayham to figure out how to get the first piece."

The God of Mischief then disappeared and the wolf god left for the City of Brandor.

When next he appeared, he was in the king's dining hall. Sam, Shalee, BJ, Helga, and Michael were sitting down to discuss who would be Sam's new advisor.

Michael had asked the king to allow him to stay in the General Absolute's position; he didn't want to be sworn in as Sam's advisor, not being an overly political man. He realized that there is a level of politics in the General's position as well, but he didn't want to be pulled out of the day-to-day dealings of the army. He knew that, to be the king's advisor, he would be involved heavily with the senate and the thought was not appealing to him.

Sam agreed to Michael's request, leaving the king with a decision to make about who his advisor would be. He was quite pleased when Mosley showed up; now he would ask the god for his opinion.

"Mosley, it's good to see you. What brings you here, my friend?"

"I have come to give you news of the whereabouts of the first piece of the Crystal Moon. I have just come from a meeting with Lasidious and the other gods where we were told the crystals is on Scorpion Island, at the center of Lake Zandra."

Both BJ and Michael began to speak at the same moment when they heard this. BJ, realizing they couldn't talk over each other, held his tongue and waited.

"Thank you BJ," Michael said, "so to continue, Lord Mosley, isn't Zandra a doomed body of water? It's haunted by the Mist Mares I believe. No one has ever even set foot on the island except for one man, named Barutomus, and he has long since died. From the writings about his exploits, the island is also covered with giant scorpions. He wrote that they have a king with a poisonous tail over eight feet long. Scorpions aren't to be toyed with. If this island is covered with these creatures, it will be a nightmare to find the Crystal."

Everyone at the table turned to BJ now to hear his response.

"I agree with the General about the scorpions," he said, "but I'm more concerned about the Mist Mares."

He turned to Sam and spoke.

"Our army can fight the scorpions and win, but the mares are haunted. Neither sword nor any other weapon known to us will kill these beasts. They walk on top of the water and are sheer evil, killing everything that has tried to cross the lake. For reasons we don't know, they don't come on the land and no one has ever seen them anywhere other than on the lake. They don't go up or down stream, they look like ghosts, and, from what I've heard, they breathe an icy mist that kills anything it touches. Some stories call them demons, others shades, and still others spirits. No one has ever been able to study their nature, but it everyone within Grayham stays clear of the lake's shores."

Sam stood after hearing both men speak and looked at Mosley.

"Is this all we know about the situation?" He asked calmly.

Mosley smiled. As expected, Sam was thinking beyond the obvious.

The god responded, "Lasidious has given me a scroll to show you. I'm not able to explain its meaning, but it's a riddle that will give you an idea of how to deal with the Water Mist Mares."

Mosley nodded his head and the scroll appeared on the table. The king opened it and placed it flat to read aloud. He wanted to make sure everyone had a chance to give input on its meaning.

❧

Water Mist Mares of Zandra.
Beautiful, but yet so deadly.
A sole reflection.
Their nature is in war.
To govern the lake from shore to shore

❧

Sam lifted his head after reading the scroll and scanned the room for clues. He had a good idea what the answer was, but he wanted to see if anyone else had a guess. He smiled at the commotion around the table and watched as everyone passed the scroll around. He knew that looking too deep into a riddle's meaning was what Lasidious had hoped they would do and, by the looks of their blank stares, they were doing exactly that. After a while he took the scroll and asked for answers. Michael spoke first.

"My king, by the looks of it, none of us have a guess as to its meaning."

Shalee looked at her husband and smiled.

"Sam Goodrich," she snapped. "You stop this right now and tell us what the meaning is. I know you figured it out as soon as you read it. Stop toying with us and give us the answer or I'll…" The sorceress tapped the butt end of Precious on the floor and smiled at her lover without finishing her statement.

Other than Shalee, the only people in the room who understood her actions were BJ, Helga and the king himself. BJ and Helga laughed.

BJ said, "Well, you have to admire her tact, sire. Only your queen would say something like that to you in a meeting of this magnitude."

"Agreed, BJ," Sam replied as he winked at his lovely, pregnant wife. "You've got to love our queen; she's quite the handful."

Michael and Mosley looked at each other, then shrugged the shoulders.

"Okay, well the answer is that the power of the Mist Mares is in a reflection. The problem that we need to figure out is which one holds the power. If we kill that specific one, the others will most likely either die or become harmless."

"What do you mean by a reflection, sire?" Michael asked.

"I'm referring to the sole reflection of the mare that is created by the water beneath its feet. I believe this is the source of their power. The problem is: which mare is it?"

Mosley smiled and announced that he could not help any further. He said his farewells and disappeared.

After he was gone, BJ looked at the group and said, "I swear to you that the gods meddle in our lives way too much. I liked my life better when I didn't have to worry about such things and I just trained fighters."

"Well, just think of how much more *interesting* your life will be now that I have decided on you for my advisor," Sam said. "You'll have to deal with the gods and the senate."

Helga screamed, jumped from her chair and ran around the table. She pulled BJ from his chair and hugged him as Michael looked at Sam. It was clear to see that the king's General Absolute had a question, so Sam motioned for him to speak.

"Sire," he said, carefully choosing his words, "I'd like to understand your decision to make BJ your advisor. I'd like to know, and I mean no offence by this BJ, exactly what qualifies a teacher of weaponry to perform these duties?"

Sam smiled. "No offense taken. Let's just say, General that I feel he'll do a good job. I'm making my decision on a gut feeling. I'm sure you know what I mean. When you're in a battle and the fighting is chaotic, it's your instincts that help you make your decisions. You know and trust those feelings despite what everyone else thinks. I want you to support this and understand that it is my instinct that tells me this is a good thing."

Michael stood from the table and bowed to his king indicating he understood and accepted Sam's decision. "Shall I prepare for our advance on Lake Zandra? The Scorpion King's Island is small enough that we should be able to take just one of our Legions and hunt for the Crystal. I'll prepare the army and leave the problem of the Mist Mares up to you, if that's okay with you, sire."

Sam agreed.

"I'll send word ahead of us to tell Branson, the Legion leader of the City of Cottle, to be ready within three Peaks of Bailem for our arrival," Michael said. "We can leave tomorrow as it will take us two Peaks of Bailem by hippogriff to get there. We can march to Lake Zandra and prepare to cross to the island from its southern shores taking about another five Peaks of Bailem, maybe fewer if everything goes well and the army is prepared. We can use the cities' newly-built harvest wagons to carry as many boats as we can fit on them. The rest will need to be shouldered by the men. Since this city is close to the Ocean of Utopia's shores, they should be done taking their crops to the coast, so by the time we get there, everyone should be ready and the large wagons will come in handy. What do you think, sire?"

Sam was impressed with this quick decision-making.

"It sounds like a fine plan, General. BJ will stay here and run Brandor in my absence while Shalee and I go with Michael to retrieve the Crystal. If there are no further questions, I say we get moving."

Helga jumped from her seat. "What about me, sire? I also have some abilities that could be useful. I did train your wife to use her magic, you know. I should come with you in case there is a magical emergency."

Sam laughed.

"A magical emergency, aye, well…" He would have objected but he watched as Shalee gave Helga a high five and knew it would be a waste of time. "I guess it's settled then. Let's get moving."

Two Peaks of Bailem Later

LASIDIOUS appeared to Yaloom in his home as he wanted to find out what the evil team leader was planning to do with the scroll that he had been given.

"What do you want, Lasidious?" Yaloom snapped.

"I want to know when you're going to tell somebody about the scroll I gave you. For the last two days, I've watched you and all you've done is sit here and look at the words on it. What's the problem?"

Lasidious watched Yaloom move to look over the railing at his waterfall.

"I can't figure out what its meaning is and it's bothering me," he said as he played with the flawless, gem covered rings on his fingers. "I'll find George as soon as I figure it out."

Lasidious blew, his voice filled with anger.

"Are you so stupid that you'll allow your ignorance of the scroll's meaning to stop you from giving George an extra two days to go after the Crystal? You're wasting valuable time trying to satisfy your own pride. Meanwhile, your chances to collect the Crystal are fading. The King of Brandor is on his way to the City of Cottle right now to meet with his army and march to the lake."

Mieonus appeared. The yellow gown she wore was stunning and complimented her olive skin. She quickly pushed her brunette hair from her face and agreed with Lasidious.

"I've been telling you the same thing for the last two days, Yaloom... but he won't listen to me. I agree with you, Lasidious, he doesn't need to know the scrolls meaning to allow George to see it, but he won't move from this spot."

Lasidious screamed loudly as he called for the Book of Immortality to make an appearance. It was only a brief moment before the Book appeared and the god began to speak.

"I've called you here to let you know I've decided to take the team lead away from Yaloom and give it to Mieonus. It's obvious he doesn't have the intellect or the ambition to lead his team to victory. A change needs to be made."

Mieonus ran across the room, grabbed the scroll from the table and disappeared to meet with George.

Yaloom exploded with anger as this happened. "I have the mind to—"

"To what? Even if we weren't governed by the Book's laws, you aren't powerful enough to challenge me. I'd destroy you. You're pathetic and always will be."

Yaloom started to raise his hands to send his power against Lasidious, when the Book floated between them. "I suggest you think about your actions, Yaloom. If you do this, I'll retaliate and you will be destroyed."

Lasidious laughed wickedly in the background, taunting Yaloom to use his powers. He wanted the Book to destroy his enemy, so he made degrading statements to instigate an attack. After listening to this verbal assault, the God of Greed managed to calm himself. Disappointed, Lasidious vanished.

Bloodvain's Throne Room

MIEONUS appeared in the barbarian king's throne room when the only person besides the guards was Senchae. The guards took their defensive positions, preparing to attack whereupon the goddess held up her hand and caused everything in the room except the king, to stop moving.

"Senchae, where's George?"

"Who are you to enter my throne room and demand information from *me*?"

"I'm Mieonus," she replied.

Senchae held her gaze, despite his confusion, and responded, "Is this name supposed to mean something to me?"

He realized the woman in front of him was using similar magic as George's so he didn't want to be too bold. He'd been aggressive around this kind of magic before and it nearly cost him his son's life, not to mention his own.

Mieonus was annoyed the king didn't recognize her as a goddess.

"You're wasting my time, Barbarian,' she snapped, "Now where's George?"

"I'm here," the mage replied, entering the room. "How can I help you this fine day . . . and to whom do I have the pleasure of speaking with?"

As always, George was charismatic toward a woman he didn't know.

"My name is Mieonus, and I'm here to give you this scroll."

George was not familiar with the name, but he was sweet to her, careful not to ruin a chance to gain an advantage.

"It's nice to meet you, Mieonus. May I say you look lovely? So what's this scroll that you're referring to?"

The goddess enjoyed his compliment and tossed him the scroll. "This should have been given to you two days ago. Brandor has a head start and I'm sorry for that. It's the key to get past the Water Mist Mares of Lake Zandra."

She watched as George opened it and read the contents of the riddle.

Looked up at her he said, "Should I understand what this means?"

"I can't answer your question regarding this riddle. It's for you to figure out. All I can tell you is that Lasidious has placed the first missing piece of the Crystal Moon on Scorpion Island."

George looked at the Barbarian king to see if this rang a bell. "Do you know where this Scorpion Island is, Senchae?"

"I know it's at the center of Lake Zandra in the Kingdom of Brandor. My people haven't spent much time in that area and I can't tell you much about it. However, I do know the lake is haunted and it's said there are demon horses that live on the lake's waters."

Mieonus was taken back at the king's lack of knowledge, let

alone his total ignorance of the Mist Mares. She knew she couldn't say anything to assist them so in reality, the visit was a complete waste of time; she excused herself and vanished.

Senchae looked at George and shrugged his shoulders. "I wonder what that was all about... do you know anything about this missing piece of the Crystal Moon? The Crystal Moon is what keeps all the planets that the gods—"

"—Yes, I know, I know... it keeps the worlds separated," the mage said. "If it isn't put back together soon, everything will end. It's missing. Does this riddle mean anything to you?"

The Barbarian looked at the scroll but shook his head no, as George expected. All the king could say is that he knew the lake was haunted and that part of its shores bordered the Serpent King's kingdom. The mage sent a guard to retrieve his pack and when he returned with it, George studied his map to find the lake. He realized he could make it there within six Peaks of Bailem if he left right now and it would also give him a chance to do some reconnaissance. After thinking for a while, he came up with a plan.

Before George gave his orders, he motioned for all the king's guards to clear the room. The mage was not the king but the Barbarians had no confusion as to who was running things. As long as George kept Senchae's pride intact and gave his orders out of earshot of the king's subjects, he could do whatever he wanted.

Once they were gone, George said, "Senchae, I want you to gather the army and prepare for war. From the way it sounds, there won't be much the army can do to collect this piece of the Crystal since you don't know where it is. The Serpent King isn't due to arrive here for another seven Peaks of Bailem so I'll leave now and teleport to the City of Champions. From there I'll circle the east side of the lake to its southern shores and see if I can gather some information. If we're lucky, I'll be able to learn more about these demon mares."

George paused, waiting to see if the Barbarian king understood the plan; then continued... "I'll make it back in time to meet with the Serpent King, then teleport the Serpent back to his home, or at least as close to his home as I possibly can, where we'll mobilize his snake army. If Brandor can retrieve the Crystal before we can,

I'll attack the Kingdom of Brandor from the west with the Serpent King's army and work our way to the east."

The mage paused again but this time for a different reason. He knew his friend Kepler was watching from the shadows and had crept in closer to listen to their conversation. George had put a spell on Kepler that indicated when the beast was around. He didn't like the idea that the demon cat could hide in the smallest of shadows without him knowing about it. The way his brothers had appeared outside the Cave of Sorrow the day Kroger died was eerie to say the least. He knew the beast was his ally, but he also knew the cat was a master manipulator like he was... and manipulators always had to be alert to other manipulators.

"Kepler, my friend, if you wanted to listen to what I was saying, you only had to walk in and make yourself at home. I keep no secrets from you... we're partners, remember?"

The cat emerged from the shadows. "How did you know I was there, George? And since when did you start having conversations without me present?"

The mage laughed.

"Relax, some lady appeared and threw me this scroll. I assume she was one of the gods, but I didn't confirm it. Her name was Mieonus, does it ring a bell?"

"Yes, she is the Goddess of Hate," Kepler responded. "What's the message she gave you?"

George held it up and said, "It's about the Mist Mares of Lake Zandra, but Senchae doesn't know what it means. I was about to leave to gather some information on this situation. Apparently the first piece of the Crystal Moon is located on an island at the center of the lake."

Kepler shook his head. "Well, it's a good thing I showed up then. I know something of the Mist Mares. I also know the island is covered with giant scorpions. We will have no problem moving around on the island if you can keep us from being seen by the Scorpion King and his creepy subjects. It's the Mist Mares we have to worry about. They can see everything that is unseen to the naked eye. I know this first hand as I tried to take a drink from the lake one night when I was traveling; they charged me. Somehow they saw me but I was able to run back from the lake's shores to get away from them. They stopped before coming on the land. If they could have left the waters, they would have. I've never seen such anger in a beast. They must be bound to the lake somehow. If you can get us past them, we'll have an easy chance to get the Crystal. The shortest distance to the island is from the north side of the lake, so that's where we should go. If we can get past the mares, it will only be a half-day swim. I hope you're in good shape."

"Swim, who needs to swim? George said, "I'll create an ice raft and we can sail across. The only problem I really have is with this riddle... I don't know what it means. Apparently it holds the key to getting past our demon pony problem."

George lowered it to the floor and spread it out so they could read it together.

"This seems very straight-forward to me," Kepler said with pride. "The reflection of one of the mares holds the key to their power. The real problem you have is which one, but I think I know the answer to that, too. When I watched the mares from the shores that night, I noticed one of them always stayed a few hundred feet away from the others. Every once in a while the herd would send another to take its place. This mare would stay clear of the rest of them until another was sent to take its place. If you could figure out a way to hold this creature in one spot and disturb the water beneath it, there would be no reflection for it to retrieve its powers from, then we could cross. The good thing is that this mare was always the same distance from the others and followed the herd. I can draw their attention and you can see if this brings the other one close enough for you to use your magic."

George bent down after looking at his map.

"This is good," George smiled. "We will go to Athena's home tonight and in the morning teleport to the City of Champions to depart for Zandra's northern shore. We'll have two days to find the Crystal before the Serpent King arrives. Senchae can have his scouts keep the snakes busy and you could get Maldwin to help them with this for me until we get back, if you don't mind?"

George leaned in and hugged his demon friend around the neck. Since the giant cat's next was shoulder level, it wasn't hard to do.

"You're turning out to be a regular Book of Knowledge, Kepler. What would I do without you?"

"I'm glad you're happy with me, George," the demon responded uneasily, "but do you think you could stop with all this touchy feely stuff? It's kind of appalling to have a human be so caring towards me after I've spent so many years eating your kind. My brothers have been making fun of me."

This was now George's opportunity to poke his own kind of fun at the jaguar. With the same voice he used to speak to his dog back on Earth, he slowly walked towards Kepler in a stalking manner. The cat backed up as his friend came closer.

"Doesn't my furry little demon Kepler love his Georgy Worgy? He needs kisses—oh yes he does—come here and give daddy kisses. Daddy George loves you so much . . . oh, yes he does."

The Barbarian king laughed as he watched George chase the demon out of the room trying to hug him.

The Grayham Inquirer

When inquiring minds need to know where their favorite characters are.

GEORGE left the City of Bloodvain, teleporting with Kepler and one of his tiger subjects to Athena's home. His wife's pregnancy was causing her some emotional stress, so rather than leaving in the morning; George decided to stay to pamper her, reinforcing his love for Athena.

Neither the mage nor Kepler knew that this late start would be to their benefit. They would not teleport to the City of Champions until Early Bailem the following day

SAM'S hippogriff already landed along with the others. As Michael had ordered, the king's army was ready. Immediately, they began their march toward Lake Zandra, which would take nearly five Peaks of Bailem.

Shalee and Helga were preparing for their journey with the king. Shalee gave her friend the cape she took from Double D the day he died knowing that the Island of the Scorpion King was going to be a nasty place and they would need every advantage they could find including the invisibility cape. The army would be busy fighting the giant bugs while Shalee helped Sam fight with the army; then Helga could use the cape to search for the Crystal.

The ladies did not tell Sam of their plan; they wanted to surprise him with the news once Helga re-

turned with the Crystal. Shalee gave her friend the other half of a *pendant necklace* she had made and the ladies embraced. Soon they were riding with the army on horseback.

LASIDIOUS was on his way to the World of Luvelles. He was not going there to meet with Celestria, but rather to talk with the Head Master, Brayson Id. He would appear to the Head Master looking like, Amar, the Head Masters good friend and old, Mystic-Learner!

There were many details which needed to be discussed and planning the future was in order to continue to create diversions to keep the god's attentions away from his soon to be, newborn son. Amar was the only man capable of pulling this off, but since Amar was dead, thanks to George's handy work, Lasidious would have to make it appear as if he was still alive.

BJ sat on the throne, pretending to be the king. He asked everyone to leave the room, then lowered himself into the chair to get an idea of how Sam felt. As it turned out, he pushed his luck a bit too far by having the cook bring him his meal where he sat. When the woman arrived, she scolded BJ and pulled him from the room by his ear. She dragged the advisor into the royal dining hall and sat him in a chair.

When BJ tried to object, the woman, almost 20 years his senior, instructed him to be silent and eat his dinner without causing her further trouble. The advisor had to smile. He had always been taught to respect his elders... he ate without question.

BJ fell asleep later that night having wonderful dreams of Helga. In his visions, they were standing near a brook which peacefully cascaded down a small embankment and into a shallow pool. Sam stood in front of them with Shalee standing to Helga's left as her maid of honor. To BJ's right, Michael, the General Absolute handed him the ring he would use to promise his love to Helga for all time. The ceremony was short, but lovely and the kiss between the two of them celebrating their union was full of promise. It was the best dream BJ had ever had.

Thank you for reading the Grayham Inquirer

Chapter 36

May the Best Man Win

Five Peaks of Bailem later

SAM, Michael, Shalee and Helga stood on the shores of Lake Zandra. It wasn't long after the waters had been disturbed that the Water Mist Mares appeared and, as night approached, the king asked the General to have the army set up camp.

Michael did as instructed and established a post at a safe distance away to watch the ghostly beings throughout the night. He ordered some of the men to disturb the waters of the lake by throwing rocks, allowing them to observe the behavior of the mares. Despite the aggressive nature of these creatures, they were beautiful, like spirits hovering above the lake's surface as they threatened the army. Their hoofs never touched the water, nor did the mares come ashore. Their bodies moved with a graceful deadliness that complemented the glow of their white coats as the light faded.

The cries of the beasts sounded like any normal horse, but every now and then, a shriek penetrated the air from one that had been isolated a few hundred feet away. Every time this cry occurred, Sam noticed another member of the herd would move to take its place as if relieving it from guard duty. By Early Bailem, Sam had the solution to their problem.

Lake Zandra's Northern Shore

GEORGE, Kepler, and the accompanying tiger arrived on the north shores, opposite of Sam's army. Kepler was disturbing the waters waiting for the Mist Mares to appear, but nothing was happening.

"This doesn't make any sense," Kepler said. "They should be here by now—these creatures are fast. It doesn't matter where they are on the lake, they should be here by now."

"I don't know where they're at, or why they aren't here, but I know that I can teleport us all back to shore if they come. Let's get going and make a run for it."

"And exactly how do you intend to run across water?"

"Not literally run, dummy. Watch this."

The mage touched the water and an ice raft began to form. Once they were aboard, George lowered his hand into the water and conjured a powerful wind with his fingertips. The big sheet of ice glided through the water toward the island.

Back on the Southern Shore

MICHAEL ordered the army to prepare the boats for crossing. Now all that remained was for Sam and Shalee to figure out the problem with the mares.

"Shalee," Sam said, "Come here for a minute. Do you see the mare that keeps to itself isolated from the rest of the herd?"

"I do."

"Use your magic to hold the beast in place. I'll use my bow to disturb the waters beneath it and we'll see what happens then."

Shalee tried, "Damn!"

"What is it? What's wrong?"

"I can't reach it. It's too far offshore... I need to get closer."

"General, have the men throw stones into the water down shore. I need them to keep the herd's attention while the queen moves closer to the waterline."

"Yes, sire."

The herd took the bait and Shalee made it to the water's edge, waving her hands through the air. This time the mare was in range and it became stuck in place as a result of the queen's magic.

The ghostly horse cried for the others. They charged at Shalee as she teleported away from the water's edge, barely vanishing in time to avoid the herd's deadly mist.

"Holy crap," Shalee yelled. "That was too close. I felt the chill!"

Sam replied, "Maybe this isn't such a good idea. I don't want to get us killed going after the Crystal. Maybe I should take the army home."

Shalee grabbed his arm and pulled him away from everyone.

"Look, you and I both know we need this piece of the Crystal to save the worlds from destruction. It was a close call, but this is our lives now. We're just going to have to buck up and get the job done."

"I know, but I feel so overwhelmed. If you get hurt, I'll fall apart. You're the only thing keeping me together through all of this. I'm really not cut out for this, Shalee. I try to put on a strong face, but all I want to do is go home. I wish I could wake up and this whole crazy world would be nothing more than a bad dream. I miss home babe and I just don't want to do this anymore."

"I know and I understand how you feel. I miss home too, but it's gone and you and I are stuck here, whether we like it or not. You're strong, Sam, Bassorine saw to that. I should not be telling you this, but the reason you're so gifted is because Bassorine made sure that you were blessed. Haven't you ever wondered why you have the abilities to remember the things that you do. Don't you ever wonder why you learn so quickly? Haven't you ever wondered why you were so athletically inclined? All this is because of Bassorine. He asked our gods of Earth to give you the abilities you have. You and I were selected to come to Grayham before we were born. I want to tell you more, but I can't. I need you to be strong. Without your strength, I also would've fallen apart a long time ago. I look up to you and so does this army. Show them why the gods chose you!"

"How long have you known this?"

"How long doesn't matter... I can't tell you anymore right now. What matters is that you and I have no Earth to go home to and this isn't a dream we can wake up from. And unless we figure this mess out, we may not have this home either. Sam . . . I need to feed from your strength." The sorceress lifted his chin. "There's some good news though, that I think will make you happy."

Sam took a deep breath. "And what would that be?"

"The mare is still bound by my magic."

"Since when did you become such a leader, Shalee?"

"How about we finish this conversation later, maybe when we are alone?" She pinched his butt. "Now get to work!"

Sam lifted his bow and aimed at the feet of the bound mare. As soon as the water beneath its feet was disturbed, the others shimmered as if losing their form. He waited for the water to settle; once again the herd solidified as they screamed with anger.

"Did you see that, General?" Sam yelled. "Get over here! Watch this."

Again Sam shot the bow and again the herd shimmered.

"General, the herd is affected when the water beneath this single mare is disturbed. I want all the archers to aim for this spot."

"Yes, sire!"

Soon the herd of mist mares no longer had the power to maintain their form and faded into nothingness, leaving only the lead ghostly mare spirit to be captured.

Sam looked at Shalee. "Okay, now that we've got just the one mare to deal with, how long do you think your magic will hold her there?"

Shalee sighed. "Not long enough for the army to cross the lake, I'm afraid. And we still have to get us all back again as well."

"That's not quite what I had in mind." The king thought a moment. "Okay, the mare is unable to come on land, so if we put it on the dirt, maybe it will lose its power."

Shalee grabbed his arm as he started to walk off. "You don't need to go out there. Besides, he may still be able to use his icy breath. Let me bring it here."

The sorceress raised her hand and the ghostly mare floated toward them. The archers adjusted their aim to keep the waters beneath it disturbed. Everyone cleared a circle for Shalee to set the mare down, being careful to stay far enough away so the misty breath from the ghostly beast could not reach them. As she began to lower the mare to the ground, the creature cried, filling the air with a horrid shriek. The men grabbed their ears in pain. The cry was so loud that Shalee lost her concentration and the beast fell to the earth. As soon as the first hoof touched the ground, a brilliant burst of light shot into the sky. Even though it was now only the

Peak of Bailem, it could be seen for miles around. The army was thrown to their backs as a burst of forced air smashed into them.

The rest of the herd reappeared and hurried off of the lake's surface, running past the army. Their hoofs now touched the ground as they ran freely across the countryside with a trampling thunder. Grayham now had its first pack of wild ghostly mares.

Sam quickly made sure no one was hurt.

"It seems that they no longer have the ability to kill... they ran right through us. I just might have to hunt them down and figure out a way to capture one of them as my own for a mount."

Shalee slapped his arm. "Hey, don't forget to capture me one too."

Michael picked himself up and rubbed his eyes. "I've never, in my entire life seen anything so amazing. When that mare exploded, it had to be the brightest light ever created."

Sam tapped on the General's shoulders after brushing himself off. He pointed to the sun and said. "What about that light?"

"Very funny, sire; maybe you should try your hand at theatre some day."

"What? I've already tried theatre. Didn't you enjoy my performance with Double D back in Brandor?"

Michael rolled his eyes and shouted for the men to ready their boats. Sam smiled at his reaction and took Shalee by the hand, leading her to one of the boats where they both jumped in. It was not long before the entire legion was rowing to Scorpion Island. As they crossed, Shalee winked at Helga and gave her the thumbs up. The elderly sorceress smiled and draped the cape over her shoulders. She would put the hood up once she set foot on the island and begin looking for the Crystal.

George, Kepler and the Tiger Approach the Island

GEORGE waved his free hand over the group as they drew closer to the island. Each of them vanished as they prepared for their secret invasion of the Scorpion King's kingdom. They all had seen the bright flash to the south but could only guess at its origination, so they blew it off without much discussion.

The icy raft ran onto the shore and the rocks crunched into the ice, making plenty of noise, alerting three giant scorpions who turned quickly to investigate. Everyone exited the raft and moved away from the poisonous creatures stealthily, observing the creature's movements and being careful not to make any further noise.

George was awed by their size, but he was not so taken that he felt the need to get a better look. They were massive and, from where he stood, what he could see was enough. Their tails were at least six or seven feet long with stingers sharpened to a fine point while their mouths seemed to have two mandible-like scissors. Their big, beady eyes gave him chills and he was sure they would zoom in on him at any moment. The top of their shell-like backs were waist high and the pinchers at the end of their two front appendages could easily tear a man in half. He had never seen a scorpion up close and just these three were more than he ever wanted to see again. The mage motioned for the group to stay quiet and move on.

The shores of the island were rocky, but, as they traveled inland, the ground became more like desert. They kept attracting attention to themselves as the sand was flipping up into the air with each footstep, and their footprints left a trail right to them.

They needed a diversion so George released the magic that kept the extra tiger hidden. Once the cat was visible, the beast became the scorpion's new target. The big cat took off running as the scorpions gave chase. Once they were far enough away, George spoke.

"I think the tiger should be quick enough to outrun them for a while, don't you?"

"That was mean, George. But I love it," Kepler said. "Let's pick up the pace while the going is good."

"Yeah, let's go."

They both ran within his spell of invisibility. Eventually, after much searching, they found a cave leading deep into the ground. The sand gave way to a much harder surface where they no longer had to worry about leaving tracks. Slowly, they began their descent into the hole. George used his magic to help him see through the darkness.

Sam's Army Has Landed
The South Side of Scorpion Island

SAM jumped from the boat while the general ordered the army to form ranks. Suddenly the tiger crested the hill running towards them with over 600 giant scorpions in tow behind him.

"Prepare for battle," Sam cried as he grabbed Kael. "Val arrna, coia, ngw, vara poy. " Kael burst into flames, extended his length an additional eight feet and put an area of protection 15 feet around the king to protect him from the scorpion venom.

The men gave their battle cries and prepared for the massive collision that was about to take place. Shalee waved her hand over Sam and Michael and toughened their skin against the scorpions' stingers, then lifted her staff into the air and shouted, "Val arrna, coia korons." The air filled with meteoric balls of fire that fell to the top of the hill killing 47 of the giant arachnids in the blast. Scorpion body parts went flying in many different directions as Sam's army screamed with excitement at the power of their queen.

The tiger, seeing the group ahead, hoped to find a way to shake the angry scorpions that chased him. The beast was frightened, even though he had a lead, knowing full well that a giant sting from one scorpion's tail could end his life. As he got close to the army, the cat spun around to face the charging horde, signaling to the army that he intended to fight beside them.

Sam yelled, "General, protect the cat. Shalee, use your magic to capture it."

The sorceress did as instructed. Lifting the cat into the air with just a wave of her hand, she sent the beast floating after placing him safely in one of the boats.

The queen turned and readied herself to assist the army. "Are you ready, Helga?"

"Don't worry about me, child, I'm ready."

Shalee watched as Helga put the hood of Double D's old cape

over her head and disappeared. The older sorceress began to walk around the oncoming scorpions as Shalee sent another wave of fiery meteors crashing into the skittish horde of poisoners, sending the body parts of another 53 scorpions flying in countless directions. Again the army cried out as the General ordered the soldiers to attack. An enormous eruption filled the air as Sam's legion of men, 2,533 strong, ran into the battle. The Sword of Truth and Might screamed for blood as Sam charged into the horror joining his brave men.

George and Kepler are Holding Tight

THE CRIES of Sam's army echoed off the cave walls as George and Kepler descended deeper and deeper into the giant underground lair of the Scorpion King. Suddenly, they found themselves pushed up against the cave's wall, although still invisible, George used a protective barrier to protect them. The scorpions were responding to the screams above ground, George estimated that over 800 of them had passed by their unseen position. Whatever was happening up top was commanding a lot of attention and eventually the cave was empty allowing the two to walk about wherever they wanted.

The cave was dark and dismal, and smelled of waste. It was impossible to take a step without getting garesh all over their feet and shoes. Eventually they found a branch of the cave that split off with a pedestal at the end of the narrow pathway. George walked slowly towards it.

"Kepler, hide in the shadows while I go to investigate the area."

"I don't like this, George. I think we should stay together."

"Just relax . . . how does a demon as huge as you get so scared?"

"I'm not scared. I'm sensible. Splitting up isn't smart."

"I'm only going to be 50 feet away. I'll be right back. I want to see if the Crystal is here. Just stay put and keep an eye out, okay? Come get me if you see anything."

"Okay, but hurry!"

George moved in to stand over the pedestal. To his surprise a piece of the Crystal, just like the one he had just before falling through the floor back at the Temple of the Gods, rested on top of it. He lifted it from its resting spot—keeping his magic at the ready.

Once the mage saw everything was okay, he called Kepler and touched the cat's back. Both of them closed their eyes and when they reopened them, they were still standing beside the pedestal.

"Garesh," George whispered.

"What is it?"

"I have used too much power. It'll be awhile before I can get us out of here."

"This isn't good. Those creepy things could come back anytime now."

"I know, let's think a minute."

The mage scanned the area to create a plan. He still had two unused snare scrolls from his trip to the Cave of Sorrows so he pulled them out.

"Just stay away from the areas I use these scrolls on. Their magic should stop any wandering scorpions and give us a chance to kill them. We can hide until I have the power to get us out of here."

Helga Begins Her Descent

HELGA, now in the cave as well, was thoroughly disgusted by the rank smell, and lifted her robe to keep it from touching the garesh-covered floor. Despite her revulsion, she moved quickly, having discovered the cave by following the scorpions' trails from the southern shores. The way in was surprisingly easy since it appeared to be clear of the poisonous creatures—but she still wore the cape's hood just in case and proceeded with caution.

Before long, she too found the narrow pathway leading to the pedestal.

"This has to be it," she whispered. "Shalee is going to be so proud, and I can't wait to see Sam's face."

Slowly, she tiptoed towards the pedestal, scanning the cave to make sure she was alone. It appeared that none of the scorpions were present. But without knowing it, she gave her position away to the demon jaguar hiding in the shadows. Kepler's ears snapped to attention and his demon eyes searched the cave. He saw nothing, but the cat knew something was out there. He lifted his nose and searched for a scent... woman. Her unique smell said she was moving toward the pedestal. The demon gave a wry smile as he waited.

He didn't have to wait for long as the woman whispered curses as she found herself trapped in George's snare.

"Damn, damn... I can't believe this! How could I be so stupid!" She kept her voice low to avoid attention; unaware that a cat listened trying to determine the height and place the voice was coming from.

Kepler crouched with a low growl, preparing to attack with a quick strike to her head... when suddenly a large scorpion rounded the corner. The monster was nearly a foot longer in its poison-filled tail than the others had been. This had to be their king.

Helga knew her whispers had attracted the beast but she was still invisible which helped keep her position hidden.

Oh no . . . It must have heard me, she thought. Stay still and don't make another noise old girl. Maybe it will go away.

Still, Helga began to panic as the monstrous Scorpion King scurried towards her. She stood as still as she possibly could, but the sorceress knew that as the creature grew closer, it would run right into her. If she stayed quiet maybe the beast would just bump into her and move on.

She wanted to use her staff's magic, but would have to remove the hood of the cape and reveal herself to do it. The cape's power would not allow for destructive magic since it was strictly designed for stealth.

She had seen the numbers of these scorpions and knew that her power was not enough to hold them all off. If she lowered her hood and spoke the words of power necessary to kill this one, the others would come and she would be in a worse situation than she was in now. She decided to stay silent and hope for the best.

George watched from behind the pedestal as the scorpion approached. He could see the size difference and it was unnerving. He was hiding behind the pillar, and could not leave until enough power had been restored, to teleport him and Kepler out. He could not see Helga, nor had he heard her when she became trapped. All he knew was that he might have to use more of his power if the beast did not cross one of the snares' locations soon. He readied his sword to kill the creature, encouraged by the path the scorpion had chosen.

Suddenly the mage was aware of Kepler's presence and he waited to see what the jaguar's intent was. He had told the demon to hide near the scorpion, but given the current situation, it was obvious why the cat had moved.

Kepler whispered to his friend from the shadows. "There's a woman. She must be using a spell to keep herself from being seen. She's stuck in your snare George... the scorpion's going to run into her."

George smiled, but did not respond. Sure enough, the giant insect made contact with the invisible woman, and the mage listened as she made a fatal mistake.

"Ohhh," Helga squealed, then immediately cupped her hand over her mouth. She watched with horror as the Scorpion King took a defensive position as began to use his massive pinchers to feel around.

Please move on... please move on, she thought. *Just move on, there's nothing here for you to feed on.*

Helga watched the first three passes of the giant's powerful claws miss her... but the fourth pass found her leg. The beast began to squeeze, creating tremendous pain. Now the sorceress ripped her hood away and began to speak her words of power.

Her command started with her staff's name, a name that her teacher had hated when she was a younger sorceress in training. Her teacher exploded when Helga gave the staff a name longer than one syllable, telling her the name took too much time to be spoken. On this day, the sorceress would realize the consequences of her mistake. She had named her staff, 'Your Majesty.' Helga gave her staff the name out of ignorance and a sense of fun, never realizing the seriousness she might one day have to face. Once pronounced, the staff's name couldn't be changed.

"Your Majesty, Na—" Helga was stopped in the middle of her command. The scorpion's massive stinger barreled its way through the air as she spoke and buried itself deep within her chest. She would have finished speaking her final word but the force of the collision knocked the air out of her. The word was lost forever as the poison filled her body. The last thing the sorceress would ever see would not be the love of her life, BJ or Sam or Shalee, but would be the beady eyes of the killer insect as it moved in to take her face in its mandibles to rip it apart.

Back on the Southern Shore of the Island

SHALEE'S body count was growing. She sent magical arrows covered with fire into the masses of the Scorpion King's army and the scorpions were falling, body parts of both beast and man were everywhere. The ground was saturated with both the blood of men and the oozing, green slime which acted as the scorpion's life-force. By the end of the fight, the sorceress would kill over 356 of these giant insects, but not without a few casualties to Sam's army.

Sam's men had slain another 703 of the giants, as the king and General continued to plow their way through the enemy. The magic Shalee had used to toughen their skin prevented the scorpions' stingers from penetrating their bodies and her husband's sword cut through the beasts like butter. Michael stayed within the 15-foot radius of Kael's protection, and fought beside his king. Both he and Sam were tearing through the enemy like forces of nature.

Sam had released a feverish thrill as Kael sliced through the giant beasts, causing them to scream horribly. Back and forth, back and forth, he swung Kael's extended blade of fire through the air as the Sword of the Gods cut through their numbers. Once in awhile the sword would pass, without ill effect, through Michael and the other members of his army who fought near him.

"Now this is what I call a fight," he screamed to his General as they moved toward the top of the hill.

"Agreed, sire," Michael shouted, catching one of the tails in his hand and severing it with his blade. He gave a downward thrust to the giant's back and listened to its nightmarish squeal as it died. "That was 37, sire."

"That's it? I'm at 71." A moment later he screamed again. "Make that 74."

The General shook his head and kept fighting. A long while later the fighting finally stopped as the last giant scorpion lay dead. In total, the king had lost 502 men; another 143 lay wounded. Sixty-three of those men would not live through the night as the poison injected into their bodies was far too toxic. The General ordered the healers to attend to them just the same, as the rest of the men stacked the dead on the boats to be taken home.

Meanwhile, Shalee was worried about Helga; she had hoped the older woman would have returned by now. She figured she would tell Sam and then go look for her.

"We have a problem."

"What's that?" Sam asked, tossing one of the giant's stingers to the ground.

"Helga was wearing the assassin's cape and she went to go find the Crystal. I'm worried about her."

"What? Why would she do that? Where did she go?"

"I think that I've made a bad decision. She went to find the Crystal, but I don't know where."

"Dang it, Shalee!" Sam shouted.

Sam immediately assembled 100 of his men and began to follow the scorpions' tracks to the cave. Shalee had to use her magic to keep up with the group, her fear for Helga's safety increased as they ran.

They entered the cave. Shalee commanded the darkness to give way to the light. The king led the way and, after awhile they found the area where Helga had been snared. The Scorpion King had severed Helga's legs and tried to back out of the area while dragging her body. The giant insect had become caught in the second snare and was still working hard to get free.

Sam tried to stop his wife from turning the corner once he saw the bloody mess. "You don't want to go in there. Why don't you let me handle this one? I'll come back to the boat shortly, okay?"

The queen could see the sorrow in his eyes but needed to look for herself. She pushed past him and, as she rounded the corner, lifted her hands to her mouth.

"NO, NO, NO... Helga NO!" she screamed as she quickly thrust her right hand forward. Thousands of iron-like needles flew from her fingertips and buried deep into the Scorpion King's body. The cave filled with the monster's piercing cries as it fell heavily to the floor, jerking with its last breath 'til it finally became still... and quite dead.

George watched from behind the pillar as Shalee took the insect's life. He realized his power to teleport had finally returned, but this scene was too priceless to leave. He wanted to watch it to its conclusion... an Academy Award-winning shot—if only he had a camera. He could already see Shalee's pain as she knelt down beside what was left of her friend's mutilated body. The only part remaining of the woman that could be identified was a pendant necklace. George watched Shalee lift from the cave's floor.

"I gave this to her, Sam. I gave it to her only eight days ago." Shalee cried as she continued. "This is my fault. She would've never been here if I hadn't agreed to it. Sam, I killed her! I should've stopped her from using the cape!" She buried her face in her bloodied hands and sobbed as the king lifted her from the floor.

"I'm so sorry, Shalee," George said, feigning his sincerity as he came out from behind the pedestal.

Shalee spun around out of Sam's arms sending her magic in his direction. George held up his hand and diverted the power, the needles pierced deep into the cave walls.

"It's me, Shalee. Relax. It's George."

Sam grabbed his wife's arms to keep her from doing anything else. "George, what're you doing here? Are you here for ..." Sam hesitated and chose not to continue.

"Well, if I were to take a guess, I'm here for the same thing you are. Sorry about your friend, Shalee. I was hidden behind the pedestal when she died. I wish I could have stopped it, but I needed to save my powers for myself."

The mage stood next to the hidden demon.

"Why would you be after the Crystal, George? And what powers are you talking about?"

"Well, Sam, it appears you and I are on opposite sides. I now command the Kingdom of Bloodvain. I think you saw me redirect Shalee's power just now, so I think that's a good example of the power I'm referring to. Shalee knows I should be dead right now, but she isn't powerful enough to hurt me."

"You're right, George. You should be dead. Where did you get that kind of power? I'm sorry by the way . . . I was startled," Shalee said. "I would never have tried to hurt you. What do you mean you command the Kingdom of Bloodvain?"

"It's okay, Shalee, I forgive you. But, like I said, we fight for different sides now, so at this point, it looks like we're enemies. Kinda sucks when you think about it... but hey, it's all about getting my daughter back. And this, my old friends, is the only way I know to make that happen."

Sam shook his head. "George, your daughter, what are you talking about? She's dead like the rest of our families."

"NO . . . she's not dead! I can save her. I can bring her back, Sam. I know how to do it!"

"George, they all died when Earth was destroyed. I know it's hard to believe. Hell, I still hurt when I think about it too. We can talk this through and fix whatever it is you need help with."

"You're wrong . . . you can't help me." George lifted the Crystal into the air and screamed. "I'm not wrong, Sam. My baby girl can be saved and there's nothing you can do to help me. May the best man win! No offense, big guy, it's just business and this is the only way to get my Abbie back." With that, the mage closed his eyes and disappeared with the hidden Kepler.

Shalee collapsed to the floor hysterically. "Sam, what is going on? None of this makes any sense. How could George be our enemy—what did we ever do to him?"

Shalee looked down at the pieces of Helga's body as she held the pendant to her heart and wished with everything in her that it would fix the pain. A moment later, she fainted from the pressure as Sam caught her in his arms and held her tight.

The Grayham Inquirer

When inquiring minds need to know where their favorite characters are.

THE NIGHT after George collected the Crystal from Scorpion Island, he and Kepler appeared in the Barbarian King's throne room. The mage opened his pack to place the Crystal inside but to his surprise, the object glowed as he let it go. He was not sure what to think. When he showed Kepler what was happening, the demon did not know what to make of it either.

SAM took his grieving wife out of the cave and ordered his men to collect what was left of Helga's body. They traveled to the southern shores of the island where Michael commanded Branson, the legion Leader, to take the men back to the City of Cottle to light the fires for the celebrations of their passing.

The king informed the General that Shalee would be teleporting the three of them and Helga's body back to Brandor. They would return to Cottle in five Peaks of Bailem to pay their respects when the army arrived. Once all this had been accomplished, Shalee instructed them to close their eyes and touch one another. When the group opened their eyes, they found themselves in the couple's royal bedroom chambers. She asked Michael to have the morticians clean up the remains of Helga's body and have her friend brought back in a closed casket by

morning. Shalee wanted to allow BJ one more restful night of sleep before giving him the bad news. She didn't want the king's advisor seeing his lost love in this condition.

LASIDIOUS had been watching from his home far beneath the surface of the Peaks of Angels. When the images appeared in the cube-shaped fireplace within the green flames, he watched the events on Scorpion Island. He was elated at George's luck, never guessing the mage would end up with this piece of the Crystal Moon. It certainly made things more interesting, and an adjustment in future plans was now necessary.

Lasidious knew the others were going to be furious when he informed them that George already had the second piece. He still had it since his arrival on Grayham, even George did not know it. Lasidious remembered that Sam had told Mosley that George fell through the floor with it, but the wolf never asked about it. He never had any intentions of taking the Crystal from George. He simply made sure it had stayed invisible to the mage and the other gods until it was time to reveal the second piece of the Crystal's location.

This invisible piece was in George's pack. As Lasidious watched from the fire, he could see George had questions about the Crystal and he knew that the time for explanations would have to wait. He would avoid making an appearance in the mage's dreams until he addressed the gods tomorrow at Late Bailem.

With George having both pieces of the Crystal, the power to control the worlds was strengthened now that they were together. It would be at least another year before the worlds would begin to drift.

His visit to the World of Luvelles had been a productive one. His conversation, looking like Amar, with the Head Master of that world was encouraging. It was just a matter of time before his plan with the Elf would be implemented.

CELESTRIA was now only 20 Peaks of Bailem from having the baby. She could hardly wait to hold her son for the first time. She also looked forward to seeing Lasidious again once the baby was left in the care of the elven witches.

ATHENA was having some serious morning sickness and her mother was rubbing her back while talking her through it. Mary wished George was here, but unfortunately he would not be around much until the baby was born. She would just have to deal with it. She had no idea that George had been coming to see her daughter. The couple had managed to keep this secret well.

BJ is approaching Sam's throne room. One of the castle servants had been sent by the king just after breakfast to fetch him. For the last two days, the advisor to the king had been preparing the home that both he and Helga would share. This was the home that every advisor to the king was provided and it was grand. He could not wait to see his beautiful, sweet love. BJ had gone into the city while the army and his friends were away and purchased an extraordinarily beautiful wedding ring. He was so looking forward to being her husband.

Thank you for reading the Grayham Inquirer

Chapter 37

What a Tangled Web George Weaves

The City of Brandor
The King's Throne Room

BJ was as joyful as a man could possibly be when he walked in to see Sam with his head held high. As he entered he searched the throne room. He saw Sam, Shalee, Michael, the king's guards and finally, the closed casket. His eyes stopped on the coffin and a chill ran down his spine. His happiness was stolen from him within a single breath and there was nothing he could do or say about it. He turned to look at Shalee. A thousand unanswered questions filled his eyes. The queen's legs crumbled as she collapsed beneath the pressure of his silent accusations and experienced a guilty feeling that she had never felt before as her eyes met BJ's.

Sam managed to catch his queen just in time, then ordered the servants to take her to their bedroom chambers. Once they were gone, the king turned to look at BJ's hopeless face, watching as his friend slowly walked across the room.

Not a single word was spoken as the king's advisor knelt next to the coffin, lowering his forehead to rest against its cold surface. An intense feeling of despair filled every last cell of BJ's body, a pain so deep it tore at his soul as he fell into a fetal position.

Sam rushed to BJ's side. The king watched as his advisor's strong, scarred-up hand opened up. The ring meant to symbolize his greatest happiness—a happiness that BJ had intended to cherish for the rest of his life—rolled from his palm and fell to the floor as nothing more than a useless trinket.

BJ wept in agony.

At Athena and George's Home in Lethwitch

GEORGE popped in quickly to give his wife a kiss and a cuddle. He was scheduled to meet with the Serpent King at Late Bailem and knew exactly what he was going to tell Seth.

He was sitting at the table when Athena walked in with her mother. George quickly stood up and greeted them.

"Hey, I happened to be in the neighborhood," he joked. "I wanted to tell you that our family should be together permanently not long from now. How are you, Mom?"

Athena ran across the room and threw herself into her husband's arms.

Mary said, "I'm better now that you're here. This young lady is doing nothing but throwing everything up. I can't wait until this phase of her pregnancy passes. Your wife is unbearable at the moment."

George tilted the head of his beautiful Athena back from his chest and looked her in the eyes. "Are you still being a little priss?"

Mary did not give her daughter the chance to answer. She spoke for her. "Hah, you could say that again. You keep her for awhile, I'm leaving. I'll see you tomorrow, little girl."

"So how long are you here for?" Athena asked.

"I have a meeting to go to tonight up north, but it won't be anything that will take all night. I'll be able to come back home once it's over. Other than that, I'm all yours tonight and all day tomorrow."

Athena quickly pried away from George's grasp and ran towards a pail sitting near the front door, and began to throw up. Her morning sickness was now a morning, midday, and night sickness as well.

The God World of Ancients Sovereign

THE GODS had all traveled to the Hall of Judgment and were once again sitting at the table that the golden stand of the Book of

Immortality rested on. It was just after Late Bailem when Lasidious finally appeared.

"I'm sure we all watched the events of the first piece of the Crystal take place with eagerness. I was impressed at how it all ended up," he said gloating a little.

Mieonus jumped into the conversation. "So am I . . . I thought for sure when I left that idiot barbarian's throne room that there was no chance George would capture the first piece."

"Well, when you have Brandor doing all the work to kill the scorpions," Mosley added, "what do you expect? The back door was left wide open for him to walk right in and take it. I have to say that the fight between the Scorpions and Brandor was most impressive to watch. No matter how I feel about it, George won the Crystal fair and square."

"It was impressive to watch Shalee's power, too, "Lasidious said. "I wish I knew what Bassorine did. I've never seen a sorceress gain so much power so fast."

The wolf grinned and Lasidious caught a glimpse of it. "You know something don't you?" the God of Mischief questioned.

"You know what it is that Bassorine did, but you're not going to tell me, are you?"

"You give me too much credit, Lasidious," Mosley responded. "I don't know anything more than you do, but it does make me happy to know that I have a chess piece that can hold a candle to George."

"Agreed," Alistar said. "It was sad to see Shalee's friend die though. I'm sure this will set her back some."

"Mosley," Lasidious said, ignoring Alistar's sentiment, "Do you remember back before you became a god, the day you and Bassorine appeared before Sam and Shalee, in the temple?"

"I do," the wolf responded.

"I know you also remember I said that two pieces of the Crystal would be placed on Grayham."

"I do."

"Do you remember when Sam and Shalee said that three of them had appeared in the Temple of the Gods and that George had fallen through the floor?"

"What are you getting at, Lasidious?"

"Give me a moment, I'm getting there... just relax. I was about to ask you if you also remembered that George was the one who picked up a piece of the Crystal, causing the rest of the Crystal Moon to vanish..."

"I do remember that he was the one to touch the Crystal. What does this have to do with where you put—"

Mosley stopped mid-sentence. After a moment, he began to laugh in his wolfish way. "You can't be serious." He looked at Lasidious and it was clear to both of them that he had it figured out.

"What's so funny, Mosley?" Alistar said, acting as if didn't already know. He winked at Lasidious and smiled, careful not to allow the others to see the exchange.

Mosley responded, "I'm not laughing at anything other than the irony that I've known this whole time where the second piece of the Crystal was, and I hadn't thought of it 'til now."

"So where is it?" Mieonus snapped impatiently.

Mosley turned and looked at her. "Well, Lasidious said the Crystal would be on Grayham and it is. It's been with George this whole time."

Mieonus's team exploded with laughter while the other four members of Mosley's team began swearing at the God of Mischief. All Lasidious could do was stand at the head of the table and grin. He had expected a mixed reaction from this crowd and now that it was happening, he was enjoying every minute of it.

George's Meets with the Serpent King

GEORGE teleported to the home the barbarian king maintained south of Bloodvain. As planned, the scouts brought the snakes there for their meeting. The Serpent King was told that George was the king and he had arrived only minutes ago to greet them.

"So, you're the new King of Bloodvain?" Seth said in his hissing voice as he watched the human enter the room.

It took the mage a moment to gather his thoughts. He had never spoken with a snake before, and this particular one had a body over 40 feet long. His fangs were large, sharp, and intimidating and had an aura of evil that made George quiver inside, however he refused to show this weakness.

Seth saw that George was staring at him and hissed again. "Is there something wrong with you that would cause you to stare at your guests so rudely?"

George, realizing what he was doing, apologized. He moved to the fireplace and took a seat on its hearth. This home of Senchae's was more of the same: mounted animal trophies everywhere in yet another stupid log cabin. The mage was thankful that none of the trophies involved a snake of any kind. George sat down.

"I'm glad you were able to come and visit with me, Seth. You have a problem heading your way and I wish to help you with it."

The snake slithered into a better position in which to converse. "What makes you think I need your help with any problem that may be headed into my kingdom?"

"The Island of the Scorpion King was attacked by Brandor. They'll be headed your way soon. From what I know of your numbers, you can't defend yourselves against Brandor. Tell me if I'm right."

"I don't believe you. Brandor's army couldn't get past the mares."

Every time the snake hissed his words, George found himself leaning forward as if waiting for the rest of them to be spit out.

"You're wrong. They destroyed the mares."

"You expect me to believe this? I know they're deadly. How did they kill them?" The serpent adjusted his coils as he waited for the response.

George decided that he would turn up the heat a little on the conversation and spoke more forcefully this time.

"I don't care if you believe me, Seth. I know that I speak the truth. If you don't want my help, leave and don't come back. You can die like both the scorpions and the mares did. Do I need to show you before you'll listen to me?"

"So it appears that I don't have much choice but to believe you. It's a safe question to ask, since you know it's impossible do to this."

"Not impossible, Serpent King, I can take you to the island now if you like." George stood from his seat and waited for the reply. Seth studied the man's face prior to answering. "I have no desire to travel this evening."

George rolled his eyes. "I'll take us there. You don't even need to move from the spot you're in. Just close your eyes and we'll go."

Seth coiled his body even tighter than before and his guard did as well. "So you expect me to just close my eyes? Do you think I'm stupid? You're up to something, King of the Barbarians."

George had heard enough. He waved his hand and put his magical bonds on the Serpent King and his guard. "If I wanted to hurt you, Seth, I could've done that already. There's nothing you could've done to stop me. Do you want my help or not?" The mage waved his hand again and released just the snake's wicked tongue.

The snake tried with all his might to break George's magic but could not move. After awhile he finally realized he could speak.

"Release me, and I'll accept your help."

"Send your guards from the room!"

Once the creature did as instructed, George waved his hand to release the guard. The snake slithered off as it collected the others to leave.

"Look, Seth, all you need to do is close your eyes, I'll take care of the rest. When you open them we'll be on Scorpion Island."

Seth was astonished when he opened his eyes. "Magic has never been used on me before. Are we really here?"

"This is the place. I'll release you, Seth. You need to understand that I can do far greater magic than what you've just witnessed. I don't want to be put in a position that would cause me to use any of it on you."

"I understand."

George released him, and allowed the serpent to investigate the island's southern shores.

The mage followed Seth until the snake believed that he was indeed on the island. Giant scorpion's bodies lay everywhere, the bloody mess finally convincing the Serpent King of where he was. George looked at his map, and saw that the snake's kingdom was south-southwest of their current position. He moved to the shore and once again created an ice raft, then instructed Seth to board it.

Once on the other side, George spoke. "Okay, I've shown you everything that I've said is true."

"This is correct. I trust you."

"I trust we are allies?"

"Yes, Barbarian King, we are allies."

"Splendid, it's time for you to go home. Begin your preparations for war. The Kingdom of Brandor will be attacking soon. Make no mistake, the Barbarian Kingdom will help you, but you will be at war before I can get my army here. Prepare a good battle plan. You know your lands... take advantage of it. Make the armies of Brandor come to you. Fight them from inside your underground kingdom, don't fight above ground. You will lose the war if you do. Once the time is right my army will attack as well."

"Thank you. My kind will forever be in your debt. I must go now and prepare."

George closed his eyes to teleport and when he opened them again, he was standing by his sleeping wife. He smiled as he looked at her peaceful beauty, then climbed in to take his place beside her.

Soon after the mage was asleep, Lasidious appeared in his dreams. He had been dreaming of his beautiful little Abbie when the god appeared. He was glad to see the god because of the business he needed to attend to, but also angry since the dream of his baby girl was so pleasant.

"Damn, Lasidious," George snapped. "You just interrupted a good dream of Abbie."

"I'm sorry, George, but I've got something important to tell you. You actually have both pieces of the Crystal Moon that are on Grayham in your presence."

"I was wondering why the Crystal began to glow when I put it in my pack. Is the other one in there as well?"

"It is, and you've had it the whole time. I have kept it hidden from you until now. When you get up and open your pack, you will be able to see them both. Do you understand that this will bring war to your doorstep, George?"

"I've already thought of this. When I got the first piece of the

Crystal, Sam and Shalee were there. They know that I have it. I figured that this would make them attack Bloodvain, but I've got an idea. I'm going to bring the fight to the doorstep of the Serpent King instead. I've already taken the king to Scorpion Island to show him what Brandor is capable of. He's now willing to align himself with Bloodvain as he thinks Brandor is going to attack him."

Lasidious was unsure about George's new information.

How do you intend to get Brandor to attack the Serpent's Kingdom when you have both the Crystals? I only told the snake they were going to attack him so he would go north to see you in Bloodvain. I don't see Brandor attacking Seth's underground city. There's no reason to do such a thing."

"You're wrong... It makes sense really, when you know what I know. I have a plan, Lasidious, but it requires a small amount of help from you."

"George, I've told you before that I can't help you with any direct event that will change the balance of power."

"I know that, I don't need you to do anything that would affect the balance of power. All I need you to do is ask the three gods who were with you when I threatened Senchae with his son's life to show up with you tomorrow night in the Barbarian King's throne room. I have a few things to say that the gods will find interesting. Could you make sure they are there, or at least are watching, when I say what I have to say?"

Lasidious smiled. "I sense a plan of genius coming... all right I'll grant your request. May I know what this plan is or do I have to wait?"

"You can wait. Just be there by Late Bailem and I assure you that you won't be dissatisfied. Once I leave Bloodvain, I'll be heading to Gessler Village. Bring the gods to the Bloody Trough Inn to hear the rest of my plan, I'll be at the bar drinking. Just keep them from following me inside the shed when I take a leak... maybe bump into a chair or something to let me know you're there."

Lasidious agreed to follow through and left George to enjoy the rest of his dream. In the morning, the mage woke up with his expectant wife and attended to her as she once again began throwing up.

The God World of Ancients Sovereign

LASIDIOUS called Mosley, Yaloom, and Mieonus to the Hall of Judgment. He wanted to make sure they would go with him to Bloodvain's throne room.

"How are you all today?" Lasidious asked.

The three gods and the Book of Immortality (who always rested in the hall) said they were fine but also demanded the God of Mischief get down to business.

"I want to know if any of you heard what George said to the Serpent King last night."

"I did," Mosley responded. "Why?"

"Well, did you get everything I got out of that meeting?" Lasidious sat at the table and played with the Book's golden stand, waiting for a response.

Mosley thought a moment and answered. "Nothing more than George telling him Brandor was going to attack the snake's kingdom and for them to fight underground."

Lasidious had not known this information, but he did not let on about his ignorance.

"So I see a problem with his plan, don't you?"

The wolf moved to the head of the table and sat on his haunches on the floor. "I see many flaws in this plan. Brandor has no intention of attacking Seth. Why would they fight the Serpent King's army when George possesses both pieces of the Crystal? Sam will attack Bloodvain, not the Serpent City."

"I agree with you Mosley, but I also overheard George telling the Barbarian King that he needed to meet with him tonight. I thought maybe the five of us could listen in on that meeting. It will be intriguing to see what he's planning."

The Book of Immortality floated over to the god. The thin slit in his binding opened for him to speak.

"Do you want me to attend as well?"

"Sure, why not," Lasidious responded, "all you do is sit here and collect dust. Maybe you should get out and get some fresh air in those pages of yours."

The Book thought about this.

"I don't see any reason why I can't go. When shall I appear?" Lasidious patted the Book's cover.

"Be in the throne room just before Late Bailem. When George appears to the king we can watch this meeting and remain unseen as we have done before."

Late Bailem: Bloodvain's Throne Room

LASIDIOUS, Mieonus, Mosley and the Book of Immortality arrived in their invisible form at the Barbarian King's throne room and stood behind the king's throne.

Yaloom stayed home stating that he no longer cared what happened. But, in spite of the god's anger towards Lasidious for the way he had treated him, his curiosity got the better of him, so he watched the meeting from his waterfall.

Senchae, his guards, and the new general of his army, Corvin Hurthon, were in attendance with a few of the army's military officers. George appeared in the center of the room with Kepler and his brothers beside him.

"Thank you all for coming," George announced without wasting any time. "I've called you here to let you know I intend to make sure that the battle for the pieces of the Crystal is fought without any chance of us losing them. I'll be traveling to the Serpent King's kingdom to hide the two crystal pieces there until we can defeat the Kingdom of Brandor."

Senchae interrupted, "How will you keep the Crystals from being used by the snakes as a bargaining tool to create an alliance with Brandor?"

"I'll hide the crystals within the Serpent King's underground kingdom but Seth will not know that he has them."

George paused for effect.

"I have things I must do and won't be able to be contacted by anyone for the next 15 Peaks of Bailem. I will be creating other alliances. We must be sure we have enough of an army to crush Brandor."

"Where will you go, George?" Senchae asked.

"My king, I think where I go from here is a matter best left between you and me. These are things that these brave men around us do not need to worry about. They have much to do to prepare for war. Let us speak of this at another time."

Senchae liked the diplomacy his advisor was displaying.

"I'm sure you're right; we'll speak of this later."

Senchae realized George had no intention of telling him anything, but the mage made everyone feel that he respected his position and this was good enough for the king.

George looked into the many eyes around the room, watching to make sure the men liked the idea of using the snakes to fight Brandor. After a brief question and answer session, he made his exit.

"Sounds like he's worried that Brandor will defeat the Barbarians," Mosley said after he watched George disappear. He turned and faced Lasidious. "Let's all meet back at the Hall of Judgment to discuss this further." Everyone agreed and then vanished.

Soon Lasidious had his feet up on the table in the royal hall. He leaned back, enjoying his position of power. The Book of Immortality took its place on the golden stand while Mieonus stood behind the God of Mischief, rubbing his shoulders.

Mosley spoke first as he lay down on the table.

"Like I was saying before, it sounds like he's worried that he'll be defeated by Brandor. He wants to make sure he doesn't lose the crystals and, I must say, hiding them in the Serpent King's city is a great idea. Sam will never know that they're there. I wonder what George did after he left the meeting? Why does he need 15 Peaks of Bailem before he can make another appearance before the king?"

"That's what I want to know," Lasidious said. The God of Mischief was happy that Mosley had spoken. It would make the job of getting them all to the Bloody Trough easier. "I say we go find out." The god waved his hand and a map of Grayham appeared. He told the map to search for George and it revealed him in Gessler Village.

"I like your new toy," Mieonus said after seeing how easily it found the mage. "When did you create that?"

"You know me. I'm always tinkering on something. Shall we go?" All of them agreed and once again disappeared.

When George opened his eyes, he and the cats were underneath the Bloody Trough. It was good that they had appeared in the spot they did as there were two horses drinking underneath the inn on the opposite side of the wall, the presence of the three jaguars would have scared the life out of them. Instead the demons hid themselves within the shadows and waited for George, staying quiet.

The mage walked into the inn, found a seat at the bar, ordered his ale, and waited for Lasidious and the others to show up. After a bit he started to relax and began to enjoy his drink.

Mosley was the first to appear outside the inn. Once the others arrived, they all entered the inn together, unseen as before. Finding a spot to sit, they watched to see what the mage was up to.

"Why would we want to stay and watch him drink?" Mieonus said. "All he's here for is some ale... this isn't any fun."

"We don't know why George is here since we've barely arrived, so leaving now would be stupid," Lasidious said. "But he generally has some kind of plan; maybe he's meeting someone here.

Let's see what happens. It's not like we have anything better to do ourselves... I'll summon us a drink."

The god waved his hand across the table and soon everyone who could drink had frosty ale.

The Book of Immortality, feeling a bit left out, opened its thin binding slit to speak.

"I wish you all would've created me with the ability to enjoy a good drink. I've always wondered what food and many of the liquids you pour down your throats taste like. I hear you talk about it and I find myself curious at times."

After a brief debate, the three gods agreed that it would not do any harm to give the Book a set of taste buds, eyes, rosy cheeks, arms, teeth, a tongue, nose and stomach inside its pages. They decided that the waste that would normally exit a human body would be stored in the form of excess random letters towards the back of its heavy binding. The Book would have to open itself up to this area and dump the letters to the ground every so often when this page was full. This was the first book that the gods had ever created that could eat and drink. The idea that the Book would be dropping its pile of letters all over the ground gave all of the gods a good laugh. They wondered if this pile of text would have an odor.

As they laughed, Lasidious used the distraction to make sure George knew they were there. He moved one of the chairs just a bit to make a noise, acting as if it was unintentional. Everyone in the room turned to look in the direction of what they thought to be an empty table.

"Do you think he knows we're here?" Mieonus asked as she watched George stare in their direction.

Mosley chided. "Between Yaloom falling in the fire and you bumping into chairs, we might as well put up a sign that says,

'Hey, George, the gods are watching you'."

All the gods laughed as they watched George turn back around to face the bar. Soon a man walked in and sat down to order a drink and the gods watched as a conversation between the big man and George began. The mage ordered another drink and, after a while, excused himself in the middle of the conversation to go empty his bladder. He would leave more than once for this and each time Lasidious kept the gods busy. This was an easy task because they were all having such a good time.

George walked to the back of the inn and, each time he entered the shed where Double D had killed the big Barbarian, he poured his glass of ale on the ground. He figured he would do this a couple more times before putting his plan into action, which was to act drunk and shoot off his mouth. He would disclose that the two pieces of the Crystal Moon were going to be hidden in the

Serpent's Kingdom. After a few moments, he went back in to his seat and continued with his activities, secretly pleased with the sign Lasidious had given him alerting him to the god's presence. After a few more ales, George stepped up his drunken act, singing out the whereabouts the Crystal Moon.

"Hey, big man, did you know the Crystal Moon has been stolen from the Temple of the Gods?" He raised his voice so everyone could hear. "I know where two of the pieces are right now. I have them on me. See, look, I have them right here, yep I do." Lifting them high into the air, he continued as he stumbled around. "I spoke with the Serpent King. Shhhh, don't tell, but he's going to let me hide these two crystals in his underground city."

Lasidious acted surprised. "What is he doing? He's going to ruin his plan. Why would he do this?"

Mieonus replied, "I don't know, but he's your puppet, not mine."

"Be quiet," Mosley snapped. "Listen!"

George continued.

"My buddy Sam is now the king. I'm sure you've all heard about this. I don't have to tell any of you that he would be so pissed off if he knew I had these." The mage fell on his butt as he put both crystals back in his pack and continued speaking from his seat on the floor.

"I bet he would pay a reward if he knew I was taking them to the Serpent King's city. You know what? That bastard is too cheap to see that this information is worth good coin. Maybe I should go and explain it to him. I bet everyone here thinks this information is worth good coin, right?"

George stumbled up to a big man and threw his arm around him. The mage noticed that the bar now had many interested ears. All he had to do now was play up the story a little longer and someone would confront him. He took some coin from his pocket and started throwing it around.

"If I were a king, I'd pay for this information, but Sam is too stupid to do that." George moved away from the big guy, making sure he fell to the floor again. "Does anyone want to go to Serpent City with me? Oops, that's right; none of you can teleport like I can. You're all pathetic. I don't know why I'm hanging out with any of you spineless idiots."

As he picked himself up from the floor, a voice from across the room called out to him. "I'd be careful who you call names, mister. It seems to me that a small man like yourself would be an easy target for a killing if he didn't watch his tongue."

George turned to find the source of the threat. Standing near the door of the inn was an intimidating-looking man who was clearly a Barbarian. With his clothes made of furs and protruding muscles, George couldn't have picked a better person to finish his drunken act on if he had hand-picked him himself. The mage stumbled in his direction as he spoke.

"I bet you think that you're the one who could kill me, don't you?" George said as he slurred his words. "I have bigger fish to fry than you. You're just a stupid Barbarian."

The gods watched in disbelief as George stumbled around acting like a drunken fool.

"He's so drunk he's being careless and stupid," Mosley said.

"I can't believe this," Lasidious said. "I think my buddy George has a screw loose in that head of his. He's picking a fight with the biggest guy in the bar. George is going to kill him and he'll need to leave. Is anyone in a betting mood?"

All the gods wanted in on the action.

"I say he kills the Barbarian and heads for the Serpent's Kingdom to hide the crystal," Mosley said.

"I think he'll kill the Barbarian," Mieonus stated, "then go sleep off his intoxication before going to the snake's city."

The Book of Immortality decided to bet as well. "I think he'll kill the Barbarian and teleport to Scorpion Island. He'll hide the crystals there since no one would ever think he'd do something like that. The island's empty so there's no chance anyone would go there to look for it. You know the people of Brandor won't want to go there after all the men they lost in the battle. I think George is still sober and this is just an act to draw Brandor to Seth's city of Snakes. He's counting on someone to run and tell Sam about his secret hiding spot for the crystals."

Lasidious laughed.

"Wow, I have to admit that, that's pretty deep." The god thought a minute and realized they had never given the Book a name. It was odd to be chatting with it and unable to address it in any kind

of formal manner. "I agree with Mieonus, but something is bug-
ging me."

"What's that?" Mosley asked.

"It's silly, I suppose, but do you realize we've all been sitting
here talking to the Book and it feels like it's one of us? Do you
know what I mean? I feel like it's a part of the gang. Maybe we
should give it a name." Lasidious looked at the Book and continued. Would you like a man or woman's name?"

"That's a great idea," Mieonus said. "I agree we should name
it. It is awkward now that you mention it."

The feeling was mutual. Everyone was in agreement.

George had turned the big Barbarian to stone and left the bar,
but the gods were enjoying their conversation far too much to
care, and dismissed the killing with little more than a glance. They
would finish their conversation and track the mage down in a bit.

Finally, after a good while, the Book spoke. "I think I like the
name Thomas."

"Thomas?" Lasidious questioned. "Why not something that
suits the power you possess? Don't you think that's a weak
name?"

Mieonus jumped in to the conversation.

"How about using the names Dagan or Drake? Those seem
much more powerful and would suit you better."

The Book did not like their choices and declined.

Mosley added a name to the mix as well.

"Thomas does sound weak. You're far too powerful for a name
like that. How about the name Draco? It is what the dragons of
Dragonia name some of their young. That's a powerful name."

The Book declined again. "There's a reason why I chose this
name. Of all the souls within my many, many pages, he's the one
who stands out above all the rest. This specific Thomas that I'm
referring to was from Earth, and died when it was destroyed."

Lasidious interrupted. "It seems like we've heard a lot about
Earth lately. See what happens when we introduce earthlings into
Grayham?"

The Book of Immortality laughed. "I've grown to know Thomas's soul quite well since I collected him. Granted, he was one of
the billions I collected when I left to gather them all and he ac-

companied me as I traveled. This young boy's soul gave me much-needed company. He was ten years old and liked a game called football. I have had many conversations with him and—"

"—So you liked the child," Lasidious interrupted, "but the name you choose will be with you for an eternity. At least make it a strong one. Don't settle for something feeble like Thomas."

The Book finished his story.

"The child's one concern when he found out he died—" Mieonus interrupted this time.

"—We aren't going to call you Thomas. So you might as well pick something stronger than that. Give us another one."

Mosley jumped in. "I understand this Thomas is a good soul, but you're far too powerful for such a name. You need an extremely strong name."

Illustrated By: Ian Ferrebee

The Book thought a moment longer and spit out another one. "How does Gabriel sound?"

All the gods agreed this time... it was a good name. And, since it was a man's name, the gods adjusted the Book's new facial features to appear more masculine. Mosley tried it on for size. "So, Gabriel, it's nice to meet you."

The wolf laughed at how silly it seemed to refer to the Book as a real person.

"It's a boy, everyone," Mieonus screamed. "But the baby has a square head. Don't tell the mother, she'll want to put it back on the shelf."

The joke made for a good chuckle. Then Mosley changed the subject.

"So Gabriel, maybe we should go look for George and see who won the bet."

The Book Gabriel agreed, and the gods all checked Lasidious's map to see where the mage had gone. The God of Deception thought back to his conversation with George the night he sat with him near the fire, remembering they had been outside of Lethwitch within the trees of the Enchanted Forest. He told George his daughter was the only soul saved from the darkness of space around the destroyed Earth. He was glad George had not heard their current conversation that *all* the souls had been saved. Every soul that ever existed, no matter where they were from, had been gathered by the Book. Even the souls from the destroyed Heaven and Hell had been placed within Gabriel's pages.

As it turned out, the Book was right: George was inside the cave on Scorpion Island. They all decided they would join the mage, but this time they would not stay hidden.

Now, having all arrived, the gods stood behind the unsuspecting man. Lasidious was the first to speak.

"Nice act, George," the God of Mischief said. "I actually thought you were drunk."

George whirled around as Lasidious spoke and sent his magic flying. The god caught the arrows in his hand like a small irritation. The mage quickly regrouped once he saw who it was and apologized, questioning the god.

"What are you doing here, Lasidious? Why are they with you?"

Kepler and his brothers stayed in the shadows as they watched Mosley jump into the conversation.

"Relax, George. I have to admit that you had me fooled at that bar back in Gessler. I actually thought you were drunk when you told everyone in the bar that you stole the crystals. I believed you were going to hide them in the Serpent King's underground city. Bravo, bravo, you're very creative. I'll give you that much."

"Yes, very well played, George," Mieonus cut in. "You'd make a fine god. I must say that your deception will keep Brandor busy for quite a while. You don't have to worry about us saying anything to ruin your plan. The level of scheming that you've accomplished will affect the balance of power. I also say, Bravo!"

The Book or better yet, Gabriel... now floated over and said, "You're a far cry from the soul that I have within my pages. Your daughter isn't deceitful like you are. I find it hard to believe that your daughter's gentle spirit was given to you to be her father. How could your Gods of Earth expect a man with such an evil heart to raise her? Abbie is nothing like you, George . . . nothing like you at all, and yet she still loves you!"

George dropped to his knees at the thought of his daughter. He was about to ask Gabriel a question about her, but Lasidious cut in. "George," he said in a louder than normal tone. The mage picked up on his subtle hint and dropped the subject. "So what's next, my friend? What happens in this cave stays in this cave."

George chuckled

"Sounds like Vegas."

The gods looked puzzled.

"Oh, forget it. Since when do you all watch me?" the mage asked as if he had no clue they had been there. "I guess little old me must be turning heads, aye?"

"Yes, you are," Gabriel said. "So what's next in your plan?"

"Well," the mage shifted his feet, "It sure seems strange to be talking to a book, but I'll tell you. I'm going to the home of the Minotaur King in Minotaur Hills and tell him that Brandor has decided to kill his subjects. I'm going to tell them that Sam's army has already killed the Scorpion King and, if I have to, I'll show them. After that, I intend to do the same thing with the Bear King. I'll go to the caves of the Bear Clan and make sure they feel the threat as well. I'll let both of them know that Brandor intends to attack the Serpent King's city next. If they wait until the armies of Brandor have crossed into his kingdom's borders, they can attack from behind. This should thin the herd a bit, don't you think?"

Mosley responded. "No wonder he needs 15 Peaks of Bailem before he can return to Bloodvain."

"Wow, you guys really *are* watching me close. Yes, I need all 15 days. I have two more inns to visit tonight before I've finish weaving my little web. So, if you don't mind, I need to bury these crystals and get out of here."

All the gods agreed that they were going to learn nothing more, and that George's plan was very sound. They all agreed to meet at the Hall of Judgment and vanished. Just before Lasidious left, he gave George a wink, and told him to keep up the good work.

Chapter 38

A Ticket Out of Here

GEORGE buried the two pieces of the Crystal Moon behind the pedestal once the gods were gone from the cave of the dead Scorpion King. He patted the top of the podium's smooth surface and looked at the blood-stained area of earth beyond it. The mage thought of how the giant insect had torn apart Shalee's friend, the memory replaying in his mind as he stood there. It seemed like a sad but necessary incident.

George's plan now was to recreate the events that happened at the Bloody Trough Inn twice more. He teleported outside the City of Champions and made his way to a hole-in-the-wall tavern. Once there, he changed his mind on the amount of stops he would have to make after seeing the men who were drinking... this would be his last stop, he couldn't believe his luck. Some of Brandor's soldiers were there celebrating with their buddy on his last night of being a single man.

George decided that the future groom, who also happened to be an officer in Sam's army, would be his target. So, just like at the Bloody Trough, he delivered his message that he was going to hide the two pieces of the crystal in the Serpent King's underground city giving a performance that was as good as gold. Before he left the bar, the future husband had been turned into a piece of solid stone art. The mage also threatened his friends, friends who happened to be just as highly ranked as the groom. Now he was sure his message about the crystal's pieces would get back to Sam.

Then the mage left with the demon cats, teleporting south of the City of Bloodvain.

"Keller, go into the city and inform the king that I want him to mobilize the army and head to the western shores of Southern

Grayham. Also, tell Senchae that once they get to their destination, he needs to march the army south and stop north of the Serpent King's borders to set up camp. The army needs to mobilize quickly so Sam's scouts will deliver word that Senchae is after the crystals. Let's hope that Sam takes the bait and takes his army to the Serpent's Kingdom.

"And finally, take this note to Senchae. Hurry, once you return we will go to Athena's. We will sleep through the day and go to Angel's Village at night."

He had a goal over the next nine Peaks of Bailem to meet with the Minotaur King and the Bear Clan King. He would arrange it so both kings believed that Brandor had decided to destroy all of the beasts who rule their own kind. He would take both of the kings to look at Scorpion Island and show them the dead body of the Scorpion King. With the snakes, bears, Minotaurs, Barbarians, Kepler's Skeleton Warriors, and his big cats attacking from all directions, Brandor's army would crumble and George would be able to take control of Grayham after the war.

Once home in Lethwich, he called to Athena, "Honey, I'm home."

Athena ran into the room and jumped into his arms. "Oh, I missed you. So how long are you here for this time?"

"I have to leave soon. I'll be gone for a while, but I'll be able to have the family together real soon. You won't have to work if you don't want to. The family can come with us as well."

Athena hugged him, "So where will we be living?"

George took a deep breath. "In City View, I think you'll love it there and so will the family if they come."

"George, that city is full of Barbarians. What about our safety? What about our baby's safety? My family won't want to go."

"There's no reason to worry. I'm beloved within the Barbarian Kingdom for the work that I do. No one will harm us. We will be safe, and so will your family."

Athena shook her head. "I'll follow you anywhere as I promised, but I don't think my family will go with us... and that will be hard for me."

"You're forgetting I can teleport you home. Besides, I'll talk to your family. I'm sure they'll want to come. Don't you worry, okay? I got it all under control. Have I ever let you down yet? Do you trust me?"

"Of course I trust you." She led him into the bedroom. "Let me show you how much," she said with a grin of promise.

After a good while George lay back on the bed exhausted from their activities and snuggled his wife. He had chosen to move them all to City View because this was the one place in the Barbarian Kingdom that would not see war. If Sam believed his lies about where the crystals were hidden, the war would not extend this far to the east. Although he did not plan for Lethwitch to see war either, he knew that his face would draw attention. It would be impossible to live here. When he visited Athena, he would not leave the walls of their home until they moved.

It was just before the Peak of Bailem when he finally fell asleep. Kepler and his brothers were hidden in the Enchanted Forest where George would meet with them at dusk and teleport to Angel's Village.

The Next Day, Outside the City of Brandor, on The Shores of The Ocean of Utopia

AFTER SAYING GOODBYE, BJ left with Helga's body in the back of Sam's royal wagon. He wanted to find a spot on the coast to light the fire to honor her passing. BJ's heart was heavy; he had loved Helga more than he had ever loved any other.

Sam and Shalee were traveling back to the City of Cottle to attend the passing celebrations of *all* the men who died on Scorpion Island. Shalee was going to stay behind and go with BJ, but the king's advisor wanted to be alone. When the queen tried to object, Sam pulled her aside and suggested she let him go. He told her it would be a good time for BJ to begin the healing process. The king explained that he needed his advisor's head back in the game as soon as possible. Sam told his queen and BJ that he was sorry for his callousness, but he had to think about the good of the kingdom. BJ's face showed his distain, despite acting as if he understood Sam's position.

The wagon held the coffin on one side and the wood for her pyre on the other. This was the second time BJ had to say goodbye to a woman in his life. The problem was that, this time around, his heart was totally destroyed. He was lost. His first relationship had not had any of the same passion he shared with Helga and his sorrow was unbearable. He decided he would continue to travel for as long as it took to find a spot that complimented his lost love's beauty.

When BJ found the perfect spot, he jumped down from the wagon and made his final judgment. The sands of the beach were white and clean. The trees that sat back from the shoreline and created an alcove of privacy. The waves crashed softly against the shore. There seemed to be a peacefulness that BJ knew he and Helga would have enjoyed together if she were still alive. Within this alcove there were two boulders that sat close to one another. They would serve as the perfect spot to light the fire to celebrate her passing.

As he lifted the wood from the wagon, BJ's heart seemed to become heavier with each step. Never had he felt so overcome with sadness. The longing for his love to return and claim that an evil joke had been played consumed his thoughts. He stacked the wood the way Helga deserved, he would not settle for anything less than perfection with the placement of each plank. BJ was losing himself with each piece that he set down. His heart was falling into a pit of helplessness from which he could not crawl out.

He carried Helga's coffin from the wagon and lifted it onto the pile. He made sure that it was centered; adjusting it nearly a hundred times before he felt its placement to be perfect.

The night was approaching and BJ watched the sunset cast its beautiful array of colors into the darkening sky. It would be the last moment he and Helga could share together. The urge to hold her just one last time as the sun descended behind the horizon pulled at him.

He used an iron bar to break the lock that secured the coffin shut. Slowly he lifted the latch, not knowing that his lover lay torn apart inside. This had been a detail that both Sam and Shalee had avoided telling him.

BJ paused, unsure if this was the right thing to do. But thinking it through, he convinced himself that Helga would have enjoyed the idea of him holding her one last time before lighting the fire of her passing. He lifted the lid and looked inside to see his beautiful love's pieces. His face turned from one full of compassionate love, to one of horror and excruciating agony.

He took a step back from the coffin losing his balance and falling to the sandy beach below. He hurried away from the hellish nightmare and collapsed into the cascading waters that flowed on to the shore, crying uncontrollably. Raising his head to the heavens he screamed, cursing the gods for stealing his happiness... cursing Sam for allowing his lover to go into the mouth of danger... cursing Shalee for not being there for Helga when she needed her most.

Eventually, after anguish and cries of despair, BJ stood and retrieved his dagger. He grabbed a container of oil and poured it over much of the perfectly stacked wood on a single side beneath the coffin, but only on this one side. He cleared a place next to Helga and lay tightly next to her pieces inside the coffin. With a lit torch in one hand, he plunged the dagger into his stomach with the other. Dropping the torch onto the wood below he lay back to wait for the dagger's wound to end his life.

But the flames spread much quicker than BJ had anticipated. In his grief and confused state he had used too much oil. His eyes had not closed forever before the intense heat consumed the coffin. His horrific screams filled the night sky before his soul finally left for the Book of Immortality's pages.

George Meets the Minotaur King

GEORGE spent the last four and a half days putting his plans together, including Kepler in his ideas. The demon would act as his interpreter; he had turned into quite the tour guide as well, getting them wherever they needed to go. The group realized that the time needed to implement their plans was tight, critical in fact, in order to make this war happen in the Serpent's Kingdom.

George used his power to strengthen Kepler's body and had

ridden him for most of the last four Peaks of Bailem. The jaguar's brothers tagged along and teased Kepler as he complained about the saddle the mage had created. Despite the taunting of his brothers, the demon was accepting of his demeaning task because he liked helping George.

They now were approaching the hilly pastures where the Minotaur King was grazing. George put a magical wall of force around the group as he rode Kepler into the area as the group's intrusion was not welcomed. The part bull, part human subjects of the Minotaur King bellowed at the intruders as they cross the pasture.

The appearance of the Minotaurs was something George had never seen before. These creatures had large bullheads attached to human torsos, and human-looking arms. The bottom half of the beasts were strong cow-like legs with large hooves as feet. They stood upright and walked like any normal man would whether male or female. It was odd to watch them reach down near their hooves, tear the grass from the earth with their hands, place it near their mouth and scoop the plant in with their large cow-like tongues to consume it.

As they got closer to the king, the beasts became aggressive and attacked. The big bull-headed men bounced off George's magic like a child's ball bounced off a wall. The mage laughed as the confused beasts picked themselves up off the ground, dazed from the collision against the invisible shield. Soon Kepler stood in front of the Minotaur King. After watching his strongest subjects fail to break through George's magic, the king decided to address the mage.

The demon jaguar translated as the beast king spoke, asking if George was a god since he had great powers. George allowed Kepler to confirm that he was, in fact, a god.

"Kepler, tell him my name and ask him his."

Kepler did and said, "He said his name is, if I'm translating it right, Horace."

"Horace? Was his mother angry when she named him?"

"This might not be the time for jokes, George. A little tact might work better."

"Explain that it would be wise for him to send out his scouts to watch for Brandor's army… and tell the king that Brandor is going to kill all the beasts that have any royal structure. Inform Horace that the Scorpion King is already dead. It is only a matter of time until he's next. Assure him that Brandor's next target will be the Serpent King's underground city and let him know I can show him some of Brandor's handy work."

Illustrated By: Ian Ferrebee

Kepler spoke with the Minotaur King and George nodded as the beast bellowed angrily at what he had been told.

Kepler turned to translate. "He's angry, George, very angry. He wants to know if you have any real proof and, if so, why have you not brought it to him."

"Tell him I can take him to the Scorpion King's island and show him the king's dead body."

Kepler again translated.

"He said he's willing to go and is ready to leave."

"Tell him to close his eyes."

Once done, the mage teleported the group to the location of the Scorpion King's body. When they appeared, they were next to the pedestal where the mage pointed to the giant body of the insect. The Minotaur bellowed angrily and walked up and out of the cave to take a look around the rest of the island. George was quick to direct him to the southern shores watching the Minotaur's anger grow as he witnessed the gruesome scene.

"Kepler, ask him if he knows anything about the Water Mist Mares."

Kepler spoke to the king and then said, "He does know of them and that they are very powerful."

"Well, then tell the King that the mares are dead thanks to Brandor. Tell him I can prove it."

"George, are we starting this tell me, to tell him, to tell me, to tell you thing again? You're killing me."

"Aw, just shut up and tell him!"

Kepler obeyed and informed George that Horace understood that, if Brandor could defeat these ghostly spirits, there was too much power in their army.

"Tell him I don't want him to attack Brandor right away. They'll need to wait until Brandor attacks the Serpent King... and make sure he understands I have a plan. If he attacks Brandor from behind, he'll have assistance. The Barbarian King's army will be marching from the northern side of the Serpent's Kingdom and will be his allies for this war. Tell him the Barbarians are already marching."

"He wants to know why the Barbarians would help them."

"Tell him it is because they don't want to see Brandor gain too much power and once this war is over, they'll go back to their kingdom in the north. They want to weaken Brandor's army, and a good way to do this is by keeping Brandor from killing all the beasts of Grayham."

Kepler translated.

"He agrees with your logic, George. He also doesn't want Brandor to have this kind of power."

When all was settled, George continued. "Make sure he knows the bears of the Bear Clan will be fighting as their allies also. Tell him I'll try and bring the Bear King to see him soon. They'll be able to devise a plan and work together."

Sam's Throne Room

SAM walked into his throne room with the General in tow. The king was angered and disturbed as he spoke.

"What do you mean he has hidden the pieces of the Crystal Moon in the Serpent King's underground kingdom?"

Michael answered.

"Sire, I'm sorry, but I have only just received this information myself. One of our officers from the City of Champions has come to Brandor to deliver this message to you himself."

Sam snapped again.

"So bring him in, damnit. Why is he in the hallway? He can't very well talk to me out there, now can he?"

Sam had a heavy heart. His emotions were getting the best of him as he barked his orders at Michael. No one had ever seen the king act this way and as a result, they were all walking on eggshells around him.

Both Sam and Shalee had just learned that BJ's remains had been found with a hunting knife at the center of the pile of ash. His friend had committed suicide and, from the looks of it, the advisor had been dead for days. The scouts said that he was found on the beach where he had lit the fire for Helga's passing and from the looks of it, he had taken a spot next to her in the coffin.

Joshua, the officer who traveled to Brandor to deliver the information regarding the Crystal Moon, was now standing in front of the king waiting. He was anxious because Sam was standing with his back to him unaware of his presence.

Eventually Sam tried to clear his mind of all thoughts concerning BJ as he addressed his officer.

"So they tell me you heard a drunken man bragging he had two pieces of the Crystal Moon, and that he was going to take them to the Serpent King's underground city to hide them. Is this right?"

"Yes, sire," Joshua responded.

Sam sat on his throne and took a deep breath. His face turned hard as he responded. "Joshua, will you please tell me why a group of officers in my army were not able to stop this man and bring him to me? Were you all too drunk? What were you doing in that tavern in the first place?"

After hearing the king's tone, Joshua swallowed hard before he responded.

"We were celebrating our friend's last night of being a single man, sire. We tried to stop the man who spoke those traitorous words, but he wielded magic like I've never seen before. He turned our friend to stone. We weren't strong enough to stop him."

Sam knew it was George, but why would he act this way? Once again he responded coldly to his officer. "Why would this man say such things, Joshua? Does it make sense for him to divulge such critical information? What else do you know?"

"My king, the man was drunk when he said these things. When he came into the tavern, he was happy about something and started buying everyone drinks. It was not until much later, after he became intoxicated, that he began to speak carelessly. The boys and I tried to take him into custody, but his magic was strong. He told us that he knew you from a place called Earth, and he called you some words I've never heard before."

This piqued Sam's curiosity and he asked, "What were these words, Joshua?"

"Sire, I don't know that I'd want to say them with so many people present."

Sam leaned over and looked him in the eye. "You've found me on a day that I don't have patience for things you want. I'd tell me now if I were you."

Again Joshua swallowed hard. "Yes, Sire. The man said that you had garesh for brains and that you were a spoiled, weak donkey. He said he was smarter than you and that you could stick all the languages that you speak up your . . . well I think he meant your butt, sire. He called you . . . I think it was, the rear-end of a horse. Shall I continue, sire... there were many other, much stronger sounding words also?"

Sam leaned back in his chair and laughed. "I bet he did, Joshua, I bet he did! That sounds like a drunken man." Everyone in the throne room looked at each other in confusion. They all personally would have been embarrassed by the things Joshua said, but their king just laughed it off.

After a minute, the king stood and motioned for Michael to come forward. "What do we know of the Barbarians? When we were in the cave, George said he was running things up there. Has there been any movement of their army?"

Michael responded, "Sire, we should be getting word back from our scouts within days. I dispatched them after we left the island and told them to report back four Peaks of Bailem from now. I have sent other scouts every two Peaks of Bailem since then to make sure we get updated information. If the first set of scouts doesn't know anything, the others are sure to find something out."

Sam formulated a plan.

"I want the first five legions of the army to stay here and protect Brandor. I want the other five and what's left of the eleventh legion to assemble at the City of Champions. If the information the scouts bring back suggests that George is really going to hide the Crystals, we will attack the Serpent's Kingdom. If it's not accurate, we will head north and attack the City of Bloodvain. I'm not about to wait here for something to happen. You have only eight Peaks of Bailem to do this, General. Do not fail or I'll lead the army myself!"

Sam did not wait to hear Michael's reaction and stormed out of the room. He knew it was possible to make his orders work but right now his main concern was to make sure that Shalee was okay. He knew his queen would be grieving. Since he had arrived in Grayham, both of them had seen far too much death. The fact that they now had to grieve for someone else they cared so much for was going to be hard. He would take his queen and go with her to where BJ had died. He was sure that their friends would want them to stand over their ashes and say goodbye.

Two Peaks of Bailem Later

AFTER smoothing everything over with the Minotaur King, George left for the Bear King's cave. He rode Kepler, moving along with his brothers, into the caves and, as before, it made a strong impression. The conversation was similar to the one they had with the Minotaur King also including a trip to Scorpion Island. When the big bear, Groth, saw the Scorpion King's body, he too became angered. The Kodiak-looking bear walked through the southern shore, speechless at the massacre. George made sure he pointed out that Brandor had also killed the Water Mist Mares. Groth's reaction was just like that of the Minotaur's.

The beast felt that Brandor's army was too strong and something had to be done. After all this, the mage brought the bear with them to the top of the Minotaur King's pasture where Kepler translated for both beasts. After a while, Horace and Groth had formulated a plan to fight together with the assistance of Kepler's translations. They would also fight alongside Kepler's Skeleton Warriors and his giant cats would be joining the fight alongside the barbarians. This pleased both of the beast kings.

Between the 9,000 barbarians, 1,500 bears, 1,100 Minotaurs, 300 giant cats, 2,100 snakes and the 400 Skeleton Warriors, the forces attacking Brandor's army would be over 14,400 strong.

The mage took the bear home after watching his plan fall seamlessly into place. He asked Kepler to say goodbye to Groth and watched as the mighty Bear King rose up to show his appreciation for George's help.

Illustrated By: Angela Woods

George took the cats with him to the north side of Lethwitch to speak with them before heading into town to spend the evening with Athena.

George gave Koffler another message for the Barbarian King, telling Senchae to attack from the north of the Serpent King's city once Brandor arrives. He wrote that there would be reinforcements in the form of bears, Minotaurs, Skeletons, and cats, all of which would flank Brandor and come at them from all sides. This would be Senchae's greatest victory and the glory would rest on the great Barbarian King's shoulders. He would go down in history as the man who defeated Brandor. The mage figured this would be enough of an ego boost to solidify this part of his plans. He told Koffler to be swift in his journey, and that he would give the demon something special once he returned. He would teleport the giant cat to Angel's Village and then retire for the night.

George would have been proud of Senchae if he knew what the big Barbarian had done—he sent a few of his scouts to collect the unicorns and had them join them for the battle. It was an unexpected use of force that the mage had not counted on. By the time 50 unicorns had joined the battle, Sam would be facing a hellish army of many different kinds of beings, all of them with a unique style of fighting.

Kepler, while waiting for George to return from Lethwitch, went into the Enchanted Forest to send out his orders. He already had sent one of his tigers to gather all the giant cats of the land, instructing them to move only at night and travel toward Lake Zandra, running as fast as they could and staying out of sight. They were to hide north of Zandra until after Brandor entered the Serpent's Kingdom. After this happened, they were to circle west of the lake and join the Barbarians for the attack heading south.

Kepler also sent 400 Skeleton Warriors to join the fight by sending another one of his raven friends with a message for the leader of his skeleton army. The verbal message included code words that only the bony skeleton commander knew. They too were to travel day and night and stay away from populated areas. He wanted them to join the cats at Zandra. Once Brandor entered the Serpent's Kingdom, they were to circle east of the lake to attack with the bears and Minotaurs.

Two Peaks of Bailem later

GEORGE collected Athena's family and teleported them in small groups to Gessler Village. He paid the innkeeper enough coin to clear everyone out of the place, intending to keep her family there until he had regained enough of his power to accompany them to City View.

Since they would never set foot in Lethwitch again, George also retrieved Maldwin from his mother-in-law's barn. Kepler told the rat that it was time to get his family. George was keeping his promise and Maldwin was happy. He sent Keller from Lethwitch to the Cave of Sorrow to retrieve the rodent's family and bring them all to City View to join them. There would be enough time before they arrived for George to figure out a place for them to live, figuring there had to be a cave where they could stay until he finished building something special.

The journey to move Athena's family to the Barbarian city would take over 12 Peaks of Bailem. Before they could leave the inn, George would need to recover from the massive power drain from teleporting the family to Gessler in the first place. Rest was mandatory, not an option.

George slept next to his wife while Kepler and Maldwin kept watch over the Bloody Trough's doors to ensure the family's safety. They would all be leaving in the morning for City View.

He had just fallen asleep when Lasidious appeared to him in a dream.

"Hello, George, I've been watching you. I'm impressed at what you have done but . . . you're needed somewhere else. Going to City View isn't where I need you in order to get your daughter back."

"Okay, I'm tired and can hardly move. I need rest, Lasidious. What do I need to do in order to get Abbie back?"

Lasidious refreshed his soul.

"I have replenished your strength. I need you to sleep later, my friend. I need you to go to the World of Luvelles. There's work to do, George, but it has to be your choice."

"What? Why would I want to go there? I just now got myself into a good position here. What about my wife and her family?"

"I have taken care of that problem. Your wife and her family will be able to go with you. I also have made arrangements for Kepler to go."

"What about Kepler's brothers and Maldwin? I can't leave them behind. Hell, Kepler won't go without his brothers anyway." George thought a second before continuing. "I promised Maldwin a good home for his family and Keller has gone to get them. Koffler is delivering a message to the Barbarian King, so this is terrible timing, Lasidious, just terrible, man!"

"Do I detect a soft spot in that cold heart of yours, George? You don't need to worry about Kepler. He's a demon. As far as Maldwin goes, I'll personally make sure his family has an amazing home inside the Cliffs of Latasef. I'll make sure they are protected and I'll even create them a tree that grows cheese. It won't be safe for you and your family here, George. You'll be a hunted man. I'd rather you use your skills elsewhere. You've proven to be an asset to me and now the gods are very interested in everything that is happening on Grayham. You've masterfully manipulated this world and your daughter will be with you soon because of it. I swear to you, George that it won't be long before I have the power to do so."

"So how do I get to Luvelles?"

"You need to teleport you and your family to Merchant Island and find a man named Hesston Bangs. He will put you all into a special container that will be carried by the Merchant Angels to Luvelles. Once you're there, I'd like you to travel to the village of Floren. You will need to find an elven witch family named Rolfe from the Clan of Ashdown. They'll have a new baby living with them. I want you to go there, kill the family, and raise the baby as your nephew. The baby will be born by the time you arrive and this may come as a shock to you... but this baby is my son. It is this boy who will give me the power to get your daughter back, but not until he's a little older."

"Holy garesh, Lasidious, that's crazy, man! You want me to raise your child as my own nephew? So how will I convince Athena's sister to go along with something like this? That's heavy news to be springing on her just out of the blue like that... I mean, how would I break this kind of news to her? I can just see it now.

Hey… Susanne… Oh, by the way, you have a kid that you forgot about. That's just freaking nuts, man. Don't get me wrong, Lasidious, I'd be honored to take care of your kid. But how do I do it?"

"I'm sure you'll figure it out."

"Sure… just leave it up to me… nice, man. I better get a really sweet house out of this to babysit in. I want something that reminds me of Earth too. You've been in my head enough to know what I like. I want the whole family to have houses of their own. Do we have a deal?"

"I'm sure I can manage that, George."

"Right on… then it's settled, so how will I get everyone to Merchant Island? I've never seen the place before. What about the crystals I've buried?"

"I want you to take both pieces of the Crystal Moon with you. I'll be hiding the third piece on Luvelles, but I'll reveal its location to you later. As far as Athena's family goes, have Maldwin prepare their minds to perceive the baby as one of their own before you leave this inn. Use his visions to make them believe that my son is Susanne's child. I'm sure you know how to make this happen. The Head Master of Luvelles is expecting you, but he thinks that Amar has referred you to study under him while you're there."

"Why would he think that? Amar is dead."

Lasidious gave an evil grin. "Let's just say someone who looked like Amar appeared to him and told him how powerful you are. The Head Master was happy to see his old student and, based on his recommendation, made preparations for you and your family to come. You'll have your nice houses, and yes, I'll make sure they're built to your style. Amar also told the headmaster to give you plenty of coin when you arrive. It's waiting for you at an inn called Kebble's Kettle.

"You'll be rich, but we'll have to work hard to keep the gods busy. I need you to make a mess, just like the one you did here and keep the gods' attention off of my son. I think the safest place for my boy is going to be right under the gods' noses. They don't have any clue if Susanne has a child or not. It will seem normal for you to call my son your nephew. This will be a great deception and you'll be a part of it."

George cut in.

"You still haven't told me how to get to Merchant Island. And don't you think that Amar visiting the headmaster after he was dead will throw red flags up to the gods regarding the timing of these events?"

Lasidious laughed.

"Head Master Brayson thinks he saw Amar a while ago, before he died. He has no clue Amar is dead. The timing will be fine. He was easy to manipulate. I'll have to show you how I did it someday. Besides, the gods won't be thinking about Amar. Out of sight... out of mind, you just have to love that.

"This next part is really going to get your goat. You have the ability to look through Kepler's eyes and see into his mind if he allows you to. The demon has been to Merchant Island so you can find a spot to teleport to by using his memories. The cat never forgets anything, so it will be safe to teleport based on what he remembers. You have grown close enough to the demon for him to trust you inside his mind. Just ask him for permission and explain why you need to do it. Open your own mind, George, and I'll show you how to do this."

George asked smugly, "How could you have forgotten to tell me something this useful? Do you realize how much more I could've accomplished if you'd told me this sooner? I could've teleported everywhere and not wasted time walking all over this ridiculous place."

"Who said I forgot? I'm sure you could have made a bigger mess here on Grayham, but I think the one you've made already will do just fine. I need you to hurry to Merchant Island. You'll be leaving for Luvelles in two Peaks of Bailem. You're scheduled to be transported by the Merchant Angels that night. You can sleep and regain your powers on the way. The trip will take two Peaks of Bailem as well and this should give you plenty of time to rest."

George thought a moment.

"I think this will work. I'll get the Crystals and stay here until Late Bailem tomorrow. Maldwin can make the family understand that Susanne has a child and we can leave for Merchant Island after dark to find this Hesston Bangs. Luvelles, here we come. Wow, we have a ticket out of here. I'm relieved now that I think about it. Now, will you please tell me where to find this, Hesston?"

Lasidious smiled. "Tell Kepler that Hesston works at the docks of the Merchant Angels during the day. They only appear at night to gather everything that needs to be transported to the other worlds. This will give you most of the day to get into the container that has been prepared for you and your family. Amar took good care of you, don't you think?"

Lasidious laughed with George as he continued. "Kepler will know where to go once he hears this information. I'll speak with you again once you're on Luvelles and have my son with you but it may be a while before this happens so be patient, my friend. Until then, have a good trip, George. It won't be long before your Abbie will be with you."

Lasidious imparted beautiful visions of Abbie into George's mind as he left him drifting off back to sleep.

The Grayham Inquirer

When inquiring minds need to know where their favorite characters are.

GEORGE, his family, and Kepler have gone to the World of Luvelles. The ride provided by the Merchant Angels to this new world was a dark and dismal one. The container was barely large enough to hold them all. But despite the fact that everyone had to sit in their own bodily waste in the darkness, everyone remained in good spirits.

George led the group to the Village of Floren but had no idea how to find Headmaster Brayson. The only thing he knew for sure was he had an elven witch family to kill and a nephew to take care of. Susanne and the family now believed that Susanne had a son, their minds manipulated by Maldwin before leaving Gessler. Even Athena was now talking about a baby she had never met before.

Maldwin's visions were specific—after the baby was born, there were health issues that had to be dealt with. The family now believed that George had rushed the child to Luvelles to receive the attention he needed for his survival. But there was one detail about the baby's birth that Maldwin's vision never delivered into the families' minds, a detail George never thought about, one that could possibly cause problems later.

KEPLER had left word for his brothers to govern their pass within the Mountains of Latasef. As it turned out, Lasidious had been right about the demon. The jaguar was more than happy to leave his brothers behind.

CELESTRIA gave birth. She had cleaned the child up and after holding him, handed the beautiful baby boy to the elven witches and left for her home on Ancient's Sovereign. Once home, she waved her hand over her belly, removing all evidence that she had gone through a pregnancy and waited for Lasidious.

SAM asked Shalee to stay behind in Brandor. She was not handling the stress of losing BJ and Helga very well. She had been crying for days and the healers warned Sam that, if she did not calm down, the baby could be in danger. As a doctor, he knew they were right. Her depression made her a prime candidate for a miscarriage and he was not about to risk his baby or his queen, despite the asset she would be in battle. When Shalee tried to object, Sam would not even consider it.

After arriving in the City of Champions, Sam received word from his scouts that the army of the Barbarian King was headed south to the Serpent King's city along the west coast. By the sounds of the reports, the Barbarians and the snakes would be outmatched in this war. Days ago he had ordered Michael to turn the army in the direction of the snake's underground home. The army had crossed the Snake River, and was now two Peaks of Bailem from the underground city where the Crystals were said to be hidden.

Thank you for reading the final edition of The Grayham Inquirer

Chapter 39

Surrounded

Griffon Cliffs
Below the Temple of the Gods

MOSLEY was with the Griffon, Soresym, within the cliffs of Griffon Falls, below the Temple of the Gods.

"Sam is walking into a trap and there's nothing I can do about it. To have the power of the gods and be able to do nothing because of our laws is frustrating," he said.

"Trap . . . what are you referring to?" Soresym said looking out across the beauty of the valley below. "I have heard nothing."

"You do know that Sam is now the King of Brandor?"

"I do. *That* kind of information travels fast."

"Well, he's leading Brandor's army to the Serpent King's underground city. He has no idea that he's about to be attacked from all sides. The bears are working with the Minotaurs and are planning to attack from behind once they cross into Seth's Kingdom. The Barbarians are approaching from the north and the serpents from the south. But this isn't the worst of it. The unicorns travel with the Barbarians, along with Kepler's giant cats and his skeletons travel with the Minotaurs. Sam has no idea that he's about to be caught in the middle and I'm unable to help him."

Soresym looked confused. "Why would the Minotaurs . . . or the bears, for that matter, break their alliance with Brandor—Brandor has done nothing but allow them to live in peace. The kings of Brandor have allowed their kind to compete in the arenas as well. This doesn't make sense."

"The Crystal Moon has been stolen and has been hidden in—"

"Stolen?" the griffon interrupted. "How?"

"How isn't important. What's important is that it's missing and its pieces are now scattered throughout the worlds... two of the pieces are on Grayham. The bears and Minotaurs have been deceived. They believe that Brandor plans to attack and kill all the beasts of Grayham."

"Why would they think this?"

"Brandor went to the Scorpion King's Island to retrieve one of the missing pieces of the Crystal Moon. When they got there, the scorpions attacked and there was no chance of negotiations. All of the scorpions were destroyed in this battle but Brandor was still unable to retrieve this piece."

"What do you mean—unable? Why would there be a piece of the Crystal Moon there?"

"Lasidious decided to place it there to start a war."

"And why would Lasidious do that?"

"Again, my friend, "why" isn't important. Lasidious does things for his own reasons. What's important is that a man named George got to the Crystal first and took it. George also has another piece of the Crystal and has claimed to have hidden both pieces within the Serpent's underground city. Brandor is going there to fight for them."

"I was wondering why the temple had been sealed. It was good to keep the faithful from knowing this. Panic would have filled the land."

"It looks like Sam is going to lose his life trying to retrieve these pieces. I've been watching Grayham carefully and have seen the movements of all the armies."

Soresym shrieked. "Sam is a good human. It isn't his time to die. The gods must do something to stop this."

"The laws of the gods will not allow us to intervene. Soresym, you're mighty and the leader of your kind—yet even you are still bound by your own laws. I'm sure you can understand."

"What I understand is that Sam is the king that Brandor has always needed. I've come to know him as I've traveled with him. Something must be done."

"But who is left to help? I must be going, my friend; there are matters I must attend to. All we can do now is hope that Sam is strong enough to survive this battle." Mosley vanished.

The griffon sighed and looked out across the valley in deep thought.

The Home of Lasidious and Celestria

"CELESTRIA, George masterfully manipulated this world. He was always two steps ahead of everything that was going on and made the most unlikely of allies to do it," Lasidious said as he lay in bed with his goddess.

"I so missed your smile while I was gone," the goddess said, rolling over and cupping his face with her hands. "I can't tell you how many times I thought of what fun you must be having with all your scheming. So you decided to send George to take care of our baby on Luvelles?"

"I did!"

"I like the idea that his wife's sister, Susanne, is the one who'll be acting as his mother until we bring him home. I hope George gives him a good name."

"If I know George, our son will be given a strong name."

"So, exactly what's going on with the war? Will it be enough to keep the attention of the gods?"

Lasidious kissed her forehead and said, "I made sure that I kept the gods with me for four Peaks of Bailem after I appeared to George. Mosley managed to get away from me at times, but I don't think he knows anything useful. I ran the others everywhere with me. I have a good idea on how everyone is thinking. Between watching Sam, the Bear King, Minotaur, Serpent, and Barbarian kings, and the creatures that Kepler commands closing in on one another, I'd say that we were busy. Believe me, none of the gods have any knowledge that George has left for Merchant Island with Athena's family. It will be a while before they figure it out."

"It is comforting to hear your confidence."

"I'm glad you're comforted. The Headmaster of Luvelles isn't scheduled to meet with George for quite some time. After he kills the elven witches, there will be no reason to use his magic and draw attention to them all. George should arrive in Floren and have them all dead before the war ends. I don't think the gods will take their attentions off the war over the death of a few witches."

Celestria snuggled up to the God of Mischief. "I knew you had it all under control. Please don't ever make me have another child without using my powers again. I don't think I could do it again. The witches drove me crazy. But on a positive note, I did learn how to bake again." Both the gods enjoyed these simple thoughts as they kissed and embraced.

The next morning, Lasidious awoke, leaving his goddess lying in bed, and vanished to meet with Maldwin. As instructed, the rat was taking his family to the Cliffs of Latasef.

"Maldwin, we need to speak," the god said in the rat's language.

Maldwin replied. "Who are you?"

"A friend; George informed me of his promise to give you a wonderful new home."

"Where is George anyway? Kepler's brother said to make sure I took my family west to the Cliffs of Latasef, but I have no clue where to go once I get there."

Lasidious smiled. "George saw to it that you were taken care of. He has asked me to make sure that a home like no other is provided for you. Follow the mountains to the east until you come to a small opening before the edge of the cliffs. What you'll find there is an amazing home—with a nice surprise inside. I've protected this home so your family will always be safe."

Maldwin twitched his nose with excitement. "Thank you. When you see George, please tell him thank you for me as well."

"You can tell him yourself. I'm sure this isn't the last time you'll see him."

With that said, the god vanished.

The Next Day on The World of Luvelles

WHEN GEORGE arrived in the Village of Floren with Athena's family, it was past Late Bailem. The mage loved this new world. Everything he had seen since his arrival had some sort of magical influence used to create it. The magic here was much, much stronger than anything on Grayham and, in some places, the air smelled of it.

Their journey had taken them through other villages that were similar in size to Floren, but they did not appear on his map. The general look and feel of these homes and villages was more to George's liking with even the smaller homes constructed, or rather created, in such a way that they exuded class. Magic was used for many things that did not exist on Grayham and George was very happy to have a cold drink instead of warm ale.

As George entered the inn with Athena's family, Kepler didn't hide. All along the way, they had seen others walking throughout the countryside with various types of animals at their sides. The inn was called Kebble's Kettle, and George was amused at the quaint originality of the name.

The people of Luvelles seemed to be, for the most part, very pleasant, but both George and Kepler noticed there was also a dark side. Some of the people they met on their journeys seemed two-faced, despite their sweet outward appearance. George was a master at picking up on this since he was this kind of person himself.

The inn was comfortable, almost like an upscale motel back on Earth, with many magical upgrades. The walls looked as if they were created out of some sort of construction material, but upon further investigation, seemed to be organic. It was as if they were alive and it felt strange to pass his hand across them as the tiny little hairs which lined their surface, hairs that couldn't be seen until closely inspected, tickled George's palm as he passed it across them. It was as if the walls themselves held within them a natural warmth, just like a human body holds its own heat.

This is fascinating, he thought. *It's like the building is alive, but still with the appearance of a regular building. I really need to look into how this is done while were here. The magic on the world must be extremely powerful.*

Aside from a small check-in counter that was to the left of the entrance, the dining area and the tavern filled the rest of a spacious room. When patrons ordered drinks they simply reached out and pulled them from mid-air as the drinks floated themselves over to their tables. There was a vaulted ceiling five stories high and the colors of the inn were earth tones, and very pleasing to the eye.

No stairs lead up to the remaining levels of the structure nor were there any elevators. George watched as a woman stepped up onto a small circular platform and then simply appeared on the balcony of the next floor up. As George stood there looking up, a dustpan flew by his head and asked to be excused as it made it was to the far side of the room, allowing a small broom to push dirt from the floor onto its surface. The dustpan then lifted from the floor and disappeared through a large set of double doors.

You've got to be kidding me! Even the cleaning is done by magic. I hope our new homes are like this also!

"Hello, friend," the innkeeper said after watching them a while. "I see we need a number of beds for the night."

A short, wobbly man, barely able to see over the counter, climbed up a set of booster steps to look George in the eye. He had narrow, long, pointy ears and a pudgy nose with a billowing pipe pinched between his teeth. The pipe smelled of a sweet, cherry-flavored tobacco that had stained his graying mustache a yellowish-brown over the seasons, complementing his rosy cheeks. George found the tobacco scent pleasant and could not help but notice how the points of the man's long ears poked through his graying hair. He smiled as he approached the counter.

"Yes thank you, my name is George and this is my family . . . and yourself?"

"Well, if you saw the sign, then you know my name," he said with a jolly grin. "I'm Kebble and you can call me, well Kebble works," he said with a laugh. "Everyone in this village calls me Kebble. Welcome to Kebble's Kettle. So what can Kebble do for you today?"

The short man was amused with himself and George turned to look at Kepler as if to say—*Is this guy for real?* He reached out to shake the Elf's hand.

Kebble eventually stopped laughing and took his hand. Slowly he counted everyone in George's group, needing to do it three times since he kept losing count. After a while he said, "I see you need enough beds for 31 people and one giant kitty."

Kepler snapped, "I'm not a kitty. My name is Kepler and we need beds for 34 humans and one jaguar"... thinking to himself, *What an idiot.*

"Whoa," Kebble responded. "Looks like you have a testy little pussycat on your hands there, George. You can keep him in your room, but we have special places for our Goswigs to relieve themselves outside. If you'd like, you can take Kepler outside to the sandbox to the right of the inn."

"Goswigs," George repeated with a confused look on his face. "What's a Goswig?"

Kebble stopped a moment and looked at the human. "You don't know what a Goswig is?"

"Should I know what a Goswig is?"

"Well of course, if you travel with one, then you should know something so trivial." Kebble pointed to Kepler.

"Kepler isn't a Goswig. He's a friend of mine. I'm new to this world and have no clue what you're talking about. I recently arrived by the Merchant Angels."

Kebble became excited. The happy man's fat cheeks wrinkled as his smile widened.

"You must be here by the authority of the Headmaster. What an honor to meet you, George. Allow me to give you complimentary rooms for your first night. Indeed, I actually have your package waiting for you as Headmaster Brayson requested."

"Good, but maybe you and I can speak of this later. I'd like to get my family settled."

"By all means, I also have a package for someone named Mary. Is she also in your group?"

Mary heard her name and approached the counter. "I'm Mary, but I doubt that you'd have a package for me. I have only just arrived on this world a short while ago."

Kebble grinned, "I think we'll let the package decide if you're the correct Mary that it seeks."

"What?" Mary said confused, "I don't understand!"

"You don't need to understand. Give me your hand and I'll show you."

Mary held out her arm and Kebble took her hand. His hand was much smaller than hers as he pulled it close, pushing her fingertips against the note that had been placed on the side of the package. Sure enough, the paper changed color from a bright yellow to a passionate red indicating the package was truly for her.

Kebble puffed on his pipe as he nodded.

"Yep, this is your package, madam. The card is never wrong. Someone has their eye on you."

Mary was not sure if she should be happy or scared. She had never had anything like this happen to her before.

"Thank you, Kebble... I think!"

"You're welcome, my lady." The chubby elf turned his attention back to George. "You must be a very talented apprentice to be given such an honor. To be invited to come to this world by the Headmaster is a rare thing. I'm also sure that you'll be assigned a Goswig someday and you'll be able to learn about them for yourself."

"Oh, my goodness, Mother," Athena shouted, seeing what was in the package that Mary had opened.

"I know . . . have you ever seen anything so beautiful?" Mary said, as she was now holding up an incredibly elegant dinner gown. "This is my favorite color... and it's my size. Should I be happy? How is it possible that someone could know so much about me? Kebble, do you know who sent me this package?"

"I do, but I can't say anything. I'll say this however . . . you have nothing to worry about. Your admirer isn't a threat to you or your family's safety."

Kebble once again turned to George.

"As I was going to say earlier," the happy elf leaned in and whispered to George (although Kepler still managed to hear him)....
"Just make sure that your big kitty doesn't pee on the floor. I normally don't allow real animals to enter the inn, but I'll make an exception since you're new to this world. I know how hard it is to keep a real animal in line. Filthy little critters, don't you agree?"

George could feel the jaguar's agitation but thanked Kebble for his generosity anyway and asked for their rooms. Each of them stepped onto the platform and appeared in front of their doors on the fourth level. Once in the room, George familiarized himself with it.

"Athena, I'll be back. I'm going to go and get Susanne's baby."

"Oh, that's wonderful, take me with you!"

He had to think quickly. He still needed to kill the witches so taking Athena was impossible. "You know, babe, I kind of need some alone time. I'll make it up to you later, okay?"

"No problem, hurry back with...? With . . . with, ummm, I can't remember the baby's name, honey. I'm such a terrible aunt."

"Garrin, his name is Garrin," George replied as he kissed her. "Tell your sister that I'll be back soon. I'm sure that you're going to be the best aunt on this world, sweetheart! The whole family will be happy to see the little guy."

The mage took Kepler with him, once again standing on the circular platform as they left the inn. George hated lying to Athena, but he could not figure a way around this one. The lie was necessary to get Abbie back. If he had to raise this child of the gods to get her soul released from the Book of Immortality, then so be it. But he would be damned before he would allow lying to his beautiful wife to become a habit. He wanted desperately to protect their relationship from such deceptions.

Once downstairs, he asked Kebble if he knew of the elven witch family called Rolfe. The innkeeper knew them and said they were from the Clan of Ashdown, telling George how to get to their home, and that the walk was not far.

"Thanks, Kebble... I'll go and visit them one of these days. I'll find you in the morning and get the package you have for me."

"That will be fine. I have a safe place for you to store things if you need it. I wouldn't want to be keeping that much coin on me if I were you, especially not in this village. We have many different characters that come through here. I'm sure you understand what I mean. The Headmaster himself asked me to provide this for you."

"Great, thanks Kebble."

Once they were outside and walking to the witches' home, Kepler spoke. "Kebble irritates me. Can you believe the nerve of that guy? You know I hate the word kitty ever since you killed the Saber Lord and tortured him. I have half a mind to go back in there and eat him. Tell the kitty not to pee on the floors! Real animals are filthy little critters! The nerve of that guy… it makes me sick! It's too bad that he wasn't evil, or I would have my first skeleton on this world."

George patted his big furry back. "Once we kill these witches, you and I need to lay low for a while until we are contacted by the Headmaster so let's not do anything until we have further instructions from Lasidious. Please tell me you agree and will deal with the changes for awhile."

"I agree, but I refuse to use his stupid sandbox. I'll go find some bushes like any self-respecting jaguar should."

George smiled quietly to himself as they continued their midnight walk towards the witches' home.

As George stood over the dead, stone bodies of the elven witch family, studying their lifeless faces. Both he and Kepler had made quick work of them, and the mage used his powers to keep them silent as well. After a moment of staring at their handiwork George looked for the baby. He found the god-child in one of the bedrooms and lifted baby Garrin into his arms.

On his way back out of the room, he waved his free hand over the pile of stone. It crumbled to the floor in a mound of unrecognizable rubble. George commanded a wind to enter the home to gather the pile of powdered stone and the dust was carried out of the village and scattered into an open field.

George looked at the baby. "Hey, little guy," he said, holding the child's hand in the palm of his own. "My name is Uncle George and I'm going to take good care of you. Let's go find your mom."

The mage reached down and touched Kepler's back, teleporting them all back to his room at the inn, where he handed the baby to Athena. He smiled at the joy that the newborn brought to his wife's face. Soon the entire family was in their room, loving and googling over the god-child, Garrin.

War Has Begun
The Serpent's Kingdom

TWO Peaks of Bailem earlier, Sam's army had crossed the Snake River into the Serpent King's kingdom. They passed through an enormous mire, it was cold, wet, mossy, waist deep in spots, and slowed the pace of every legion. The army had not been able to sleep that first night due to the awful conditions. It was a dreadful place, full of predators, which under normal circumstances, would have attacked any single man. However, due to the size of the army, these same predators fled for their own safety—all, that is, except the leeches. They attached themselves to many of the men's bodies and were unable to be removed until the men were on dry land. They pressed on to find solid ground and when a tent could be pitched, the men burned the slimy little blood suckers, tearing them away from their skin. Not long after, they finally found sleep.

The underground city of the Serpent King rested inside an enormous area of seemingly-impenetrable lava stone. Sam could not figure out how these massive serpents burrowed into this type of earth, but, since his arrival on Grayham, he had seen many things that he would have never thought possible.

The General Absolute was nervous about the army making camp in such a vulnerable position, worried about a surprise attack by the serpents, but none ever came... it was as if the snakes wanted to stay below ground and wait for Brandor to come to them—or better yet, perhaps they didn't know the army was coming. Either way, none of this bothered Sam—he had an idea and had come prepared.

Two days later, the Peak of Bailem had arrived.

"General, I want a report," Sam ordered.

"Sire, the four legions you ordered to meet the Barbarian army should be in position by morning. I have sent Dreston and his legion into the serpent's city and we have 1,500 men left to assist Dreston once he flushes the snakes out."

Both Sam and Michael sat on horseback. They had hoped to find a tactical location in which to command the army, but the terrain was fairly flat, with tall trees making an advantage practically impossible. The trees burrowed their heavy trunks through the lava stone, so a clear line of sight could not be found. Both men would need to rely on their scouts to bring them updated information.

Dreston and his legion of men slowly descended into one of the many openings of Seth's underground, reptilian hideaway, with torches held high and swords drawn. Eventually they came to an impasse with no room to move. To their left was a drop into darkness with no visible bottom and to the right, more of the same. The path of lava stone before them was narrow, no wider than 20 feet, an impossible crossing for 2,500 men. The cavern's ceiling could not be seen, their torches' flames not strong enough to penetrate the darkness. This spot would have to do.

Up till this point, there had been no sign of the snakes—not even a single hiss had been heard. The men had descended nearly 500 feet without any confrontation... something was not right; this was too easy.

"Okay men, this will have to do, we can't go any further," Dreston whispered as he held up his rugged, scar-covered hand. He was a strong man, with nine different previous engagements with some of the Barbarian's scouting parties under his belt. His legion was the king's finest and his men were known for their fearless acceptance of impossible tasks. Today's task was no exception.

"Lieutenant, bring the barrels forward and place them every 20 paces on either side of this ledge. I want each lid opened and the wicks set. We'll burn these slithering little suckers out of here."

Each barrel held 100 pounds of a crude oil called Solsum. It was a flammable, slow burning substance which all of Grayham use to light their homes at night. When used in mass quantities, the smoke was toxic. In total, 60 barrels would be dropped, 30 on each side.

The barrels were now in position and three men were assigned to each to ensure they were successfully pushed into the pit. Dreston moved to the edge and held his torch over the side.

Something moved, trying to escape the light, moving inward, towards the ledge they now stood on—beneath their feet. Dreston knew instantly they were all in danger. This was an ambush. They were exactly where the slithering beasts wanted them.

He signaled to light the wicks and the torches were lowered. Taking hold of the hand of one of his men, leaning out over the ledge, what he saw gave urgency. Hundreds of holes covered the surface of the walls below and twice as many eyes were beginning to climb towards them.

Dreston shouted, "Get those damn barrels over the edge now—prepare for battle. They're coming! Retreat to the surface as we fight." He finished his orders just as the first of the giant snakes crested the ledge and began using its long, powerful body in a whip-like fashion, knocking many of the men off. Their hopeless cries echoed throughout the cavern as they disappeared into the darkness below.

Some of the barrels were caught in the serpent's coils as they fell, the liquid splashed onto their cold-blooded bodies and burst into flames. The heat caused a frenzied reaction that worked both against Dreston's men and their own kind. As they burned, they flailed wildly, knocking both serpents and men alike to their deaths.

Dreston called for battle, pulling his sword from the eye of his first kill. He turned to look for another as two fangs surrounded his lower body from behind. Agony filled his eyes as the serpent snatched him up and slung him from side to side.

The legion leader's leg gave under the pressure and shredded at the hip as if it was nothing more than an overcooked piece of beef being picked apart. The serpent quickly swallowed the appendage and turned to find the rest of his delicacy. Dreston landed hard, his arm breaking beneath the weight of his body as his fall knocked two more of his men from the ledge. The coils of the giant snake encompassed his body without further hesitation. The legionnaire maintained his wit and with his last ounce of heart—he thrust his blade upward as the serpent's mouth closed in over his head. The creature cried out in a bloodcurdling, hissing scream, its body twisting into a tight ball of death as the smoke from the exploded barrels of oil billowed upward from the depths of the darkness.

The serpents began to disappear as the toxic fumes turned into a thick black fog. The remaining men who could still move began to retreat above ground.

$$\infty\quad\infty$$

"Sire," the first scout shouted as he stopped in front of Sam. "The Barbarians travel with the giant cats of the north. They're fighting together side-by-side and that isn't the worst of it. The unicorns were hidden within their numbers. I saw them appear. They are magical beasts, sire. They have enough power to destroy us all!"

"How many cats and how many unicorns are there, soldier?"

"Hundreds of giant cats and at least 40 or maybe 50 unicorns," the man answered. "We can't fight this kind of force. All our men will die for sure. Sire, we need to retreat and establish a new plan."

Sam thought for a moment and then agreed. "General, sound the horns and let's get out of here."

Michael had not given the order before the second scout rushed up from behind them, screaming and nearly out of breath.

"Sire," the scout said as he bent over to capture the air he needed to continue, "The Minotaurs are marching behind us and will be here shortly. They travel with the undead skeletons of the demon cat, Kepler. They number close to 2,000 strong. These skeletons can't be killed, sire. They've already killed four other scouts, but I was able to break away and remain unseen."

Sam shifted his mount towards Michael. "Why would the Minotaurs be fighting against us? I was told that they were our allies!"

Michael shook his head in confusion.

"This doesn't make any sense. For them to be marching with the skeletons is, well, I don't know—I'm at a loss!"

"General, let's retreat to the southern shores. We'll work our way home from there. Sound the horn."

Michael began to raise the horn to his mouth when yet again another voice called to them. "My king, the bears are coming," the third scout screamed as he approached on horseback.

"General, I thought the bears were our allies also," Sam snapped. "What the hell is going on here?"

"They are our allies. This is a great blessing. We can use this to our advantage. We can ask for their assistance. Maybe they saw us coming to fight the snakes and wanted to help."

"No, my king," the scout cut in abruptly. "The bears have already killed two of us and are coming as enemies. They're over 1,000 strong, sire—they are angered." Sam looked at Michael. "Do you have any bright ideas, General? It appears that we're surrounded."

"I don't… the majority of our army is too far north to stop this kind of a force. Today appears to be a good day to die, sire." The General ripped his sword from its sheath and held it high. "It has been a pleasure to know you, my King, but the time for plans and words has passed. I say we fight like rabid dogs and die like men. To die beside you, Sam, will be my honor."

The king lifted Kael high into the air and commanded the Sword of the Gods to bring forth its fire. The blade screamed with joy at the thought of the pain they were about to inflict.

"Michael, I believe you're right, it is a good day to die."

Sam thought of Shalee and his unborn baby. He knew there would be many wonderful things that he would miss. The first steps, first smile, first words, and the joy they would all bring to his wife's face. He could only hope that his queen would be strong enough to handle raising their baby on her own. He looked into the sky and was about to shout out his love for her, but as he did, he noticed a dark, fluttering cloud approaching.

"General, what do you make of that cloud?" Sam shouted as he steadied his mount.

"My lord, it is the griffons. They are powerful. It looks as if every creature in Grayham is coming for us now, sire."

"Don't be so quick to judge, General." Sam lifted Kael high into the air and commanded the blade to burn with a bright light.

"Soresym!" he screamed. He could only hope the Griffon had not come to fight against him.

From high above, Soresym's eagle eyes spotted the King of Brandor's signal. Before altering his course, he ordered his family of over 100 griffons and 200 hippogriffs into battle.

The pure white, magical unicorns had been ordered to act as the first wave of Senchae's attack, ahead of both the giant cats of Kepler and the Barbarian King's army. They were a powerful force, despite numbering only 50 strong. As the magical steeds galloped into battle, lightning shot from their horns and arched between the men of Brandor's army with an intense heat. The joints of their plate armor were welded solid as they fell to the ground, charred and lifeless.

The magic was overwhelming, indefensible, and Brandor's men retreated, dodging from side-to-side to avoid an electrical death. But on this day, at this very spot, Nathan, a sergeant, and four of his men would hold their ground. They would not run. They had found an alcove within the lava rock to hide, and were waiting for the unicorns to pass.

Nathan's father, Thomas, had been a tactician of war for most of his life and had advised the late King of Brandor, Keldwin, for many seasons. Thomas was essential when it came to planning different battle strategies to protect the kingdom from the possibility of attack. These strategies had been embedded into Nathan's nature as a small child and he recognized a helpless situation when he saw one. He knew that their current location was without an exit strategy, but he would not go down without a fight. The sergeant and his men could at least narrow the odds before they died.

The five men slowly crept up from behind the magical steeds with all their armor removed to ensure a surprise attack. From a stealth-like run, their blades plunged deep into the sides of an equal number of unsuspecting unicorns, and as quickly as the men killed the beasts, they chopped off their horns and clenched them in their hands.

Realizing what was happening, the rest of the magical steeds began their assault against Nathan's small group.

Nathan shouted, "Hold the horns tight. They'll protect us from their magic. Stand ready, ready your blades and fight together no matter what. No surrender!" he screamed. Are you with me?"

"NO SURRENDER!" the men yelled, shouting bravely in the

direction of the unicorns—a shout dismissed as nothing more than mild irritation.

The steeds methodically encircled the small group. Lightning, fireballs, and storms of ice were all used against them, but the horn's magical resistances kept them safe. The eyes of the unicorns were full of rage, knowing their magic was useless against their own power. They began to scuff their hooves across the lava stone and tightened the circle around Nathan's group. The men were trapped.

Suddenly, Soresym's mighty griffon family began to plow into the top the unicorn's backs. One after another—like meteors they fell, their wings folded against their bodies to increase their speed. Before impact, razor-sharp talons and lion-like claws were extended as they drove the magical and now lifeless steeds into the cold hard ground. Blood sprayed in all direction as if bombs of red liquid had been dropped from a tremendous height. The force of the spray stung Nathan's face at impact.

The pained screams of the unsuspecting unicorns filled the air, only to be equally matched by the griffons as they shrieked gleefully. The smallest of the winged attackers—weighing over 2,000 pounds—buried their talons deep into the flesh and severed the unicorns' spines. Thirty unicorns perished with no chance to defend themselves. The others, though injured badly, responded by using their magic to teleport home to the Dark Forest. The strongest threat to Brandor had been disbanded in a matter of only a few short moments.

Nathan's men held their swords high and cheered for their winged allies. It was now time to turn their attention to the next big threat. Kepler's feline subjects were the next wave they must face, which included the support of the Barbarian archers.

Brandor's army stopped their retreat and rejoined the battle. Nathan and his men climbed back into their alcove of stone to retrieve their armor. Once again the mighty griffons and their family of hippogriffs torpedoed out of the sky into battle. Ten of the giant cats perished—another 30 lay injured and unable to fight. But this time, the winged army was not without casualty. The giant cats were ready, their quick reflexes allowing them to avoid the crushing weight of the griffons. The cats responded by leaping onto their backs and tearing into their flesh with their mighty claws.

Barbarian archers filled the air with arrows, causing little damage to the griffons—their thick hides protecting them as they descended for another attack, but the hippogriffs were not so fortunate. Their hides were not as resistant to the projectiles and 38 hippogriffs fell in an uncontrolled spiral, their blood staining the ground as they splattered.

The griffons snatched the giant cats, carried them high into the air and used their bodies as projectiles against the Barbarian archers. The men of the north were in tight formation and could not avoid being crushed beneath their weight.

Soresym shrieked as he landed in front of Sam.

"It looks as if I've come at a time of need, King of Brandor." Sam let out a sigh of relief.

"Soresym, my friend, I can't tell you how happy I am that you're here. We're outnumbered, and surrounded… I really could use your help."

"It's your lucky day! I must've taken a liking to you, Sam. I find you intriguing and can see the value in protecting your position as King of Brandor."

Soresym shrieked again, "The unicorns are no longer a concern for your army, but I fear the hippogriffs are no match for the Barbarian's weapons."

The griffon shifted and looked over his back as he scanned the area. "Order your army to the north and assist your other legions against the Barbarians. We'll deal with the serpents since they have no air-born weapons. I, on the other hand, will fly south and speak with the Bear King. I'll convince him to fight *with* us. The Minotaurs should also stop their attack once they realize I'm fighting at your side."

"I'll do that, my friend. It also might be a good idea to separate the horns from the unicorn's bodies and fly with them into battle against the serpents. I've just now received word that the snakes are coming to the surface. We are smoking them out of their caves, but they are far more powerful than I initially imagined. The unicorn horns are said to make poisonous creatures burst into flames so it should make your fight with them much easier."

Soresym raised his massive eagle head and called out in a language Sam could not understand. Another griffon, flying overhead, responded and departed for the others to relay the orders to gather the horns and fly south.

Sam shouted, "General, take the troops north and join the attack against the Barbarians." He turned his attention back to Soresym. "I'm in your debt. I don't know how you knew I was in trouble, but you're a sight for sore eyes."

"Sam, I suggest we speak of this later; there's a fight to be won." With that said, the griffon launched into the air and headed toward the Bear King, Groth.

The serpents were making quick work of Dreston's men as they fled from the underground city. Their 40-foot bodies out-slithered the running men and delivered their deadly poison. For every one serpent to fall, five men died. The battle was looking hopeless for the 520 men left alive—of just over 2,500 that entered, but relief soon came.

With swords held high and voices raised, they watch as the snakes burst into flames. The griffons, along with the hippogriffs, descended on the serpents with unicorn horns grasped in their talons. With each swooping pass, their slithering bodies disintegrated into piles of ash. The serpents' retreat was inevitable and they hurried to the safety of their underground city, only to realize the toxic fumes would not allow it; but to stay topside was hopeless against such a power as well. Seth called for his army's surrender.

Groth, the Bear King, stopped his army when Soresym landed in front of him. The griffon spoke in the bear's own language.

"Groth, stop your attack! You have been deceived. Brandor isn't your enemy. We must work together to stop the Minotaurs from attacking Brandor's army. You've been misled. The Barbarians and the skeleton army are your real enemies. Brandor doesn't have plans to attack your kind."

Groth grunted heavily, "I saw the body of the Scorpion King with my own eyes. How do you explain that? Brandor attacked his island!"

Soresym thought back to the conversation he had with Mosley. The wolf god had told him everything. "Yes, Brandor was there, but with good reason. Brandor was there because they had no choice. Brandor has never had a plan to attack you—or the Minotaurs. I tell you again that you have been deceived. This war isn't necessary."

"Why would Brandor attack the Scorpion King then?" The bear shifted anxiously. "If it wasn't an act of war against all beasts, then what was it?"

"It was necessary. It was necessary to save our world. A piece of the Crystal Moon was taken and hidden in the Scorpion King's home. Brandor went there to save us all. They wouldn't have attacked if the scorpions had peacefully greeted them. I assure you of this on my honor. You know that I live in the service of the gods. I wouldn't lie to you. We don't have time to debate this. I'll give you further details later, but, for now, Groth, I'm asking you to join me in talking with the Minotaurs. Don't fight this war against Brandor."

Groth growled, thought a moment and then responded. "Carry me with you and I'll stand by your side. If what you say is true, then a lie has been told to us all and we need to stop the skeletons' advance against Brandor."

Groth turned to face his army. "We must head north to join the Minotaurs. Go now, I'll be back soon." Facing Soresym, he continued. "Shall we go, griffon?"

Soresym took the bear into his massive talons and carried him to find the Minotaur King.

Horace, the Minotaur King, and his army were following the southern edge of Lake Zandra. He was about to give the order to charge when Soresym finally landed with the Bear King in front of him. The Minotaur lifted his hand, stopping his army and shouted in his own language.

"What is the meaning of this, griffon? Why do you carry Groth with you? There's blood to be spilled. He should be with his army."

Soresym took note—the leader of the skeleton army was at the Minotaur's side. This gave him pause and he was careful to speak with the Minotaur in his own language so the bony warrior could not understand.

The griffon translated everything for the Bear King explaining the deception. Soon Horace raised his head into the air and bellowed with anger. The skeleton leader waited. There was anxiousness within the skeleton commander, but he had been instructed to attack Brandor's army at the Minotaurs' sides. The bony commander would not move until the bullish king ordered the army to continue.

After a moment the Minotaur King shouted for his scouts. Once they arrived, he ordered them to quietly spread the word to his army that the skeletons were traitors and wait for the order to be given to attack.

Soresym interrupted, "The skeletons will not die. A plan is in order before you dispatch your men."

Meanwhile, Sam shouted his orders. "General, sound the horn and pull the troops back. Night is coming. We will regroup and attack the Barbarians as a single unit in the morning. The Barbarians will most likely follow our lead and also regroup. We'll attack at first light. Signal the griffons and the hippogriffs to land and rest among us."

"Yes, sire!"

Once Sam's orders had been carried out, Michael approached his king. "Sire, the Barbarians have begun to regroup. They are also setting up camp. They won't attack in the dark. We have an opportunity to use this to our advantage."

"What advantage is that, General?"

"I have spoken with Goss. He is the brother of Soresym and one of the respected leaders of the griffons. I have asked him to come to a meeting."

"Okay, but how will this give us an advantage?"

Goss landed.

"Because, King of Brandor, my kind can see in the darkness. We shall have an advantage from this alone, but also one of the fastest of our kind will arrive shortly with your queen. I can't imagine why you would have left her in Brandor."

"I left her because she's pregnant! Damn it, I don't want her here. Whose bright idea was this? I swear, it better not be you Michael!"

"No, sire—blame your queen."

"What do you mean by, blame the queen? I don't want the future of our kingdom to be on this battle field."

Goss sat next to the king. "If you don't win this battle, there will be no future for Brandor. Your queen is strong and Soresym has informed me of her sorcery."

"How could Soresym know how strong her sorcery is? He has never seen it."

"Let's just agree that he has been informed—how, matters not. Your queen will be helpful in this battle. Besides, she was on her way to join you anyway. She was just south of Angel's Village when we found her. Your queen had already ignored your orders and was on her way here to help. Soresym convinced her to wait until we had a chance to fly her in safely."

"How could she possibly—"

A screech from above filled the air as the gusts from a large set of wings stirred the earth. Sam watched as Shalee landed a short distance from him and he hurried to help her down.

"Shalee, I asked you to stay home—we can't risk our baby like this."

"Well, I missed you too. Don't you think I know I'm pregnant? I can tell you're glad to see me."

Sam sighed heavily. "You know I'm happy to see you. I just don't want you to get hurt."

"Me? Get hurt? From what I've heard, you could have died today. Without the griffons, I wouldn't have a husband. Don't you tell *me* about the danger! You walked right into a trap—a trap George set, I might add. You're lucky that a little birdie decided to make sure you had some extra help. I'm here and I don't care what you say—I'm not leaving, so you might as well let me use my magic. Besides, I was going stir crazy in Brandor. That's why I teleported to Angel's village and hitched a ride. I can't keep crying, Sam. I need to be here with you."

"I'm the king, Shalee. I want you to go home. I won't let you stay and risk our baby's life."

Shalee walked up to her king. She leaned over and whispered in his ear so the others could not hear. "If you think I'm leaving, you're nuts . . . I'll teleport you home and return without you if you want to play the king card with me, stud. I'm here to help whether you like it or not. All I've done since you left is cry about Helga and BJ's deaths. I need to help, Sam, and I need you to believe in me right now. I can't go home. I'll use my magic to fight from a distance."

Sam pulled her close and hugged her. "Promise me that you'll teleport someplace safe if you get into trouble. I couldn't bear the thought of losing you. We've lost so much already."

"I promise," she responded before kissing him.

"Sire," Michael said. "I hate to interrupt, but we need to plan!"

Goss interjected, "Yes, this is truly a tender moment, but we should be planning. We griffons can see at night. Have your army gather as many heavy pieces of lava stone as you can. We will fly through the night and drop them from above. I'll take your queen on my back and head north of the Barbarian's camp. She can send her fires down on them. This should keep their army from resting through the night and give Brandor an advantage. We should be able to kill a fair number of them before dawn."

"Sire, this is a good plan. The queen will be safe while on the griffon's back. She'll be hidden within the darkness. Her magic will kill many as it falls from the sky and she'll never set foot on the ground. If we're lucky, the Barbarians will retreat before morning."

Sam thought for a moment. "General, you fly with the queen. If you feel she's in danger, I want you to have Goss fly her to safety. She has the future of Brandor in her womb and I'll not risk her life."

"Yes, sire!"

Shalee kissed Sam.

"Thank you!"

As the griffon ascended into the night, Shalee lifted Precious high into the air, her voice strong as she commanded fire to begin raining from the sky. The camp of the Barbarians began to burn as the griffons and hippogriffs released the lava rocks.

Panic filled the camp as the men of the north scattered for their lives. Bodies fell lifeless, both burned, and crushed.

The Barbarian King looked to the sky, realized the hopelessness of the situation and shouted for his new general. "General, order the army to attack the camp of Brandor. We need to mix among them so the griffons will have no choice but to stop dropping their rocks."

Shalee observed the Barbarian's army's movements. She teleported from Goss's back and appeared next to Sam. "The Barbarians are headed this way. They didn't retreat like we thought they would. They'll be here soon. You need to prepare!"

Sam shouted. "General, prepare the army—we attack now!"

"Yes, sire!"

Four hundred bony warriors' skulls shouted from their piles, ordering their limbs to make their way back to their torsos. The shifting of the piles caused a frightful, clattering noise as the bones bumped against one another. Despite this noise, both the bears and Minotaurs seemed to enjoy the spectacle. They had easily torn apart their opposition, and it was now a matter of figuring out what to do with their bones.

"Charge," Sam shouted as he ordered the army into battle. Kael screamed with glee, his sharp edges begging for action. Kael quieted once he realized that Sam would be keeping watch from the top of a small mound of lava stone—away from the battle.

Shalee had hitched a ride on Goss's back, sending her fireballs into the advancing Barbarian army, wanting to inflict as much damage as she could before they collided with Brandor.

Swords, maces, shields and bodies slammed hard into one another as the full force of Brandor's army met the large men of Bloodvain. Bodies fell, blood saturated the earth and the griffons, along with the hippogriffs, once again descended from the rear of the Barbarians horde, smashing them like grapes.

Soon the fight was too tight for the flying beasts to be effective and they had to pull back. Goss landed next to Sam. "We can no longer assist. It is up to you from here on out. My kind is large and fighting in close combat would hurt your men, not just the Barbarians. We will keep watch and attack when we can!"

"Thank you, my friend," Sam replied. "Brandor owes you a debt. Shalee, stay with me, I need your help."

"Any friend of Soresym is a friend of all griffons. Consider it our pleasure. We will be watching from above." With that, Goss took to the sky.

"Shalee, I need you to use your power on my eyes. I need to be able to see farther than I do now. I need to be able to see in the dark!"

"Why?"

"Trust me—just do it . . . please!" Sam lifted his bow and began firing his arrows into the night.

Michael lifted his sword high, despite his exhaustion. His plate armor was severely battered, and in some places had fallen from his body due to the abuse of the countless confrontations he had survived throughout the night. His blue eyes were bloodshot and it took every last ounce of his will to stand in front of Senchae Bloodvain and call him onto the battle field.

"SENCHAE, King of the Barbarians, I challenge you! You and I can settle the outcome of this war!"

The Peak of Bailem had come and gone. It was now time for the General Absolute to create his legacy—or solidify his death, but either way, this action would stop the fighting around him.

Senchae lowered himself from his mount and moved to take his position in front of Michael. The barbarian stood two feet taller than the General Absolute and outweighed him by nearly 300 pounds. His armor was covered with blood. Michael was a large man, but appeared diminutive compared to the Barbarian King's size.

The horn of the Barbarian general sounded and both armies began to turn their attention towards the two men. Senchae spoke, "I admire your courage. I'd like to know the name of the man that I'm about to kill."

It took everything within Michael to claim his bravery. "I'm Michael, the General Absolute to the Kingdom of Brandor… and it isn't I who will be dying today, Senchae."

The men of Brandor that had gathered and managed to hear the General's response, cheered.

Senchae waited patiently for the noise to die. "Ha, today will be the last time you address a king by his first name."

Senchae lifted his heavy blade and began his advance. His army began to stomp their feet as the fight began. A large circle of men, both Barbarian and human alike, had accumulated and had stopped fighting to watch the battle.

With shield in one hand and sword in the other, Michael began to circle. He engaged, rolling forward, and slicing at one of Senchae's legs. The king lifted his leg, avoiding the blade as it passed beneath him.

"I see that you have quickness about you, but it won't do you any good!"

"It is true… and I will not miss again."

"Who said there will be an, again?" The barbarian lunged forward and smashed his two-handed sword hard into Michael's shield. The force sent the General backwards and to the ground.

Senchae followed this assault by kicking Michael hard across the side of his chest as he tried to recover and lift himself from the ground.

The leader of Brandor's army cried out as he heard two of his ribs crack. Senchae backed off.

"To think that once you die, I'll command your army. Your men will serve me, General."

Michael gathered his last bit of strength and lunged toward Senchae with his blade extended. The barbarian stepped to the side and grabbed him, lifting him high into the air and threw him against a tree. The General Absolute fell to the ground, spitting blood.

"I must say, I never would've thought that someone from the south could have this much heart, General. It's a shame that you must die now."

The Barbarian King lifted his blade high. The heavy metal began its decent, but suddenly, the tip of an arrow exited the front of the Barbarian King's throat. Senchae's eyes glossed over and he began to gasp for air. He stumbled a bit before falling to his knees as Michael pulled himself to his feet and lifted his blade, plunging it deep into the Barbarian King's heart as he screamed, "Attack!"

Brandor's army reacted, fueled with a renewed vigor. Their blades moved with swift conviction as the battle commenced.

From across the battlefield, Sam lowered the Bow of Accuracy to his side. He grasped Kael and summoned the blade's extended fire and charged down the mound of lava stone and into the chaos.

It was not until Early Bailem the next day when Sam found Soresym. The last thing Sam imagined that he would ever see would be the hundreds of skeleton's arms inching along the ground as they tried to return to their torsos. To his delight, he saw three piles being carefully watched—one for the skeletons' heads, a second for their torsos and a third for their arms and legs. The separated limbs were continually being tossed back onto the pile as they tirelessly tried to reunite with their bodies. The bony heads were becoming more frustrated and screamed yet another order with each failed attempt.

The Bear and Minotaur Kings met with Sam, along with Soresym. Sam was the first to speak as Soresym translated his words. "My Lords, it appears there has been a grievous misunderstanding. It's good to know that we've been able to solve this problem without more bloodshed."

Groth responded, "Why did you attack the Scorpion King's Island?"

Sam took a deep breath. "I was told one of the Crystal Moon's pieces was in his cave. I needed to get the piece of the Crystal and find a way to save our world. I took my army with me in case the king attacked—which he did. I didn't want that to happen, but I knew unless we found all the pieces of the Crystal Moon, this world would cease to exist."

After a time, the shock of the Crystal Moon being stolen had settled. Horace spoke. "If we can help in any way, we are at your service."

"We are as well," Groth added.

Sam thought a moment. "We need to go into the Serpent's underground city to find the first two pieces of the Crystal Moon. They have been hidden there. We will be able to use the unicorn's horns to drive the serpents back if need be, but, for now, we have some bones to deal with. Any idea on what we should do to kill these things? We can't just leave them here."

Soresym agreed, "We need to separate their parts and make sure they'll never be able to rejoin one another. I know of no other way to stop them. If they're allowed to rejoin, they'll attack Brandor as ordered by Kepler. They won't stop until this has been accomplished."

Sam sighed, and then lifted Kael into the air. "You're the Sword of the Gods. Do you know of a way to kill these things?"

Kael responded, "I do! You need to set them on fire. This is the only way to destroy them."

"That's it? It's that simple?"

"Simple if you know the answer, I suppose. Put my blade into the pile and command my flame. I'll do the rest."

Sam looked at Soresym, shrugged his shoulders and moved to the pile. He commanded Kael to produce his flame and soon all three piles of bones were ablaze. The cries of the skulls sounded hellish as their souls rose one by one into the air and penetrated the pages of the Book of Immortality.

Sam turned to Soresym.

"We need to find Kepler. He's responsible for creating these creatures and needs to be stopped. Will you have the griffons and the hippogriffs take to the air and search for him? I want to make sure we put an end to his life and stop this kind of evil from ever running free again within Grayham."

The griffon thought a moment.

"I'll do this, but it is not my kind that will destroy him. We'll bring him to you. You'll need to pass this judgment yourself. As the King of Brandor, your people need to see this. This will send a message throughout all of Grayham that you intend to have a peaceful kingdom. I also suggest that you finish what you've started. Go north into the Barbarian kingdom and bring all of Grayham under one peaceful rule."

"I agree, but first we have some snakes to deal with."

"The snakes are of no concern. They have surrendered. You will be able to search for the Crystal's pieces without interference!"

Meanwhile,
The Home of Lasidious and Celestria

CELESTRIA backed away from the green flames within their fireplace, the visions of Grayham fading as she turned to cup her lover's face in the palms of her hands.

"So, my love, I can't wait to see Sam and Shalee's faces when they realize Seth doesn't have the crystals."

Lasidious sat down and put his feet on the stone table. "Yes, I think it will be entertaining. I must admit, I wasn't expecting the griffons to help. I would guess Mosley had something to do with it. But I think there's enough confusion on Grayham to keep the gods watching for a while.

"Our baby is safe and in Susanne's care. It's time to turn our attention to Luvelles. Everything is going better than we could have hoped for. The next stage of our plan is ready to be implemented! But first let's offer George a well-deserved rest. I'm sure, in due time, he'll make us proud once again."

The End

www.worldsofthecrystalmoon.com
www.phillipjones.com

email: worldsofthecrystalmoon@gmail.com

**Keep reading for a SNEAK PEEK
inside the pages of Book 2.**

Book 2
Crystal Moon

Magic of Luvelles

BLACK SKIES threatened the land below as the clouds continued to rumble with their raged-filled curses. The morning had been unkind to the World of Luvelles, punishing the terrain with pebble-sized hail and earth-scarring strikes of electrical fury. The forest had taken the brunt of the storm with the high winds abusing many of the tall evergreen-looking trees causing their branches to fall heavily to the ground. Countless mud-filled puddles could hardly be avoided as they stained the white dress of a severely injured woman.

Shalee Goodrich, powerful sorceress and queen to the Kingdom of Brandor, grit her teeth in agony. Her moans could be heard as she crawled along the muddy road leading away from the swamp. The open wound across her abdomen marked an easy trail for the dark figure stalking her to follow. Her flight had slowed and now, the once sporadic speckled drops of blood were turning into smaller coin-shaped areas of saturated earth.

The hunter knew his prey was beginning to tire. He smiled as he bent down, rubbing his hand across the stained dirt.

"You can't run forever," he whispered. "Your blood gives you away! It didn't have to end this way. I'm going to miss you, my love!" Methodically, he rubbed the essence of her life between his finger tips and tasted it.

Shalee pulled herself off the road and into the forest. Her forearms were torn from the gravel embedded in her skin. Her teeth chattered uncontrollably as her body continued to lose its heat but she managed to force herself into an upright position against a large stone. The blade of her assailant had made a clean cut. She tried using her magic to cauterize the wound—but failed.

Why can't I use my magic, she thought. Her mind screamed for answers, but none could be found. Again she closed her eyes and tried to teleport—nothing—there was no escape. *I've got to get out of here, he's gonna kill me.*

It wasn't long before her attacker stood above her, looking down with eyes full of evil intent.